UWE JOHNSON

ANNIVERSARIES

From the Life of Gesine Cresspahl

Translated by Leila Vennewitz

A Helen and Kurt Wolff Book

Harcourt   Brace   Jovanovich

New York and London

This volume encompasses Volume One and part of Volume Two
of the German original, Jahrestage 1 and 2.
For all translations into foreign languages, the author
prepared a cut version, on which this text is based.

Printed in the United States of America

Library of Congress Cataloging in Publication Data

Johnson, Uwe, 1934–
    Anniversaries: from the life of Gesine Cresspahl.

    Translation of v. 1 and part of v. 2 of Jahrestage.
    "A Helen and Kurt Wolff book."
    I. Title.
PT2670.O36J3213   1975   833'.9'14   74–20942
ISBN 0–15–107560–3

First edition

B C D E

My thanks to

Peter Suhrkamp

Helen Wolff

177868

TRANSLATOR'S NOTE

As always, I am deeply indebted to my husband, William Vennewitz, for his never-failing advice, encouragement, and assistance.

I have also benefited from the close co-operation of the author, as well as from the patience and understanding of our editor, Helen Wolff. Inevitably there have been aspects of the translation needing clarification, and the consensus among us has been to preserve as far as possible the idiosyncrasies and flavor of Uwe Johnson's style, a decision that has had some unorthodox results: for example, the baptizing of German street and hotel names with English versions is intended as a counterpart to Uwe Johnson's own delight in rendering many American and English idioms into German in the original.

Furthermore, I am indebted to the author for supplying me with the actual clippings from the New York *Times* that cover the articles and news items he mentions, thus giving me direct access to the original sources of which he himself has made use.

LEILA VENNEWITZ

ANNIVERSARIES

August 1967–February 1968

*L*ong waves sweep slanting against the beach, hump muscled backs, raise trembling combs that tip over at the greenest summit. The taut roll, already streaked with white, enfolds a hollow space of air that is crushed by the clear mass as if a secret had been created and destroyed there. The bursting wave knocks children off their feet, whirls them around, drags them flat over the gravelly bottom. Beyond the surf the waves tug at the swimmer, pulling her on outstretched hands over their backs. The wind is only a flutter, with a wind as slack as this the Baltic had petered out in a ripple. The word for the short waves of the Baltic was choppity.

The village lies on a narrow spit off the New Jersey coast, a two-hour train ride from New York. The authorities have fenced off the wide sandy beach, and access is permitted to outsiders at a charge of forty dollars for the season; uniformed pensioners loiter around the entrances eyeing the visitors' clothing for registration tags. The Atlantic is open to the inhabitants of the summer homes which, under their angled roofs, with verandas, two-storied galleries, and bright awnings, perch comfortably on the stone embankment well above the hurricane mark. The local dark-skinned domestics fill a church of their own, but Negroes may not buy houses here or rent apartments or lie on the white coarse-grained sand. Jews are not welcome here either. She is not sure whether, in the years before 1933, Jews were allowed to rent houses in the fishing village beyond Jerichow; she cannot remember seeing any notice prohibiting them in the years that followed. Here she has borrowed a bungalow from friends for ten days, on the bay side. The people next door take in the mail and read the picture postcards that the child writes to "Dear Miss C." from summer camp, but they persist in addressing her as "Mrs. Cresspahl" and very likely take her for another Catholic of Irish descent.

Ge-sine Cress-pahl
I'll kick your heels and make you fall

The sky has been bright for a long time, blue with white clouds, the horizon hazy. The light weighs heavily on her eyelids. Between the expensive beach chairs and blankets there is plenty of unoccupied beach; from neighboring conversations words penetrate sleep as if from a time past. The sand is still heavy with yesterday's rain and can be patted into firm soft cushions. Across the sky, tiny airplanes string ribbons of words boosting drinks and stores and restaurants. Farther out, above the close-packed herd of sport-fishing boats, two

jet fighters are practicing navigation. The surf crashes into the explosion of a heavy shell, is thrown together with the spattering sounds
produced each evening by the village movie house in war films. She is
wakened by a few drops of rain, and once again the gray-blue
shingled surface of a sloping roof in the darkling light reminds her of
a furry thatched roof somewhere in Mecklenburg, on another coast.

To the Village Council of Rande, near Jerichow, Mecklenburg.

Dear Sirs: As a former resident of Jerichow and at one time
a regular visitor to Rande, I would appreciate knowing the number of summer tourists of the Jewish faith who visited Rande in
the years preceding 1933.
Thanking you for your assistance.

In the evening the beach is wet and hard, riddled with pores,
and presses the slivers of shell more sharply against the sole of her
feet. The receding waves strike her ankles so hard that she keeps
tripping. When she stands still, the water hollows the ground out
from under her feet in two troughs, then covers them again with a
swirl. After rain like this the Baltic would wash a gentle, even edging
against the shore. When the kids ran along the beach beside the
Baltic, they used to play a trick on the leader: one of them would
give the foot just leaving the ground a swift sideways kick, hooking it
behind the heel of the other leg—hers, child that she was, and the
first tumble was a mystery. She walks toward the lighthouse, whose
recurring flash slices narrow wedges out of the blue shadow. Every
few steps she tries to let herself be thrown off balance by the waves,
but she cannot recapture that sensation between tripping and hitting
the ground.

*Can you teach me that trick, Miss C.? Maybe nobody knows it
here.*

Along the Israeli-Jordanian front there has been more shooting.
In New Haven citizens of African descent are said to be smashing
store windows and throwing fire bombs.
Next morning the first shore train to New York is drawn up in
the open beside the bay, decrepit equipment with mortgage plates
under the name of the railroad company. Jakob would never have
allowed such dilapidated coaches to leave the siding. The streaky
windows frame pictures, white clapboard houses in gray light, private
marinas in lagoons, sleepy breakfast terraces shaded by heavy foliage,

river mouths, last glimpses of the sea beyond breakwaters, the views of past vacations. Had they been vacations? In the summer of 1942 Cresspahl had put her on the train at Gneez for Ribnitz and explained how she was to get from the station to the harbor. She was so upset by the separation that it never occurred to her to be scared of the journey. She had thought the coastal steamer in Ribnitz Harbor looked like a fat black duck. As they moved out into Saal Sound she had kept the Ribnitz church spire in sight, added the Körkwitz one, then learned the Neuhaus dunes by heart, and had stood looking back all the way to Althagen to be sure not to miss the route back to the station, to Jerichow.

In the summer of 1942 Cresspahl preferred to have the child out of the way. In 1951 he had got her out of his way, sent her to southeast Mecklenburg, five hours from Jerichow. The station at Wendisch Burg lay above the town; from the end of the blue-gray gritty platform you could see the eastern edge of Lower Lake, lusterless in the afternoon. Not until she reached the barrier did she notice that all the time she had been standing there, undecided, Klaus Niebuhr had been watching her, not saying a word, comfortably leaning against the iron rail, nine years older than the child she remembered. He had brought along a girl called Babendererde, one of those people who smile at random, and Gesine gave a wary nod when Klaus introduced her. Besides, she was afraid he knew why Cresspahl did not want her in Jerichow for the time being. You could hardly call it a vacation.

The train rumbles leisurely up to little station squares; commuters in business suits emerge from the dimness beneath the roofs, each alone with his brief case; on the train they lower their seat backs and settle down to sleep. Now the sun is licking the rooftops, throwing fistfuls of light over the lower-lying countryside. The branch line between Gneez and Jerichow led at a distance past villages; the stations were like children's red blocks with gabled, tarred roofs, a scattering of people waiting outside with shopping bags. The high-school students positioned themselves on the platforms in such a way that by the time they got to Gneez they were all in a group in the third and fourth compartments behind the baggage car. It was along this route that Jakob learned the railway business. In his black smock Jakob looked down from his caboose so tolerantly onto the group of school kids, as if unwilling to recognize Cresspahl's daughter. At nineteen perhaps he still classified people by their social status. From New Jersey's scummy brown marshes across long-legged trestle bridges the train sways into the Palisades and down into the tunnel beneath the Hudson to New York, and she has already been standing quite a while among the weekenders and commuters lined up in the center aisle, occasionally moving forward six inches all poised for the race to the train door, the escalator, the labyrinthine construction fences of Pennsylvania Station, over to the West Side subway, the Flushing line, onto the escalator, out from under the blue vaulting to the corner of 42nd Street by Grand Central Station. She must not reach her desk more than an hour late, and that only today, after her vacation.

August 21, 1967 Monday

Clearing skies in North Vietnam enabled the Air Force to attack targets north of Hanoi. The Navy bombed the coast with aircraft and fired eight-inch shells into the demilitarized zone. In the south, four helicopters were shot down. The racial disorders in New Haven continued yesterday with arson, broken store windows, looting; an additional 112 persons have been arrested.

Beside the stack of newspapers waits a little cast-iron dish, and the vendor's arched hand swoops down over it before she has even had time to throw down the coin. The man's eyes are hostile; people have snatched his money once too often in passing by on the street.

So that's what I let my neck be shot up for, lady.

The body of the American who failed to return to his Prague hotel last Wednesday evening was found yesterday afternoon in the Vltava River. Mr. Jordan, aged 59, was an official of the Jewish charity organization JOINT. He had gone out to buy a newspaper.

The bottom of Lexington Avenue is still in shadow. She remembers the taxis jostling each other in the morning on the wide street, prevented from turning by a traffic light, its red exploited by pedestrians to cross the one-way street going east, its green allowing them to hold up the waiting cars. She does not hesitate to defy the traffic signal. She has been coming here since time out of mind, elbows pressed to her sides, intent on the rhythm of the people walking next to her. She avoids the blind beggar clinking his outstretched mug, grunting surlily. Again she cannot make out what he says. She is walking too slowly, her gaze wanders, she is preoccupied with her return. Ever since she has been out of town the wail of sirens has been suspended between the high, windowed towers, swelling, dying away, raucously erupting beyond more distant blocks. From the side streets fierce hot light strikes across the avenue. Her eyes on the dazzling cement, she walks along beside a black-marble base façade that mirrors the colors of faces, painted metal, canopies, shirts, store windows, dresses, in muted echo. She turns aside into a white-lit passage from which ammonia steams into the open, released bite by bite through the narrow spring door. This entrance is known only to the staff.

She is now thirty-four. Her child is almost ten. She has been living in New York for six years. She has been working at this bank since 1964.

I imagine: under her eyes the tiny grooves were paler than the tanned skin of her face. Her hair, almost black, cut short all around, has become lighter. She looked half asleep; she has not spoken much to anybody for some time. She did not remove her sunglasses until she had passed beyond the glinting door panel. She never wears her sunglasses pushed back into her hair.

She was barely amused by the rage of the drivers who are victimized day after day by a traffic light on Lexington Avenue. She had arrived in this country by car, a Swedish sedan that had been eaten away by snow salt for two years at the foot of 96th Street, across from the three garages. She has always taken the subway to work.

I imagine: during the lunch hour she again reads that yesterday afternoon a man was rowing on the river in Prague and, on reaching the May First Bridge, found lodged in one of the water barriers a Jew from New York who had left his hotel to buy a newspaper. (She has heard that in Prague English-language newspapers are sold only in hotels.)

You American? Hlavní nádraží dříve, this station, before, Wilsonovo nádraží. Sta-shun. Woodrow Wilson!

She would have had to say Yes, since she had an American passport in her handbag. She has forgotten the name in the passport. That was in 1962.

I imagine: in the evening, under a sky already stripped of light, she emerges from the 96th Street subway station onto Broadway and sees, framed in the arch below Riverside Drive, a green open space, beyond the frayed greenery of the park the flat river whose hidden shore makes the river seem to spread out like a lake in an August forest in dry, scorched silence.

She lives on Riverside Drive in three rooms, below the treetops. The indoor light is pierced with green. To the north, in the midst of dense clouds of leaves, she can see the lamps on the bridge, beyond them the lights on the parkway. Dusk sharpens the lights. The sound of engines runs together in the distance and pounds in steady waves through the window, like ocean breakers. From Jerichow it was an hour's walk to the beach, past the marsh and then through the fields.

August 22, 1967   Tuesday

Over mainland China two jet fighters of the U. S. Navy were shot down yesterday. The Department of Defense declares 32 men officially dead in Vietnam. The Marine Corps has killed 109 North Vietnamese. The bunch in the south promises completely honest elections.

Yesterday in New Haven once again store windows were smashed and fires started. The police wore blue helmets, carried rifles, fired tear gas. Meanwhile 284 citizens were arrested, mostly Negroes and Puerto Ricans.

The newsstand on Broadway, at the southwest corner of 96th Street, is a green tent built around a core of aluminum cases. On the left are the local magazines laid out in overlapping rows; on the right by the entrance the stacks of daily papers; on the right outside the European imports, secured with encrusted weights. The stand is a weather forecast for the people living around the corner; when it adds more roof with poles and canvas, rain may be expected. The old man in the greasy cap who works the morning shift feels entitled to his moods. His right hand is deformed; but he insists on customers' placing the money between his crooked fingers, and every morning he works at pressing coins out of the hollow of his crippled hand with a fat thumb. This morning he does not return her greeting.

He knows this customer: she arrives every workday at ten past eight from 96th Street; she always brings the right change; she tries to read the headlines of the New York *Times* as she tugs the paper from under the weight. She usually walks empty-handed to work; the paper tucked under her elbow, she runs down into the subway, always to the same train (which he almost immediately hears, through the grating in the center of Broadway, as it enters the station). She says good morning as if she had learned it at one of those schools up north; but she was not born in this country. The vendor also knows this customer's child, from Saturdays, when the two of them walk along the street with their shopping cart; the child, a ten-year-old girl with the same smooth round head but with sandy foreign braids, says good morning as if she had learned it at P. S. 75 a block farther along, and comes secretly on Sunday morning to pick up a paper consisting entirely of comic strips. The customer knows nothing of this, or that the child seldom has to pay. The customer buys no paper other than the New York *Times*.

Tomorrow for a change you won't say good morning, lady. All these fancy manners.

On weekdays Gesine Cresspahl buys the New York *Times* at the stand because the delivery boy might miss her breakfast time. On the platform she folds the paper lengthwise once and once again so that she can keep hold of it in the crush through the subway doors and, squeezed between elbows and shoulders, read the first page of the eight-column spread from top to bottom, swept along under the street for fifteen minutes until she can continue on foot. When she flies to Europe she has her neighbor keep his copies; on her return she spends many weekends recouping lost New York days from foot-high piles. During her lunch break she clears her desk and reads the pages following the front page, elbows propped against the edge of the desk, in the European manner. On a visit to Chicago she hurried for two miles along a snow-swept street of blind apartment houses until she hunted down the out-of-date New York city edition in a pro-Chinese bookstore, as if only what was printed elsewhere were to be believed. On the way home from work the three lengthwise folds are so firmly creased that the columns open up obediently, fold under on the right, swing over to the left, like the keys of an instrument under the fingers of one hand; the other hand is needed to hold on to the strap in the overcrowded, swaying car. Once, after midnight, she walked through the hot side streets, cautiously, looking straight ahead, past knots of whispering people and a brawl over a drunk or unconscious woman, over to Broadway, at this hour crowded with policemen, prostitutes, drug addicts, to buy the earliest edition of the New York *Times* and open it up under the acetylene lamp on the pointed roof of the kiosk and find the news item, which was truer now than the sensational headline that she had not been willing to believe when she saw it in the afternoon papers (that was when Mrs. Enzensberger had tried to finish off the Vice-President in Berlin with bombs made of pudding powder). She keeps the crumpled, flapping paper under her arm until she is inside her apartment, and over supper she rereads the financial reports, although now for professional reasons. When a day at the beach has caused her to miss the paper, she keeps an eye that evening on the subway floor and on every trash can she passes, looking for a discarded, tattered, stained New York *Times* of the day, as if it alone provided proof of the day. She has come to treat the New York *Times* as a person, and to study the great gray bundle gives her a sense of the presence of someone, of a conversation with someone to whom she listens and replies with the courtesy, the surreptitious doubt, the hidden grimace, the forgiving smile, and the gestures, that nowadays she would show toward an aunt, a collective, unrelated, imaginary one: toward her concept of an aunt.

August 23, 1967   Wednesday

Yesterday the Air Force flew 132 missions over North Vietnam. A caption under a picture of the wreckage of an airplane in Hanoi states that the Communists claim this to be aircraft shot down by them. The photo was important enough for the front page, but it is not until page 6, overshadowed by news from Jerusalem, that we find the official announcements of the death of forty servicemen, only the dead from New York and surrounding areas being mentioned by name, fifteen lines of local news.

During the night five hundred policemen patrolled the Negro neighborhoods of New Haven, searched automobiles, trained searchlights on windows, arrested one hundred people. And had she been at Foley Square yesterday afternoon she could have heard a radical Negro leader shout that there was a war on with the whites and guns were needed, as she walked down West 95th Street toward the still moistly hazy picture of the park with the river in the middle. She imagines she has watched the faces of the policemen, one of whom is to be seen under the raised black fist in the paper, with a skeptical, almost hardened expression, as if he were still savoring the aftertaste of the recent brawl.

In August 1931 Cresspahl was sitting in a shady garden at the mouth of the Trave, his back to the Baltic, reading a five-day-old English newspaper.

He was then in his forties, with heavy bones and a firm stomach above his belt, broad in the shoulders. In his gray-green corduroy knickerbocker suit he looked more rustic than the summer visitors around him; he behaved with caution and his hands were massive, but the waiter noticed him raise his hand and soon placed the beer beside his hand, vouchsafing a few phrases. To these Cresspahl replied with a low, absent-minded growl. He looked beyond his crumpled newspaper toward a table in the sunlit center of the garden at which a family from Mecklenburg was sitting, but in an abstracted way, as if he had had enough of his obsolete news. At that time he was full in the face, with a dry skin, already tough. His long head was narrower at the brow. His hair was still fair, short, growing in little whorls. He had an alert, cryptic expression, and his lips were thrust slightly forward, as on the photograph in the passport I stole from him twenty years later.

He had left England five days earlier. In Mecklenburg he had given away his sister at her wedding to Martin Niebuhr, a foreman with the Department of Waterways. He had paid for the dinner at the Ratskeller in Waren. He had observed Niebuhr for two days before giving him a thousand marks, as a loan. He was paid up on his father's grave in the Malchow cemetery for twenty years in advance. He had left a pension for his mother. Had he not bought himself out? He had visited a cousin in the Holstein area and helped him bring in the harvest one day. He had had his passport renewed for five years, as required by the naturalization regulations. He still had twenty-five pounds in his pocket and did not want to spend much of it until he was back in Richmond, in his workshop full of expensive equipment, among his reliable customers, in his two rooms in Manor Grove, in the house for which he had made an offer. On this trip he had seen again where he had been as a child, where he had learned his craft, where he had been called up for the war, where the Kapp putschists had locked him up in a potato cellar, where the Nazis were now having street battles with the Communists. He did not intend to come again.

The air was dry and swift-moving. The warm shadows flickered. The sea wind tossed scraps of the open-air concert into the garden. It was a time of peace. The photograph is the color of chamois leather, yellowing. What did Cresspahl see in my mother?

In 1931 my mother was twenty-five, the youngest of Papenbrock's daughters. In family photos she stands at the back, hands clasped, head slightly to one side, unsmiling. One could tell she had never worked other than to please herself. She was about medium height, like me, wore our hair in a knot on the nape of her neck, dark hair, falling loosely around her small, docile, somewhat sallow face. She was looking worried now. She seldom raised her eyes from the tablecloth and kneaded her fingers as if she were at a loss. She was the only one to notice that the man, who was watching her levelly without nodding, had followed them from the Priwall ferry to the linen draper's, to the nearest free table in the garden. Old Mr. Papenbrock leaned back with his whole weight in his chair and nagged at the waiter, or his wife, when other tables were served. My grandmother, silly sheep, said, as if she were in church: "Yes, Albert. Of course, Albert." The waiter stood beside Cresspahl and said: "Not that I know of. Weekend. A lot come up from Mecklenburg. Good families. Yes, sir."

I was pretty, Gesine.
And yet he looked more like a workman.
We had an eye for such things, Gesine.

Cresspahl was waiting for the ferry to Priwall when the Papenbrocks came and stood in the front row; on the ferry he stood leaning against the barrier, with his back to them. On the other side he let them go past him to Albert's delivery truck and soon disappeared among the people walking along under the dense foliage of the residential street. In the evening Cresspahl drove back to Mecklenburg in a rented car, through Priwall, past Pötenitz Bay, along the coast to Jerichow. When my father's boat sailed from Hamburg for England, he took a room at the Lübeck Arms in Jerichow.

Gesine Cresspahl is sometimes invited for lunch to an Italian restaurant on Third Avenue. Behind the building there is a garden surrounded by ivy-covered brick walls. The tables under the colored umbrellas are spread with red-and-white-checked cloths, the noise from the street is muffled by the roof, and the talk is about the Chinese. What are the Chinese up to?

The Chinese are setting fire to the British Mission in Peking and beating up the Chargé d'Affaires. That's what the Chinese are up to.

August 24, 1967   Thursday

Five fighter planes have been shot down over North Vietnam. Seventeen military personnel are officially dead in the south, and one of them was Anthony M. Galeno of the Bronx.

In the Bronx the police have seized an arsenal that included grenades, handguns, dynamite, gunpowder, hand grenades, rifles, shotguns, pistols, percussion caps. The four collectors, private patriots, wanted first to kill the Communist Herbert Aptheker and then to save the nation from the rest of its enemies.

When Gesine Cresspahl arrived in this city in the spring of 1961, it was to be for two years. The porter had set the child on his cart and pushed it with a flourish through the dilapidated shed of the

French Line; the child put both hands behind her back when he extended his and took off his cap. Marie was almost four. After six days at sea she had given up hoping for the Rhine, the kindergarten in Düsseldorf, her grandmother, in the new country. Gesine still thought of Marie as "the child," the child had almost no defense against her. She was worried that this move might be frustrated by the child, who was blinking, scowling and scared, under her white hood at the dirty light of West 48th Street.

She had twenty days in which to find a place to live, and on every one of them the child fought against New York. The hotel found a German-speaking baby-sitter for her, a stiff-necked elderly woman from the Black Forest in a pitch-black dress all frills and rows of buttons, who could sing songs by Uhland in a thin soprano, but the emigrant had retained more of her dialect than of the High German that was spoken in Freudenstadt twenty-five years ago; the child did not answer her.

The child walked about the city with Gesine, never letting go of her hand, stood pressed close to her in buses and subways, watchful to the point of suspicion, and it was late afternoon before she let herself be lulled to sleep by the monotonous rhythm of travel. She drew her head down between her shoulders when Gesine read to her from the For Rent advertisements in the New York *Times*; she cared nothing about attended elevators, or about air-conditioning units; she asked about ships. She looked around with a kind of satisfaction in the apartments that Gesine could afford, stingily truncated and shabbily furnished rooms, three windows to the dingy courtyard and one to the bare, hard façade opposite, expensive because free of Negro neighbors; they could not compare with the windows looking out on the garden in Düsseldorf; she had a right to something better than that.

The child would have nothing to do with English, she endured the greetings and cries and flattery in snack bars in the bus in the hotel lobby as if she had been deprived of her sense of hearing, when she did reply it was only with a reluctant angry shake of the head and lowered eyelids. She was so quietly obsessed with going back, over and over again she was called well brought up. She began to refuse food because the bread, the fruit, the meat, tasted different. Gesine resorted to bribery and told her she could watch the cartoons on television; the child turned away from the screen, not defiantly. The child stood by the window looking down into the street, darkened by high-rise façades, where everything was different: the garish packs of taxis, the uniformed, whistling doormen under their canopies, the

American flag above the Harvard Club, policemen toying with their clubs, the white steam rising from the vents of heating ducts, shining in the alien night. She asked about airplanes. Gesine was relieved when, after many days of watching, the child asked why some of the people here have dark skins, or why old women from the Black Forest are Jews; most of the conversation was wordless, in the eyes, in the mind:

would you ever give up, for my sake?
Give me these two years. Then we'll go to West Germany for as long as you like.
You mean you're thinking of giving up.

On the twelfth day, for the child's sake, Gesine gave up searching in Manhattan and moved to the residential quarter of Queens. The train climbed out of the tunnel under the East River onto the high stilts across from the United Nations Building, and the child, discouraged and stubborn, looked at the superhumanly high jagged skyline of the other shore and then at the humble, low, boxlike buildings, the single-story wasteland (as a poet says) to the right and left of the railway. But in Flushing they found boulevards, wide between grassy slopes, shaded by old trees, rustically bordered by well-spaced white clapboard houses with slate roofs, and Gesine no longer apologized tacitly to her child. The child said: "Wouldn't it be nicer to go and look for a house by a beach?"

The real-estate agent in the main street was over fifty, sedate, soft-spoken, a white man. When he removed his glasses he looked experienced. Age gave him the appearance of reliability. He could offer furnished apartments in the treed areas, with steps down to gardens, with swimming pools around the corner. Gesine could afford to live here. The man smiled at the child who, rigid with indignation, regarded the move as a fait accompli. He spoke about the area, described it as respectable and Jewish, saying: "Don't worry, we'll keep the shwartzes out all right." In one movement Gesine swept the child from the chair, her purse from the desk, and was on the sidewalk, taking good care to bang the glass door with a crash against the frame.

That evening they sat in a restaurant at Idlewild Airport watching the aircraft move out onto the runways, start out over the ocean against the darkening sky. She tried to explain to the child that the agent had taken her for a Jew, for a better person than a Negro woman. The child wanted to know what she had meant, "You bastard of a Jew," and realized that miracles can happen, saw the suitcase with her toys from the hotel being driven up, felt she was already on a plane, tomorrow she would be home. Gesine was ready to give up. You can't live among such people.

The West German Government is planning to lift the statute of limitations for all murder and genocide perpetrated during the Nazi period, perhaps.

Light artillery can be ordered through the mails, but for a pistol one needs a license, and she does not dare go to the police.

August 25, 1967   Friday

Since last night rain has been falling on the city, muffling the rumble of cars on the parkway along the Hudson to a subdued hiss. This morning she has been wakened by the swish of tires on the streaming asphalt beneath the window. The rainy light has hung dusk between the office blocks on Third Avenue. The small stores at the feet of the high rises cast a modest, village light into the wetness. When she switched on the fluorescent panel in her office ceiling, the light, compressed by the dark, momentarily painted a homelike atmosphere in the sharp-angled cell. This is the day the child is coming home from summer camp.

In the evening the brows of the bank, not far above her floor, are draped with fog. Seen from the street, the board-room windows blink waterily, sinking ships.

That evening she waits for the child in the coffee shop of the bus terminal at George Washington Bridge, smoking, in desultory conversation with the waitress, the newspaper secured by her elbow. The paper is creased just as it was when she fished it out from under the kiosk's rain canopy, saved up for the hour of waiting. She allows herself to choose reports from the Contents instead of starting with the front page.

A federal court has indicted twenty-five persons in connection with the $407,000 in traveler's checks that disappeared last summer from Kennedy International Airport. They have the one who resold the checks for a quarter of their value, also the one who disposed of them for half, as well as those who cashed them, but they have not got the person who actually kicked them off the baggage truck; on July 11 the presumed tipster was found shot to death in a ditch outside Monticello, New York. The Mafia is busy on the telephone.

The child has sent her a postcard with her arrival time, a photograph showing her with some other children in a rowboat. Marie has one leg dangling in the water, and around her shin she has a wide, blackish bandage. Her expression is fearless, calm among the grimaces of the others. She bashed her shin against the binding of her water ski. Her height is four foot ten. Her handwriting has the curves and loops of the American model. In multiplying she writes the multiplier below, not beside, the multiplicand. She thinks in Fahrenheit, gallons, miles. Her English is superior to Gesine's in articulation, modulation, accent. German is for her a foreign language that she uses to her mother out of politeness, with a flat intonation, American-shaped vowels, often at a loss for a word. When she unthinkingly speaks English, Gesine does not always understand her. When she reaches fifteen she wants to be baptized, and she has persuaded the nuns at the private school on upper Riverside Drive to call her M'ree instead of Mary. Actually she was supposed to be expelled from this school for refusing to take off the GET OUT OF VIETNAM lapel button in class. As soon as she gets home, she pulls off the navy-blue school uniform with the crest on the left breast pocket; she likes best to wear tight pants made of white broadcloth, the hems of which she cuts off with a kitchen knife, and sneakers. She has given up scarcely one of the friendships made during her six years here; she still talks about Edmondo from Spanish Harlem who even in kindergarten could express his feelings only in blows and in 1963 was placed in an institution for life. She has stayed overnight in a number of apartments on Riverside Drive and West End Avenue. She is much in demand as a baby-sitter but is strict with the children, sometimes quite rough. She has the Manhattan subway system in her head; she could take a job with Information. What she types in her room she keeps in a folder tied with knots that defy counterfeit. She goes secretly to Gesine's box of photographs; she has used her pocket money to have a copy made of one picture showing Jakob and Jöche standing in front of the school for locomotive engineers in Güstrow. She has forgotten her friends in Düsseldorf. West Berlin is known to her from the newspaper. Many stores on Broadway owe her tribute, Maxie's with peaches, Schustek with sliced sausage, the liquor store with chewing gum. She bobs up and down over a slip of the tongue when she has said that Negroes are Negroes after all; she bobs up and down and makes a pushing gesture toward Gesine with outstretched upright palms, saying: "O.K.! O.K.!"

The second page of the paper carries a picture of an American pilot pointing on a map to where he shot down two North Vietnamese pilots; he is shown in profile, his lips drawn back over his teeth, his smile seems slack and satisfied. The official American dead are to be found today on page 12, seven lines unrelated to the news above. "Long Island Man Among War Dead," says the heading. The report states that there are twenty-eight.

Marie says:
They're my braids, not your braids, and I'll cut them off when I like.
My grandfather was well off.
Mrs. Kellogg shaves her legs.
I can stand the sight of blood. I want to be a doctor.
My mother thinks Negroes have equal rights, and at that point she stops thinking.
Negroes have a different anatomy from ours.
President Johnson is in the hands of the Pentagon.
James Fenimore Cooper is the greatest.
My father was a delegate to the International Conference on Railway Timetables in Lisbon. He represented the German Democratic Republic.
Düsseldorf-Lohausen is a hub of international air traffic.
My friends in England write me twelve times a year.
My mother is in banking.
My mother comes from a small town on the Baltic; one mustn't rub it in.
My mother has the most beautiful legs on the whole Number 5 bus above 72nd Street.
Fathers have such a hungry look.
Bring our boys home!
Sister Magdalena is an old bag.
John Vliet Lindsay is the greatest.
My mother and I always fly on the same plane so that we would die together.
If John Kennedy were alive, everything would be better.
My best friends are Pamela, Edmondo, Rebecca, Paul and Michelle, Stephen, Annie, Kathy, Ivan, Martha Johnson, David W., Paul-Erik, Mayor Lindsay, Mary-Anne, Claire and Richard, Mr. Robinson, Esmeralda and Bill, Mr. Maxie Fruit Market, Mr. Schustek, Timothy Shuldiner, Dmitri Weiszand, Jonas, D. E., and Senator Robert F. Kennedy.
My mother knows the Swedish ambassador.
Go ahead and get married, only I don't want a father.

I can speak Spanish better than my mother.

After two years my mother wanted to go back to Germany, and I said: "We're staying."

Among the national news items the New York *Times* also refers to the death of an industrial tycoon who started out in 1895 as a delivery boy at a dollar and a half a week and died leaving a fortune of two and a half billion dollars, and the paper devotes over two hundred lines to his memory.

The child walks past the glass wall of the restaurant. She has not turned her head, walks on in the midst of the crowd of parents and good-by proceedings. She is thinner; her skin is dry and tanned. She looks more than ten. She is wearing the Vietnam button on the collar of her windbreaker. Her braids swing slightly from side to side when she tries to look behind her in the glass panels of the exit. She stops and turns, and her left shoulder does not slide away from under Gesine's outstretched hand.

"Ich habe dich gesehen," she says, each syllable stressed, each word equally slow. She repeats: "I saw you," and this time a single, triumphant soprano tone rests on the word "saw." She does not resemble her father.

August 26, 1967   Saturday

Two U. S. Army sergeants have been arrested on charges of passing secret documents to Mr. Popov of the Soviet Embassy and Mr. Kiryev of the United Nations, in shopping centers, in restaurants, just like in the movies, and the gentlemen have left the country by air.

During attacks in North Vietnam American fighter-bombers came within 18 miles of China, and they lost the 660th plane, and the Secretary of Defense tells the astonished senators that North Vietnam cannot "be bombed to the negotiating table."

Prices have gone up so much that in July we had to pay 4.6 per cent more for fruit and vegetables than in June, and a member of the American Nazi Party shot his leader when the latter took his washing to a coin laundry, in Arlington, Virginia, and soap flakes swirled around the dead man.

Would she have stayed here, if not in the apartment on the street beside the river? She is not likely to have stayed had she not, after giving up the search, found the slender advertisement promising three rooms on Riverside Drive, "all facing the Hudson," available for a year at $124 a month. The voice on the telephone showed surprise at Gesine's questions. Certainly the apartment was overrun with applicants, "but we're waiting for someone we like." Children were allowed in the building. "If you happen to be colored, come anyway, don't worry."

During her first visit to New York Gesine had ridden a Number 5 bus down Riverside Drive, the inner edge of an extended artificial landscape that starts off with a promenade by the river, followed inland by a parkway with divided lanes and landscaped approach loops, and then by a spacious, hilly park fifty blocks long with monuments, playgrounds, sports grounds, lawns, and bench-bordered paths. Only then is the park framed by the street itself, bent at many points, curving over gentle humps in the road, stretching out narrow exit fingers behind more islands of green to the houses, unique in Manhattan, a horticultural display, a street with a view of the trees, the water, the landscape. At that time Gesine had wanted to live someday in one of these high bastions of prosperity, richly orna- mented in the Oriental, Italian, Egyptian, unfailingly magnificent style, their dignity rather increased through wind and weather, and she had imagined the street was beyond what she could afford.

Broadway, where it crosses 96th Street, is a market place of mostly small buildings, with many customers dropping in off the street at the Irish bar, the drugstore on the southwest corner, the food store across the way, at the newsstand, and, then as today, tattered men stood against building façades, stolen-goods receivers and thieves, drunks, lunatics, many of them black, unemployed, sick, some begging. The languages on this Broadway are varied, a confused interplay of accents from every continent with versions of American; passing by, one hears Spanish from Puerto Rico and Cuba, West Indian French, Japanese, Chinese, Yiddish, Russian, the jargons of illegal pursuits, and again and again German as it was spoken thirty years previously in East Prussia, Berlin, Franconia, Saxony, Hesse. The child heard a high-bosomed matron, old-fashioned in a flowered dress with bows, lecturing in German the little man creeping along beside her under his black hat, and the child halted, lost in a daydream, temporarily unaware of the tugging of Gesine's hand. It was a palish morning, with many people on the street moving along carefully against the moisture-laden air, and the intersection promis- ing the memory of Italy for many mornings to come. Ninety-seventh Street, sloping to the west, was murky between the decrepit, ema- ciated hotels, dirty with slimy refuse in the gutters, stained sacks and battered garbage pails on the sidewalks, and at the bottom it opened out onto a broad curving field formed by the flowing surface of Riverside Drive, grassy slopes, densely wooded summer park. On the playground, children were jumping around under the glittering jets of water. In the shade by the park fence, family groups lay and sat on the cool grass. Beyond the full-blown leafy treetops hung the blue-gray prospect of the other shore, of the mile-wide river. They stood for a while facing the buff brick building around whose base wound a strip of an exotic bull pattern. To live in this place seemed so far from reality, Gesine began to divide up her money into bribery sums, saw herself in complicated, dangerous negotiations.

The apartment begins with a tiny entrance hall, the left side of which contains a kitchenette in the wall and ends with the massive refrigerator. On the right it opens into a large room where two girls were packing paperbacks into cartons. They were about Gesine's age, one with a Danish, one with a Swiss accent, and they greeted the child first, solemnly and politely, as a person. This room has two windows facing the light open space across the street, onto the park. To the right the apartment continues with a smaller room behind curtained glass doors, with one window facing the park. The Danish girl had her bed in here. On the other side of the hall, next to the bathroom, which has a window facing the park, is the Swiss girl's former room behind a solid door, with a window on the park. In winter the steep New Jersey shore is visible through the bare branches, and the breadth of the river, the hazy air, can blur the architectural wasteland on the other side to an illusion of unspoiled countryside, to a vision of spaciousness and distance. The two girls were stewardesses who were being transferred to Europe. They wanted to leave their furniture behind for a year. They wanted to hand over the apartment at once. It was to cost nothing more than the rent. They asked Marie if she would like to stay here, and Marie used an English word: "Yes." The building manager, a heavy-set, dignified Negro with a resplendent British accent, gave change to the last cent for Gesine's down payment. The girls took them out for a meal, accepted their help in packing, and helped them to bring their luggage from the hotel, and the child seemed sad when they drove off that night to the airport. They did not return after a year, but we visit the Danish girl on our vacation. We had an apartment, and asked no more questions. During the seven years many handmade pieces of furniture have replaced the factory ones, first in Marie's room, the Danish one, then in the middle one, black-brown wood, a lime-green, glass-fronted bookcase, blue monk's-cloth curtains, a fluffy rug on which the child, lying on her stomach, reads aloud from the newspaper, her chin on her hands, swinging her legs. All day long an even expanse of swishing rain envelops the apartment.

Marie has been collecting pictures from the newspaper, and today she cuts out the one showing, in the foreground, the body of the Nazi leader collapsed beside his car, in the background, on the roof of the coin laundry, a policeman at the spot from which the other Nazi had fired. "Rabbi Lelyveld," she reads aloud, "says that Rockwell was a nuisance rather than a menace." The child goes on, in English, in a didactic tone: "I understand the distinction the Rabbi makes and what he doesn't want to say."

August 27, 1967   Sunday

The East Germans in power say: We are now introducing the five-day, 43¾-hour week, a unique socialist achievement. The American Nazi Party says: Our leader's body belongs to the Party. The wife of the arrested sergeant says: I don't believe it, my husband's not a spy. The New York *Times* says: In the United States the 40-hour week was introduced in 1938.

And once again the weather in North Vietnam had improved sufficiently for bombing raids, and the Pentagon implies that the others are using Communist China as a sanctuary for their aircraft, and yesterday morning three men raided the Schuyler Arms Hotel on 98th Street, shot and wounded the night porter, and got away with $68. That was about 3 A.M., two blocks from here.

And the New York *Times* devotes more than eight full columns, 184 inches, to Stalin's daughter, starting with the front page. So this unfilial daughter of Attila sits among the Goths on Long Island in a garden under a black oak tree and says: On the whole she is in favor of freedom.

She says, so the New York *Times* tells us: "I believe that when people have freedom to do whatever they want, and to express whatever they like, and to have even freedom to have riots—they do it."

She is referring to the Negro riots in Detroit.

So she was wearing a simple white dress and beige shoes as she expressed her thoughts in a relaxed, cheerful manner among a group of friends and journalists. The New York *Times* deems it necessary for us to know this.

This hope of salvation says: "I like dogs better than cats. I used to have a dog—but no more."

When asked whether she had a bank account, the daughter of

the leader of the socialist camp replies "Yes." Then she giggles and asks in return: "Do you?"

The New York *Times* acquaints us with the fact that the refugee-by-choice has had to learn how to write checks.

The daughter of the greatest socialist statesman says: "Although I always felt a personal attachment to my father, I was never an admirer of what was called 'Stalinism' as a system."

Then she asked for a glass of water, "with ice, please."

And when she spoke of her children she lowered her voice, looking off into the woods beyond the garden.

She says: "The chief evil influence in my father's life was what made him leave his priesthood and become a Marxist."

She says: "I think a religious feeling is inborn, just as a person is born to be a poet."

The New York *Times*, says the New York *Times*, will start on September 10 to publish excerpts from the book by Stalin's daughter. It says so neither at the beginning nor at the end, it says so casually and peripherally. The New York *Times* has confidence in its readers.

August 28, 1967   Monday

In a report on co-ordinated attacks by the Vietcong throughout the southern part of the country, the New York *Times* cites losses for that side (killed or wounded) as follows: in CanTho 268 (later 248), in Hoian 79, in Hue 1, in QuangDa and Dienban 53 or more, near Pleiku moderate, in Banme Thuot 13, near Saigon light, giving a total of 355.

In the early thirties Jerichow was one of the smallest towns in the state of Mecklenburg-Schwerin, a market town of 2,151 inhabitants lying inland from the Baltic between Lübeck and Wismar, a little place of low brick buildings fringing a cobbled road and extending from a two-story town hall with fake classical fluting to a Romanesque church with a spire like a bishop's miter: it is high and pointed, with smaller gables on all four sides.

Around the market square to the north, toward the sea, were a hotel, the mayor's office, a bank, the credit union, Wollenberg's hardward store, Papenbrock's house and business, the old town, with side streets branching off from here, Kattrepel, Short Street, the Bäk, School Street, Station Street. The south end, around church and cemetery, was where the original town had been, five alleyways between timbered houses, until it burned down in 1732, rebuilt only in the nineteenth century with squat brick houses, shoulder to shoulder under modest roofs, today the site of the post office, the co-op store, the brickyard beyond the cemetery, the brickyard owner's house. Around the town there were still many barns, the side streets soon turned into paths, and some of the store windows on the main street were flanked by wooden farmyard gates. There, on three hundred acres, lived farmer-townsmen, merchants, artisans. Cresspahl came from the south, along the road from Gneez, and drove through the main street past the market square out of Jerichow, for now he was expecting to see the town. Here the town came to an end, there were fields all the way to the sea.

Jerichow was not a town. It had a town charter dating from 1240, it had a town council, it was supplied with electricity from the Herrenwyk power plant, it had a dial telephone system, a railway, but Jerichow belonged to the nobility whose estates surrounded it. This had not been a result of the fire. The nobility had taken the farms of the peasants who had made the land arable, incorporated them into their own fields, made the peasants serfs; and the feeble ruling house of Mecklenburg, up to its ears in debt, had confirmed the nobility in these rights by way of the reciprocal inheritance treaty of 1755. Of the villages that had made Jerichow strong, only three tiny, humble settlements remained. In this corner of the world the nobility ruled over its day laborers as employer, mayor, magistrate, risen to fame as robber barons, to prosperity as entrepreneurs. Jerichow had now almost reverted to its original state—village in a clearing. It was excluded from shipping because of the great ports and its distance from the sea. At the place that could have been a port for Jerichow there was now the fishing village of Rande, at the turn of the century already rich enough for hotels warranting such names as the Archduke, the City of Hamburg. Jerichow had remained a station on the way to Rande, and the diligences of earlier days, like the buses of today, yielded no free-spending summer visitors here. Trade did not come via the narrow country roads; the highways bypassed it far to the south. Jerichow suited the nobility the way it was, as an office, a warehouse, a trading post, a place from which to ship their wheat and sugar beets. The nobility did not need a town. Jerichow got its railway to Gneez on the main line between Hamburg and Stettin because the local nobility needed transportation. Jerichow was too poor to build sewers; the nobility did not need them. There was no movie in Jerichow; the nobility did not approve of this invention. Jerichow's industry, the brickworks, was in the hands of the nobility.

The nobility owned the bank, most of the buildings, the Lübeck Arms. The Lübeck Arms had a septic tank. The nobility bought spare parts for their machines in Jerichow, used the administration, the police, the attorneys, Papenbrock's granaries, but their more important business was conducted in Lübeck; they sent their children to boarding schools in Prussia, held church services in their own chapels, and had themselves buried behind their country seats. At harvest time, when it was too far to go to Ratzeburg or Schwerin, they drove to the Lübeck Arms in the evening and played cards at their own table, pompous, genial, droning men, wallowing in their Low German dialect. Because of the Lübeck license number on his car, they took Cresspahl sitting over his beer for a traveling salesman.

Jerichow called its main street, the narrow cutting that dated from its origins as a forest clearing, Town Street.

At breakfast Cresspahl inquired about the weather. He went into the little stores, bought stationery or good-quality shirts, and asked a few casual questions. He stood for a while on the path behind the yard of Heinz Zoll, who did the cabinetwork around here, and had a good look at the lumber stored in his open shed. He began having his beer at Peter Wulff's inn. Peter Wulff was his age, less stout in those days, a lackadaisical, taciturn innkeeper who observed Cresspahl's patient waiting just as this customer observed him. Cresspahl wrote a postcard to Richmond and gave it to the hotel porter to mail. He went to see Jansen the attorney. He walked to Rande and had dinner at the City of Hamburg Hotel. He read all the advertisements in the *Gneezer Tageblatt* on the page for Jerichow and the surrounding area. He did not slacken his pace when he passed Papenbrock's gate, but his walks took him past it, and before long he knew that the young man in charge of unloading sacks in the yard was Horst Papenbrock, the son and heir, then thirty-one years old. Between receding chin and receding forehead Horst's face was as pointed as a fish. Cresspahl could see old Papenbrock through the open window, sitting at his desk, sweating above his comfortable, sensitive stomach, nodding with such strenuous politeness that he seemed to be bowing while sitting down. Evidently he did not like bargaining, or bargaining for long, with high-class clientele, this Papenbrock who was so stingy that he refused to own a private car and drove his family to Travemünde for coffee and cakes in his delivery truck. My mother did not see Cresspahl. He saw my grandmother helping behind the counter in the bakery, a deferential, spry old lady with rather a cloying manner of speech, especially with children. Here Cresspahl would nod through the open door as he passed.

and I never was a silly sheep, Gesine.
They threw you onto your side, they tied your hooves together, they pinned your neck to the threshing floor with their knees, they ripped off your fleece with blunt shears, and you never opened your mouth, Louise née Utecht from Hageböck Street in Güstrow, you silly sheep.

Cresspahl knew that Horst Papenbrock and Griem the farmer were Nazis and had to go to Gneez for their brawls because the Social Democrats in Jerichow were their neighbors, relatives, town councilors. He knew that Papenbrock, with his grain business, his bakery, his rural deliveries, was the richest man in Jerichow, and that he also lent money. He knew that the only historical monument here was a Napoleonic redoubt, on the coast, five miles away. He knew that Jerichow could not support more than one cabinetmaker.

August 29, 1967   Tuesday

On Third Avenue, north of 42nd Street, houses dating from the last century have been left standing, four and five stories of what were once elegant façades of brownstone or expensive brick, but greasy soot has lodged in the stone, the windows are smeared and dusty, and only the street level is occupied, by small businesses, cafés, bars, obscuring the dead buildings above them with their neon signs and awnings. They have all they can do to take care of customers coming in off the street; there is hardly any steady local trade. The future of the street is to be the steel and glass office buildings that are recessed above block-wide, ten-story bottoms, and which from the twentieth floor up are stacked in identical layers, still sixty feet wide at the fiftieth floor. The tinted glass and metal between the strips of window may be dark blue, gray, green, yellow; some buildings also have brick columns stuck onto the supporting beams; a further difference is the names on the street-level marble veneer. The buildings are easily demolishable, and their names have been neither chiseled nor embedded in the walls, but cemented or screwed on, for convenient removal.

The building in which Miss Cresspahl earns her living consists of a twelve-story plinth extending the width of the block, surmounted by a recessed terrace, and topped by a smooth tower. The glass between the shining ribs is bordered with blue-gray strips. Most of the windows are slatted with Venetian blinds, but a little fluorescent light manages to shimmer through the cracks. From across the street she should be able, with head thrown back, to make out her two windows, but she invariably loses count. At street level half the outer layer of the building has been furnished as an ordinary bank behind giant-sized show windows that are neither tinted nor ribbed nor draped and draw the eye in toward the imitation-leather sofas and chairs, low tables, desks on islands of carpet, rows of tellers' windows under the eye of automatic cameras, the highly polished steel door of the vault. The bank, a living room as big as a station waiting room, is still empty. In the other half of the building at street level is a restaurant that shields its customers from the light of day with pale-green curtains. The building's main entrance with its four swinging doors sucks in so many people from the sidewalk that the hurrying pedestrians get out of step. Behind a wall of pale marble the foyer opens to the left into three elevator lanes; the far end leads to the preserve of the building management; the wall on the right is occupied by a long counter with newspapers, candy, and cigarettes. Each elevator lane is individually controlled by a supervisor in a blue-gray uniform with the company's name embroidered in script on the left breast pocket. She manages a nod to him. As she enters one of the elevators, whose green light indicates that it is going up, she looks at the street number let into the floor to show the passenger whether he is in the wrong building. Among the twenty-five or so occupants she sees not one familiar face today. As the double steel doors snap shut in front of her, it is nine minutes to nine.

"And how was the office today, Gesine?"

Mrs. Williams is back, and she didn't make it to Greece after all because she was scared of the military. A third circular urges employees to lock their desks during lunch hour and to take their handbags with them whenever they leave the office, because of recurrent thefts on the tenth floor. The latest rumor is that we have bought Xerox. My boss had to fly to Hawaii this afternoon; his son is being sent there from South Vietnam to recuperate.

"Anything in the newspaper?"

Mahalia Jackson is in the hospital in West Berlin.

August 31, 1967   Thursday

The Vietcong continue their raids in the south. The Soviets are conducting a secret trial of three authors. The Chinese force the British Chargé d'Affaires in Peking to bend his head by pulling his hair; in retaliation, they say. Six more cemeteries have rejected the body of the Nazi leader; the party has now cremated him and is maintaining an armed guard over the ashes.

What kind of person does Gesine have in mind when she thinks of the New York *Times* as Auntie?

An elderly person. At the high school in Gneez teachers used to be called that, ladies advanced in years, educated in the humanities, earnestly deploring the trend of the times, in private conversation only, with no solution either. Once they had wanted to alter the trend of the times by studying at old Imperial universities, by going camping and canoeing with men without a marriage license, by earning their own living to the dismay of their middle-class families, whose articles of faith they later, as they themselves grew old, gray-haired, tramping about on sturdy soles and perhaps in slacks, defended against the changing times: it is not right to hoist Revolution into the saddle; perhaps she hasn't had enough riding lessons. One has to think of the horse, too. True, if made in class, a statement such as this would have meant dismissal. They were called Auntie indulgently, not unkindly, not without pity. (The name Auntie for kindergarten teachers, those guardian-heroines, was spiteful. Unathletic boys, timid girls, were called Auntie, with contempt.) However, to Gesine the New York *Times* seems like an aunt from a good family. The family has built up a fortune on the labors of others, but not ruthlessly, just in tune with the times. The family has rendered services to all governments, and all governments are on record. Family tradition is carried on in this surviving aunt. Gesine visualizes age, a lean figure, the face deeply lined, the mouth curved in bitterness, but the clothes dark and elegant, the hair still piled high, a harsh voice, smiles only in the corners of the eyes. An access of rage never. In her bearing, her stance, she flirts with her age; it is the token of her experience. She has been around, she has looked life in its narrow-lipped face; there is no fooling her. She has had her affairs, but she was most certainly not an adventuress, everything took place with propriety in the best hotels in Europe; that is all in the past. She so obviously claims respect that she almost invites its refusal. She tends to be obstinate, a bit of a nuisance in fact, when she feels excluded by younger people. She likes to see young people having fun so long as she is the one to dole out the fun. Gesine imagines a living room, a drawing room, furnished in Empire style, where the aunt holds court. Everything is very decorous, the elders are listened to first. There is tea, there is whisky. After that there is tea. The old lovers come to remember, the younger generation to be instructed. The staff is fanatically discreet. Auntie smokes (cigarillos), she is not above hard liquor; she enjoys a joke as long as she is not forced, in the public interest, to call it unacceptable. She keeps abreast of the times. She can cook, she can bake. Auntie has remained single, an indication that she is without peer. She gives advice on marital problems, she can imagine what marriage is like (the job of a music critic being to criticize music, not to write symphonies. Or even sonatas). She is up-to-date. (In her own family Gesine has no such aunt.) This is a person whom you can persuade to go along with anything any day the law requires it.

Nevertheless this person is something more than merely agreeable.

Her manners are useful, they set a good example.

She never raises her voice, she delivers a discourse.

On fifteen by twenty-three inches, in eight columns, she offers a free choice of over twenty stories.

She waits before calling an accused person guilty. Of the city's two murders a day she mentions only the instructive ones.

She never calls the President by his first name, but a murder victim she does.

She refers to hearsay as hearsay.

She grants those whom she despises an opportunity to be heard.

She addresses sportsmen in the language of sportsmen.

And she calls attention to changing Nature.

She helps the poor by charitable donations, and she examines poverty by scientific methods.

She decries disproportionate sentencing.

She is at least compassionate.

She is impartial toward all forms of religion.

She preserves the purity of the language, even correcting her clients' advertisements.

She offers the reader a maximum of two advertisement pages with no news item (except Sundays).

She never swears, nor does she take the name of the Lord in vain.

She occasionally admits to errors.

She can restrain herself and call a murderer a controversial character, from brigadier general up.

She learned good manners in the nursery. Why should we not trust her?

September 1, 1967   Friday

The American commander in South Vietnam says: The North Vietnamese are lying. Radio Hanoi claims American losses (dead, wounded, missing) for the first six months of this year to be 110,000. He says the figure is 37,038.

As of today, the divorce law of 1787 is no longer valid. Anyone marrying now must wait two years before being free again.

"You don't have to marry me," says D. E. "I just want you to live with me."

D. E. sends flowers, telegrams, theater tickets, books. He takes Marie out to dinner, has made friends with Esther, listens to Mr. Robinson's stories about his military service in West Germany. D. E. lives in New Jersey, but he spends a lot of time in the bars around 96th Street on Broadway, two blocks from Riverside Drive. On the telephone he can almost always say: "I'm right around the corner." D. E. is close to forty, a tall fellow who wears Irish tweed and Italian jackets, with a long, fleshy, patient face above which he wears his hair long and parted, as if to hide his age. D. E. weighs two hundred and twenty-four pounds and moves nimbly on small feet. D. E. drives a powerful English car, his suits are in carefully chosen colors, D. E. does not want for much. D. E. works for the war industry.

D. E. says: "I work in Defense."

Gesine first heard D. E.'s name in Wendisch Burg, in 1953. He had gone to the same school from which Klaus Niebuhr and the Babendererde girl had resigned that spring, and he was to be barred from studying physics in East Berlin after standing up at a faculty meeting and calling the Babendererde case an example of violation of constitutional rights in the German Democratic Republic (on the part of the Government of the German Democratic Republic). Not then and there, but after the June rebellion, he left the country. No doubt he made up his mind with the aid of a list of pros and cons similar to the kind he draws up today when unable to make up his mind about cars or houses or political opinions. On one side of that list had been Wendisch Burg, the East German brand of socialism, and a dragged-out affair with Eva Mau. The other side of his balance sheet showed: Prospects for my continuing education are not favorable here. Thus he had not had to make up his own mind.

Gesine had first seen him at the Marienfeld refugee camp in West Berlin, a skinny youth with a straight, narrow head and, at that time, fair hair, who showed an absent-minded solicitude for her by questioning her about Jerichow and holding forth on political theory with much recourse to the language of physics. The only topic that presented no problem for them was the Babendererde case. He made no effort to have himself allocated to the same town as Gesine. She saw him for only two days before he was flown out to West Germany. He was said to have told the board of admissions: I decided in favor of the lesser evil. So they let him go to Stuttgart, he wrote his doctoral thesis in Hanover, from West Germany he went to England, and he was bought into the U. S. A. in 1960. He did write postcards, sometimes letters, mainly concerned with the exploits and adventures of Eva Mau, and from Stuttgart young Mrs. Niebuhr wrote accounts of D. E.'s fleeting affairs in an admiring, almost respectful tone. To this day the Babendererde girl speaks of D. E. as of an older relative, as if she owed him a debt of gratitude. Gesine had been in New York for eleven months before he found her as he was leafing through the telephone directory and invited her to their first dinner, a bulky, taciturn, somewhat pompous fellow who proposed marriage to her after he had met Marie.

D. E. works for a firm in an industrial park in New Jersey that is involved in the DEW Line. D E W stands for Distant Early Warning, a line consisting of radar stations surrounding the NATO territories and designed to give warning of Soviet rockets in time for an American counterattack. He must have promised the military more than his favoring of the lesser evil before they allowed him to take up this work and regarded their secrets as safe with him. He scarcely works in the scientific end now; he is a technician. By this time he is earning twenty-five thousand dollars a year, and part of his job consists of inspection trips to England, Italy, France, Denmark, Norway, with an embassy representative waiting at the passport control. According to D. E., his colleague in Soviet Russia is confined at a military airport and carries on a black-market business in technical literature. His firm can count on government orders for the improved systems of the seventies, and D. E. can count on the confidence that the firm places in his abilities. D. E. does his best to reduce these abilities by the regular consumption of alcohol.

The home D. E. offers us stands beside a broad stream in a

wooded area of New Jersey. It is an old colonial house of white clapboard, with a blue slate roof. He now owns almost half of it. The house is looked after by D. E.'s mother, a shy, bony woman with a passion for housework who has learned her English from her maids. D. E. was one of the few who had the foresight to get their families out of East Germany before the open frontier in Berlin was closed. The place consists of a few scattered houses, and D. E.'s mother has derived her image of the United States from a similarity with the countryside around Wendisch Burg, and most of all from television programs. She is so proud of her son that she wants to be buried where he has found success. Her behavior toward Gesine is cautious, almost formal, as if she had fears to dispel. She sighs over D. E. when he goes off into his study in the evening with the French red wine he buys by the case from an importer, but she says nothing, and every morning she puts out two bottles for him. D. E. sits at his steel chunk of a desk, a ponderous, melancholy figure in the night, and telephones to the island of Manhattan. He says: Dear Miss Mary, quite contrary, why don't you come and see me, the weekend is so long. I'll make you a barbecue in the garden, I'll drive you to the beach. He says: If she doesn't want to, let me come and see you both.

You just don't want to be alone when you die.
But with me there the child would be taken care of.

Unfortunately, D. E. has got around the child. Marie laughs at the funny faces he makes, especially the one of hurt dignity, at his display of drawling Mecklenburg dialect, at his mimicking of Southern or New England accents, and she envies him his English, for in languages D. E. is a parrot. Marie believes his tales full of unexpected twists, about the woman who beat a policeman over the head with her shoe outside St. Patrick's Cathedral, about his cats, who can count, about the vice-presidents of his firm who wage war on each other on the eighth floor. Marie invents codes, now that he has taught her coding systems. Marie admires his behavior in restaurants, and the fact that he can afford restaurants on the fifty-second floor. At night Marie opens her door a crack when D. E. sits among his bottles after dinner and talks, about laser beams, about the political history of Mecklenburg, about Tom's bar. Marie regards the two guest rooms upstairs in D. E.'s house as their personal, inalienable property. Even his name has been given to him by her because she enjoys the slight hiccup between D and E. She does not mind his drinking (he doesn't lie around on the emergency-exit steps of the movie on 97th Street, in rags, scaly with dirt and beard, snoring hoarsely, one hand still grasping the bottle in the brown-paper bag, he's not a Broadway bum, he's a professor). Once when D. E. told them he was coming over, Marie went to the telephone and ordered a supply of red wine and Gauloise cigarettes, paying for it out of the housekeeping money. But D. E. arrives with grocery bags on each arm, flowers tucked under one armpit, chocolate bars wedged between his fingers, and his droning voice is audible from the corridor, kidding Mr. Robinson, and Mr. Robinson waits in the open elevator door to watch D. E. go into the Cresspahl apartment, head raised, sniffing the air, calling out in awed wonder: "Ah, that go-od Mecklenbu-urgian cooking!" And Marie laughs.

September 2, 1967   Saturday

During the night, until early in the morning, the cars crept bumper to bumper beside the river into the long weekend, sending short waves of muffled sound through the open windows on Riverside Drive. D. E. insisted on comparing it to artillery fire. Now the weekenders have left silence in their wake, and up to 660 of them, it is predicted, will have died in traffic accidents by the time Labor Day is over.

The morning is cool, light, dry in the park. This playground, sprinkled with white light, belongs to Gesine's very beginnings in New York; it was here that Marie brought her in touch with her first neighbors. This morning she sits on one of the benches at the edge of the arena and looks down on the half-naked children running around in the intersecting jets of water that spout from three nozzles. She is waiting for Mrs. Ferwalter, who spends Sabbath mornings here in the summertime. By half turning around she can see through the leaves the blue-curtained window behind which D. E. is sleeping off his wine, spread naked right across the bed, his arms along his sides, breathing shallowly through pouting lips, alone in the apartment.

Mrs. Ferwalter is a short, obese woman, mother of Rebecca, a sturdy person with a taste for loose-fitting red dresses. Her cheekbones are wide-set, her forehead is narrow above almost black eyes and eyebrows, and the curve of her head as it tapers toward a narrow chin recalls the face of her girlhood. Now it is swaddled in age, immobilized in a rigid expression of disgust of which she is unaware. She was born in 1922; she looks like a woman of sixty. Six years ago on this playground Mrs. Ferwalter heard Gesine talking German to her child, and she got up from the next bench, approached on her plump legs, heavy-footed, and sat down beside Gesine. "Maybe mein Kind can play mit yours," she said good-naturedly, with an accent that sounded almost Russian. She looked like someone who is recovering from a dangerous illness. Her coarse brown hair was short, unevenly cut as after a skull operation. She wore a sleeveless dress, and as she leaned on the bench with her arm to sit down Gesine saw the number tattooed on the inside of her left forearm. Her eyes went to the woman's pudgy legs but found no relief in the prominent varicose veins.

"I'm from Germany," Gesine had said, and Mrs. Ferwalter had replied, sighing over the dry heat, or nostalgically: "I could tell. Europe . . ."

She had already summoned Rebecca, then five years old, a well-behaved child with her mother's hair, doll-like with her small suspicious mouth, her dark eyebrows, wide starched collar, neatly pressed jacket and skirt, and, doll-like, jerkily, she bobbed a curtsy to Gesine. Marie approached warily, step by step, turning aside from time to time but unable to control her curiosity. The two children stood with their hands behind their backs and looked at each other with disdain, but Mrs. Ferwalter ordered severely: "Go and play nicely!" and Rebecca obediently led the strange child over to the swings. Mrs. Ferwalter began to praise Marie: "Your child is so quiet. She doesn't race around. She doesn't scream at her mother. She's not American. She's European. They know how to bring up children in Europe," she had said in her broken English, broken German, gazing after the children with eyes that narrowed, almost blinked, her small lips pursed in the strain of disgust.

Mrs. Ferwalter comes from a Ruthenian village, in eastern Slovakia, "where the Jews lived like in a nest." She stresses that it was a "good" village. The Christians tolerated those of the other faith, and the fifteen-year-old girl was not molested by the teen-age boys at the Christian end of the village, even in the evening. We can't ask her about her parents. "I wasn't pretty. They said I was cute." "My hair hung down below my waist." In 1944 she was handed over to the Germans, probably by the Hungarians (we can't ask her about that). The Germans took her to the Mauthausen concentration camp. "One of the wardresses, she was so kind, she had five kids, and she had to do all those things, you know." She meant an SS female guard. We can't ask her about that. In a photo taken in 1946 she has the face of a thirty-five-year-old woman, smooth-skinned. She tried to stay in Czechoslovakia and in 1947 married a saddler with a small leather-goods business in Budweis. The Communist putsch made the country where she had grown up unsafe, and in 1958, by way of Turkey, Israel, and Canada, she arrived in the United States. The doctors call the fat in her shoulders, her neck, throughout her whole body, a symptom of the concentration-camp syndrome. Part of this syndrome is her restlessness, her sleeplessness, and a permanent inflammation of the respiratory tract with which she can cope only by sucking the mucus into her throat with a harsh, scraping sound. We haven't asked her about all this. During the six years she has spoken of these things, casually and incidentally, the way one mentions fragments of one's life to friends.

Mrs. Ferwalter was the first of the European emigrants on Riverside Drive to advise Gesine about the neighborhood; she suggested a kindergarten for Marie, pointed out stores with imported food, warned her of shops run by "bad" Jews, and consistently drew attention to all the "European" elements on Manhattan's Upper West Side. She is homesick for the taste of Budweis bread, and perhaps she has clung to Gesine during these six years, with telephone calls and walks and chats in Riverside Park, because this German woman knows the taste of the bread she misses.

On Saturday mornings she waits in the park for her husband and son, who have gone to the synagogue. She herself takes liberties with her God, but she sees to it that Rebecca does not desecrate the Sabbath by starting to run around with other children or getting too close to the ice-cream man. When she calls out to her daughter her voice is audible across the whole playground, a shrill screech, and Rebecca trails morosely round and round the bench from which Mrs. Ferwalter governs. But when Mrs. Ferwalter thinks herself unobserved she leans toward Gesine and says, with a wink in Rebecca's direction and a conspiratorial smile: "She knows how to walk, that child. She's got long legs, that child." She has Gesine read aloud to her from the paper; she would never spend money on a paper. Rebecca's school costs money, and her husband doesn't earn much as the manager of a small shoe store on Broadway. She moves her legs this way and that, crosses her ankles, shifts about on the bench. She cannot sit still. She nods with her fat chin, disgusted, revolted, by the news that the Soviets have expelled two United States diplomats because the United States has barred two Soviet diplomats. She nods, as if she knew all about espionage.

Mrs. Ferwalter has got to her feet and walked to the playground entrance where, between her husband and son, both ceremoniously attired in black suits and squat black felt hats, Marie is pushing the cart with next week's groceries, straining and thin-lipped with responsibility, and Mrs. Ferwalter leads Marie over to the playground, one arm laid tenderly about her shoulders, and presents her to Gesine, crying: "She's a sport! Just like a real Czech!"

Now her mouth is relaxed, and her eyes are wide open.

September 3, 1967   Sunday

On a day like today, thirty-six years ago. On a white day like this, cool under a hard blue sky, in clean, swift-moving air. On the beach promenade in Rande, beside the gray and green sea, across from the sharp and lowering outline of the Holstein coast. Keep to the sunny side under the fluttering leaves. Cresspahl's voice must have been a deep bass at that time, with throaty initial vowels, in the Low German dialect of Malchow; my mother's, small, flexible, a high contralto. Now and again a High German expression escapes her: "God willing," or "for Mother's sake." She has dropped behind her parents, and Louise Papenbrock keeps turning her head over her shoulder toward the stranger who might be asking her daughter the time.

> *But what's going to come of it?*
> *Why don't we wait and see?*
> *But you've got something in mind.*
> *That's what I'm waiting to see.*

Front page. From the New York *Times* correspondent in Bonn. Ilse Koch, "the Beast of Buchenwald," was found dead in her cell yesterday. Her neck hung in a noose made from sheets and tied to the door latch. She was sixty.

> *My name is Cresspahl. I am forty-three. My father was a wheelwright on the Bobzin estate near Malchow and is dead. My mother has a livelihood in Malchow. I am a carpenter.*
> *A cabinetmaker.*
> *I can also make cartwheels.*
> *I am twenty-five and am to marry someone in Lübeck.*

Ilse Koch, a plump person with vivid green eyes and flaming red hair (according to the New York *Times*), born in Dresden, in 1937 married a friend of Hitler's, the commandant of the Buchenwald concentration camp, in a spectacular pagan night ceremony that took place outdoors. The Kochs then lived in a mansion not far from the camp.

Would you care to be my wife?
Well, I learned my English at a boarding school, with a Rostock accent.

51,572 anti-Nazis, Jews, and forced laborers from all over Europe died in Buchenwald. On her morning rides Ilse Koch beat prisoners with her riding crop, she gave orders for beatings and executions, and compelled prisoners to take part in orgies of a sadistic and perverse nature. She ordered the killing of tattooed camp inmates for her collection: she made lamps from their bones, and lampshades, gloves, and book covers from their skin.

Are we going to change our name when we become British subjects?
If you like.
I'd rather keep your name.

During the trial of Ilse Koch in 1947 a Dr. Konrad Morgen, former SS investigator, prosecutor, and judge, was interrogated. In 1943 he had been ordered by the SS to examine the Koch case. According to his findings she was an incurable moral degenerate, a perverted, nymphomaniacal, hysterical, power-mad she-devil. Her handicrafts disappeared after this investigation. Karl Koch was shot by the Nazis in the last days of the war.

My older brother didn't turn out well, he's in South America.
My sister is married and living in Krakow
    to an attorney who embezzles trust funds.
And Horst isn't exactly his dad's pride and joy. Unfortunately I'm now the favorite child and being sent to the city. You must tell them you earn four thousand marks a year.
I can say six.
And that Hitler is an Austrian.
Tell Horst that?
My father.
If you like.

During her detention Ilse Koch became pregnant, so the Allies sentenced her to life imprisonment only. Later the sentence was reduced to four years (in the opinion of one witness: because she had helped supply the Allies with incriminatory material for the Nuremberg trial). The West Germans arrested her in 1949 when she was released from Landsberg Prison and in a new trial sentenced her to life imprisonment.

Do you sleep with a pillow? Do you believe in God? Is Richmond far from the sea?

In October 1966 the Bavarian Government rejected Ilse Koch's application for a pension. In 1962 Ilse Koch had also applied to the European Commission for Human Rights.

Do you want children, Heinrich Cresspahl?

September 4, 1967   Monday, Labor Day

Are we to believe this? That more than three hundred Czechoslovak intellectuals have launched an appeal to the West to join in a protest campaign against their own censorship authorities, and of all people to the author John Steinbeck? We don't think we will believe this. Steinbeck has visited the war in Vietnam, and what he saw there did not displease him. Nevertheless the New York *Times* seems to believe the report and publishes it on the front page.

The Vietcong have marked election day in South Vietnam by staging terrorist attacks and shellings against the voters in twenty-one provinces. At least twenty-six civilians are dead. The Americans carried out bombing raids near Hanoi.

The New York *Times* draws our attention to the weather. As evidence it publishes a picture taken at the corner of 89th Street and Riverside Drive, massed treetops around a monument glittering in the sunshine, almost no pedestrians, some parked cars. Nearer, Arcadia, to thee.

The city is silent. The ear misses the sound of car engines, helicopters, sirens. The light is as white as it was yesterday. Above the city, the wind from the Great Lakes has driven all the soiled clouds out onto the Atlantic, for two days the chimney stacks have not been smoking, and the air is clear, cool, and swift. It is the first weekend this year with no rain. From Riverside Drive, across the whole width of the Hudson, the brownish cubes and cylinders are clearly and unmistakably visible on the New Jersey shore, modern architecture, the ruined view that in the 1880's was to be pre-empted for Riverside Drive.

The houses on this street, scarcely one less than ten stories high, were built for the new aristocracy of the nineteenth century, for the new money, railway money, mine money, natural-gas money, oil money, speculation money, the money of the industrial explosion. Riverside Drive was to surpass Fifth Avenue as a residential area, with its baronial entrances, impressive foyers, eight-room suites, servants' quarters, concealed service entrances, uniformed staff, with the private view of the river, the wilderness of swelling treetops on the distant steep shore, of Nature. On all of Riverside Drive there is not a business, not a store, only two or three hotels, though even these are residential hotels for permanent guests. Where commerce did dwell, it wished to be aristocratic. Here lived such figures as William Randolph Hearst, in fact he lived on three floors that he later converted into a hall three stories high and containing his private elevator, then added more floors until he bought all twelve, in 1913. In those days an address on Riverside Drive spelled fortune and credit, power and princely rank. It was a street for White Anglo-Saxon Protestants. After World War I they were joined by those Jews from Harlem who found their formerly exclusive quarters no longer appropriate to their station in life, as well as by the immigrants from the Lower East Side whose incomes had meanwhile become adequate for the prestige of this address, emigrants who had made it. During the thirties the Jews from Germany arrived, at first with all their household belongings in crates, then with no baggage, then from the German-occupied territories of Europe, and after the war came the survivors of the concentration camps, and finally the citizens of the state of Israel, inveterate Europeans who had been unable to cope with the siege and the climate of Israel, with the result that on Riverside Drive and West End Avenue behind it a Jewish colony had gathered, linked by religion, linked by blood ties, linked by the memory of Europe.

The Belgians used to call me Madame, *and the Americans call me* Darling. *In Europe children bow when they meet grownups. My family had been in Germany for five hundred years. My father used to come home with a long loaf of French bread under his arm. My father was—.*

Your father was killed by the Germans, Mrs. Blumenroth.
My father died young, Mrs. Cresspahl.

Riverside Drive did not surpass Fifth Avenue as a residential area; President Kennedy's widow does not live here. Retired people live here, middle-income families, white-collar workers, students. Countess Seydlitz lives here. Ellison the writer lives here. (The helper at Schustek the butcher's would refuse to move here; he believes in having his own lawn in front of his own house.) Most of the buildings still consider themselves above having dark-skinned citizens as tenants; Negroes are permitted to manage them, maintain them, operate the elevator, polish the brass. And in these monuments to prosperity age lurks like a neglected disease. Some of the elegant suites have been converted into economical bachelor apartments, and many of the neighbors complain of leaky heating systems, rattles in the plumbing, a series of defects in the elevators, and in the lobbies that soft membrane of dirt on the marble paneling and antiquated furniture that by now defies water and broom. In some buildings the rents have been frozen by law since the war. Doormen, who not only greet tenants but are also supposed to scare away burglars and kidnappers, are a rare sight these days, and as often as not the manned elevators have been replaced by automatic ones in which the occupants eye a stranger with caution. Apartments are still in demand here and are rented as soon as they become vacant. The ceilings are high, the floor plan is old-fashioned, the walls muffle sound; the management attends to garbage and repairs. The street is considered almost safe. (On the park benches there is much talk these days of the homosexuals who hang around in summertime at the Soldiers' and Sailors' Monument and call it the wedding cake.) And the street is among the quiet ones. It sees two parades a year at most. Long grass grows in the pavement cracks. During two seasons of the year the noise of motors from the Hudson Parkway is filtered through the park foliage, and except during the rush hour Riverside Drive is a street of local traffic, empty and silent at night until 6 A.M., when the first people drive to work and the hollow whistle from the railway under the contours of the park will penetrate shallower sleep tomorrow morning. This is where we live.

September 5, 1967 Tuesday

At six thirty yesterday evening four policemen patrolling one of the Brooklyn ghettos came upon four or five young Negroes who were attacking an old white man. They managed to seize one youth, and they shot another in the back of the head. A crowd rushed up hurling bottles and rocks at the police with shouts of "Kill him!" A liquor store was looted by youths, other store windows were smashed. The police removed their barricades around the area some time before midnight, but just after eleven 15 Molotov cocktails exploded in the street. The youth who was shot had already been dead for two hours. Richard Ross, aged fourteen.

The Soviet Union is believed to have delivered 500 million dollars' worth of arms to developing countries since 1955.

Sometimes the bank's elevators dip a little as they start to rise, as if the machines were genuflecting. Nearly twenty people in the ascending elevator listen to two girls complaining doggedly but not angrily about the corner store. While it is true that the place has not raised the price of coffee, it has recently started using smaller containers; Gesine meets the amused glances of her neighbors, who start exchanging nods. The little movements of the neck make them look like people just waking up. All the buttons on the panel beside the door are lit up, the elevator will stop at every floor. "That's right, a local," she agrees, smiling, absent-minded. In the lighted slots over the doors the firm's name appears twelve times, twelve times the same three words with the red five-stroke symbol, without naming the departments, except for the third floor: Reception. On the third floor visitors are screened and the records of minor transactions kept. On the fourth floor the two girls with their coffee containers in paper bags get out, and again some of the occupants smile, as if something predictable had occurred. On the fourth floor are the accounting machines. Her first job in this country had been at an accounting machine, a yard-wide work surface, third on the left in a row of twelve, at a calculating machine whose rattle detached itself from the miasma of noise in the big room and penetrated her ear with a strangely individual note. On the fifth floor are the stationery supplies and the central mailing office. She has not been on the fifth floor since Mrs. Williams began providing her with paper, pencils, and typewriter ribbons. At first she put up a resistance to being waited on; then she realized that Mrs. Williams enjoyed these errands spread over the day. The sixth floor, called East and West after the coasts, was where she had started out in this building, at a metal filing cabinet in the general office, visible from all four sides, at a typewriter, and at the extension telephone of one of the department heads. On the seventh floor are the cafeteria and conference rooms. The larger coffee mugs are still being used in the cafeteria, and many get out here to take advantage of this. On the eighth floor are the engineering and personnel departments; on the ninth the bank's memory; on the tenth the legal department and library. From the elevator's frosted-glass sky a loose tube casts small flickers of darkness, as in a thunderstorm; blurred background music mingles with the clatter of the sliding door and the ping of the signal in the corridor. On the eleventh floor Gesine gets out and turns west. The building is divided into two halves by the passenger and service elevator shafts, and this floor houses the South American department in its eastern section and part of Western Europe in its western section. (Although in Europe the eleventh floor would have been the tenth, in her own mind it is already the eleventh.) The heavy door wheezes and slaps shut behind her.

> Good morning, Jee-zine.
> Good morning.

September 6, 1967   Wednesday

Fifty-four Americans and 160 North Vietnamese have been killed since yesterday morning in actions in the Queson Valley, 136 North Vietnamese at Tamky, three Americans near Nuibaden Mountain, 16 Vietnamese near CanTho, five Americans and 37 Vietnamese at Conthien, 34 Vietnamese in Quang Ngai Province.

Last night Negroes in the Brownsville section of Brooklyn again hurled rocks, bottles, and Molotov cocktails at police and firemen. The air was thick with the smoke of ignited trash cans and piles of rubbish. Mayor Lindsay met with ghetto spokesmen at a police station. The New York *Times* mentions that he wore a blue suit and a blue knit sport shirt.

In the early hours of yesterday morning a man rushed into the Bluebird Tavern in the Bronx, fired eight rifle shots, and left the place without saying a word. One dead, two wounded.

In 1920, during the Kapp putsch, Baron Stephan le Fort, retired cavalry captain, owner of the Boek estate (6,479 acres), fired a cannon at the town of Waren-on-the-Müritz because the workers had taken over the town. The shell hole in the wall of the town hall can be seen to this day. When the farm laborers in the area heard tell of five dead in Waren, they set out with shotguns and scythes and searched the surrounding estates for the rifles, machine guns, and ammunition supplied by the Reichswehr at Güstrow to the estate owners. Papenbrock, the tenant of the Vietsen estate, retained as tutors, apprentices, and a secretary five volunteers who had fought in the Baltic States, and he sent these men away through the back garden when the gardener came running up with news of the enemy's approach. Papenbrock, then fifty-two, took up a position on the front steps, shoulders thrown back, stomach propped up by his belt, in breeches and boots, and said: "Gentlemen. I give you my word as an officer. There are no arms in my house. However, if you still want to make a search, please be quiet in the girls' room so as not to wake them up."

My mother, a child of fourteen, stood on the bare hall floor in her ankle-length white nightgown, winding her hair around her wrist and glancing back and forth between Papenbrock, her sister Hilde, and the farm laborers who were questioning her in Low German dialect. Papenbrock's expression alternated between threatening and affectionate. At last, taking a deep breath and with downcast eyes, she said: "In there." Behind the massive oak linen cupboard in the girls' room, in a blocked-up doorway, hung nine infantry rifles and two hundred and ten rounds of ammunition in belts. My mother was put on bread and water for two weeks. Papenbrock spoke of betrayal by his own flesh and blood. His wife spoke of the Christian's love of truth. Papenbrock's hand flashed out to her cheek, and he did not go to church all summer. On the surrounding estates there was talk about Papenbrock's honor as an officer. In 1922 Papenbrock gave up the tenancy.

In Vietsen each of us girls had her own maid.

Then there were the maids for the ironing room, the kitchen, and the laundry room, the housemaids, and the housekeeper.

For a time Louise Papenbrock had a private chaplain.

When Papenbrock wished to travel he would telephone the stationmaster of the village railway station and have the desired train stopped for him out in the field by the estate. The man would say: Yes, sir. For two chickens at Christmas.

And on his return Papenbrock would pull the emergency cord when he reached the estate, pay the two-hundred-mark fine, and climb into the carriage that Fritz had driven up along the cart track in time to meet the train.

Fritz moved with the family to Jerichow. He died there.

When Robert was seventeen, Hilde always had to wake him two hours before school started so that Louise Papenbrock wouldn't find the maid in his bed.

The maid's name was Gerda and she was my age. She married someone in the village when she got pregnant.

And Papenbrock paid for the outfitting of the bride.

And once again Louise Papenbrock couldn't understand her husband.

Robert rode a horse to death in a race with a car.

When Robert wanted to ride to Teterow in an hour I took the horse by the halter and led it to the stable. As he walked beside me he kept saying, very softly because of the stableboys: "Give me that horse." In the stable the light was dim, it was an evening of low cloud just before rain, and I couldn't see him take his revolver out of his pocket. He said: "Give me that horse, or I'll shoot."

"Go ahead, shoot."

I ducked, in fun, and all I lost was one hair.

And the horse reared on its hind legs. As a mount it had been ruined.

"Don't tell Mother," he said.

Mother never found out.

Your Uncle Robert would arrive at school drunk, run up debts in restaurants, shoot at sparrows in town and hit windowpanes. When he got a teacher's daughter into trouble he had to be sent to Parchim. In Parchim

he took a room in the Count Moltke Hotel.

And strolled through the town carrying a little silverheaded cane.

At the Golden Grape on Long Street he sat over roast duck and red wine and, catching sight of the school principal and his wife through the window, invited the shocked couple in for roast duck and red wine. That was the end of him in Parchim.

From Parchim on I'm not too sure.

From Parchim he went to Hamburg.

With three marks in silver from Parchim to Hamburg?

The first thing Robert did was to sell two borrowed horses without the owner's consent, then he got blind drunk. And then he went to Hamburg.

In Vietsen the story was: He's learning the import-export business in Rio de Janeiro.

In Vietsen they said: Open the door, the grain merchants, the Jews, are coming.

In Vietsen your great-grandmother was still alive. She always killed the geese.

Henriette was her name. She came from an aristocratic family.

She would use French expressions like: bureau, bain-marie. Or: wash-lavoir.

While the house was being searched one of the farmhands said to me: "Put something on your feet, child."

Papenbrock gave up Vietsen because the nobility had cut him dead since 1920.

Papenbrock's lease of Vietsen was not renewed because he hadn't drained the land as required by the contract.

Because they all laughed about the girls' room.

Because he hadn't drained the land.

We don't know, Gesine.

Why do you want to know, Gesine?

Because of Cresspahl. Why did Cresspahl want to take up with a family like that?

September 7, 1967   Thursday

The news vendor on Broadway, at the southwest corner of 96th Street, prefers his customers to place their dimes in his hand rather than beside the stack of papers, as if his mutilated fingers could function like whole ones. On the subway stairs, whose metal strips are more worn on the left, footsteps have to be shortened. It is as well to hold the token between thumb and forefinger five paces before reaching the turnstile. After the passage under the local train tracks through to the south platform, the first door of the last car stops one and a half paces from the stair rail. The train has come through Harlem, the seats are tightly packed with dark-skinned sleepers. The New York *Times* must be folded in the remaining seconds before the jolt of departure, before the passenger braces himself against the swaying of the train by grabbing the strap that hangs over each seat. In the morning the passages and stairs below Times Square are divided by chains and subway guards into lanes for the streams of pedestrians between the four subway lines; below the three platforms of the shuttle train to Grand Central the center lane is considered the most advantageous. At this hour it is almost impossible for passengers to avoid touching each other. In Detroit automobile workers are on strike against Ford. Years ago, in the grand concourse of the station, under the blue-and-gold starry sky of the barrel-shaped dome, an express train for Chicago was being announced; never since then has she managed to hit just that moment.

From the floor of the concourse, sleepy commuters thread their way out eastward to Lexington Avenue, not yet alert enough to battle for taxis. Meanwhile, of the seven hundred faces she has seen this morning almost all are forgotten. Now begin the smiles.

She has learned this now and is only rarely taken aback by the smile on the receptionist's face that every morning promptly mounts, sags, slips off. She feels she is too slow for the elaborate, unvarying exchange of hello, how are you, reply, counter-question, counter-reply, good-by; she finds it hard to get all this over with in the four paces of a corridor encounter. This she has not learned. But the smiles make her feel protected, and she brightens hers up to the point of hilarity.

That's our German girl; but Germans are different.

The department consists of an inner core of office cubicles separated by frosted glass, a general office with groups of desks, and an outer rim of offices with outside windows. Beyond the steel door, which snaps shut behind her, she passes the reception desk, four desks on the left, three inside offices on the right. She walks as if deep in thought past Mrs. Agnolo's machines, feigning a conversation with the next desk; Mrs. Agnolo has a son in Vietnam. Yesterday 36 Americans and 142 Vietnamese died near Danang. She dreads the morning when the news of his death will be brought to the office; the boy still has four more months to serve. Most of the inside offices are already white with fluorescent lighting, the chairs in the general office are all occupied, but the girls are still opening up their desks, rummaging around in their handbags, showing each other newspaper ads. In two minutes a web of typewriter noise will hang in the air, suddenly, as if switched on. Outside her cubicle a removable brown plastic nameplate is fastened to a slot on the wall, the name "Miss Cresspahl" imprinted on it in white. The cubicle measures twelve by ten feet and has wall-to-wall carpeting, a steel cabinet, desk, typewriter stand, transcriber, telephone, swivel chair, filing baskets, visitor's chair. At eleven the coffee cart arrives, at twelve the staff goes for lunch, at five the stenographers may leave, at six the switchboard closes down, at eight the elevators stop running. As Miss Cresspahl takes the mail from the In tray on Mrs. Williams' desk she glances through the open door at the slats of the Venetian blinds, framed in blue frosted glass, of the building across the street, at the mirror into which this day will plunge, leaving no trace, until darkness falls.

September 8, 1967   Friday

The Secretary of Defense explains the kind of barrier he plans to build on the northern frontier of South Vietnam. He speaks of barbed wire, land mines, and sophisticated electronic devices; he says nothing.

The New York *Times*, anxious to be of service, describes the future curtailments in factories supplying Ford: at stake is an annual five billion dollars' worth of supplies that risk not being produced. Pickets are not being molested. Thirty years ago at the River Rouge plant in Dearborn, Michigan, there were riots, street fighting, and shooting. Thirty years ago a child of Cresspahl's fell into the rain barrel behind his house.

"You have a memory like a man, Mrs. Cresspahl!" says James Shuldiner, his thoughts elsewhere. It is broad daylight, in a Scandinavian sandwich bar on Second Avenue, at a narrow little side table, cheek by jowl with listeners, and Mr. Shuldiner has not once invited Mrs. Cresspahl, in the evening, to one of those velvet-dark restaurants in the East Fifties, to a tablecloth, to discreetly tendered bills, and to intimacies. James Shuldiner is of slight build, moist-eyed, brooding, with awkward movements, stiff, beneath a shock of almost black hair still resembling the high-school student of eleven years ago, a boy from Union City who was of no use to either gang, beaten up by both gangs, and who after the last vacation headed straight for the Army, Mr. Shuldiner, a worried tax expert who would admit to pride in a masculine memory. He did not place his hand on hers, he looks not at the lady but at his egg salad, he has become conscious of a new worry. Nevertheless he waits.

"Thank you, kind sir," she says.

Mrs. Cresspahl takes no pride in her memory. Mr. Shuldiner is staggered that she can cite the Cash and Carry legislation of 1937 that permitted the United States to supply armaments to warring nations; Mr. Shuldiner does not insist on calling her by her first name, he enlarges not on his own problems but on those of international politics. She had searched for the year 1937 and again found nothing but a static, isolated fragment such as the storehouse of memory arbitrarily selects for her, preserved in quantities beyond her control, only occasionally responsive to command and intention:

In 1937 Stalin caused a large number of his General Staff to be executed, in 1937 Hitler completed his war plans,

one has to buy at least one of Pete Seeger's records now that the TV authorities have blacklisted him because of an antimilitarist song,

(says Marie),

today's edition of the New York *Times* is No. 40,039,

since the day before yesterday the following words can be seen written by hand on a billboard in the subway at 96th Street and Broadway: Fuck the Jews,

her memory has helped her through school exams, tests, interrogations, it enables her to get through her daily work, one man regards it as an ornament; what mattered to her was a function of memory, recollection, not the storehouse but reproduction, return to the past, repetition of what has been: to be inside that again, to enter into that again. There is no such thing.

If only memory could contain the past in the receptacles we use to sort the elements of present reality! But the multilayered sieve of earthly time and causality and chronology and logic that we use for thinking is not served by the brain, where it remembers the past. (Our conceptual terms are not even valid at the site of our thinking; this is what we are supposed to conduct our lives with.) Reproduction is the very thing for which the repository of memory is not designed, the evocation of an event just what it resists. At a nudge, prompted by even partial congruence, by the random and the absurd, it will volunteer facts, figures, foreign speech, unrelated gestures; offer it a smell combining tar, rot, and fresh sea breeze, the faint whiff from Gustafsson's famous fish salad, and ask for the contents of the void that was once reality, life-awareness, action: it will refuse to supply them. The filter allows scraps, splinters, broken glass, shavings, to trickle through and scatter themselves without meaning over the plundered and spaceless image, obliterating the traces of the sought-for scene, leaving us blind with open eyes. The piece of the past that is ours because we were there remains hidden in a secret, locked against Ali Baba's magic word, inimical, unapproachable, mute, and enticing like a great gray cat behind the windowpane, seen from very far below as with a child's eyes.

Never mind the cat.

Mr. Shuldiner broke off in his presentation of the most recent infringements of international law as Mrs. Cresspahl picked up her purse, her hand gripping the back of the fat black bag as if it were the neck of a cat, slung the purse over her wrist, and said something in a German dialect. He allows her to explain, not offended, leaning forward like an attentive listener:

"That's what my father said when I was scared of a cat sitting under the table. She settled down across the leather of his clogs and went to sleep. That must have been in 1937 too. That was the day I fell into the rain barrel."

"And your mother, was your mother looking on?" asked Mr. Shuldiner eagerly.

Lisbeth, I'll kill you.

"My mother was not looking on. I'm sorry. I was daydreaming, Mr. Shuldiner."

James Shuldiner dutifully accompanied Mrs. Cresspahl along Second Avenue into one store after another, an embarrassed spectator of her attempts to buy one apple. Apples are sold in high-class stores in packages, also by the pound, not singly. After Mrs. Cresspahl has succeeded in at least stealing an apple in a supermarket, he tries to say good-by. He watches her bite into it and says: "I like your dress, Mrs. Cresspahl." He will not tell her this time either why he telephoned her. He walks up the sloping street, a thin, rather bent person, black and white in a business suit. He may be shaking his head.

If a cat was lying on the sill inside the kitchen window I must have climbed onto an upturned bucket and from there onto the rain barrel. If the lid of the barrel was missing my mother must have been standing close by. If Cresspahl pulled me out she must have been watching. What can I do about it!

September 9, 1967 Saturday

Justice almost prevails in New York this morning. The air is motionless. The air cannot move under stationary heat masses in the upper atmosphere, since yesterday it has been unable to rise into the cold and shed the dirt pumped into it by the city from power plants, gasworks, chimney stacks, car motors, jet engines, and ships: the inversion has clamped an impenetrable dome over the city. The accumulated dirt from soot, fly ash, hydrocarbons, carbon monoxide, sulfur dioxide, nitrous oxide, is no respecter of persons and seeps through cracks of windows into eyes, into skin folds, dries out throats, shrivels mucous membranes, exerts pressure on the heart, blackens tea and seasons food, creates additional work for lung specialists, shoe shiners, car washers, window cleaners, and for Mr. Fang Liu, in his basement shop off Broadway, who now accepts the Cresspahl laundry from Marie with deft, eager gestures. Few people can hide behind sealed double glass and high-powered air conditioners: imprisoned in their bare, fusty towers on the East Side, they miss the lurid clouds painted by the humidity beyond Riverside Park, miss the dun rags of haze draping the Hudson. In every store on Broadway in which Marie walks around with her shopping cart the mere word "pollution" will invariably yield her some conversation as well as the New Yorkers' pride in the unparalleled difficulty of life in New York, mutual sympathy, sighs can be exchanged and smiles bartered when she pushes her hair back from her perspiring brow with her forearm. Outside, on the hot, darkened street, she will feel as if her face were plunging into a wall of steaming water.

For Marie often goes shopping on Broadway on Saturdays. In the early morning she creeps barefoot up to Gesine's bed, steals her alarm clock, and tiptoes to the door, letting it click shut behind her against carefully balancing fingertips, although she suspects that Gesine was holding her breath like someone awake who has been lying on her back for quite a while, her arms crossed behind her head, listening.

For six years ago the four-year-old child clung to Gesine at the swinging doors to the kindergarten, drummed screaming with rage against the doors of the elevator into which her mother had disappeared, often lay on the classroom floor during playtime, silent and sad, deaf to persuasion, her face turned to the door. The head kindergarten teacher complained to Gesine over the telephone, and after three weeks she brought her a list of the most essential words that the child had refused to learn. Among these were ones such as hand and foot, get up, touch, look for, and Gesine began buying West German newspapers again, to look at the employment ads. The child listened to the English she spoke with a polite frown, never letting her out of her sight, and she realized that for Marie English stood for the outside world, all those alien things that should at least not follow them into their home. However, she did not want to promise the child a reward for learning. She would not permit herself to feel sorry for the child when she sent her off by herself to the ice-cream truck at the park entrance and had to watch Marie, her hands clutching the quarter behind her, moving half a step back for each step forward, shoved aside by other children, unnoticed by the driver until he turned away to drive on. Marie even denied the English she did know. At the supermarket she let the cashier place a dollar bill in front of her and ask who the stout dignified gentleman in the middle was; and although the customers standing behind prompted her either aloud or in whispers, Marie waited, sullen and silent, to see whether these people would finally relent and speak German. (Outside on the street she said indignantly: "George Washington! As if I didn't know! And I didn't know a single one of those ladies!") For her this had been a test of her self-confidence. It was not until they went on a trip up the Hudson and she let two boys draw her into a game of tag up and down the passageways and stairs of the many-storied houselike steamer that she betrayed herself: unseeing she ran past Gesine between the rows of chairs and said, as if to a stranger: "Excuse me!"; later she was discovered on the stairs up to the bridge telling the astonished gaping boys about Düsseldorf and the Rhine in the bubbling mixture of truncated German words and acoustical curves into which she had converted the intonation of the radio announcers. But that evening the boys flew back to their riverless city in Ohio, and again Marie was jostled by the kids on the playground and teased about the thick-lipped rumbling sounds that she took for the American medium of exchange. The children had learned from TV movies how to brace a stiff arm against a wall to corner a victim, and Gesine entered the fray and snatched Marie away because the child was not defending herself.

But Marie, now piloting a whole week's groceries between the clattering steel doors of the elevator, is involved in a vociferous conversation with Mr. Robinson, and again Mr. Robinson leaves the elevator door open and watches intently as the child pushes her way into the Cresspahl apartment and repeats her story about the bum who tried to make off with the contents of her shopping cart on Broadway. "And I didn't bother with being a lady!" At Schustek's she was waited on not by one of the helpers but by Mr. Schustek in person, and she tasted three kinds of sausage before buying any. Gesine stands for a long time in the aisles of a supermarket, is susceptible to goods in new packages, her purchases are prompted by curiosity, by appetite; the child walks straight between the lures, blind to posters, deaf to radio commercials, raising and lowering her eyelids at the same steady rate, and she places not one ounce, not one package, into her shopping cart that is not on her list. Today the child caught the cashier to whom she once refused information about George Washington ringing up twenty-one cents too much, and the cashier apologized, without argument, to the child and the customers within earshot. The child tries to show Gesine the face one listening customer made, a woman who had previously been forever shooting off her mouth about the cheating going on at the cash registers and is now indignant over a ten-year-old girl exposing the swindle; the matron's sour disgust distorts the child's face right up to her hairline. And the child has not forgotten today's New York *Times*, a neat firm bundle, undisturbed in its machine folds, the consciousness of the day. She places the paper beside Gesine's breakfast as if it were a gift.

The Secretary of State does not exclude the possibility that Red China will enter the war in Southeast Asia. However, he would consider that a most ill-advised decision.

And not until page 48, among financial and real-estate items, did the circumspect medium disclose that in the first six months of the year over 500 civilians were killed in North Vietnam by U. S. assaults, by 77,000 tons of explosives in March alone.

"And the twenty-one cents," says the child after accounting for her purchases, in the rough, catarrhal voice acquired from six years in New York's polluted air, "the twenty-one cents I gave to the beggars, sixteen to the one with blue hair, and five to the one at 98th Street."

September 10, 1967   Sunday

Our agriculture needs tax relief! And anyway the Treasury should accept tax payments in kind! The tariff laws must be changed! The state ought to control the middleman's profits instead! If only Berlin would cut back imports at least!

That, complains Papenbrock Senior, is the only way to tide the Mecklenburg aristocracy over the year 1931!

The old man was not even shouting, or trying to hide the asthma during the intervals to which his cigar compelled him; he lay back limply in his armchair, eyes half closed, in the slanting reddish sunbeams that blinded his office windows. He merely wanted to gain time with his visitor, a fellow by the name of Cresspahl who had written on a sheet of hotel letter paper from the Lübeck Arms asking for an interview. The visitor behaved, moreover, as if he were seriously concerned with the problems of the East Elbian nobility.

"As for the tax debts of those aristocratic gentlemen, I imagine they're not worth the paper they're written on," said Cresspahl solemnly, in the same formal Low German, sitting bolt upright on the visitors' sofa, his gaze resting on Papenbrock's bald head as it reflected the evening light. Blink as he might, the father of the fiancée could find nothing disrespectful about him.

Papenbrock wondered how to cope with the man. The man was strong, not running to fat, not to be bullied. The man had been able to afford a room at the Lübeck Arms for a whole week now. In the telegram he had received from England there was mention of substantial orders, although Frieda Klütz, the telegraph operator in Jerichow, had not been able to prepare an exact translation of these dealings for Papenbrock. His daughter talked about three thousand pounds in an account with the Surrey Bank of Richmond, and Papenbrock had swallowed his contemptuous snort, for cash merited respect. The man had not bothered to impress his future father-in-law with an account in Jerichow, he had learned from the German banking crash in July. The man had served in the Army; he had been promoted to sergeant by Papenbrock's comrades on the Russian front. The man was from Mecklenburg. But Papenbrock could not bring himself to accept the man.

"If you as a shrewd businessman support the aristocrats' program . . . ," said Cresspahl provocatively, thrusting his shoulders slightly forward as if eager to hear about Papenbrock's contacts in the ministries of Mecklenburg-Schwerin.

Papenbrock still hesitated to reveal his friends to this Cresspahl. The latter came from a region in the southeast where Papenbrock had once lost the tenancy of an estate. This Cresspahl might have sat behind a desk in the town hall of Waren when Papenbrock was forced to hand over his rifles to a workers' committee. Meanwhile this Cresspahl had lived for ten years outside the country, in the Netherlands, in England, among those who had won the war, and even Captain Papenbrock (Ret.) found it hard to render such a son-in-law palatable to his Stahlhelm cronies. The fellow did not even behave as if a few years ago Papenbrock might have been his superior officer. This man, despite the respectability accruing to him by virtue of his thrifty spending in Jerichow, nevertheless sat in Peter Wulff's back parlor, after closing time, talking to people who came by bicycle from Wismar and of whom not even the district police knew where they spent the night.

Papenbrock did not feel like making friends with a man who went without a hat, who let himself be seen on the terrace of the Archduke Hotel in Rande with a Dr. Semig. It was all very well for Dr. Semig to have two diplomas hanging on his wall and to parade his war medals through the main street on the Emperor's birthday: Papenbrock considered it sufficient to pay Semig's veterinary bills, and by return mail at that. But Semig was capable of sitting outside a Christian hotel under a striped umbrella drinking cognac in the company of summer visitors and expounding the world to strangers.

And Papenbrock wondered how to cope with this Cresspahl. This fellow allowed one to invite him after dinner, this fellow allowed Papenbrock to smoke his cigar alone, he did not insist on the glass of claret merited by the occasion, it was impossible to insult him. The fellow had money, almost as much as his Lübeck rival. But maybe he wouldn't go as far as to invite Dr. Semig to the wedding. And Papenbrock slid out of his chair, groped around in the room, now almost pitch dark, reached down with all of his sixty-three years under the desk, set the open bottle on the desk, poured, and said, abruptly switching from dialect to High German: "Mr. Cresspahl . . . ," signaled to my nonplused father to rise, and began: "Mr. Cresspahl, so we're going to become relatives. Tell me, son, what kind of a first name did they give you?"

Lisbeth Papenbrock had done a good job with my grandfather.

Gesine Cresspahl is spending this Sunday on Staten Island, in Tottenville, later on the Midland Beach boardwalk. The child has insisted on waiting out the rain here. To the northeast, across the bay of the Atlantic, the weather-blurred towers of Brooklyn can be seen, glinting white under rifts in the clouds. Beyond those palaces of the sea, in the two-story slums, people are killing each other.

Because of the outing she has missed the New York *Times*. In a trash basket she sees a remnant of today's edition with a large picture uppermost. It shows, rather indistinctly, a plump, dark-haired little girl of about fourteen being held in the arms of a casually dressed man who is just giving her a kiss. The man has a mustache, his shirt collar is not American. He bears a resemblance to Stalin in his best years.

"And then?" asks the child. "Then your mother got engaged like they do in Europe?"

Then she got engaged to Heinrich Cresspahl, cabinetmaker from Richmond. Louise had secretly reset the table in the dining room and was polishing the glasses when the men arrived from the office. Holding the cloth, she grasped Cresspahl's hand, tried to look him in the eye, and spoke of God's indispensable approval. Cresspahl did not take this seriously, and Papenbrock, blinking as he turned aside, withdrew to his wine cellar. Once again my mother revealed herself to Papenbrock as his favorite daughter, moving around the table as she served, quietly, unassuming, content. Louise Papenbrock wept when it seemed appropriate. Papenbrock drank cognac and Moselle wine by turns and talked about the handsome children that his daughter and Cresspahl would bring into the world,

but make sure the girls don't have your bones, Heinrich Cresspahl, prost!

and talked about Heinz Zoll, the Jerichow carpenter whom he would buy out. And my mother sat down beside him and looked at Cresspahl as if she were asking him to do something, but Cresspahl shook his head, and she said, a trifle anxiously but at the same time archly: "We're not staying, Dad." And Papenbrock clutched at his heart, where her hand already was, and grinned, a bit embarrassed because he had betrayed how great the shock was and, for that very reason, deliberately exaggerated it.

"And Horst Papenbrock?" asked the child.

Horst Papenbrock was not there. My mother had made sure of that. He was at a Nazi get-together in Gneez.

September 11, 1967   Monday

In yesterday's edition of the New York *Times* Stalin's daughter described "The Death of My Father," in today's "Life with My Father and Mother." The world's finest newspaper bolsters the memoirs of the defectress with photographs not provided or authorized by the author; today's is a picture from 1935 showing Stalin thumbing his nose at his chief bodyguard's camera.

And we've been loyal to the paper for six years! At one time we were at the mercy of the chained dog of the East German military base; inside the outer fence it was confined in a wire-mesh kraal, thus prevented from ever making friends with a civilian and forcing it to become a hypochondriacal, introverted, highly irascible type who, even when it was raining cats and dogs, would stand outside its kennel barking hysterically, and if it was not zeal that made its voice crack, it was the "New Germany's" voice breaking; at one time we were dependent on the democratic virtues of elderly spinsters, the diligence, the argumentativeness, the hypocrisy, the abstract conscience, the self-righteousness, of old maids who had remained untouched for so long that they were by that time ready to deny any and all sexual intercourse: the Establishment press within the confines of the West German military base. And we were sure: never could we totally despise an honest old aunt like the New York *Times*. And in 1961 we had the choice between her and the *Herald Tribune!* Between the conservative dark attire of hard work and devotion to duty, and on the other hand the more attractive layout, the more entertaining pictures, of a figure who, although also no longer young, appeared with ribbon around her pale hair, bows at her neck, fashionable colors around her hips, and little boots from the Via Condotti; we had no alternative.

Not like a blind chicken finding a lost grain but like the watchful magpie stealing silver, so again in 1961 the New York *Times* could be relied upon to look through a millstone and foresee the Berlin Wall, and to describe both for us in secondhand phrases, firsthand quotations, with glosses, photographs, preliminary summaries, in the minor narrative forms; and when the rhapsodic subject had been fitted together in all its strands and the outer layer of the dividing fence removed, she assembled all her descriptive resources in an epic spate, and in daily reports from the construction site supplied installments of the story that to her had already become history. How could we have doubted her? At that time she cost only five cents. For five cents not only paper printed on both sides but the justified expectation that this housewife is not going to sweep news items under the carpet, that she regards dirty linen as an occasion for doing the laundry, that every closet may be opened and in none of them will hang a skeleton! This trustworthy person has equipped us with reasons for living in New York! Here for the first time we could add logic to the reasons for our presence and say that a local newspaper places news from Germany in proper relationship to world news: a minor relationship, thus helping and persuading us to accept reality with the expectations and judgments for which our parents had already prepared us! It was not just a matter of convenience. We have become accustomed to her as to a person with a place in the household, and not as a poor relation living on charity or a few remaining privileges. We had no wish to change her: in her eyes the welfare and profit of her country take precedence over all else, we used this criterion to filter her prejudices; often her country's egoism ignores her scruples and censure, and we felt reminded of the tragic heroes of the German classics who were forever either behind or ahead of the times. Our attitude toward her strictly followed Brecht's suggestion, and we offered her co-operation and consideration: what mattered most to us was her experience. We observed that she advised the King of Greece to improve his country with a putsch and that it was not the King but his generals who were able to interpret the oracle of Times Square, but cunning is the very least that we will concede elderly aunts. And are we not indebted to her for promptly recognizing the fact that in Greece too the Western bloc was hobnobbing with Fascists? She remained true to herself and unhesitatingly voiced her disgust at the torture of politically controversial Greeks. And it is not the proprietors of the paper, on instructions from monopolies and political parties, who systematically design the image of the present,

they write what the subscribers expect; but you, Gesine, you're naïve,

as Countess Seydlitz remarks. Mrs. Albert Seydlitz says that Gesine, in her distrust of bourgeois traditions, also sneers unintentionally at traditions that are merely abused but still essential to mankind. We must not nourish our lives on bread alone; we need proofs, too, child.

To be on close terms with Auntie Times is a necessity for us, and we are glad to pay our respects to age as well. She sets our table with the latest trends, we redouble our thanks and admire her cultivated gestures. We find it almost touching the way she takes pains to keep us on a minimum level of knowledge by preceding a report from Cobh with the information that Cobh is in southeast Ireland, near Cork, in County Cork, and was at one time famous as a port of call for transatlantic liners. We respect her objectivity and let her call herself "a New York newspaper." A purveyor of detail, yes, but a counselor of confusion, no. Anxiously, yet not without affection, we observe her attempts at least to acknowledge changes in popular taste when all of a sudden on July 3, 1966, she replaces her typefaces with larger ones or, unexpectedly on February 21, 1967, carries the date on the masthead in cursive instead of upright; it suits her, and we trust her sense of proportion and propriety. One thing, we dearly hope, she will not do to us: not for the most modern, far-out Madison Avenue custom creation will she abandon her austere eight-column front page, not for the most British of all Roman types will she remove the uncial fraktur from her brow, the adornment of age, the monument to the past, as indispensable as the art nouveau motifs above the glass-shod feet of Manhattan buildings. Such buildings are no match for the wrecking balls of pure-profit calculation, she it is who holds the two centuries together. Meanwhile, conservatively enough, she is asking ten cents for her services, and we would gladly volunteer thirty.

We raise our hat today to Mr. William S. Greenawalt of Brooklyn. Well over two weeks ago he wrote a letter to the editor of the New York *Times* asking: If the Sanitation Commissioner can keep his white sanitation trucks white, why can't the Transit Authority keep its red subway trains red?

And the New York *Times* has judged this also to be another of those things that are fit to print.

September 12, 1967   Tuesday

Mrs. Cresspahl is requested to be available this afternoon to be driven to Kennedy Airport, where there will be a letter requiring translation. An hour before closing time, Mrs. Cresspahl is called for by a man in livery, a heavyset, elderly Negro who, with the solemnity of a footman, introduces himself as the chauffeur of Mr. De Rosny, the Vice-President, designates her as the latter's interpreter, and adds: "I am Arthur." His short tightly curled hair is streaked with white, and while speaking he holds his uniform cap over his left chest. Mrs. Cresspahl's attempt to shake hands with him is thwarted, he has already stepped aside. Taken aback, she tells him her first name, halfheartedly, and he replies gravely, indulgently: "That's quite all right, Mrs. Cresspahl."

Mrs. Cresspahl has to walk behind him as if behind a servant. His uniform, his measured tread, his unseeing expression, momentarily silence the day's-end chatter among the typewriters in the general office, he leaves her no time to say good-by, he is already holding open the door to the main corridor and lets her pass through like some invisible object. At the elevator he insists on carrying her brief case. On the way down, alone with her, he comments on the weather, his face turned toward the indicator panel, ignores her replies, and repeats: "Yes, ma'am," until they reach the basement and he can bow to her and to De Rosny's car, shut the door, and put on his cap. She feels as if she is being handed over, carted off, locked in, like a parcel to be delivered.

The Vice-President's car, from the outside a black monster fifteen feet long, is the shell for a private first-class compartment, a completely upholstered cabin with four seats, telephone, reading lamp, writing shelf. The cabin is insulated from the outer world by tinted glass and a thick panel behind the driver's seat, also, it seems, by such a smooth suspension system that the interior betrays neither the leap with which the vehicle mounts the exit ramp onto 46th Street, nor its spurts across Second Avenue down into the broad trench leading to the tiled tubes of the East River Tunnel. This is one of Mrs. Cresspahl's favorite routes, now that she is used to the white light and the constricting vault under the East River; it is the route that spells travel. It is an exit from the city, for the street widens steadily between the industrial plants of Brooklyn, the well-spaced apartment houses, and finally the Long Island expressways, until, where the cemeteries are, the sky is suspended almost unbroken over the horizon. Grouped about in fields, the stones of the interment communities re-create the rising and dipping of the original landscape, low flickers under dusty conifers. The graveyards are cities, protected by walls, threaded with pleasant curving streets, densely built up with narrow tombstones, like the old brownstone houses of Manhattan, then opening up once more into green parks where solitary palaces of the dead reflect the levels of earthly possessions. Finally the scabs and scars of industrial exploitation and land speculation have been supplanted by opulent countryside on both sides of the exit road, by landscaped lawns and woods, almost all the way to the ring of passenger terminals, to the concrete corrals in which cars have been rounded up in serried ranks, a stationary glinting herd. Yet for Mrs. Cresspahl there was no pleasure in this trip. She would have preferred it if the man at the wheel had not held his thick neck so motionless, if he had let down the panel, turned around just once and admitted to a surname. But at the International Arrivals terminal Arthur reached the door ahead of her, ushering her in with a bow, unmistakably a rich man's chauffeur who once again removes his cap, rests his eyes for an instant, without expression, on her face, and repeats in his respectful husky voice: "Yes, ma'am. Certainly, ma'am."

If you don't like this country, why don't you choose another one?

Inside the terminal, suspended above the baggage claim area, there is a glassed-in deck that permits a full view of the moving belts in the Customs aisles, a quarter-view of the baggage carrousels, an eighth-view of the passport-control exits, so that passengers below can be picked out from above. The heavy teak beam against the glass is closely packed with the propped elbows of those who have come to meet passengers, on Gesine's left those of an Italian family, against her other shoulder those of an Indian couple, all looking down in comfort on the weary, crumpled, confused passengers and on the contents of their open bags in which the Customs officials are feeling around with firm, knowing fingers. Gesine is expecting a white man of about sixty, a flabby, gray, indistinct face, a man in loose gray garments, a banker but one who will nevertheless open up his leather bags alongside the Customs cash registers. She remembers her employer from the original interview she had with him three years ago, from good mornings nodded in the elevator lanes, and most clearly as a passport photo in the company's promotional literature. The passport photo is all that enables her to recognize the man, now coming into view on the far side of the inspection area, his unopened suitcases on a porter's trolley beside him, escorted by a uniformed official through an automatic door and saluted by a policeman, not of French descent after all, it seems, but one of those Irishmen. The person Mrs. Cresspahl intercepts at the foot of the stairs is an agile man in a suit of very blue linen, a thin stooping figure whose firm muscles support the flesh of his cheeks in creases, a deliverer of long convoluted sentences who thanks Mrs. Cresspahl in one of them for coming, patronizingly orders the porter around, and with old-world courtesy ushers Mrs. Cresspahl through the automatic doors, pays off the porter with a precisely calculated additional 11 per cent, and advances with no show of amazement toward Arthur. For Arthur has been patrolling the airport ring road in his black chariot for the last fifty minutes and punctually to the minute draws up at the curb beside his boss's canvas baggage. "Hello there, Arthur!" this boss says, and Arthur, his cap on his head, smiling under the thick dark-brown folds of his forehead, with white teeth, says: "Well, Chief!"

On the way back the panel behind Arthur's seat in the limousine is lowered, he keeps only one hand on the wheel, the other arm rests along the back of his seat so he can turn around more easily, De Rosny sits conveniently in the opposite corner, and they exchange news.

Mr. De Rosny hasn't flown straight through from Honolulu, of course. He stopped over in California, he had this suit made in Italy, he put up with Paris cooking for two days, he managed to get a seat on an American airline, he is looking forward to seeing New York again. How about you, Arthur?

Arthur has bought his wife a new washing machine. His second-youngest son has passed his medical exam, not with honors but with good marks. Arthur has spent the weekend in Connecticut, he sure likes that back yard of his. His wife is upset because of the teachers' strikes, the younger kids are missing school, although the teachers' demands, especially for smaller classes and higher pay . . .

"And how did you get along with her?" says the boss, tilting his chin toward Mrs. Cresspahl. "She was O.K.," says Arthur, and for an instant Mrs. Cresspahl catches his eye in the rear-view mirror. He does not wink at her, just makes a tiny, reassuring movement of his eyelids.

I might have known the boss would put his arm around your shoulders, hold the door open for you, let you choose your seat. Gesine, or whatever your name is.
O.K., Arthur. And go to hell, Arthur.

September 13, 1967   Wednesday

Federal Judge Dudley B. Bonsal has ordered the subway to permit the display of antiwar posters; on account of the Fourteenth Amendment.

Gesine's ten days beside the Atlantic have by now been eclipsed by three weeks in the city, and the behavior patterns of the other employees are beginning to close in on her again. Once again she moves the hands of her watch and clocks five minutes ahead, so as not to arrive late at the office. She ignores these five minutes both going to sleep and getting up, only when delayed in the subway does she consciously rely on the reserve. She converts occasional disruptions in the subway service into a negative rule with which to safeguard her way to the office against lost minutes, and she mentally saves up any further minutes of less than five that accrue from finishing breakfast early or not trusting her watch. She keeps track of her time reserve by listening to the radio while simultaneously discrediting this balance because she distrusts the casualness of the announcer:

Well, folks, if you wanted to be out of the house by half past, you're now only seven minutes late:

Furthermore, she tries to reduce her tested average of thirty-five minutes between home and typewriter by hurried transfers and reckless interpretation of traffic lights, but without crediting herself with the gain. Now and then the accumulated reserve sends her off from Upper West Side as early as ten past eight, often bringing her at eight thirty past the obstinate clock in Grand Central Station

This is the clock that wakes up America!

and more than once it had been eight forty-five when she reached the electric clock in the office, its spindly seconds-hand paring away her margin. In the fifteen minutes gained she could unfold the newspaper, but she would feel it was petty to start punctually at 09 hours 0 seconds, so she sets to work on the In tray. The tempo of her work is not affected by her hoarding of minutes, for assignments are handed to her as they come; there are even half hours during which Mrs. Cresspahl reads dictionaries, studiously bending over the page, her door open. . . . Not until ten to five does she begin to restore her hoarded minutes to normal time. And yet she easily loses one or two of the real time units so that it is usually five forty before she reaches the door of her apartment. This discrepancy of one twelfth of an hour she considers a genuine loss, regardless of whether Marie has been waiting or not.

The management has not installed time clocks, and in the regular circulars to the staff the word punctuality does not occur. Gesine is no more devoted to this firm than to previous employers. She cannot even manage a stab of conscience when she is two minutes late in the morning. Others may interpret her early arrival as zeal, an excess of zeal even, yet she is unable to give up this juggling with imaginary time. There is nothing else for her to rely on. She lets Mrs. Williams tease her about the Teutonic virtue of punctuality, she lets D. E. carry on about traumatic punishments for being late to school. All she has is this check that appears on her desk in a sealed envelope at the end and middle of each month, eight thousand dollars a year before income tax; the check cannot compare with an employees' union, which could go on strike like the workers against Ford, the railwaymen against the Long Island Railroad, the teachers against the city. She can be given two weeks' notice at any time, and she has only five months' salary in a savings account to pay Marie's school fees until she finds another job. She is determined not to pass up a single insurance, not even the punctual appearance at her place of work, the visual presence.

And confidential overtime at the Waldorf Astoria Towers . . . a hundred feet above the evening emptiness of Lexington Avenue, a hundred feet outdoors above tipsy businessmen, strayed tourists, cabs majestically patrolling the evil-smelling canal of the street . . . in

the fusty air of air conditioners, air of grandmothers' closets, closets
full of curios and treasures . . . overtime for Vice-President De
Rosny, who is conducted to his suite like a popular visiting prince, for
whom the hotel sends up a bar with fresh ice, a second television set,
an electric typewriter in a kind of cradle on wheels . . . overtime for
the translation of a letter from Prague, in Polish-French, about night-
clubs, 16-millimeter movies, a girl called Maria-Sofia, about interna-
tional dollar credits . . . overtime with cocktails . . . overtime and
being driven home in a black coach, through the reddish glow of the
West Forties, under the arching jets of open hydrants, along the
West Side Highway, high up beside the gray steaming Hudson, the
mist-wrapped farther shore, on past swept raked Riverside Park,
across the world . . . hours beyond working hours beyond the terms
of normal work . . . ?

It was an outing. It was amusing. It was strange. It was overtime,
without pay.

September 14, 1967   Thursday

In an interview concerning yesterday's battles around Dongson, Lieutenant Colonel William Rockety speaks of a North Vietnamese who
penetrated as far as the American mortar batteries and killed two
Marine infantrymen before being killed. "One Vietnamese," Lieutenant Colonel Rockety tells the New York *Times*, "really courageous—or crazy."

In the last two years the intensification of the Vietnam war has
created more than a million jobs in the United States. This applies to
all branches of industry except shipbuilding and construction and
represents nearly a quarter of the total increase in job opportunities.

How far was Cresspahl from disgust as he squandered day after
day at Jerichow in August 1931, a healthy man idling in the midst of
the harvest, blinded by his entanglement with his image of Papenbrock's youngest daughter as if she were the only possible woman his
life could need?

Cresspahl must have been disgusted by the repetition. At sixteen, yes, the world could still be blotted out by a girl's nearness, her
breath, the look in her eyes, the feel of her skin, her voice; at sixteen,
yes, his purpose and plan and future may once have been overlaid by
the dogged, confident desire for a fifteen-year-old girl who became so
much his aim and object that he thought of her no longer as the
boss's granddaughter but only as the inescapable necessity, the confidence in an obscure design for the whole of his future life: at sixteen,

as a carpenter's apprentice in Malchow-by-the-lake, at the turn of the century; but in 1931, in Jerichow near Gneez, at forty-three?

Is not repetition intolerable: that one's need for a person should sift and resift one's consciousness through the same old sieve, that long-forgotten feelings should return afresh, that imagination should once again tirelessly interpret and extend the mere externals of a person to every conceivable correspondence between her and him, that the voids in the real person should be concealed without warning by the image of the person, that at the mere sight of her the heart should beat faster, as tremulously as at the mere sight of someone else these five, twelve, twenty-eight years past, as if some unimaginable reality were to be revealed here, something as yet untouched, as yet unfelt? He must have forgotten himself.

Standing, a powerful figure with stalwart arms, sleepy and good-natured on the market square beside the town scales, watching cart after cart drive onto them, walking along by hot weary horses, leaving behind the teamsters sitting crouched in sweat, as if work were to be looked at. Beside the town scales he was not close enough to Papenbrock's house to seem to be waiting, but close enough to see a window move.

Going for a drive, as innocent as any summer visitor, in the veterinarian's carriage, past the hay wagon crunching along the unpaved shoulder of the road, an observer of the scenery, on holiday, persistently but casually bringing the conversation around to the local grain trade, and from everything Dr. Semig said about Papenbrock being a smart businessman hearing only, "You'll be happy with that girl, Cresspahl. Lucky, I tell you."

Strolling, an idle lounger in collar and tie, past the rows of reapers in the broiling wheatfields, away from the pounding of the threshing machines, as if on holiday under the hard taut sky along the paths around Jerichow, from manor to manor, from the steep shoreline to the Gräfin Forest, around the marsh, through every street in the town, merely because Papenbrock's daughter had grown up here: here he wanted to acquaint himself with what she had to give up.

Sitting down, an explorer, in the station tavern, the Nazis' hangout, to drink the sour beer and wait for Horst Papenbrock until he turned up on the third evening, and letting him sound off about the Dawes Plan and last September's Reichstag election, and leading him on to drink, pint after pint of Kniesenack beer downed with schnapps, and dragging Papenbrock's lurching, merry, maudlin son and heir across the market square at midnight and propping him up

against his father's gate, and going in to Peter Wulff's back parlor to
tell him all about it, only slightly drunk, in very good spirits, completely satisfied.

Traveling to Hamburg for the day and coming back and making
a modest appearance in an English shirt bought at Ladage & Oehlke,
in a business suit, hatless, on his way to Papenbrock's house and
office; amusing the people of Jerichow for weeks with his love affair,
his head full of the secret that existed between him and Lisbeth
Papenbrock, for no one's eyes but hers and his.

A Protestant. Protestants.

*A fellow must have money if he can waste that much time on his
feelings.*

With Nazis. Sits there drinking with a Nazi.

Well, it's not the money he's after.

*You haven't the guts. You wouldn't make a fool of yourself
before two thousand people.*

That's how he sees his life: a religious girl.

Yes, she wouldn't have you, Stoffregen.

*She'll never come back. She'll go with him wherever he says. She
took his hand the moment they left the market square and started
out on the path across the fields.*

*They were lying there in the woods. He didn't hear me ride by
on my bike, and she had her eyes open.*

*On the hillside. Where you can see a bit of sea, over toward the
cliff.*

One woman warned him. After closing time Meta Wulff joined
Peter and Cresspahl in the back parlor and began talking about
Pastor Methling, and about Lisbeth, who invariably sat in the second
row in church, below the pulpit. Wulff growled at her to stop, but
Meta, a fisherman's daughter from the Dievenow, slapped him below
the shoulder and rubbed his back and went on talking about the
Bible classes that Papenbrock's daughter held for children in the
church hall above and beyond the call of Christian duty. All Cresspahl got out of this was: she's even good with children.

September 15, 1967   Friday

This summer is over.

During the past week 2,376 people died fighting in Vietnam.
Yesterday the Soviet Russians denied they were mistreating one of

their authors at a labor camp. Schoolteachers are still on strike. South Korea is considering a plan to put up an electronic wire fence along its northern frontier. The wife of Jan Szymczak of Brooklyn, who arrived in the United States from Poland only last February, has left him; as of today, he will no longer be responsible even for her debts.

This summer is over. This summer, Tshombe, who made millions out of the revolution, was abducted to Algeria, and his former friends are sharpening the guillotine. This summer saw the beginning of the thirty-third military conflict since the end of World War II, the office cubicles on the bank's upper floors were overpopulated by transistor voices reporting from Israel, doors that had never been closed since the building went up were left on the latch, and Mr. Shuldiner talked all through one lunch about Jewish imperialism; on Broadway the slight figures with their round beards, their ringlets, their mournful expressions, jumped when their neighbors showed their respect with a slap on the shoulder, and had trouble following the political discussion on the sidewalk, and one of them, while taking flight into the 86th Street station, ran into Mrs. Cresspahl, who had been listening to the debate from five paces away—"I'm no hero, I'm a theologian," he said. During the victory parade on Riverside Drive, Marie walked beside Rebecca Ferwalter at the end of one of the ranks as if she belonged there, not wearing blue and white but waving a little flag, the Star of David. Kosygin drove north along Third Avenue in a black funeral car, and the spectators in their air-conditioned office towers could not open their windows to wave to him. But then he went to see Niagara Falls after all. Nikita Sergeevich Khrushchev made one more appearance on television, an old, worn-out man carrying on about bygone deeds. On the wall between our windows hangs the photograph of a California housewife who learned of her son's death by telegram; for the benefit of the photographer she sits down again and pretends to read it. In six months private crime has increased by 17 per cent. If there are two murders a day in New York, when must one of them strike Mrs. Cresspahl? Which night will the windowpane shatter, a shadow under the overpass rise up with a knife, an arm around her neck drag her from the street into a basement entrance? Three Finger Brown, head of a Mafia family, has died in his bed, and the police photographed the mourners at the graveside. Negroes have revolted in twenty-two cities; to date their dead have numbered 86, and meanwhile the New York police has 32,365 men. We sat on the Hudson promenade, surrounded by men fishing, families picnicking, people playing tennis, and looked across the sludgy surging river into the

stifled red light of evening, listening to the civil war in New Jersey
that had free access to Manhattan along the railway tracks and roads
under the river. Late one night came a call from West Berlin, from
Anita, who has the bar, and she had wanted to know: Still alive,
Gesine? If only we knew whether John Kennedy was killed by a
lunatic or on orders. The Air Force is losing micromines along the
Florida beaches and has no idea how. Railroads, telephone companies, automobile plants, schools, were the object of strikes. It's got
nothing to do with us, we're guests here, we're not to blame. We're
not to blame yet. In Vietnam more Americans are being killed than
South Vietnamese, and General Westmoreland has ordered more.
The legislators are laughing themselves sick over a law against the rat
plague in the slums. De Gaulle promises freedom to Quebec. Over
and over again the great powers photograph the far side of the moon.
Krupp has died, and Ilse Koch has committed suicide. One of the
inventors of the gas chamber, a fat German in his mid-fifties, was to
be seen entering the dock in a Stuttgart courtroom. This summer is
over, that is the past of our future, these are our expectations of life.
Yet underneath Broadway, at the 86th Street station, when an
express goes thundering northward on the center tracks, we look at
the unmoving, unseeing people through the windows flashing by and
dread the day when we might cease to be one of them, a future in
which our life in New York might exist only in nostalgia.

September 16, 1967   Saturday

Saturday is South Ferry Day. South Ferry Day is considered to have
officially begun when Marie announces their departure for the Battery at noon.

Her first sight of the ferries between the southern tip of Manhattan and Staten Island had been from the tourist deck of the
France, in the days when she had still to be lifted up to the railing.
She stared hostilely at Manhattan's skyscraper cactus growing to
gigantic proportions instead of diminishing to human ones; with
curiosity she watched the ferryboats quartering New York Harbor
beside the transatlantic liner, many-storied houses painted orange
with blue trim, racing along like fire engines. She nodded, dazed,
when Gesine could not tell her what they were; on an outing she
recognized the type at a second glance, although the ferry doors had
obscured the exterior for her like blinkers.

The Staten Island Ferry had been her first wish in New York, desired ardently enough for her to wait time after time and without nag-

ging for it to come true: the trip by the Brooklyn express to Chambers Street, jogging along on the local as far as the screeching loop of the subway around the South Ferry station, emerging from underground into the big waiting room, all without haste or hurry. But when the great doors were rolled back along the walls she started to tug Gesine by the hand through the passages and over the gangplanks to the vessel, as if in all that space for three thousand people she might miss the one spot that was uniquely hers. In those days when she drew pictures of New York for her Düsseldorf friends she used to represent it as one huge harbor for window-studded orange floating caves containing a kindergarten next to great numbers of cars. In those days she still let people ask her why she spent Gesine's free day on trips with the South Ferry: because it is a house that drives; because it is a street between the islands that takes itself across; because it is a restaurant in which you can travel without having to pay the price of leaving home.

And at the South Ferry turnstiles she was allowed for the first time in this city to pay her own fare; here she was accepted among the citizens.

Meanwhile she invariably starts off her use of the vessel on the car deck, supervising the ferry people as they untie the hawsers and close the grilles, until the men take off their gloves and stroll through the car tunnel to the other bow. In the smoking lounges below and on the main deck she goes in search of the shoeshine man with whom she has a standing order for her Sunday shoes and carries on a running, skeptical conversation about his concession and his life on the ferry. And at the snack bar, among the tourists on the foredeck, among the family parties and old-age pensioners and children between the rows of scratched brown benches, there are enough people to be observed so carefully and politely that if she should be spoken to she can casually move away. She moves away along the passage, absorbed in looking, a lanky child wearing braids and a faded windbreaker, frayed white pants and shiny best brown shoes. She says nothing about what makes her follow the Negro girl of her own age who was carrying around a two-year-old child on her hip, one hand holding the ice-cream cone teasingly to the infant's quivering querulous mouth; she says nothing about the old man with the crossword puzzle who asked her the French for lobby (she gave it to him). When she thinks no one is looking, but only then, she turns her head and walks a few casual steps behind the child playing mother. When confronted with a policeman, as with any official uniform, she steps aside as she has been doing ever since seeing pictures of American soldiers in the Dominican Republic in 1965; policemen are the only people to whom her sole response is a crooked, uncertain smile. Occasionally, keeping a tactful distance, she circles the bench where her mother sits turning the pages of the newspaper. With a formal nod she conveys that she does not intend to disturb her. During the forty-five minutes it takes from Manhattan to Staten Island and back, she has covered the hundred yards from bow to bow several times.

But Marie waits for the return trip, when the ferry is once more level with South Brooklyn, before taking Gesine up onto the top deck and identifying the ships lying in the gloomy mist outside the Narrows, the fort on Governors Island, and the barracks erected by the Army beside the classical red and white buildings from the last century; she lets her face be scoured by the swift wet wind on which the fringes of Hurricane Dora are approaching the hanging cables of the three bridges over the darkening East River. She says: "Thank you very much for taking me," gravely and without batting an eyelid, as if she had needed to be supervised on the South Ferry. It has never occurred to her to ride the South Ferry alone.

Then we went to Rande and took the excursion steamer to Travemünde. She came along as far as Hamburg. She wasn't sad.

We were very tired, we were very merry—
We had gone back and forth all night on the ferry.

September 17, 1967   Sunday

At noon yesterday in London's Bayswater Road a man could be seen being dragged into a car against his will by four others. He was heard calling for the police. In the afternoon Scotland Yard sent squad cars to Heathrow that blocked the runway and prevented an Aeroflot aircraft from taking off. After a tug-of-war with the captain and crew, the police removed from the surrounded machine a young Soviet physicist who had been studying at Birmingham University for the past eight months. When interrogated by the British he did not seem very coherent. A Soviet Embassy spokesman explained that Mr. Tkachenko had wished to leave England earlier than planned on account of nervous exhaustion, and that the Embassy doctor had given him an injection. (At which point Mr. Tkachenko called for the police.)

Cresspahl, back in London at the start of the thirty-sixth tax week in 1931, now began preparing in all earnestness for life with

Papenbrock's youngest daughter. The two helpers with whom he normally carried on his carpentry business now frequently saw him standing in the yard that was enclosed by back yards, his eyes on the brick paving or turned toward the smokestack of the Richmond gasworks, one hand on the back of his neck, deep in thought without ever wondering what he was doing. But since they had both worked for him, and usually beside him, for over a year, they merely pointed the boss out to one another with a smile as he stood there in the heat like a blind man, for minutes on end, until it dawned on him that the planing indoors had stopped. The younger helper, whose name was Perceval, went on a tour of reconnaissance late one evening, but all he had to report was that the boss had been hard at it in the workshop until midnight. After that they offered to work overtime. But Cresspahl had no intention of firing either of them.

The firm did not belong to Cresspahl. The firm, Pascal & Son, belonged to Albert A. Gosling, Esq. Albert A. Gosling was a wiry, nervous little man, part-owner of a piece-goods business in Uxbridge, and had become Pascal's legal heir. Reggie Pascal, without issue and himself the Son in the firm's name, had intended the business to go to the carpenters' guild in Richmond. As a distant relative, Gosling had contested the disposition and, being a retailer, all he saw in the workshop was a piece of property to be sold. The lawyers, Messrs. Burse, Dunaway & Salomon, who represented their alternately warlike and wormlike client without enthusiasm, got the better of themselves and explained that the firm of Pascal & Son, which for a generation had served a steady middle-class and aristocratic clientèle, represented capital. When Albert A. Gosling showed that at least he understood that capital yielded interest, Messrs. Burse, Dunaway & Salomon advertised in the *Richmond and Twickenham Times* for a master carpenter who would be prepared to act as manager for a carpentry business. Cresspahl noticed the advertisement when he returned with Mrs. Trowbridge from a trip to Dorking and invited her to supper at Short's "Greyhound" in George Street, Richmond. Or was it she who had noticed the advertisement?

Throughout the spring of 1929, Albert Gosling, wearing a new bowler hat, would appear at the workshop and try to check up on Cresspahl. However, since he could not tell a vise from a file, he would talk about his childhood veneration of Reggie Pascal (whose bones in Sheen Cemetery he had nevertheless failed to visit) and ask for payments on account. His whining insinuations made Cresspahl's workmen feel uncomfortable, and Cresspahl insisted on the accounts' going through the lawyers. Burse, Dunaway & Salomon jointly im-

plored Gosling to leave the workshop in peace; at one point Dunaway
became so enraged that he pushed the file clear across his desk and
almost over the edge. Gosling invested his profits in new custom-
made suits and, his beard now a neat Vandyke, spent more time
hanging around Paddington Station with young blades than in the
shop with his wife at Uxbridge; when he did come to Richmond it
was to sit in respectable bar parlors inveighing against the Germans,
in fighting whom he claimed to have risked his life. Cresspahl was
told of this not only by waiters but also by Perceval, at that time an
apprentice. (Perceval would have liked to see his master hit back just
once.) Mr. Smith supplied the information that during the war
Gosling had counted caps at the Dartmouth naval supply base.
Salomon, who as the junior partner of Burse and Dunaway had been
saddled with the Pascal file, had taken a liking to the stubborn craftsman from "Michelinburg" who did not insist on talking about the
Depression or the Jews, and his personal advice to him would have
been to resign as manager had not his loyalty to his client, in the face
of Cresspahl's handsome profits, triumphed in the end. Cresspahl
had met members of the Jewish faith not only as dealers in the
villages around Malchow but also as noncoms on the Western front,
and he had no trouble getting used to Arthur Salomon, who showed
such unabashed pride in his Oxford accent, his conservative black, his
office furnished in rosewood, the legal tomes behind his small, alert,
disillusioned head. Cresspahl instructed him to feign an offer for
Pascal's property, although at a lower price. Then he had him draft a
settlement for Mrs. Elizabeth Trowbridge.

It was perhaps for three weeks that his memory retained the
sight of a small-town girl waving from the St. Pauli wharf, the whole
trip from Hamburg to Kingston-on-Hull as far as King's Cross Station, one full day and ten hours, and then another twenty days at
work, and still during his last supper with Elizabeth Trowbridge.
Then Lisbeth Papenbrock sent him a product of Horst Stellmann,
the Gneez photographer, Portraits A Specialty: a girl, not striking in
appearance, with her hair parted in the middle and combed down
over her ears, Lisbeth Papenbrock with her hands folded in front of
her stomach, posed against Stellmann's curiously gathered draperies.
She is looking cautiously and in amusement at the portrait camera
where Stellmann is writhing under his black cloth, and her lips are
slightly parted. Cresspahl instantly forgot all previous images.

A wee bit odd
Is loved by God.

September 18, 1967   Monday

Where we live Broadway is old. Our Broadway begins at 72nd Street, where it meets Amsterdam Avenue and cuts across Verdi Square. Here a spacious center strip, bordered at the intersections with benches and in some instances shrubs, divides Broadway into two wide boulevards. On either side of the street, elephantine specimens of Renaissance architecture rear up, and far to the north the many-windowed buildings under their rhapsodic moldings bear witness to the feverish confidence in real estate that started galloping off around 1900, at the time the subway was built under Broadway. There are hotels, movie houses, apartment houses, dating from an age in which profits were invested, when art nouveau or Italian scrollwork around the knees and brows of buildings was still designed to proclaim their worth. The boom did not suffice for closed ranks of these ornate monsters; between them, humble and four-storied, crouch the more cautiously calculated apartment houses that made less effort to hide their fire escapes, and now their age betrays them. Few hotels have been able to retain their affluent customers and preserve the reputation promised by the façade; by and large they now provide shelter for permanent residents, penurious old-age pensioners, scarcely anyone with children. The apartment houses need not advertise their vacancies for long: although their address carries no prestige they are well served with subway stations and bus lines in all four directions. But for forty years not one new building has gone up on this street and, despite the galaxy of lights from the stores at the foot of the façades, Broadway recalls views from the days when horses still trotted in front of vehicles and the residents spoke of the "boulevard."

And old people stand motionless on the traffic islands along Broadway, step cautiously forward onto the quickly usurped crosswalks, hover at the edge of a crowd surrounding a peddler, kill time over a cup of coffee in automats: discarded people. These people failed to save their property from the Nazis and get it out of Europe; they received no substantial compensation, they cannot prolong a comfortable middle-class past in the polished apartments along Riverside Drive, they live by themselves. Discarded by their children, the survivors of long marriages, solitarily they live out the last warm days on Broadway, but still close to movement, traffic, bustle, until it is time to go back to their furnished rooms, to the old-people's homes on West End Avenue. These are not old gentlemen taking a rest after a well-planned walk, or old ladies savoring the delights of impulse-buying, as they sit on benches along Broadway, these are wards of state welfare, and little more than their clean clothes and erect posture divides them from the ragged black-skinned man behind them sweating out some noxious liquor on the reverberating subway gratings. And the desire to chat with neighbors is tempered by reluctance. The *Novoje Slovo*, from which two are jointly reading about the state of the world, is not adequate, it is not enough for solidarity that their mothers were neighbors in Ruthenian villages, and what kind of intimacy can spring from discussing their marriages and the careers of their children if the children do not come, either to visit or to meet them in cheap cafés where water is free, and sometimes cream and sugar too? Nor can it even be said that with twenty cents and years of loyalty they have a claim on society for a rendezvous, for when their automat's lease expires the proprietors move on, looking for customers with less time, more cash. The only thing left is the benches.

September 19, 1967 Tuesday

For your child, Gesine Cresspahl, it had to be a private kindergarten, and you didn't mind its being held in a church donated to God by a Rockefeller in memory of his mother, in spacious, clean classrooms high above Riverside Park and the Hudson, with teachers who were paid well to be patient with middle-class children, Mrs. Jeuken, Mrs. Davidoff, who made Marie believe in a world in which kindness, lack of envy, and obedience pay off; for that you skimped and saved the month and a half's salary, and your excuse was that "things must be made easy for her to learn the new language." Weren't you teaching your child to expect a lot?

The British have turned back the runaway physicist to the Soviets. Both sides are now agreed that he is a sick man, and each power reproaches the other with lack of proper behavior.

But your child, Gesine Cresspahl, even when she was six did not go to a public school, to one of those shabby brick buildings that reek of fiscal avarice, to overcrowded classrooms where the children of the poor sleep off the quarrels of their parents, where underpaid teachers have to be more concerned with self-defense than with teaching, to a world where what counts is the blow, the cut and thrust. Didn't you

*like the broken benches, the stinking toilets, the bleak cement yards
behind stout wire netting? Or was your child not to be deprived of
instruction because of walkouts like this six-day-old one that today is
keeping four fifths of New York's teachers out of school, a strike in
which the issues are not only salaries but new schools, smaller classes,
rights to disciplinary action against disruptive children? In a school
for Marie are the police not to appear and drive delegates from the
colored community out of the building? Are there some things you
know that you want to keep your child from knowing?*

"When Patrolman Clarke was led from the floor with his head
bandaged, some of the women demonstrators shouted: 'I hope you
die.' "

*So the only place good enough for your child, Mrs. Cresspahl,
was a private school on the northern slopes of Riverside Drive, and a
Catholic one at that, a concrete pile of finest cut and costly work-
manship, listed in the record of contemporary architecture, an institution with a two-year waiting list and fees running to three of your
salaries. You were not put off by the discreet bus that takes the
children past and away from the slums to unalloyed knowledge; you
were not embarrassed by the school uniform, the navy-blue blazer
with the gold crest on the breast pocket. Your child is already to be
treated as a separate and independent person, her abilities are to be
recognized and developed as early as possible; but why by people
wearing long brown habits with a white cord around the waist and
limited intelligence under the coif? True, with a certificate from this
institution the child will be admitted to the elite universities, unlike
the graduates of P.S. 75, and she will have friends in the wealthy
families to which she does not belong. Why this pretense, when two
fees in arrears are enough to explode it?*

The East Germans have told the West Germans (according to
the New York *Times* correspondent): Overcome your militarism,
and your neo-Fascism, and the power of your monopolies; then we'll
negotiate with you.

*And when your child, Mrs. Cresspahl, goes for a medical
checkup she does not go to a city clinic, need not wait in the lousy
moldy corridors beside people lying there bleeding, or unconscious, or
mentally defective, your child goes to a doctor's office on Park*

Avenue, announced like a lady, greeted like a friend, fifteen dollars a visit, forty dollars a blood count. Your child knows her doctor by name, writes him letters, dares to call him on the telephone. Your child's doctor earned his outstanding marks not at a state university but at Harvard, and for your child the doctor will make a house call. Where else could you find that, a New York doctor, gross annual income over a hundred thousand, making a house call for a slight temperature and discussing the treatment in a leisurely conversation, relaxed and idle in his chair, not the professional man, the business-man, more like a friend paying a social call? For your child the best is just good enough, Mrs. Cresspahl? Why for your child? There's some mail for you too, Gesine.

Dear Mr./Mrs./Miss Cresspahl:

I have been called up without notice for active military service. Kindly settle any outstanding accounts with my attorney. You may be sure I will inform you of my return. . . .

Washington, Sept. 18 (AP)

The Defense Department identified today the following men killed in action in Vietnam: Second Lieut. William D. Huyler Jr. of Short Hills, N. J.; Specialist 4 Harold J. Canan of Oceanside, L. I., and Pvt. Laifeit Grier of Brooklyn, of the Army, and Lance Cpl. James P. Braswell Jr. of the Bronx and Pfc. Robert C. Wallace of Plattsburgh, N. Y., of the Marines.

September 20, 1967   Wednesday

Thirty-six years ago yesterday or the day after tomorrow, Lisbeth Papenbrock took the streetcar to Fuhlsbüttel, picked up the airline ticket that had been ordered in advance, boarded the aircraft for London, landed in Bremen, landed in Amsterdam, landed nine hours later at Croydon, and was driven in an open taxi to Richmond, a worn-out, excited traveler who stared with parted lips at the reddish colors of the streets dulled by the afternoon fog, and was almost surprised to find that the New Star and Garter Hotel existed not only in Grieben's guidebook but also at Richmond Hill (eight shillings. Twenty per cent unemployment in England). When the cab driver drove off grumbling over the tip, she almost ran after him. She did not want to begin here by making mistakes.

It was dark by now, thick coal-black night when she stood in the yard outside Cresspahl's workshop. She took her time, watching him as he worked, a sturdy fellow in a shirt and no collar who had neglected the yellow stubble of his beard for days and, swearing under his breath, was busy with some heavy clamps. Now and again he would grimace, deep in thought, so sure was he of being alone. When at last he came to the door with his pipe he could not see who it was, and saw who it was.

They were very moved. All the words he had offered her about the house and about Salomon and about Richmond instantly took on for her the shape of his stairs, his kitchen, his room, and the smoke-stacks of the gasworks beyond the window. His visit to Jerichow steadily increased in reality. Already she was afraid of losing him; she hoped she would die before he did.

Cresspahl was taken aback. (He did not mind the money she had squandered on this trip; in fact he was uneasy at their having agreed to live within a careful budget.) He was taken aback at the sudden impulses which, after this one, he would have to expect of her. It staggered him to find how blindly she believed she was keeping pace with him; while he was still being chafed by a sense of strangeness and distance, she no longer felt any separation at all. She seemed to him like a child running an egg-and-spoon race who is so carried away that it forgets that its playmates also want, by fair means or foul, to bring their fragile burden to its destination; he felt an added obligation to make sure that it arrived intact. Now he was superior to her not only in age. She had made herself dependent. He had not wanted that.

During the day she let him work, and by evening he had thought so much on her behalf that he began to talk incessantly. Each was so sure of the other that they started talking back, not only in fun. They would tenderly recite the times and places at which they might have met earlier: in 1914 at the Whitsun market in Malchow, in 1920 at the town hall of Waren, in 1923 in Amsterdam, in August 1931 for just one minute at the station in Schwerin. All losses seemed un-thinkable; now they had made it.

They invited each other out (the German foreign-currency restriction of 100 marks having just been abolished), and when Cresspahl wanted to take her to Schmidt's in Charlotte Street for a German meal she asked to be taken to an English restaurant. (Leslie Danzmann had given her one of her dresses.) He handed her the menu to choose from. She gathered that she was to practice her English, and he saw the waiter tuck a smile into his mustache. (Not so long ago he had been dining with Elizabeth Trowbridge at the White Horse in Dorking. The White Horse was another thing he would have had to sacrifice.) She was not intending to educate him when she brought him a safety razor, she wanted to give that impression. She was so full of high spirits, on the top of a double-decker tram at the peak rush hour, that people sitting nearby had smiles for her, for Cresspahl too. Once, with her purse lying on the table, she had paid a bill and covered his tobacco pouch with her hand and put it in her handbag so that he would not have to carry it, so that later he could ask her for it, so that later she would have something to give him.

He had made a table, a light and sturdy oak frame, that would seat them and four children. That was fine with her. He showed her his designs for beds, but she ordered one in which they could lie together. That was fine with him.

She told him about her walks in Richmond, what she thought of the various shops. The winding main street reminded her of Gneez, each building with a different façade, and the smallness of the shops, the often overcrowded sidewalks. (He did not look at her; he did not notice that she went on at length about the parish church.) He wanted to show his gratitude and asked about Jerichow, and she told derogatory stories about Jerichow:

Molten the baker had a hand-painted sign in his window: Germans, Eat German Bread! At home she would not have thought of laughing at it, but standing in front of a bakery window in George Street she was seized with a fit of the giggles.

(She did not tell him that Pastor Methling had thundered from the pulpit against the surveying of Jerichow land for a Catholic church. "So come to church on Reformation Day in your top hats!" he had shouted. Since Jerichow's trades were preparing for big orders to follow from this commission, Pahl the tailor had to put a new top hat in his window every day. The craftsmen of Jerichow were indeed planning to show Pastor Methling his top hats, although not for his reasons.)

She made her brother look ridiculous in order to please Cresspahl: Horst Papenbrock, who turned up for supper in brown shirt and Sam Browne belt, who walked up and down the main street with Griem, likewise in uniform, merely because the German Government had lifted the ban against the Brownshirts: as a public demonstration. Horst Papenbrock, who can never amount to anything with the Brownshirts because his father won't come across with a truck for propaganda trips into the countryside. Horst Papenbrock, who ac-

quires a small, almost soft voice when he begs his father for donations to the Brownshirts.

*Dad, you surely can't want your son to run around like an
ordinary Storm Trooper.*
Berlin's lifted the ban against you. That'll do to go on with.

And what has the New York *Times* picked today from the life of
Stalin's daughter for our particular attention? "It was May. Flowers
were in bloom outside the dacha. 'So you want to get married, do
you?' he remarked. For a long time he stared at the trees and said
nothing. 'Yes, it's spring,' he remarked all of a sudden. 'To hell with
you. Do as you like.' " (1944)

*I wanted to sleep with you before we got married, Heinrich
Cresspahl. In a bed, I mean.*

September 21, 1967   Thursday

Our building on Riverside Drive has another entrance in the basement where 96th Street approaches the underpass, an unsuspected
lead-gray door after the open caverns of the three garages and before
the dark approach to the overpass, a passage opening between angle
walls. Beyond the open door, which today has sucked in damp brown
leaves from the park, all the others are locked: the door to the inside
fire stairs, the one to the elevators, the others hiding maintenance
equipment and garbage incinerator. This evening the low passage is
too narrow for Mrs. Cresspahl; she is not patient as she presses the
button that summons Mr. Robinson to the basement, not because
she is wet through, not because she would have a hard time defending herself with shopping bags in both arms: in just such a passage
(reports the New York *Times*)
in the basement of a building on West 181st Street

near Fort Washington Avenue
*always right beside us: whenever we transferred from the subway
to the express buses, whenever we took out-of-town visitors to George
Washington Bridge, whenever we ate chicken Jewish-style, not far
from just such a respectable building of bricks held together by once
elegant sandstone decoration, a few steps from that basement, always
right beside us,*

Mr. Hartnett, the building superintendent, yesterday found two steamer trunks with tags reading "Property of Anne Solomon." Her widower knew nothing about any such trunks and left it to Mr. Hartnett to open them. One was empty. The other contained the bodies of three infants, tightly wrapped in tarpaper and evening newspapers of January 1920, March 1922, and October 1923, as well preserved as mummies. According to Mr. Solomon, who did not marry Anne until 1933, she had previously been a domestic in White Plains. She must have waited until 1935, after moving to 181st Street, before secretly storing the trunk in the basement, then to live over it until 1954, the year of her own death.

"An American mother," says Mr. Robinson, noticing Mrs. Cresspahl's eyes on the *Daily News* spread out on the stool beside him in the elevator. He stands facing the grille door while he takes her up from basement level. "An American mother," he says in his thin hard Spanish voice: "the first time at fourteen, then at sixteen, then at seventeen, and at twenty-seven she finally got married. What was there left for her to tell Jacob Solomon?"

Mr. Robinson, "Robinson of the aquiline profile," for the past two years one of the three elevator operators in this building, soon began to greet Mrs. Cresspahl with utterances that sounded like *Auff'iddezen* or *goodnmong'* and has reluctantly resigned himself to her English replies. Mr. Robinson had spent youthful years in Germany. He believes he understands this foreign lady.

"The scenery in Germany, *wunneba*," he would say. He repeated this sentence willingly in order to suppress other ones; he wanted to give the German lady pleasure. For while it was true that the Cuban refugee had bought his civil rights more quickly by volunteering for the Army, and in North Carolina was still grateful for his training as a low-frequency technician, in the restricted zone around the Schwarzer Berg near Grafenwöhr he found that a mirror was being held up to him by the Army. In the mirror of the Army he became aware of his red skin, almost as red as an American Indian's, and of his black hair covering his head in short shining waves down onto the nape of his neck, so stiff that they never got out of place under his patting fingers. Private 4th class Robinson had first to be reprimanded for getting into a fight with some pink-skinned soldiers outside the Bayreuth railroad station before he learned to go drinking with dark-skinned soldiers in the dirtier bars where the rum was more expensive and the girls showed their contempt more openly and at higher prices. The scenery was the forest of the Upper Palatinate that he could see at night from the window of the radar truck near Flossenbürg on the Czechoslovak border.

Flossenbürg concentration camp can best be described as a factory dealing in death. Vicious killings of Jews were the order of the day, poison injections and shootings in the back of the neck were daily occurrences.

For his final year Private Robinson had himself transferred to West Berlin. To West Berlin too, as everywhere abroad, the Army exported the ghettos it prohibited in its military zones at home; in West Berlin too, the bars for second-class Americans were drearier, more often a target for the police, and more expensive than the taverns for ordinary citizens. And in Berlin the Germans laughed at the foreigners parading down Clay Avenue on July Fourth in their armored equipment, hands held flat under their chins, sitting like ramrods in impractical attitudes, staring fiercely ahead like dolls in toy vehicles. In Berlin he knew a girl who wanted to learn some of his English. With his English from the streets of the Bronx the girl was not understood by Americans who had learned theirs in a school. Private Robinson had been thinking of a love affair. Berlin could not hold him in Germany. The Army could not hold him.

"And it might have been a girl friend who planted the steamer trunk with the mummies in Anne Solomon's basement," says Mr. Robinson, low-frequency technician, elevator operator, electrician, plumber, house painter, dealer in used television sets, superintendent of the storage basement (who does not recognize Mrs. Cresspahl when he meets her on Broadway in the company of smartly dressed Negroes, heavyset men of uncommonly cheerful disposition), a person who cannot be questioned, cannot be fully understood. He precedes Mrs. Cresspahl out of the elevator and presses her bell until Marie opens the door, today only the width of the chain, carefully and not altogether relieved by the sight of him.

"We did as you said," he promises the child, who keeps him there with a questioning, expectant look. "We searched all over. Puedes estar segura. En nuestra casa no hay cementerio particular."

As he turns away he winks at Mrs. Cresspahl. While he winks he raises his hand and pats the skin at the corner of his left eye, several times, with careful fingers, as always when we are quite sure he is lying.

September 22, 1967   Friday

The Secretary of State has allowed his daughter to marry a Negro, who is also, incidentally, a second lieutenant in the Air Force Reserve and has applied for service in Vietnam.

Since 1961, approximately 13,365 U. S. citizens have been killed in action in Vietnam.

September 23, 1967   Saturday

In 1931, ten eggs cost 78 pfennigs, a pound of butter one mark thirty. St. Peter's Church in Jerichow had the following scale of charges: for wedding decorations and cleaning up afterward, two marks; for ringing the bells at the approach of the bridal car, three marks; for lighting altar candles, one mark; for choir and organ during the ceremony, three marks; and it sold admission tickets to others than members of the wedding party for twenty-five pfennigs. All fees payable in advance. From this catalogue Lisbeth Papenbrock had ordered everything except the invitation cards and the tiresome singing; on Reformation Day after lunch she actually found herself being driven in one of Swenson's black rental cars through the main street to the church; her feelings were mixed. She had anticipated the sensation so often, now the hope of it trembled and broke, not only under the stares from both sidewalks as she sat in the slow-moving car, stares that seemed to her barely polite, not only under the grim silence of the family, who since yesterday evening had been split with quarrels in all directions: Louise Papenbrock with her husband and the bride because the wedding procession was not to arrive on foot; Papenbrock with his oldest daughter because the husband she had brought along was not only bankrupt but drunk; she in turn with Horst because he could not hold his tongue about the anonymous letters Cresspahl was said to have received; Horst with his father because the latter would not allow him to wear his Brownshirt uniform to the ceremony (although Pastor Methling had been willing to regard a delegation of uniformed Storm Troopers as a patriotic demonstration), because his Krakow brother-in-law had once again been helped out of his debts, because Lisbeth's dowry came off his inheritance; Lisbeth with Horst because he had called Cresspahl's relatives common; Papenbrock with everyone because they had tried to force him to invite his oldest son in "Rio de Janeiro";

what was really worrying her was Cresspahl's acquiescent behavior. She did not think this was right. He had agreed to having the wedding on Reformation Day, the announcements prepared for the *Rostocker Zeitung* and the *Gneezer Tageblatt* and the *Lübecker Generalanzeiger* had been returned from Richmond without a single change, he had allowed her to have her way with the topic for the sermon ("No man, having put his hand to the plough, and looking back, is fit for the kingdom of God"; Luke 9, 62), he had, to be sure, insisted on Dr. Semig being invited but not the Wulffs, he had finally accepted the loan of a hat from Papenbrock so as to be wearing something he could take off at the church door, all this in exchange for the assurance and confidence that at seven thirty the Number 2 express would rescue the two of them from Jerichow and take them to Hamburg. But if he wanted a deal, why not credit her with something for the will to move to a foreign country, which, when all was said and done, remained the greater sacrifice?

I'm doing it for you, Cresspahl. You're the one I'm doing it for. But do you see that?

This is the first photo: the bridegroom with my mother against the churchyard wall, her face abbreviated to eyes and lips, unrecognizable beneath the border of the long veil that drew a line across her forehead and above that followed and exposed the outline of her head in an absurd and fragile-looking pot shape, he (long since hatless) to her right, his left arm behind her back but not touching her, a farmer disguised in his loose-fitting black suit (from Ladage & Oehlke, Alster Arcades, Hamburg), an outsider with lips offering a stolid pout rather than a smile, a stranger trusting in the Stettin-Hamburg express. Next comes a picture of Cresspahl's mother, an old lady with twisted shoulders whose grimace of happiness over the stumps of yellow teeth miscarries under the arid graying hair, so hard is she straining to hear in her worn-out, overworked body, our Grannikins, eighteen months before her death. Placed next to her is Gertrud Niebuhr, her second child, embarrassed and awkward at the honor and the advantage, who will wait to get home before reliving the celebration in the most animated of words, and Martin Niebuhr, friendly and stiff in his unaired Sunday suit, and Peter Niebuhr, forestry student from Berlin, his eyes invisible behind his glinting spectacles, standing there as if he had found himself in some all too distant land. All these people could speak only a very southern variety of Low German. And facing them Stellmann shifts his tripod farther and farther back, extends one hand with three beseeching fingers from under the black cloth, entreating with sharp commands more synchronized facial expressions. And then there is one in which the semicircle of assembled relatives, including the minister, appears against a black background of numerous stalwart men, each under a black top hat. These men had not got into the wedding picture out of spite but had allowed a modicum of pleasure to creep into their stony solemn expressions, as if on this Reformation Day Someone, and not one of them, mark you, had been made to look a proper fool.

This picture is one I never saw.

The other is a photograph, stuck onto varnished cardboard and bearing the engraved address of Stellmann the photographer, the view of a long table under flashlight and lamplight reflected in the table centerpieces and the meat platters. When I saw this picture, it had hardly been handled. But the sepia in its cardboard folder had turned almost dark brown and blurred the outlines of the faces. I recognized Papenbrock by his pear-shaped skull, also by the rather servile severity with which he leaned toward the lady on his right. This lady, in a suit that looked like a uniform and was designed to emphasize her square shoulders, may have been a relative of the Bothmers and was called Isa. The woman on Papenbrock's other side I know to be my mother; I have been told this. This time she is wearing what may be a green blouse drawn in at the neck with a narrow white cord; the photograph catches her with one hand behind her head touching the hair that has been done up in the form of a casque, so that she is laughing, with pleasure at her gaucheness but as though the laugh did not suit her. This was the face that mine resembled in 1956. The photograph is spoiled by Cresspahl's having turned half his broad back toward the lens, in conversation with the attorney from Krakow who has drunk up Hilde Papenbrock's patrimony and is inflicting one misfortune after another on her; and this is the man, disbarred from the Mecklenburg Legal Society, thrusting his dark head forward as bold as brass, gay but perhaps only artful with his screwed-up eyes, his firm cheeks, whom Cresspahl is toasting in cognac. Next to these two the camera has caught a man in the act of leaving: Semig with the rabbit head, Semig with the wide flat brush to the front of his shorn rabbit head, Semig with the crooked lips and the wrinkled nose, but it is not that he has to sneeze; he is just trying to look friendly. Semig left before the guests had finished their coffee. He stopped behind my mother and bent over her shoulder, not for long, for seven words (You'll be happy with that girl,

Cresspahl). He nodded to the others as he left the room, and for long after, the Bothmers, as well as the Papenbrocks, talked of his behavior as being surprisingly tactful for a Jew, and a professional man at that. Pastor Methling was annoyed with Semig because now he could not decently remain seated. The minute he was out the door the schnapps bottles appeared on the table, and when my mother and Cresspahl reached Hamburg by the Number 2 express at nine fifteen and walked across to the Reichshof Hotel,

"they were married," says Marie. (Saturday is South Ferry Day, when so proclaimed by Marie.)

September 25, 1967   Monday

How come: she wonders, he wonders, we wonder. How come she is suspended, seat belt fastened, tilted back, in a three-engined jet, stacked over Pennsylvania? But the massed clouds in the foreground and the level strata to the north earlier on recall the Arctic (pictures of the Arctic), the edges imagined somewhat sharper, icier. Only her watch knew it was afternoon; the white radiance under the blue sphere just kept repeating "light, light." The aircraft is at an angle of about forty degrees, apparently aiming at a blue sea-hazy hole in which browny-yellow patches of dirt indicate human settlements. The wing slanting against the swelling cloud clusters was the only sign of the plane's repeated curve. That must have been April 1962, when she was obtaining American visas for European passports; after a few weeks the passports would come back from Milan in registered envelopes as if none of them had ever traveled to East Germany. That morning in Minneapolis, in the mirror facing the bed, her whole body had looked yellow, one night closer to death. It is the sun, sinking into the cloud cover, that coats the wing in glowing fire. Gradually the white sculpture of the sky is being leveled to a bluish tufted expanse. The captain reports, grumbling for the passengers' sake, on new instructions from ground control in New York. New York, will we ever get there? The stewardesses served the second round of Bloody Marys, raw vodka floating on the tomato juice. A girl can afford weekend trips like this only with blank airline tickets such as those issued to important stockholders. She can't cross the Atlantic with these tickets, and the Pacific only as far as Hawaii. In Milan, Vito Genovese lived for a time next door to Karsch. In Minneapolis, on Foshay Tower, there had been two women and a man who turned their eyes toward the forests and dotted lakes in the north whenever other tourists pushed past them behind. (Je vous assure que vos papiers d'identité ne serviront pas aux buts anti-communistes.) Where was the child? The child was at Mrs. Ferwalter's. No, on an eleventh floor. The child mustn't forget to buy the New York *Times.* The child, the two last Cresspahl eyes, as a survivor. The aircraft is now circling below the clouds, over a twilit coastal area, pinpoints of lighted windows, cars not discernible. One of those echoing sonorous voices will say into the phone: Marie, do you have a father, a grand-mother, any relatives? Be brave now, or else! Without warning the aircraft begins to race, swooping low over the Atlantic in the direc-tion of Brooklyn, close to shrouded Verrazano Bridge, the Empire State Building rearing solitary in the night, vaporizing under its braided lights. Coney Island, a whirl of colored lights. Chains of headlights on the expressways. Blue street lights swathed in mist. Slow taxiing on the approaches, waiting to enter the main runways. Once a deep tunnel teeming with cars caught her eye beyond the wing. In the pigeonholes for passengers' mail there is no message under the letter C. The downtown bus is marking time, stuck in traffic. The gravestones to left and right flicker past under city lights. The tunnel, the tiled Hades beneath the river. At the terminal, numbers for taxis are handed out. This town won't last much longer. What's so special about First Avenue? This town may last another two hundred years. (The doorman on the ground level of Foshay Tower stood there so anxiously, so reproachfully, as if he himself were Foshay, who in the end lost everything, shares and cash and tower.) At 96th Street the railroad emerges from under Park Avenue: the rich live on stilts. Central Park is totally black. In the middle there is not only a stable for police horses but a pistol range for the police. A return ticket to Minneapolis. Maybe the child has kept the tea warm and put the papers on the table, with a note saying DON'T CHANGE THE ALARM. Although wind-swept Singer Bowl in Queens may have been filled yesterday with striking public-school teachers, for Marie there is private school tomorrow. Now let's read the agony column. "My wife having left my bed and board I am no longer responsible for her maintenance."

"Gesine, wake up. Where were you?"

"A few years ago."

September 26, 1967   Tuesday

"Despite the forecast of milder days ahead, there was a feeling of autumn in the air. And it wasn't entirely welcome.

" 'It looks like fall is really here,' said a gas station proprietor in Upper Montclair. 'I don't know how many more winters I can stand.' " ©

Cresspahl did not get very old.

Time and again the soft white-gray light over the brilliant green squadron of trees, where the marshes used to be. He couldn't see that well any more. Time and again the smell of the green leaves, still strong and fresh, with the west wind. So much hurtful hoping. Now there was a brown patch of spindly stalks in the hollow, and the smell of mold, until the ground starts to freeze.

The town was no bigger than it had been decades ago. He could walk from one end to the other, take its measure, look at the children. For the others were dead.

A few days ago a topping of snow had fallen; it would have taken a long time to turn everything white, had it not melted away. Outside the Jerichow post office two four-year-olds were collecting the flakes in the bigger one's cap, showing the passersby, Cresspahl, too: Snow.

Winter. Kern's granddaughter had told him about one winter when the ice slabs had piled up at the foot of the cliff. One could walk on the Baltic. For Elke Kern this had been a First Time.

That piece of ground behind the milk-can stand that his wife had called the garden, he wanted to dig that over again. When his wife died, the fence rotted away, the chickens devoured the garden and scratched it all up. After that he had torn down the wire.

One can go to the cemetery, if one feels like doing as many things as possible for the Last Time. But he didn't remember the woman.

Jakob now, he remembered him. Jakob's grave he did visit. Jakob he did talk to. Well, Jakob. How are things? Yes, Cresspahl. I'm lying here on display, you know. Creutz fixed up the grave as a showpiece, and now he's always bringing customers to me, and every time he says: I hope I lie in as fine a grave one day. And then they buy.

Be seeing you, Jakob.

Where the stove has warmed the floor, the cat lies all night, stretched to her full length. She is listening.

She is listening to the pocket watch on the table, to the creaking of the chair.

America is too far away for me to imagine.

When Jöche wakes up he sends his wife to see how I'm doing. Whether I'm still alive.

In Malchow it was still only master craftsmen who were allowed to place another master craftsman on the hearse and lower him into his grave. The clothmakers and shoemakers both have their own hearses.

In February, before the start of this century, there used to be stalls in the Malchow market square selling special cinnamon buns stuffed with almonds and currants, shaped like a jester's cap. Seventy-four's old enough.

Now Jöche's bicycle was propped against the milk-can stand. On the rack hung the rugs from Jöche's parlor. Against the house, the crates of empty beer bottles. Jöche had left the railroad for the brewery. Where does he put all that beer.

Oh, they managed well enough. Jöche had split enough firewood for two winters. Jöche had dug over the ground after all. He wants to sow grass?

September 27, 1967   Wednesday

On Monday yet another bus driver in Harlem was attacked, the second such incident recently. As on the preceding Tuesday, two light-skinned Negroes boarded the bus during rush hour, one grabbed the change money ($28.80) while the other put a knife to the driver's throat. The slashes he received had to be closed with seven stitches. The other passengers fled the bus in panic, if only to avoid having to testify against the robbers. From now on, plain-clothes police will ride the buses in Harlem.

The East Germans want to sell a few hours of film here about captured pilots in Hanoi. Their idea of a price is half a million dollars.

So now life had begun in earnest, eh, Lisbeth Papenbrock?

And with no one to help her. Mrs. Jones, who used to give a lick and a promise to Cresspahl's two rooms and now still came to do the laundry, she couldn't give her any advice about the Richmond butchers and greengrocers, she did her shopping at Brixton station. And Mrs. Jones regarded her as the lady of the house, avoided unseemly conversations that would have forced her to call a spade a spade. Besides, she couldn't understand what Mrs. Jones was saying.

Mrs. Jones would say: Such a special face, beaming at her grandchild, who had flat cheeks like hers and looked as calculatingly out of narrow eyes, pressed her lips to the same thin line, as she did. Lisbeth Papenbrock had understood her to say: Such a special faith. The sound of this English was something she had to repeat over and over again to herself, until a memory from her schooldays more or less fell into place. This language was spoken so fast. And although the inflection appeared limited to a single high tone, actually it often dived down and swooped up again and changed the meanings. She could not blame Mary Hahn for this; Mary Hahn had seen to it that they learned a Scottish English at the Rostock finishing school. And however clearly and slowly she tried to speak, the sales people still paused as they weighed her purchases and looked at her mouth. Cresspahl, who has as much English as a Puerto Rican after two years in New York, Cresspahl they understood.

And she lacked the vocabulary! She could carry on a conversation about John Galsworthy or Sir Thomas Beecham, but she had to point to a casserole or a sieve. Every evening she had Cresspahl translate the recipe for the next day from *Frieda Ihlefeld's Book of Home Cooking* (9th edition, published by Friedrich Bahn, Schwerin, Mecklenburg), but Cresspahl did not have much experience in the jargon of the kitchen, and he did not own a dictionary. (A dictionary was something they had to buy, too. That wasn't exactly saving.) And then she still had to go to the workshop when she was out shopping and ask for the word for bread crumbs, very embarrassed in front of the helpers, to whom Cresspahl proceeded to explain what she wanted by describing the process and making appropriate gestures. And then she had to convert her weights into English ones. And in the restaurants, at the hotel, she had not been expected to watch her sixpences; in Richmond she was expected to watch her pennies.

And Cresspahl never saw that she needed comforting! Cresspahl would come cheerfully upstairs to meals, stretch his legs out under the table, and compliment her on the food. And she noticed a new thing about him: he was able to close his ears. Anything he did not want to hear ran off his alert friendly face like water. He would look at her, the corners of his mouth betraying his pleasure at the sight, he would look just a fraction past her eyes, he never heard her complain. He had not behaved like this while she was still Lisbeth Papenbrock. This made it impossible for her to maintain an argument.

Heinrich, listen, some bad news. Pastor Methling wants to retire at sixty-eight, he must be ill.

He's an employee. With his pension, why should he work longer than he has to.

Heinrich Cresspahl! Let me tell you something! He is laboring for the Lord, and there you go mocking a sick man.

He's lived a healthy life. And if the Lord rewards him for his labors, then he's getting a special deal from his employer.

After the first quarrel about the church she set his plate down before him but did not eat with him. Between meals she went out of the house to punish him, far away into town. She shivered in the alien November. The similarity of the historic buildings with the way she had imagined them was oppressive. Swarms of birds above the rooftops in Parliament Street; she was less at home here than they. A soldier of the Household Cavalry, holding his sword in front of his nose, was marching up and down with ponderous tread among the pedestrians, looking like some enormous cock with his helmet hiding most of his face and his apparent ability to erect the plumage on his helmet. That was another thing she found it impossible to learn: that in the Union Jack a white-bordered red cross of St. George lies on a white diagonal cross of St. Andrew on a blue ground over a red diagonal cross of St. Patrick. On the lawn between Westminster Abbey and St. Margaret's there were poppy graveyards for the military and the paramilitary and other bodies like the fire brigade; little wooden crosses with red rosettes were being offered for sale, already sharpened for sticking in the ground. This was how the poppies had been blooming at the end of the war in Flanders. This was not in memory of the dead on her side. And when she finally did return to Cresspahl, past miles and miles of identical semidetached houses with identical alternately square and curved balconies, identical painted columns, under the white and yellow street lamps, her feet in the wet leaves, it did not seem right to her that her Christian duty should bid her forgive Cresspahl. She found that hard to do for his sake. She felt at a disadvantage.

Cresspahl thought: It's enough to apologize with an embrace. (Besides, he had no idea what for.)

September 28, 1967   Thursday

In the morning, in the first shadowy expanse of the five glass door panels, I see the reflections of the other side of the street, bathed in white light, and the framed image with its signs, store windows, passers-by, is reproachful, like some peaceable creature, when I let a fifth of it swing away by opening one door. In the second expanse, that of the inner doors, the reflection is less distinct, all but disintegrating in the equal sections of the doors as they swing beside me, bouncing back again as it mirrors the pale marble surfaces of the lobby, and now it is a picture of shadows, motionless and moving, overhung by darkness as by treetops, and between the gliding images of shadow people the background has deepened, white ocean light seen under green foliage, boats on the water, indelible and familiar outlines, names fraught with time, and only when I lose the picture at the fluorescent-lit corner of the elevator does my memory surround the agreeable sight and moment and instant with a sharp border of danger and disaster.

A day like this, swathed in the mist hanging over the opposite shore, over the colors of withering leaves beside the half-seen water, promises a morning in Wendisch Burg, sailing weather for a morning fourteen years ago, creates a longing for a day that was not like that, fashions for me a past that I have never lived, turns me into a false person divided from self by the tricks of memory.

Conversation in the elevator: So-and-so has got married, and the next day he had to report anyway for military service.

I wouldn't know.

Vietnam probably.

(Eleven people listening.)

Showers in the evening.

September 29, 1967   Friday

That's right. That's what we expect. In its first section our good old New York *Times* hasn't a word to say about the hole that was shot yesterday in the front window of the Franklin Society Federal Savings and Loan office. First do your homework, then you may play, says Grete Selenbinder, courtesy aunt, auntie of the keys, auntie of the tears. Homework is: the air battles over Hanoi; the teachers' vote on their new contract with the city; the Czechoslovak Government's depriving its writers of a journal; the leader of the left wing of the League of German Socialist Students in West Berlin being one Rudi Dutschke. "Dutschke is sometimes called 'Red Rud' or 'Revolutionary Rudy,' but he is no classic Marxist." That takes care of that.

Now you may play. On the first page of its second section, with epic photos and elegant type covering 102 square inches, the *Times* takes up a comfortable position and with clever wordplay assists obtuse readers to grasp the action: "Two Midtown Bandits Ricochet and Retreat When Bullets Fly." Immediately, however, Auntie controls our pure lust for pleasure by passing judgment from the very beginning: the two men have bungled the bank holdup "from inept start to ignominious finish." First mistake: they were conspicuous. Walked into the bank, 441 Lexington Avenue, with brown paper bags under their arms, the kind we use for shopping, and with their narrow-brimmed hats pulled low toward their noses. Second mistake: in their nervousness they hit a guard over the head when he questioned them. Third, insufficient reconnaissance of the terrain: when another guard started shooting, one of the robbers tried to tug open a door that only opened outward. When they finally solved this puzzle they dashed out and vanished on Lexington Avenue (what's more, into the heavy crowds on Lexington Avenue, for the benefit of newspaper subscribers not familiar with the locale). Fourth mistake: they left a clue. They lost their hats and also left behind the paper bags in which they had intended to carry away their loot.

And now the New York *Times*, as a reward after analysis, re-enacts the whole story:

It was about 10 A.M.

441, that's on East 44th Street.

It was quiet in the bank.

Only ten customers.

The guard is wearing a uniform. He is struck down.

They turn toward the counter.

One of them has a pistol.

He points the pistol at the office manager, the latter having stepped forward.

Some of the tellers scream and throw themselves to the floor behind the counter. From behind the counter a plain-clothes guard shoots at the thugs.

They do not understand where the shots are coming from.

They panic, they flee.

Of the three shots fired, one made the hole in the front window.

Beneath the hole, in front of the window (seen from inside), stand at least eleven men, all solemn, almost grim, deep in thought.

This is what we mean, the New York *Times*'s great scholarly gesture, her sober yet pithy contribution to the sociology of bank robbery.

And that is how a lady of the old school behaves: she may condescend to document a bank holdup, but rowdiness she will not tolerate.

The crumbs fall from the table at which she discusses her subjects with such significance. We, compelled to absence by work, taste in them the traces of a rescue from our remoteness from Asian places and the house next door. We imagine that she is saving up for us the life we have missed, still warm and fresh, as if we could catch up with it.

On Lexington Avenue the sidewalks are even narrower than on

other streets, more than on other streets pedestrians elbow their way along, before and after office hours, praying for a taxi, cursing at a bus, their hearts set on the next shuttle to Times Square. But we won't cross the street to look at the hole in the window: we have the photo tucked under our arm. Outside Grand Central, sticking out into the surging stream of pedestrians and forcing it into half the space, two news vendors have set up their stand, and those who are pushed into the gutter by the resultant buffetings can hear them barking: Wall Street. Latest. Wall Street. Latest, and, more softly: Thank you sir. Thank you sir. It is done in a flash; coin and paper almost meet in one hand, and those who have both full get the paper stuck under their arm. Inside the Graybar Building, in the twilit approach to Grand Central, two men stand behind a counter made of crates, with exactly the same papers, mute, dejected, not obscured by customers, and even those people who have not yet acquired the latest news from Wall Street do not stop, as if there were something suspect about such unpretentiously displayed goods. We buy neither here nor there, we are waiting for the New York *Times*.

In order to get his gun-control law through Congress, President Johnson has agreed to permit the states to allow the mail-order sale of rifles and shotguns. It does not always have to be revolvers.

September 30, 1967   Saturday, South Ferry Day

The opening of the schools after the two-week walkout did not take place quite without incident. As one teacher was entering her school in Brooklyn, someone in a passing car yelled at her: "Dirty Jew!" She happens to be of Irish descent. A million dollars' worth of stock certificates stolen. Fifteen years in an East German penitentiary for an American photographer. The West German Government replies to a letter from the East German Government as if it had not read it.

"Was she homesick, your mother, that Lisbeth Papenbrock, in Richmond?" asks the child.

"She was trapped. She had used up all her christening presents, her own money, on the airplane trip from the Baltic, on purchases for her own kitchen. She had to have a double boiler, of course, just like her mother's in Jerichow."

"In Jerichow the only thing she could have been sure of was ridicule, right? She wanted to make the grade, I guess."

"And finally the townsfolk of Richmond themselves insisted on

this Mrs. Cresspahl's coming to terms with them. She was a customer, and when she can't express what she wants you just pull open
all six drawers of rice and explain the various kinds to her and list the
recipes they are suitable for; she's sure to take one of them. And by
the time the counter is full of pots and pans for boiling, braising,
roasting, steaming, she's bound to recognize one of them as what she
wants and buy it. And, not being shy by nature, she soon started
behaving like her mother, who was capable of saying to sales clerks:
You can take that one away, don't bother to show me cheap stuff like
that. (Although Louise Papenbrock would do this only when Albert
was out of earshot. Albert didn't like people to guess what he was
worth by the way she behaved)."

"How about the people who weren't trying to sell her things?"

"Perceval and Jim started by being embarrassed at eating with
the boss and his wife, and all they liked about her Mecklenburg
cooking at first was that it meant they could save money at the fish-
and-chips stall. After a while she learned how to prepare mutton.
(The butcher could soon tell whether a customer was a good cook,
and he didn't lie to this one when he recommended something.)
Then there was Mrs. Jones with her squinting granddaughter, she
stayed on if only out of curiosity. And street urchins, a shivering
ragged mob, they could rely on her for a slice of bread. When they
hung around the entrance to Kew Gardens she always paid the
admission for one, preferably a girl. A dinner for Salomon. It was true
that Salomon only stayed for an hour, but he did come."

"And was she as hard up as we are?"

"It went against the grain for her to ask Cresspahl for more than
the housekeeping money they had budgeted for; besides, it hurt her
pride. But she did have a bit more to spend than we do, and she also
had the still unfamiliar dignity of the young housewife who is
managing a husband's money for the first time. And she didn't like
the house behind the gasworks, the house with the workshop. She
wanted a new house, just for living in, something with a bay window
or a balcony, with a garden at the back ("for the children"). This
meant putting eight hundred pounds, for lifetime possession, on the
real-estate agent's desk. Cresspahl left it up to her to eke at least half
that amount out of her housekeeping money. He could have given
her the down payment for a house like that right away out of his
savings; but he didn't let on. He wanted to give her time, the way you
give a child time."

"And what did she write home?"

"She boasted. In describing Richmond she wrote about the park, the old-established shops on George Street, riders in the park, parades of the East Surreys in their red tunics, the skating on the rink by Richmond Bridge. She said nothing about the rotting buildings in their own neighborhood where the working classes were imprisoned. If she prospered in a foreign country, at least Jerichow should see it as an enviable foreign country. Here you could buy imported groceries, coffee, tea, cocoa, chocolate powder, infinitely cheaper. She also wrote: that in the October elections the Communists hadn't got in a single one of their twenty-six candidates, and that twenty-one got no more than an eighth of the votes in their constituencies, thus forfeiting their deposits. (She didn't write that Cresspahl considered Prime Minister MacDonald a traitor to the Labour Party because he had agreed to a curtailment of unemployment benefits.) Once they had dinner out, at the Original Maids of Honour Restaurant, for three shillings a head; she wrote about restaurants as if they went there every week."

"Did she give him her letters to read?"

"She gave him her letters to read, and he took them to mean she was happy. He looked at her kindly, obliquely, slightly from below, a shade uneasily, but in such a way that she didn't notice him looking."

"Did Cresspahl still get anonymous letters from Jerichow?"

"She got an anonymous letter, postmarked W. C. 1. It was typewritten and regretted their lack of participation in social life. On the other hand, the writer went on, she would get along very nicely with Mrs. Trowbridge."

"That letter she didn't show to Cresspahl."

"That one she kept to herself. She had never breathed a word to him about Midshipman Herbert Wehmke. She didn't intend to keep it from him forever, but for a while longer yet."

"Want to bet?" says the child. "Want to bet there's going to be a bang? Want to bet?"

For many ferry captains aim too late for the slip, so that the heavy vessel bangs into the wall of wooden piles at the entrance, the first time hard, then with a more subdued sound. Then the groaning of the timbers in the swirling water can be heard.

October 1, 1967   Sunday; heating season opens

Now once again the dreams of early morning are punctuated by the throes of the hot water sent up by Mr. Robinson from the basement in exposed pipes through floor after floor. The water recoils from the cold air, rebounds on all sides from the unequal pressure, so that in sleep an old man seems to loom up beside the head of the bed; he has an iron gullet, a jagged pipe in his throat, he breathes with razor blades, devours glass and scrap iron. Little pebbles continue to bounce up and down, ricocheting back and forth. Restricted without warning, the water's breath pounds in hasty alarm against the metal. The regular rhythm disintegrates in feeble, expiring heartbeats. The fellow has no intention of dying, he shoves a barbed-wire broom down his throat, making rasping, tickling, grating noises that sound positively comfortable. For a final cleanup he sends in little men with sharp hammers who check the whole length of the pipe with deliberate, unevenly spaced blows, alternately using the pointed and blunt ends. In a series of sweeping heaves they are all coughed up, to land with a thump on the floor, chirping as if their bones were breaking. Slowly the fellow rinses his mouth, not with one mouthful but with single drops that hop around like fleas. A mass of broken glass rattles downward, the fragments tinkling against each other but without ever reaching the bottom with the anticipated deafening crash. The fragments have coagulated into glass balls with which someone is gargling. Now he is clearing his throat. He thinks no one is listening, he hawks repeatedly, copiously. Finally, he coughs it all up, with vigorous jerks of his shoulders. Finally, sleep is so threadbare that the images tear even as they unwind. It is not a dream, it is the heating getting under way in the morning. The heating season has opened.

Dear Building Management, year after year I find these noises quite unacceptable.

That's right, Mrs. Cresspahl.

But not in New York.

In New York the people in the slums have to hammer on the heating pipes till noon before the janitor will start up the furnace.

Is it true that the insides of this seventy-year-old building of ours are rotten through and through?

No doubt about it, Mrs. Cresspahl. They are rotten, through and through. It's the mortgages, they're eating their way through from top to bottom. And a very good morning to you, Mrs. Cresspahl.

Later, when the heating has subdued its agitation to a helpless hissing in the radiator valves, the other sounds of Sunday emerge. There is the rustling with which the fallen leaves yield to the shoes of strollers. There is the alarm clock in one of the apartments above us announcing that church is due to start in an hour. There is the wavering hodgepodge from the classical radio programs. There is the whisper of the wind in the park, bringing the bored conversation of children in through the window. There is the gentle click of the park worker bearing down with all his weight on the chains of the children's swings, one after the other, in order to prevent a tragedy this day too.

We mean the quiet park worker, the one who is six foot six, thin and taciturn, who greets the children as if they were his employers. We don't mean his summer helper, the Puerto Rican, the one who paraded the green Parks Department work clothes among the mothers like a uniform, his gloves tucked in his belt like an army water flask, hollering with the kids, strutting up and down until everyone had noticed him. We mean the Negro whose overalls show he has been working, who usually has his gloves on his hands when he sweeps up the rubbish and dead leaves, under and behind the benches too, as if this were his own garden, while the other one, proud also of the touches of gray in his hair, entertained the ladies. The other one could read and write, he need not work here any more. The Negro has stayed on. He greets the adult visitors to the playground as old acquaintances, not familiarly but with a casual, almost indulgent smile. We don't even know his first name.

Among the other early sounds of Sunday is the groaning of the elevator cable as Esmeralda takes the boy from the West End News Service up to the thirteenth floor. He then proceeds to leap down the reverberating iron staircase behind the elevator shaft, three steps at a time, distributing the New York *Times* on floor after floor, five pounds of paper that land with a solid slap outside the numbered doors, including Apartment 204. Mrs. Cresspahl does not want to miss the Sunday edition again: since yesterday she has been a customer of this ragged Negro boy who any moment now will bang the heavy front door behind him, unburdened for the few paces separating him from his wagon with its heavy load.

The park across from the windows is now flooded with the October sunshine that adds a touch of the incredible to all the colors, to the sprinkling of yellow leaves on the grass, to the elephant hide of the bare plane trees, to the bright tangle of brambles on the upper promenade, to the cold Hudson, to the streaks of forest haze on the opposite shore, to the steely sky. The sense of Sunday has coincided with a Sunday. It is an almost innocent picture in which children and strollers dwell as if harmless. It is an illusion, and feels like home.

October 2, 1967   Monday

Dej Bůh štěstí
is painted in colored fraktur on the fluorescent-white showcase
dividing into two halves the front part of the restaurant "U Svatého
Václava." The restaurant is tucked away on Manhattan's East Side,
in the seventies, in the midst of the Hungarian and German quarters.
The approach from the Lexington subway is across Third and Second
Avenues, alongside dilapidated tenements, over cracked paving, past
storekeepers guarding their displays, under the eyes of neighbors
chatting on front steps, on through garbage and among scar-
encrusted cats, to a small house whose street level gives no indication
of a restaurant. The blue door with its rectangles thinly outlined in
white and red betokens the colors of the Czechoslovak Republic, and
Czech is the language spoken by the customers inside at the widely
spaced tables, intimately, loud enough to be overheard, as if these
were still the days when middle-class folk enjoyed themselves in
Prague's Malá Strana. The regulars are elderly, formally dressed,
dignified; couples silenced by marriage as well as that solitary gentleman moving his lips above his raised glass as if he were talking to the
dead, who alone can still recognize his pasty old man's face. Younger
and more casually dressed are the delegates of the Czechoslovak Socialist Republic to the United Nations, administrators as well as the
spies of the new power. Here, uninhibited by the presence of now
powerless refugees and compatriots, they feed the same longing for
Bohemian, Czech, or other Continental cooking. Presumably they all
know what "Dej Bůh štěstí" means; we don't, and even Dmitri
Weiszand won't attempt to translate it.

Dmitri Weiszand, Mrs. and Miss Cresspahl's host this evening,
is embarrassed. He should know what it means. For this man with
the Slav cheekbones, the strong East European accent, the affable
manner, is Polish by birth, a close neighbor of the Czechs but not of
their language. But then he is Polish only by birth. When in 1939 the
Soviet Union, as arranged, annexed Eastern Poland, part of the
Nazis' loot, it also swept up Weiszand the child and switched his
citizenship, and in school, which remained otherwise unchanged,
taught him Russian as well as another difficult subject called patrio-
tism. He had had to resign himself to the back row. When the
Germans reclaimed their loot two years later, they also acquired
Weiszand the schoolboy, but they had no citizenship for him, and
there wasn't even a school for him to learn Czech. Later, as an

expedient and for two years, he was a German, and the Americans, when they let him in, entered that in his papers as his origin. His knowledge of German probably amounts to about ten words. And this Mr. Weiszand with his youthful shock of brown hair, his plump face, his expression and complexion barely touched by age, is in his forties, a graduate of several camps in Eastern Europe in which he might have learned French, Romanian, Italian, Dutch, and Czech too for that matter, but the teachers were not on their toes, and when he was landed in New Jersey he arrived without brothers or sisters or parents, and to remember them was as repugnant to him as the Russian and Polish they had spoken. "I have a friend who is a professor of Slavonic studies," says Mr. Weiszand, embarrassed. "He'll find out for us, dej Bůh štěstí."

Marie does not like going to the St. Wenceslas Restaurant; it is one of Gesine's preferences that she is willing to indulge. She cannot enjoy the conversation at the next table. The space between the tables, the white tablecloths, the napkins folded into bishops' miters, all remind her of going to Europe; but she does not want to leave this country. The story of St. Wenceslas, who was put to death by his brother Boleslav on September 28, 935, the management's reminder of halcyon days in Prague's Malá Strana, printed on the back of the menu; she finds things are too remote. The young students working here as waiters still have their native accent; she finds them too obliging. D. E. would not like going to such a restaurant either. Besides, she has had to wear her red velvet dress with the lace collar for the occasion. She feels ill at ease eating the unfamiliar roast pork with the foreign dumplings, shifting her knife and fork awkwardly about, listening impatiently to the abortive exchange of remarks between Dmitri and Gesine.

"How do you feel about the way Stalin's daughter is behaving?" says Gesine, and Marie realizes that the question has slipped out inadvertently, that she wishes she had not asked it, and indeed Mr. Weiszand's amiable expression turns the tiniest bit stiff, and he gets no farther than: "Well, of course, for a while I was one of Stalin's floating possessions, but . . .," and Marie yields to her boredom and begins, carefully, craning her neck, to read the New York *Times*.

"(Reuters)—The newspaper *Bild am Sonntag* said today that Stalin's eldest son was shot by the Nazis in 1944 after refusing to make an anti-Soviet speech to Russian workers at an armaments factory in Berlin."

But Marie cannot bear Gesine's raised eyebrows, her sidelong glance, not admonishing, merely anxious, and she sets out to make up for her behavior. She walks between the tables to the bar by the entrance, frowning under the watchful eyes of the other customers, and has a discussion with the old man at the cash register. He is dressed all in black, his face is so impassive, his eyes rarely move, and she does not like approaching him. But he answers her as if she were an adult, he does not encourage the onlookers to smile at her, and while supplying the information in a flat impersonal voice he offers her the bowl with the olives.

"I'll tell you what it means, dej Bůh štěstí," Marie says at the table. She says it twice, first in English, to restore Mr. Weiszand's faith in her politeness, then in German, as a peace offering to Gesine: " 'God send thee happiness,' that's what it means."

October 3, 1967   *Tuesday*

Emmy Creutz, wife of the cemetery gardener in Jerichow, sends her account, as she does every October. Dear Mrs. Cresspahl, the covering of your graves for the winter will cost six marks each, including bouquets. The annual charge for perpetual care is also due, three graves @ 20 marks.

From Saigon the New York *Times* reports bombing raids on North Vietnam. In seven raids in only three days, B-52 bombers have produced 110 secondary explosions. During a raid northwest of Conthien, the bombs produced 44 secondary explosions and three large fires that left the entire area in flames.

Emmy Creutz encloses photographs of the graves with her account, as evidence. Lisbeth Cresspahl's metal cross has still not been scraped and repainted. Rust stains have seeped down from the metal lettering on the boulder dumped onto Cresspahl's skull by the town of Jerichow. The slab with Jakob's name, which is supposed to be lying on his mound, is still standing in front of it, like a price tag. The very idea of Emmy Creutz leaving the appearance of the cemetery to the customers.

Erich Rajakovich, in charge of deportations at The Hague from 1941 to 1943, has been captured on the Istrian peninsula. He is wanted by the Netherlands for the murder of 100,000 Jews (estimated).

The pictures of the Jerichow graves show their condition in August, a mass of withered flower colors, no dark shades. Ivy, which we wanted for all three, grows only over Lisbeth Cresspahl. But the Creutzes have to consider their business. The other two lie in the midday sun; wrote Emmy Creutz: ivy will never grow there. It cannot be claimed that ivy needs much attention.

In honor of the Soviet revolution, the New York *Times* reports on the effects of the purges carried out on Stalin's orders among his comrades by Beria and Alexander N. Poskrebyshev. Poskrebyshev was reliable. He did not lift a finger when his wife, a long-time member of the Party, was shot.

Emmy Creutz claims that our overpayment for the financial year 1966/67 has been used up by planting pansies (so that there's always something in bloom on the grave, Mrs. Cresspahl). She thinks of a grave as a garden. For the balance and as an advance on the 1968/69 account, she requests further payment in kind.

General Poskrebyshev died his own death last fall, in comfort in the Kremlin Hospital. His memory remained unimpaired. While there he told a story about his friend Beria: asked whether a certain prominent Communist was still "sitting" (i.e., in jail), Beria laughed: "No," he said. "He isn't sitting any more. He's lying flat on the floor." When General Poskrebyshev told this story he likewise roared with laughter.

As a fee Emmy Creutz would like the following: 1 man's turtleneck sweater (Silastik), maroon, size 38 to 40, 1 no-iron shirt, size 16½, and 1 man's parka, size 44, nylon, lined, not too short, I leave the color to you, Mrs. Cresspahl. Emmy Creutz can only have learned of the existence of these articles from West German television commericals.

Asked about another victim, General Poskrebyshev screwed up his face and said: "Must have been shot. We didn't start using poison until 1940 or thereabouts."

This takes up a Saturday morning in the department stores around Herald Square. Then we have to send the parcel to Ite Milenius in Lübeck so that Emmy Creutz won't have to pay duty on goods from the United States. Ite Milenius has to obtain disinfection certificates, otherwise clothing is confiscated for the benefit of the German Democratic Republic. Ite Milenius then has to pack the articles in three small parcels and send them to Emmy, Erich, and Jürgen Creutz in Jerichow because the German Democratic Republic does not permit the sending of three articles of clothing in one parcel. In return for this Ite Milenius will now supply us with a list of what she would like for Christmas.

In Darmstadt the trial began yesterday of eleven members of SS "Sonderkommando A 4" who participated in 1941 in the murder of some 80,000 Soviet citizens, of whom 70,000 were Jews. In Kiev they drove 33,771 men, women, and children to the edge of the Babi Yar ravine, shot them, and pushed them over the edge, all in less than thirty-six hours.

Who's going to wear the maroon sweater, I wonder, Creutz, who is seventy-one, or Jürgen, deputy commander of the Schwerin military sector, an officer in the East German Army and an opponent of West German commercial television? Perhaps he wants to wear it with his dress uniform.

In July 72 per cent of the American public were still in favor of continuing the war in Vietnam, in August the figure was still 61 per cent. Now it has dropped to 58 per cent.

Amalie Creutz, the first wife, hanged herself in October 1945, in her bedroom. She did it in broad daylight, at midday, perhaps in the hope that she would be found in time by the two workmen for whom she cooked. She was three months pregnant, by one of the eleven Soviet soldiers who had raped her in the Gräfin Forest. Mayor Cresspahl's appeal to have an abortion performed was rejected by the hospital in Gneez and the health authorities in Schwerin. (And Cresspahl was arrested by the Red Army counterintelligence.) Amalie Creutz was afraid of her husband, still a prisoner-of-war in France. She was afraid that public opinion in Jerichow would prevent Creutz from believing her. Jakob's mother helped bury her. In 1950 Creutz married one of his workers, Emmy Burbach from Reichenberg in Silesia, a widow. She was twelve years younger than he, and at first he was glad to let her take over the management of the business from him. At one time he used to write at the top of her accounting letters to Cresspahl's daughter: Dear Gesine, and put at the bottom: Affectionately, Erich Creutz. Now the letter says: Yours truly, Emmy Creutz.

Then we have Marie Abs' grave, in Hanover, West Germany. That's maintained by automatic bank remittances. If the sun fell out of the sky, we'd all be sitting in the dark.

October 4, 1967   Wednesday

Jewish New Year, Rosh Hashanah, begins today at sundown and lasts until Friday evening. To mark the celebration, alternate side-of-the-street parking regulations will be suspended for the duration.

Rajakovic must have escaped to Austria. The Yugoslav police had warned, not arrested him. (Moreover, Rajakovic denies the allegation that he amassed his fortune by supplying the Communist bloc with strategic goods.)

According to the analysis of Gunnar Myrdal, Swedish expert in social crises, the United States must spend "trillions of dollars and at least one generation" in a realistic, nonracial attack on the country's poverty. Marie isn't nervous at all, in a country like this.

Lisbeth Cresspahl was nervous in England. She was scared of the unemployed who came marching on London as part of the National Unemployed Workers Movement from Wales, the North of England, and Scotland, a ragged throng of men who, even to her eyes, bore the marks of poor diet and wretched housing. She stood in a sparse line of onlookers at Charing Cross, a respectable housewife in a new coat, a fox collar around her neck, fashionable shoes on her feet, staring rather foolishly, very shocked, at the Hunger March. She could not yet grasp the fact that all the demonstrators wanted was to draw attention to their plight, she did not trust their patient, peaceable behavior. Besides, the N. U. W. M. had been organized by the Communist Party. She had once had to deliver a message for Perceval and came face to face with the Ritchett parents, people of Cresspahl's age, unkempt, malodorous, who almost rudely tried to prevent her from entering the house. She would have liked merely to pity the boy for having to return from work to slovenly parents, a neglected home. It was a long time before she accepted the fact that a protracted life with neither work nor income produces this kind of indifference, of which indeed the Ritchetts were as ashamed as if it had been their personal failure. Then she found out that Perceval was also supporting his parents on his wages, as well as his brothers and sisters, the Labour Office in Richmond being in some doubt as to their destitution. Now she could picture more of these disintegrating homes behind the uncurtained windows in working-class streets, and could almost understand the defiance of people for whom there was no provision and whose efforts at preserving an illusion of respectability, with an occasional shave and bargain-basement clothing, were limited to street and pub. She did not dare approach the Ritchetts with charity; they had instilled shame into her too.

Raise the boy's wages, Cresspahl.

Take it out of your housekeeping money, Lisbeth, and don't let the competition find out.

As long as she had been called Papenbrock, she had been secure. For justice, she had brought with her not a concept but a sense. That sense, counseled by the Protestant faith, permitted differences, although not blatant ones, of course. Poverty in Mecklenburg had been hidden from her: in the backwardness of the Mecklenburg soul, in the Papenbrock family's confidence in its right to a privileged existence, in regular donations to the church, in stupid sayings such as virtue is its own reward, or, nobody ever starves to death on the land. There she had never felt threatened. Here she did, for from Cresspahl's remarks she had gathered that they were both just keeping their heads above water on the fringe of the Depression due to the lucky circumstance that the better-off classes still had money to spend on the repairing and restoring of heirloom furniture. He also tried to explain to her what he remembered from meetings of the Labour Party: that unemployment had been caused by a decline in exports in all important branches of England's industry, and that some mechanism was at work there. Moreover, he seemed to believe that British policy was sacrificing its own working class to its concern for the value of the pound abroad. She did not like the sound of this. It meant that their situation depended on economic laws and actual people rather than on destiny. She might have surrendered to destiny. She felt trapped. For charity beyond a reasonable degree of benevolence would have cut into her housekeeping money, injured the dream of a home of their own. So she was unjust, and she believed this injustice would be followed by divine punishment, earthly though its first manifestation might be. How could they both continue to live indefinitely in a country in which the churches and squares were hung and adorned with monuments to the dead in the war against the Germans? How much longer would Cresspahl be allowed to work in a country in which craftsmen advertised with assurances like ONLY BRITISH MATERIALS USED. ONLY BRITISH LABOUR EMPLOYED; what security did they have here? And in her heart of hearts she kept thinking: It's not all that bad in Germany. When confronted by capitalism for the first time she regarded it as something foreign.

That pert manner of hers, she's got that from you, Lisbeth.

You've got that from me, Gesine. And make sure your child doesn't try to find excuses for you one day the way you do for me.

October 5, 1967   Thursday

This is a recorded message.

D. E.,

This tape is extolled in advertisements as being "free of static"; perhaps you actually can hear in the background the terrific rainstorm that's washing our windows. For we had been having a long long Indian summer, and now it's over.

Here's some news that will sadden you: the St. Louis Cardinals have defeated your Boston Red Sox two to one, and it seems it wasn't even an exciting game. How about that?

Now to Marie. Marie insists on my continuing my account of how it was when Grandmother married Grandfather. Her questions sharpen my imagination, and her listening looks attentive. She sits at the table with her hands framing her face, looking like the Mecklenburg coat of arms, your ox's head. But what she wants to know is not the past, not even her own. For her these are a presentation of possibilities from which she believes herself immune, and in another sense stories. (I haven't actually asked her.) This is how we spend some of our evenings.

My storytelling often seems to me like a bare skeleton, I lack the flesh to cover it with, I have searched for a coat for it: in the Institute for the Preservation of British Customs. It is housed on Madison Avenue at 83rd Street, not far from the sumptuous funeral home where the departure rites for members of New York's Social Register are performed. On account of the high-class neighborhood, the Institute's windows have been sealed and the façade has been given a face-lifting, and inside the walls are paneled in red and hung with eighteenth-century paintings. The worn armchairs must have been flown in from a London club, or else some artist has converted them to their present venerable condition. The staff behaves as though this mansion were open to the plebs merely because the owner has fallen on hard times, and female plebs are channeled along a back staircase to the archives.

At this Institute there is a microfilm of the *Richmond and Twickenham Times,* from the first issue in 1873 to the present day. The newspaper calls itself a "Journal of local news, society, art, and literature," and, with its title fraktur and starting off with the births, marriages, and deaths columns, is a distant relative of the old London *Times,* but a small-town relative with sensational, rather vulgar advertising on the front page, at least in its 59th year of publication, Richmond, 1932.

Here we find Kellogg's Corn Flakes being promoted, the very ones Marie has for breakfast today. How the brand names survive us! After each war they reappear in full strength, Junkers & Ruh, Siemens, Linde, Du Pont, General Motors. You would call this one of my disjointed thoughts. What I meant, though, was not a thought at all, but a feeling. An emotion, you would say.

Almost every issue of the *Richmond and Twickenham Times* contains an advertisement, on the front page, in boldface, for Gosling & Sons, Richmond's Leading Emporium, and now you will suppose that I called Pascal's heir after them. But I cannot change his name, that's what he was called, Albert Gosling, patriot and denouncer.

This isn't how we spend all our evenings. On Monday D. W. invited us to the Czech place, and I must admit you're right, he keeps confusing the person with the country of origin. For him I am Germany, the old one and the two present ones, for him I sometimes have no face at all but a national pigment instead, to him I am responsible for the West German state railways and for the West German Nazis. But it is not for lack of fastidiousness that I share his table, you and your fastidiousness. I would like to know what else he wants from me.

Did the report on the shrapnel bombs appear in the Danish newspapers too? In the New York *Times* it says that two tiny children were led in at a press conference in Hanoi, survivors of the attack of September 27, one wounded so terribly in the face that he was unable to speak. Marie can't get over this. "D. E. has to do something about it," she says.

This weekend you won't be able to phone us; we'll be in Vermont. Your mother, on the phone she sounds quite amicable. Mr. Robinson has been asking after you. And so, with kindest regards,

Any unauthorized person listening to this tape is asked kindly to return it, postage paid, to Gesine Cresspahl, Apartment 204, 243 Riverside Drive, New York, N.Y., Telephone 212 749-2857.

This goes for you too, D. E. But you should tell it something about your own affairs too.

And because you want me to say it, I'll say it: When there's no one else at home, you're the best.

The New York *Times* radio station has just announced something for you: In the second game of the World Series, thanks to Yastrzemski, your Boston Red Sox beat the St. Louis Cardinals five nil. You'll be able to figure out what that means.

October 6, 1967   *Friday*

Yesterday in Miami five masked gunmen entered the home of the Du Ponts (33 rooms, golf putting green, tennis court, swimming pool) and after a leisurely two and a half hours left it with goods to the value of a million and a half dollars, polite to the end. When the

Du Ponts, whom the gunmen had tied up, said they felt cold, a blanket was pulled over them, and when Mr. Du Pont's leg itched, one of the men scratched it for him. When Mr. and Mrs. Du Pont speak of them their tone is not unfriendly.

"I can't see what she had to complain about in Richmond," says the child, referring to her grandmother, "your mother."

"You can't compare it with the Richmond of 1932. The kind of cases that came before the courts in those days were burglaries, drunken brawls, crossing the yellow line on the highway, motoring offenses in general."

"And the beauties of Richmond," says the child, leading her on.

"And the enterprising town of Richmond, lying in the affectionate embrace of a bend in the south bank of the Thames, hugged between it and the barrier of Richmond Hill and thus unable to spread out in land speculations so that in this enclosure it had to lay one stone carefully on another, upper-class homes and mansions arranged in terraces around Richmond Hill, a market town, town of gardeners, site of Elizabeth I's death, that gave its name to towns all over the world, Richmond, Kentucky, Richmond, Indiana, Richmond, Virginia. . . ."

"I've done my homework," says the child, in English, ingratiatingly.

"She did try, our Lisbeth Cresspahl. There was Richmond Bridge, for instance, captured in paintings a thousand times over, even by Turner, an object of history and culture, a hundred yards of bridge between the town and the noble buildings of east Twickenham, late eighteenth century, idyllically surrounded by pleasure craft, excursion steamers. What Lisbeth Cresspahl saw was five arches of white stone, surmounted by a curving paved surface, she was courteous enough to know the sight by heart; it did not move her. True, she walked almost every day to Richmond Park (always via Queen's Road rather than Hill Rise, because of the former brewery where disabled soldiers made the poppies for all of England), she often stood beside Thatched Cottage and took in the mandatory view of the Thames below, across steeply sloping lawns, between formal and pleasing groups of trees to the shrubs along the shore, the island thickets, the water that turned blue in the evening shadows; and in her letters she also listed all the distant things that were visible on clear days: Windsor Castle, the Berkshire Downs, St. Anne's Hill, the Hog's Back beyond the clouds of chestnut blossoms above

Bushey Park with its tame deer; it did not console her. The countryside had been laid out wastefully, untilled, awesome in the antiquity
of its culture, forbidding in its majesty, alien. So she went there
alone, not for the view but to be alone. It disquieted her to think
that the only way she might take root here would be by an effort of
will."

"Nothing had been kept from her."

"Cresspahl had prepared her. He had described himself as a kind
of foreman, and really that's all he was, he didn't deserve the reproach that was on the tip of her tongue. He had not described the
gasworks area as respectable, and she had learned to put up with the
gasometer, its pink now painted halfway up a dirty brown and
peeling off above that in great rusty triangles; yet she was hurt by the
arrogance of the *Richmond and Twickenham Times,* which took it
for granted 'that it is not in a part of Richmond where the residents
are likely to object.' She should not have expected the solid citizens
of Richmond to include her in their neighborly activities, she did not
like the feeling of being thus truly alone, below the middle class,
hardly above the lower, and a foreigner to boot. Cresspahl had suggested she take advantage of church functions to get to know people;
she had shouted at him, furious with herself because she was at sea in
the liturgy and ritual here. Now she thought it cruel of him to change
the subject at the very mention of church, quite calmly and in perfect
good humor, as if this were an area reserved solely for her and on
which he was not entitled to encroach. To put an end to this dis-
agreement, she bought herself a King James Bible at Hiscoke's
secondhand bookstore on Hill Street; Cresspahl picked up the leather-
bound volume and put it down again without a word or any indication that he understood she was making an effort. Sometimes she
would have liked to attack him with: You've got everything you
wanted! and was appalled by her own reply: That I wanted; it disquieted her to be prone to such urges. She put off going to the Aliens'
Registration Bureau, often for several days; she did not like to see the
official turn the pages of their two passports as though they were
about to expire. She had not reached that point yet. And Cresspahl
saw nothing! In June he took her to the Royal Horse Show, proud
and content to have Lisbeth Papenbrock on his arm, and that's how
they looked in the photo she had to send to Germany: a confident,
happy couple, not the way she felt. On one occasion she saw
Cresspahl through an open door, standing at a bar, glass in hand,
chatting with the man next to him, as serenely as if he had no need

of her, as remote as if she would never reach him. She could not even reproach him with spending too much money at the pub. But there were many minor grievances that she could reasonably and justly express, and she felt so frustrated that she wrote some of them down so as to be able to look at them, and possibly understand them, at some later date. During a storm in August (12th, Friday morning), with dangerous lightning and tropical rain, she was obsessed with the thought of dying, and she was so terrified to think that Cresspahl might find the concealed notebook after her death that she secretly threw it into the wood-shavings stove in the workshop. She was always making new resolutions, and again and again she would find herself arguing with Cresspahl, be unable to extricate herself, and she would turn away speechless and remain for days trapped in a silence that in front of the workmen she would hide in convulsive garrulity. But alone with Cresspahl and the cat she could not have spoken casually even to the cat. Cresspahl could do that too, live side by side with her without a word and without a look, after several attempts to placate her had been ignored, and what held them together during such rifts were the established mealtimes, getting-up time, and only a touchy, mercurial time for reconciliation, and not a word beforehand, in the North German way."

"That's the North German way?" asks the child. "I haven't inherited that," says Marie, convinced and relieved.

13,643 United States servicemen killed to date in Vietnam. Is it possible that they still do not form a large proportion of the 200 million citizens of the United States?

October 7, 1967   Saturday

It was Marie who chose the rental car in which the Cresspahls leave Manhattan this morning; a sedan disguised as a sports car, named after the tough horses of Spanish descent that used to roam the plains of America, and it had to wait, pawing the ground, in the traffic jams and construction sites of the Cross Bronx Expressway before it was able to reach the interchange above St. Raymond's Cemetery and the finger of the Bruckner Expressway, when it could trot off to the north, to the New England Thruway. It was for Marie's benefit that the Cresspahls drove slowly along West End Avenue, as if in a parade, to give the kids she played with a chance to see her as a child with a car; in fact it was Marie who had decided on this weekend for a visit to Vermont. She does not know this, she has had to get her way step by step in the face of simulated opposition from Gesine.

When I tried to meet you halfway, you still never noticed, Gesine.
You didn't mind my thinking you harsh, Cresspahl. It suited you.

And Marie contentedly observes the tracks of the New York Central Railroad beside Federal Highway 95, the stations at New Rochelle, Larchmont, Mamaroneck, where others are going off for the weekend; she makes no response to the people looking out of the Greyhound buses cruising past the low yellow car like battleships; but she overdoes the businesslike air with which she reads the road map, hands Gesine the coins at the toll barriers, wrinkles her nose in disapproval as the two young fellows in the Oldsmobile pass the Cresspahl car a second time, for fun: the child is playing a game. The game of going for a drive.

"If this Lisbeth Cresspahl, your mother," she says. She is staring straight ahead at the four lanes, frowning with concentration.

"Your grandmother," says Gesine. But this prompts no reaction from the child.

"If she burned her book of complaints against Cresspahl. How do you know she did?"

"She began a new one. It's at home in the safety deposit box."

"In New York? At the Hanover Trust?"

"In Düsseldorf."

"Can't you make something like that for me?" asks the child, hurriedly, for fear of not succeeding: "Not complaints. Things you've been thinking about just now, things I won't understand till later on. And complaints."

"On paper, with the date and the weather?"

"On tape, like the letters we send."

"For when I'm dead?"

"Yes. For when you're dead."

It is Marie who, beyond Springfield, Mass., pilots them along narrow back roads, through the country of Polish tobacco growers, an area of low houses in scattered settlements, past Emily Dickinson's birthplace, then above the Connecticut River, mostly within view of the wide-spreading water asleep between the fir trees on the high banks. In the southeast corner of Vermont, between Massachusetts and New Hampshire, in the outskirts of a village built almost entirely of wood, in a damp orchard, she finds their hosts' white clapboard house, full of years and peace beside a crimson barn painted by previous generations with the blood of slaughtered animals. Marie rejects that idea.

Then the door of the kitchen extension bursts open to let out a pack of small children, laughing and dirty, who rush over to Marie. She stands among them rather stiff-legged, conscious of the dignity of her age, a visitor from New York City. Is this what she came for?

October 8, 1967   Sunday

"Where did you first meet these Fleurys?" asks the child, not as soon as they leave but sixty miles farther on, after an ominous silence, not reproachfully. Last year Marie still spoke of "Annie," although less familiarly of "Frederick."

We have known Annie Fleury for five years, from the days when she was still called Killainen and was a guide at the United Nations Building, explaining the works of art and symbols to tourists; at that time scarcely over twenty, a plump, lively creature with apple-blossom coloring who turned up one day looking very disappointed when we opened the door to her. For the Cresspahls' name does not appear over the doorbell, and she had expected to see the former occupants of Apartment 204. She is also from the Baltic, from the Gulf of Bothnia, the child of farmers, and she had gone to Helsinki and Geneva with the aid of grants. She could laugh so hard at her stories, her forgetfulness, her two left hands, that we kept her. Once we hurt her feelings because we called the Protestant Church a "Corporation with Limited Liability," but she was saddened for us rather than herself, and she came again, brought some Scandinavian toys for the child, stayed overnight, a friend who insisted on making herself useful. In those days she still mimicked the American formalities that precede a date, and in her bag she carried the picture of a boy who was waiting for her in Kaskinen, Finland, a wholesaler's son who would have been happy to have a multilingual secretary for a wife. She did not accept a TV correspondent, or the soap distributor from St. Louis, she accepted F. F. Fleury of Boston, a specialist in Romance languages who earns his living with his typewriter. He promised her the right kind of life, a life in the country, and we did not like his way of speaking French because, like Pauly Möllendorff in Gneez, he wrenched his voice in articulating foreign words as if he were remolding himself, not merely his mouth, and we received the wedding invitation too late to have made it even by plane. When we visit them in their Vermont farmhouse, for which his translations have in fact enabled him to find the down payment, he does not show up until late in the day, letting the afternoon wear on in his attic room while we fix up the house with Annie for Sunday. For not only is the house a venerable museum piece, it is so old that in some spots it is falling apart and, because Mr. Fleury does not display the energy here that he has often enough demonstrated in college football, our friend gets behind with her housework, what with three children,

"F. F. Fleury, Jr., the boxer," says Marie;
"Annina S., the apple child," says Marie;
"Francis R., bandylegs," says Marie;

and because she has not only to discuss the "choice passages" of Mr. Fleury's daily quota in the evening but also to make a clean copy of them during the day. She seemed cheerful enough as she went about her housework and cooking, and although we were by ourselves, all the children being out in the damp woods, she did not attempt to complain, only she seemed hardly aware of F. F. Fleury when he turned up in the kitchen, handed him a drink without a word, fixed one fresh drink after another, unasked, five by suppertime, a number throughout the meal and after, until he finally emerged from his stubborn, violent silence into the argument to which Annie submitted without resistance, sitting there leaning slightly forward, with strangely squared shoulders, her hands between her knees, almost elated, as if now the expected were happening: the quarrel about anything at all, about the state of the bathroom or the war in Vietnam.

The New York *Times* has come to Vermont to meet us, thick piles in a village store where a grumpy old woman was roused by welcome curiosity because our car bore the blue and yellow New York license plates, and we came so early, slipping away secretly in the cold morning from the house of friends.

And the Cresspahls exchange compliments. "You're a good driver," says the child. She only says it because now, early in the gray afternoon, we have reached the West hundreds of Manhattan, the tattered Puerto Rican children playing on the dirty pavement, on the broken front steps of the houses. She says it because we are coming home.

October 9, 1967 Monday

When Fred Wright, handyman, returned yesterday morning to the basement on Avenue B where he sleeps, he found next to the furnace the bodies of eighteen-year-old Linda Rae Fitzpatrick and twenty-one-year-old James H. Hutchinson, both naked, lying on their stomachs, beaten to death, their heads smashed in. The girl, from a wealthy Connecticut family, had been trying out life among the hippies and jobless in Manhattan's East Village for only a few weeks; the boy was known there as a cheap source of LSD, marijuana, and barbiturates. He was known as "Groovy."

Another picture shows a young girl surrounded by dense foliage. Black hair, black clothes, somewhat preoccupied in her seriousness, she is driving a downed U.S. pilot before her with her nice little rifle. He is hanging his head as if his neck tendons had been torn.

During the day, a tendency to showers.

Without closing her eyes Lisbeth Cresspahl could see her mother writing the letters that she received from Jerichow during that November of 1932. The old lady would be sitting at the kitchen table where, as she considered what she would say, she could see the granary wall, still frequently painted by the low-lying sun with tones of yellow and the shadows of swaying branches. She would pause for a long time, casting about for the anecdotes of the week, her head raised to the cool light from the yard in an austere, unseeing gaze. All the Biblical quotations and appeals to God that she tucked away in her letter would be embellished by Papenbrock on Sunday with frivolous underlinings and exclamation marks. The conflict between the two of them had long since been reduced to teasing, and latterly Lisbeth Cresspahl had the feeling that she was not far from a similar understanding with Cresspahl.

And every Monday afternoon, whether or not the sea wind was sweeping wide swaths of rain through the main street, Louise Papenbrock would walk to the post office with her letter for England, look each person on the sidewalk straight in the eye, take her place in the lineup at the post office, the letter in full view in her hand, and invariably ask Mr. Knever, the head post-office clerk, to weigh it and calculate the postage, with the result that the letter scale at Papenbrock's office became the subject of talk in Jerichow. In this way she wanted people to know that she had two married daughters, and although one of them was under police observation near Krakow, the other was well off and respected and, what was more, living abroad.

The vaguer she was about the news from Krakow, the easier it was to imagine it. Just what one would expect of Hilde Papenbrock. She did not take sides against her husband, Dr. Paepcke, former attorney and notary, not even when he used his father-in-law's positively final loan to lease a brickyard instead of to make good the funds he had embezzled. She let herself be persuaded that this would provide them with sufficient profits to take care of their debts, and allowed her anxiety to be offset by trips to Berlin, visits to one country estate after another, gala nights at the Kurhotel Krasemann on the lake. Rumor had it that she adored her Alexander; the truth was simply that she did not want him to miss any fun. As a child, when she had been naughty her eyelids would flutter, for a few seconds escaping her vigilance. Now, one wet night with no thunderstorm, the brickyard burned down. The Paepckes could prove they had been at the local movie, but by the time they drove up to their house just before midnight the police were already there, refused an invitation to come in for a drink, and, because of the insurance policy the Paepckes had just increased, wanted to charge them with having been on the premises and committing arson. Hilde Paepcke was asked whether she knew about any candles. She then denied this too quickly and emphatically.

It's not my family, Cresspahl.
It's our family now, Lisbeth.
In the end you may have to provide bail too.
I'm not going to provide bail for stupidity. They put a candle on a brick floor. Any child could see how the fire had started.

The news of Horst Papenbrock was that the threatening encroachment on his inheritance had made him quite tractable. He was depressed, too, over the loss in votes suffered by the Nazis in the Reichstag election of November 6; he would have liked his gang to go right to the top in one sweep. He even tried to make up with the sister who had forsaken Germany for England, and enclosed a picture of a girl in one of his letters. This was a buxom brunette, almost appealing in her youthfulness had she not worn such a grim expression. Elisabeth Lieplow was her name, from Kröpelin. She was wearing a sleeveless white T-shirt, on her bosom the emblem of the

League of German Girls, with the swastika. He would like the photo back, but old man Papenbrock was not to see it, for the time being.

And Lisbeth Cresspahl wrote a terse postscript to a detailed letter about the state of business and Richmond Park and recipes— "In March," she wrote—"early March. Cresspahl wants a girl. And if I win the boy will be called Heinrich."

"Henry you mean."
"Henry I mean, Cresspahl."

That year Adolf Hitler, through the good offices of a government official in the state of Brunswick, acquired citizenship in the German Reich.

October 11, 1967   Wednesday

How it rained last night! It had been spattering against the window-panes since midday, and when the offices closed it came pouring down in thick sheets onto Third Avenue, onto the newspapers and handbags held by the pedestrians over their heads. Across from the subway entrance on 42nd Street, the rain halted us with a broad black puddle at the curb, and the police with an interminable red light. Just before ten the park all at once fell quiet, not a drop more was to be heard. But the lamplight between the scarred trunks of plane trees was caught in blurred halos, the air was not clear.

The letters Cresspahl received from Jerichow in that November of 1932 were from people in Peter Wulff's back parlor, kidding him about their beer and his wedded bliss, together with stories built up sentence by sentence from the casual mention of first names as well as clippings from newspapers. But they did not write about themselves: they wrote about the Communists from Gneez and Gadebusch who were trying to butter them up in evening get-togethers and meetings. But these Social Democrats out of office could not forgive them the previous August, when the Communists had joined forces with the Nazis in voting against the Prussian Government. After all, they had talked then, hadn't they, about the "boss system" in the Socialist Government? Now suddenly they were suggesting an alliance against the Nazis. But German Social Democrats have their own notions of dignity, you'll see.

But they don't stand a ghost of a chance, Cresspahl. Let's not get involved.

The cause of this political battle in Jerichow was a brand of cigarettes called "Drummer" manufactured by a Dresden firm. The factory had made a deal with the Nazis and enclosed in each package the picture of a National Socialist politician. Böhnhase, the tobacconist on Town Street across from Papenbrock's granary, had a nice display of them on his counter. So then the Communists sought support from the Social Democrats for the brands *they* manufactured in Berlin, without success. One of them decided to approach Böhnhase personally. Böhnhase refused to handle the brand known as "Collective" because he did not know what the word meant. But he did place a trial order for a brand called "Red Type," and Böhnhase supported the German National People's Party and wasn't going to let the Social Democrats tell him what to do. "Red Type" had become popular among farm laborers and farmers because the name somehow reminded them of potatoes and beets.

On the road to Rande, a young shoemaker, a dues-paying member of the Hitler Youth, had been so thoroughly beaten up that it took him three hours to crawl back to the hospital in Jerichow. The district police officer was away on vacation, and the municipal police claimed they were too busy. The aristocracy did not object. In for a penny, in for a pound, Kleinschulte was supposed to have said, and not in the back room of the Lübeck Arms either, but at a meeting of the town council, for the record. The boy, still hospitalized with a broken arm, felt uneasy about all the publicity being given him for his "martydom" by the Jerichow branch of the Nazi Party, and when he saw his picture in the *Gneezer Tageblatt* for the second time he let himself down that night by two sheets onto the street and disappeared from the area. Erich Schulz was his name, one of the Schulzes from Jerichow-Ausbau, the hamlet east of the Rande highway.

"We have them here too," wrote Cresspahl. "Fascists they call themselves here. Their headquarters are in Chelsea, they've got guards posted at the entrance and troop-transport vehicles in the yard. They're playing at soldiers. But I don't think they're allowed to kill yet. D'you know someone called Elizabeth Lieplow from Kröpelin? Drop me a line so we'll stay in touch."

October 12, 1967   Thursday, Columbus Day

Because of the holiday, the bank's service area is closed to the public. On all the upper floors, however, the offices are open. At noon the basement restaurant was so full that waiting customers were breathing down the necks of the seated ones, and the waitresses snatched away the used plates so hastily that reading the paper was out of the question. Nor could we choose our regular waitress, the lively one, the absent-minded one, the solicitous one, who can moan so ecstatically and say as if to a fellow sufferer: Oh, Gesine . . .

The New York *Times* has received a report from La Paz that the agitator Guevara probably lived for twenty-four hours after his capture before being killed. Seven bullet wounds, mortal ones in both lungs, one directly through the heart.

The Soviet Union has replaced 80 per cent of the Arabs' war matériel lost during the June war. According to the Israelis, who are requesting the Western powers for permission to purchase arms.

And mail service is normal too. The tape from Greece has already been unpacked, inserted into the machine set up in readiness by Marie. She is waiting at the other end of the table for the playback, in happy but solicitous anticipation. She has already listened to it twice.

To phone number SIX AUKS, New York. To the rightful occupants of Apartment 204. Dear colleagues and school friends, patriots and traitors, you six crested auks, guillemots, Icelandic giant auks, parakeet- and rhinoceros-auklets, Greetings.

Dear Mary. Not contrary but just the way you said it would be. When I arrived they were all there, and in Copenhagen I went to your hotel and had a room high up where the rooms are forever flying over the crooked red roofs it smelled of America in the corridors not Hilton but Sheraton Boston. The Danes were in a huff a West German a defense expert has chosen Jutland as the ideal unsinkable aircraft carrier for the Federal Republic let them sink themselves so much for state secrets. My Danish I don't know there's something rotten.

Ran race with a ground hostess at Kastrup on the roller treads they have that's right Marie roller treads. Two East German aircraft standing in the rain forlorn puppies so what. On the contrary Communism is good for you inquire about it just ask for it.

Germany, no. Could tell you how to sink them if need be just perfect nothing but Swiss on the aircraft large family returning home my French I don't know a bit off. Lake Constance at the Überlingen end like putrefying soup then Switzerland colors of blue white green clean enough for lab tests.

Zürich between planes the snack bar was besieged by a group of traveling musicians from New Orleans or was it Birmingham two girls fragile as birds dressed like your great-grandmother as a child Henriette von Heintz is that right and they wanted Sprite no luck the men hamburgers no luck so I translated their wishes into something approximate the waitress said And what would the colored gentleman like that floored me. There's no getting away from the stink a moment before I had almost felt homesick.

You can have your Karsch. No reply to my first telegram in the newspaper big article the Karsch analysis of the German Quandt concern one of the brass has just crashed here near Turin Karsch a guide for Italian industry to the West German pundits in the financial pages so what in answer to my second telegram tells me to go to a café at the Scala after a two-hour wait I left and for that I flew to Milan. Milano.

Public indignation in Italy because the Coca-Cola Company keeps its flavor a secret infringes against local laws Coke wants a new law in West Germany they already have one only two people know the Coke formula head chemists in Atlanta are never allowed to fly in the same plane otherwise Coke itself wouldn't know what it consists of the Italian chemists feel frustrated they'd dearly like to have one of the two drums of concentrate that are flown in from Atlanta. No other state secrets.

What you now hear is the unmistakable unique sound of a DC-9 engine flying toward the Albanian coast it's turning aside now after all I'm not supposed to say it I won't say it of course I can live without you both only I don't like it thanks for your snide remarks about my Boston Red Sox the day will come losing altitude as we head for Athens.

Dear Censor: This message is open not coded my Greek I don't know needs brushing up a bit there's no more to it than that kindly take care when rewinding damages will be claimed for every obliterated comma. Sorry for the interruption, Marie. I won't say it. Yours D. E. End of message.

October 13, 1967   Friday; Yom Kippur, Jewish Day of Atonement

---

For a long time now, Manhattan buses have been displaying ludicrous slogans along their flanks either side of their route numbers, at night we would see their fluorescent white shining beneath our windows and exhorting the public: WELCOME A STRANGER, a balding Latin American type extending a hand of welcome; DECRY COMPLACENCY as a contrast to a sleepy-eyed sybarite; BE KIND . . . BE GENTLE, as a lamb, for example. The advice was not practicable, we merely took note of it. Now they are a reality, for the New York *Times*, the official organ, reports on them. The Transit Authority received delivery of new buses so early that it was unable to sell the advertising space. This was the true situation. The exhortation to good works means no more than THIS SPACE IS AVAILABLE.

According to the earnest belief of Secretary of State Dean Rusk, for the United States to back out of its obligations in South Vietnam would subject that country to mortal danger. Moreover, he is not in the least afraid of the antiwar intellectuals; Einstein, he said, was a genius in mathematical physics, an amateur in music, and a baby in politics.

The Soviet Union has increased its military budget for the coming year by 15 per cent, to 16.7 billion rubles.

Was anything apparent early in 1933?

Cresspahl sent Peter Wulff in Jerichow/M. a clipping from the *News Chronicle* from the first week in January because it said that Germany would have a good year, if the signs were not misleading. Germany's anticipated economic recovery would put an end to the Red menace. This was the kind of thing they sent one another as an innuendo, as a query, as banter. Neither of them believed in a recovery. As far as the *Gneezer Tageblatt* was concerned, Peter believed the official announcements and half the local news.

Wulff had found out something about Elizabeth Lieplow from Kröpelin. She was a troop leader in the League of German Girls, and at the village of Beckhorst adjoining the Beckhorst estate she had made herself unpleasantly conspicuous, not because she made her group of girls parade in the uniform that was still banned, but because she did so on a Sunday morning and instructed her subordinates to undress for gym on Beckhorst Common, half an hour before church time, so that the churchgoers all had to pass by a whole lot of scantily clad girls jerking about as they did the splits and backbends. In this letter he said nothing about Horst Papenbrock because he knew Lisbeth would read what he wrote.

Had we been breakfasting yesterday morning at the 52nd Street Café between Sixth Avenue and Broadway, we too would have seen six men and a woman, all Negroes in their late twenties, turn up with a sawed-off shotgun and a knife and take $3,150 from the cash registers and the customers' pockets, then spray the victims from black aerosol containers with a gas that renders a person incapable of fighting, running, or seeing. The effect was similar to that of Mace. Mace is a gas sold in black cans but only to the police and military services. The New York *Times* implies a question.

Today is Yom Kippur. Since sunset the Jews have been sitting and kneeling in their synagogues and temples, occupied with prayer, fasting, and rendering account. "Kol Nidre" is how the prayer for forgiveness starts. Marie has long wanted to accompany her friend Rebecca to an event of this kind, but even without Mrs. Ferwalter's veto Rebecca would not take her. We have never yet been invited to a meal at the Ferwalters'. We are good friends. For them we will always be goys.

October 14, 1967   Saturday

True, our home on Manhattan's Upper West Side is imaginary. The process of addiction to the area has been solely on our side, we cannot expect the others to reciprocate. And yet, an hour's walk through the neighborhood inoculates us for years against moving away. The bus driver who stops for us today in the pouring rain does not mind our waving him on and raises three fingers in greeting toward the door as it snaps shut; although halted almost at once by the light changing to red, his gaze in the rear-view mirror follows us without anger, his expression is friendly, as if we were neighbors. We would miss him. The city's utility post at the corner of Riverside Drive and 97th Street, we would not like to be without it. Again and again we count its burdens, greet it like a friend. For not only does it carry a whipcord thicker at one end with which it pulls the light across us (as a poet has said): it also bears the signs for both streets, two sets of traffic lights, and the one-way street sign, as well as at the very top a little yellow light to indicate the fire alarm attached as a final load to its middle. For us, 97th Street is crowded with the past, with presence. In the house on the north corner, behind a second-floor window, is where Caroline keeps her sewing machine, that's where we go to sew. On the south side, between sidewalk and houses, deep alleyways have been hollowed out, and the Puerto Rican children on the basement steps are there not to play but on the way into their homes. Down there is where they live. Across the street an old Jewish woman stopped us once, years ago, and complained about the decline of the neighborhood (in the old days, she said, it had been so high-class and Jewish); she was confused, as if she had been living for a long time without a mirror. Four to five paces on the uneven cement of the far sidewalk, that's her place now. "They've destroyed everything," she complained, swaying ever so slightly on her stiff legs. Perhaps she meant that these apartment houses at the west end of 97th Street had been built as respectable addresses, for established middle-class families, like her own maybe, who wished to demonstrate their financial stability with bay windows and stone ornaments applied to the yellow brick façades. To her, not only the open garbage cans flanking the substantial entrances were disgusting, but also the throb of blaring record players issuing from the upper stories that invariably comes to meet us like something we had been expecting. We know these songs about a Caribbean sky, we have already heard them on the transistor radio that Esmeralda takes up and down through our building in her elevator; nothing of ours is destroyed by this music. True, the youths on the front steps near West End Avenue let us cross their line of vision as if we were not right in front of their eyes; even Marie takes only covert looks at them, to read from their lips the Spanish that, when heard, she does not quite grasp. No, these husky young men lounging in doorways have expressed neither anger nor envy at us. In our childish battles in Jerichow, in our childish fear, we, after all, could rely on being rescued by parents.

And you want to live in one of these hotels, when you're on your last legs?

Just look at this child, Cresspahl. Now she's promised me a house on Staten Island for my old age.

These hotels, if they promise twenty-four-hour telephone service it must mean they're expecting you to call for help.

Don't show off, Cresspahl. Just because you've all had the experience of dying. I won't need your help for that.

On Broadway, at the shoe repair, at the flower shop, in the little delicatessens, at Schustek's, we are asked about our health, our vacations, school, and we also use this lubricant of the consumer society and express admiration for Schustek's skill in aiming his cleaver between the pork ribs or complain about the weather. At Schustek's we are valued customers, he would supply us for weeks on credit. Mr. Schustek can still speak a little Westphalian German, and his two Puerto Rican helpers understand and speak enough Yiddish for the customers of this store. The Sabbath holds no fears for him, and Mrs. Ferwalter does not buy here. On these sidewalks we can tell the neighborhood people from the visitors and are greeted by them with the subdued, fleeting glance that only just betokens recognition. We speak to the man on the afternoon shift at the newsstand only when he speaks to us. For last winter, bundled up and stamping his feet against the cold, he compared the weather with a January in Berlin, and we said: We've been to Berlin too. At that he pulled out a hip flask and watched us in silence from indifferent, wide-open eyes as he drank, until we finally moved off. We had recalled his situation in Berlin too vividly to his memory. All we know about the old gentleman who nods to us through the cafeteria window is that he regularly calls out to us: Hi, darling! He is very carefully dressed in his antiquated garments, and through the gap in his jacket we see that the waistband of his pants reaches almost to his nipples. His gaze across the raised cup was quite empty, full of some other sight. That's how Cresspahl could sit after the war, present and yet far removed into a time now existing only in the mind. Now the beggar with the blue-black hair is approaching us across 96th Street, and we escape into "Good Eats," where we are addressed as neighbors who have been missed and have been missing too long. The East German kids in my class call that perpetuating capitalism. Are we to say: Charlie, do you want only our money? Charlie will say: You want one of my three-decker sandwiches, the way only I can make them, and, as you say, for your money, Gesine. Right? See? And the kid wants toast with maple syrup, same as always. Yeah, it's seventeen months now since the house across the street burned down. A ruin, at an intersection like that! Suits me, the cafeteria over there being out of business. Guess it'll stay that way. They won't rebuild that fast, because of the insurance companies. They won't want to stick their necks out, our neighborhood's too unsafe for them.

October 15, 1967   Sunday

"All the News" is what the New York *Times* promises us in the inscription on its West Side plant as we drive north toward it on the expressway beside the river. All the News, it promises, and it is a little while before the qualifying words move within the scope of the windshield: That's Fit to Print. It is hard to define what news must be in order for the New York *Times* to print it: suitable, proper, worthwhile, or whatever. For a long time the paper avoided giving any clue to its formula, and today it provides a hint with the headline to a report on *The Worker*, the Communist paper, with only two editions a week and a paid circulation of not more than 14,218. All the News That Fits the Line, says the New York *Times* of the other paper, only news that suits the Party line, while the New York *Times*, its self-confidence unshaken, displays a heading of less specific promise.

Marie's homework is entitled "I Look Out the Window." She has been sitting half the morning by the window at the typewriter on which she is typing a rough copy of her essay. As she reflects, her hands slipping down onto her knees, her back gets rounder and rounder and, her head on one side, she looks with such concentration into Riverside Park that she fails to notice a glance, hear a footstep. Perhaps she is trying to describe the playground, by this time plainly visible through the bare plane trees. The playground across from our building, surrounded on the outside and protected on the inside by old, tall-crested trees, is a wide, multilevel expanse, starting at its north end with a long area for slides, seesaws, sandboxes, fenced-off groups of swings, surrounded by green benches, which are often damaged. This is followed by an arena inside a high wall, its infield encircled by an iron-pipe railing, and from here steps lead up to a level where there are rows of benches, garden tables, and a little château of a maintenance building from which in turn more steps lead, up to the highest level, where the park is some twelve feet higher than at the south end of the playground. She might be saying: that the tables will soon be moved inside. She might be saying: that the buxom supervisor, the one with the red-cheeked peasant's face, stopped working here weeks ago and is now using her deft stubby fingers, to the sound of the same lilting Irish voice, to wipe children's noses and apply Band-Aids somewhere else. Marie might be describing: how the colors are in layers under the clear sky, the blue terrace of the steep New Jersey shore between the softer color of the vegetation and the sharper gray of the river, all scattered with the sand-colored twigs and sparse patches of leaves on the upper promenade, and then at the lower edge of the picture the piercing colors of the automobiles next to the somber formality of the shadowed park fence. She might be saying: that Rebecca Ferwalter can now be heard under the window uttering a nasal cry in which one can only guess at a name. But Marie and her friend agree to meet later that afternoon, and Marie goes on clicking away on the typewriter keys before pulling out the last sheet and laying the draft beside Gesine's newspaper, without emphasis, rather preoccupied in fact, as if her mind were still working on what she had been seeing.

"I look out the window. The window is the big pane of plate glass of 'Good Eats,' at 96th Street and Broadway looking south. The time is an evening in late May last year. The building across the street is on fire. The building consists of two floors, with a cafeteria, drugstore, and offices. The smoke was not billowing, it was coming out of the empty windows like breath or fog, so white. Spectators were crowding the sidewalks, mostly colored people, but showing consideration for each other. They wanted everyone to have a good look. I could see over the shoulders of those outside the window. Their murmurings became louder when the jets of water uncovered flames on the second floor. The fire hid in the floor until it betrayed itself again with smoke. The streams of water, as thick as a man's arm, were raised up by the engine down below; others penetrated the building from above from a hoist and mechanical ladders. Numerous vehicles had assembled at the intersection, the red trucks of the Fire Department, private and city ambulances, white and green radio cars of the police. In the middle of the south side of the road stood two men all by themselves, not in uniform. They behaved as if they owned the fire. The people on the stools next to me craned their necks while they were chewing. They could not lean on their elbows all the time. Sometimes one of them would wobble, when he was bumped by the policemen pushing their way through to the telephones at the rear. Beyond the window the water was washing the front of the building and tearing off the wood of the shutters. High above the roof the four big billboards were still lighted up. This was the first time I had seen them. The pavement looked dry, although none of the hoses closed tight around the hydrants. A block away from the intersection the pavement looked as if it were steaming. Policemen were standing there with flashlights, directing cars to one side; the drivers had no idea what was happening. All the side streets were jammed with restless headlights. My mother says it reminds her of war."

"I didn't say that."
"You did too."
"No. In the morning I said: When the building was boarded up by the police with yellow planks and the firemen were inspecting the charred wood and soaked rubble, when the air was dry again: I said, it smelled of war."
"We're not supposed to write about smells."
"Can you write: It looks something like that?"

Marie sniffs in disapproval as she alters the sentence. Tomorrow Sister Magdalene will ask her whether she had been thinking of Vietnam. And so there'll be something to talk about at the next PTA meeting. You are not bringing your child up properly, Mrs. Cresspahl.

October 16, 1967   Monday

Cresspahl suspected nothing.

He thought Lisbeth Papenbrock had settled down in Richmond, in England. Now when she heard the telephone ring she no longer turned around to him but picked it up almost without hesitation and struggled through the whole conversation with scarcely a single misunderstanding in the foreign language. English had crept into her German sentences—"aber das's'n full-time job," she had said innocently enough, unaware that she had mixed the two until Cresspahl suddenly looked up. "Or nicht—?" she said, her head on one side, embarrassed and teasing, so he would not put the error into words. At such moments he believed he was thinking what she was thinking. He had watched her surreptitiously at the Royalty Kinema while Buster Keaton in *Speak Easily* blossomed from a professor of Greek mythology into the manager of a musical-comedy company; he was confident of her quiet, informed laughter. She had been talked into going to the Christmas party of the Richmond Anglo-German Circle at the Station Hotel, she had submitted to the singing of all the German carols, from "Silent Night" to the salutation to the Christmas tree, as if to some boring ritual, and she had persuaded him to take her home at the appearance of the new club member, Santa Claus, carrying his sack, with the result that the President, Mrs. Allen, was obliged to send Mrs. Cresspahl's gift (a baby's celluloid rattle) to her by mail. He gathered that she now had less need of German atmosphere.

He had come to trust her interest in Richmond affairs. When she voiced approval at Ham being incorporated into Richmond, when she mentioned Mayor Reid as if the name had been familiar for years, it had sounded as if Richmond were now her town, in whose external changes, at least, she was involved. She had told him about the work being done to Richmond Bridge, one pylon of which, on the Middlesex side, needed reinforcing, about the work of the diver at the bottom of the Thames, secured by ropes, signal lines, and air tubes, about the troop of children on the river path passing critical judgment as each sack of cement was lowered and shifting their dreams of a career below water level. December 1932 had been unusually warm, with a lot of sunshine, and from all her walks she had brought back something from the town, not homesickness for Jerichow. She had come out of the bakery with her coat unbuttoned, so that for a moment her protruding stomach was noticeable on the sidewalk, and an old soul whom she took for a beggarwoman had said to her: God bless you, dearie. She put away the sixpence that the old woman, disappointed, had waved aside. When Wright Brothers, the big store on George Street, filled its upper windows with Bargain Sale signs, owing to the magnificent corner building being renovated and equipped with new electric elevators and a new tearoom, Mrs. Cresspahl dialed Richmond 3601 and asked the sales clerk to put aside for her, at the sale price, the baby layette she had had her eye on before the crowds appeared. Furthermore, she had become interested in Richmond in a manner learned as a Papenbrock daughter: she had read up on the town's history, and in the remains of the old Tudor palace she could show Cresspahl the very window from which, on March 24, 1603, the ring was thrown to the waiting horseman as a sign that Elizabeth, Queen of England and Ireland, had finally succumbed to her cold and that the way was open for James VI of Scotland. Lisbeth Cresspahl evidently knew this James well enough to call him a roué. Now everything had been arranged, nursing home, doctor, and household help starting February 10, 1933 (not Mrs. Jones, who had wanted to give up two other jobs to take this on), a trained nanny who could also cook. Cresspahl had heard it said that when men become fathers for the first time they behave ridiculously, so he watched to see whether he made his wife laugh when he stopped her from picking up anything heavy or supervised her diet according to the doctor's orders. He did not make her laugh. Sometimes she seemed not to hear him, but to be already listening to the child under her folded hands. But there had been no more strained silences since last fall. Quite often he thought to himself: It's going to be all right.

Once, in January, he came upon her in a side street off George Street. Pavement and sidewalks were almost empty. She could have seen him approaching. She was walking slowly, a step at a time, one hand on her hip, looking not ahead but up at the buildings. She seemed to be searching for something above the elaborately ornamented and domed attics. Her face was almost immobile. Her skin was cold and reddened by the wind. Her gaze was strangely clear, revealing no thought. She walked past him, although he had stopped. If there had to be a choice between her and the child, he would have decided against the child.

Then, at the end of January, she asked him to telephone Moxon, Salt & Co. in Regent Street. They were the agents for North German Lloyd, and she wanted a steamer ticket to Hamburg. Cresspahl was caught so unawares that he was on the brink of answering her at once. Then he saw that she had prepared herself for the argument as if for a job to be got through, and that she would sit there indefinitely, as she was now, a little slumped, her forearms on her knees supporting her stomach, submissive and unyielding. He said cautiously: "You can't have both, a child at your old home and me too in Jerichow." And she replied, not unkindly: "How does the child concern you, Cresspahl?"

"That's how I came to be born in Jerichow."

"Would you have liked it much better to be born in Richmond?" says the child, says Marie. She is sitting at the supper table, her fists supporting her chin, eager for the answer.

"I'll say I would. And to have grown up there, and never left England."

"That I can't understand. Oh. Oh, I see. Oh well, sorry."

October 17, 1967 Tuesday

GIRLS SAY YES TO MEN WHO SAY NO (on a sign at a demonstration in San Francisco against the wartime draft). For the second time in three days the U. S. Navy has bombed one of its own positions.

Prague sources have informed the New York *Times* that Miss Zdena Hendrych, daughter of the Party's Number 2 man, stole a Central Committee document from her father's desk to please her lover, the writer Jan Beneš. The document is now in the hands of émigrés in Paris, Beneš has been sent to jail for five years, and Father Hendrych is fulminating against writers. Except that Vaculik, Liehm, Klima, Kundera, Prochazka, have not smuggled the truth across the borders but merely displayed fragments of it publicly inside the country.

"Over here!" says Sam. "Step right up! Hi there, sweetie! Two teas with, one coffee without! Who're you trying to tell! Let's go! Three Danish, yes ma'am! Here's yours, Jee-zine!"

Sam looks after the counter at the far end of the building's cafeteria, where take-out orders are filled. In the morning, just before the offices open, the crowd of people waiting is at its densest, customers arriving on each other's heels from the sidewalk as well as from inside the bank, so that he talks almost incessantly, almost impatient when he can't keep his voice busy. It is impossible to tell Sam's age. At times a confidential exchange of words places him on the level of the young stenos, of whom he knows not only the first names but their circumstances; more often his heavy, work-dulled face makes him seem nearer fifty. He is stocky, sturdy, fat in a very solid way. His gaze seems to rivet the customer he is addressing; in his few idle moments the eyes behind the cheap spectacles seem heavy, sad. His thin, pajamalike jacket usually hangs crooked owing to his rapid movements, and above the edge of his undershirt a little yellow medallion swings to and fro as if propelled. His voice changes in volume like a machine; his casual conversational tone of greeting is followed by the sharp hoarse bark with which he passes on the order to the short-order kitchen behind him and later by the precisely articulated calling out of the orders as they are completed. But he is not only an announcer, he also takes money and gives change, pulls the bags through the hatch, and from his three wall telephones takes new orders to which in turn he has to staple the accompanying cash slips, identifying them with swift squiggles that all begin with the same flat curve whose meaning only becomes manifest in a long, variously executed tail. Sometimes he has one hand too few. He never complains; only when he presses the back of one hand against his receding hairline does something like pain become apparent. The first few times we saw him he looked overburdened; meanwhile he seems to enjoy his work, if only because he can do it so well. He addresses the customers who work in the building no differently from the messengers, mostly colored or shabby white men who deliver the telephone orders to the various floors in the bank and the surrounding buildings, except that he sometimes throws in an encouraging word. It sounds like: Good boy, like the nursery, and yet the weary bag-distributors quite often acknowledge his intention with a long-suffering smile. Nor does he draw his clientele indiscriminately into conversation; his customers must feel inclined for a chat. He calls them his dear Jennifer, he wishes them an extra specially good morning, he admires the girls' hairdos and notices a new sweater at first glance, and the advice he most frequently dispenses is: Take it easy. He can straighten up from his writing position with an almost solicitous look and say: Well, anything to go with the coffee today? This is not a hard-sell tactic, and never does he extort a customer's loyalty with so much as two words that might be an invitation to come back. That's why we come back and let him help us start the day. We owe you a debt of gratitude, Sam.

By early afternoon, when the flock of tables has been tidied up and waits forlornly by the street window, and even the swivel chairs around the three horseshoe counters are sparsely occupied, Sam receives only telephone orders, coffee for the hungover and ice for the

early drinkers, and at the same time he chats with the customers
perched at his counter as they eat. Telephone and cash register leave
him in peace for minutes at a time, but he does not sit down, he
stoops over the low counter, checking his cash. Bundle after bundle
of green bills appear in his hands, and the way it slips through his
fingers he seems to be washing his hands with it.

"Looks pretty good," says Mrs. Cresspahl. "Oh, Gesine," says
Sam, listlessly, wearily, and now she notices something stiff, jerky,
about his movements that is hidden during rush hour. She also
notices for the first time the deep clefts in his fleshy forehead, the
pallor of illness beneath the sweat. "This joint," he says:

(and he is not an employee here. He is not being exploited here.
The whole place is his baby, he pays the rent, has built it up, is
responsible for the wages of three cooks, nine waitresses, two cashiers,
he's the boss here)

"This joint, shall I tell you how I'm going to get out of here? If I
get out of here. In a box, I tell you. In a box!"

In one of those rounded metal containers the police use to
remove corpses, shortly after two men in narrow-brimmed black felt
hats took their guns out of brown paper bags and shot Sam down.

No. He will have a revolver beside the cash register. Sam's not
going to let anyone rob him of a single day's take.

So there will be time to get a coffin after all, not the final one
but a plain interim city coffin, after Sam has collapsed in front of the
short-order kitchen, a little surprised but not angry at the pain that
without warning mounts from his heart through his left arm into his
brain and blacks it out. Let's hope his glasses don't drop off as he
falls, so we may be spared the face hidden behind them. That's how
it will be.

"So what," says Sam patiently. Perhaps he was used to being
beaten up as a child.

"Don't be so scared, Jee-zine!"

October 18, 1967   Wednesday

The Jewish Feast of Tabernacles—Succoth—will begin today at
sundown. It will be observed by Orthodox and Conservative Jews for
nine days, and by Reform Jews for eight days. The holiday is en-
joined in the Bible, "that your descendants may know that I caused
the Israelites to live in booths when I brought them out of the land
of Egypt." (Leviticus, xxiii, 43)

Dear Red Cross Anita. Old chum.

I've copied this out for you from the New York *Times,* because this is the kind of thing the boy you want to get out of East Germany should know about, if he not only *is* Jewish but looks it to such an extent that you feel you can't use any passport that does not indicate the religion as Jewish.

For six years I've had them as neighbors and can't distinguish them from others. Maybe an eye for this sort of thing does exist, as a gift. I don't have it. Have the East German police been trained in this field?

I've found someone who looks like the person in your photo. Except that he's twenty, not nineteen. He grew up, as you specified, speaking French, and has Belgian citizenship. He is on a visit to his grandparents, two blocks from our corner, and, since we know old Mr. and Mrs. Faure from the Broadway and Riverside Drive neighborhood, they have vouched for me. Actually it's because of Marie that they trust me. They are taking the child as a guarantee. Unfortunately they think we are involved in this transportation business to the West out of love for the Jews, and are touched. The boy who gave me his passport is co-operating for reasons he believes to be political.

It was just by chance that I managed to arrange this so promptly, and I wouldn't risk Grandma Faure's confidence for any other motive. This one I'll accept. Let's hope it really is that way: that your nineteen-year-old couldn't take the anti-Israeli propaganda in the German Democratic Republic after the June war and opened his big mouth, that he was kicked out of school and the security police now have their eye on him. A boy like that has to be got out, if only to be amazed. Let's hope it's got nothing to do with love.

For that I wouldn't lift a finger today. At the time, Anita, just after the Wall was built clear across Berlin, you must admit our sympathy made real suckers out of us. When your poor wretches turned up carrying on about their love for someone cut off in the other part of the country, how often did you shut them up by agreeing, so as not to have to listen to all that soulful junk. We all ought to have paid more attention. Some of them, after all, simply felt outraged because the G. D. R. was being unfair in withholding the object of their affections. Some wanted to get their fiancées or mistresses over to prove their virility to them in this department too. Remember the poet from Munich who wept all over your bosom? Two months after the girl he had asked for was delivered to him, he threw her out. Remember Dietbert B., the photographer, the man of the world? To listen to them talk, separation from their beloved was killing them, they just had to be together, at any price, and in actual fact there wasn't enough to keep them together any place. It turned out that absolute, unconditional love was possible only in the capitalist boom. What bullshit!

Part II.

No. I'm not homesick for Germany. And Marie most certainly isn't. She's even embarrassed when someone finds out she was born in Düsseldorf and not New York. And the building in Düsseldorf, my first very own apartment, has been torn down. I'd like to be sitting once more under your gray glass roof that rattles when the incoming jets roar overhead on their flight path; not in order to be in West Berlin, but to see your faces and find out what you're all up to.

Around the corner from us, on West End Avenue, is the Hotel Marseilles, a crenellated tower from the medieval period called turn-of-the-century; it has air conditioners sticking out of the windows like rows of false teeth, and offers Bar & Restaurant & T. V. in Every Room & Swimming Pool. When Marie and I were out for a walk last Saturday, I found myself saying: "That's where she could stay, Anita the Red." It was another few steps before I realized what I had said, and that it's possible. To celebrate your Ph.D. we'll invite you over and share the expense. For instance, I'd like to tell you a queer experience I had, something that happened in Minneapolis. And we would get you to start reading the New York *Times*, the most experienced person in the world, the first to fly the Atlantic, the first to fly over the South Pole, the Firm You Can Trust.

Sincerely yours,

G. C.

October 19, 1967 **Thursday**

The New York *Times* is having an argument with another paper. It had presented the Bolshevik Revolution, on the occasion of the latter's fiftieth birthday, with the statement that the exploitation of man had not ended but had been transferred to the world's greatest employer, the Soviet state. *Pravda* retorts that it is impossible to back up such an assertion, there being no evidence with which to do so.

What did Cresspahl care about the bold headlines in British newspapers announcing the appointment of a Herr Hitler as Chancellor of the German Reich! They weren't getting excited about it, they considered the leader of the biggest party to be in the right spot, under the watchful eye of the assembled Right; stock market quiet, the mark gaining slightly in relation to sterling. But Cresspahl's wife had gone off across the Channel, in the midst of a cold wave from Russia, thirty-one weeks pregnant. True, England was having the coldest weather in seven years, but Dassow Lake near Lübeck was frozen over. There the fishermen were walking to work and hacking holes in the remote bays. "I'm cold," she had said. Whereupon she went off into the cold.

To Cresspahl's amazement, however, everyone seemed to think it quite natural for a young wife to go home for her first confinement. Now that it affected him, he did not find it natural. He overheard a conversation between his helpers. They were discussing Mrs. Cresspahl. Perceval was enumerating all the household chores he had had to do for former bosses' wives. Once Mrs. Cresspahl had made him knead some gingerbread dough for a whole hour. But later she had placed a bowl of the freshly baked cookies in the workshop. "You could have knocked me down with a feather," said Perceval. "But the boss," he went, "look at the face he's making these days. Proper disgruntled he looks, like a real old skinflint. Can't make it out. I'd be glad to have a kid from her!" and Mr. Smith said kindly: "Shut up, T. P." Mr. Smith, emaciated by drink, still had plenty of tough strength in his long arms, and when he looked at the younger man between bushy eyebrows and over the steel rims of his spectacles he could silence him all he wanted. Until now Cresspahl had not been comfortable to see Mr. Smith so devoted in his pursuit of alcohol, but that evening he sent out for some beer. This was not because Mr. Smith was relieving him of some of the burden of educating Perceval.

What Cresspahl saw that night in the bare Petersham Road, in the whistling wind of the Channel storms, was Lisbeth's face behind the windowpane of the train as it drew out of Victoria Station. While searching for a final possible remark he had been of so little help that she had settled matters with the porter and conductor before he had even got his mouth open. She showed him that she would have sufficient help on the journey and, what was more, that she knew how to use it. He also gathered that here she was doing something alone, without him, against him. She had pulled herself up by both arms into the carriage. She stood behind the window, her arms hanging down, as if to open the window required too much effort. She looked at nothing but him. It was a different face. She seemed younger, and too young for her new experiences. She had a girl's face again, somewhat undecided around the eyes, a bit stubborn. In his memory, in the darkness of the deserted, unheated room, it remained motionless until it wavered with the jerk of the moving train and slipped away to one side.

By the time he had been without her for three weeks, he was fairly convinced that she had gone to Jerichow with his approval, if not at his prompting, at least without an argument. He was now quite relaxed about it, and so, in his memory, was she.

October 20, 1967   Friday

Last week's U.S. casualties in Vietnam bring the total figures to 13,907 dead and 88,502 wounded since January 1, 1961.

The students of Brooklyn College who were demonstrating against the presence of two Navy recruiting officers have received rough treatment from the police. One of the New York *Times* pictures shows a policeman, his mouth wide open, giving vent to his feelings by bringing his club down on a smaller, girlish-looking figure. The photo would serve to identify him.

An antiwar demonstration is planned for the weekend in Washington, D. C. Troops of the 82nd Airborne Division have arrived there to protect the Pentagon.

En route from London to Jerichow, Cresspahl wanted to skip a train in Lübeck. He felt obligated to hurry to Jerichow. He did not want to obey this dictate. When he had mounted the awkward stairs and reached the station's upper level, he could look down on the Stettin express, via Gneez, with a connection to Jerichow. He knew he ought to hurry to Jerichow. He had a nagging sense of future guilt. He preferred that to the prospect of Papenbrock's house, of Louise Papenbrock and the sham piety with which she would lead him to the door of the room where meanwhile the presence of a newborn infant could be assumed. He was not yet ready for that room. Besides, he was not even expected there. He had heard it said that in the first few days of life babies cannot see that well anyway. By the time he had got rid of his suitcase the postponement seemed to him successful and almost transformed into a vacation.

The Customs fellows in Hamburg had put on an extraordinary exhibition. They had called him by name in congratulating him on his return to Germany. Had he not been dressed as if for a funeral they might even have punched him in the ribs. It happened to be an ordinary working day, March 2, 1933, a Thursday, and he wanted to look around the Free Hansa City of Lübeck to see if the people there had also taken leave of their senses.

Each station exit was partially blocked by pairs of uniformed men: one man in the familiar green of the police and one in the uniform of the Storm Troopers, each inspecting wallets. But the city policeman whose job it was to pass people along to his colleague often stepped nonchalantly away from him, as if embarrassed, so that the checkup among the jostling travelers took on the appearance of a not too serious, almost indecent procedure. Nevertheless Cresspahl assumed a co-operative demeanor (such as he had employed all his life in his encounters with officialdom), as if he were prepared to wait patiently for the Brownshirt to paw through his papers, like those of the two youths who under their tweed caps looked more like hairdresser's apprentices than workers. However, the policeman in his black shako signaled to him with a furious jerk of the chin that the search did not apply to people in black clothes and polished shoes who had come to Lübeck on a visit, and out on the sidewalk Cresspahl once more caught his disgusted, almost imploring look. The policeman seemed nauseated by the private army of this fellow Hitler, and Cresspahl very nearly nodded to him in sympathy.

Erwin Plath lived in the suburb of North St. Lorenz, in a side street off Schwartau Avenue, not far from the boundary slaughterhouse, and Cresspahl stood in some surprise outside the dignified, neatly painted gabled house before knocking. The woman rushed at him as if she had been standing behind the door. "My husband's not here!" she screamed. "My husband's not here!" she repeated, and Cresspahl stepped back onto the sidewalk so that she could have a better look at him. This didn't help her. Her husband wasn't there! she shouted, as if she wanted all the neighbors to hear. Cresspahl slowly undid the two top buttons of his overcoat, partly in bewilderment but also because his collar felt tight, and suddenly she whispered something. He gathered that Erwin would be at Hindenburg House that afternoon "to join in." "My husband's not here!" she said in a loud voice, and Cresspahl did not even attempt a reply. Back on Schwartau Avenue he permitted himself a shake of the head. Erwin had told him years ago in Hamburg about a stubborn but goodnatured wife, and not about a scared girl trying to put on an act.

On the railway bridge, instead of turning right he kept straight on toward Ebert Square, crossed the city moat, rounded the Holsten Gate in its earth bowl, and disappeared into the heart of the city. There was not much to see there. He inspected the crammed furniture stores, and he did not need to be told that unemployment was still hurting the instalment business, that consequently the sawmills were holding back in their buying, and that in this city nobody was waiting for someone like himself. Standing there, a sturdy fellow in his Sunday best, his hands behind his back, looking at placards and store windows and newspaper displays, walking leisurely down Broad Street, up King Street, the short curls on his bare head exposed to the soft flowing air, somewhat curious, still not amazed.

Then he saw something, but time began to pass so swiftly that by the next day he no longer believed it all. At Hindenburg House a funeral procession came marching toward him, with muffled drums, naval and swastika flags, and at the rear, far behind the blue and brown uniforms, the undeniable figure of Erwin plodding along, a bit stooped, as if they were not the same age after all, with a kind of fixed stare as if he actually were helping to accompany someone to his grave. The only thing was, what had a .dues-paying member of the Social Democrat Party to do with a deceased lieutenant-commander, with a cortege of Storm Troopers? Erwin ignored him as he joined the ranks and adopted the appropriate dazed expression, and they jogged along wordlessly side by side as far as the Old Cemetery, mourners to their fingertips. Not until the procession had swung into the central avenue did Erwin turn off onto a side path, his handkerchief raised to his face to brush away some invisible object, so that no one particularly noticed him. Later Cresspahl found him at the very edge of the cemetery, behind the wall of a mausoleum, jittery, looking over his shoulder, whispering, not cheerful, not kidding around, not the man Cresspahl had known for twenty years. Erwin was waiting for somebody. It was not Cresspahl. At heart he was waiting for the police, only he would have liked to meet someone else first.

So it was Cresspahl who rode back from the cemetery with Erwin's envelopes, on the back platform of a Number 2 streetcar down Israelsdorf Avenue across the square known as the Klingenberg to Kronsford Avenue. The address was in a street of prosperous houses, with elegant stucco between the timbering or recherché art nouveau brickwork. In one of these houses, in a velvet- and mahogany-darkened room, Cresspahl was able to hand over the two passports, since papers for abroad is what they were. The people around the polished family dining table seemed to be playing school, impatiently, hastily, as if they really had more urgent matters to attend to. The question was whether the Communists had set fire to the Reichstag, or Hitler's Storm Troopers. The question was also whether the Social Democrats could now reconcile aid to the Communists with their dignity. For the Mecklenburg state delegates of the German Communist Party, Warncke, Schröder, Quandt, Schuldt, were in flight, and there was reason to fear that Ernst Thälmann might soon be ringing the doorbell. There were rumors that Thäl-mann was on his way to Denmark. Still, the Communists had once made a pact with the Nazis against the Social Democrats. Could they ever be forgiven the phrase "Social Fascists"? The leader of the discussion was a little runt of a man, the square mustache under his nose never moved and he held his polished round skull to one side as if he were asleep, but when he awoke he started declaiming like an irate, implacable schoolteacher. Cresspahl did not witness the outcome of the dispute because he rode back to town with two other men, in different streetcars in fact, and this time on a Number 1 via Ratzeburg Avenue.

At the Klingenberg he saw neither of the men who had left ahead of him, not that he minded much, for they had still not given him a chance to tell them about his dissociation from the German Socialist Party since 1922. After a while he went off to the alleyway where Erwin had said he would wait for him, and sat for a long time in vain by a window opening out onto a back yard, in the parlor of an old woman who treated him as one among many adolescents who get themselves into trouble out of sheer mischief. It was apparent that she was used to such visits. She spoke nothing but dialect. She forced upon him a plaice fried in very little butter. Then she tried to prevent him from leaving, appealing to him in the gentlest of tones as if she had not previously seemed to be quite quarrelsome. She reminded him of his mother; he wanted to laugh. Outside his attention was caught by some drunks because they were standing around so apathetically and joylessly. On Johannis Street a crowd pushed him close to a brawl that was just getting under way with light punches between three men. After each impact they would take another half-step forward, arching their shoulders back like boastful children, until one of them intercepted a blow to his upper arm and with his free hand hit the attacker under the chin. They were still quarreling about the parade two weeks earlier of the Reichsbanner, the Socialist veterans' organization, that the Storm Troopers had halted by blocking the street, on the pretext that there had been shooting there, also that someone had shouted an insult to Reich Chancellor Hitler; the two dead men, however, were later identified as members of the Reichsbanner. (And last night a Nazi torchlight parade had allegedly been fired on from the rooftops.) The policeman outside the Reich Bank gazed steadfastly northward, even his hearing did not make his head turn around, he was apparently occupied with the renewed ban on tearing off twigs and pussywillows either inadvertently or deliberately. Toward evening Cresspahl came through the street called the Schüsselbuden, and on noticing the consular plaque of His Britannic Majesty King George V on the wall of Number 17 he had a sense of two different realities, and would rather have been in only one. At the Salt Depots, on his way to the station, Erwin Plath intercepted him. He was now holding himself quite erect, a self-respecting citizen out for a stroll, and he talked in a loud voice about a Sunday excursion he was planning to Ratzeburg, by motorboat on the Wakenitz. But he could not refrain from looking over his shoulder, and he was still waiting. Someone had been asking for him at home that noon. Cresspahl declined to accompany him there, but at the station he found that at that late hour there was no train to Gneez, let alone Jerichow, and when he knocked once more at Erwin's door he was arrested by the police who shot out of the dark hallway and drove him to the police station in a car that had already struck him as too luxurious for that street. The police were willing to bring food to his cell in exchange for his money, the British supplements to his passport being at least to that extent effective, but otherwise they had no idea what to do with this phlegmatic fellow who claimed merely to have skipped a train in Lübeck and who sat stiffly on his stool, huddled in his coat as if afraid of soiling the black cloth against the walls. In those days the Lübeck police still attached importance to cleanliness and suspected him of an intended insult. So it was early morning before they took him along for questioning, and still he did not want to extricate himself by using his father-in-law's business reputation in Lübeck. He was convinced that the only way to get out of this was to play dumb. He insisted on a confrontation with his friend Erwin Plath, that being the man he had come to visit, and now time was running out and he wanted a chance at least to see him. Finally they brought Erwin in and made him stand in the opposite corner of the office. Erwin looked slightly the worse for wear about the shoulders, but he was frankly cheerful now, as if the long wait were over at last and the event less upsetting than the prospect of it. The Commissar, scintillating after a good night's rest, embarked on a long interrogation, cunningly starting off with the question: Where had the gentlemen first met, to be such good friends? And Cresspahl drew himself up and almost knocked the dumfounded interrogator off his swivel chair with the ringing cry: "24th Holstein Artillery Regiment in Güstrow, 2nd Battery!" After the first syllable Erwin joined in, and at the proper place Cresspahl gave him time to echo: "5th Battery!" said Erwin.

Over breakfast in Gerda Plath's kitchen, Erwin was back to his waiting. "Whoever can that have been, yesterday noon, the man you sent me a message about to Hindenburg House," he mused, massaging the back of his neck. "Someone who knew the sign of the two coat buttons," he said, looking past Cresspahl, from whom he could expect no help here. Gerda shot an inadvertent glance at Cresspahl, who until now had treated her with marked reserve, and at that moment each realized that yesterday someone failed to turn up, someone else who had known the sign for a sign. "There's one," she said, cocking her elbow toward Cresspahl. They both watched Erwin's face where delight was struggling with the other realization. Then he said, very slowly: "Well, I'll be damned."

That morning, Friday, the third of March, 1933, Gesine Cresspahl was born in Jerichow.

October 21, 1967 Saturday, South Ferry Day

"So Cresspahl, your father, my grandfather," says Marie, "didn't reach you in Jerichow till the afternoon of March 3, 1933."

"Early afternoon, at the same time as the leader of the Communist Party of Germany, Ernst Thälmann, allowed himself to be discovered and arrested in a small room on Lützow Street in Berlin. And he didn't have a ticket to Denmark on him either."

"And Cresspahl wasn't drunk."

"Not visibly. He had helped Erwin Plath to get through not only that morning in Lübeck but also a quart of extra strong kümmel and half a case of beer, and Gerda Plath wouldn't let him go until he had done honor to her coffee. She wanted to send a sober husband to that Mrs. Cresspahl. So when he arrived in Jerichow, walking along Station Street and under the first sixteen of Papenbrock's windows, erect and rather slowly, he was the widest-awake drunk you can imagine."

"Consequently in a good mood," says Marie.

"A blind man who saw everything without being able to remember it. A deaf man who could hear a cat run by without identifying the sound. Jerichow seemed to him very noisy. There was music in the square. There were more people in the square than he remembered inhabitants. Papenbrock's door to the square was locked."

"Cresspahl hadn't been told."

"He felt sure he had read the *Gneezer Tageblatt* in the train. He felt sure there had been no birth announcement of any Cresspahl in the paper. He returned to Station Street and found Papenbrock's gate in the high brick wall and a door into the house. In the warm passageway, behind all the brown doors, there was silence. The silence overwhelmed him, making his ears buzz as if he were under water."

"Families like that take an afternoon nap," says Marie.

"Lisbeth lay asleep in her hair in the room over Papenbrock's office that a week ago had been a front parlor. She slept propped up on pillows, her mouth open, breathing heavily against the overheated air, surrounded by the stately formal furniture as if on her deathbed."

"Now about the child."

"The child lay in a rustic wooden cradle against the wall between the two windows that faced the square. The child was tucked in under a pile of feather quilts. The child was sleeping on its right ear, between lightly clenched fists. Its breath could be seen but not smelled. The chin still protruded, the forehead receded steeply under the few dark hairs. It was a fully mature infant, with complete fingernails, reddish-blue skin, and only a few crow's-feet at the corners of its eyes."

"You can't know that about yourself," says Marie, stating a fact, not in protest.

"I've been told that no one noticed Cresspahl. All of a sudden the house awoke and dispatched one envoy after another to the two sleepers. Along came Mother Laabs, the district midwife. Along came Louise Papenbrock with hot-water bottles for the child. Along came the servants, cook, housemaids, coachman, hired hands, to offer their congratulations. Edith arrived with her two children and proved to them that the new baby had been brought by the stork, for at the foot of the cradle he had also left some Lübeck marzipan in two twists of gold paper. Edith of all people. Along came Albert Papenbrock, a grandfather, in his stocking feet, carrying the tea on the best tray, the way Lisbeth had learned to make it in Richmond. They didn't have much use for the fellow standing by the north window. Louise Papenbrock gave him a satisfied and imperious nod; she had postponed her revenge. To the people from the stable and the granary he seemed suitably dazed. Edith's children curtsied and looked him straight in the eye until he came across with sixpence. Albert was the only one to put his arm around his shoulders and say something to him in gurgling tones, perhaps he was trying to laugh, and drew him almost tenderly into the next room and set him down in front of a bottle of claret and drank a glass too, his face still puckered up like a child in need of consolation. But before that Dr. Berling came in and whacked Cresspahl on the shoulder.

*Well, you old rascal. Can't say you tried very hard. It's not a
boy, eh?*

When can she travel?

Go to England?

Go home.

That's for the mother to decide. Ask her in three weeks.

Not before?

*Have some sense, man. Why go back to England? Now that
Germany's at last coming into her own again?*

You can't tell that from a distance.

"Now something about married life."

"Cresspahl had caught his wife's eye as he walked past the head
of her bed into the next room. In any case he wanted to wait until
they were alone. At first the red wine merely made him drowsy. For a
time he couldn't rid himself of the vision of Horst Papenbrock in
the uniform of Hitler's Storm Troopers raising his glass to him and
checking off a series of items on his bent fingers, like a math teacher
enthusiastically proving a proposition. Then he managed to forget
him and think about Meta Wulff instead. With Meta Wulff he
could talk quite innocuously; he told her about the night in the
Lübeck police cell. When Dr. Semig appeared, there was already no
doubt he was seeing him, although at the sight of him he had let slip
an exclamation that he would have liked to take back if only he could
find it in some corner of his memory. Then, after the second bottle,
he had drunk himself sober. The afternoon music on the square, that
had been the band of the 162nd Storm Troopers' Banner from
Lübeck. Horst Papenbrock's figures had been the arrests of Communist functionaries: in Rostock 27, in Schwerin and Wismar and
Güstrow 10 each, in rural Mecklenburg 58. The noise under the
windows came from one of the loudspeakers set up on Town Street
and the square by Schmidt's House of Music to relay Hitler's speech
from Hamburg. That flickering light between the gabled roofs came
from the torches being borne by Storm Trooper and Stahlhelm
detachments to illuminate their uniforms on their march to the Rifle
Club, and that gentle current of air issued from the door now
unlocked by Papenbrock because he thought he had nothing to fear
for his property from this bunch. The blaze and sparks in the
billowing smoke at the other end of town came from the pyre of
burning torches, and the singing from the low-hanging night came

also from Papenbrock as he groped his way upstairs contentedly humming to himself,

To thee I've surrendered
With heart and with hand
Thou land of love and life
Belovèd Fatherland

and as Cresspahl bolted his door he found himself thinking in English, the way he pronounced it: Aw-right. We won't surrender. Not a hand, not a stone, not a leg. Whether you call us loyal or loved, you want something from us, and we won't give it to you. The child was a girl, so that in turn he owed something to Lisbeth; but even supposing the child had not recognized him, at least it had looked at him."

"Your mother, Lisbeth," says Marie. "Tell me how she felt about it."

"That's beyond me."

"Can't you think what she was thinking?"

"No, nor how. I've ceased to understand her."

That was today, in the late afternoon, when the ferry was already halfway back to New York Harbor. Marie had been called over by a Japanese gentleman who handed her his camera, with suave apologies, and Marie had posed him and his family with expert instructions and hand signals in front of the towers of Manhattan before absorbing the vibrations of the deck in her flexed knees and clicking the visitors' proof of their world tour into their own camera. As she went ashore, over the gangplanks and steps and down the ramp beside the ferry building, she responded three times to the tourists' friendly glances, not with smiles but with a very slight bow from the shoulders and recognition in her eyes. "Welcome a Stranger," I said, and although she obviously recognized the quotation from the Transit Authority buses she replied, almost grave, almost gay: "Sure, Gesine. Welcome a Stranger."

October 22, 1967 Sunday

Well, start, Gesine.
No, you start.
Why weren't you at yesterday's demonstration in Washington?

Because I don't believe in it. The President's policy in Vietnam isn't going to be affected by the protests of minorities.

There were fifty thousand demonstrators.

Against two hundred million U. S. citizens. And President Johnson gave a luncheon.

The New York Times *devoted a quarter of its front page and almost two inside pages to the demonstrations here and abroad.*

The New York Times *happens to report events too.*

Publicity in the New York Times *might alter the opinion of the nation.*

We don't even know what the paper has in mind with its photos. The front-page picture of the three U. S. marshals using their white clubs to strike a man lying on the ground, is that intended to arouse the indignation of its subscribers? And the one next to it of the youth yelling his head off, is that to draw attention to the anti-Establishment beard, the disguising sunglasses, the distorted mouth?

Publicizing the opposition to the Vietnam war through the news media, mightn't that mean a chance for the opposition?

A chance.

For you even a chance has to be a sure thing, hasn't it.

A bit.

Were you scared of the white clubs, Gesine? Admit it, you're relieved you weren't one of those who were driven out of the Pentagon by military police with rifle butts, down the steps. That blood on the steps, it isn't yours.

If I'm crippled I can't look after the child.

The child, the child. Your authorized excuse.

My authorized excuse.

You're afraid of going to jail.

What use am I to anyone in jail? Yes, I'd be afraid of going to jail, any jail, in any country.

Norman Mailer was arrested yesterday at the Pentagon.

For "technical violation" of a police line. Want to bet he's already back home in Brooklyn Heights?

He's declared himself an opponent of U. S. policy in Vietnam.

He was also there in his professional capacity: soon he'll be selling us his experiences.

What you didn't like was the Vietcong flag in the parade.

I couldn't care less about the Vietcong. All I want is the withdrawal of foreign troops from Vietnam.

Of our troops.

Of foreign troops.

The marijuana fumes from your fellow demonstrators would have made you doubt the cause.

Would the cause be easier to identify under the influence of drugs?

One small flaw in the beauty of the deed, and you won't commit it.

Not only the deed would come back to me but also the flaw.

And so you wouldn't want to remember the deed.

And so a rejection of North American expansion in Asia would be twisted into approval of Soviet expansion.

You're talking like a goddamn intellectual.

And you're talking like people who are no longer around.

You just didn't want to make the effort. You didn't like to go as an over-thirty. You didn't like to be conspicuous and be seen among a whole lot of school kids, students, young people.

Who was I to join in with? The flower children? The Music and Art high school?

You didn't want to be spotted as an outsider.

It's true I would have felt I had to disguise myself.

For once you wouldn't have been alone.

That wonderful sense of intimacy around the campfires in front of the Pentagon, I don't have that sense any more. Being surrounded by soldiers with fixed bayonets held professionally on their hips, that wouldn't have lured me into thoughts of heroism in the face of danger. The smell of wood smoke and tear gas in the air, that wouldn't have made me think of the sufferings that are scientifically forecast to precede the inevitable victory. The community singing of "Down by the Riverside," even while I was there the prospect of remembering it would have been enough to make me feel uncomfortable.

Just so you won't be embarrassed, either now or later.

Just so I don't do anything I can't bear to remember.

You would have been bothered by the burning of police barricades in the campfires at night.

The destruction of public property had not been one of the points at issue. That doesn't make taxpayers any more sympathetic to peace marches.

They're your taxes, too, that are being sent to the front.

Should I rather pay taxes for Britain's African arms deals, for West Germany's armaments industry, for the Soviet Union's occupation costs?

Yesterday, when you came off the ferry, you didn't understand

*what the little demonstration in Battery Park was about. You didn't
know why so many cars, and buses and police cars too, were driving
in broad daylight with their headlights or parking lights on.*

*They drove around like that too when John F. Kennedy was
killed.*

*Yesterday they did it to show solidarity with the nation's war in
Vietnam.*

*I admit, in my case ignorance was bliss. But that's a feeling that
will go away in time.*

That's what Edith said too.

And then she had her fifth child.

*And you're satisfied that all you know about yesterday's demon-
strations here and in the rest of the world is what you read in the
papers? Is that any way to live, instead of being there, joining in,
getting involved, taking action?*

*It's what I've been left with: to find out about things. At least to
live with my eyes open.*

*Gesine, why weren't you at yesterday's demonstration in Wash-
ington?*

I won't say.

But you can say it to us.

Not even in my thoughts.

Then there's only one thing left.

As long as I don't complete the thought, it doesn't exist.

October 23, 1967   Monday

---

*So you want to keep your mouth shut today, Gesine? Hold your
tongue? Not utter a word?*

*It's supposed to be typical of New York. One man has described
a record of twenty-one days' silence. It's supposed to be typical of
alienation in New York.*

Why do you want to remain silent, Gesine?

I don't feel like talking.

Conversations about work won't count. We don't count Marie
either, although she walked to the door without a word after surprising Gesine by putting an arm around her, briefly but emphatically, so
that the feeling of her body from knees to shoulders lasted for several
seconds. (Don't ask me anything, Marie.)

The encounter with Jason passed off without a word, without
even a grimace. Where the iron stairs around the elevator shaft open

toward the building's staff room, Jason appeared in the doorway, massive, black, somber, saturnine, momentarily blocking out the noise from radios and television, withdrawn into the darkness behind his eyes. (Lovely day, Jason.)

The mechanics in the middle garage are pretty much awake, they call out, greet Mrs. Cresspahl as their sister, one of them whistles. (I wear my skirts as short as I like.)

At the corner of 96th Street and West End Avenue the police car has drawn up and deposited the policeman who five mornings a week supervises the route of the school kids going to Emily Dickinson. Striding toward the middle of the intersection and firmly pulling on his white gloves, he eyes the pedestrians on the sidewalk who, embarrassed and annoyed, for once have to obey the traffic light. (Sure, Officer.)

Behind the window of his "Good Eats" Charlie stands stock-still, his head with its gray brush crowning the high forehead turned unseeing toward Broadway, forgetful of his hands scooping a hamburger onto a spatula. In the corner of the window stands a printed, grease-spotted card recommending Charlie's cooking to the customers of a West German travel agency. (How do the Jews in the office above you feel about that, Charlie?)

The old man at the newsstand has his hands in his apron pocket, watching this customer exchange coin for paper as intently as if he were trying to read her lips. (Today I'm the one who's forgotten to say good morning.) That wasn't easy. She almost went back to make it up to him with a remark about the weather. (Has *Der Spiegel* arrived yet?)

On the way down the foul-smelling subway steps, a woman detaches herself from the wall like some dream-figure, quietly and unfashionably dressed, not sufficiently interesting for the male subway users, saying, "Dearie, darling, don't you have a dime for me?" (I could recommend you an excellent poem by Brecht, you housewife-run-amok.)

The A express is jam-packed today and feels more crowded every minute with the rambling monologue of a black man who raises his hoarse drawling voice to the ceiling, his neck arched back as if he were drowning: "They wanna corrupt the Negro! They're intendin' and meanin' and plannin' t'corrupt the Negro with sex!" (Who are you trying to tell?)

In the concourse of Grand Central Station a dignified old lady in a lace blouse and black tailored suit is trying all the telephone coin-returns for overlooked nickels and dimes, senses that she is being observed and asks us in the sprightly tones of an expensive college about the train from Montreal. (Call Information, Madam.)

At Sam's we have to trust him to know our standing order by heart, and indeed the jostling at his counter prevents the usual exchange of greetings as he hands over the bag to us; perhaps his nod, the melancholy glance away from his barking mouth, was not meant for us. (Hi, Sam. Tea with lemon. Thanks Sam. Don't work too hard, Sam. So long, Sam.)

So we manage to get to the first elevator lane in silence, to the eleventh floor, past the girls in the typing pool, to our desk, and after two hours' silence in front of the humming, clacking machine Amanda settles down in the other chair, equipped with steaming coffee and lighted cigarette for an extended visit, and wants to know how we are. She insists on being told. Now the game has been lost. "Can't you see I'm jumping for joy?" says Mrs. Cresspahl.

On the way home we made another attempt at silence. Marie was standing by the railing around the subway exit at 96th Street, a somewhat anxious, determined child who permits a few more wordless steps before the day has to be put right.

"Are you still sad, Gesine?"
"No."
"D'you remember what you were sad about?"
"No."
"It's these goddamn Mondays, Gesine. Sometimes I hate everything too, Gesine."

October 24, 1967   Tuesday

While Robert Smith, of 470 Sheffield Avenue, Brooklyn, was having a loud argument with his wife Clarice yesterday afternoon, their six-year-old son Randy went to the closet, took out his father's .22-caliber rifle, loaded it, took aim, and shot his father in the chest. His father will never have another row with his mother.

In 1933 in Jerichow Cresspahl felt he was being treated as if he were to be kept out of a row. In the morning, in the downstairs hall, he let his attention wander for a moment and before he knew it was being embraced by Louise Papenbrock. At breakfast old man Papenbrock waited until he knew his wife was busy upstairs with the child ("with the children"), then sent Edith to the Lübeck Arms for two pitchers of Kniesenack beer and poured himself and Cresspahl a stiff schnapps as well; he was not only grateful for the chance to take things easy for a change but also relieved to find that this son-in-law could handle his liquor. He had not been aware of this. Papenbrock and Cresspahl walked down Town Street and up again, so they would be seen, and they went into the stores and were congratulated by Molten the baker and Pahl the tailor and by Böhnhase, and over schnapps at the counter or in the back room they agreed, depending on the circumstances, that either the retailers or the tradesmen were the backbone of the middle classes and that the Nazis apparently were aware of this. Even Stoffregen did not run away when Papenbrock buttonholed him and claimed his congratulations. Cresspahl could not understand why the man seemed so ill at ease and depressed. By the time they reached the mayor's office Papenbrock was pretty red in the face and not averse to little outbursts of anger against his wife Louise, but Louise recalled earlier days on the Vietsen estate and did not once send to the Lübeck Arms, where by this time eight solid citizens were drinking the health of the newborn child. Papenbrock was also being congratulated on his son, who, thanks to an event known as a change-over, had got himself into a position of political power, but Dr. Erdamer, the mayor, refrained, and Papenbrock tried to discourage them with a wave of his long, thickened hand. Horst had appropriated a police detachment in Gneez and, with the aid of the authority and lists given him by the district administrator, was searching out Communist activities known as machinations. Papenbrock's emotions fluctuated between pride in the boy, who had now, say what you like, learned to give orders in a forceful, paramilitary way, and anxiety that he would have to answer for the steps taken by his offspring, including any toward Dr. Erdamer, for Dr. Erdamer was not only a Social Democrat but on Horst's list of those who were to be "kicked out." For the time being he wanted to keep Cresspahl out of all this, just for a few more days, and Cresspahl suspected nothing.

A row would have suited him nicely. It was not only the foolish hilarity of the womenfolk in Papenbrock's house as they used the pretext of the baby's arrival to try to oust the men ("My husband's in the hospital. We've just had a baby"); he had wanted it all to be so different: a private room in a clinic, medical supervision, trained nurses, no visitors outside the family, and a semblance of hygiene. Now his wife was lying in state in the front parlor, obliged to put up with the formal visits of family friends, and the baby got picked up and shown to the visitors' children and put down again and picked up, affectionately patted by earthy germ-laden fingers, and would develop a headache like the one Cresspahl already had from the flower arrangements in the dry overheated air. Nor did he manage to talk normally with Lisbeth (except during the first night, which he spent on the floor beside her bed, his hands clasped behind his head, talking softly, until she forgot her sudden fear and was able to fall asleep). She did not agree on a date for traveling, but neither did she disagree with him. When he looked at the child blindly, helplessly, sipping drops of sugar water from his cracked finger, he was conscious of a violent sense of urgency.

On Sunday afternoon, while the loudspeakers of the Schmidt House of Music were emitting the latest figures from the Reichstag election, interspersed with recorded classical music, to rattle against the windowpanes, the child was given a name. In the *Gneezer Tageblatt* it had been announced merely as "a healthy girl." Lisbeth Cresspahl had been expecting a boy, and the only name she had decided on in advance was Henry, and Cresspahl had not expected to get his way before she did for once. She asked him for suggestions. She was sitting half upright, propped against three pillows, looking at him, attentive, almost gay. Her eyes seemed darker than usual, she had not yet regained her color, nor was the loose hair around her face as light as usual. She considered the ideas he slowly, hesitatingly, put forward, opened her lips, chewed the air. She seemed to be tasting them. The child was certainly not to be called Elisabeth—"which Lisbeth would you want to come when you called one of us: both, Cresspahl?" She quite understood that for a second name he could consider Louise only out of politeness to Papenbrock's wife, and not willingly. She mentioned his sister's name. Cresspahl said slowly that he thought it must be a name which would summon no one else. "Gesine," he said almost unthinkingly, and wished he could have taken it back. "Yes," said Lisbeth, compliantly, kindly, so that he was obliged to regard it as a gift. He was sitting on the edge of her bed, at the foot end. Without so much as a glance at the cradle she prodded his hip lightly with one foot under the cover, saying: "Gesine Henriette."

Is that you, Gesine?
That's me, Gesine.
1904 in Malchow am See?
I was fifteen. He was sixteen. I was Redebrecht's granddaughter.
What did you look like, Gesine?
I wore my hair in braids around my head. I was blonde. He always wanted me to unpin my braids. The first time I went upstairs in the middle of the night to the window, my hair hanging loose.

There had been no prior arrangement or suggestion. But he was
standing there.

Gesine, are you dead too?

Not necessarily, Gesine. I would only be seventy-nine. The old
woman who stood in your way at the Wendisch Burg station in 1952,
that might have been me. The old woman with the stick sitting on
the bench outside the old people's home in Hamburg, maybe that
was me. You can imagine that, can't you, Gesine.

I can, Gesine.

October 25, 1967   Wednesday

The Soviets have now decided after all to be annoyed about the flight
of their secret agent Runge to the West; they admit he exists; and
they call him an unscrupulous criminal. And they publish the existence of an American agent who defected to them from New Delhi.
John Smith is his name.

"Gesine, I'm worried about one of the kids."

"A girl I know?"

"No. A girl in my class."

"Does she sit next to you?"

"She's been put next to me."

"A girl from another school?"

"From Harlem."

"Is that the trouble?"

"The trouble is she's colored."

"Mind what you say, Marie."

"O.K. O.K.!"

"You should say: A black girl."

"Sure, Gesine. Sure."

Some pupils from the Polish, Bulgarian, and Czechoslovakian
embassies have been beaten up and intimidated at Lincoln Junior
High School in Washington, D. C. One boy had to be taken to a
hospital. The State Department informs us: "This is very bad for our
image overseas."

"She's the only black girl."

"Call her by her name."

"Francine is the only black girl in our class, and out of all twenty-
one girls Sister Magdalena had to pick on me."

"You're embarrassed."

"No. It's because it's so pointless. She's an exception."

"An exception among Negroes?"

"An exception to life in this country. She's an alibi-black."

"Marie Cresspahl, explain yourself."

"An alibi-black is someone who's allowed to enter our school for nothing."

"So the institution won't lose its federal subsidy."

"So that a farce is made of the law."

"D'you think there should be room for all Negroes in your schools, for the sake of justice?"

"It's unjust that until then I should have to do the alibi-black's work for all twenty-one of us."

The playwright LeRoi Jones, charged in New Jersey on account of two revolvers found in his car during the July riots, denounced the white judge and the white prospective jurors as his oppressors. He was then handcuffed.

"It's too much for you, Marie."

"It is a bit much. Francine's behind in math, she can't write proper English, she doesn't know where Montreal is."

"And she's never been taken along for a weekend to Montreal, like one child I know personally."

"Francine can't even learn. She remembers so little, and even that she gets mixed up."

"Maybe she's got no place at home to study, no peace and quiet, no time."

"That's not my fault."

"Welcome a Stranger."

"That's what I've been doing, ever since Labor Day. This is the seventh week I've been checking her notes, going over tests with her in break, listening to her repeat her lessons, explaining her homework again over the phone. That's not what I mind. What I call work is something else."

"What do you call work?"

"Work is this being friendly."

"Is she friendly?"

"The first few weeks she was stiff with nervousness. She wouldn't even raise her eyes. Even today she still needs to screw up her courage or a dig in the ribs to speak up. But with me she doesn't force herself any more."

"She thanked you."

"I told her not to bother."

"She's become friendly."

"And I have to be friendly in return! Otherwise I can't help her. Otherwise she's hurt. And . . ."

"You don't like her."

"Right, I find her ugly."

"What Negroes don't you find ugly?"

"Jason. Esther. Shakespeare."

"Because they look like the ones on TV."

"I don't watch TV behind your back."

"Sorry."

"Now she says right to my face: she likes me. Next thing she'll be putting her arms around me in the morning and when school's out. Now she wants all of me."

"She's been taken in by the alibi."

"I don't intend to go on paying for that."

"In what way are you paying?"

"With Marilyn. With Marcia. With Deborah. They think it's more than decency that makes me help Francine. They think what Francine thinks: that I do it for love. I want out."

Seven years ago a family of four spent only $5,790 to maintain a life without luxury in New York. Since then the United States Bureau of Labor Statistics has added only home-ownership to that standard of living. This, together with increased prices and taxes, means an expenditure of $10,195 for the same family in 1966, 71 per cent more. Maybe we won't make it here after all.

"Why didn't you bring this up till now?"

"I was waiting for the weather to improve."

"What weather?"

"Yours, Gesine. Talk about the Negro situation, and you can count on a prickly reaction from Mrs. Cresspahl."

"You don't want to tell Francine?"

"No. I can't."

"Then let her go on thinking what she thinks, and just remember why it is you're helping her."

"How about my real friends?"

"You can let them know how you feel by asking them to help with Francine."

"That wouldn't be lying?"

"Not out-and-out lying."

"O.K. That lets me out. Thanks."

"Don't you mind our having all this on tape now?"

"No. By the way, I'd like to invite Francine over sometime. When I have my Halloween party."

"Now you're trying to fool the tape."

"And you never fool anyone, Gesine. Not even tapes."

"Maybe I'm better at it."

"Sorry. I didn't mean you. I meant: when I recognize a thought, even before I've quite spoken it, have I really thought it before? Was I serious when perhaps I thought it? Am I remembering it, or the wish to think it? Tell me, Gesine."

That evening, almost as soon as we got home, a horde of thunderstorms and rain showers swept out of the west toward our windows, spilled itself swiftly and violently onto the city, from five until shortly after midnight. It's turned cold now.

October 26, 1967   Thursday

The Soviets still cannot accept the defection of their secret agent Runge, unless it be an invention and a stupid joke of the competition's, and the East Germans are even claiming him as a (criminal and fugitive) citizen. In a countermove the London competition is displaying genuine photocopies of Runge's Soviet passports, identity cards, and documents.

Dr. Gallup has been questioning the nation once again. Forty-six out of a hundred confided to him that they regretted United States involvement in Vietnam. In 1965 there were only half as many.

Cresspahl met with some difficulty in registering the birth of his child. The town hall was under guard.

Horst Papenbrock had not begun his seizure of power in the market square. When he returned from attempting to ferret out Communists in Gneez on the Monday after the Reichstag election, he had caught none, his day seemed incomplete, and his eye fell on the Jerichow school flagpole. He thought the pole looked bare. Late that afternoon the Storm Troopers assembled on the square, some of them less than enthusiastic about standing around erect and mute, and marched off to the right onto School Street, not singing and rather wavering, like a tank with a drunken driver winding its way between

the low buildings and the dogs, and ran up the flag of the National
Socialist movement on the school playground. They left behind a
double guard consisting of the two men who at this stage could
display not merely presence of mind but also a fairly complete
uniform. The mayor waited until dusk before dispatching the police.
The municipal police consisted of Ete Helms, likewise not much over
twenty and looking forward to going off duty shortly, so that he did
not mind being sent off and delayed buttoning his tunic until he was
standing in Papenbrock's hallway and asking for the young gentleman. Horst had had a bottle of kümmel by his plate of ham and for
a few minutes played the superior officer toward the younger man,
until he learned that Dr. Erdamer, the mayor, had said: "Stupid
nonsense" (to himself, as he closed the door). Five minutes later
Horst was protecting the double guard with drawn pistol, and Ete
Helms stood until almost midnight beside the playground fence, alert
now, his hands at his belt, envious of the Nazis' hot-coffee supply, impressed by the smart changing of the guard every hour, not quite comfortable among the onlookers, who had not enjoyed so much nocturnal
diversion for years and were having fun stepping forward each time he
ordered them to step back. Just before midnight Dr. Erdamer had the
good sense to yield to Geesche Helms's requests and send her husband
home to bed, so that for the Storm Troopers and the gaping crowd
the fun went out of the salutes and the marching and they vacated the
playground, but it had been Horst Papenbrock's victory all the same.

For next morning the guard of honor, although without the
police, was again drawn up on the playground when the children
arrived for school. That duty had been assigned to Walter Griem by
Horst, while the latter gave orders for the Nazi flag to be hoisted on
the town-hall roof and posted two uniformed sentries, one on each
side of the flight of entrance steps. Dr. Erdamer had a good view of
them from his window over the steps, also of the Stahlhelm members
who had meanwhile insinuated themselves into this sentry duty. On
his desk lay Monday's *Lübecker Generalanzeiger*. The newspaper's
heading stated that it would appear every morning except Monday.
Its appearance today, a Monday, was in honor of the Reichstag election and because of the nature of the results. In the electoral district
of Mecklenburg the Social Democrats had lost one seat, leaving 120.
The Communists were down from 100 to 81 seats. But the Mecklenburg soul, not being content with a mere 195 Nazis in the Reichstag,
had augmented them by 93. In his hands was that day's *Lübecker
Generalanzeiger*. He had read the headline so often that the bold

fraktur was transformed as he read it from its own implications into alien ones. "Lübeck No Longer Red!" the paper exulted. But in the Senate of the Free Hansa City of Lübeck there never had been any Communists; what was meant was Social Democrats. What was meant was himself. In eight and a half years of administrative service he had habitually dissociated the term "red" from himself and applied it to the Communists, who had wanted to smash the Republic, not make it prosper. This he had tried to do in small Mecklenburg towns, and it was not the inhabitants and not his Party that had prompted him to move on but more favorable offers. He had cleaned up not only Jerichow's town hall, but the road to the sea, the fire station at the gasworks, the Labor Office, as well as the weed-choked lots in the northwest part of the town that he had turned into the beginnings of a residential area. He had needed neither his law degree from the University of Leipzig nor his career nor his Party book to gain respect; in Jerichow as in other places he had always been on friendly terms with the aristocracy and the prosperous townspeople and had seen eye to eye with them not only in the forms of social behavior but also in the decency that these forms were supposed to harbor. He no longer understood the local aristocracy. He understood their point of view, the economic interests of those who preferred to wait out the political storms in the security of their estates, but it bothered him that they should sit there so calmly instead of ordering their hired hands to kick the Nazi bullyboys off the day laborers' settlements, that they should fail to proclaim, either personally or through the church, that they had no desire for the National Socialist plebs to succeed. The church's attitude bothered him. It bothered him that Papenbrock did not give his son a good drubbing. He had always agreed with Papenbrock, not only over a bottle of wine but also on the resolutions to be passed at town-council meetings. Papenbrock had been too much of a gentleman to stand for election; Papenbrock had nevertheless enjoyed having a finger in every pie being baked in the town hall. Now he was allowing his offspring to run up a red flag with a swastika on the town hall and guard it with an armed man who aimed his weapon at Ete Helms as soon as the latter peeked around the edge of the dormer window, and it was not birdshot that he would be firing either. His colleagues in the Senate of the Free Hansa City of Lübeck had shown him the way: those who were members of the German Socialist Party had resigned, although the Reichstag election had nothing whatever to do with the composition of the state legislature. It was unconstitutional. It was against the law. And he had always been in small towns. Now he would never advance to the ministerial level in the state capital, Schwerin. In Jerichow his daughter had lost a friend, that Lisbeth Papenbrock married to that Englishman Cresspahl. He had lost responsibility for the village stabbings, the exchange of bullets at night between the Reichsbanner veterans' organization and the Storm Troopers' auxiliary police. He had lost the weekly wrangle with the Nazi town councilors over Dr. Semig the Jew. He had lost the people who that Sunday night had stood by Schmidt's loudspeakers until eleven o'clock, waiting for the election results, merry in the warm air, as if intoxicated by each new figure. They behaved as if not only the police were being abolished but the tax department too. He had been unable to get hold of anyone by telephone at the Party office in Schwerin, or even Gneez. When he opened the town-council meeting that afternoon he was still undecided. Then the Jerichow Social Democrats resigned: Upahl, Stoffregen, Piep, Piepenbrink. Even Stoffregen. Erdamer was now forty-three. When he rose, his shoulders quite naturally assumed the bearing of an officer. He held his chin too high to be able to look at any of those seated. He could feel the brief, then lowered glances at his bony, close-cropped head, at his eyes almost blinded by overstrain, at the contemptuous twitch in one corner of his mouth, and he was sure they were watching him, not without concern, as he went through the door. On the threshold above the entrance steps he saw Cresspahl approaching the square, that son-in-law of Papenbrock's who was obviously coming to register the birth of his child, the child whose health they had drunk together as recently as Saturday. He decided not to tell him that the Registrar was busy taking minutes at the council meeting. As he began walking, a fairly erect, arrogant figure wearing riding boots under his long topcoat, his footsteps were no longer being guided by any decision. Now he was walking between the two sentries, without seeing them (otherwise he might have addressed them by family and first names), he had passed between them before the two fellows had converted Horst Papenbrock's order, now not so self-confident after all, into a fumbling present-arms maneuver, he had passed Cresspahl without noticing him, and Cresspahl stood there halted in three movements: starting to pass the time of day, bursting out indignantly at Horst, taking the first half-step to catch up with Erdamer, in the middle of the square, in full view of onlookers, at a loss, open-mouthed, with a deaf yet listening expression, like a trapped rabbit waiting for the blow less than a breath away from the back of its neck.

Hold your tongue, Gesine. Hold your tongue.

October 27, 1967   Friday

is the day on which the New York *Times* announces: One tends to forget things that are associated with unpleasant experiences.

This has been proved to the New York *Times* by an experiment undertaken by two researchers at Princeton with sixteen undergraduates. The subjects of the experiment volunteered and had no idea of the purpose of the study. First they were taught a language of ten "nonsense syllables" of three letters each, and then they were given English-word equivalents for each of these syllables, for instance "memory" for DAX. Then they were given a second list with ten other English words that were subtly associated with those on the first list. The words on the second list were projected onto a screen, just as the vocabularly of the first list had been. But during the showing of some of the words on the second list an electric shock was administered to the volunteers' hands. The current formed a bridge across the associations to the invented equivalents and burned up the connection. The painless equivalents were retained in the students' memories. There is your proof. If you don't believe it, pay ten cents. Ten cents is the price of the New York *Times*. Sitting beside us on the visitor's chair, perched on the edge with eagerness, hat askew, talking and talking and keeping us from our work.

A service to our customers, Gesine.
News from the World of Science.
A contribution to your problem, Gesine. Because you're concerned about the process of forgetting.
Of remembering.
For years we just took it for granted.
At last two men turn up in Princeton and tell us what's what.
That they've proved it.
Think they have.
Have, Gesine.
What prompted them to prove this particular point?
A popular notion.
"What's unimportant to me, I remember."
No. "What hurts gets forgotten."
Why is this superstition worth investigating?
So we may be able to make use of it.

What kind of forgetting are they talking about, à la Vienna, à la London, à la Chicago?

Just plain blotting out, Gesine. Simply the annihilation of what was known.

To be exploited for political purposes.

No morally thinking person will . . .

But science wouldn't hesitate.

For the time being it has merely observed a learning process.

As applied to a maximum of sixteen people.

Who are volunteers, consequently above suspicion.

Consequently not even selected according to their ability to remember or forget.

Who know nothing about the nature of the test, consequently convincing.

Who consequently don't even have a motive for remembering and forgetting.

Oh yes they do. A few dollars.

To whom the learning process itself promises only moderate pleasure or profit.

Who are at least all the same age.

A Granny Prüss would not only have noticed the electric shock, she would have rummaged around in her memory for the circumstances. Granny Prüss is vindictive.

The result of the learning process is subjected to a genuine alternative.

You feel a shock, you forget; you feel comfortable, you remember. Some alternative.

But a significant one.

As significant as the cow that gets shock after shock from the electrified fence. The cow is simply incapable of remembering.

In the case of your cows, Gesine, the shock was the learning objective.

In the case of human beings, the process of forgetting is supposed to be transferred, right?

Indirectly, don't you see?

With only ten word-links.

Still.

That are all notched at the same spot.

The break is genuine, Gesine. The break is still genuine, whatever you say.

The New York Times calls the arbitrary grouping of thirty letters in rows of three "a language."

Just as science does, Gesine. Strictly according to science.

A language of unrelated words.

Science is sure to have its carefully weighed reasons.

The learning of languages requires the application of what has already been learned.

In that case the process of forgetting would entail too much effort.

In that case it would have some value.

But semantics were not the object of the exercise, Gesine.

The maturing period in the memory has been ignored.

A process of forgetting has been proved.

But there wasn't even a desire to remember a useless vocabulary.

Each person was given the democratically equal choice between the possibilities of remembering something or forgetting something.

Blind reaction.

Automatic reaction.

The alternative was loaded at one end with pain.

The loaded possibility was destroyed.

The proof of the pudding.

No pudding, Gesine. A functional model of the most delicate behavioristic origin.

Bioveristic?

Don't be so cheeky, Gesine. The New York Times is unequivocal.

Science must know what it's doing.

Quite right, Gesine. Where would we be without science. Where would the United States be without its scientists.

Who use an experiment to prove an experiment.

And that, whether negatively or positively, pain is associated with memory.

Somehow.

"Unequivocally," Gesine. The scientists say so themselves.

Auntie Times is protecting herself with quotations.

Quotations are evidence of reliability in reporting statements.

But words were burned, weren't they?

Only words, Gesine. No one suffered any harm.

And suppose another newspaper were to write the word "words" with the letters t, h, i, n, g, s ?

It would be an unforgivable misrepresentation to its readers, a sin against the spirit of journalism, inexcusable for all time.

And why does the New York Times do it?

All the better to grab you with.
And why do you have such big teeth?

October 28, 1967   Saturday

"Saturday!" says Marie. "Saturday!" she says. "South Ferry Day."

October 29, 1967   Sunday. Change from Daylight Saving to Standard Time

Where we live, at the northern boundary of our neighborhood, stands the church of St. John the Divine, the largest Gothic cathedral in the world, three blocks wide, from 111th to 113th Street along Amsterdam Avenue, begun 1891, no further construction since 1941, not complete without the planned central dome and the two towers at the west end. We have always called it the Cathedral of St. John the Unfinished. Now it is to stay that way, as long as the Right Rev. Horace W. B. Donegan is Bishop of New York, until the anguish of the unadvantaged citizens in the surrounding slums has been relieved. Those are two different dates.

"I don't get it," says Marie. "How come I've gained an hour just because the clocks have been altered?"

"Because you had an hour's less sleep on April 30. Daylight Saving Time got you out of bed too soon."

"And if I've forgotten that, is it still real?"

October 30, 1967   Monday

The first sound was the slapping of the elevator ropes. As if the chains were hitting the walls of the shaft.

Above Riverside Park a brightly colored bird was making a flapping rocking sound. Then it lifted its tail and hung in the wind over the Hudson crying Arr-Arr. It was not a helicopter from Station ABC, it was your electric shaver flying away, its motor has had just about enough of its casing. Sir.

You can tell me all you want about recessed roller friction: the subway trains rumble, and the compressed-air opening of the doors is a human sigh of relief even though it needs the passengers waiting in front of them to make it that. Inside, but not until the train stops, all the overhead straps bounce lightly back against their springs. Then the passengers start raising their hands and elbows and, holding newspapers, handbags, brown paper bags, squeeze around each other until all are facing the car exit, in the hope that, as every day, the door will obey the valves and roll away, one half into each side.

Car horns are tuned to a uniform note modified by the brick and concrete canals through which, against walls, under bridges, it ricochets upward. Police sirens, adjustable from a polite whine to the howling of dervishes, are almost an element of the air. They are followed by the automobiles with the beds for the dead.

Obsessed screeching on the tracks under Park Avenue in the forties. The approach to Grand Central is a bottleneck. Who wants to go on seeing all those trains beneath his feet? Are they anything more than a memorial?

Inside the elevator the buttons, cushioned receptacles for pressure, yield to a touch with a mysterious click, as if to a kind action, and express their thanks by turning yellow.

When the thermostats instruct the air-conditioning blowers to pause, everyone dies a little because something familiar is missing, something they can now no longer describe. But for a while the ribs of the machine have completely stopped spewing out cold air. As if someone would never breathe again.

The coins dance merrily in the top of the coin collector that restrains the bus drivers from a particular kind of dishonesty. And the nickels tendered by the driver as change for a quarter since the fares went up sound thicker; now I can hear the silver in those dimes I used to get.

The hospitable clatter of cheap cutlery on the counters, the almost brutal slapping down of the bill, the almost sisterly care with which the plate is set before you: There you are, dear.

And again that gusto with which, on behalf of the Transit Authority, the machines swallow subway coin after subway coin in their comfortably grinding gullets prompted by passengers into chewing motion at the rate of five a minute by the three-armed turnstiles, or six a minute, that would be some 1,600 an hour at four turnstiles, that's too many, and yet it's more than that. And again that heavy rumbling sound, audible through all the swaying and jolting and braking, that betrays the excessive weight of the payload and is reflected at the base of the skull in a feeling of almost ominous pressure.

At the bar the man behind the counter sets down your drink with an uneven clink, half the base of the glass following the other half. With an air of hesitation he scoops up the coins lying in readiness on the counter and lets the prepared selection of three coins bounce through two fingers onto the counter top before taking three inaudible steps and ringing them up by pressing three keys. As they activate the cash register they echo in the ears of some customers like thunderclaps; the drawer flies open, and the hand slapping it shut strikes a note of doom. Sir.

"Don't hurry away, Mrs. Cresspahl." "Oh there you are, Gesine."

Late at night, the window raised halfway up. A defenseless ear to which speeding cars patiently and ever again expound the Doppler effect or without subtlety hammer in rapid noise, an ear for which buses starting up create a new world of sound and annihilate the purely remembered one. Expressway traffic, filtered through branches dense as hair, tests wind-strengths of four to six, conveys groundswell and receding breakers, suspends pauses in the wind, and sends up waves like water; the comparison with the Baltic shuts it out with no compensation.

In Queens, four blocks recently blew up with a noise appropriate to the explosion of a gas main, and those standing by those living near those living in Queens told the paper: It was like something from outer space, like a catastrophe, inhuman somehow.

It is the same noise I hear now from the next apartment, from the evening news over ABC-TV from Vietnam. It is like something from outer space, it is catastrophic like antiaircraft shrapnel just before the unexpected, dull, earth-shattering impact of the bombs, it is humanly possible. Sir.

October 31, 1967 Tuesday

March 1933 was, in its own right, a season in Jerichow. The wind might blow from the sea into the town, but in it fluttered streamers of rested earth, of coming blossom. Seagulls were in the air, frolicking aircraft. Fat plump pigeons warmed themselves in the lee of the chimneys, slid off in leisurely gliding flights, streaked the red flag on the town-hall roof with their droppings. The sparrows told the world they were being taken care of. The light made the bricks warm, painted the stucco of the town hall yellow, made the grayed wood of the yard gateways come alive. To look at it all, it would be easy to think nothing had been smashed. It'll be all right. It'll all straighten out. Now all we have to do is get the child registered so it will have papers for Richmond. Then we'll stick it in a basket and carry it home, each taking one handle.

If Papenbrock was asked, Brüshaver, the new pastor, was lax.

He did not call without being invited. He did not wear his cassock outdoors, he walked along Town Street in a suit that was not even black, a man of forty who already walked with a stoop, narrow in the shoulders, with a little square mustache, and such a faraway look in his eyes that his prompt response to a greeting came as a surprise. It was disappointing to see him take his cassock out of his bag as he stood in the hall and change his clothes as if he had come to do a repair job, not perform an incomprehensible act. They did say, though, that dying in his presence was tolerable. But people like Miss Käthe Klupsch, people with established seats in the front pew below the pulpit, missed Pastor Methling's noisy fervor and described Brüshaver's manner as like a doctor's, not only at the sickbed. And Brüshaver spoke, he did not preach, he did not raise his voice, he did not wave his arms about. He behaved as if the church were his business. He did not utter threats when religious duties were over-looked; he would mention the oversight in a casual way. He issued no challenges, neither as to the hats on the pew ends nor as to the fully recovered new mothers who had not yet been churched. Methling, his predecessor, had always put on a show when he let beggars stand ten feet outside his door and threw them used clothing, berating them soundly as he did so and not without sniffing for alcohol fumes; at the Brüshavers' they were quietly asked into the house and could put on the donated garments indoors, and they would emerge onto the street as decent citizens. And Brüshaver stayed home. He did not turn up at the Lübeck Arms. What incensed Papenbrock most was the way in which Brüshaver read out the Protestant Church's appeal in connection with the March elections. ("For fourteen years the powers of the Catholic Center Party, the Social Democrat Party, and the Communist Party, with their *international* ties . . . Now in the struggle against them, Germany's renewal is to begin *from within.*") "Like someone reading a financial statement!" Papenbrock had grumbled. It had not been solemn enough for his taste and had nearly spoiled his pleasure in going to vote.

Brüshaver was not at home. Cresspahl was received by his wife, a mere girl she seemed to him, not just because she had barely turned thirty but because of her supple, offhand movements, because her blond braids were pinned so loosely around her head, because she seemed too young and too bright among the somber books and furniture of the pastor's study. And she did not quite manage to treat Cresspahl as the helpless young father. She tried, but not even the dignity of being the official deputy was of much help to her. When she took down particulars and dates her pose resembled a schoolgirl's.

She leaned so close to the book, she pressed her forefinger down so hard without realizing it. "And the day?" she asked, her pencil posed above Brüshaver's engagement calendar. Suddenly he realized that she had been watching him appraisingly, yet incuriously, all the time. What he had taken for friendliness was an illusion created by her youth. She was another of those who wanted to make him atone for the sins of the Papenbrock family. But meanwhile he had spent too long looking at her steadily and co-operatively; he found it hard to be unfriendly now.

"Wednesday morning we have the Voss funeral, Voss of Rande, who got beaten to death by the Nazis. After that it would be all right, Wednesday at eleven," she said. She was not looking at him now, she was looking at the calendar, bouncing her pencil over daily columns; then, without looking up, she entered Lisbeth's request for a church christening (no charge) for Sunday, March 12. She said good-by to him in the hall, took down her apron again from the hook, let him go alone to the door.

A home christening on the very first morning, Cresspahl.
It costs two marks, not all the world.
And the child would have been ready to travel.
Lisbeth had not had permission from Dr. Berling.
And she wanted to make quite sure. She wanted to extend your stay in Germany with a religious commitment as well.
A home christening just wasn't enough for her.
She's put one over on you, Cresspahl.
I didn't want to think that, Gesine. But you'll find out.

November 1, 1967 Wednesday

Last night a group of Negroes celebrated Halloween in Montefiore Cemetery in Queens, upsetting gravestones and hurling stones and eggs at cars. When the police arrived, first with one radio car, then with forty, the crowd numbered three hundred youths, all "colored," as some people insist on saying, who pelted the agents of law and order with rocks and bottles.

On Broadway too, in our neighborhood, bands of children were running around wearing witches' cloaks, witches' hats, their faces painted and blackened, but beneath the paint and charcoal their skin was pink, so that even a policeman was not immune. Deep in thought, the man was strolling along the sidewalk, the bulge of his pistol flipping up and down on his hip, his club twirling at his wrist, and he suspected nothing when five children in disguise surrounded him, capering and yelling, and gave him the choice of Trick or Treat, until he began to feel around in his hip pocket for coins, embarrassed, deterred from defending himself by the gaze of grown-up passers-by, who not only were watching to make sure he behaved like a friend and helper but wanted with their own eyes to see a policeman publicly forking out honest-to-goodness money. One of the children, standing at the edge of the surprise attack, gesticulating and chanting in some embarrassment, a girl of Marie's height, was wearing a long yellow cloak with black tiger stripes, such as Marie had made over the weekend. The face had been blackened and the hair hidden under a black hood, and seen from a distance it could not be Marie. Marie had wanted to arrange her own party for Halloween, All Hallows, All Saints, a party at home, and her friend Francine was to be allowed to come.

The howling mob had already gone through Maxie's store, and the one whom the customers and helpers call Max stood thunderstruck in the midst of his neatly displayed fruit and vegetables, for lying on the ground in the sawdust were trampled pears and grapes, flung down by disappointed kids who would rather have been given money. In the doorway, next to the hanging scale, one of the rearguard was still busy fleecing an old lady. She was adventurously dressed in bold colors, each item somewhat remote from current fashion, and in her strands of whitish hair there was a bluish shimmer, and she had a foreign look, not quite all there. It was queer the way she talked. She had obviously been collecting change in preparation for today, and she talked without stopping about the wonderful privilege and opportunity afforded by Halloween to give the dear innocent kiddies pleasure, and Max's helpers looked on in disapproval as she dug coin after coin out of the depths of her shabby handbag, not only nickels but quarters too, blissfully chattering away, with no eyes for the decidedly challenging, extortionate expressions of the kiddies in front of her. Hardly had she left, shaking her head and muttering to herself, when the helpers turned on the youngsters and shooed them onto the street, and although they had not previously considered this customer crazy, since she did after all shop for and buy vegetables, they made the typical German gesture behind her back to show she was nuts. Max did not mention Marie. For six years Max had been greeting the child with "Hey, blondie!" and giving her peaches or apples; Marie had consumed fruit by the hundredweight in his store, and if he had noticed her among the Halloween gang he would have said something. "And the grapes that aren't good enough for this generation have been air-freighted in from California!" he had said. "Maine or Long Island potatoes, Mrs. Cresspahl?"

The victimized policeman was now standing outside Sloane's Supermarket, his back to the wall, very erect, not approachable. The twirling of his club no longer looked playful, but professional, and however vacant and equable his gaze appeared no child would venture near him now.

On the east side of West End Avenue a troop of witch-children were moving uphill, carrying plastic pumpkins on sticks, their arms around each other's necks, almost rhythmically in step, very small beside the dark-red and gray elephantine buildings, very innocent as they sang in their immature voices:

One little, two little, three little witches
Fly over haystacks, fly over ditches,
Fly to the moon without any hitches:
Hi-ho, Halloween is here . . . ,

until they turned in under the awning of Marcia's entrance, marching past a startled doorman into the lobby with the shrill, urgent, chivying battlecry of Trick or Treat! Trick or Treat! and this time there was no mistaking Marie, red boots, yellow cloak, black hood, a child that gives up her own party and prefers to go to someone else's rather than invite a child of a different color to her home.

And the child who came home in the black darkness had stood for fifteen minutes outside in the corridor before feeling able to use her key. When she made up her mind, she had rolled her Halloween costume into an unrecognizable bundle under her arm and walked without a word past the table, with no eyes for supper, to her room, pulling the French doors behind her and closing them very quietly, and not a sound was heard from her until next morning. This is the second day she has used lack of appetite as an excuse, has withdrawn immediately behind her own doors, and in general behaves in a taciturn although not sulky manner (which she once believed she had not inherited), although also, like a child, in unconcealed amazement, as if there were something she did not understand.

It wasn't like that.
Tell that to Francine.
It wasn't like that. Marcia invited us before I could invite anybody.
And one can't take colored children to Marcia's.
It wasn't my party.

You promised Francine.
It was you I promised, and she doesn't know anything about it.
I know about it.
Besides, it wasn't a promise. I thought I might do it.
And why couldn't it be done?
Can't you see I'm ashamed?
Is it a pleasant feeling?
This is the second day you think I'm lying.
How was it then?
I don't know why I did it.
Shall I try and tell you?
No. Then I'd think it was the truth.
How much do you know so far?
Not the truth, anyway.

The truth is, as could be read today on Third Avenue on the roof and side of a delivery truck:

The truth is that NU Skin Lotion is the best way to protect your skin.

That's the truth, and the advice on how to save one's skin is free.

November 2, 1967   Thursday

Let it be known to one and all, I, Elinor S. Donati love my husband dearly, and as such hope to remain Mrs. William R. Donati forever and ever.

Are we to say: Congratulations? To: Mrs. William R. Donati, whoever that may be, c/o The New York *Times*, Department of Public Notices.

On March 11, 1933, Albert Papenbrock, grain dealer and bakery owner in Jerichow, Mecklenburg-Schwerin, presented his granddaughter Gesine H. Cresspahl with a gift. He deeded a farm on the edge of town to her, with land, barn, and outbuildings, to be administered by her father, Heinrich Cresspahl, cabinetmaker, Richmond, Greater London, until she came of age.

Lisbeth. Lisbeth. Lisbeth.
Think of the child, Cresspahl.
Lisbeth. Lisbeth.
We owe it to the child, Cresspahl.
Lisbeth.

Suppose something happened to us, Cresspahl.

That's not why you left for Germany, Lisbeth.

With your knowledge, Cresspahl.

That's not why I came.

You're here now.

And I didn't want to come.

It was your duty, your obligation, to come.

And if I hadn't?

Then it would be up to you to decide now.

I'm not staying in Germany.

But we own a piece of it now.

I don't need a piece of it.

But I do, Cresspahl.

In the birth announcement you put: Jerichow and Richmond.

Because that's the way it is.

Because you wanted to show off, Lisbeth.

It won't do any harm.

In Lübeck they arrested me.

A misunderstanding.

My understanding was different.

In Mecklenburg we've had Nazis in the government ever since last summer.

Crackpots.

See?

Trigger-happy heroes.

See? Why should they concern us, Cresspahl?

You're related to one.

All the better.

Your father provides the house and your brother the connections.

Anyone else would be glad.

Not me.

Oh Cresspahl, your pride.

Financially it's madness.

Papenbrock's bought out Zoll. Zoll's going to Gneez to work for the Party.

He too. You too?

Cresspahl, you've got your Fascists in London too.

Not in the Government.

Not yet.

Never.

Are you willing to gamble, when your child's at stake?

Lisbeth, we wouldn't be foreigners much longer.
But long enough.
Lisbeth, the child would be a British subject.
Not right away.
Was this why she had to be born in Jerichow?
Yes.
Yes?
Cresspahl, it wasn't the place for me.
You wanted a house in Richmond.
And now I want one here.
You got along all right in Richmond.
I didn't even like the colors.
The colors. Lisbeth.
Yes. The red. The blue. On the ships, the letter boxes, the uniforms. Such cold colors.
The colors of that painter, Con . . .
John Constable. That was a painter. Those were painted landscapes.
You liked them.
As art, not for living with.
Whose idea was this?
Papenbrock's.
Lisbeth.
I asked him.
When?
When the baby was born.
Lisbeth. Lisbeth.
Oh Cresspahl. When I arrived from England.
Lisbeth. Lisbeth. Lisbeth.
You talk as if we still had a choice.
We.
I mean it, Cresspahl. We.

Papenbrock informed his son-in-law of the gift in the presence of his daughter. He was confident that at the bedside of newly confined mothers no one shouts. Furthermore, he had planned to monitor the young couple's first comments. Actually Cresspahl's first comment was that the idea needed thinking over. That he then left the room with a quite casual glance in Lisbeth Cresspahl's direction was something Papenbrock had not expected. He was still sure of getting his way, but the hope of deriving pleasure from it was gone.

November 3, 1967 Friday

The Chancellor of West Germany, a former member and civil servant of the Nazis, has appointed a former member and civil servant of the Nazis as his Government's new press chief.

They'll never learn. They look at the hand with which they slap their surviving victims, and can't understand, said Uwe Johnson the writer. Then he got slapped.

For Johnson the writer also failed to understand. Only nine months ago, on January 16, he took his seat one evening behind the long green table set up by the Jewish American Congress in the ballroom of the Hotel Roosevelt, appeared next to the leonine head of Rabbi Joachim Prinz (formerly of Berlin-Dahlem), and waited to tell the Jews of New York something about the election results of the West German Nazi Party.

Where did you sit, Gesine?
Close enough to be able to see you, Comrade Writer.
At the back.
Yes, way back, close to a door.

Such speakers from Germany have to be introduced as they deserve. This one was introduced by an official of the Jewish American Congress with the story of a friend who recently intended to fly by Lufthansa from Philadelphia to Düsseldorf and asked for kosher food when he made his reservation. When he was buckled into the Germans' aircraft they had no kosher food for him, but from the English Channel on they did what was known in World War I as loop-the-loop. "I said to my friend: Did you have to tell them you're a Jew?"

The roomful of Jews laughed, not maliciously, they seemed in a way delighted. The wave of merriment bypassed islands, individual listeners who quietly and narrowly observed the German on the platform as he polished the bowl of his pipe in the palm of his hand. Then another wave of laughter swept through the hall when the public-address system broke down and Rabbi Joachim Prinz (formerly of Berlin-Dahlem) comically raised his arms and cried in a thundering voice of desperation: "They're everywhere (the Germans. The Nazis)! They're even here!"

The German who in fact was there behaved as if he grasped not only the American language but even the mood being prepared for him among the audience. He looked up with curiosity at the cheerful, unworried speaker who was introducing him to the Jews. Seen from the hall, his uptilted face wore a severe, humorless expression. And yet actually the jokes were quite funny. Invited to the podium, Johnson did not consider leaving the gathering (after expressing his thanks for the introduction) but embarked in all seriousness on his talk, not, it must be said, with the end of the Middle Ages, but nevertheless with the year 1945 and the subsequent formation of two German states. But he failed to achieve the New England intonation that he may have intended to use for this occasion and lapsed into the wrong vowels, the wrong emphasis, into the pseudo-British accent that his school had allowed him to get away with.

"Ladies and gentlemen," said Johnson. The front half of the hall showered him with not yet unanimous cries of "Louder!" "My thanks to the J. A. C. for their invitation to deliver," said Johnson. Now the back half of the hall adjusted to the rhythm of the front half, lagging only slightly behind in the cry of "Louder!!" "Let me begin with, and even mention, the East German Republic, also known as the German Democratic Republic," said Johnson, and this time he broke into the next wave of shouting from the hall, took advantage of the excellently functioning sound system, and transmitted his full vocal power through all the loudspeakers, intolerably loud: "YOU'RE NOT GOING TO MAKE ME SHOUT, ladies and gentlemen!" After he had shouted, the audience appeared to doze off and left him in the belief that he could be heard, and understood.

Sorry, Gesine.

Not at all. You produced nothing more sensible during the entire evening.

D'you suppose they wanted to see whether I could defend myself?

Are you always that slow in the uptake?

At no time did they applaud him, not even when he could no longer refrain from mentioning the appointment of a Nazi as Chancellor of West Germany. "It wasn't meant as a slap in the face of surviving victims, though the world felt it was." It was simply a lack of understanding, he went on, of the fact that every German government of this century will be measured by its distance from the Nazi Establishment. The Chancellor had not been elected because of his connection with the Nazis, this aspect of the matter is supposed to have been forgotten. Johnson would have done better to say nothing about what had been forgotten. And anyway his sentences were too long, too German, and although now and again he mastered fragments of the American intonation he seemed at a disadvantage. It was impossible to credit him with understanding, let alone explaining, the country for whose explanation he had allowed himself to be made answerable; he had not yet grasped that time and place had deprived him of the innocence of a tourist guide and twisted every analytical word on his lips into a defensive one. Perhaps he realized something of this during the ensuing speech by Charles G. Moerdler (formerly of Leipzig, Saxony), before whose lips technology now really did break down and who was not once exhorted from the hall to speak louder. True, Mr. Moerdler was not only one of themselves but the Commissioner of Buildings in New York City, who also saw to it that he was remembered by the signatories to his resolution as a name in future election lists. Johnson sat slumped behind the green table, both hands shielding his manuscript, the spotlights reflecting from his bald head, and he scanned the audience from time to time briefly over the rims of his glasses. Strangely enough he was wearing, with his conventional business shirt, a black-leather jacket such as otherwise only Negroes wear, some Negroes, the Negro with the woolly beard and the flashing eyes in the sleepy face whom we saw Wednesday evening in the West Side subway, though more at ease in his tight-fitting shiny leather outfit and with one hand in his pocket concealing something angular.

Who's telling this story, Gesine?
We both are. Surely that's obvious, Johnson.

The writer was then given a lesson in reality. Employees of the hotel set up two microphones in the central aisle of the ballroom, and behind each one of them waited ten or eleven people to comment on Johnson's presentations, considerations, revelations. And they said: My mother. Theresienstadt. My entire family. Treblinka. My children. Birkenau. My life. Auschwitz. My sister. Bergen-Belsen. Ninety-seven years old. Mauthausen. At the age of two, four, and five. Maidanek.

"He didn't do it," said the Rabbi.
"He's one of them," they said.
"You're not being asked to forgive him," said the Rabbi.
"We're not going to forgive him," they said.

"You're being asked to talk to him," said the Rabbi.

"You talk to us, Rabbi," they said.

"He's a guest," said the Rabbi.

"Outside he's an enemy," they said.

"Be sensible, folks," said the Rabbi.

"He's doing nothing about the new Nazis," they said.

"How is he supposed to in his profession?" said the Rabbi.

"He's not supposed to do it in his profession but as a human being," they said.

"You heard what he said," said the Rabbi.

"He ought to be ashamed, just the same," they said.

"Have you any further comments, Mr. Johnson?" said the Rabbi.

"It has all been said," said Johnson.

"Thank you, Mr. Johnson," said the Rabbi.

The Chancellor of West Germany, member of the Nazi Party, accomplice of the murderers of the Jews, has remembered a friend from the same government department. And while it is true that the latter did not join the Nazi Party until 1938, the fact remains that he never resigned his membership. Just the man to be press chief of the West German Government. The West German Government desires friendship with the American people, with 5,936,000 Jews in North America, two million alone in the city in which we live.

November 4, 1967   Saturday, South Ferry Day

The Secretary of Defense has received a report that the Soviet Union will soon be able to put a bomb into orbit that can be slowed down at any point during its path, detectable only three minutes before the explosion, with a payload equivalent to three million tons of TNT, a splendid blockbuster.

"As if a fist were to crash into the harbor," says Marie. She looks calculatingly into the glittering rain shower across the water, as if estimating the height of the fountain that would send the ferry, with her on it, the steamers on the hazy horizon, the barges and the train ferries with their freight cars, and the sleek Coast Guard greyhounds, all shooting up into the sky.

"And Staten Island, and Long Island, and Manhattan, and great chunks of New Jersey, New York, and Connecticut."

"Are you trying to scare me?"

"No."

"Then don't tell me in advance," she says. She is leaning her elbows on the railing of the outer deck, her face turned to the wind to be washed. Sensitive to the weather, her face is smoothed over, covered up, as if by another skin. If her eyes were closed she would look blind now. Only the little fair hairs creeping out at her temples from under the hood invite recognition. But she is waiting. She knows for sure that from behind the curtain of mist Staten Island city hall will emerge, as indestructible in reality as in recollection. "I wouldn't want to live anywhere but New York," she says.

Cresspahl did not want even to consider a life in Jerichow. It would have been a life with the Papenbrocks.

In taking up with the Papenbrocks two years earlier, he had been secretly convinced of never having to become involved with them either emotionally or in business. What he liked about Lisbeth were the ways in which she seemed to differ from her family. Now he was being forced into closer acquaintance with the family.

From Horst Papenbrock he had expected hostility. Now, at the few meals that his duties allowed him to take at home, Horst was behaving with something like discretion. He asked Cresspahl to call him by his first name but addressed him by his last name; here he was acting the younger man. He made no attempt to talk about his exploits with the Storm Troopers; not once did he insist on joining in the conversation at table, not even when the granary, of which he had been placed in charge, was under discussion. Sat quietly in front of his plate, his left hand relaxed on his lap, carefully sipping his soup, keeping his eyes lowered as if the liquid were a mirror or a message. He seemed to be not so much tired as cogitating. When Edith told him that one of his men was waiting in the hall, he altered his bearing as he rose, threw back his shoulders, lifted his chin, strode to the door as if on a stage, the hand that held the napkin dangling at his side so that the linen brushed his brown boots. On his return from the conversation that, to those at table, had rung strangely sharp and clipped from beyond the door, his doll-like face, even the pointed triangle that was his nose, bore a look of pleasure, an all-pervading pleasure, with a smile as if at some anticipated delight, and this time he was firmly clasping his napkin and slapping his boots with it, crisply yet with his mind elsewhere. He had obviously not had much practice in expressing delight. The workers in Papenbrock's yard and granary had not treated him as the boss but had

adopted the old man's nickname for him, Sonny. Papenbrock's boy
Sonny. These days they turned aside when the military tone he
adopted in giving orders made them want to laugh. As yet he was in
no hurry to assert his discipline in the granary. At the inn, Cresspahl
had heard someone say that young Papenbrock had been driving the
car from which Voss had been thrown onto the street, not clubbed,
incidentally, but whipped to death. The speaker did not know Cresspahl, and when a dig in the ribs drew his attention to this relative of
Papenbrock's at the next table he had looked him straight in the eye
as much as to say he wasn't scared of a fight. Cresspahl had half a
mind, only the occasion did not appeal to him. Horst denied having
had anything to do with Voss: he didn't concern himself with small
beer. Small beer, Cresspahl was given to understand, was for Horst
the settling of old scores, old enmities, old injuries, rather than the
National Socialist cause that Horst talked about, not persistently but
when occasion called for it, in a shy, halting manner as if the subject
were sacred. There must certainly have been enough girls in and
around Jerichow who had preferred to do others the favor rather than
Horst. Cresspahl did not care to be responsible for him, whether in
or out of uniform, so he turned aside even Horst's respectful inquiries
about his war service, dismissing him with preoccupied silence, barely
supportable offhandedness, as if Horst were a puppy. Why bother
about good will he had no intention of using?

The old man he could accept. He could not entirely accept
Papenbrock's constant attempts to draw his son-in-law into a game in
which drinks had regularly to be consumed behind Louise's back. He
could barely accept the old man discussing, if not explicitly the
Cresspahls' return to Germany, nevertheless the people in Jerichow,
Gneez, and Schwerin who had in the past paid respectful attention to
Papenbrock's aspirations (this was Papenbrock's notion of tact. He
did not want to confuse Cresspahl but to help him make up his
mind). Cresspahl found it hard to accept the way the old man would
eye his son, his youngest chick, in a gloomy yet potentially gleeful
manner, the strict yet indulgent father, still undecided as to whether
Horst's relations with the new power were good or bad for business,
but at heart unhesitatingly prepared to accept either decision. For the
time being, all Horst wanted from his father was a truck, but before
Papenbrock would lend his firm's name to the Storm Troopers he
wanted to have it explained, over and over again, how the national
revival was involved in this. What Papenbrock insisted most on
hearing from Horst was those parts of the Nazi program that
threatened the department stores and large landowners, and under

his amused gaze, in Horst's embarrassed recital, the future of the Nazis came to seem unreal, anyway not dangerous. What he really could not accept was Papenbrock's wanting to know in detail how Cresspahl had managed to achieve such a sizable account at the Surrey Bank in Richmond, and whether Lisbeth's figures of 1931 had been anywhere near accurate. That was unacceptable. It was amusing to watch Papenbrock proving his shrewdness as a businessman toward his family too, when, for instance, he alluded vaguely to shoemakers' daughters yet did not admit to ever having heard of Horst's Miss Lieplow, which prompted a surly, barely dutiful look from Horst, like someone who has stumbled on a hidden obstacle. Papenbrock had already enjoyed placing difficulties in the way of his prodigal son, but in the case of this offspring his enjoyment might not be quite so outspoken. His daughters, on the other hand, had always been able to "twist him around their little fingers." Things were to be made easy for his daughters to like him. That was acceptable. Otherwise he could accept Papenbrock.

Hilde he could accept very nicely. Hilde Paepcke had left her husband behind in Krakow, involved in his disputes with the fire-insurance people who were in no mind to forget about the candles; Hilde wanted to see Lisbeth's baby, she wanted to be the baby's godmother, she wanted to visit her old home. Hilde was pregnant. She wanted to have children before Alexander got kicked out of respectable society once and for all; she wanted to "salvage some of the assets." So she unburdened herself to Cresspahl when they went for walks in Rande, arm in arm, in an intimacy that was both sudden and tacit. When it finally dawned on Cresspahl that there was nothing accidental about the way she allowed her breast and hips to touch him, they reached agreement in a lighthearted sidelong look of complete candor, and Hilde said gaily, without a trace of regret: "Makes your heart bleed, doesn't it!" "The things one misses in life," said Cresspahl. On his own initiative he invited Hilde and Alexander to visit them in Richmond.

He still would not admit to regret at having resisted bringing Louise Papenbrock to England, although in that case Lisbeth would have remained at home and the child would have been born where it was going to live. Louise Papenbrock in his house, that could not have gone off without a row. In Jerichow he at least had no right to contradict her. For however naïvely Papenbrock may have seen himself as head of the household, it was Louise who ruled it, the old man on a loose rein, the children on a shorter one. The bottle of kümmel that Papenbrock consumed in great secrecy was replaced by

Louise with a fresh one. The amount contributed to the church by the Papenbrock household was determined by Louise, and she let Pastor Brüshaver feel that she disapproved of the lack of fervor in his sermons. The food that appeared on the table was what she considered proper, and the length of grace corresponded to her mood. She had had a bed made up for Cresspahl in Lisbeth's old room, far away from Lisbeth and the baby, at the end of the third floor, without ever consulting him as to his wishes. And Louise had completely readjusted the household to the baby's birth; all her arrangements drew a fence around Lisbeth that Cresspahl had to climb, not with permission but when instructed. He was even denied a chance to complain; for Louise Papenbrock had already brought four children into the world with her hot-water bottles and overheated stoves. On the contrary, gratitude was demanded of him.

He was scarcely ever alone with Lisbeth, and never without expecting their solitude to be disturbed.

The day before the christening was to take place, Gertrud Niebuhr telephoned Jerichow. She insisted on taking Cresspahl, who answered the telephone, for Papenbrock, whose voice she had expected. "Mr. Papenbrock!" she said to him, excited by the sending of her voice out into the great world, and it transpired that she had misplaced Cresspahl's address in Richmond, scatterbrain that she was. She wanted to write to him. She wanted to tell him that Mother was "not too well." No, nothing serious. "Heinrich, it can't be you talking! You're supposed to be in England!"

The day of the christening Cresspahl took the train via Blankenberg and Sternberg and Goldberg to Malchow, away from Jerichow, with a sense of relief that would long weigh on his conscience.

He had not looked at the house for the child Gesine.

Today is a great day for the New York *Times*. It has calculated its circulation for October and reports: a record of 8,256,618 lines of advertising copy sold! A record 963,130 weekday copies! A record 1,588,091 Sunday copies! This announcement appears on a page for which the paper might otherwise have been paid six thousand dollars. But it refuses to be petty in its rejoicing.

November 5, 1967 Sunday

The North Vietnamese Defense Minister wrote an article in which he publicly acknowledged China's support in the war. He resisted the insistent requests of the Soviets to delete that sentence. So now it has appeared in the *Krasnaya Zvezda,* so now it is true in the Soviet Union too.

We walked down Broadway from our building as far as 79th Street and back through Riverside Park, along the promenade and the street, and Marjorie was nowhere to be seen.

She is not called Marjorie. We don't know her name. We don't know her. She came into our lives last winter, a girl waiting at 97th Street for a Number 5 bus. There was a biting wind that day, cold enough to chill one to the marrow from waiting. She was not standing hunched and miserable with the cold; she made a careful and delicate pantomime out of feeling cold. It looked as if she were feeling cold in a spirit of comradeship. We spoke only a few words to her, and at once she confided in us: she was glad, she said, not to have missed this weather. She uttered it as a truth, and since it was her truth it did not sound importunate. So trustful is she.

So charmingly can she live. The word beautiful, it still applies to her. Under ponderous capes she can hide the fact that for sixteen years she has grown the right way, very slender, not thin, with long legs that attract the glances even of passing females. It is her face. Her face gives information about her that never disappoints, need never be taken back. She has a pale, transparent skin (one shade less than pink), and she wears her black-brown cloud of hair to below her shoulder blades, she has minutely indicated eyebrows and great dark eyes; those are her resources. We look at her mouth because it is young, we look at her lips because of their quite conscious, deliberate smile. The smile is serious, it is considered. It means something, it can be understood. It is friendly. What is granted to other people on feast days, she can live on without stint.

She sees us, she beams. She talks with her black eyes, and we believe her. There is no explaining why she should be happy to see us; we accept it without mental argument. As she comes down Riverside Drive surrounded by her chattering, laughing girl friends, she is already looking at us in a way that is personal, for us alone, a way that says she would like to whisper in our ear: It makes me feel good to see you both. It is not even embarrassing. There is no doubt about it. She hangs her truth over us like a cloak. As yet she can only express what she is. She has a way of turning toward us, attentive, light-hearted, almost deferential in her participation, in a lovely gesture that ripples from shoulders and neck and is reflected in our sensation of a physical touch. She embraces us with her eyes each time as if she recognized us, not only her image of us but also what we might be.

Whenever we see her, she has some new way of presenting herself. She comes wearing a big, wide-brimmed hat, she wants it to be noticed, she wants to amuse us. And she wears the buttons that challenge the rest of humanity (Bring Our Boys Home! Support the Police: Bribe Your Friend and Helper!), but stuck into the crown of her hat, onto her handbag. And her hair, one day she ties it up with a four-inch ribbon, then she is satisfied with a rubber band, the next time she has used a whole handful of hairpins to crisscross her hair into place. Just as one day she wears only mauve stockings, so the next day she can wear only copper-green ones, no other color would do. She walks along Broadway in a dress her grandmother wore at the beginning of the century in Scarborough-on-Sea (not Scarborough), a billowing, ruched affair; she has hit on a fresh new fashion, although not intentionally. It is a genuine dress from a genuine closet belonging to her real grandmother. She says so.

She boarded the Number 5 bus in which we were sitting. She was delighted. We left the bus, as she did, at 87th Street. She thought that was splendid. We turned side by side into 87th Street. She could not get over her satisfaction. We told her our destination. She told us her destination. She could not have expected more from this day, that on top of everything else we had friends on the same street. Suddenly she halted and shouted a name up past the eighteen floors, ringing and triumphant, rejoicing in the strength in her throat, waved to us with the whole of her long arm, shouted the name of her friend, waved, lifted her radiant face to the sky.

In our neighborhood it is only habit that makes us jump when someone taps us on the shoulder from behind. For when it is a double tap, done with very light, straight fingers, it is she. Her face is not furrowed by a grimace, it is relaxed and open in anticipation of the coming pleasure. "Hi!" she says, and she could make it clear to the most obdurate foreigner: This is a greeting. It is one of the most sensible, natural, credible kinds of greeting. She demonstrates it, so you will know how to do it.

A person out of the Arabian Nights.

When school has tired her, two large spots appear on her cheeks, unquestionably red, danger signals.

This winter she stood at the corner of Broadway and 96th Street, where the icy wind from the Hudson can sweep unimpeded up the hill, and sniffed the weather, her delicate, vulnerable profile raised oblivious to all else, and she said, knowingly and mysteriously: "It's over now." With her face, and still more her neck tendons, she can convey a feeling, intact and recognizable, and express herself beyond her words in a language that is regarded as lost. What she was saying was: There may still be ice, there may be more snow, the new season is in the air and will grow there. The earth has remembered. Consider, Mrs. Cresspahl. Consider this smell.

She does not know our name. We do not know her name. She wants nothing from us. We cannot want anything from her. It is pointless.

If ever, Mrs. Cresspahl, the City of New York has caused you harm or suffering, I am authorized to tell you: It was not meant to happen. It was the result of an oversight. We are sorry, and I will console you.

Today she was nowhere in sight.

November 6, 1967   Monday

Cresspahl found his mother in a village southeast of Malchow, in a strange bed. She had not shrunk in death, but when he lifted her she felt like a sleeping child in his arms.

November 7, 1967   Tuesday

"I don't believe it!" cried Mrs. Erichson. She saw us at her door and said I don't believe it, an expression of delight in her face, feigned rejection in her voice, as if she did not see us, as if the telephone could not announce reality, as if Manhattan's bus terminal had to burn down that very Monday evening, as if the Hudson were going to swallow up the Lincoln Tunnel today of all days, as if in addition to all that Federal Highway 80 would collapse into the New Jersey marshes, so that there had never been any reliable prospect of our turning up for supper. "I don't believe it!" she said, more gently, merely to savor once more the blend of the evidence of her eyes and the spice of doubt, while she was already drawing us into the hall. It was intended to express delight. It is a Mecklenburg way of greeting a visitor or a piece of news. This is what old people in Mecklenburg do.

Now do try to feel at home, Gesine Cresspahl. And you did laugh, against your will.

D. E. has faked the house. Not only has he used new beams and clamps to make the sagging shingled framework as sturdy again as a young house, he has also changed its life-style. The colonial furniture in hall and living rooms is in too good condition, too valuable, for a farmhouse. Behind the handmade doors there are unexpected, brightly lit cells equipped with the latest inventions of the science of sanitation. The old lamps never shone that bright. The discreet grilles in the century-old hallways may well be genuine brass, but an automatic heating system sends warm air through them into the exhibition of antiques. Every item in the house is subject to a plan; the leather cushions may be askew, a telephone may lie forgotten in the middle of the rug, a cat may be asleep on a typewriter, the New York *Times* would thoroughly approve of the house as an example of tradition and technology in interior decoration. From the ground up the house has been redesigned, divided into one communal and three separate areas: one for Mrs. Erichson on the ground floor next to the utility rooms and the living area for all the occupants, one for D. E. on the east side of the floor above, and a third on the same level. The latter has its own staircase, a series of brown doors along a passage of white paint and muslin curtains, separated from the remainder of this floor by a door that has been allowed on this side to retain its original bolt and lock. It is here that D. E. sets down our suitcases, not inside a room but in the passage, beside the door.

This is where you could live, Gesine Cresspahl. At least try to feel at home.

The house has its routine, the routine runs like a clock, routine that merely tells the guests the time without restricting them. D. E. spends the hour before supper sitting on a stool at the breakfast counter by the kitchen window, chatting with his mother over his Copenhagen beer; yesterday evening Marie sat across from him, her chin cupped firmly in her hands, gathering information on the notions of the layers of the original earth that Dr. Andriya Mohorovičič fell for in 1908, and on the American project to drill holes in the ocean floor in his honor, Moholes. Blending with the comforting sound of roasting pans being shifted and the refrigerator door clicking, the voices penetrated the beams and were indistinctly audible upstairs, too intimate for peace of mind. Outside, the wind was busy grasping fistfuls of bare branches, clenching and unclenching its fist, pausing to recover its breath. Under the darkness of the sky, the interior of the house swelled, expanded with light and warmth and human life. When Marie entered, a cat on her shoulder, fuzzily silhouetted by the lamplight behind her, I confused her with the child I was dreaming about, the child I once was.

Sure you don't need any more sleep, Gesine? You can have supper whenever you like. In this house the guests' wishes are law.

In this house the guests' wishes are all anticipated. Even at supper D. E. did not insist on telling his own stories but with discreet questions, counterquestions, interjected questions, persuaded his mother to talk about the past, so that the old lady became wide-awake in the night and raised her head. Her great gray bird's eyes held the listeners' gaze, made lowered lids uncomfortable. She wanted to see her stories reflected; she did not want to exert herself for nothing. About her father driving to the Güstrow wool market in 1911. Her face is creviced with age. Everywhere the skin is criss-crossed with deep sharp lines, deeper than the wind of seventy years could have carved them. About the farmer's daughter who was not supposed to marry someone in the town, and not a hairdresser. The deep-dyed pouches under her eyes make her face seem still thinner, the skin withered, the cheeks hollow. She looks as if she were living on her very last ounce of strength; but last summer she passed her driver's test, she still chops her own wood. How the Depression affected the hairdressing business in Wendisch Burg. About Brand the shoemaker having his hair cut for friendship's sake and for friendship's sake wanting to pay only half-price. We will remember that shoemaker. After 1933 things improved for Erichson's Hair Stylists, two girls on the ladies' side, soon three assistants on the gentlemen's. Her own hair looks like a snow-white board that has been bleached under water, scored by water, then broken off into jagged splinters. Presumably she uses nothing but water these days. Conversations at the hairdresser's. She hadn't thought much of Hitler. She says that to please me, to please D. E. No, by conviction she was a royalist, she would have liked to see the ruling house of Mecklenburg restored to power. So D. E. had been a child whose job it was to sweep up the hair in the shop. At the Mecklenburg maneuvers of the new Wehrmacht she had been only ten steps away from Mussolini. Mussolini in Mecklenburg? She had gone shopping for Jews when they no longer dared go out on the streets of Wendisch Burg, yet they had been professional people. If one could only believe that. One would like to think so. Grateful letters from Mexico City.

Are you sure? Just as old Mr. Erichson had suddenly started to write affectionate letters home from a labor camp near Stalingrad. That we'll believe. Good night, Mrs. Erichson.

The morning really does begin with a holiday feeling. In New York it is Election Day, banks and stock exchange and schools and liquor stores are closed. The sounds from the house do not rupture the last sleep. They are so familiar that behind closed eyes they turn into images. That muffled click-click is Mrs. Erichson putting the rubbed-up table silver away into its velvet compartments. That brief double slam is the girl from the village who comes to help in the mornings; when her hands are full she pulls the door shut behind her with a twist of her ankle. There is a child too, singing the Coca-Cola jingle. The child wouldn't mind staying here, an hour and a half from New York. From far away, close to the outermost layer of the house, comes the murmur of D. E.'s typewriter. That's where money is being earned, it would be enough for us. Now there are three voices singing in the kitchen; Marie appears to be conducting as they ask of Fate how in the world the Coca-Cola Company does it. We are favorites here. One step out into the passage, and they will start preparing a second breakfast. On the table there will be not only the Philadelphia *Inquirer* but the New York *Times*. This is how D. E. sees my life.

November 8, 1967   Wednesday

Among the critics of the American war in Vietnam is one with the rank of lieutenant general of the paratroop forces. James M. Gavin is thinking not so much of the people of Vietnam. He simply regards the war as too costly for the American nation.

The number of unemployed has risen from 4.1% to 4.3%, the highest level in two years. This represents 3.8% among whites. This represents 8.8% among Negroes. But only a tenth of the country's citizens are Negroes.

Paul Zapp, aged sixty-three, has been arrested in Bebra, Hessen. He is responsible for the murder of at least 6,400 Jews in the occupied areas of the Soviet Union. Until the day before yesterday an assumed name was all he needed.

Cresspahl returned from Machow and went to look at the house that had been offered to his child. On the way through Town Street people looked at him with curiosity and greeted him spontaneously, on their own initiative, even strangers. Papenbrock had placed an announcement of the death of Grete Cresspahl, née Niemann, in the *Gneezer Tageblatt*. Probably he wanted to keep his son-in-law attached to Jerichow, even though he had to begin with the memory of the Jerichow townsfolk. Cresspahl knew nothing of the announcement.

At the south end of Town Street, on the right, stands the parsonage, red brick, white trim, mossy tiled roof. The other side of the garden wall is the churchyard wall. On the two halves of the iron gate children can swing in semicircles. Then the wall takes a sharp turn to the right, westward, running beside a sandy path known as the churchyard path, or the brickyard path, because of the long red drying shed on its other side, the masonry more monotonous than the enclosure of the dead with its slanting coping stones and green glazed domes. Opposite the middle of the brickyard wall there is a bay in the churchyard wall with a narrow little door and the big arched doors of the mortuary, so flimsily built that it had to be stuccoed. At the spot where on the left the brickyard gate indicates the big work yard, one can look across Creutz's fence on the right. The land belongs to the church; the church has leased it to Creutz since it does not need it yet for the dead. Look over your right shoulder: no trace of the dead. Through the overgrown elder bushes along Creutz's boundary there are glimpses of the church's brick walls. It is from here that the gabled spire looks tallest. Across from the brickyard entrance and set back a little stands the house of the brickyard owner, next to Creutz's leased property and in a neat garden behind a white iron fence. The ceremonial flagpole surrounded by flowerbeds has seen days when it flew the flags of the fugitive Kaiser. Beyond this point there are no more buildings. The path runs between meadows and fields, dipping and rising toward the west, until it peters out, not even reaching a village. Now, facing the sea, the marsh comes into view. There, to the left beyond a weed-choked plot of grass, stands a low farmhouse under a blackened sloping roof. This is my home.

Cresspahl did not begin by entering the house. Some of the windowpanes had been smashed. For the time being this was all he needed to know.

The farmers who had developed this land had at one time been so wealthy that they even had their barn built of brick. The barn, set at right angles, was taller than the house and roofed with overlapping tarpaper. The north side of the barn was almost all door, two lofty wooden panels, eroded by the sea wind, one of them containing a door for people. Inside, the bays had been swept clean. Toward the end the farmers had been thrifty. All they had left behind was useless junk: a twisted beet cutter, broken shafts, barrels for sauerkraut, and, in perfect condition with its paint gleaming, the dashboard of a Sunday carriage. The stables in the eastern half stank of rotting straw. There were stalls for pigs, sheep, crib space for twelve head of cattle, four horses. Since the day they were driven away, the wind had dwelled here. The building was so chilled through that there was trace of neither lovers nor cats. The manure heap must have stood there for three years to dry up like that. The stables had been equipped with electric light. But anyone who tried the switch felt the current streak right up into his shoulder, making his arm shudder. The predecessors were trying to say: Our misfortune is all yours now.

Behind the house there was a black tree full of starlings.

To the south, west, north, it was empty around the farm. Only the wind spoke. To the north there was a hole between earth and sky, a strip of the Baltic.

1. If one wanted to, one could replace two thirds of the door with glass. That would let in enough light for carpentry work.

2. Most of the restoring could be done by Cresspahl himself, if he wanted to.

3. If one wanted to, one could force the occupants of the surrounding homes to put up with the noise of sawing during usual working hours.

If one wanted to.

It is not right to leave New York for even a single day. Right away we have missed the first snowflakes in the city. Today the weather is behaving with cold sunshine as if butter wouldn't melt in its mouth.

November 9, 1967   Thursday

Yesterday Adolf Heinz Beckerle went on trial in Frankfurt charged with aiding, as Hitler's envoy in Bulgaria, in the deportation of 11,343 Jews to death camps. On the contrary he maintains that 40,000 Bulgarian Jews owed their survival to him. Charged with him is Fritz Gebhard von Hahn, a former colleague of the West German Chancellor's, on account of 20,000 Greek Jews.

This is a brief report appearing way below the New York *Times'* outermost petticoat. She makes no bones about venting her opinion of the Mayor's plan to accept commercial sponsorship for a half-hour TV program. The old lady gives His Honor John Vliet Lindsay an arseful. "It is a matter of propriety!" she cries, and lets fly at him again. She is certainly not lacking in vigor.

It is Thursday, and the wrong-number experts are at it again, starting right after lunch. The first one, still inexperienced in the business, merely wanted to know whether Marie was RIverside 9-2857. She replied sternly that he was speaking to 749-2857, and although the numbers 7 and 4 correspond to R and I on the dial, the man was so taken aback that he hung up. "As if he didn't know about American phones," reports Marie, gleefully. She regards it as a brand-new trick, and she has invented it.

At first we had to look after the telephone bequeathed to us by Mesdames Bøtersen and Bertoux. It responded to a number starting with MOnument, and rang very often. In Germany telephone bells had been implacable and shrill; here a gentle tinkle issued from the telephone, as persistent and delicate as the movements of a cat stretching after a nap. Men inquired after Ingrid and wanted to speak to Françoise, and Françoise was to take Ingrid along to the Gran Ticino, and scarcely one of them could grasp the fact that both girls now lived in post-office boxes at the airports of Kastrup and Geneva, and quite a few of them were keen to know the first name offered by the new voice in the microphone. Then the telephone company performed an operation on the instrument, removing its soul from its casing and placing it in storage for a temporary rest.

After that, RI 9-2857 was installed in the apartment, if only to provide a line to Dr. Brewster's practice, to a children's hospital. But the child wanted to play at learning to use the phone and was soon the first to lift the yoke of the whimpering instrument from its neck and ask in the American way: Who is it? instead of: Who's there? And it was at this telephone that Marie learned to lie, under supervision. For then strangers came on the line and wanted to hear not only that they had dialed the Cresspahl number but also whether the Cresspahl apartment was on the 3rd or 13th floor, was numbered 13A or 134, because the telephone directory does not yet relieve criminals of the finer details of preparing a break-in, and Marie would not only describe the position of Apartment 204 for them but trustingly supply the added information: I'm alone. So now an Uncle Humphrey had to be invented, a boor and a bully who allegedly slept in the next room, for whom Marie built a matchbox house under the telephone, and the strangers had no desire to get into conversation with Uncle Humphrey. Then D. E. found us while idly turning the pages of the Manhattan directory, and we had our name removed from it and are glad to pay the charge.

We are left with those who throw dice to make up a phone number, and those who after profound study discover a gap between 749-2856 and 749-2858, and those who dial direct from San Francisco to the east coast merely to tell us what time it is there and what the weather is like, and those who inadvertently dial the wrong number and only want to apologize. The situation will not get really bad until direct dialing under the Atlantic becomes possible and German millionaires are presented with a new game. Then we will be totally dependent on Marie, who has recently begun to trust in the absurd and fends off unwanted calls with the statement: This is an unlisted number. This is an unlisted number. Even obstinate callers are confused.

Once, as recently as late last September, our telephone started responding to the kind of connection that was used in the fifties in West Berlin. The membrane at the other end of the line was animated not by words but by breathing. No matter how even it was, at one point the air-stream always began to rattle, making the sound ominous. Nothing but breathing.

Voices you hear enough.
If only the dead would keep their mouths shut.

Once, only two weeks ago, a woman's voice rattled off something, impersonally, as if from a card index: "Your name is Gesine Cresspahl, born March 3, 1933, in Jerichow, a resident of the United States since April 28, 1961." "Yes," I said, got only a click in response, and wished I had pretended to be someone else.

"This is a nonworking number," says Marie now in a mechanical voice, like a worn-out tape: "This is a nonworking number." Then, not willingly, not convinced, she holds out the receiver to me over her shoulder, saying: "Some fellow called Karsch, doesn't know where we live, doesn't know me . . . how am I supposed to know! You've never told me anything about him!"

"I'm going to borrow that child someday," says Karsch.

"Where are you, Karsch?"

"I'd rather not say," says Karsch.

"D'you need anything, Karsch?"

"It's not that bad," he says. "Good-by," he says. "'By."

He said nothing about calling again. Apart from the fact that Thursday is the day when the wrong-number experts strike most often.

November 10, 1967   *Friday*

President Johnson arrived secretly in the city last night. Five hundred policemen surrounded the Americana Hotel; they were posted on the roofs of buildings around the hotel, and a further 100 were in the ballroom in which the President was telling the Jewish trade-union leaders that the nation was risking a far more terrible war in the future if it failed to see through the present one in a small and distant country in Southeast Asia. Page 1.

On page 17, below the bus problems of White Plains and the assurance that the Mayor of Albany was not guilty of drunken driving, the New York *Times* publishes the war's official dead, eleven and a half lines.

The main item on page 1, however, is the picture of the West German passport used by the Soviet agent Runge. Not only does the newspaper tell us everything that is known about his life, it also describes the structure of the Soviet secret service, complete with chart, so that we now know who is responsible for the "bloody business": Rodin, alias Nikolai B. Korovin. The postal address, though, is not given.

Lisbeth Cresspahl was not to be spared her mother-in-law's funeral. Her sister Hilde spent a whole afternoon telling her about it.

Papenbrock had had misgivings about his family's not being seen in the cortege. He had at least sent Hilde to join the mourners.

On her arrival the coffin was still open. It had been set up in the passageway of the Schmoog farmhouse. Berta Niemann had been friends with Erna Lübbe since 1873, a friendship that continued when Erna married an heir to the farm and Berta married a wheelwright who worked on the village estate. She had been on a visit to her friend.

For two days she lay in her friend's bed, not agitated, mostly asleep. She was so tired that she let herself be waited on. When she opened her eyes, Mrs. Schmoog thought she saw disappointment in them because it was not someone else standing by the bed. When Cresspahl bent to enter the little room, the Schmoogs thought she was still alive. So at the moment of death she had been alone.

On the brow of its thatched roof the Schmoog farmhouse displays two crossed horses' heads and the figures of a year in the early eighteenth century. The roof comes low down over the half-timbered walls. The stables for cows and horses led off from the front part of the passageway. Now the passageway had been swept spotless, with water, making the beaten earth look like uneven stone. The coffin had the place of honor. Anyone on the way to parlor or kitchen had to acknowledge its presence.

When the mourners from the village had gathered together it suddenly became noticeable that Mrs. Schmoog was chatting quite naturally, almost brightly, with her friend's son. Mrs. Schmoog was no older than the deceased. She had now had an opportunity to show both her husband and the hired help how she would like her own death handled.

The coffin was about to be closed when the assembled guests moved apart to free a wide space for an old man who walked with stooped back and bent knees. He had shrunk very much. He removed his top hat before even stepping into the passageway. He had never spoken another word to Berta Niemann since she married Heinrich Cresspahl, nor even passed the time of day with the Schmoogs, partly because of their friendship with the new Mrs. Cresspahl and partly because of a quarrel around 1890 over a strip of field. Since the war the old man had hardly appeared in public, even in the village. He was not embarrassed. He walked slowly over to the coffin. He stood for a long time beside the coffin. He tried to straighten his back. Then from the nape of his neck it could be seen that he had nodded to the dead woman. Then he turned around and shook hands with the dead woman's daughter, then the son, then the relatives.

Then he crossed over to the Schmoogs and shook hands with everyone, including the sons, daughters-in-law, grandchildren.

Then everyone crowded around the coffin so that the pastor could not watch. Cresspahl placed the lid on the coffin. Then they helped him screw it lightly down.

It was two hours to Malchow, at walking pace. The village had lent its hearse. Not many wreaths were propped against the coffin. Nevertheless the wreath from the Papenbrock family looked more meager than the others.

In Malchow the coffin was carried into the church by: Martin Niebuhr, Peter Niebuhr, Alexander Paepcke, Günter Schmoog, Paul Schmoog, Heinz Mootsaak. Inside the church they left Cresspahl to himself so that he could lay his mother down properly once more. When he came out through the doorway, the six men went inside without him and screwed down the lid of the coffin, firmly this time. Then the service began.

Cresspahl was affable to everyone, including Hilde. At Meinin-

ger's on Long Street she sat next to him. He behaved like someone
who has finished a job. At one point he stood up and thanked
everyone for coming. After that he looked on without impatience at
the eating and drinking going on around him. This was one more bill
to be paid. Then he could go.

Hilde deliberately reduced her sister to tears. It suited her that
Cresspahl should get his way.

She did not just tell her how it had been. She expressed herself
in vague reproaches, as if her younger sister could still be scared on
moral grounds. By the time Cresspahl returned to Jerichow, Hilde
had brought her sister to the point where he had to console Lisbeth
for his own loss. Now she would have gone with him to the station
had he asked her to.

November 11, 1967   Saturday, Veterans' Day

Karsch may have been talked into believing that on American telephone dials an R differs from a 7, but he did not overlook the fact
that there is no mail delivery when the participators in past wars are
marching. His letter was brought by a man in chauffeur's uniform.
The man did not pause even momentarily for a tip and gave no hint
at all of being accustomed to entering better maintained buildings
than this one. The letter is not from Karsch. It is from the Italian
delegation to the United Nations and contains written instructions to
the security guards to allow the bearer of this letter and one child
access to the building through the service entrance, and it is signed by
a Dr. Pompa.

Marie is disappointed. The security guards at the United Nations Building are Americans, they may even be from the Bronx or
Manhattan, the escalators look like those she can see in any modern-
ized subway station, the restaurant is run by a wholly terrestrial hotel
chain, and not even the long bar is sacred. Mr. Karsch is going to
have a hard time with the child.

Dr. Pompa and Mr. Karsch come walking along the foyer like
twins, both very tall and imposing in their casual suits, both walking
like people who are afraid of treading on small objects, both irrevocably well on in years and possibly only intelligible to each other.
Except that Dr. Pompa's skin clings firmly and comfortably to his
face, his eyes are commanding, and he still watches his smile.
Karsch's face is quite soft. He takes care where he looks, he is
cautious, he is far from wanting to see everything. Now he see us.

Ti voglio bene.
Ti voglio bene.

It is Karsch, and we can embrace him unhesitatingly, a person who is changing in our direction. It is not possible that one should still be able to trust someone, after many years, not doubtfully, not tentatively, in the wholly confident delight of reunion. It is possible. It is Karsch, who keeps his back straight when he is introduced to a child, not patronizing, grave, formal almost, so that Marie is hard put to it to find cause for offense. It is Karsch, the first to notice at table that this child does not understand Italian and without ado switches to his unemphatic British, which in turn is not alien to Dr. Pompa. It is Karsch, whom the waiters approach like doctors, who talks to them unblushingly with his fingers, and with his hands. It is Karsch, who discusses flying-weather conditions as long as Dr. Pompa is present, who asks us what we have been doing as soon as the outsider has left, who tells us what he is has been doing without self-pity. He still lives alone in two rooms in Milan. They are no longer the rooms next to Vito Genovese; it is not his own house. Karsch has come to New York to work on a book.

He looks ill. His hair has turned almost white, with a few darker streaks. He wears it long, it clusters in little tufts around his temples. With this, and the creases in his custom-made jacket, the crooked tie from the shop next to the Scala, he involuntarily betrays that he has no one to look after him. He is not sad. His glasses are framed in thin glittering steel and the reflections from them hide his eyes. He does not want to hide, he does not want to appear much in public. And when Karsch pours some more red wine, the bottle's lifted neck passes over his glass. Karsch no longer drinks.

"What's the book about?" Marie says at last, oblivious of discourtesy and how to behave toward strangers in a restaurant. A stranger cannot see that she is worked up, that her fingertips are trembling.

"About families, family clans, family visits," says Karsch.

"In Italy?"

"Italy, and your country," says Karsch.

"Why don't you write about Germany?"

"It is not one of the hallmarks of the German nation to read its books as soon as they are published," says Karsch, in private amusement, not over Marie.

"And you want to be read immediately, right?" says Marie severely, still sounding like an interrogator. She is not in the least intimidated by Karsch's lazy nod.

"What kind of families are they?" she asks. Karsch taps the middle of the folded New York *Times* that contains a report on the stolen-credit-card racket being run until recently by the Mafia families, the Gallos in Brooklyn and the Gambinos.

Did you have any trouble with those people, Karsch?
A bit, Gesine.
Now you don't want to show that we know you so you are hiding us in the U. N. Building.
Well, the food was all right, wasn't it, Gesine?
Dear solicitous old Karsch.
I'd rather you told me what kind of jealousy is eating that child of yours, Gesine.

For Marie wants to know who pays for these trips of Karsch's across the Atlantic, whether Karsch really settles his bills himself, whether it is true that he gets no assistance in this from any government or any university, whether he really makes a living by the way he lives, whether he really does manage everything differently from D. E. She has become carried away in her excitement, and a stranger cannot see that she would give much to be able to hide behind perfect manners. She finally achieves this when she says good-by. It is a promise that is meant as an apology. "Next time you call us, I'll remember you," she says.

Her gaze follows Karsch as he ambles innocently away down the foyer, preoccupied and forgetful under his rumpled hair, nodded to by colleagues, drawn into conversations with a friendly clasp of his arm, a man with many friends, some of them famous, and she states with conviction that she hates him. She avoids Gesine's eyes. She pulls her coat collar up so high that she can make the points reach the corners of her eyes, as if accidentally. "I hate him!" she says. "I hate him!"

November 13, 1967   Monday

The rumor of Franco's murder that traveled with the snack cart through every floor of the bank this morning could not survive in the fresh air. He is alive.

"Too bad," says Amanda. "And we've a list as long as my arm, haven't we, Gesine?"

Amanda means the list of still extant dictators waiting for their assassination. Amanda is Mrs. Williams, and today Mrs. Williams goes home by a different route, so does Mrs. Cresspahl, and they both meet again in the bus that staggers up Third Avenue like an exhausted animal. Amanda's voice is not penetratingly loud, but she does not mind being overheard. She would not even help to finance an assassination attempt, she would fight tooth and nail to avoid looking at a dictator bleeding from a gun wound; she is not implying the actual step, all she is doing is taking a stand on the side of her own convictions. She believes we see eye to eye with her over this. The whole day, since early morning, has not been able to starve out her affability; just as she has greeted every visitor to the department and every passing vice-president, from nine o'clock to closing time, with boundless or subdued delight, so now a recurrent smile continues to flit across her young, only twenty-eight-year-old face, like an ingrained habit, like a curtain being constantly raised and then bouncing back into place before the entire stage has been exposed. A year and a half ago Mr. Kennicott II, the personnel manager, introduced her to the department as Amanda, so she was on a first-name basis with everyone, Naomi here and Jocelyn there, with the exception of her superiors. Then on the fifth day she was not at her telephone when the payroll department asked to speak to a Mrs. Williams and was not known by this name to Naomi, or to Jocelyn, only to Mrs. Cresspahl, who had recently committed the faux pas of calling her by her last name. This kind of thing does not offend Amanda, she overlooks the blunder as if it were an inadvertent discourtesy. Her affability is not indiscriminate. When she hands out the fortnightly checks to the girls in her typing pool, she does so with comments about the boat that has been refloated, or the chimney that is smoking again; but Mrs. Cresspahl's she lays down in a sealed envelope as if it had come by mail, placing it beside the In tray, however, and if her expression is congratulatory it is not familiar. Differences in work and remuneration are handled by her discreetly. She writes Mrs. Cresspahl's letters, she gives her own instructions to her typists; her manner toward everyone follows the forms of request and consultation, except with the male heads of the department. She is as desirous of information about the private lives of others as she is to report on her own: in moderation, fino a un certo punto. She comes from one of the swarms of suburban homes near St. Paul, she tells tales of winters in Minnesota; she flies back for her father's funeral and mentions the incident three months later, casually, thus avoiding the emotional reaction of outsiders. She married a student who is now working as a psychologist for the New York Police Department; she inadvertently recommended joining the police force as a way of avoiding being drafted into the Vietnam war. She is working as a senior secretary merely to be able to furnish their Bleecker Street apartment completely in Scandinavian style, or for the next summer vacation in southern Europe; she would not admit to not wanting to think of having children of her own without adequate reserves. She knows the truth about Mrs. Cresspahl's status and in the presence of others accords her the title of married woman as a protection, she passes on the lunch invitations of various men in an amused fashion that does not even show curiosity, let alone approval, she knows about Marie's troubles with the language and the mental outlook, if not the sinister ones then certainly the ridiculous; there are times when it almost seems as if she knew her personally. It is agreeable to be observed in her company, even on the M 101 bus during rush hour. People standing near them are refreshed by her tireless, still girlish voice, approve of her glib tongue, observe discreetly or with frank regret her plump, sturdy legs, then her generous outlines in the close-fitting paramilitary coat, finally her wide, half-awake face that conveys naïveté to anyone overlooking the intermittent tightening of the lips, the narrowing of the eyes to a single point. In the friendly atmosphere she generates there is room for more than herself alone. Now she is talking about the handbag thefts on the South American floor in her astonished, didactic, flippant tone, hanging perfectly relaxed on the strap, absorbing without irritation the vehicle's sudden jolts, amused by the hesitant looks of the seated men. She is a jolly person. Isn't she a friend? Ask her for money, and she will figure out how long she can manage without it. Invite her to a meal, she will show pleasure and not annoyance at the tiresome waste of time before she can leave. Load her with errands, she will deny being caused any trouble. Ask her to lie for you, she will do it. How is it we are so certain that there is only speech between us, and no communication? How can there be something lacking? Even we, after all, perceive the well-meaning superiority of the former student when she mentions the Williamsburg clergyman who in his sermon yesterday demanded of the President "some logical, straight-forward explanation of United States involvement in Vietnam." Amanda is amused by the demand. "Maybe he wanted to take advantage of the President's sitting in the front pew," she says, and her bemused malice is directed at both, at the clergyman as well as at the powerful sheep in his flock.

"I don't know much about clergymen," says Mrs. Cresspahl,

suddenly so obsessed with dissociating herself that she has not even foreseen Amanda's precautionary apology and has to exert more effort to ward this off than the expected riposte would have required. This puts a crimp in the conversation.

Meanwhile, ever since the sixties in fact, the driver has given up pulling in to the sidewalk, although the people on his bus are now no longer so crowded together but are standing almost apart; he stops only when required by the bell, although traffic from the business district is meanwhile thinning out. In this area dispatchers are stationed every twenty blocks, checking and making notes of how the schedule is being maintained, and the driver has to make up for his delays and get back onto schedule. Besides, it turns out that Amanda has summed this one up in one passing glance. The ring of indifference and tolerance with which he showed himself to be armed against the lack of skill of private-car drivers, the right-of-way of the police, and the usual traffic jams, his armor, is beginning to crack and by the time he goes off duty may burst under the pressure of accumulated, repressed rage. "Move along now, ladies," he says, in a tone that invites the remaining passengers to partake of his ill-humor. Earlier, beneath the selfsame cap pushed to the back of his head, he had looked ready for a bit of fun. Mrs. Williams and Mrs. Cresspahl stand in the nineties at Third Avenue, neither wishing to explain to the other why she took a northbound bus to get to Greenwich Village or an East Side bus to get to West Side.

"How cold it's turned again," says Mrs. Williams. She stamps her icy feet, she wants this conversation to end on a note of agreement. Toward the east the island slopes steeply down to the darkly reflecting bowl of the East River, where Hell Gate is.

"Excuse me," says Mrs. Cresspahl. This can be taken to mean the haste with which she runs away from the green light across the street, or something else.

"I'm sorry, my dear, sorry, Mrs. Williams."

But that's the way it is, we are not imagining her voice.

November 14, 1967   Tuesday

Senator Robert F. Kennedy, not in Government, does not share the Government's opinion, at least in regard to Vietnam. "Despite the killing and destruction," he writes, "we are in no better position now than we were a year ago—and we will not be in any better position a

year from now," and furthermore he recommends negotiating with
the Vietcong. However, the Government denies that any chance for
negotiation has been passed up.

Che Guevara, traveler in revolutions, has allowed not only
himself to be captured in Bolivia but also his diary.

By the third weekend in March 1933, Cresspahl had spent
precisely his fourteenth day in Mecklenburg, and his calls on several
people in Jerichow were taken to be farewell visits. The man could
not possibly continue to rely on his workshop back there in England
carrying on indefinitely without him. This was obvious to them.

Cresspahl walked past Dr. Erdamer's house without glancing
over the shrubs, although he could hear doors opening and closing
and he thought he heard the daughter calling his name. Then he was
sure he had, but still he did not turn around. It was not altogether a
mystery to him why the suspended mayor wanted to alter his behavior. The meeting of the town councilors had passed a unanimous vote
not only approving but commending his actions for the year 1931/32.
This may have been because they would have liked to persuade him
to continue, at least provisionally, to manage the town's affairs, but it
was certainly due to pressure from old Mr. Papenbrock. Furthermore,
Papenbrock had seen to it that the mayor's release from office was
reformulated into a personal request. Now Erdamer sent his daughter, hatless and coatless, out onto the street to catch up with Papenbrock's son-in-law, who did not want to accept anything more
on his father-in-law's account; not this, anyway.

It was not the custom to ask Papenbrock. On the estates, sometimes in the administration offices of Schwerin, he was obliged to
explain what he wanted, just to make sure. Not in Jerichow. In
Jerichow it was still enough for him to want things a certain way.
Hence he was not always fully understood. He had wanted to prevent
an impropriety because it would have injured a civil servant, a professional man, a person of his own social level. As far as Maass, Böhnhase, Pahl, Methfessel, business, and the trades were concerned,
Papenbrock had decided "to draw the line." If he demanded decent
behavior, to whom could this apply more than to his son, Sonny? It
fitted in with all the tales of how Papenbrock was said to have let his
offspring know who was boss, although no one had actually been
present. Not only had Papenbrock lent neither word nor property to
Horst's Storm Troopers: with his German National People's Party he
was part of the new Government. Papenbrock's voice still carried
weight, and whoever had been turned over by his son to the courts in

Gneez, the old man had doubtless taken steps toward his speedy release, as in the case of Sass, the Customs official, who was said to have insulted the new Reich Chancellor, and of the Communist tailor's apprentice in whose room a Storm Trooper's uniform had been found. And when the Mecklenburg state legislature ordered the old Imperial black-white-and-red flag, along with the Swastika flag, to be hoisted on all public buildings from March 13 to 15, who saw to it that the (merely tolerated, not even authorized) Mecklenburg state flag was also run up and, what was more, to the same height? Papenbrock. True, he had declined to state what it was for, but it was as much as to say that within a year the state of Mecklenburg-Schwerin would have weathered this seventh Reich Government like all the rest. So here came Papenbrock's son-in-law, evidently to say good-by. Not only was he not a business rival, but he had not appeared in public anywhere in the company of his brother-in-law. Let's give the fellow a drink and wish him a pleasant journey.

Dr. Semig was out on a case. The door was answered by Dora Semig, née Köster from Schwerin, so like her husband that the sight of her immediately recalled his appearance: both tall, slender and firm of build, with rather stiff, dry-skinned faces that were nevertheless capable of agile, soft, friendly movements. That was how he knew Semig's wife. Today she kept her lips tightly together, her gaze straight ahead, she refused to greet Cresspahl even after recognizing him. He was standing one step below her. She held firmly on to the door. She seemed hostile rather than scared. During the night of March 13, at two o'clock, there had been a ring at the door of Dr. Spiegel, a Jewish attorney in Kiel. In response to shouts of "Police! Police!" Mrs. Spiegel had opened up. The shouters were not from the police and killed Dr. Spiegel with a bullet through the temple. The Semigs' maid had thereupon given notice. Dora Semig had been brought up to have maids. She had never had to come to the door herself. She looked so dour that Cresspahl did not quite believe her. He took half a step back so as to glance into the courtyard. Semig's carriage was not in the courtyard. Now Cresspahl was making Dora laugh. It began in a small way, against her will. Then her lips parted slightly in the middle. Then, very slowly, the corners of her eyes began to crinkle. Then she laughed. She was not even offended when Cresspahl said he had no time to wait for Semig.

He called on a number of people, among them Wulff. Like the others, Wulff had foreseen Cresspahl's departure. Besides, Cresspahl did not want to drink alone. Wulff set down a glass for himself rather sharply on the bar counter, with satisfied fury, the way he did everything that afternoon, whether directing Elli Wagenführ from table to table with sidelong glances or holding out his empty glass to Cresspahl with a grimace as if he had tasted something bitter. Elli Wagenführ had known Peter Wulff for at least six months from her evening job in the bar and, when occasion demanded, could give him the rough side of her tongue as well as she could rap customers over the knuckles; but today she spoke to him only to pass on orders, and when she had to go behind the bar she stayed firmly at the sink. Wulff did not care whether Cresspahl had something to discuss or not, he had plenty to talk about himself. The Communist member of the state legislature had let himself be captured at Neustrelitz. The local branch of the German Communist Party in Krakow am See had dissolved voluntarily and sent all the membership books and documents to the Mecklenburg State Criminal Department, with the assertion: "We've had enough!" "We've had enough!" added Peter Wulff, in High German and as if he were imitating a High German. "It sure stinks!" he said in dialect, as incensed as a man who, although he has predicted it all, is not that pleased, in fact somewhat annoyed, to have been right. He abused Warncke and every Communist he could think of with short biographical sketches, whether he had to cite the lapses of their grandfathers or their own bedwettings at a tender age. They had so deeply disappointed him that he felt injured beyond all expectation. It was as if he were giving reality to a dissociation that until then had existed in words only. He was talking now like someone getting ready for a journey, an enterprise that, while not without danger, was entertaining, as if it were at last getting under way, as if now at least the waiting were over, as if he were anticipating the coming day with grim pleasure; but he did so casually, paying little attention to Cresspahl, for he had written him off for the future, and even beyond the weekend for that matter.

It never dawned on him that Cresspahl might want something of him. Cresspahl stood unobtrusively facing him, one hand in his trouser pocket, leaning lightly with the other against the edge of the bar, his head erect and his face immobile. He watched Wulff and gave no sign of response either with a frown, or with his eyes, or with the corners of his mouth. Wulff may have been thinking that Cresspahl had wound up all his affairs. He had never known him for a talkative man. It was all Wulff could do to search for a suitable remark about the death of the other man's mother; he had no wish to be put even more on the spot by the occasion of this leavetaking. He refilled their glasses, raising his first to indicate that this round was his, and said: "I'm not doing this for my own sake, said the wolf."

"But a lamb tastes all right anyway, says he," said Cresspahl.

He had not looked to anyone like a man who, while not actually in need of advice, would certainly have welcomed some.

November 15, 1971   Wednesday

"I don't like what comes next," says Marie. "Can't you change it?"

"Can't you tell it differently?" says Marie. "Is it really true that in those days every English child had to be christened?"

"But the child was in Germany, in the country, in Mecklenburg."

"And again Cresspahl did it for the sake of that Lisbeth."

"He did it for his wife's sake, and he even arranged for a church ceremony for Sunday, March 19, 1933. This time he got the pastor himself rather than Mrs. Brüshaver. As Cresspahl watched him sitting at his desk he could understand some people calling Brüshaver a bureaucrat. He marked down the date, although it was only two days away, he entered the fee received in a ledger, his actions were those of a bookkeeper whose firm has been given an order. That is how he looked to Cresspahl. Brüshaver was a broad stocky fellow who did not look robust. That flesh on his body, it was not fatty or greasy, it even clung firmly to him, it just seemed so noticeable. His hands lay so limply on the desk. His cheeks did not sag, his chin was no more than round, yet his skin was stretched tight over flesh. It moved so little, it had not done much work. Sad flesh. Cresspahl was not looking at him through the eyes of someone who earns his living with his hands; besides, he had noticed that the garden behind the parsonage had been freshly dug over, none too neatly but deep enough. They were roughly of an age; the other man's face did not readily betray his age, perhaps the eyes did though, by the unwavering concentration in his gaze, so fixed that it conveyed not only attentiveness but actual observation. It irritated Cresspahl that Brüshaver's thoughts should be obviously occupied permanently with something else that did not concern the other man, like a doctor withholding an ominous diagnosis from a patient. Like a doctor! people said. And how small his lips were, as ingenuous as a child's. There was a kind of expertise in the way he moved his lips as he wrote down the baptismal text, as if he were savoring something and had once again found more to understand than is to be read in verse 6 of the 71st Psalm. At least he knew his job and could find the place. This was all Cresspahl had to say in his favor.

"Say it in English, if you must say it at all," says Marie.

"By thee have I been holden up from the womb: thou art he that took me out of my mother's bowels; my praise shall be continually of thee."

"Blood and thunder!" says Marie in ringing tones. But the tape merely simulates her indignation, her laughter follows unexpectedly, making the adjusted modulation reverberate with her heartfelt merriment. "My foot!" she says.

"Ought that to have been changed?"

"No. But I don't like him changing your name."

"Nobody's changed my name, Marie."

"Is your name Gesine Henriette C. then?"

"No."

"See, Gesine Lisbeth? In telling a story one has to think of everything."

"Maybe he just wanted to save up the name Henry for the next child. One of the next children."

"Maybe he wanted to do that Lisbeth of yours a further favor."

"Maybe it was his way of buying her consent to having Dr. Semig stand godfather."

"He hadn't named him at the previous appointment. Whatever happened to Alexander Paepcke?"

"Paepcke had a case at the Güstrow courthouse too early the next morning. But there were many who would have stood in for him."

"After that week it had to be a Jew."

"A Christian, Marie. A Christian. After this new declaration Brüshaver turned another of his stares on his client as if he had been so busy listening to him and looking at him that his ears and eyes had deceived him, until Cresspahl patiently reiterated the facts: "Mr. Semig is not a Jew, even his grandfather was baptized, and the Kösters won't have given their daughter away blindly"—all in that relaxed, obliging tone with which on other occasions he offered a fight, and Brüshaver nodded. He did not nod with his whole head, he moved his creaseless eyelids in a brief indication of assent, adding: "People do talk, Mr. Cresspahl. A lot of nonsense, if you ask me, Mr. Cresspahl."

"I don't like it," says Marie.

"You mean Cresspahl inviting the Jerichow vet to a christening?"

"If he wanted to pick a fight with Jerichow, he should have been in Jerichow. He should have stayed."

"D'you want me to change that?"

"I want you to tell it differently."

"We'll present it a little differently."

"Don't forget the child on display at Papenbrock's house."

"It was now up to Cresspahl to disabuse the pastor of the notion that they were agreed on all points except the one in which the church was only required to assist. When Brüshaver read out the baptismal text, just to be on the safe side, Cresspahl misunderstood this for a question, hesitated over his answer, and finally said: "No." It was said humorously, yet also as a rebuke for a ridiculous and unwarranted assumption, and signified partly that Lisbeth Papenbrock looked up her own Bible texts, and partly that Cresspahl did not expect from the church . . . that he did not think the church . . . that the church and he did not . . .

"And thirdly," says Marie, "that he was not exactly in urgent need of friends. That he did not need friendships in Jerichow. Why doesn't he leave!"

"Put the child under his arm and go to Hamburg and give it a piece of his steak and a drink of his beer?"

"I see," says Marie. "A man with a baby. That wouldn't do."

"He no longer had any alternative. The only place he could keep the child, and his wife, now was in Jerichow. Richmond, Lisbeth's foreign country, was out.

"What made him so sure?"

"She'd told him."

"Weren't things done the way the husbands wanted in that country of Mecklenburg?"

"It was customary, Marie."

"Why didn't he say to her: Take the baby, pull yourself together, follow me?"

"You're not normally in favor of violence, Marie."

"He wasn't worried about avoiding violence. He was scared."

"He was scared of losing her."

"He was chicken! He didn't want to find out what she might be capable of if the worst came to the worst!"

November 16, 1967   Thursday

Mr. Josiah Thompson is among those who did not believe the official report on the death of President Kennedy. When he came up with three assassins instead of the officially acknowledged murderer, he received a visit from agents of the FBI. They warned him that any-

thing he said might be held against him. So he said nothing.
Thereupon they left. Now he has no idea what they wanted to ask
him.

The address recommended to us by Mrs. Ferwalter is on the
East Side in one of the nineties toward the East River. At the
beginning of the street behind iron grilles are arrayed the dead
hopes once placed by the retail trade in the street's inhabitants:
semidemolished store counters, broken glass, packing trash. There are
scarcely any children standing about on the street. The abandoned
cars had been sitting here like this a month ago, a bit rustier now, a
bit more thoroughly cannibalized. The street is barely alive, people
come here from other neighborhoods and throw their cumbersome
junk, from sofas to refrigerators, down beside the trash cans whose
bellies are too empty even to stink. The building cowers pitifully in a
row of four-story relatives, moribund. The front steps look un-
trodden. The door is open, wedged back at an angle indicating that
fear for personal property is a thing of the past, there is now only
indifference. Most of the windows keep out the daylight with dusty
shades. Ten years ago, maybe, because the front was not faced with
sandstone, the owner attempted to paint the bricks a watery blue;
since then the building has received no further help. In the entrance
hall there is not yet the kind of dirt that is deliberately created, there
is only dust and sticky dampness, the blend of decay. Beyond the
doors is a sickroom silence, and they have an expressionless look, as if
little cooking were done here these days. On the fourth floor Mr.
Kreslil has pinned his visiting card to his door, a piece of yellowed
elegant pasteboard, artistically printed thirty years ago. He does not
indicate that he gives lessons in Czechoslovakian, and he has canceled
the abbreviation for "Professor" with a neat, unemotional stroke.

The apartment is defended by an old woman whose name, as we
learn by degrees, is Jitka Kvatshkova.

The first time we went there she required our name and some
reassuring words to be repeated many times before she would unhook
the door chain. She is short. With all her plumpness she looks
harried and on the run. She has increased the height of her head by
twisting her hair tightly into a flat topknot, making her low steep
forehead seem overburdened. The look in her eyes does not relax
when she recognizes the visitor, they continue to search for the
unbidden guest on the stairs, for danger. Her accent is so foreign that
at first we could only guess from her gestures that we were to wait.
She found it so hard to believe she had been understood that her

manner seemed severe. Around her hips there is a rustling as of many petticoats as she moves to the nearest door, her hand already extended as if she were bent on an outburst of anger. Beyond the door, however, she speaks softly, quite humbly. The visitor invariably has to wait to be announced. The room in which we wait is used sometimes as a kitchen and at night for sleeping. The chair in which we wait is an armchair, its seat almost worn through, the arms still warm from Mrs. Kvatshkova's hands. On our second visit we tiptoed to the television set facing the chair. It was still warm. By now she is used to us; besides, television programs have taught her what to say in this country to arriving and departing guests, but the best she can do is a smile that begins simultaneously in various areas of her face, running together to form a continuous, entirely convincing gesture. Once, too, she touched our arm and with a distressed shake of the head sympathized with our weariness, taking us back to Jakob's mother, who used to accompany Cresspahl's sleepy child to the morning school train in the dark. Nevertheless, she insists on the ritual of announcement. This bare room is hers, she lives in it, she works in it, but for outsiders it is supposedly Professor Kreslil's anteroom; she pretends to be the housekeeper and not the woman who lives with him, perhaps because long ago in České Budějovice that was how they handled the situation.

Like Ottje Stoffregen in Jerichow. After the war Ottje Stoffregen lived in a room above the pharmacy, and in the kitchen he kept a woman refugee from Pomerania whose job it was to negotiate with him over the admittance of visitors, as if he were sitting at a lion-footed desk engaged in his work and not poring over the volumes of journals in which he had been permitted to publish until 1938. He would then rise to his feet as if absorbed in pressing thoughts, come toward the visitor with outstretched hand, with a glad but preoccupied smile, and he was a gaunt figure like Professor Kreslil, whose suits hung loose and crooked on him, except that Stoffregen's English materials were not shabby even after ten years' wear, while Professor Kreslil's clothes looked more as if they came from that Bohemian forest through which the party of the working class had chased a lone sheep, and Kreslil merely cannot afford a dentist to fill out his cheeks with proper dentures, while they had knocked out Stoffregen's teeth; he wore the gaps like a decoration as if he had to act the witch in the fairy tale, his grin always slipped to one side into a familiarity that could not be trusted. Not like Stoffregen. With his formal mode of address, his bowing, Kreslil ought to be in a dark suit sitting at the best table at the St. Wenceslas Restaurant, and has not yet seen the inside of it, his colors are different too, the color of his healthy pink scalp and his shock of hair whitened by age, while Stoffregen was yellow, and Stoffregen was above giving lessons, there was nothing to learn from Stoffregen; Kreslil has prepared his desk as for a teaching banquet, with plenty of pencils and paper and open textbooks, his own books stand way behind him on the shelf, five blue volumes by one Anatol Kreslil, all with the same indecipherable title, and Kreslil sits up straight, correctly, the way it used to be learned in school, carefully clears his throat, starts reviewing the homework from the last lesson, smiles encouragingly behind his rimless bifocals, looking forward to my knowledge, and we are indeed able to recite that our houses are far from the railway station, naše domy jsou daleko od nádraží, and we lack whatever it is we need to make these words come easily . . ., and at school there had been a time when I wanted to stop learning the language of the occupying power and for a whole school year never got beyond the story of the little old grandpa and the rebellious turnip, and he pulled, and he pulled, tjeshil, tjeshil, a nje vytjeshil, and again and again Kreslil's Czech makes me start speaking in my Russian and he withdraws behind a pinched, severe expression, watching me with this disapproval while I sleep, it is a refresher course in the history of socialism, I have seen myself sleeping in one of Blach's pictures, shoulders slightly hunched, neck limp and face sagging, as if I were dead, for a single German word Kreslil wakes me from my ten-dollar sleep and conducts me past the horrified Mrs. Kvatshkova to the door, I didn't speak Russian, didn't speak German, I don't say a thing, how can I fall asleep here. How can I sleep in the home of these people. Wake me up.

November 17, 1967   Friday

He is not the man. The old man wandering the streets of Panama peddling combs, wine, and old clothes is not Heinrich Müller. If the chief of Hitler's secret police is still alive, he is at large.

On the third page, where the New York *Times* usually publishes news pictures from Vietnam, there is a photograph today of the 75-foot cage at Catanzara in which Italian justice is holding 121 members of the Mafia during a trial. If Karsch can stay in this country now, he must have his people in Calabria.

Avenarius Kollmorgen was looking forward to an enjoyable evening. He sat often enough by himself at night. He had read of the renunciations of old age; he did not find that this applied to him with either people or pleasures. Not that he needed people, all he needed was their company. He did not want his emotions involved. He had dissociated himself from his parents by graduating in law, rather than arts as they would have liked. He had recovered from having a first name carried by others to literary and philosophical fame as a family name; and he did not even want Richard Wagner for a grandfather. The self-image he had created was not that "Avi" of Wismar High School, not that "Arius" of Erlangen University, but that perfectly genuine and secretive Avenarius Kollmorgen who had ceased to bother others with explanations of himself. This Avenarius he knew to be a gentle and vulnerable creature. All right, so he had not made his mark in any of the arts. Very well, so he had left Rostock for a much smaller seaside town where he was not easy to find. True, he lived alone. To what woman could he have explained himself? The children who shouted jingles after him, the Jerichow townsfolk who were amused by his gait and his idiosyncrasies of speech? What did he care if they thought he was crafty, arrogant, a screwball in fact? That wasn't such a bad disguise. And the reason he so rarely entered the Lübeck Arms was not that the steps were rather too steep for his rather short legs; he simply did not like what the licensee did to the wines. The fellow bought dubious vintages. And he stored bottles on the sunny side of the cellar. Such things had never been served up in the Kollmorgen home. And he was not very good with people en masse. He had little to talk about because he knew so many secrets that the borderline between them and open matters sometimes became blurred. No, what he needed was individuals to whom, in his own home, he could assign a chair and his rules, people who were unable to defend themselves against unhurried observation, analysis, and assessment by Avenarius K. And from time to time, of course, visitors were welcome as an alibi for the neighbors, who almost every morning saw more empty bottles accumulating in the yard. So it suited him nicely when Albert Papenbrock turned up with his son-in-law for a discussion about the strange gift to a two-week-old child, despite its being a Saturday evening. Papenbrock was getting on in years, mind you. Possibly as the evening wore on he would reveal weaknesses that a Kollmorgen was still far from having to fear. And he had been curious about the son-in-law for a long time. In 1931 the latter had not come to him but had gone to Dr. Jansen. Funny, in the literal sense of the word. Nothing wrong with his colleague Jansen, by the way. Kollmorgen got up from his Seneca and marched to the kitchen, erect enough to tip backward, and chased Geesche Helms's sister out of the house. However inquisitive she was, she never managed to find the vintages for which she was sent. So the sturdy little attorney went down the cellar stairs, with a sigh of satisfaction over the little job that would yield such copious reward.

When he had seated his clients in armchairs, rotund traps from which they would not so easily escape, they seemed to him to be still agreed. Papenbrock had come for a pleasant evening, hardly for lengthy business negotiations. As soon as he had his cigar going, he tilted his chin toward the bottles arrayed on one side, and a Kollmorgen does not wait to be asked. The other man—Cresspahl, wasn't it?—sat rather more upright, unlike a visitor, looking rather sleepy with his pipe, his thoughts evidently elsewhere. He appeared to be waiting. No wonder. Kollmorgen could hardly stand it himself. The preliminaries took time, but unfortunately were indispensable. First the weather. For the middle of March the weather was not too bad. This also took care of the prospects of good business, secondly. Thirdly, the family. Better not. Politics. Certainly not. The agenda, then. It can't be much longer now. Hopefully Dr. Kollmorgen spread out the pages of his draft on his plump capacious thighs, leaned his elbows comfortably on the padded chair arms, and began his discourse. He rocked back and forth from a sense of well-being and anticipation. In order to keep his daughter's husband in this country, Papenbrock was giving his granddaughter a piece of land that would not become hers until March 3, 1954. He, Kollmorgen, would not live to see that day, so today he must make sure he got all the entertainment to which he was entitled. "And the other children?" he asked.

He held his round, flat-backed, bulging head very high, jerked fierce eyebrows upward, behaved with all the gravity he could muster. Let the clients do their worst, he was ready for them. In the case of several children the estate could only be divided up according to its financial value. The various majority dates would have to be taken into consideration, as well as a whole series of legal proceedings, not to mention the bureaucratic ones. The question was justified, there was nothing they could do about it. This . . . Cresspahl, wasn't it? betrayed no sign of annoyance, merely nodded quietly, his head on one side, the way amateur chess players comment on their opponent's opening as if to say it would just barely do and a different one would be better. What a pity that by this time Avenarius lived too much out of the world to make friends with a person at least to the point where they could play chess together. Then he noticed Papenbrock's hand as, holding the full glass, it paused in midair and twitched to one side so that a drop spurted over the rim. Papenbrock had come unprepared. It was no use his trying to wipe out that impression now with a puff of smoke and the mention of restrictive clauses. Let Papenbrock think he had recovered himself. Let him be amused at what he thought of as Kollmorgen's mannerisms. That was just fine.

Since in this case the child's mother is voluntarily renouncing her legacy, should the child die the deeded property reverts first to the mother, only then to the father, and after that to the deeder. As administrator, the father is not entitled to borrow against the deeded property or to encumber it with a mortgage. From the usufruct he is to defray the costs of maintenance of buildings and land and pay all taxes and local rates. The property is protected from top to bottom and on all sides from the owner's father. That's how you want it, gentlemen, isn't it?

"There'll be nothing in it for us," said Cresspahl, without bitterness, no less quietly than Papenbrock had been listening to the terms.

Papenbrock hoisted himself upright, in two attempts, in order to look his son-in-law straight in the face, not just surprised but hurt. In an aggrieved tone he named the sum he had already spent on the property, with a slight upward rounding as a matter of fact, although every phase of the purchase had gone through Dr. Kollmorgen's office. In his delight Avenarius tried to pour some more wine into Cresspahl's glass. Cresspahl's glass was not yet sufficiently empty.

"Maintenance!" said Cresspahl. "The condition that place is in, the wind can take care of that."

He offered no protest when Papenbrock, with barely restrained fervor, brought up the subject of a certain account with the Surrey Bank of Richmond; he dismissed it with a casual nod, and it was borne in on Papenbrock that the account was indeed as substantial as Lisbeth had said, possibly even more so by this time. This made him stumble in his calculations, and meanwhile Avenarius was reveling in the certainty that Papenbrock had been counting on the sentiments of family kinship. He made a mental note of this error, above his fat hairy right ear, for later delectation. He could not afford to miss anything of what was going on right now. There was no need for him to pit the two men against each other. Observation, innocent undisturbed observation, was his greatest delight. Papenbrock had been acting as if he wanted to make his son-in-law an indirect gift so as not to hurt his feelings, hence by way of Cresspahl's daughter. This Cresspahl, however, was sheltering behind his obligation to examine the gift for its advantages to his daughter. Avenarius could not have conceived of anything better. He leaned back unassumingly, clasped his hands over his stomach while continuing to rock on his elbows, and turned his head from one to the other to be sure not to miss a single strike or hit. What he liked best was the way this . . . Cresspahl handled things. His manner was not challenging, as the affair might have warranted, but slow and thorough, as of someone who had promised to think the matter over. Now he had finished thinking it over. Papenbrock had immediately snatched the piece of paper on which Cresspahl had made his calculations, with the result that he was torn between Cresspahl's figures and what Cresspahl was saying. Kollmorgen regretted this, for Papenbrock was thus not aware of the full acuteness of his failure. Cresspahl, on the other hand, could state from memory that at the present time the property was of no substantial market value. Nevertheless, he said, to sell it would still be the more sensible course. The money could be held in a trust account until the child came of age, preferably divided equally between a German and a British one to allow for divergences in economic trends and to facilitate matters for the trustee in the usufruct and the fulfillment of the obligations arising out of the gift. In this way the gift would at least not entail any additional expense. As regards the latter, it could hardly be desirable for the trustee to apply his cash resources to an enterprise over which he had no disposal rights. The way things stood now, it wasn't an enterprise at all. It was far too early to start talking about maintenance, but there was plenty to say about rehabilitation. Rehabilitation was up to the donor, if he seriously wanted to do the child a favor. But it was also at the discretion of the donor. It was for him to decide whether he wanted it carried out by persons authorized by himself or by the child's legal representative; in any event it would be for his account because undertaken for the benefit of the recipient of the gift. After the deeded property had been restored to normal condition, it still would not meet the requirements of the administrator's craft, and even then a business had still to be established and built up, and then, said Cresspahl courteously, in the tone of a good-natured promise: "Then we'll talk about my money."

Long after midnight Avenarius Kollmorgen was still pacing his three rooms, not so erect now, and sometimes hugging himself a little with pleasure. He carried his glass as he walked, sipping knowledgeably, and as he swallowed the wine he would lift a serene, joyous face to the ceiling. He had observed Papenbrock in defeat. Prompted by emotion, Papenbrock had assigned a great deal of money, more than he had intended. Papenbrock had believed his son-in-law to be at such a disadvantage that he had not reckoned with the encumbrance to himself. Now Avenarius knew rather more about Papenbrock. His image had rounded out. He knew all about images, there was always some point at which they ceased to tally with the persons concerned, this he knew from personal experience, but while people could not apply their image of Avenarius Kollmorgen to him, he knew very well how to make use of his image of them. Oh yes. His favorite recollection was the moment at which Papenbrock had grasped the situation and set down his half-empty glass and taken leave of his hopes of an evening's chat among congenial men. It had been a splendid evening for Avenarius K. Even the private army of that Austrian, that . . . Hitler, had for once refrained from bawling and shouting and thus disturbing a spectacle that had turned out to surpass Avenarius' fondest dreams. The top-heavy, stocky little man stopped by one of the windows, stuck his powerful head between the curtains, and contemplated the market square as it lay before him in the darkness like a giant stage, hemmed in by the gabled houses gleaming whitely. One day a stage like that should be set up for Avenarius, for all the spectators between Wismar and Lübeck, enabling him for once to present himself as the wise yet deeply sensitive creature he really was. They would not understand. He did not need their efforts to understand him. They were doomed to misjudge him. He was willing to remain content with his solitude. It left him free to pursue the superb entertainment that only he could contrive from the banal business affairs of others. Still, to be fair: he had had no reason to expect such an evening. He had no right to that degree of pleasure. But if he had no right to that, neither did he to another bottle of Pommard; but since he had been granted the one, he must provide himself with the other. Otherwise there would be no order in this world, and order was to be found only with him. Down to the cellar, Avenarius.

November 18, 1967   Saturday, South Ferry Day,

---

perhaps the last this year. For last night the second snowstorm in less than a week moved through New York State and New England, and although it bypassed the city with some rain and occasional snow flurries the temperature continues to remain in the lower forties. Gesine still subtracts 32, multiplies the remainder by 5, and divides it by 9, to arrive with her 6° Centigrade at the same result as Marie, who has always been able to translate 42° Fahrenheit into a sensation: It's cold.

Marie does not say this. Both going and coming on the ferry she trots around the outer decks; during the return trip to Manhattan she even keeps to the windward side, although Gesine is sitting indoors on the other side. So she cannot be seen. So she has no need to show herself. So she has no need to talk. Yesterday she put the mail down beside the telephone without sorting it into friends, strangers, and junk mail, as if she had not looked through the envelopes and in particular had not noticed the letter with the school's official imprint. She withdrew as if by chance into her room whenever Gesine approached the telephone, and it is only a possibility that she overheard the appointment made with Sister Magdalena this morning. Two can play at this game. Gesine leaves it to her to start a conversation, just as Marie has been leaving it to Gesine for the past four hours. Now, level with Liberty Island, she returns to the saloon, rubbing her hands, hunched up, that's how cold she is. She says nothing about school but talks about the Statue of Liberty erected in New York Harbor by Frédéric Auguste Bartholdi in the image of his beloved mother. "She's got feet like a goose," says Marie.

 She has to sit down beside Gesine, slightly beyond her direct line of vision, before making up her mind. "O.K., so I'm sorry," she says. She has pushed her hood to the back of her neck but ignores her braid, which has become caught in the fuzzy blue wool. She leans forward, her elbows on her thighs, and she even shakes her head like a man who regrets some foolish action although at heart he is not willing to take the blame for it since he cannot fathom his behavior. "Except I don't understand how they found out!" she says.

 Sister Magdalena did not seem particularly indignant. She had set out the cups and saucers in her tiny room on the top floor of the school's new wing, in the wood-paneled cubicle that, despite the orderliness of bed and desk, still suggested a furnished rented room, a purely temporary abode. Sister Magdalena was wearing the same grayish-black dress in which on other days she taught, in which, so Marie guessed, she also slept, "on her back, too, without moving." She was so hard to make out from the little bit of face that her vows permitted her to reveal to secular persons because, to compound the difficulty, she barely moved it. She kept it firmly in that tolerant expression in which severity and kindness can live side by side, and was not aware that she prompted thoughts of the Paris fashion models with their shaven heads. Sister Magdalena is thirty or fifty or forty years old; even the age of her voice is concealed by an invariable tone of combined deference and firmness. With her teacup, her hostess manners, she was trying to endow the occasion with the air of an innocuous visit; but she sat stiffly on her chair, knees together, shoes together, and even the loosely clasped hands left no doubt that this was a summons.

She had a complaint to make about Marie. She presented her complaint in the guise of anxiety about the child, of sympathy, in that pedagogic language that conceals statements and intentions behind expressions from life outside the school, with digressions and cross-references in which any direct question becomes enmeshed like a fly caught in a spider's web. She began by saying that children express their feelings. She went on to describe the differences between the various feelings. She elaborated on the varying degrees of control that children have over their feelings. She circumvented puberty by describing it as "a more than spiritual change." So Marie had expressed her feelings, was that it? That was not it. True, she had attempted to express her feelings. In a history class she had voiced an indignation over the treatment of the Indians by the conquerors of America that had interrupted the course of the lesson and necessitated a discussion that, despite possible psychological gains, had nevertheless jeopardized the maintenance of the syllabus. Not only had she woven a totally irrelevant allusion to the Vietnam war into an essay she had written entitled "I Look Out the Window," but during school breaks she had made it difficult, indeed almost impossible, for other pupils to clarify their feelings about the war in question. She had become aggressive. Was that the cause for complaint? No. It was rather a tendency of the pupil to partisanship, to an almost moral solidarity with the underdog in historical processes. No one could deny that the war in Vietnam was a tragedy, but so were other events in human history, and the school's objective was to convey not the unjust aspects of any one subject but the content of the subject itself. A child who was prepared to get worked up over established facts might become a threat to the community of life and learning as envisioned by the school constitution. Was that it? No, Mrs. Cresspahl. All Sister Magdalena was concerned about was the spiritual well-being of this child.

How are we to explain this to Marie? Are we to reproach her with: Marie, you are too biased? Marie, you have got to change that?

Sister Magdalena had carried on without pause in her terraced digressions, gentle and remorseless. Interjected questions stung her like wasps, she was quite unprepared for interruptions to her discourse, and when she indicated by the mildest creasing of her brow and tightening of the corners of her mouth that she was being caused great distress, what she really intended to convey was reproach. She extended this expression to a wry smile meant to bemoan her human frailty, a halfhearted pretense at an apology. This was her way of avoiding answers. She appeared to be asking questions, but not directly. She spoke of the hardships and deprivations from which working parents suffer, particularly in that they have to pass them on to their children. Especially in the case of single, separated parents, the renouncing of authority might have other and worse consequences for the children than those that are desired and, to a point, laudable. It might be fit for some families, but not all, for children to address their parents by first names rather than as parents. The result was a familiarity, an illusory equality, that was more likely to wreak havoc in a child's emotions than to develop them. Sister Magdalena never once became concrete, even the school psychiatrist was mentioned simply as a mutual acquaintance who had, of course, performed outstanding services in his profession as well as in the field of human behavior. These were statements, but their general distillation yielded no factual information. It was as if she wished to make do with impressions. We could explain nothing to her. The only thing to do was to offer her out-and-out play-acting in simple terms: anxiety about Marie's place in the school, concern for Sister Magdalena's obviously sleepless nights, the eager determination to improve; all in the vague hope of at least some measure of credibility. It was not a barefaced lie. Sister Magdalena is the home-room teacher, and after a summons to her the next step is one to the school principal's office. The institution is swamped with applications for every grade, just because the curriculum is so sound, and it will be of no help to us that we have not requested a grant but pay the full fees, considering the other candidates can boast of the sacrament of baptism, which Marie cannot produce. The third summons to the principal's office is tantamount to the child's dismissal from school. Against the judgments of a teacher who has taught the Fifth Grade exclusively for the past eleven years, there is no appeal. Not long ago the institution expelled a child with a congenital hip defect because she ultimately proved incapable of conforming to the teachers' conceptions of a desirable child. The lie resided elsewhere: in the amicable forms of the conversation, in our expected and unquestioned respect for Sister Magdalena's psychological competence, and included our unwavering cordiality as we parted at the elevator door, from which Sister Magdalena refused to budge until the arrival of the elevator. Out on the street, if she wore a secular hat, we would not recognize her. "It was such a pleasure to have a talk with you, Mrs. Cresspahl." "Not at all. The pleasure was mine, Sister Magdalena."

> *Forgive me, Jakob.*
> *O. K., Gesine. What for?*
> *For saying, "We are not living apart."*
> *The way it is.*
> *For saying, "He is dead."*
> *That always helps, doesn't it, Gesine?*
> *Forgive me, Jakob.*
> *Take the child away from there, Gesine.*
> *Where to, Jakob? To the moon?*
> *Dublin, Gesine. London. Copenhagen.*

Are we to give Marie orders: Kindly respect my authority? Are we to threaten her with the bogeyman? With the psychiatrist? With the Notice of Expulsion? Are we to demand of her: Don't tell your friends at school what we discuss at home?

The child is so lost in thought that she forgoes the pleasure of watching the ferry enter the slip, although for several minutes the throttling of the engines has been increasing the hull's vibration and most of the passengers have crowded toward the doors and stairs in wedge-shaped clusters. "I don't get it," she says. "I was alone in the classroom when I wrote it on the blackboard, and Sister Magdalena erased it during the next lesson without asking."

"What did you write on the blackboard?"

This is hard for the child. She does not exactly squirm, but she wavers, she holds her head to one side, the other side. "Bugs Bunny for President," she finally admits. "Can I apologize to the old monster in writing, or must I do it personally?"

The New York *Times* is not of the opinion that President Johnson does his job worse than the cartoon figure Bugs Bunny, who is forever concocting inventions, ostensibly for the good of mankind but in fact to their disadvantage and detriment. On page 1 the New York *Times* publishes three photographs of the President's press conference and a report almost two pages long: how he stepped out from behind the podium, waved his arms, chopped the air, drew imaginary lines with his fingers, how his voice fluctuated between high-volume anger and quiet, self-deprecating gentleness, how he walked up and down in front of the camera like a revival preacher.

The real Johnson. His comment on the critics of his conduct of the war was: He did not want to call them unpatriotic, but they were living in glass houses.

November 19, 1967   Sunday

At last we are relieved of our trade secret: the devaluation of the pound is in the New York *Times*.

Marie wants to know what a church christening is like. She is disappointed to learn that only a little warmed water was brushed across the baby's forehead, and that parents and godparents promised the church to bring up the future person according to the wishes of the church. In return for this, the church's appointee confirms the child's name. Told like this, it might discourage Marie from her plan of having the ceremony repeated in five years on her own person.

This had in fact been the entire content of the service at St. Peter's Church in Jerichow on March 19, 1933. Some of the congregation remained seated beneath the sleepy organ strains that the organist, Julie Westphal, had intended as a sign for them to leave the church; a few even moved into the vacated front pews of the aristocracy beneath the disapproving eye of the verger who under Methling's regime would have been allowed not only to intervene but to demand payment of the admission fee. Old Bastian was not happy about the new pastor. Lax, this Brüshaver. Warming the christening water, what an idea: Mollycoddling right from the start, not to mention the extra work for Pauli Bastian in his old age. Pauli kept his face stiff as a board while the Cresspahls and the Papenbrocks entered the center aisle with the baby, and the creases centering around his nose formed a pattern not suitable for decorating a nursery. Cresspahl carried the baby, rather high at his chest and with great concentration, until he could return it to the mother at the altar. The women were all in the best of moods. Louise Papenbrock had nodded more gently on finding herself in the front pew beside Dora Semig, who had after all been a Miss Köster from Schwerin. Semig's wife watched the ritual with the child as if all the participants were bent on making her laugh, and as if her power to resist the urge were rapidly vanishing. Hilde Paepcke could not keep her head still, looked up at Cresspahl, signaled to Lisbeth with her eyes, with her lips, not as the older sister but like a child joining in the game; for Hilde Paepcke was rehearsing the christening ceremony for the child she was carrying in her belly. Lisbeth, my mother, your grandmother, did not show much expression in her face, but one could tell from the way she looked at Brüshaver, and from her ready, instantaneous joining in the prayers and responses, that she was celebrating a solemn feast, that she had got everything she wanted. Of Louise Papenbrock it could be said without reservation that her face was not under control and that possibly the prestige of this christening embellished the memory of earlier ones in her life, or at least made them more bearable. We will say nothing of such ladies as Käthe Klupsch, for whom the affair was insufficiently dramatic and tearful. Cresspahl's expression showed nothing. He had his work-face. The other godfather, Dr. Arthur Semig, Veterinary Surgeon, held his hands loosely clasped in front of him and was unashamedly enjoying himself. He stood beside Lisbeth Cresspahl looking down on the baby's head, which was turned toward him, on the eyelids twitching in half-sleep, the lips pleasurably opening and closing, the cat's paws, as they are called in German, what you call crow's feet, at the corners of the eyes, and the grown man was as intrigued with the child, he wrinkled his nose as unself-consciously,

"as Mr. Fang Liu," says Marie.
"As only Chinese can behave toward strange children."

Papenbrock sat there as if he were monarch of all he surveyed, but a dissatisfied one under whose nose something obnoxious was going on. He was not seething with rage at Cresspahl, although this is what Cresspahl assumed. The previous evening Papenbrock had exchanged Avenarius Kollmorgen and his red wine for Lindemann and his Moselle wine at the Lübeck Arms and had stayed on beyond closing time merely to brood in silence in Cresspahl's company. Cresspahl was prepared to sit out the stubborn silence if it was helping Papenbrock over his defeat; he had no idea that the older man was comparing him silently with Horst Papenbrock and the way the latter spent his time, and that he was giving serious consideration to his will. Papenbrock was now not giving his full attention to what was going on. He was sufficiently involved for the moisture in the inner corners of his eyes to become a nuisance, but instead of dabbing at it with pleasure, like Louise Papenbrock, he wiped it brusqely away, as if it were one more annoyance. He did not hear the baby sneeze, they had to tell him later. He had made a start early that morning. He had waited to see whether Horst would turn up for breakfast in his Storm Trooper's uniform. The moment he saw the brown boots he began to roar, to the consternation of Horst, who was not aware of being observed. Horst insisted he was going to wear his uniform to church. Papenbrock pushed back his plate, very slowly, with manifest regret. This put Horst in the wrong, because he was forcing his aged father to let the fried eggs get cold. As he rose to his feet, Papenbrock began to shout. Cresspahl had been sitting with bent head, like everyone else around the table, and he almost admired the old man. He shouted without any effort at all, one insult after another occurring to him, against people who lack respect for the dignity of a religious ceremony, who don't do their job, who can think of nothing but stupid antics ("Stupid antics?" said Horst, pale, calm, outraged, believing it was the symbols of the new state that were under attack. "That's right!" roared Papenbrock: "Holding hands with shoemakers' daughters!") all in a spate of obscene dialect, so that Horst did not have the courage to plead on Elisabeth Lieplow's behalf that, although she did come from Kröpelin, the town of shoemakers, she was certainly not the daughter of a shoemaker but of an official in the tax department. As he left, the door slammed behind him. When he returned, wearing his black Sunday suit, Papenbrock sent him to feed the horses, and this time Horst showed neither rebellion nor threats even in his face, and it is hard to stomp off in dress shoes. Now, beside the old man in the pew, although still under observation, he signaled his independence by an appearance of boredom, believing himself to have weathered Papenbrock's mood. He continued to believe this until lunchtime, although it did strike him that, while the dish with the roast goose was passed to him several times, the white wine was not. Actually Papenbrock's manner was peaceable enough, almost as if he were bent on enjoying himself. He made three speeches, one directed at Lisbeth, one at Hilde, one at the child sleeping off the exertions of the outing at a safe distance from him. The third Christian name, Albertine, had been more than he had a right to expect, he is supposed to have said (according to Mrs. Brüshaver). Then he asked the question: whether one was required to forgive one's children, possibly everything. Not even Louise felt like replying to this, but Louise Papenbrock saw something coming. She hunched her shoulders a little, clasping her hands in her lap to be ready to pray if necessary. But Papenbrock insisted on a reply. Finally he turned point-blank to Brüshaver, and the new pastor, caught raising his glass, behaved once again as if he knew all about the internal disputes of this family. He gestured a toast, he gave a little nod, but in such a way that his assent yielded the very springboard Papenbrock wanted. He reminded his family of that Reformation Day in 1931 when every last one of them had reproached him with being "hardhearted," merely because he had not wanted to invite the son in "Rio de Janeiro." Brüshaver now stared into his glass, and Semig wished he could leave the room. "Lisbeth has a child, Hilde's expecting one," said Papenbrock, not without satisfaction at his logical train of thought. "You're going," he said, without even turning to Horst.

Horst protested in vain. He couldn't speak Brazilian: it was pointed out that the language was Portuguese and could be learned. He would have difficulty locating his vanished older brother: then he must try all the harder to find him. That might take a year: Papenbrock could manage without him for two years. It would cost a mint of money: Papenbrock had the money. Horst could not extricate himself. His sisters gave him no support, partly to make him atone for many injuries, partly because they were taken in by Papenbrock's magnanimity. Furthermore, they were moved, and considered Horst's attempts at refusal a disgrace. Louise Papenbrock cried because it seemed the thing to do. Cresspahl found himself almost against his will siding with the older Papenbrock. The old man had no faith in the new Reich Government and no desire to be involved in a collapse of the regime as a result of Horst's activities with the Brownshirts. It was also possible that he wanted to protect Horst by sending him around the world. It was amusing to watch Horst. Horst believed there was a choice between going and staying; but actually his choice was between the Nazis and his inheritance, and if he chose bourgeois property he might get only half of it, the vanished Robert Papenbrock the other half, and Horst was to co-operate, in Portuguese. And Horst did not dare bring up the subject of the Brownshirts, among whom he would meanwhile be deprived of promotion and glory. It was amusing, but there were moments when to Cresspahl the people around the table seemed like strangers. He felt like an outsider, and indeed his packed bag stood by the front door waiting once again for the train connecting with the Number 2 express for Hamburg. Except that this time he was traveling alone, and for the last time.

Representatives of businesses along Fifth Avenue have staged a parade along Fifth Avenue to protest against parades along Fifth Avenue. The merchants lose half a million dollars whenever there is a parade and suggest that the parades be rerouted to the streets on the west side of Central Park, West End Avenue, and Riverside Drive. We'll show them.

November 20, 1967   Monday

In order to protect the dollar from the consequences of the devaluation of the British pound, the Federal Reserve System has increased the discount rate to 4.5 per cent. Here again the New York *Times* would like to prevent readers from skirting this news merely because they do not understand it, so the paper explains it once more: the discount rate is the amount commercial banks pay to borrow from the Federal Reserve System, and the New York *Times* repeats the lesson in the summary of events of the day. And for this we have taken courses in economics at Columbia University. The Spanish Government has also devaluated its currency. This week work will be harder at the bank than last week.

It began yesterday morning. Marie could be heard on the telephone in the living room. She answered very briefly, it sounded each time like Yes. The docility in her voice was amazing. Then she could no longer be heard, but neither could the click of the disconnection. When I went to look, she was standing with her back to the telephone and holding the receiver at arm's length. She gave a deep sigh when it was taken from her. The dialing tone was audible. Her eyelids were lowered, she was working her knuckles, she was trying out what she would say. "It was Karsch," she said.

But then it had not been Karsch. A strange man had been asking for him. He was not in this apartment. The man knew that. Not only did he know where Karsch was, he also promised he would stay there unless he were replaced by two thousand dollars. Moreover, the matter was urgent. He had called Marie "Sister," just the way she imagines the Mafia does. The things children dream up. The stories children tell.

Marie did not defend her story. She went to the green desk bequeathed to us by the Danish girl, reached into the top drawer between the passports, and took out the travel money, spread it out on the table, and began sorting it:

SFr. 187.00
£9/11/-
DM 15.00
Lire 40,000

The story was not diminished in its second telling. The stranger wanted cash, in small denominations, by this evening. At one point he had let Karsch's voice speak into the telephone; it had sounded a bit blurred, as if on tape. So Marie had asked him about the meal he had ordered a week ago at the U. N. restaurant, and he told her exactly, down to the Idaho potatoes. The stranger had spoken of himself as "we." As if Karsch were sitting tied to a chair, blindfolded, guarded by expert gunmen. The things children think possible.

Marie listened patiently to every objection, but with a preoccupied expression, as she walked from room to room in the apartment, systematically, with no detours. It was as if she wanted her own actions to compensate for the time being wasted by her mother. She took the housekeeping money from the tea canister in the kitchen closet and spread it out beside the foreign currency. Then she brought the cashbox with her own savings. There was finally a total of $450 on the table, including the foreign bills. Where can one change foreign currency on a Sunday in New York!

"Kennedy Airport," said Marie. Her face had become quite small. She was so worried, at least *she* did not doubt her story. It was too late to laugh, she would not even have been offended by it now; at most she might have thought it inane. We don't know anyone who would lend us $1,550 on a Sunday with no questions asked.

"D. E.," said Marie.

"Can you let us have a lot of money, D. E.?" said Marie on the telephone, not in the least shy, and she promptly named the figure of two thousand. D. E. made Marie cheer up. She answered him in a brisk, jaunty tone, with D. E.'s help she had already sighted land in the future. That was more than I had been able to do. Three times she said Yes, then the conversation was over. She brought me my coat, she pushed me out the door. Everyone else believed it.

D. E. made it no more real, nor did the galloping of the empty Sunday trains underground. Even a D. E. will not be able to cash a personal check on a holiday. In the West Side express a family sat close side by side, father mother son and small daughter, all spick and span, the girl prepared with tight braids for half a day at the movies on 42nd Street, the best Sunday outing within the budget of the jobless, the Negroes. At least they could believe in their destination. The cavern under Times Square was as empty and silent as a small-town market square. As I ran for the shuttle train a group of schoolgirls deflected half the looks of surprise that followed me. Then it wasn't surprising at all, this train likewise promptly slid its doors together, began trotting off. In the concourse of Grand Central, all the bums and policemen seemed to be waking up. For a moment I saw myself from the height of the blue dome, a tiny figure running diagonally across a piazza from the General Electric corner, making a slight detour for the hub that was the information booth, until the escalators carry the little figure high up into the Pan American Building. The elevator ascended as if it wanted to fly through the sixtieth floor into the sky. On the flat roof over the roofs, the ocean wind struggled with the gusts scattered by the rotary blades of the helicopter. Even when level with the top of the Chrysler Building, 1,046 feet above the street, we can think of no comparison for the semicircular overlapping slices: how could we have thought of onion slices from down below? South Brooklyn was buried under uniform square flat roofs, each surrounded by leafless hedgerows. To the south the Atlantic was crocheting delicate fringes to the land, arms behind dikes, eyes separated by seawalls behind peninsulas, curlicues like handwriting in the marshes. A shaft of sunlight whipped across the cemeteries, flickering over the headstones as in a speeded-up secret film. After nine minutes, Kennedy International Airport spread itself obligingly beneath the machine. The only fear was for Marie. If Karsch wants to play with the Mafia people, why does he also have to give them our phone number! Here at the southwesternmost corner of the Pan Am Building is our rendezvous. A likely story. The fourth helicopter to come hopping up in the boisterous wind was the one from Newark Airport. D. E. looked disguised in his blue cloth hat, which he wore perched on the top of his head as if for a joke. But his expression was grim enough, he looked fiercely around. It was the first time we had ever seen him upset, nonplussed, worried. "And thanks for the excellent weather," said D. E.

The whole time in the bus, right up to the doors of the terminal, he talked about obstacles on the way over, not in his usual, rapid, wisecracking manner. He spoke slowly, with irritable pauses, as if his thoughts were keeping pace with writing. The other passengers might well have taken us for a bored married couple in conversation before departure. On the way to the airport, then, he had stopped at Oscar's to pick up something he had forgotten. Oscar runs the booth at the fork, and just as he has many times sold D. E. alcohol illegally on a Sunday, so he will have lent him some cash. D. E. had also got gas "where we always get gas." That is another of his friends who will cash his personal checks. So the bills won't arouse suspicion. He was sorry, but he had parked his car rather carelessly at Newark Airport and badly needed someone to drive it away. On the sidewalk outside the SAS departure building, D. E. handed over an airmail letter for mailing and a ring with car keys. He would not leave without an embrace. He did it in the Russian manner, like a quotation from the Russian, but he spent more time over it than a quotation takes, with both arms around my shoulders, for one cheek, for the other, the first one again. "Look after the kid!" said D. E. morosely before moving away, a powerful fellow, stooped with dislike for traveling, with no desire for Copenhagen. He invariably says Copenhagen, he also says Reykjavik; it is more likely to be Baffin Island, if not Greenland even. Come back soon, D. E. Have a good trip, D. E. Nobody seemed to answer the number six auks in Manhattan. Marie waited for the fifth ring before lifting the receiver. Now she was speaking lightly again, impetuously, excitedly, like a child. "I'll wait for you at New York Central, third wicket from the left," she said, substituting a click for the reply she did not wish to hear. She wants to go along, we'll have to get that idea out of her head. The Manhattan-bound helicopter carried very few passengers. Shielded by seatbacks, I opened the flap of the airmail envelope. It contained a quantity of bills, all under fifty dollars, most of them dirty enough to have been used for wiping the floor. And it wasn't two thousand, it was two thousand four hundred. Just like D. E., overdoes it every time.

"We'll mail it to ourselves," said Marie in the Grand Central concourse, a somewhat preoccupied child who kept glancing over Gesine's shoulder and looking around to see if they were being watched and wishing she had eyes in the back of her head. "In an airmail envelope, from New York 10017 to New York 10025?" I asked. But the question did not put Marie off, she said: "If I don't tell you the address, you can whistle for your Karsch: as D. E. so rightly says."

"You're trying to blackmail me."
"I want to go along."
"You must be brave."
"I can't be brave at home all by myself, waiting. With you, close to you, I'd be a bit braver. I promise."
"Promise then."

So far it hadn't cost too much: two subway tickets, fifteen dollars for the flight to Jamaica Bay, only three dollars for the taxi to West Side Air Terminal, five dollars for the bus to Newark Airport. In Newark we sent the surplus money by telegram to our home address. Driving D. E.'s Bentley took some getting used to. The first address was a coffee shop in a service center on Federal Highway

1, just beyond Elizabeth, New Jersey. There really was a slip of paper in the telephone directory there. From then on it was like a montage of all the final thirds of kidnapping movies: they sent us back to Newark, they wanted us in Passaic, they wished to see us in East Orange, we were to park for half an hour in front of Newark Airport. After a while they decided to call us up at the various rendezvous to which they summoned us. Now each rendezvous was becoming dirtier, drearier, more movielike than the last. Even Marie began to get bored. The men were positively apologetic; they had hardly believed their eyes when they saw the Bentley drive up. They still did not know our name. But tomorrow they will know who the car belongs to. This went on until early evening. Meanwhile Marie asked about a christening in Jerichow thirty-four years ago and about the peculiarities of the Portuguese language, and, what was more, seemed to be listening to what she was told. In the riot quarter of Newark a man got into the car and sat down on the back seat. At first he refused to believe he had negotiated with Marie. Then he called her a "fast kid." I wish he weren't right. It was so dark he could not be recognized. He did not speak jargon, not even incorrectly. Had the voice been on tape we could have told that the speaker had been brought up by Italian parents; in the flesh, at the backs of our necks, the voice was unobtrusive, nondescript, could have come from our neighborhood in fact. The man was speaking for Mr. Karsh. It was an honest business deal. For Mr. Karsh had certainly not been kidnapped. He had gone on his own two feet and of his own free will to the place where he now was. He had not been explicitly invited, and the discourtesy, indeed the impropriety, of his behavior had been pointed out to him. Mr. Karsh had asked permission to compensate for the disagreeable impression he had made. A price had been named. Mr. Karsh had accepted the price. It was a one-time transaction, although not feasible without consent on all sides.

"Have you any complaints, lady?"

"None at all," said Gesine.

"How about you, young lady?"

"Of course not," said Marie. "But I wish you'd hurry up. I have to go to school tomorrow morning."

When the man on the back seat had counted the bills, he stuffed them into the envelope, tucked in the flap, and said: "Not quite."

"What do you mean, not quite!" said Marie. She was feigning

outrage. Not long ago she had been expressing doubts as to the favorable outcome of the enterprise. Two thousand dollars seemed to her too small a price for a living human being, and she is right, such petty amounts are not usual in the trade. Now all she showed was rage over a failure to live up to a bargain.

"We had some expenses," said the partner. "Gas . . ."

That came to another thirteen dollars. Then we were given a door key and the description of a location. The location was a half-burned-out row of stores in Newark. The riot fires had eaten away the plastic blinds, the store signs, the tubes and display signs, blackened the façades. The door was that of a barbershop, between a coin laundry and a wrecked liquor store. The key fitted. Beneath the dampness of evening, the smell of ashes and charred wood had risen again. Inside nothing was recognizable. Footsteps landed on splintered glass. The glass crackled as from strangers' footsteps when Marie ran outside. She is relying a hundred per cent on D. E.; if she needs a flashlight he will have one for her. When the light in his car went on, the outline of the car seemed to expand with well-being. The only car in driving condition on the deserted street, it looked undefended, not defensible. Marie returned with D. E.'s flashlight. She found the door to a room at the back. Here the windows were not broken, and the air was close and overheated. Here, in one of two barber's chairs, was a prone figure, bound with leather straps around chest, stomach, and legs. They had let the back down as far as it would go and raised the foot supports. It may not have been too intolerable for someone used to sleeping on his back, although not for a whole day. It was one of those situations in which for a few moments I am unable to move. The fact that I want to move forward makes no difference. The figure did not move, and our entrance had been by no means quiet. In her rage Marie forgot all precautions as she ripped the blindfold from his eyes. That woke Karsch up.

During the whole drive to Newark Airport and the bus terminal in Manhattan, Karsch behaved in a ridiculously shamefaced manner. When we parted he tried to apologize. We couldn't accept that. He tried to thank us. Marie couldn't accept that.

"I didn't do it for you!" said Marie.

Now it is almost eleven the next morning, and it is all over. Now the Newark police are looking for D. E.'s car, reported stolen from Newark Airport yesterday evening by Mrs. Erichson. The police won't start searching right away at the airport.

Now comes Karsch's call from London. Karsch is speaking from a hotel in Gloucester Road, only a few steps from the station through which the line to Richmond-upon-Thames passes. There not only Karsch would be safe.

Now the chauffeur from the Italian delegation comes to negotiate with Amanda for a personal interview with Mrs. Cresspahl. Once again he gives no indication that he is accustomed to entering buildings of quite a different kind. He gives no sign of recognition. His manner is so formal that he gets in his own way. He holds his cap tucked under his arm over the left breast, but this makes it difficult for him to take the impressive-looking envelope out of his left pocket with the other hand. Amanda, outside at her typewriter desk, placed at an angle, has a good view of the scene. She is twinkling with amusement. The envelope contains Dr. Pompa's personal check for two thousand dollars and not a cent more. A gentleman does not care for debts.

Now the "census clock" in the Commerce Department in Washington, which records a net gain of one new United States citizen every fourteen and a half seconds, moves on one step. Now there are 200 million.

November 21, 1967   Tuesday

The New York *Times* lauds the reaction of the nation's financial markets to the British currency crisis; it speaks of a cool and orderly performance. Chicago's largest bank has increased its minimum interest rate by half of 1 per cent to 6 per cent.

It was not 11 P.M. yesterday after all when the clock in Washington recorded the two-hundred-millionth citizen of the United States. To enable the President to see it, the milestone was delayed by three minutes. The figure is out of date anyway. In 1960 at least 5.7 per cent had already been missed; the Negro group probably by 9.5 per cent. Helpfully, the New York *Times* points to the 790 millions of mainland China.

So it was Potsdam Day, March 21, 1933, a Tuesday, on which a madman by the name of Hitler, bowing humbly, accepted the German Reich from an old field marshal, the day on which Cresspahl returned to Richmond, south of London. The fool. Let's hope he realized what he was doing the moment he said good-by to Germany.

"One's not supposed to insult one's father," says Marie.

"You've seen Richmond."

"It didn't turn me on," says Marie.

We have seen it. It was a November in London. What else do we remember? We had arrived from Geneva, and Marie was so carried away by her joy at being once more among people who spoke English that at Heathrow she tried to board the bus to the Airline Terminal on the right-hand side. Then it was explained to her. In town we searched Victoria Station for the spot where in January 1933 Lisbeth Cresspahl negotiated for the last time with an English porter. What else do we remember? Marie compared the London Underground with the subway that she regards as her own. She thought the escalators went too far down into the ground, and in the trains she felt trapped because the tunnel roofs came so close to the tops of the cars. The next evening D. E. flew in from his radar convention at Brussels and moved us into one of his hostelries, an American one. For a long time our opinion of British accommodation for impecunious foreigners continued to be: the inhabitants only dare do this when the Queen is not in town; for otherwise how could she enjoy a single quiet night's sleep? But the Queen was in residence.

We traveled to Richmond by the District Line, first through an open stone cutting beside brown and dusty cables that looked as if they had been laid in more leisurely times sixty years ago and not temporarily patched up after a German air raid. Then light from aboveground entered the train, etched black and brown in the colors of an English November. The blocks of flats could be ignored, my parents had not seen those. The changing pictures in the windows were accompanied by the monotonous series of billboards on which Barclays Bank and the Midland Bank carried on a stylized war, with promises that only by a stretch of the imagination could be called moral. Were there boats on the Thames? There was fog. I should have known the order of the stations by heart: Ravenscourt Park, Stamford Brook, Turnham Green, Gunnersbury, Kew Gardens, Richmond, and back to Upminster. Instead I had to buy a street map in Richmond; I didn't even know whether Cresspahl had turned left or right outside the station. The woman in her kiosk called me "Dearie." Cresspahl had turned to the left, across the railway bridge to the Quadrant, then into Sheen Road, possibly taking a short cut through Waterloo Place, past the thrifty old stone cottages where he could have waited for death. Lisbeth Cresspahl may have waited in one of the little houses along Sheen Road, all the same size, two-storied, with the same double bay window that needs its own roof; we might even find her in William Hickey's old-age home, just before Manor Road forks to the left and toward the spot where her husband once had a workshop. Cresspahl was only seventy-four when he died, that much we know; but she would have survived here, and one of those red pillar-boxes with the handleless saucepan lids is where she might to this day have been mailing letters to New York: Dear Daughter.

The English would pretty soon have put us behind barbed wire, daughter dear.

But it would have been only for seven years.

When they came the second time to take Mr. Mayer to the internment camp, he excused himself for a moment, went into the next room, and

I don't want to hear about it.

Just because I did the same?

Would you have done it in Richmond too, all because of a few years in an aliens' camp?

I never reached that point during my lifetime, daughter. I've no means of knowing, or promising.

We did not undertake this journey alone, D. E. came along too, and he began by turning the trip into a thorough inspection of Richmond, taking us around the Green, to Maids of Honour Row, to the Old Palace, and to Ham House, all upper-class objects, the preserve of nobility and culture, that my parents would have avoided. So he resigned himself to the town's middle-class parts. He did not put his questions into words; he gave me a sidelong look, as if I secretly knew all about the Tower House restaurant beside the bridge, so weatherbeaten it looked as if even thirty-five years ago it had been no place for customers, let alone my mother. On the river path he and Marie walked ahead of me, each busy with the other and hand in hand; he turned partly around, as if to make sure I was still following. Perhaps she walked here in the winter of 1932, carefully, with her heavy stomach, among the excited children watching a diver at work. The river path was quite empty, all the shrubs were bare. Gosling's department store was still there, at the corner of King Street. Wright Bros.' department store still had the same telephone number: Richmond 3601. I would rather have walked past Short's Greyhound Restaurant; but D. E. had been recommended the address of 24 George Street. All the picture postcards of Richmond showed summer scenes: clouds of lilac beside the wharf, swelling clusters of leaves outside the opulent houses on the water side of Hill Street, old people in deck chairs on sunny lawns beside a greenish Thames,

Sunday crowds on the other side around the Castle Restaurant building that looked as gay as a circus but in reality stood there bare in the wind, hunched and shivering under its threadbare colors. I saw none of that. What Marie knows best of Richmond is a large barnlike dollhouse in a store at the corner of Paradise Street and Church Walk, and it was not easy to dissuade D. E. from buying it for many pounds, for 220 dollars, and having it sent to America. Wherever we went, the local inhabitants took us for American tourists. By the window of a Chinese restaurant on Sheen Road sat two elderly women, old-age pensioners, exchanging gentle banter with the proprietor, who was carrying a two-year-old boy on his hip. She might possibly have tried out Oriental food in her old age. Thus, and ultimately with women friends in Richmond after all, she would have sat by the window whiling away the time. And she would have learned to pronounce the word "tea" as "tye." Things might have worked out after all with the parish church. I would have had red knees from the constant wind off the river, like that little girl walking into town and still wearing knee-socks in winter. I would be someone else, except for my name. I would not be German; I would talk about the Germans in an alien and remote plural. I would bear the guilt of a different nation.

At first it was hard to recognize. For Reggie Pascal's workshop could not have been on Manor Road. As far as the railway tracks there were bored-looking single-family houses behind neatly separated front gardens, barely startled by passing cars. At the tracks the road was blocked by wire-mesh gates with large red circles in the middle that opened and closed like a trap. A narrow footbridge was suspended over the railway, and from there we could see it. Reggie Pascal's workshop could have been in the triangle of ground formed by the District Line and the Southern Railway and Manor Road, across from the gasworks. Maybe all the old buildings have been torn down. When Cresspahl gave up the business they tore down the old houses and yards, at the spot where the Baltic Timber Company sells hard and soft lumber, also in short lengths, inquiries welcome. Supposing I had grown up here, among these smells of wood and gas that do not mingle, each in its own place. At fifteen I would still have been envious of the people who could live in the tiny "Railway Cottage" across the tracks. This would have been one of my most persistent memories: standing on the bridge above the Southern Railway line, above the rattling trains, amiably spitting onto the carriage roofs. I would come back and have to look each time for the gasometer that to the child had seemed so huge. Meanwhile they have painted it. I would come back to Sheen Cemetery, very grassy toward the north. There would have been room there in the white flicker of skimpily carved crosses and figures. Had they died here, I could visit my parents. Had they lived here, we would have spent more of our lives together.

"Richmond didn't turn me on," says Marie.

November 22, 1967   Wednesday

Some hippies have a house in east Denver that they call "Provo," as a sign that they wish to provoke the Establishment. There Carol Metherd, aged 24, cut the heart out of the body of her two-year-old son William and inserted a soft-drink bottle with a broken neck into the cavity. Presumably she is under the influence of drugs; she says nothing, stares at the wall.

A trip with D. E. runs like clockwork, including the one to England and Ireland and home again the year before last. Give him your airplane ticket, he will check the cost, and an airline once had to refund him two dollars. Let Marie mention an evening in the Rainbow Room on the 65th floor in New York, and the next day at noon she finds herself high above London in the restaurant of the Post Office Tower and has no inkling even at the foot of the building. The child prefers to be surprised. While Marie was still busy with her friends in South London, the lunch-table conversation turned to Cresspahl's time in the Netherlands, and three hours later we were walking along the Brouwersgracht in Amsterdam; and not once had we had to hurry; and he paid not with his credit card but by having the tickets rewritten, and a pretty generous rewriting it had to be. Mention a hotel not far from Stephen's Green of which you have forgotten both name and street, and there we all were in Dublin the next morning, and the hotel porter greeted him by name. He tips, but not too generously. That was how we traveled through Ireland, and invariably the bags were at the station, the trains were about to leave, the taxis were waiting at the door.

In Limerick we had the third morning free, and D. E. drove us to a place called Kilkee built around a harbor that hugs a green piece of the Atlantic, and still we were in plenty of time at Shannon Airport for him to have his two bottles of wine with lunch and a chat with a Customs official about the prospects of a Third World War (the man would have liked to bet). Then we were airborne, and the machine was in fact a DC-8, and except for us there were only five passengers so that a crash would not have been worth while, and nine hours later we were home. Marie likes his way of looking after others. Another person, although even his unexpressed wishes might be fulfilled by such sleight of hand, would still rather be allowed to watch and see how it is done.

It is not his will that he is asserting; it is what I have expressed. We live together, each in his own place, and this again he has turned into an arrangement that is more dominated by his need for completed solutions than by my distrust of final settlements: what was planned as loose has become firm, and he would be capable, moreover, of demonstrating my error to me. True, he does make suggestions. One suggestion was the excursion to Kilkee, that horseshoe of houses, almost all one story high, that looked more rustic than maritime, around a patch of captured ocean, with one or two summer hotels, a low village with the everlasting wind for a neighbor, its back to Europe, its face to the Atlantic clear across to the coast of America. At the western end of the horseshoe, on Marine Parade, stood a house that was empty behind its solid front steps, sound walls enclosing five rooms, protected from the full force of the gales by the Duggerna Rocks. For D. E. it was a possibility. Not only could he pay for it, but by next year he would succeed in transforming the house into a system of gadgets that would serve the occupants from every angle; by the time we moved in, at least the local tradesmen would have had nice things to say about us. It would have been three quarters of an hour to Shannon Airport, once every eight weeks I could have driven there, a wife waiting for a husband to come home from work. Marie would have got used to a school in Limerick. The place is quiet in the fall, in winter, in spring; less than fifteen hundred people live there. From the bathing place called New-found-out, a stretch of grass from which one can dive forty feet into the sea, a path winds over the rocks, past the bay where the *Intrinsic* went down in January 1836, to Look-Out Hill over two hundred feet above the sea. There the seasons would once again teach me the changes in the colors of the water. In winter the nights would be very high and black. From my walk at night I would return chilled to the marrow, as if to Cresspahl's house. The towns would be very far away; almost a world away. This is what D. E. believes: that I need a house of my own. He did not put the question into words: before we flew on, we made one last trip there. No doubt he has made a note of the names of the real-estate agents in County Clare, Ireland, and of how to reach them by telephone; perhaps he is still waiting.

What he would like is "to live with us." We do not even share the same background now. He does not regard his past, the people and the country, Schusting Brand and Wendisch Burg, as reality. He has turned his memory into knowledge. That life of his with others in Mecklenburg, only fourteen years ago after all, has been tidied away as if into archives in which he keeps files on people and towns up to date, or closes them when deaths occur. It is all still there, of course, to be summoned on demand, only it is not alive. He no longer lives with these things. After only a few years in the States he began using the four dots for the ratio sign in his lectures instead of the German two, the oblique stroke for division instead of the horizontal one, as if he had never learned it any other way in Wendisch Burg, and when he wrote on the blackboard his block letters came out in the American style, flowing anonymous characters. He is not a good teacher. His delivery deceived the students because of its chatty tone; anyone who started making written instead of mental notes was lost. D. E. had no desire to commit himself to anything more than that this was the known extent of physical knowledge, with the tacit addition: for the time being that's the best we can do. Questions, slowness on the part of his students, he endured with apparent good humor, he also seemed willing to help; but the delay pained him nonetheless. Incidentally, during the lecture he had forgotten there was a guest among the students; he had to recall me to himself, in spite of having recognized me. At the college he was respected, he was on friendly terms with two or three gifted students who thought they could privately pick his brains in the cafeteria. In his field he feels most at ease with his peers. His peers not only rank equally with him in technical know-how and ideas, whether, exempli gratia, D. E.'s monitor stations in Alaska and Greenland are earmarked for work other than defense: they let themselves be convinced of the existence of an opposition between the arms systems of the United States and the U. S. S. R., and after that his peers are not susceptible to moral attempts at disruption. An occasion involving moral issues was one of the few times D. E. almost blew up. He did not actually shout, but his speech became angry, arrogant. He wanted to express contempt. In his opinion, morality is the business of the administrators of power who proclaim it, and not the concern of their dependents, whose business is survival. A man who does not work visibly in defense, even if only in the bakery of his army camp, is working for defense; the difference is purely subjective, objectively trifling. Nevertheless his peers are capable of discussing the case of Klaus Fuchs, the atom spy, in terms not of the phenomenon of loyalty but of the psychological knots of the traitor. Moreover, they know with wonderful certainty that none of them will ever be treated as a war criminal and each of them will be considered a specialist; this removes any inhibitions. At the same time: all D. E.'s friends in his field are interested in the socialist thing. For them it is a theoretical exercise, the playing with an unavailable alternative; the roots of this are not biographical. There must be some marriages among them that were contracted at an age when youthful scientists join a party. What they really want, in the abstract, is to have a complete revolution handed to them, humane in its execution, humanistic in its effect. It is an attitude that long ago renounced individual protest and hence any basic change in conditions; it can live beautifully on its proofs while at the same time resembling the type of thinking formerly known as "petty bourgeois," the kind of which D. E. jokingly accuses me.

He does so jokingly. He does not presume to know me. When I do something that he considers peculiar to me, he smiles and recognizes something, but he does so openly. He makes no secret of what he has observed. If he has acquired any image of me at all, it is of scarcely more than my needs (as he understands them). He shows many sides that are bearable, most of them amusing. He does not discuss Marie's father with her, or even with me; yet he knows everything about Jakob's life that can be learned from correspondence with friends in Mecklenburg. He too has his highly personal prejudices and trots them out as careful observations or unquestionable facts. For instance, he calls the DC-8 the most efficient of all aircraft, yet knows no more about flying than what is required for a license to fly a single-engine propeller plane. He plays the North American game of showing off one's money, he shows off a house, he shows off a Bentley; but the house is being paid for in installments, the car is secondhand, and he does his flying with borrowed machines. He invariably enjoys keeping the neighbors in the dark about his finances. His demeanor is equable; he never loses his temper. He claims no prescriptive rights from his visits to us; he comes as a guest. He is not jealous, only of what goes on in my mind; he would like to be the only person, or at least the first, to know. There are many things that only he knows. What more does he want? Can't he rest on the laurels of his famous love affairs and enjoy the comforts of visiting a family where there is already a child, a child, moreover, who has always understood him? He says: No. Am I, at my leisure, financed by him, to make what he cannot make: a life for one person only? He would reply: As far as I'm concerned. He would even spare me the pretenses of social life. He does not even want children by me. Were I to let him put me in a cage, it would be built according to my specifications, down to all the charge accounts and credit cards I could wish for. The only thing is, what does he need someone in his life for?

Marie could endure it. She could endure living with him in an apartment, in a house. They were walking along beside the Thames near Richmond as they always do, side by side ahead of me, without a care in the world. Not only was she proud of the black coat with the fur collar that he had bought her on Regent Street; she was also content to be seen in the company of this distinguished-looking gentleman. They laughed as they talked, and the very turn of Marie's head toward him shows how she enjoys the exchange of banter. Marie walked with her hands clasped behind her, because that was what he did.

That I believe. The rest I don't believe.

D. E. telephoned today from the north, on a strangely resonant line that brought his voice right into the room. He is in a different time zone, yet he managed to hit the exact quarter-hour in which our household has been put to bed, although Marie not yet. He took his time. He dawdled away the conversation with inquiries about Karsch and the weather, and the monitoring service will scarcely have noticed that toward the end we were roundly rebuked. It had been a mistake to report the theft of his car to the Newark police, because the license plates were false, presumably exchanged "where we always get gas." "Happy Thanksgiving," says D. E. amiably, after instructing us to spend the holiday on a trip to a gas station across the Hudson. Marie, who finishes off the conversation, brings me the tidbit of information that "Amen" will do just as well as "over and out," with God as with people, when talking by radiotelephone. Once again he has taught her something and, what's more, something she can use only with him.

It is true, we did not look at the car's license plates. It is true, the Mafia has friends in the New Jersey police. It is true, once again he has thought of everything, and we had doubted his superintelligence. It is all true, and it is almost unbearable.

The Government finally admits that it actually held 25,000 soldiers in readiness for the Washington demonstrations last month in order to prevent riots in the capital's slums. Not only troops were to clear the people from the streets, huge bulldozers were also lined up for this purpose.

November 23, 1967   Thursday

It is the fourth Thursday in November, according to law Thanksgiving Day, for the 327th time in the United States. But we had a job to do in New Jersey and were being rushed along under the streets through which Macy's parade would travel, as it did every year, from 77th Street on Central Park West to Herald Square, gigantic blown-up figures of American folklore, from Donald Duck to Smokey the Bear, brandished by children dressed as pierrots, accompanied by raucous rousing music, for the purpose of giving thanks to the Lord our God. The Mafia was evidently still stunned by yesterday's raid carried out by agents of the Internal Revenue department on a telephone exchange in Brooklyn where Joseph (Butch) Musumeci, under the protection of Albert (Kid Blast) Gallo, accepted bets on the results of football, baseball, and horse racing in New York, with an estimated annual turnover of 11 million dollars. Now the participants have been charged with failing to purchase the fifty-dollar federal gambling-tax stamp, and at Newark Airport stood D. E.'s car, untouched, with—it was quite true—false license plates, somewhat dirtier and still wet from this morning's rain. And neither Karsch's business partners nor the honorable police of the State of New Jersey obstructed us on our way to the gas station "where we always get gas." We were expected by an elderly mechanic who kept wiping his shovel-shaped black hands on two rags yet offered neither hand to us. His chief concern was to prevent us from explaining anything to him; and he would not let us watch him. After fifteen minutes he drove the Bentley with D. E.'s proper inviolable identification out of the repair shop again and even refused a tip for working on a holiday. All that dignity, patience, and gravity that he showed in his face was once regarded by us as the hallmark of honesty; this is how he has managed to survive to the age of seventy. When we left he shook hands with Marie, with a rather embarrassed smile, as if he were trying to warn her of something, and Marie bobbed a vestigial curtsy, thanked him gravely, and addressed him as Sir. Sometimes, when I am not looking, she can treat Negroes arrogantly, imperiously; but she would not dare any such thing toward a friend of D. E.'s. "It's always a pleasure to be of service to a real gentleman," said the gas-station attendant about D. E., perhaps as a message for him. It would be silly to say that D. E. has no secrets from us; we shall keep a few things from him. That afternoon we were back on Broadway, the part we live on.

We emerged from the subway on the east side of 96th Street, and I recognized Francine's look from seeing it so often. I did not know her name. She was standing close to the window of a junk store; there was something permanent about her posture, as if she were going to stay there all day, on strangely stiff legs, her arms hanging down, tense. She was keeping an impassive eye on the stairwell as if she were merely counting the people one by one, with no interest in their differences. When she recognized Marie her eyes suddenly focused on her, and her immobile weary face relaxed, prepared itself for an expression. But she waited for Marie's nod, and she returned the greeting with such hesitation that it looked as if she were afraid this response was already going too far. I recognized the look. Many afternoons around this time, when working people are returning to the area, this girl had been standing at this exit, almost as tall as Marie, a "colored girl," and she always looked at me as if expecting me, and immediately turned her face aside. Once she followed me, at a distance, from window to window of the delicatessen stores, across 97th and 98th streets and right across Broadway, and she had disappeared, as if she had had some other objective after all. Then I forgot her again, and in the forgetting only the details of her face remained, the color that is known as chocolate, the hair that is not permitted to grow kinky but is twisted into curious little braids, the eyes that though open are vacant, very full protruding lips that may show grief, or not grief. "That was Francine," said Marie.

Marie said:
Sometimes she spends half the afternoon there.
She stands there because she can't go home.
At home she shares a room with three kids, as well as her mother.
The kids are two brothers, fifteen and a year and a half, and a sister of fourteen. They're only half-brothers and sisters, she has her own father.
None of the fathers are there. Otherwise the mothers wouldn't get any welfare, that's the law.
I expect she's there today because it's a holiday.
On holidays the father of her youngest brother sometimes comes and brings wine and drinks it with her mother and sleeps with her mother in one bed.
It doesn't bother her any more, except maybe on a holiday. Roast turkey, pie, maybe she doesn't want to see that they don't have those things at home.

Her pocket money is twenty cents every two weeks, when the welfare check arrives.

There was a time when she used to stand at the subway station waiting for her father. She doesn't know what he looks like, he never came back after she was born. She knows he's called Benjamin, and she's sure she would recognize him.

Her mother tells her nothing about this father. Once she blabbed. That's how Francine knows that twelve years ago he had a room in a hotel on West 102nd Street.

When she's at home she has to do her homework on a tray on her lap.

What bothers her most is her little brother, the one by the fourth father. She has to change his diapers, carry him around, put him to bed.

Her mother doesn't look after the kids. She has the TV going all day, from first thing in the morning.

When her mother doesn't have a visitor at night, the oldest brother sleeps in her bed and Francine with her sister and the baby in the other.

There are only two beds in the room. The oldest brother has to sleep with the mother ever since he tried to do it with Francine's sister.

You know what I mean.

He did it one more time with her, and the mother gave him a beating. That was a week ago, and since then he hasn't been home.

Maybe Francine's waiting for this brother at the subway.

But she doesn't squirt poison into her arm the way he does.

He began doing that two years ago, when he was twelve and a half.

They're mostly boys in a gang, they sit in a bunch on the roofs and do it together.

Then he taught Francine's sister how to do it.

She's scared now.

She's scared because she thinks she's pregnant.

At first she did it lots of times with a boy friend in the toilet so she'd get pregnant. She wanted a baby so the welfare would give her her own account and she could live without the family all by herself in her own room.

But now she doesn't want a baby any more. She figures she doesn't know enough yet to tell the child.

Francine says she doesn't use the needle.

Francine says there's a gang of girls in her building and they hold a knife to your throat if you refuse to use the needle the way all the others do.

That's why Francine likes to stand on Broadway where there are policemen around.

She only goes upstairs when there's a grownup on the stairs whom she trusts.

But she doesn't trust very many. Lots of them are on drugs or vermouth or on . . . I don't know what it's called.

The building's on West 103rd Street, right around the corner from us.

The old apartments there have all been turned into single rooms, with a family living in each one.

The landlord sits in his apartment with the door open. It's like an office, with a counter. Only instead of glass in front of the counter there's a wire grille instead. They have to pass the rent to him through the grille.

That's as far as I went with her.

It's not that I'm scared of the room. We've got cockroaches too. Or of the oldest brother. I'm scared her mother will be mad at me. As if it was all my fault.

Francine's doing much better in school now.

I showed her the public library on 100th Street and took her there because she didn't want to go alone. The librarian gave her a card right away and told her she can read there and write too, during regular library hours. They're not open all the time, of course.

Now Francine's grateful to me again, said Marie.

November 24, 1967   Friday

The dollar is taking another beating. In London and Paris they are buying gold like crazy. The New York *Times*, incidentally, estimates the amount of private American capital invested in Europe since 1958 at ten billion dollars and describes the spread of the American way of life from Sweden to Spain. As examples of European influence in the United States it cites the appreciation of a Château Mouton Rothschild or a Spanish Riscal, as well as a sense that there is something to be said for the European obsession with bidets.

Marie refuses to approve of Cresspahl's having wangled a further eight months in Richmond, Greater London. She insists that people should live together once they are married. Here she has conceptions of order.

For eight months Cresspahl could watch from the outside how

the Nazis were setting up their state. He must have taken it all in. Since he had been living in towns he had read newspapers, although in a more rustic manner: only when the day's work was done, when he could be sure that no useful task awaited him, slowly, as recreation almost, and with a deep-rooted suspicion that reserved for his own eyes proof of the truth of the news. But he had actually seen the things of which reports from Germany continued to inform him.

What he had missed from March onward was supplied in detail by the London papers. On March 21 the President of the German Reich decreed impunity for the crimes of the Nazis. On the same day he decreed capital punishment for misuse of the uniform or insignia of Hitler's private army and instituted special courts. Now Hindenburg had signed enough papers, now Hitler could go for the real power of the state. For the Nazis' state was not yet ready when Hitler was appointed Reich Chancellor on January 30, 1933; only his supporters thought it was. Others mark the beginning with the March elections; but Hitler had received only 43.9 per cent of the votes by then, less than half. We mark the beginning of total dictatorship with March 24. On that day the German Reichstag, or at least those members who were not under arrest, accepted the "law for the abolishment of the plight of people and nation," a law with which Parliament renounced its rights and transferred them to the new Government. From then on Hitler could invest his ideas with the force of law, so he began then and there in March with the dissolution of the individual German states, and ordered the immediate carrying out of executions, by the rope if possible. By October 1939 he had brought in 4,500 of his laws and was using the Reichstag simply as a glee club, the costliest in the world. These were the added attractions offered in March 1933 by the German Reich Government to Mr. Heinrich Cresspahl, of Richmond, England, in the event of his return.

When Perceval realized that the boss's wife was not going to return in a few days or even a few weeks, he gave notice. He would not give any reason, but avoided Cresspahl's eyes. Once he had received his reference, he stayed away from the workshop from one day to the next. During those three weeks Mr. Smith had kept the lad's nose to the grindstone so that the remaining orders could, if necessary, be filled without him; nevertheless Cresspahl began to miss the boy. Fifteen years later he could still tell people that Perceval had been one of those fellows who, for all his size and huge appetite, retained an angular, bony appearance. Very big ears. Very pale complexion through which the color would flood in a rush. When he lifted a heavy object his whole body seemed to contort; he often forgot to use more than strength on the job. His work had to be checked; maybe he didn't have what it took to be an independent carpenter. It wasn't so much his work that he enjoyed, Cresspahl would say, as praise for achievement; but praise he had to have. Now and again Cresspahl would ask about him in the town, but Perceval had not applied for a job in Richmond. The parents came to see Cresspahl and had no idea where their son was. Perceval did not come back. It was true that one night in the middle of April Cresspahl's windows on the second floor (where Lisbeth had had the sitting room) were broken, with some care, but he preferred not to believe that of Perceval. The silent departure seemed more fitting, Cresspahl thought.

Mrs. Jones came over, unasked, from Brixton and offered to run the house for him, at least until she had found out why young Mrs. Cresspahl had not returned with her husband. Cresspahl bade her good-by, pressing a pound note so blatantly into her hand that she never did return. Once a week he would go through the rooms with a broom. Where the broom did not reach, in the curtains, in the upholstery, dust accumulated and congealed with soot. Sometimes it pleased Cresspahl to think he could chop it all up. And there were already streaks on the windowpanes with which he had replaced the broken ones; he had not even wiped off his puttied fingerprints. Cresspahl had his lunch in the kitchen with Mr. Smith, sandwiches from a pub, with beer for Mr. Smith, water for Cresspahl. In his younger days Mr. Smith had gone to sea, and on one occasion the crew had forced him to substitute for an incompetent cook. On the strength of having survived that voyage, he would sometimes try his hand at bacon and eggs. But he had not learned to clean pots and pans, and when he ran out of unused utensils he gave up cooking. Sometimes Cresspahl would keep him back of an evening, for supper he used to say, but he had gin on the kitchen table. With half a pint under his belt Mr. Smith would forget all about his shyness and begin to talk. He invariably referred to Perceval as T. P. T. P. had actually talked more about the boss's baby than about Mrs. Cresspahl. "Young folks like that want to have a family," Mr. Smith would say, so distinctly and slowly that Cresspahl realized how often the thought had occurred to him. Now and again Cresspahl would consider offering him one of the vacant rooms. But Mr. Smith did not need a family and around ten o'clock would get to his feet, leaving half an inch in the bottle for good manners. He showed very little, except that at this hour he could not resist putting all his intentions into words. "I'll be on my way now," he would say. "It's high time I was gone," he would say. Then he would leave. At the door he would say: "My specs." Then he would adjust the tarnished Health Service frame on his little wizened face. Cresspahl could still hear him talking on the stairs, occasionally repeating to himself: "That's all right, Mr. Smith."

In May the German Reich Government recompensed the German industrialists' financial contributions to Hitler by a series of rewards in kind. It ordered the trade unions' day to be celebrated as the "Day of National Labor." On May 2 it occupied the offices of the trade unions. On May 10 it transferred the seized funds to an institution of its own creation, something called the "German Labor Front." The Communists had been taken care of; now it was the Social Democrats' turn. They were the only party that had not voted for Hitler's Enabling Act. Their hasty approval on May 19 of the German Reich Government's foreign policy came too late to do them any good. On May 10 their offices had been occupied, on May 22 their party was banned. That's the way to do it. These were some of the prospects held out by the German Reich Government in May 1933 to Mr. Heinrich Cresspahl, of Richmond, England, in the event of his return.

In May Cresspahl summoned Albert A. Gosling, Esq., to the workshop. He did his best to pick a quarrel with Gosling. He positively rubbed his nose in the meager entries in the order book; by May he had already stopped accepting orders. Little Mr. Gosling of the generous gestures was delighted to be able to recoup the loss by saving on Perceval's wages; Gosling the businessman. Even Mr. Smith with his morning headaches could not resist a cheerful grimace and exchanged his plane for a very fine rasp in order to sharpen his hearing. Cresspahl drew Gosling's attention to the wooden chests that he had deliberately stacked up beside the door. He did not tell him that the sturdy chests, which had not been cheap to make, were intended for Lisbeth's belongings; he quoted him shameless reductions in the price; Cresspahl's own requirements. Gosling liked the chests. He ordered one for himself, but of red cedar, with brass fittings and handles. Cresspahl brought up the subject of statements that Gosling could prove to have been made before witnesses, statements directed at Cresspahl's business conduct (he invented this on the spur of the moment). It transpired that Gosling had indeed agitated not only against Germans but against this particular German, for Gosling took off his black hat. He hooked his somewhat overlarge umbrella onto the workbench. He held out his hand to Cresspahl. He apologized. He realized the error of his ways, he said.

He was very sorry about it, now that it was the German nation that was showing the world how to put one's own house in order. He said it was deplorable that England misjudged Sir Oswald Mosley. Mosley was the leader of the British Fascists. Cresspahl gave up the idea of a quarrel with Gosling.

Had he been able to infuriate Gosling sufficiently for the latter to give him notice, he would have been free on the spot.

Cresspahl gave his notice one week later at Burse, Dunaway & Salomon's. Now it would be another six months before he could leave. If he needed time to think things over, he had allowed himself plenty.

Right, Gesine?
Or was Lisbeth to be given time to change her mind?
Right, Gesine?
You still had plans for Richmond, Cresspahl!
Right, Gesine?

November 25, 1967   Saturday

Today the New York *Times* tells us that Field Marshal Erich von Manstein, who planned Germany's blitzkrieg against France in 1940, marked his eightieth birthday yesterday in Hirschenhausen, West Germany. The item immediately follows the daily war report from Vietnam.

A couple in Chico, California, received from Vietnam a coffin containing a strange man instead of the son reported killed.

At the end of April 1933, Dr. Berling gave young Mrs. Cresspahl permission to travel to England. He spoke as though he had never advised her husband to remain in a changed Germany. He was washing his hands behind her so that all she could see of his face were the heavy bluish cheeks. She had no proof that he had had the nerve to give advice to a married daughter of an Albert Papenbrock. She was so taken aback that anyone should regard the opposite of her wishes as a sensible course of action that she did not tell him off, not even when he added: "And give my regards to that old rascal in Richmond! I know Richmond. Bushey Park, the tame deer . . . you're young yet, Mrs. Cresspahl. Make something of it."

Anyway, now she had something to write to Cresspahl about. Not everything, just the regards from Berling.

She might have put his mind at rest about the Tannebaums on Short Street. For their experience was much duller than what happened to the Jews in Wismar and Schwerin, according to the tales arriving in Jerichow. The regional headquarters of the Nazis in Gneez had, consistent with their actions everywhere else in their domain, ordered out-of-town Storm Troopers to post themselves outside the entrance to the Jewish store; the sentries might have weakened under the persuasion of friends or relatives. Prause, the regional Nazi boss, was rather vague about the rural areas. In Jerichow the news spread long before noon that Ossi Rahn and Max Breitsprecher were standing at attention, like a guard of honor, in front of Oskar Tannebaum's work pants and milking aprons, and after a while they actually were surrounded by a semicircle of spectators who had merely wanted to check out the rumor with their own eyes. Breitsprecher, a saddler from Gneez, felt uncomfortable. For one thing, he did not like standing there in public with Ossi Rahn. Ossi Rahn was so familiar to the courts in Gneez that he no longer had to give them his particulars when he was sued yet again for assault or alimony. Ossi Rahn described himself as unemployed; Breitsprecher would not have cared to employ him even to sweep the yard. Ossi Rahn had been living since 1930 in the Home for Vagrants on the outskirts of Gneez; yet in the taverns he always had money in his pocket; and in order to buy his boots he had had a collection taken up among the Storm Troopers. On the other hand, Max Breitsprecher had joined the Party as a businessman who had been promised that the power of the wholesalers and of the department-store chains would be broken; now here he was standing with handsome Ossi outside Tannebaum's store, depriving not only another businessman but also himself of customers in Jerichow. After a few hours he let Ossi march up and down on the sidewalk alone, with his slogans to the Germans whom he was exhorting to defend themselves and not buy from the Jew. When Breitsprecher came back out of the store, the shade was drawn down over the door, with a piece of paper tacked to it saying CLOSED FOR THE WEEKEND. Ossi Rahn tried to disobey an order. Ossi Rahn was hauled over the coals before the assembled civilians. Max Breitsprecher walked alone through the gathering, almost unseeing, at first incredulous when Pahl spoke to him, then very much relieved. (Pahl said: "Nice material, that uniform of yours. If it were made to measure it would fit you still better.")

Lisbeth Cresspahl hoped she would never even have to speak to Cresspahl about the remaining events of April in Jerichow. For Ossi Rahn, instead of withdrawing to Gneez, had marched off to the local Nazi headquarters in Jerichow. Not only had he denounced Breitsprecher, his superior, to Griem as having been guilty of cowardice and fraternizing with Jews while on duty: he also advanced the notion that a veterinary practice surely had some similarity with a business enterprise. Griem put four men at his disposal, and with these Ossi marched off to Dr. Semig's property. Griem would have recognized the Rammin horses and carriage in the yard and would have left; Ossi Rahn could not tell one horse from another, Ossi ordered the sentries to post themselves outside Semig's gate.

Baron von Rammin left Semig's office by way of the garden steps; he had not really registered the noise at the front of the house. To tell the truth, he was so annoyed he could hardly see straight. A few weeks previously, a good friend, Count Nagel, Beatus Nagel, had written him from Austria asking him to obtain a German remedy for "yaregg," and he, Rammin, had copied it from the letter, just as Beatus had heard it from his veterinarian, and passed along the order to Dr. Semig on a postcard. Dr. Semig had made a further inquiry over the telephone as to what was wrong with that dog in Austria, and Rammin had described how Beatus's Weimaraner was unable to stop pressing its head to the ground in a most distressing way. "Aha. Pain in the aural passage," Semig had stated in his offensively knowledgeable way, had found and obtained the medication from a basement factory in Württemberg, and would presumably have sent it, together with his account, to the Beckhorst estate, had not Rammin been coming to Jerichow this Saturday anyway and, more-over, was most curious to find out what in the world "yaregg" could mean. With his customary offensive tact, Semig had quietly handed him the little package without batting an eye when Rammin began to ask about the odd name of the disease and broke off on catching sight of the word "earache" on the label. The Baron had managed to cope fairly well with the good-bys, but when he climbed onto the coach box in Semig's yard he almost passed out in his fury. It made no difference that he bred horses, not dogs; thanks to the Austrian dialect he was now in the eyes of a professional man (Jew or no Jew) a person who could neither write nor think. The most intolerable part about it was the knowledge that this Semig would never show the postcard around, the prig, honorable to his last breath. Rammin's horses, which he had started off in the direction of Dora's vegetable garden, knew even without the aid of the reins that the only way to get out of this yard was to make a half-turn, and they considerately pulled the carriage toward the exit. Baron von Rammin saw men in brown uniforms on the street, occupied with an old woman who was refusing to yield up the basket she held tied in a cloth. Then they noticed the carriage and planted themselves in front of the gate. They called out something. They were making it difficult for the horses to obey. Now Rammin's baronial blood churned a variety of words behind his forehead, almost blinding him: the disgrace brought on by the Austrian dialect combined with the insubordinate behavior of the mercenaries of that Austrian Hitler, and mixed up with this were Weimaraner dogs and his fury at the Weimar Republic, and both horses had resigned themselves to the strange fact that on this occasion they were supposed to ride over humans and were galloping at full speed out onto the street. Ossi's subordinates saw what any fool could see; they flung themselves to opposite sides. Ossi Rahn had once seen that horses can be brought to a halt by grabbing them somewhere, but he did not know where, and in its confusion Rammin's right sorrel struck out as any good-natured person would in self-defense. Then Ossi Rahn saw no more, a well-aimed lash of the whip having closed both his eyes. Witnesses later recalled the horrifying crack of the whirling wheel as it crashed into Semig's corner stone, and that Ossi, flat on his side on the ground, merely pretended that the wheel had gone over his left leg. Von Rammin's horses raced along between the quiet gardens of the Bäk like a veritable thunderstorm, wrenching the carriage around the corner of School Street against the curb so that it half tipped over and took a while to get back onto the pavement. Then Rammin regained control of the horses. During the drive to Beckhorst he pondered on a face he had recognized among the spectators. For he had had two lucid moments: once when he caught Methfessel's eye, and once when he struck one of those faces into which he had been looking down from his horse, with the clearly formulated thought: Rabble will always come to heel. At home he was sufficiently calm to write a letter to Beatus Nagel about yaregg and the Austrian nation, from which in so doing he formally took his leave.

Ossi Rahn was still lying on the ground when Dora Semig closed both gates with her own hands. He was holding his leg and wailing. His subordinates helped him to his feet and propped him against Semig's front fence; they touched him only briefly and at once stepped aside. It was dawning on Ossi Rahn that he had been lying in the dirt at Mrs. Semig's feet. He wanted to smash up the Jew's house, no less. But none of the onlookers was paying the slightest attention to him, they were all listening to Granma Klug, who was brandishing her empty basket and shouting for her cat and enlarging shrilly on the why and wherefore and on people who steal cats, sick cats, cats that hobble about on three legs, cats the last-remaining pleasure of an old woman! Methfessel found the cat in the bushes in the front garden. It was a perfectly ordinary gray and black cat, but it did have a lot of scratches and old scars and a sore hind leg.

On Sunday Dr. and Mrs. Semig were invited to lunch by an aristocratic family called Plessen.

Within a week Methfessel the butcher lost three estates as customers. He went around in Jerichow avowing to anyone who cared to hear it again that on the day of the boycott he had only driven the long way around through the Bäk out of curiosity, like all the others, that he had looked on for only a few minutes, like all the others, that he had only stayed to search for the cat, which the others would also have done for an old woman, after all. He hoped his protestations would be repeated until they reached the ears of his offended aristocratic customers. But they were not. Methfessel started once more serving in the store himself. Then business in the store declined. He was in a quandary: if he put on the brown uniform, he would have a safe clientele that was not enough to live on. A public apology in the *Gneezer Tageblatt* would have brought the Storm Troopers down on his neck and not even aroused the sympathy of the aristocracy. Sometimes he became so confused by all this cogitation that he had to make a supreme effort and remind himself that he had done nothing, nothing at all, nothing whatever. The sole result of all his talking was that even his wife no longer believed him.

The law for the rehabilitation of the civil service threw a district magistrate, two federal railway employees, and three teachers out of a job, as well as the spa manager in Rande and Dr. Semig in Jerichow, the latter having been a civil servant in his capacity of meat inspector for the northern part of the district of Gneez. His income as meat inspector had so far enabled Semig to carry on as if nothing were the matter. He went to Gneez and called on the district council office. It was thereupon pointed out to him that as a non-Aryan he had been automatically retired as required by Paragraph 3. Semig pointed out that Clause 2 nullified Paragraph 3, Clause 1, in the case of civil servants who "had fought at the front for the German Reich or its allies during the 1914–18 war." He had deliberately worn his Iron Cross. The district veterinarian pointed out to him that the post of meat inspector had been open for one day, albeit in error, and it had been necessary to fill it. Semig pointed out that an error had to be rectified by the authority that had committed it. It was pointed out to him that an official post which had been filled could not be offered a second time. Semig pointed out the lack of any legal basis for this information. Thereupon the district veterinarian pointed to the door.

Semig went back from Gneez in the belief that it was all a matter of personal intrigue, directed solely at him personally. Lisbeth did not like to tell Cresspahl about this in a letter from Germany to England.

In May 1933, in the name and with the authorization of Baron Axel von Rammin, of Beckhorst Estate, Dr. Avenarius Kollmorgen instituted a suit in the Gneez district court against Oswald Rahn, day laborer, of the Gneez Home for Vagrants. Rahn was alleged to have frightened the plaintiff's horses, provoked a situation that constituted a traffic hazard, been responsible for the leg injury of one horse by the name of Hildegard von Etz as well as damage to one carriage wheel, and threatened the plaintiff with insulting remarks as well as danger to life and limb. When Ossi Rahn was taking a stroll late one evening on the Beckhorst estate, accompanied by some Brownshirt friends, a group of estate workers had lain in wait for him in the shadow of the barns and driven him and his cronies off the Rammin property with their cudgels; the Baron, incidentally, was away on a visit to his Thuringian properties. The next evening Ossi was caught attempting arson; in any event, all the witnesses gave evidence against him. Now he was already being held in the cellar beneath the Gneez courthouse. His cronies set out to pay a visit to Dr. Kollmorgen in Jerichow, but they were met at the door by Geesche Helms's sister, and Geesche Helms was married to the Jerichow police, and anyway Dr. Kollmorgen was out of town. Avenarius was staying at the Netherlands Arms in Schwerin, on Alexandria Street, and spent the evenings at Uhle's, at Wöhler's, at Heidtmann's, and at the Golden Grape, chatting with his friends from the Ministry of Justice and imparting to them the wisdom of wine-drinking. After a week Avenarius got his audience with Hildebrandt, the Reich Governor whom the Austrian had put in charge of the good state of Mecklenburg, and the interview turned into a copious lunch with Moselle wines brought over from Uhle's on Avenarius' recommendation. On Avenarius' return to Jerichow, the baskets of food and beer for Ossi were suddenly no longer accepted in the prison wing of the courthouse, then no more were delivered, then Ossi stopped receiving even slips of paper from his faithful Brownshirt comrades with advice on how to behave. With Baron von Rammin's permission, Dr. Kollmorgen also agreed to represent the secondary plaintiffs, for now Ossi's whole life was being exposed to public view. Ossi had used his fists not only out of political hostility but also out of sheer pleasure; that accounted for the large number of complaints. Ossi sat safely behind bars; that accounted for the detailed nature of the accusations. How Ossi had tried to strangle a hired hand's daughter during sexual intercourse. How Ossi had sold a complete game-preserve fence as kindling to the Castle Hotel in Gneez. How Ossi had regularly extorted sums of money from the prostitutes at the Castle Hotel. How Ossi beat his wife, how he let his children go hungry. It all came out, or almost all, and Avenarius, low of stature though he was, stood staunchly before the judges and spoke of the honor of the German nation, how it was personified, for example, in its elite groups, how such a group, for example, was represented by the Reich Chancellor's Brownshirts, who in turn, as had been loudly proclaimed, were determined to cauterize such a stain on their brown uniform to its very root! And where others come to a full stop, Avenarius rose lightly on his toes and gazed around the room with his solemnly shining eyes. As for Ossi's self-confidence, the *Gneezer Tageblatt* wrote that it had collapsed (like a pricked balloon). Two and a half years in jail satisfied a great many people. The aristocracy felt it only proper that it had been defended against the impudence of the rabble, and that, taking all in all, the affair was a credit to the new Government. Dr. Semig had immediately conceded that he was not competent to pass an opinion on Hildegard von Etz's swollen leg and that it was necessary for a professor of veterinary medicine to be brought from Rostock University; Semig, too, felt in some way protected by the sentence. Upper and middle classes breathed a sigh of relief because the court findings betokened assurance that the Storm Troopers could not get away with everything after all. The Brownshirts well-nigh rejoiced at the opportunity to appear in public as the enemies of injustice and the scorners of dirt, and ordered additional forms from regional headquarters for application to enter their ranks. Not everyone was satisfied. For the farm workers this single defendant was not enough. Kollmorgen began to have misgivings, partly on account of his dignity, and partly because he was being required by a number of courts to take on quite similar cases, but without being granted any further audiences with Hildebrandt. And what had the great to-do of the trial yielded for Methfessel the butcher? Nothing, if you asked him.

Not all of Ossi's exploits came to light. No one was told, for instance, of the favor Ossi had done a high-placed leader of the Brownshirts in Schwerin. Instead of being transferred to an ordinary jail he was handed over to the Storm Troopers to serve his sentence. The Storm Troopers sent him to a "concentration camp" that happened to be just across the southeastern border of Mecklenburg. There, it was said in Gneez and Jerichow, he did not work as a convict but supervised the convicts at work. Then from one day to the next his family went off to Fürstenberg, and Roswitha Rahn had paid for the tickets out of her own pocket; now the rumor was considered proved. Methfessel started drinking a bit and one evening at the tavern gave vent to his opinion on justice in the New Reich. Methfessel was taken to Fürstenberg to see it at first hand. When he returned after four weeks he refused to say a word, not even whether he had run into Ossi Rahn. Lisbeth Cresspahl did not like to write about this in a letter from Jerichow to Richmond.

Come on, tell me, Methfessel.
Can you keep your mouth shut, Frieda?
I'm your wife, aren't I? Silent as the grave.
Then don't dig yourself one.

Young Mrs. Cresspahl was so confused that she found herself doing things she had not planned to do. Once in the middle of the day she took off every stitch she had on and adjusted the big mirror in the front parlor so she could inspect herself from head to toe. You could hardly tell now that she had borne a child. She had borne the child for Cresspahl; that was one of the promises she had kept. Why wasn't that enough?

She had agreed to Cresspahl's choosing Semig as godfather for the child. Why had her consent not been enough? Now Cresspahl was sitting comfortably in England and wanted her to stand up for the Semigs in his place. Since April 11, the day of Semig's dismissal, she had shown up at his front door only once; it had not been the looks of his neighbors in the Bäk that had bothered her, it was Semig's house that she found hard to bear. It had always been quiet there, apparently the Semigs wanted to do without children; now it also lacked the moving about of the maid in the kitchen, the ringing of doorbell and telephone, the driving into the yard of carriages and carts. And Semig had a way of emerging politely from his office for ten minutes to sit in the front room, but silently, gazing absent-mindedly at his joined fingertips. He looked different too, ever since shaving off his little square mustache. And Dora emphasized her Köster blood, no matter how kindly the visitor might dismiss the injustice done to Semig as an injustice; Dora kept her gaze averted like an elderly schoolteacher turning a deaf ear toward incorrigible misbehavior. Meanwhile they could hear Semig pacing up and down in his empty office. Lisbeth had only hinted that Cresspahl might buy the car which had just been delivered to Dr. Semig and for which he now had no use. The Semigs interpreted everything as pity, whether it was the visit or an offer of help. They were so preoccupied with their misfortune that they did not even listen. Cresspahl imagined it would be easy and no more than decent to continue on friendly terms with them. He had no idea how difficult she found it.

At one time prayer had helped her. Now she had her St. Peter's Church right there and could sit in her usual place and yet returned home uncomforted. Her requests were specific and pessimistic. She prayed for Pahl not to throw himself at the Nazis like that with his made-to-measure uniforms at special prices. She prayed for Edith to be able to stop stealing from Louise Papenbrock's storeroom. She prayed for Käthe Klupsch not to denounce the Jews so blasphemously in the stores. She prayed she would have no more need of words with Cresspahl and that she might once again be tacitly understood by him. She prayed for help to be able to do the things she wanted to do.

And that you should live, Gesine.

You think I don't know the answer to that. I do know it. I won't say it.

If only she had known that new Pastor Brüshaver better, she would have liked to go to him and ask him specifically whether the Church saw sufficient wrongdoing to justify living in another country. Then she would have forced herself to think: Brüshaver says so too. But these last few weeks Brüshaver had been preaching a lot about the duties of a Christian toward others as toward himself; she found no pointers there.

She did not mean wrongdoing in the civic sense. Even Papenbrock might wander aimlessly about his house muttering something about bankrupts who feather their nests with other people's property; that wrongdoing was perpetrated by the authorities, hence legitimate. She meant wickedness, the kind of thing the Bible forbids and on which it imposes punishment.

And Cresspahl had such an advantage! In one opinion of the Nazis after another he had been proved right, although not in the one that they would start a war. It was downright silly of him to criticize the military significance in the name of the new trade union, the Labor Front. It was just that Cresspahl wanted to sit out this wrongdoing in that England of his, merely to avoid the contagion of guilt. Wasn't that selfish? Was it permissible for someone to leave his own country merely to live in safety? How could she write this to him in a letter?

Now and again she managed to raise a semblance of rage at Cresspahl. When she had confronted other men with her wishes, with possible ones or deliberately unthinkable ones, she had always been required to choose then and there between renouncing either the wish or the continued company of the men. When she insisted that the impassioned Herbert Wehmke, at age eighteen, simply abduct her from the third floor of Papenbrock's house, she had known that he would march off, emitting sparks. From Cresspahl, too, she had demanded something he could not easily do, but Cresspahl had listened to her and drawn her by her own wishes into a situation in which she had her share. He simply would not accept sole responsibility. It may have been out of respect for her; it was asking too much of her. Cresspahl demanded no more and no less of her than that she scuttle every one of her reasons and come to England with the child. Sometimes it did seem possible, and not even the gossip of the people of Jerichow could have held her back; then it occurred to her again that this would mean swallowing some of her pride.

They had agreed, of course, to remain apart until November; she had insisted on it herself, so that she too would have some sacrifice to point to. But it was something else again that Cresspahl actually never once came to see her during that time. It may have been for reasons of economy or whatever; still, in her eyes it was stubbornness.

In the latter part of June, Papenbrock acquired the habit of shaking his head at random intervals and saying: "No." The first few times he interrupted the entire conversation around the dining table. Then his family realized that he was merely summarizing his thoughts for his own benefit. For Papenbrock had ceased to be a member of the power establishment. The offices of the German National People's Party had been occupied and searched by the police in exactly the same way as those of the Communists and the Social Democrats; on June 21 it dissolved itself, on the 29th Hugenberg resigned from the Government. Papenbrock's soliloquies, his absent-minded behavior, worried Louise very much. She tried to scold him, in a playful manner she had long since forgotten, and she sat there, stiff as a poker, when old Papenbrock halted unexpectedly behind her chair, placed his hand on her shoulder and moved it back and forth a bit. He was looking into space, ignoring the others at table. The gesture had signified more than his usual forbearance. It had looked almost tender.

Early in July, Papenbrock received a telephone call from Schwerin. In Berlin, in the River Dahme near the Grünau ferry, a number of sacks containing corpses had been washed up. One of the sacks contained a man called Johannes Stelling, beaten to death. Johannes Stelling had been Prime Minister of Mecklenburg-Schwerin.

Papenbrock did not promise to attend the secret memorial service for Stelling; Papenbrock called in his children from the street.

At noon Horst Papenbrock appeared for lunch, and his packed bags stood in the hall. Horst was summoned to the office. Papenbrock bellowed at him for half an hour, just as a precaution. That afternoon Horst was on his way to Hamburg and Brazil. He had not put up much of a fight. When he said good-by to the family he had seemed strangely relieved.

It would have suited Lisbeth if Papenbrock had ordered her to go to England. But Papenbrock took no note of those wishes of his daughters that he had already fulfilled. Lisbeth had things the way she had planned them. And he had no intention of interfering in Cresspahl's affairs.

There remained Hilde. For the time being, Hilde's place was in this house. She was too frivolous for these times, and Alexander Paepcke had first to produce something substantial before being allowed to come and take her away again. In the late afternoon Papenbrock had telephoned Krakow, and the next morning Hilde was in Jerichow.

"You learn something new every day," said Papenbrock, somewhat embarrassed as he sat at breakfast with his two daughters. He did not altogether like it that his children would rather receive orders than make up their own minds. But he was content to know this now and was willing to accept it as being part of his children. He regarded it as one of their characteristics; it did not occur to him that it was a result of their upbringing.

"Hilde and I and the baby went to Rande for a swim," Lisbeth Cresspahl wrote to her husband in England. "In Rande the unemployed were put to work shoveling new sand onto the beach, it's almost like Travemünde now . . .," she wrote.

November 27, 1967 Monday

But in Richmond it was July, and Cresspahl was delighting in a tree that had matured in his yard. It was a wych elm. It had been worrying him since the spring when it started sprouting thick foliage on its lower branches and had become positively paunchy around its middle while its top continued to remain sparsely leaved and looked like a

shamefaced bald pate, and was too young for that. Then it dawned
on him that the tree was not diseased but had been forced to keep its
head in the wind while down below it had been warmed on all sides
by the surrounding house walls. In May he had still been able to see
through the top branches. But now the tree had put forth leaves all
over its body and was in fine fettle. Such were the worries my father
had in the summer of 1933.

That was in July, and already refugees from Germany were turning up at the Richmond gasworks. They arrived with greetings from
Erwin Plath, with confidential messages for Cresspahl. They were
told: When the cow loses her tail she finds out what it's for.
Wincing, they cut him short and would not listen to Cresspahl's
reasons for omitting to pay his membership dues to the Social Democrats for the past eleven years; what they wanted was a bed in a room
with a locked door. Later they talked about a "concentration camp"
near Fürstenberg where a fellow by the name of Rahn was known as
"Ossi the Benefactor," this being the way his victims had to address
him when they thanked him for beating and punishing them; one of
them knew for sure that only the other day, on July 8, Dr. Posner,
the Rostock pediatrician, had hanged himself "because he was a
Jew." When they had slept off the worst of the Nazi cellars and their
escape and their arrival, they stood around awkwardly in the hot yard,
elderly gentlemen most of them, stiff-jointed from sitting at the
Mecklenburg desks of the German Socialist Party, and displayed little
aptitude when Mr. Smith tried to teach them his brand of English.
They did not stay long. They felt uncomfortable in the home of this
Cresspahl: not just because guests, like fish, start to stink after three
days, especially strange guests. No, what was lacking was a wife. A
wife would not have put such outlandish food, and cold at that, on
the table; with a wife one could have talked about one's own wife
and family who had stayed behind in Germany. And in Cresspahl's
house it was apparently taboo to ask after wife and children. Cresspahl was equally taciturn and vague on the subject of politics,
whether it was the British Union of Fascists or the Irish Republican
Army. And one could not stand around indefinitely watching him
and that Mr. Smith of his at work, even the noise of their work
pursued one all over the premises. They soon found their way to
North Sheen station around the corner and went off in search of
their own kind in London, returning maybe once with quite a
different brand of English and returning no more.

While Cresspahl was traveling to North London one Sunday in
July 1933, someone was following closely on his heels, a short little

gentleman with an umbrella whose summer suit fitted him no better than if it had been borrowed along with the rest of his dapper appearance. Gosling had been as thunderstruck by the notice of termination of the employment contract as if he had been hit on the head by the proverbial roof tile which is said to be unjust because it falls without warning. By this time Gosling had learned to put not only two and two together but odd figures as well. He had believed Cresspahl to be safely on the leash that his foreign origin had looped around his neck. He had now very nearly grasped the fact that a property consisting of premises and machinery, even if he could not live in them and operate them himself, was less profitably transformed into cash by means of a straight sale than by employing people to work on the premises and at the machines. Sometimes he had felt he was skating on the thinnest of ice: at the thought of the time when an even smaller number of people might be able (or want) to buy the products of that labor; never had he so much as dreamed that the workers in their disloyal pigheadedness might be capable of doing him out of his regular as well as handsome remittances to his bank account. At first, having acquired a certain arrogance along with his increased income, he had not taken the letter from Burse, Dunaway & Salomon too seriously. Then with a shock of cold fear he had been forced to realize that this was not the day and age to adopt a high and mighty tone, in any case not for him; even his wife saw through his confidence.

It was annoying, it was presumptuous, it was intolerable that this German should remove the noose that had seemed so firmly in place, and it was humiliating that a personage such as Albert A. Gosling, Esq., should have to come cap in hand to a man like that. Now there was a disadvantage after all to the fact that young Ritchett no longer cost his weekly wage. (From time to time T. P. had dropped snide remarks to Gosling about what went on in the workshop, or about what Cresspahl was supposed to have implied; T. P. was hoping that Gosling would finally get clobbered.) This Mr. Smith played dumb; he was quite capable of gratefully accepting one gin after another and then ultimately losing the power of speech.

With the cunning of a big-game hunter, Gosling planned to encircle his victim and went not to Cresspahl but to Salomon to inquire about the nature of the German's "personal reasons" for giving notice. Salomon leaned his head against the inlaid lions on the back of his chair and regarded Gosling with as much astonishment as if the latter were naked, or clad in the skins of beasts. Gosling hastened to explain that actually it was not the personal aspect of

Cresspahl's reasons nor, needless to say, the reasons themselves on which he wanted information; merely whether Cresspahl's relinquishment of the position of trust was in any way connected with the person of Albert A. Gosling. Salomon allowed his gaze, which was both wounded to the quick and admonitory, to linger for a while on the hairs beneath Gosling's nose and, suddenly co-operative, promised to make inquiries. Some time later Gosling once again sat down on Salomon's visitor's chair and stretched out his legs in some embarrassment while trying at the same time to sit bolt upright. Salomon sat back relaxed and informed his client that the answer was in the affirmative. He had assumed a consoling expression that Gosling did not trust. The client desired to know whether and in what way this misunderstanding might be remedied. In this instance, Salomon informed him, the answer was in the negative. Gosling had the information repeated to him several times and now stood in front of the desk, leaning in such an intensity of rage on his umbrella that it was bent like a bow. It was useless; he was obliged with much clearing of the throat to depart.

Gosling needed no further proof that the Jew was hand in glove with the German, that he was cooking up some dire plot, was in the other fellow's pocket, and whatever else Jews are capable of. He did not dare go to Cresspahl; he did not fancy sitting through a new production of the objections and difficulties of the past few years all in a single afternoon. He wanted to construe Cresspahl's decision as the man's wish to return to his own country, because, and since, that Mr. Hitler had been introducing such sweeping changes there: just recently again with a law to prevent the passing on of hereditary diseases that allowed individuals so afflicted to apply personally for castration; on the other hand, Gosling could not understand this fellow Cresspahl's outlandish notion that for the sake of his patriotic conscience a man might give up his means of livelihood.

And Gosling was curious. He saw the German waiting on the platform at Richmond for a London train and followed him to North London as far as Seven Sisters Road and into the side street where the German rang the bell at the door of a private house. The German left after such a brief exchange that Gosling did not hope for much of a haul when he approached the door himself. It was opened by a woman, a landlady who might at one time have lived alone in what had formerly been a mansion, and Gosling believed that people who had fallen on hard times were easy prey. At first she resisted his questioning. Gosling made it relentlessly clear to her that it was a punishable offense to impede the work of the police. Now the woman became positively eager, and whenever she hesitated Gosling needed only to intensify his snarl and raise his voice. The stranger had asked after a Mrs. Trowbridge. He had not been there before. In September 1931 Mrs. Trowbridge had taken two rooms on the upper floor. She had moved out when the other tenants complained about the baby's crying. A lady, a considerate, unobtrusive person, but unfortunately with a baby that was sometimes fretful. And Mrs. Trowbridge's husband? Mrs. Trowbridge was a widow. And where had she moved to? To relatives near Bristol, but she had left no address, indeed why should she, since she kept so very much to herself.

Gosling would have been less disappointed had his detective skills sufficed to ask about the German's reaction to the fruitless information which, as it happened, had not been fruitless. So for the time being he did not discover that Cresspahl, evidently nonplused for a moment, had said: "What baby? What do you mean, a baby?"

That was in July, when the light was still pure white and without the brownish tinge with which the parching vegetation infuses the countryside in August.

November 28, 1967 Tuesday

Yesterday a representative of Dow Chemical addressed a student audience at Washington Heights and defended the manufacture of napalm and its supply to the Army. The spokesman, Dean Wakefield, began by maintaining that the war in Vietnam was not, "on the whole," a moral question. Dow Chemical, he said, was merely fulfilling its responsibility toward the national commitment of a democratic society (in Vietnam); moreover, the material was so simple to make that the Army could manufacture it itself. (The New York *Times* explains what napalm is.) Wakefield calls the members of the Krupp family "bad people." When asked whence he drew the standards he applied in making moral judgments on business enterprises, Mr. Wakefield replied: From history. "From history."

We long ago stopped buying household products made by the Dow Chemical Company. But should we also stop using the railway because it profits by the transport of war material? Should we stop using the airlines that carry troops to Vietnam? Should we renounce all purchases because they yield a tax of whose ultimate use we are ignorant? Where is the moral Switzerland to which we might emigrate?

The mail today consists of a letter with very large stamps. Each one bears the picture of an oak tree together with a person holding a book. The postmark shows a Jerichow without a w. That's where I lived for ten years. Would it be possible to go back there?

"Rande—WORKERS' SEASIDE RESORT
Town Council,
35 Street of National Unity.
Telephone: Jerichow 2 55.
November 24, 1967

Re: Your letter of August 20, 1967—
 Number of Jewish Guests at the Resort in the years preceding 1933.

Dear Miss Cresspahl:

We cannot refrain from commencing our reply to your letter with the observation that we are aware of the fact that you are a citizen of the German Democratic Republic. You are the daughter of Heinrich Cresspahl, deceased, and owner of the property at No. 3-4 Brickyard Lane, Jerichow, which remained occupied by your father until his death. Furthermore, you are still registered with the police as being of that address owing to your failure to notify the police of your departure, a fact known to us from the documents on hand.

You will appreciate that we did not take kindly to receiving a letter from you written from the United States of America, a country that is conducting a ruthless war of extermination against the brave Vietnamese people, from a citizen who not only deserted her native land at a time when it was forced to fight grimly for its survival and the efforts of every individual were essential, but has also betrayed Socialism.

These are the premises on which we are compelled to base our consideration of your inquiry.

We must commence by reminding you of the special conditions under which the German Democratic Republic lives, works, and safeguards peace. You will be aware that after almost twenty years of unremitting constructive labor our country now ranks eighth in the world in industrial production, and you will realize that hand in hand with this achievement have gone profound and revolutionary social changes, and that for the first time on German soil, in the German nation's only socialist state, men and women may look to a life of human dignity. Nevertheless, we must not lose sight of the fact that we still share a common frontier with a social system of capitalist stamp, a system in which former landowners and generals, revanchists and warmongers and, needless to say, the press barons and their accomplices, have grasped power and, consistent with their innate dispositions, are plotting day and night with the aim of damaging our young state, now that their efforts to destroy the very existence of that state have been frustrated. A frontier of this kind, however, exists not only along the borders of the territory of the German Democratic Republic, but wherever our opponents attempt to penetrate, even in the superstructure.

Under these circumstances we found ourselves asking the following question: What is the purpose of Citizen Cresspahl's inquiry? What can a person who has deserted her country for the camp of the class enemy have in mind with certain data from the prehistory of the German Democratic Republic and relating to an era preceding her birth? It certainly cannot be a case of nostalgia or personal reminiscence. It is therefore logical to assume an objective purpose. Our attention is drawn to the possibility of transforming these specific data, when observed from a simple socio-critical viewpoint even by eyes not trained in Marxist-Leninist methods, into actual occurrences with the participation and collaboration of actual persons. It would therefore require no special effort, and would be invested with a certain basic probability, for an enemy of our state to attempt, by manipulating certain—to some extent factual—data to create the impression that those persons who, in the years subsequent to 1933, either through their actions or failure to act, exerted an influence on the number of seaside-resort guests of the Jewish religion, and those persons who today are working shoulder to shoulder to build the hitherto highest-known form of human life, i.e., Socialism, are the same persons. This would be sufficient to establish the lie of latent anti-Semitism in the German Democratic Republic. No support toward the aiding and abetting of such efforts can be expected from ourselves.

We are faced here with a mentality lacking in even the most primitive knowledge of human psychology inasmuch as it disregards the thesis of the definition of consciousness by existence and of development through change. A person who, under the inhuman hegemony of Fascism, has succumbed to the temptation to participate in discriminatory acts against Jewish citizens is no longer the same person when he has consciously pondered and digested the fact of that temptation, quite apart from the circumstance that in our state such persons are barred from the leading functions of government and party. This corresponds to the policy of our state, which guarantees all minorities, be they national or religious, treatment according to the principle of equal rights. This fact is the best proof of the justification for the unremitting counteroffensive of the Ger-

man Democratic Republic against racist, supremacist, and colonialist
Zionism such as when, only six months ago, it raised its perfidious
and bloody head in the Near East.

Furthermore, we wish to inform you that the regulations of the
Department of Statistics of the District Council of Gneez prohibit
the issuing of isolated statistical information to private persons, even
when available.

Finally we wish to draw to your attention that your unlawful
departure from the territory of the German Democratic Republic
fourteen years ago has not absolved you from the obligations of a
citizen of the German Democratic Republic, and that our people and
government expect you to champion peace and understanding among
the nations and to denounce the imperialist warmongers in accor-
dance with the principles laid down by our constitution.

> May Peace Prevail!
> Schettlicht. Klug. Susemihl.
> Kraczinski. Methfessel.
> Village of Rande,
> District Council of Gneez,
> German Democratic Republic."

Sometimes Marie says of Sister Magdalena: "I wish she were in
Jericho!" It never occurs to her, so completely does she think in
English, that Jericho is a very faraway place, and not a pleasant one.
When you send someone to Jericho in English, you are sending him
to the devil, and when you merely wish someone were in Jericho you
want him to be in Timbuctoo.

November 29, 1967   Wednesday

Dear Marie,

Today I am trying for the first time to tell you something on
tape "for when I'm dead." You asked for this seven weeks ago, while
we were driving to Annie's in Vermont. Remember?

I read the *Times* today:

Oh boy.

Now you've got it on tape that I can't sing. "Like a glass with a
tiny crack in it," Julie Westphal used to say. Then she kept me in the
school choir after all. Among the second altos.

If Eisenhower were given a second chance he would invade
North Vietnam, if necessary Cambodia and Laos too. And he would
not call it an invasion of North Vietnam but "removing a thorn in

our sides." I'm telling you this because you once thought he was cute.

As a child I was inclined to lisp, now it helps me considerably, with th. Shall I try? "Removing a thorn in our sides." Can you hear it?

In the fall of 1956 they treated me like a child, like a mad-woman, in Jerichow. As if I didn't grasp their situation

Sometimes I'm so tired that I speak just as untidily as I think

My thinking doesn't seem tidy to me

The place I come from has gone

There are still some books around, you won't be able to read them. The ones in the glass bookcase. The sayings I always liked best were the ones with the words "said the lad." Foxes and cats and hedgehogs and almost all birds were supposed to be able to speak too. My favorite story was the one about the boy who sat on his bed and was so tired he couldn't even lie down. So he called his mother and asked her: "Push me over." But "the boy" was a kid who had a tough time of it.

The only horses you know are mangy ones, with flowers on their heads and moldy rags around their feet. We never drove through Central Park in a carriage, at first because of the expense, later be-cause we thought: That's for tourists.

When I drop a piece of china you say sternly: Watch your language.

Sometimes, in switching from something you claim to something you know, you talk like a horse that sees its stable door, and in your speech you gallop home like a horse with no one at the bridle.

In the days when you were learning to write, you would turn my specimen letters, which weren't always closed, into carefully closed ones, lengthen cross-strokes to join down-strokes, complete loops until the ends met.

Yesterday I explained a photograph to you. Ratzeburg 1960. "Yes, I can imagine that," you said. You always lay it on with a trowel, don't you. When I was a child I wanted so much to increase the surface on which love for one's mother can grow. I carried around a picture of her that showed her as a child. 1913. "Was that her?" I asked Cresspahl. In long long skirts. The picture was very brown. I didn't believe him. She took —. She did something to herself.

Your father died before he had any proper idea of the meaning of the words to die. I know no more than I need about your father.

And I don't trust what I know because it hasn't always been there in my memory, and then without warning it turns up as a recollection. Maybe my memory creates a sentence such as Jakob said or maybe said, might have said. Once the sentence is complete and there, memory builds the others around it, even the voices of quite different people. That scares me. All of a sudden my mind is carrying on a conversation about a conversation at which I wasn't even present, and the only true thing about it is the memory of his intonation, the way Jakob spoke

Today's sentence is . . . that I won't say it. It's a harmless sentence, no secret nothing emotional. Saying it is what would make it unbearable, uncanny

All I know about your father is what one can know about the dead. Volleyball player, socialist, subtenant. After a while objects move in front of the person, leaving only a little space in which he is supposed to have lived a life. The things that concerned him are things I can only imagine. He was concerned about his mother, but he gave her to me and left. Your father was good with girls. He was good with old women, with Cresspahl usually, with cats, with all his friends. Jakob was the only one with whom Wolfgang Bartsch could work a whole shift without a quarrel. And Jakob was good with people who were at the very end of their tether, with salesgirls in the evening, with freight-train conductresses. He was better with me than I was with anyone

If I, Marie—listen.

If I get involved with a person, their death might cause me pain. I don't want to go through that again. So I can't afford to get involved.

This doesn't apply to a child called Marie Cresspahl.

Sorry.

During the day, you see, I don't talk.

November 30, 1967 Thursday

Until recently, this was the way the Mafia operated: they would buy an ordinary tavern that was losing money, redecorate it, and keep a few homosexuals as decoys. For the past year it has no longer been a violation of the liquor laws in the State of New York to serve liquor to a declared deviate, and in town the bars patronized by sexual minorities have been yielding more and more attractive profits. Now the Mafia is beginning to sell out to regular operators and to reinvest the proceeds in private clubs for well-to-do sexual deviates, thus enjoying increased as well as faster turnover. Police informers would be

conspicuous among these customers. Things are well in hand again
now, and business is as usual.

It is true that Cresspahl failed, in the national plebiscite of
November 1933, to approve personally of the German Reich's withdrawal from the League of Nations, and in the simultaneous Reichstag elections to add his cross to the 92 per cent of Yes votes obtained
by the Nazi Party; he happened to be out of the country. He did not
even produce a child as a token of his confidence in a future under
the Nazis, as did the young parents of 1934; his child was intended to
grow up in England. Except that then he left her with the Nazis.
And when Cresspahl arrived in Jerichow at the end of November,
who had been appointed chief of the political police of Hamburg,
Lübeck, and Mecklenburg-Schwerin?

Heinrich Himmler.
Who would have thought it.
No one.
*In April came the decree to triple the Reichswehr within five
years. In September came the first "labor battle." In October the
German delegation left the Geneva Disarmament Conference. In
October the Reichswehr was alerted for sanctions by the League of
Nations. You felt very strongly about war. I thought you didn't want
to be in another war, Cresspahl. So why did you go to where there
was bound to be a war?*
But there was no sign of it yet, Gesine.
Oh yes there was.
No.
*Was it really that simple? Suddenly there were political death
sentences, but you just wanted to keep out of politics? They were
getting ready for a war, but they weren't going to call you up, you'd
been born in 1888? They may have had a phobia about the Jews,
but where you go nothing's going to happen to them? They ban all
political parties, and you belonged to one of them once, and maybe
things will work out better with a single party after all?*
Just about, Gesine.
I don't believe it.
*Hindsight's not only made you smarter, it's made you a down-
right paragon who's lost all understanding for other people. Where are
you living, Gesine? Can't you see your own war? Why don't you leave
so you can't be blamed? You know now what it's like when there's a
child. What will Marie say when she finds out?*

That dead men should keep their traps shut.
Isn't it enough that they're dead?
If I'm not to say anything, why are you talking?
I don't want to scare you, Gesine.
You just don't want to say it.
You say it.
Your wife was in Germany, and that's about all you thought of.
That's about all I thought of.

Cresspahl and Papenbrock's youngest daughter walked not only at night along the cliffs near Rande, they would walk arm in arm along the street in broad daylight too, and once again people in Jerichow were saying what a perfect love match the marriage was. One evening that Cresspahl couple couldn't even wait till they were inside Papenbrock's house and stood clasped in each other's arms in a doorway within a hundred feet of it, and when Ete Helms's footsteps paused too long the pair separated without haste and wished him good evening as calmly as you please. Ete Helms almost felt like ordering them to carry on, so he said later at home. The tales were good-natured, the curiosity was not spiteful. Maybe he, maybe she, would succeed, and they would live together in a way that was not really possible.

"Why won't you talk today," the child says finally.
"The Czech lesson has made me tired, Marie."
"Say something," she demands.
"Jen dou vode mně dál
láska mi vobešla."
"Go on!"
"Šaty měla podzimkové
a vlasy měla podzimkové
a oči měla podzimkové. . . ."
"Aha!" says Marie. "I just wanted to see whether you'd done your homework."

December 1, 1967   Friday

Yesterday's snowstorm has dressed up the trees outside the window as white sparkling strangers, swept the sky clean, and laid a dazzling mirror in Riverside Park for the unobscured sun. It left behind a wind which told everyone's bones that it is colder than six degrees below freezing, six point five to be exact. The brilliance, the chill in the air, had dressed the city in a clean change of clothes, as if it were a hardened reform-school kid being encouraged to make a new start. On Broadway, beside the steps going down into the subway, an alcohol victim had skidded on yesterday's frozen mud and withdrawn into unsuspecting sleep. Each person, no matter how hurried, stepped carefully over the prostrate figure's legs, like a horse over its fallen rider.

Instead of a letter Karsch sent us a blank check, "to cover the cost of a new telephone number." That was written in German, Marie was able to read it and considers it only right and proper. But the new number cost nothing. Our telephone company is obsessed with egotistical notions and would rather we use its services than be angry with it. Two days after the application we were "in business again," in the words of the mechanic, a man whose routine work had made him talkative and who persisted in trying to persuade us to go duck-hunting in the marshes of New Jersey. What do we do now with a blank check drawn on the Bank of the Holy Spirit in Milan?

Attached to the check are two galley sheets, apparently the last part of an article written by Karsch about his stay in the United States. So Karsch is one of those who are permitted to work in peace and to whom what they have written is sent to be reread before it is too late to correct the errors. But in this case he had not bothered with a handwritten explanation, and it is in Italian, Marie cannot read that, she wants it translated, instantly, word for word.

So before coming to New York Karsch had visited the Mafia in New England. He knows fewer people there and fewer details than his colleague Davidson, who two weeks ago published a similar report in the *Saturday Evening Post*; but it looks as though the federal police had allowed Karsch, too, to read some of the material picked up by their monitoring devices from the lips of the fathers and lieutenants of the Mafia in their own offices, and it appears from the article that Karsch, too, paid his respects to Raymond Loreda Patriarca, head of the family in the Boston area, and that with his own eyes he saw the old man sitting on warm afternoons on the steps outside one of his branch establishments, looking very stylish in his white sweater, white socks, and alligator shoes, with a fat cigar to play with and the kind of benign expression that can be worn only by someone who not only senses but sees his bodyguards close at hand. "But when a person regards himself as the Godfather, how can he fail to believe in his own innocence?" writes Karsch.

He does, it is true, describe the Mafia's sources of income, from

usury to rigged football games and horse races to its private production of LSD and the transportation of narcotics for the account of
associated families; but then as he writes his glance falls once more
on Boston Harbor and the *Constitution*, the ship named after the
American Constitution, open to the public, and Karsch reports: That
day it was closed. It is just as if he were talking to his readers, as if
he were certain of carrying out their orders. He does not include all
the details of Patriarca's career that Davidson did; but he does describe the lives of Patriarca's parents, immigrants from Italy, from
Sicily. The rumor that the Mafia wishes shortly to murder its father
because of his age and possible yielding to police interrogations
occurs in Karsch's article at a point that just fails to convict him of
insulting the Godfather. He does not omit the story of how Patriarca
once remedied a shortage of suitable employees by engaging non-
Italians without, however, instructing them in the practice and
ideology of the Mafia, in particular of omertà, and so must now not
be surprised to find the framework of his empire cracking. He offers
some sociology: how in Boston the Mafia has sunk to the level of
tavern brawls and uses noisy shooting in the streets and discoverable
corpses to settle matters that are disposed of in Chicago in discreet
silence and without trace, and that nowadays "the Boston peasants"
are being recruited for the really dirty out-of-town work. His description of the relationship between the Mafia and the New England
politicians is enough to rouse the reader to instant fury; but by now
Karsch is standing quite relaxed in Harvard Square, Cambridge, describing the streets that open onto the square and the subway kiosk
and that newsstand where side by side with the *Literaturnaya Gasyeta*
from Moscow lie newspapers from Italy.

He is mainly preoccupied, though, with children. The first is a
little girl he has watched in the Italian quarter of Boston, a nine-year-
old lady who stands behind the vegetable stall and expects the same
self-control and respectful behavior from customers that she shows
toward them; almost black eyes, usually hidden behind lids, graceful
dark sweeps of hair on her forehead, visible swallowing in the sinewy
throat, maybe scared after all.

So in Providence Karsch was beaten up by Mafia specialists. He
is not lenient with himself: he admits his defeat, and he shows no
pride in having survived the beating.

The second child was a four-year-old Swedish girl in the Copter
Club, at the top of the Pan American Building in New York, to
whom it was becoming more and more inescapable that within a few
minutes she would have to go up onto the roof and board the heli-

copter to the airport. Scared as she was, she sat down beside the gentleman sitting alone at the next table and consoled him for the fact that she would soon be flying off with her parents to the place "where our family was born from" and would have to desert him. When the flight call came, it took her by surprise after all. Pale and determined, she lugged along a heavy flight bag because that was part of the procedure, but at the foot of the escalator she turned once more and waved to the stranger, to make sure it would not occur to him to be sad at her leaving.

So Karsch went to New Jersey to follow up another rumor. He had so often heard talk of a giant grill, custom-made, on which the New Jersey Mafia was said to roast disloyal members or stubborn adversaries, that he was determined to have a try. Not only did he find the property, a spacious estate with recreation areas surrounding the seigniorial manor, he was also invited in by the master of the house, a first-generation Italian immigrant who was glad to try out his native tongue again with Karsch, enjoyed conducting him around the property, and over impeccable cocktails asked to be remembered to relatives near . . . He even ordered two of his bodyguards to accompany the visitor as far as a station of the PATH line to New York; however, on the way the two men succumbed to the temptation to milk this European a bit for their own account and, treating him with great courtesy, held him captive for two days in the back room of a barbershop in Newark. It was ludicrous, of course, to play the role of victim of two moonlighting subordinates, and the thing only became risky when it occurred to the two men that the foreigner might get them into trouble with their employer for contravening an order. Just the same, two days in shaving posture were ludicrous. It was from this situation that Karsch was rescued by the third child.

The paragraph devoted to this child does not describe her appearance; he has not even marked the passage. It only says it had again been a girl, a fourth-grade child who could not get over the fact that a grown man was more worried about the humiliating aspect of his situation than about what had led up to it; and the child had pointed out to this correspondent that he could not have prevented the incident even if he had had a gun along. This correspondent, it said, had been thoroughly cured of any romantic notions about the crime by the child's behavior. It was also clear to him now that the child wanted no thanks; solidarity fared better when merely noted.

"A tua disposizione, Fanta Giro," the article ends.

"It's all right with me if he phones again," says Marie.

December 2, 1967   Saturday

Lord Russell's tribunal for war crimes in Vietnam, meeting in Roskilde near Copenhagen, yesterday found the United States guilty on all charges: of genocide, the use of forbidden weapons, maltreatment and killing of prisoners, violence against prisoners, forced movement of prisoners, as well as aggression against Laos and Cambodia.

Jean-Paul Sartre, a member of the international tribunal at Roskilde, had already punished the United States on a previous occasion by refusing an invitation to this country two and a half years ago because its government was carrying on a war in Vietnam. Sartre's reason made every foreigner traveling to or living in the United States an accomplice.

In 1933 the Italian State Railway reduced its rates by 70 per cent in order to attract foreign tourists to the country and to a "Fascist Exhibition." Sartre bought the cheap rail tickets and visited Pisa, Florence, Bologna, Venice, Milan, Orvieto, Rome, and other towns. In Rome the philosopher complied with the conditions of the reduced fare and glanced at the glass cases in the "Fascist Exhibition" displaying revolvers and rubber truncheons of the "Fascist martyrs."

In those days Sartre read the newspapers "not well but diligently." In the fall of 1933 he went to Germany to spend a year at the Institut Français in Berlin.

The winter of 1933 was not a good time for Cresspahl to settle in Jerichow. In those days it was not yet known how to lay bricks in cold temperatures, and he could foresee that his daughter's property would not be suitable for working and living in before the following spring. True, he was now reunited with his wife under one roof, but it was Papenbrock's roof.

On the other hand, the separation from her had been good for the release of the process in which the act of missing and needing someone cleanses, scrapes, retouches, and paints the remembered image of the other person, until anticipation suppresses everything unwelcome and anchors the desired attributes and attitudes so firmly in the mind that the dream image can maintain itself for days in the face of reality; the separation had perhaps been too long for Lisbeth. Admittedly, he had arrived in Jerichow when everyone was asleep, and his knocking on Papenbrock's door may have sounded like bad news; but why had she been totally unable to recover from the shock or to stop crying until Louise Papenbrock led her back to bed? Old Papenbrock had been happily prepared to keep Cresspahl and two bottles of red wine company until the wee hours of the following day; to Cresspahl it seemed as though she had wanted to put off being alone with him. She had behaved as if his arrival meant the advent of something she had been dreading. He had tried to forget that first evening, and the very next morning saw once again what he had been wanting; and her way of giving him a teasing look, her head on one side, dovetailed so perfectly with his expectations that he made up his mind all over again to do his level best to make a success of his new start in Jerichow. But then he felt uneasy about the way she kept referring to the child as "your daughter," in a tone that implied something more than what he could see. Nor could he always make out what caused her to switch so abruptly from a gay laughing mood to one of somber brooding; he asked her once, and her reply had been almost a rebuke; she had no idea, she said, what was so gloomy about her expression, and he did not ask any more. Sometimes, too, she was so moody, impatient, touchy, that he wondered as he looked at her whether she would be in any shape to stand being told about Elizabeth Trowbridge. He put that off until later, reluctantly.

What's wrong, Lisbeth.
What makes you think there's anything wrong, Cresspahl.
I wish you'd be your old self.

Old Papenbrock was somewhat confused. It was with some difficulty that he found his way through the maze of new things and words being sent from Berlin to Jerichow: Reich Agricultural Estate, Entailed Farms, Winter Aid Program. He found something to object to in every law of the Hitler Government, but then also something acceptable. He found the ban on dividing or mortgaging entailed farms practical, while pointing out that the oldest son was not always the best farmer and that loans without security had never existed in his book. In the collections for the Winter Aid Program, he found the Austrian's words about starving compatriots humane, although he, Papenbrock, did not consider himself responsible for the starvation, and it bothered his conscience to then fork out a five-mark piece for the sake of his own reputation. At the back of his mind was always the nagging thought that the new Government had killed no less a person than a Prime Minister of Mecklenburg-Schwerin; but he thought the Reich Government might not know about that. For he had gone with some trepidation to the memorial service for Johannes

Stelling, he had shown himself quite openly in his black suit, and had they arrested him? Had they had the nerve to issue so much as a warning to an officer who had fought in the war, a pillar of the economy? Not a bit of it, my dear Cresspahl. Those people may be assumed to know how to behave. And as far as property reform was concerned, the danger was past now. Hadn't this Hitler announced on June 6 that his National Socialist revolution was over? If that's all there was to it, then it hadn't been so bad. It must have been difficult to see it in the proper light in England.

Louise had fixed up a regular apartment for the Cresspahl family in that part of the building which had been a self-contained gabled house before Papenbrock bought it because he needed the storage space in the attic. The accommodation consisted of two rooms with three windows facing Station Street, and the nursery with a window and a door to the balcony on the garden side. But Louise was not quite able to refrain from interfering with her daughter's new dignity and rights and actually made Lisbeth get up from the dinner table to fetch some forgotten object, and Lisbeth left her seat like a child. The first time Cresspahl let her go. The second time Papenbrock noticed something, and he called the maid.

Lisbeth's sister Hilde was still at the Papenbrocks', waiting to see whether her Alexander would succeed in getting back on his feet again as a solid citizen. When the sisters were together, Hilde was not as she had been in March. She was still the more self-assured of the two, carefree, gay, even-tempered; but she did not pay much attention to Cresspahl. She managed several times to revert to the topic of the mayoral election in October and to claim the required assets, if not more, for Alexander Paepcke. Old Papenbrock would then pull himself in and look so disgusted and amused that the very nose on his face seemed to express the reply he was unwilling to make to Paepcke's would-be helpful wife. Perhaps he welcomed the fact that Hilde had gradually come to regard her Alexander's missing trust funds and burned-out brickyard rather more as amusing, at any rate long-forgotten, affairs. Here was a daughter's wish Papenbrock did not grant. Paepcke placed in control of Jerichow's municipal finances: Cresspahl was tickled by the idea too, as long as it never got that far.

Cresspahl did not find it easy to take root quickly in Jerichow. It was not because the region was different from around Malchow, barer, colder, virtually treeless. It was not the alien surroundings. He had also been an alien in Malchow. In the Netherlands, in England too. Unlike Lisbeth, he did not need to know who lived behind every window. Alien surroundings had always been good for him, even if not to him. Something was missing here. Was it that the town was so small, so lonely on the flat land? Was it Avenarius Killmorgen with his tirelessly repetitive "Getting on all right, Mr. Cresspahl?" his features working conspiratorially as if to signify all manner of staggering secret information? Was it life in the home of and regulated by the habits of Albert Papenbrock? Was it being compelled to raise one's right arm whenever somebody walked along the street carrying a flag?

All through December Cresspahl's mind was still on a decision in the event that someone here should try to cross him up. He believed in his determination to scoop up Lisbeth and child and leave the country. He believed that was what he would do.

Then came Christmas.

December 4, 1967   Monday

When Guevara the agitator was dead, his murderers lashed him to the landing gear of a helicopter and flew him to Valle Grande.

Yesterday it rained from early morning until late afternoon. The snow has been washed away.

Yesterday I had a taste of dying.

The dream knew the date of death, calculated or foretold in advance. I really did have difficulty waking up, but I could recognize the sounds in the apartment on the street and those of the elevator outside our door. A coffin would have to be placed upright in the elevator.

Between now and the funeral the papers had to be sorted. On a day like this one does not wash. I was so busy with plans, Marie had to call me twice to go and help carry the coffin. Marie seemed to be carrying the heavier end. We placed the box slowly and awkwardly on a folding cot that was suddenly there under the soft brown blanket outside the door. The coffin was heavy enough for me to have been inside it, but since I was holding it from the outside and could see Marie at the other end I was only slightly uneasy.

The sorting consisted of putting large newspaper clippings, mostly pictures, in order. The clippings were dated by hand, in arranging them one had to place them one by one on the left so as to reverse the order. The sorting took place in a room that the apartment had not previously contained, a little room off to the side beyond the long wall of the living room. In the living room people were moving about, there were footsteps and talking, disturbing enough for me to misplace five sheets. While I retraced the wrong steps in the papers I saw in the doorway on the shifted sofa an unknown young man in the uniform of an American sergeant, beside him his wife, a fuzzy-haired, brown-eyed person with wild lips whom I may have once gone to school with, not in Jerichow; what bothered me was something Marie said from behind the sofa.

"Shall I wrap you in a blanket?"

On the guest cot lay the dead woman, I could see her now, a slighter and shorter figure than in life, in a limp and helpless attitude, the head already half buried in the hair. The figure wore an unfamiliar brown dress. I have never liked wearing brown.

I knew the next thought, only I could not think it: I was dead, at least since hearing the elevator, probably even since last evening. That much I had been able to take in. But now I had to go and view the corpse, before my strength failed, and become the corpse.

What has remained is the sensation of being carried, and of deafness. Sometimes I have had to repeat something to myself: this is called a candelabra, this is a fire alarm, Marie's geography notebook, the Number 5 bus. Then everything would be all right again. At the north corner of 42nd Street and Third Avenue the rains are allowed to leave ankle-deep puddles so that in avoiding them many thousands of people walk on the driving portion of the street that has been cleared by the red light; surely this is well known. How every evening at that same spot one pushes to the right in the entrance to the Flushing Line, submits uneasily to the blast of air through the swinging doors, takes one's place in the lane into which the crowd turns itself three paces before the turnstiles, how one then swings left toward the stairs, how, on reaching the lower platform, one pushes one's way forward to the exact center of the newsstand, to the level of the first door of a certain car so as to be standing, at the next stop but one, exactly opposite the spot at which the stairs lead up to the West Side Line; surely everyone knows this. That the IRT platforms seem emptier on Wednesday mornings than on other days, everyone knows this. That the IND platforms at 59th Street are fuller in the morning than in the evening is because of the people who work in the garment district in the thirties and have to punch a time clock, anyone can figure that out. That Riverside Drive makes an S in front of our house so that an endless glowworm crawls toward us, that has been thought so often.

The lamp lighting the main entrance seems new.

December 5, 1967   Tuesday

In Jerichow in December 1933 they were already saying that Cresspahl was a stubborn bastard.

For no sooner had he arrived from England than he had taken himself off, out of sight of Jerichow eyes, to the property he had scrounged out of old Papenbrock, and worked on his barn. Would come out of Papenbrock's house first thing in the morning, appear briefly in the market square and then vanish. Instead of turning into Town Street, now called Adolf Hitler Street, he would go the long way around by the school and walk along the Bäk to the very end and then back via the brickyard path. Never came any more to Wulff's tavern of an evening, wouldn't stop for anyone in the square, and who could tell what was in his mind.

They were saying the Cresspahl marriage was not such a perfect love match after all. For hardly had the fellow got his barn windproof than he took to sleeping there, while his wife lay under Papenbrock's roof. On the other hand, they said they would do the same if one quiet night all their tools had been pinched, as happened to Cresspahl. They most certainly would.

That's why others were saying you only had to look at them. Just look how Lisbeth comes out of Papenbrock's front door every day at noon with that covered basket, carrying it like a servant along Town Street, I mean Adolf Hitler Street. Surely she could let Edith do it. But she doesn't, she wants to watch her husband have his meal, quite right too. They said, and Inge Schürmann had actually seen it happen one morning, and with her own eyes too, that on his way to work Cresspahl went into Semig's house and that right after that the pair of them drove along the Bäk in Semig's new car, those few steps to the brickyard. Could it be that Arthur was teaching him how to drive? But he knew how to drive. Was it possible that a qualified veterinarian was lending Cresspahl a hand in building his barn? Surely not! But in the entrance facing the path Cresspahl had installed a new door, sturdy enough for a church, the hardest knife would break on it, and he had let in some light by glazing the south entrance, just where anyone walking by could be seen and asked about his business. That really was going a bit far, that really was unpleasant. And especially as there were two of them standing there and staring at a person, Cresspahl and Arthur Semig.

That's why they were also saying that Cresspahl was a British spy who was out to get the Führer and Reich Chancellor Hitler. Others said that His good Britannic Majesty George the Fifth wasn't a Jew at all and was a close friend of the Austrian. And anyway Cresspahl had got in touch with the carpenters' guild in Gneez, and he was registered with the roster of tradesmen in Schwerin, the newspaper said so. The newspaper says many things. Some people preferred not to believe that and thought it more likely that Cresspahl was building himself an enemy radio transmitter so he could talk to the English in the evenings. Otherwise why would he fasten wire to the barn roof? That was no ordinary lightning conductor. And the other day two rolls of wire arrived for him at the station. What does the fellow need all that wire for, radio, I tell you. No, he needs it for a fence so you can't get too close when you try to smash his windows. O.K., so we're not looking at anyone here. And anyway that Cresspahl's a stubborn bastard.

Simply puts in new panes, with his own hands. No chance of him giving any other tradesman an opportunity to earn a bit, except as a last resort. And what was Heine Freese, master glazier in Jerichow, supposed to do? He didn't get the job, but he still had to sell the glass to Cresspahl, just in order to make at least that profit. Ask the painters, ask Köpcke the builder, and they'll tell you straight out they haven't made a penny off Cresspahl. Does everything himself, he does. Knows how to do everything himself, he does. You'd do the same. I'd do the same. And it wasn't just that he was sitting on his money because he didn't have any. Käthe Klupsch knew for sure that young Mrs. Cresspahl had looked at an electric refrigerator in Schwerin, on King Street. "Santo" the things were called, kept stuff at around forty. Käthe Klupsch, of course, was just envious; what she lacked was husband she'd never managed to catch. Now, that Methfessel needed a refrigerator, you could understand that. But even Louise Papenbrock got along without one. Cresspahl probably bought the thing to please his wife. Next thing you know your own wife will be coming to you wanting these English habits! Besides, so far the fellow had put more work into his workshop than into the house. What he wanted was for people to see not how much money he had in these lousy times—businesswise I mean!—but that he needed orders. And Else tried him out and took along her aunt's sewing cabinet, kind of an heirloom it was, left it with him, wasn't much to look at. Not so as to help Cresspahl out, just from curiosity. And along he comes with Semig's delivery truck and carries it into the house for her and you could have knocked her down with a feather! Beautiful thing he'd made of it! I tell you, if you saw it in a store window you'd be sorry you couldn't afford it. How much did Cresspahl charge for it? Oh, nothing out of the way. Fair enough. But delivering orders to the house, that was downright unfair! Suppose I went to every house and delivered all the shoes I'd repaired! It's almost a crime. But the wooden boxes, you have to admit, the ones he made for the move, he could have sold them just as they stood in the freight room at the station. Beautiful things. You'd put them right in your front room. Give them a coat of paint and put them in your front room. Listen, Cresspahl'll paint them for you and charge ten marks and then put them in your front room for you.

Stubborn bastard, that Cresspahl. There's something so secretive about the fellow! Scarcely do you have an inkling that his furniture's arrived from England, and already Swenson's delivered it to Cresspahl, in a closed truck, mind you, and on a sunny day in April at that! Cresspahl must have ordered it that way. But he had to let an electrician into the house after all, and of course it's a good thing for Johannes Schmidt, but he ought to have had a better look around. Comes back and says, the walls are just whitewashed and Cresspahl's probably thinking of having wallpaper later on and the furniture's a bit new-looking, in fact the place doesn't look lived in yet. Johannes doesn't seem to have any eyes in his head. And one fine morning in May there's Lisbeth coming out of Papenbrock's house with Cresspahl, Cresspahl's carrying the baby and wearing his Sunday suit, and this time they do walk through town—I say through town, not Town Street, otherwise I guess I should have said Adolf Hitler Street, and by noon she's not back and the baby's not back and that's all you've seen of it! Now they're living there. Now he's there.

And they were saying he had done it all by himself, without Papenbrock's help. Papenbrock had other things on his mind. Like, d'you know what Hilde Papenbrock, Hilde Paepcke, got for Christmas and for when the baby was born? That's right, the brickyard lease. See what I mean? He's a Papenbrock, and looks after his children. He's smarter than us after all. Not a soul knew the brickyard lease was running out, and while other people are twiddling their thumbs Papenbrock goes off to pay a call and talks till he gets what he wants. Paepcke, Hilde's husband, he'd got into trouble all right. If they don't lock a person up, then there was nothing wrong. Well, you just wait. You just wait till the Jerichow brickyard burns down too. I didn't say anything. I didn't hear you say anything. Heil Hitler. Bugger off.

And sometimes Papenbrock did things like that just for fun, believe me. Mind you, there was always something in it for him, but he did a lot of things just to let Friedrich Jansen know what the score was, that he can be mayor and local Party leader and a drop-out law student, but that Papenbrock's Papenbrock. Still. Quite right, too. And always will be. And Jansen had plenty of other things to worry about. You don't say. I do say. He knows we know that we're doing old Lawyer Jansen in Gneez a favor by accepting his washout of a son as mayor, and mayor of Jerichow, I guess that'll be Pappy Jansen's last try. All right, so Friedrich Jansen's a Party veteran, been a member since 1927, that's why we elected him, besides we've seen him as a kid standing on one leg in the Gneez park not daring to go home because he'd shit in his pants. And now he's on the warpath, going after the municipal employees and rounding up the question-naires on Aryan descent and not one poor slob has his ready. Stoffregen was in a terrible state. Stoffregen doesn't sound quite Aryan. Does that sound Aryan to you? Stoffregen. And then luckily for him Kliefoth knew all about it. Which Clay-Foot? That Kliefoth who teaches English, the one who bought Erdamer's house, that fellow from Berlin, no from Malchow actually, I mean that's where he's from and he's teaching now at Gneez High School and takes the train every morning. That one. Oh that one. Well anyway, he hears about it and goes to see Stoffregen and tells him. And Stoffregen, Ottje, he really should have known about it himself, being a teacher, and a person does think about his name, doesn't he. I don't. That I'll believe, Hünemörder, Chicken-Murderer. And Kliefoth tells Ottje: That's Middle Low German, used to be pronounced with a long o and it comes from stöven, and that means race along and refers to the weather at the time of birth. Quite simple, eh? Middle Low German is Aryan, so Ottje's Aryan too. No, Stoffregen can't thank Kliefoth for that. That's not all there is to it! Think about it for a minute! So what does the name Stoffregen mean now! You'll never guess. Any guy that can guess I'll buy him a drink. Well? Cloudburst, that's what it means. Downpour. See? Ottje Downpour. And with a name like that he was running after Lisbeth Papenbrock and wanting to marry her. Lisbeth Stoffregen. Lisbeth Downpour, I dunno. Don't like it. Good thing she took that Cresspahl. Lisbeth Cresspahl, not too much wrong with that.

That's what they were saying, and that's the way they talked.

December 6, 1967 Wednesday

On its front page, below the date line, the New York *Times* pub-lishes a picture of the young people who sat down yesterday morning outside the U. S. Army Induction Center. The paper has not chosen a moment when the police are facing the seated demonstrators with a more friendly expression. It has taken the trouble to include a sketch map of where the demonstration took place. Anyone wishing to go to today's demonstration can find the spot with the assistance of the New York *Times*. That was probably not the intention.

What sort of things was Cresspahl wishing for the year 1934?

He wished there might be some truth in the notion that gnats prefer to stay away from walnut trees. For he now realized that there were two in front of his house, and to live where there were no gnats would be good for the child, wouldn't it. Later on the child could sleep with open windows.

That Lisbeth would stop scaring him. There were times when it was impossible to understand her. When he wanted to tackle the old range in the house and rip it out, she had wanted to keep it. She denied having wanted to cook with gas. She could say mixed-up things like: If we're not in England we won't live as if we were in England. He didn't like that, it didn't make sense. Was she sorry now that she had dragged the family away from England? Was she satisfied now that she had? Now they had gas in the house and never used it except to run the refrigerator.

That Lisbeth would start telling him again what was going on in her mind. She could shut her face so completely, it would look furious, and you couldn't reach her. And she had got into the habit of standing in front of the range and staring into the flames for minutes on end. He didn't mind about the wood being wasted in the open rings; what he minded was that she obviously didn't know why she was doing it, nor even when and that she was doing it. When he entered the kitchen she would move like a person waking up. She would give a start, place the kettle (which she had been holding all along) on the fire, and turn to Cresspahl with a little shake of the head and a smile intended as a rebuke of her own behavior.

This smile was something he wanted for some other, for any other occasion, not beside the fire. He wanted her to be always the way she was when, as the younger sister but the experienced mother, she advised Hilde on how to handle Hilde's little girl Ulrike. She was such a gay creature, using only the outward form of mockery and so implying some things one cannot express.

He wanted her to be less sensitive again. A pail banged down on the floor, a door slammed by the wind, and she acted as if she had been shot at. If she regarded a look as cold, then for her it remained a cold look, attempts to console had no effect, the attempts were rebuffed. Then she would need several hours to recover. And now they had moved as close to the church as one can come to a church, and prayer did not seem to help her. He wished she were the girl he had wanted to marry without giving it a second thought.

Many a man will loudly sing
When to him the bride they bring.
If he knew what they were bringing,
He would weep instead of singing.

That things would work out.

Cresspahl wanted to be once more at the point where he could live on his income instead of his savings. Besides, he needed some new machinery. From Heinz Zoll he had taken over a router, a combination thickness planer and jointer, a band saw, a horizontal borer, a table saw, all in such condition that the only one for which he had a kind word to say was the plane. And it hadn't been cheap. And he couldn't take full advantage of the machinery. Who would order a bedroom set, a dining table, in 1934 in Jerichow? A stepladder, if he were lucky. And that Kliefoth from Malchow had actually believed that the only place you could get a desk was in Wismar. He wouldn't have minded making him a desk. On the other hand, it was no use being snowed under with orders, his assistant didn't work the way Cresspahl was used to and he couldn't expect much from the apprentices. And, though it was hard to credit, just try and find a good journeyman carpenter. Master carpenters, now, they're to be had for the asking, but a master under a master, that never works out, you know. Sometimes he secretly wished for Mr. Smith in Jerichow. Mind you, there were times when he'd been a bit thick in the head in the morning from his gin or vermouth, but once he'd sweated out the alcohol the work flowed smoothly from under his hands, and there was no need to check it, let alone touch it up. He could not want to make a great name for himself in Mecklenburg. He could not hope for a carpentry business like Strobelberger's in Rostock, either in turnover or in reputation. A little place like this wouldn't carry that. He would have to continue for a long while making the kind of furniture you could get in department stores. No artistic cabinetwork, not a chance. All he wanted was to survive in this Germany.

He wanted Papenbrock to keep his Louise at home. If at least she came here and went to Hilde's to see the babies! But she came to dispense her pious sayings. For each and every injustice she knew a Biblical exhortation to patience and a future redress through the power of Divine justice. Such homilies left Lisbeth so composed, so serenely happy, that one could not trust her; and it didn't last. All it did was help her not to listen to him when he mentioned the name of whoever had perpetrated one of Lisbeth's "injustices," and the approximate profit margin. But here Papenbrock allowed his wife to do whatever she wished.

He wanted his brother-in-law Paepcke not to get up to any mischief with his brickyard lease. A companionable fellow, a very agreeable neighbor, but no businessman. His books were in a state that would make your hair stand on end. It was amusing, all right, to see the way Alexander would sometimes gather his family after lunch on the lawn and spend the entire afternoon waiting for the evening, drinking coffee under gay umbrellas, and later Moselle. How he could play with that baby of his! Cresspahl had never yet had that much time. And the brickyard workers had only to go to the gate and look across the street to see how the boss believed in taking things easy. This didn't bother Alexander one bit. And he would go to Gneez just for a game of tennis. And when Cresspahl put up a new flagpole for him, he wanted to pay for it. Among relatives it was fine to offer money but not to insist on paying. Alexander should have saved the money. That was something that never entered his head. It was pleasant to watch how they lived, as uninhibited as children; it was uncanny that they should have already forgotten how they had been saved by the skin of their teeth through Papenbrock. So Cresspahl hoped the brickyard would not burn down all of a sudden.

He wanted the people of Jerichow to tell him in so many words what they expected of him, not with rocks through his workshop windows.

He wanted Dora and Arthur to come to their senses and leave the country. He was now almost friends with the man, as far as that was possible with a professional man, and if Semig wasn't a Mecklenburger he himself wasn't from Malchow-on-the-Lake. He didn't want him out of the way. He merely wanted him to go to people who had nothing against him and would give him work. It was not good to watch Semig shriveling up for lack of work, like blighted wheat. And Dora was growing more and more silent and only looking like herself when she held Gesine in her arms. He wanted them to be safe. He could not tell them that.

He wanted to be wrong about the war he feared.

He wanted three more children, as agreed with Lisbeth.

He wanted all the children to survive until he died.

He wanted security for his family from financial need, from political danger, from fire and lightning.

And so at the beginning of June 1934 he went to the Jerichow town hall and asked Friedrich Jansen to give him an application form for membership in the Nazi Party.

And the next day Avenarius Kollmorgen ran into him at the freight window at the station, raised his eyebrows like a cat arching its back, nodded with deep significance, and said with the smile he thought was genteel: "Getting along all right, Mr. Cresspahl? Getting along all right?"

December 7, 1967   Thursday

If one is not permitted to go to Jerichow, the dream must invent the lie about relatives in Wismar, and the dream must invent the lie about going to the passport office up rain-leached wooden steps in a courtyard with wild vines on the walls. Anyone knowing that courtyard must have relatives in the place. Then it no longer matters that one may not leave the district of Wismar. One simply travels with someone or other who is dead. The best person would be Pius Pagenkopf: when he was alive he was a general in the Soviet Air Force and drove an old U.S. Lend-Lease Studebaker. Driving an old Studebaker along Jerichow's Town Street: that's enough to make people stop and shake their heads. My only recourse is to dart into the cemetery. Nobody's going to find me in the cemetery.

Off we go then. The bus from Rostock to Barth is quite empty, but I have never driven that road, and in fact we are now driving to Newark through the tunnel under the Hudson. At Newark Airport the aircraft is standing all alone, far out all alone on the runway, about to take off. I have a feeling that it is called TRANSALL ILYUSHIN. Seated on fish crates in the aircraft are tattered men, men in sweaters with lacy Norwegian patterns. As the plane banks after take-off one of them leans toward me, and as I recognize him he says: "Gesine, don't pretend. Don't act as if you don't know us. You're just as condemned to crash as we are."

"How about the pilot?"

"He has the choice. They've given him the choice. Once he's in the air he can make up his own mind. But that's no concern of ours."

December 8, 1967   Friday

Dear Marie. I'm going to tell your tape about today.

This morning a man was leaning limply against the wall in the elevator, and after it had gone whooshing forty feet up through the building he woke up a bit and said to me in a kind of surprised voice Jee-zine, and I addressed him with his title, to wake him up. But he still couldn't grasp that he is the boss of a considerable portion of the millions here, and in this defenseless state he was assailed by another employee who asked him how he had liked his picture in the New York *Times*. For De Rosny had allowed the New York *Times* to take pictures in his home. "That's true fame, to get onner th'women's page," he said, and behind his soundproof doors I've no doubt he lay down on the carpet and went back to sleep.

Three quarters of an hour later one of the Vice-President's secretaries phoned me. We've been invited to dinner. I would have liked to accept right then, but she is so used to fitting De Rosny into an assortment of times and places that she insisted on negotiating with me over three dates.

There's not much to tell about the office. This is the way life is there: "People whose job it is merely to go over a check list, to assess the accuracy of the figures or the wording, can't keep from discussing the whole process in depth, and as a result leave the errors untouched. Sometimes the error's caught in time, but by rights the firm should have collapsed long ago." You have to imagine this spoken with pride.

In one of the elevators the street number let into the floor has one figure missing. This catches the eye, and I still wonder whether one morning I shall actually get this building mixed up with another and not notice it till I look at the floor.

Amanda, you know about her. You know how she flirts with male visitors, constantly, and revels in it: Such horrible weather, makes no difference to a man of course, but we girls have a kind of feeling in our hair, we're ready to tear it out by the roots . . . ! That's how she talks. She doesn't mean a thing by it, and I'm sure she realizes it's nonsense, but she can't help it. And the men stand there in a daze at her desk and wonder what she's talking about and never find out and blame themselves. One of them walked away today "like a sheep," said Amanda.

I wouldn't want to live in Germany again. In West Germany they have a Nazi Party, and the Nazi Party has organized units of strong-arm boys and holds a press conference about it. And the press comes. The abbreviation for the safety squad is S. G., for "Schutzgemeinschaft," and the top Nazi can't for the life of him see any resemblance to Hitler's Storm Troopers, who also began as keepers of law and order. And they're already talking again about "blood brotherhood." I wouldn't want to live in Germany again.

This afternoon three workmen were kneeling and lying in the

bank lobby, one of them almost on his stomach, putting polish on the brass at the foot and midriff of the six glass doors (and the polish we used in Jerichow for doorplates and faucets was as proverbial as if it were part of our very lives, and is forgotten. Maybe I've really forgotten what happened in one second, and one drip later there was nothing left but the interpreted second, but the memory fails to catch that either), and they rubbed and rubbed. In another three hours the offices would be closing, and the fully loaded elevators would come whooshing down, protesting with nervous grunts and groans against the overload. By the time I got there, the afternoon's work had already been smeared by eight hundred hands.

Sometimes they coat door-size surfaces of the marble in the lobby with something that looks like plaster of Paris. Your father would have known for sure why they do this, and I don't even like to ask.

Mrs. Agnolo, I must tell you about her. Her son is a pilot, stationed in Saigon, and she counts every day of his service year in Vietnam, and tells us every day. She tells us voluntarily, without being asked, as if the boy could be helped by an incantation. She dresses as youthfully as the girls she works with in our part of the office, and she tries to imitate their behavior, whether casual or chattering, but anyone who knows about her son can tell her age, and that her make-up doesn't help. And you can see her sitting idly at her typewriter, occupied with more than filing her nails.

Today the New York *Times* publishes a picture of the new Madison Square Garden, a gigantic oval for 20,000 people under a capacious dome, in a blaze of light. The seats are still empty, or not yet ready, and I am delighted that you will have such memories of your childhood, and perhaps I'd like some similar ones for myself too.

And then in the subway I saw a Negro boy of about eight or ten, holding an unwieldy shoe-cleaning box between his legs. He had fallen asleep right there in the crowded train and let his head droop trustingly against his neighbor's arm. So she moved her shoulder forward a little, to give him support.

That's all I saw today.

December 9, 1967   Saturday

In New York, former Vice-President Richard M. Nixon implied that the struggle against racial injustice was more important than the war in Vietnam. "The war in Asia is a limited one with limited means and goals," he said. "The war at home is a war for survival of a free society." Perhaps he thinks he will find his presidential nomination in his Christmas stocking.

Families with a soldier in Vietnam may call the Red Cross at 362-0600 and make an appointment for a three-minute taped message for loved ones in the field. And the service is free, because it is Christmas.

In Irving Place, Times Square, and Rockefeller Plaza, young people demonstrated yesterday against the war. There is a branch office of Dow Chemical, the manufacturers of napalm, at 45 Rockefeller Plaza. Dow Chemical has been given a clean bill of health by the Secretary of Defense: private industry had no control over the military use of its products, he said, and in any case napalm B accounted for only half of one per cent of Dow Chemical's sales. And the demonstrators were "weeded out," as the New York *Times* sees it, by the policemen with their clubs from among the Christmas shoppers and tourists. At Rockefeller Plaza, beneath the giant, glittering, colorful Christmas tree.

By Christmas 1934 Lisbeth Cresspahl had long since been back in the arms of her church and helped out at Sunday school and was present when the Christmas tree was set up and decorated in front of the altar. And she and Pastor Brüshaver's wife had become bosom pals. Her own sister's family lived across from her, but the neighbor she saw most of was Aggie Brüshaver. She would cross the brickyard path, walk along by the fence that skirted the Paepckes' property, past the back of Hilde's house, then through Creutz's gate and along the paths between his beds and greenhouses to the back gate of the parsonage. Old Creutz did not mind this at all, in fact he rather enjoyed the association with a young woman, at least on a conversational level. And Homuth, the tenant of the church property behind the nursery, raised no objection. The two women had taken great care and trodden only a narrow path along the edge of his field; as long as they walked past there, at least the boys did not go after his turnips. Cresspahl was not worried. Maybe it did Lisbeth good to be a kind of teacher.

Brüshaver had met his second wife in the Rostock hospital, where he had undergone further surgery for the war wound to his shoulder; Aggie had been a deaconess and better prepared to assist in other people's homes than to look after one of her own, and at least in regard to cooking she learned more from Lisbeth in six months than in the three years during which she had had to interpret her successes from Brüshaver's expression. The husbands were not included in this friendship. Cresspahl thought of the other man's university education and had had enough of Arthur Semig's formalities and cultivated manners, nor did he want to get involved with someone from the same outfit as Methling; and if Brüshaver felt rejected, he showed it only by a little smile when they met on the street, an expression of what looked like secret amusement. Lisbeth did nothing about it since she wanted Brüshaver to remain the pastor, the authority; and Aggie in all seriousness regarded Cresspahl as a grumpy, unsociable type, hard to get along with, and it was he whom she blamed on the days when Lisbeth seemed low. It pleased Cresspahl to know the two women were in his kitchen; he liked to see her in a cheerful mood, when, busy with her cooking, she would push back the hair from her face with her forearm, and when she and Aggie exchanged stories about the children, about Gesine and about Aggie's Martin, Mathias, and Marlene. Cresspahl would think: They're talking about children and cooking. And so they were.

But it was through Aggie that Lisbeth learned more about the conflict between the Protestant Church and that Austrian than could possibly be known to any other member of the congregation in and around Jerichow. People listened when Brüshaver preached in his solemn, sensible, monotonous manner, and after the boycott of the Jews they found it quite fitting that the man should stress a Christian's duty to his neighbor, that was the man's job, wasn't it, that's what he was there for and what he got paid for. It had done nothing for Arthur Semig, nor did Brüshaver himself go to Tannebaum's and buy from him. But Lisbeth heard about the bickering between Church and state in the tone and detail with which the pastor and his wife discussed the matter. And it was from Aggie that she first heard that in April 1933 there had been a "dictatorship" in the Mecklenburg State Church, when Prime Minister Granzow appointed a state commissioner who took over the Church administration of Schwerin under police protection. The next thing was that Bishop Rendtorff was removed from office, and his successor was the regional director of the "German Christians," Schultz, who wanted to baptize with earth instead of water because, like the Nazis, his head swam with nebulous ideas of "blood and soil," and at Holy Communion he would actually invoke the Austrian and declare the symbolic blood of the Lord to be the blood of the martyrs of the Fascist movement.

All this information was not without danger for Lisbeth Cresspahl, née Papenbrock. In January 1934, Brüshaver had read aloud the proclamation issued by the Pastors' Emergency League that had been founded by Pastor Niemöller: we must obey God rather than man; that was a tone that really struck home with this daughter of Louise Papenbrock. Whatever the issue: whether it was refusing to complete the questionnaire with the paragraph on Aryan descent, or a religious wedding ceremony with the irreligious motto,

So far from fear,
To death so near,
Hail our S. A.,

or the purity of the Gospel message, for her the Church was always right. The Church must not be injured. The Church was being injured. In March 1934, Brüshaver was summoned to the synod headquarters in Gneez for a discussion; but Lisbeth knew from Aggie that he had been "severely cautioned" for not resigning from the Pastors' Emergency League. For Lisbeth this meant too much excitement. The excitement could be a jolly one because there was a battle under way and victory for the right was a foregone conclusion; the excitement was sometimes hysterical, desperate, because the Austrian's authorities had not the slightest intention of acknowledging that they were in the wrong; and then again it could be ludicrous, as when she was capable of humming a slogan of the Pastors' Emergency League to a tune of her own all one morning while she pumped water or peeled potatoes. It made her look so silly. Cresspahl did not like to see her weighing down her conscience in this manner with the Church's troubles, she did not even seem to realize what she was humming. He would have felt a fool to warn her about the Gestapo. Surely she must realize. And he was afraid her answer would be: Everyone must stand up for what he believes.

> *Did you find it so cold in church, Lisbeth?*
> *What d'you mean, Cresspahl.*
> *You were trembling, child.*
> *When was I trembling.*
> *While Brüshaver was telling the Christmas story.*
> *I wasn't trembling, Heinrich. You're imagining things.*

December 10, 1967   Sunday

Next week four writers are to go on trial in Moscow for intimating that they did not like the trial of writers Daniel and Sinyavsky. Three of them wrote about it, and the fourth, Vera Lashkova, is alleged to have helped with the typing. That is enough to invoke Article 70, a crime against the state, up to seven years' imprisonment, up to five years' exile.

Someone got married! The President's daughter got married! Lynda Johnson got married! She got married in the White House! She married a Marine captain! A Marine captain with an assignment for Vietnam! Relax, will you?

And Allen M. Johnson, of 54-09 Almeda Avenue, Arverne, N.Y., proclaims to all and sundry that he will no longer be responsible for the debts of his wife, i.e., Betty Johnson.

In the fall of 1934 very little meat was eaten in Jerichow, and Arthur Semig was to blame. Methfessel the butcher was to blame. The Nazis were to blame. Who was really to blame?

It all began when August Methfessel went to see Semig in September. He did not go after dark but right after lunch, and he did not walk through the gates to the clinic but planted himself by Semig's front gate and rang the bell. And since Dora Semig had recently been taking her time about opening the front door, he stood there quite a while, visible to all who lived in the Bäk or passed by there. He was holding something bulky that was pointed at one end, and it was wrapped in white paper, and might it be flowers?

Dora Semig thought the white object was flowers, and anyway she was sufficiently taken aback to lead Methfessel into the living room. But he would not sit down, stood awkwardly among the Köster family antiques, holding his offering firmly by his side. He was still standing like that when Dora returned with her husband.

Then Methfessel planted himself once more in front of them, in the attitude of an usher at a funeral parlor, and made a speech. These were times, he said, where nobody knew what kind of times they were, and often something that was said about a person was taken for something that that person couldn't by any stretch of the imagination have meant and, furthermore, hadn't even done. He did not look at Arthur and Dora as he spoke: instead he stood with his head thrust slightly forward and his gaze averted, as if his speech were written on Mrs. Semig's waxed floor. And so he hoped for now and for all time that the old times would stay old times, that was to say in one sense, and especially in the other.

Semig had no idea what he was getting at. Nor had Mrs. Semig. With a heavy sigh Methfessel sat down, placed the wrapped object on his knee, and told a tale in which Baron Rammin and Granma Klug and her cat were intimately and mutually involved. After a while Semig gave signs of having got wind of Methfessel's intentions, offered the mandatory schnapps, accepted the first refusal as final, and rose to his feet so as not to impede Methfessel's departure. Methfessel rose with surprising speed from Dora's armchair, the thin legs of which may have been causing him some anxiety, shook hands with the lady of the house, and walked to the door, but to the one leading to Semig's central passageway and his office. Arthur is said to have followed him like a lamb being led to the slaughter.

"Here," said Methfessel when the door to Semig's office had been closed. "Here!" he said, hastily unwrapping the piece of meat he had brought along. "Take a look at this!" he said, and for a moment he was once more the easygoing, canny fellow he had been before his trip to Fürstenberg. It was as if a load had been taken from him and was now in the best of hands, at any rate not in his. Sat there as if prepared, nevertheless, to offer helpful information. Dr. Semig had put on his white smock to show Methfessel that the forms were being preserved. Furthermore, he did him the favor of carrying the sample across to the table by the window where he kept his microscope, his scissors, needles, pipettes, chemicals. But even if he could have undertaken a bacteriological examination on the spot, he would not have done so in Methfessel's presence. He remained standing beside his swivel chair so that Methfessel would not actually take root. And Methfessel would not leave. Nor would he begin until given a push with an inquiry about business. From business Methfessel could finally proceed to his other matter, and now Semig had to listen to a long and involved tale of woe about the veterinarian who had recently taken over Semig's former inspection area. It was of no use whatever his trying to object to the maligning of a colleague (here Semig made no distinction, Aryan or non-Aryan). After a while he had his hand at his mouth, as usual when thinking, and then he sat down, in order to listen better.

His colleague Hauschildt had his own way of interpreting the law. He appeared to have a preference for inspecting livestock by telephone. He would demand a statement from Methfessel over the telephone as to the general condition of the animals that had been delivered, and it would seem that with time Methfessel found it difficult to come out with a particular opinion or statement, and that with time Methfessel began to mind being shouted at, even if it was over the telephone. Then Hauschildt would simply say: Go ahead, Methfessel! and hadn't been within a mile of looking at the posture of the animal or lips nostrils condition of stool genitals vagina udder breathing. Mind you, there had been occasions when Semig had also not arrived at Methfessel's stable till after dark, when he had had no other time, and been satisfied with prodding the animals awake. But in this part of the world alone he had been practicing for fifteen years, and what he could see with the naked eye wouldn't look much different under the microscope. But that Hauschildt was not long out of Veterinary Training College, and people said he had found plenty of leisure time, along with his studies, to organize a National Socialist Students' League, and people also said that at Von Meyer's he had been stymied by a prolapsed uterus. And what Methfessel had to say about Dr. Hauschildt's examining techniques was not in the textbook, and in the short time he took to phone through the result of the trichina test—well, he can hardly have got home! Dr. Hauschildt had apparently issued himself a special permit exempting him from making a trichina inspection at the slaughterhouse. And so Methfessel was scared of the law, and afraid of his conscience. It was revolting to see how submissive his beatings had made him, how cowardly. For Methfessel did not want to complain personally in Gneez. "I'm not a Party member," he said, and knew for a fact that Dr. Hauschildt was a Party member and that he and the district veterinarian were always in each other's pockets, whether in adjoining lakeside properties or sailing together or at the Ratskeller was not clear, and Methfessel even seemed nervous about knowing that much. Semig had better take the meat to Gneez, not he. "My dear Mr. Methfessel," Semig said, and August should have been able to hear that that tone was not the condescension of earlier days with which Dr. Semig had brushed aside stupid questions or naïve expectations of a reduction in fee. But Methfessel would not accept someone else's helplessness and believed he had rid himself of the problem, and left with the solemn pronouncement: "It's on your conscience now, Doctor!" In the yard he carefully avoided getting too close to Rex, although Rex had been about to offer him a paw. Rex was the name of the German shepherd dog acquired by the Semigs that spring.

For the time being, all that Methfessel got out of it was that people were saying in Jerichow that he had been willing to part with a whole roast just to be in the good books of the Jew again.

The veterinarian would have liked a few days to think it over, but if his professional ethics had not spurred him on, the warm weather would have. He wrote a rather personal letter, which might just manage to escape being filed, and sent it registered express that same evening, along with Methfessel's meat, to Schwerin, and there he really was still regarded as Dora Köster's husband and no mention was made of him in the official instructions to the district veterinarian in Gneez. The facts were stated to be "as presented by Mr. August Methfessel, master butcher of Jerichow." And Methfessel was summoned to Gneez and signed a deposition and expressed his thanks to the authorities, somewhat comforted to find that law and hygiene perhaps still meant something after all in Germany. And outside Gneez station he was picked up by some plain-clothes Storm Troopers.

Now Methfessel was a sad man. On his return from Jerichow he found his refrigerator cleaned out, the Schwerin bacteriologists having discovered *Salmonella dublin* in the liver he had submitted, a meat poisoner. Compensation, not on your life! And by this time Methfessel had reached the point where he found it quite fitting that Semig as a professional man should get off scot-free. The gang held together, it was as simple as that. Besides, he did not begrudge Semig being left in peace, until he got to Fürstenberg, where Ossi Rahn was waiting for him. After a week Methfessel had almost recovered and would have been strong enough to start slaughtering again, and had no desire to. Dr. Hauschildt now started coming very promptly, and hollering about every minute he was kept waiting, and instead of inspecting the livestock alone he had an assistant who could certify that his inspection had been carried out according to regulations. And if the veterinarian no longer overlooked a single incision when inspecting a carcass, he took his time over it and gave his student a regular lecture, and that was not the way Methfessel had imagined it. And now it was Methfessel's turn to telephone Gneez about the results, and Mrs. Hauschildt was very often unable to tell him where her husband was or how the tests had turned out. And Dr. Hauschildt had become quite fond of using the square stamp for Methfessel's meat, the one giving only qualified approval, and sometimes he even used the triangular stamp, the one classifying the meat as unfit, and by this time Methfessel lacked all ambition to prove that cattle-breeding in this part of the world could not possibly have deteriorated that much from one week to the next. The circular stamp had been the rule for his meat.

Methfessel had become morose. When the cattle trucks arrived on slaughter mornings, Methfessel would stand in his yard holding his head like a deaf man, as if it were he who had received a blow on the head and not the ox they were leading toward him.

And what a buster that man had been!
That red face of his, and that fair hair.
The whole S. A.'s not that blond.

The truck with the pigs would drive up, the pigs sleepy from the journey, pressing affectionately against each other, and now Methfessel would stand there and simply look on as his men drove the terrified animals with their brooms toward the door of the slaughter-room. Since he did not join in, it took the men longer, and the pigs had time to get wind of their comrades' blood that had run out over the threshold, and Methfessel's neighbors complained about the pitiful screaming. At first Methfessel would follow the others inside, even though he was the last, and swiftly, after a few high shrill screams, silence would fall. But then Methfessel had immediately come out again, in a daze, a great powerful man with stout arms, heavy shoulders, lowered head, a bloody knife in his hand. He would shake his head, chew his blond mustache, sunk in thought. And instead of going into the house he would hide in the woodshed, and after a while the men gave up going to fetch him. One of Else Pienagel's windows faced onto Methfessel's big yard, and that fall she often had a visitor who did nothing but stand by the window when it was slaughtering day at Methfessel's.

So for a time not much beef or pork was eaten in Jerichow, partly because Methfessel had none, and partly because Klein the butcher had for too long been regarded as the second-best, and this prejudice persisted. Thus many chickens met their end sooner than intended, and rabbits too.

Only at Cresspahls' there was still another reason. Lisbeth had noticed something about the sides of pork when Methfessel still had some to hang on the hooks in his store. The backs were curved. Over the vertebrae there were little dimples, as with people. As with Gesine too. Lisbeth suddenly had an aversion to meat.

So at Cresspahls' meat was served only when he insisted, and she would not eat any.

Now the New York *Times* is starting up again with its own brand of charity. In the likeliest and unlikeliest places it inserts the appeal: Remember the neediest! and asks for donations for a special account. Some news items look incongruous beside a refrain like that. Remember the neediest!

December 11, 1967   Monday

Marie has cut out three pictures from today's New York *Times* and intends to keep them:

The first, on the front page, brings President Kennedy's smiling widow into our home because she was going to a dinner for the Democratic Party at the Plaza Hotel.

The next presents Lynda Johnson's wedding party arranged in a semicircle, all with bowed heads, one person is even kneeling. But these people are not praying, they are watching a tape of the ceremony on television. The article closes with the refrain: Remember the neediest!

The third is a work of art and shows a poorly dressed woman with a small child in her arms, in an almost totally bare room. The floor looks broken, and the window as if it let in not only light from the courtyard but the wind too. "Many New Yorkers, such as this Puerto Rican mother and her child, face a long, cold winter with little hope, little money, and oftentimes no heat."

Edmondo Barrios, the first friend Marie had in this country, grew up in a home like that in East Harlem.

Her first reports from kindergarten contained no mention of him. What she objected to was the way children are brought up in this country. In Düsseldorf it had been permitted to attach oneself heart and soul to another child, so here too she had picked one as her favorite and taken the seat next to her and hung on her lips and followed her around (the way I follow D. E. around when he gets up to go to the refrigerator for another bottle and comes back to the table: merely so as to look at him while he speaks every sentence, which I could have heard no less clearly if I had stayed sitting down). This child was Pamela Blumenroth, and Marie refused to let anyone take Pamela away from her. But Pamela was to be taken away from her, for in the minds of the teachers a close relationship with a single partner, even among four-year-old children, was considered potentially dangerous, and at snack-time Marie was placed beside another child, Mark the Kisser, and told to play with him, and did not want him, but wanted Pamela. The idea of this training was for all the children to get to know all the other children in the class, and the word was togetherness, and for a long time Marie thought that meant enforced separation, and she behaved almost furtively when, instead of asking Mark the Kisser home for the afternoon, she deliberately invited Pamela, the friendly, alert little person who in those days had a face like an Irish peasant woman.

In order to learn to change friends as casually as she changed her socks, Marie landed up with, among others, Edmondo. Before that she had spoken of him as "the boy who likes to hit people." Then she noticed that he regularly attacked a certain group in the class, boys "with skin the same color as mine," and so it transpired that he was "colored." It seemed that this Edmondo needed no pretext at all for a quarrel: he would simply knock down any pink-skinned boy at random, sit on him, and pummel him. The victim's buddies often assumed there must be a reason for the dispute and kept to their rule of not interfering in a fight. One day Marie went over and placed a hand on his arm, saying: Stop it, in German, and not as an order but as a wish, and so as to make quite sure he understood her she smiled and shook her head, and Edmondo was so dumfounded that he forgot the fight which a moment before he had regarded as unavoidable. He followed this extraordinary person with the funny way of speaking and from then on considered her his friend and, moreover, not like the little black girls in the class, whom he continued to treat with a pasha's more or less consistent ill-humor, but like a child whom one genuinely wishes to understand, please, and protect.

As Marie's protector it might have been even easier to find opportunities for cuffing and beating up other boys, but Marie restrained him by appearing to be there solely for his benefit and acting as if David Double-U were not even in the room. And she was not scared of him either. The teachers observed the friendship between the Puerto Rican and the European child with amazement, but also relief, for now it happened less often that Edmondo threw building blocks in the hope of hitting an eye, and now they hardly ever had to drag him out of a fight that for the weaker child might have ended in a broken bone. For Edmondo was already eight and only in Marie's class because of the four-year delay in his mental development, and Edmondo attended kindergarten on a grant from the church itself and was regarded as the first subject of an experiment, and furthermore he was safe from expulsion because of the color of his skin. Unless all else failed, the church would not have liked to see its good will come under suspicion. Now that the difficult dark-skinned boy and the little German girl were together, the mornings passed almost as in a normal class, with neither extra work nor commotion, and this isolated partnership, however little it fostered togetherness, this friendship was not severed.

Marie also went to visit Edmondo in East Harlem, and life in the Barrios family was made up of the most commonplace ingredients of what everyone expects to find in this ghetto. Edmondo bore the name not of his father but of the father of his younger brother because that one had had the guts to marry Mrs. Barrios. But then he left after all, and Edmondo's father, whose first name was Rodrigo, would probably have liked to live with Edmondo's mother had this not meant that she would forfeit welfare payments, and for him to support the family himself was out of the question since he could not get a job.

He had occasionally come to see them, but not since Mrs. Barrios had become pregnant by other men for the second time. Mrs. Barrios volunteered this information to the other lady quite freely since Edmondo had told her in such detail about the other lady's daughter. She was a very pretty, rather plump person with the kind of lips known in this country as Caucasian. She wore her hair very short, like a man's brush cut, and in profile, when she raised her head, she could look full of fun, positively mischievous. Like herself, the apartment and everything in it was neat as a pin. The apartment consisted of two and a half rooms, one beyond the other. The back rooms obtained their light through the single window in the front one. Mrs. Barrios was proud of her home, which did in fact look furnished because the one large bed for all the children took up almost all the available space, and a picture of the Virgin Mary, cut out of a newspaper and pasted into a cardboard frame, lent a certain distinction to a scratched-up wall. Mrs. Barrios felt she was lucky to live as she did. The prepared, anticipated image of an apartment in East Harlem was made complete by the fact that the single window really did face onto the tracks of the New York Central Railway, which offered the tenants the spectacle of commuter trains to the country and even the Twentieth Century Limited, on elevated tracks.

Except at night, Edmondo lived on the street and in the shelter of the railway, and he used to tell Marie about this street. When he described a man with an unsteady walk as a "junkie," he did so not matter-of-factly but with visible hatred. There was something there. It was not common for someone who lived on this street to arrive with a "white" girl friend and then even enter the building, and it may have been on those stairs up to Mrs. Barrios' apartment that Marie became aware for the first time of human sexual intercourse. This embarrassed Edmondo, and his pride in his "white" friend was blighted. Mrs. Barrios could not adjust quickly enough to the middle-class custom of sending children on visits, and anyway she had no room for them, let alone toys, so she went to her welfare money and sent the children to the Apollo movie theater on 125th Street. It was Marie's first feature film, a very sad story about a lady on a sofa with a sailor "who shooted," and actually the whole thing took place in a car, or on a plane, Marie was not quite clear about that, and it got all mixed up in her dreams. That was Marie's first visit to Edmondo's home, and she often wanted to discuss it in detail, but she did not insist on a second visit.

There was a second visit, but she preferred to have Edmondo at her home. The baby-sitters who had to pick him and Marie up from kindergarten and were then responsible for him for five hours were careful to announce that they would not be able to offer their services again if this child were to pay another visit. This was understandable. In the evening Marie's room looked as if it had been subjected to a search carried out in desperate haste, as in the movies, and some of the glass panes in Marie's door were smashed, and only Marie was still intact and cheerful and a little surprised. One of the sitters reported that being around that child Edmondo was like being in the Deluge, as, for instance, when he would no longer listen to any suggestion or order and lay on the floor like a dead weight and with the limited self-gratification of a two-year-old waited for the grown-up's reaction: then you found yourself in the midst of a tidal wave with nothing solid to hang on to. Edmondo had genuinely not understood. He had been waiting for a beating; for a beating he would have stood up. Once I saw him fail to obey his mother, and Mrs. Barrios, ignoring the white middle-class members of the school outing, reached out blindly for anything to strike with and happened to grab a jump rope and tried to wreck it on the boy, who did not defend himself. The educated, the liberals, the whites, looked on pensively, and they appeared to be particularly struck by the fact that Mrs. Barrios stopped without any transition, as if she had finished a job.

We might have questioned Edmondo. His contempt for drug addicts, there was something there. His insistence on knowing whether under her skirt Marie looked like his sister, that might have helped in his cure. D. E. was the first person to observe the boy for five minutes and then pronounce him sick; and in the presence of a grownup, a white man, Edmondo had behaved very quietly and properly. It was hard to make him out. A boy who would attack any and all, often without regard to the relative strengths, what made him so scared of dogs? A man was playing with his dog in Riverside Park, and the dog, an affectionate boxer, was way off, and there was nothing in his bark but tremendous enjoyment, and Edmondo hid behind my skirt and begged and implored me to turn back and go home. Are there dogs like that in East Harlem? Do the police use dogs like that? We did not ask him. We only knew him for a year and a half. Then something happened at a summer camp for single mothers with all their children. Edmondo wore the sweatshirts stamped with the camp emblem every day. It was said he had done something with a knife. He was nine and a half then, and powerful.

The psychiatrists transferred him to a special school. The school was more of a clinic. Life had apparently infected him with a disease that doctors do not often run across. Mrs. Barrios did not have to pay a cent for him to stay there or for the therapy. At that time one could still visit him. He no longer knew who Marie was. Marie behaves as if this visit had never taken place. Then one could not visit him any more.

Even today Marie says: He never hit me. And he was so strong, he only needed to touch you and you'd fall down the stairs. He never did that to me.

Blessed be the ability to forget. Only she has not forgotten.

It seems to be raining most of the time. No wonder, it will soon be Christmas.

December 12, 1967   Tuesday

"THE GLOW OF CHRISTMASTIDE LIGHTS CITY

. . . .

"In Manhattan, happy throngs of children and adults are drawn to the newly lighted Christmas tree in Rockefeller Center and to the spectacular window displays that line the midtown area's sleek streets.

"Lord & Taylor's windows are an animated phantasmagoria of scenes from Christmas in Vienna, with tiny figurines dancing in Schoenbrunn Palace; a conductor and a diva performing in the Vienna Opera House of a century ago; the doors of St. Stephen's Cathedral opening and closing, and children romping and bellringers playing in an Alpine village.

"The windows of B. Altman are a cornucopia of great art drawn from the Metropolitan Museum and depicting, in photographic slides, the themes of joy, beauty, the festive board, children, treasures and pageant.

"Saks Fifth Avenue, which for years has ushered in the Christmas season with a display of choir boys and organ pipes, this year has emblazoned its façade with a tall Christmas tree.

. . . .

"It is quiet and warm in the Columbia Florist Shop at 200 West 231st Street. In the back of the small store, a woman prepares red Christmas candles for sale, putting little ribbons on them and setting them in their bright green bases. The busy time lies ahead, says Nick Dennis, the store manager.

" 'It's a little early yet,' he explains, pointing to Dec. 15 on a calendar. 'That's when business picks up.'

"Outside, the night has turned cold and the lights twinkle everywhere in the city and for a moment, at least . . ."

Today Francine came to see Marie. When I came home from work, both panels of Marie's door were firmly closed, muffling the sound of a strange child's voice speaking in a high, surprised tone against which Marie's suddenly sounded like a contralto.

"And you and your mother really live all alone in this apartment?"

"In three rooms?"

"Are all these books yours? Aren't some of them borrowed maybe?"

"I can't believe you've got cockroaches. There couldn't be cockroaches in an apartment like this!"

"Is this a picture of your dad?"

"Which end of the bed d'you put your head? Toward the wall? Or so that as soon as you wake up you can see the trees and the sky and the river and the New Jersey palisades?"

"Why d'you say that England's not part of Europe?"

"May I touch this book?"

"You mean he gave you a typewriter, just like that? Just because you wanted one?"

"Is he the man your mother . . . sorry! I meant to say: I'm sure he's a good man."

"Well, because he comes to visit you."

"And if Mr. Robinson says no, a person can't get into your building?"

"Not even through the basement?"

"But suppose the water main in your building breaks . . . I don't suppose that happens in a building like this."

"It does?"

"The same day? The same day?"

"And all you have to do is say thank you?"

"Your carpet must be nice to sleep on."

"You were at summer camp on Orr Island, Maine? Where they teach sailing? I was once at Green Acres. But then that's in New York State."

"Say something in your language."

"In your mother's language, I mean."

"Those five words are supposed to mean: The longer you take over a job, the harder it gets?"

"De Leng hett de Last?"

"Then she can speak three languages: her own, German, and ours!"

"More, you say? You don't say."

"What's your mother like?"

"All mothers are like that. I mean: is she dangerous?"

"It's too bad but mine's dangerous sometimes. She doesn't mean to be, but then she is."

"You're just going to stay here for Christmas? But you could go to Vermont, or to Britain . . . to Italy even?"

"I'd go to Italy if I could."

"And you're making that for your mother for Christmas? But that must cost a lot of money."

"Me make that too? I couldn't ever make that."

"It's great that you want to show me. Out of this world. But it's no use. My mother's never had anything like that."

"And she'd sell it."

"Right, the lighting. I guess the lighting will be quite hard to do."

But at this point Marie stuck her head through the door panels and saw me reading the newspaper at the table. The door was instantly closed again, there was just time for me to catch a solicitous, smiling nod from Marie. She has declared her room off limits. Everyone else may go in, D. E., Shakespeare, and Esther; not me. Marie is making something mysterious in there. I told her I did not want a surprise for Christmas, and she said: "It's not for Christmas, it's for New Year's." And it never occurs to her that I might disobey orders and take a peek. Her project involves more than work for her. It sounds like work: like knives against wood, like hammer against nails, like scraping, like scratching; she has to make her bed and see to her clothes and keep her room tidy; and every evening she puts the garbage bags out beside the freight elevator so that the scraps and rubbish from her day's work won't make me suspicious. She has promised: I may not be overjoyed about it, but it will help fill a wish I'm not aware of.

The voices in Marie's room had become unintelligible once they knew I was home. All I could make out was that they were whispering, the stage whisper of the one being hushed by the other. They emerged abruptly, and while Marie's hands behind her back closed the door on her secret again, Francine came up to say hello and good-by at the same time. She waited to see whether I would hold out my hand, and kept her eyelids lowered so as not to see whether she had an encouraging expression before her or one of a different kind. She bobbed a curtsy and said: "Good night, ma'am."

She had her coat on and, carrying her schoolbooks, was already at the apartment door. Mr. Robinson was standing in the open elevator and warmly wished me good evening, like a good friend of the family, which he is, and downstairs in the lobby stood Jason and Shakespeare, expertly and anxiously examining the floor tile which was now not only cracked but had finally crumbled irreparably into little pieces. Shakespeare was the second and Jason the third "colored" man to wish us good day, as if they really did wish it, as if we lived like good neighbors, as if we knew one another and we approved. The little black figure ran out the front door as if they were all at her heels. Because of her hurry I had once again failed to take in her face properly and only remember that she seemed to me like a child who reads a lot and is given little help in thinking about what she has read.

"She behaved as if she were scared of me, Marie."

"Sure she's scared of you. Sometimes you ask questions, Gesine . . . the strangest questions, Gesine . . . !"

"Don't trust anybody over thirty."

"It's not Francine who thinks like that, it's me. And when I think like that, I really mean something else. You know."

December 13, 1967   Wednesday

"But now he'd got all his money tied up there, I guess," says Marie.

"Right. When you think that in those days an English pound was worth 12 marks and 30 pfennigs. There can't have been much left over."

"And he had found his way there," says Marie.

He had found a way there.

At first the Gneez guild had left him, if not out in the cold, at least where he was: far away, up there on the coast. Any work there was to be had was needed by the Gneez carpenters themselves. There had been no reason for that fellow Cresspahl to come back to Germany. They had gone with their furniture samples from village to village and from one town to the next, and people had not been in any position to order, or, if they had, to pay; during those bad times he had been abroad, sitting pretty and earning money. Besides, he was a brother-in-law of Horst Papenbrock. It wouldn't do him any harm to have to stoop to repairing cartwheels and wagon shafts. And if it came to the worst he could always go to his father-in-law; where could they go? Not to the bank but into bankruptcy. And that's the truth. And Cresspahl had paid a courtesy call on Willi Böttcher, the guild master in Gneez, and not yet gone again. Böttcher's only contribution to the conversation had been many sighing Sure Sure's, all of them signifying that he did not trust the newcomer nor did he even want to discuss with him whether times were hard or not.

And Cresspahl had not liked Böttcher's son. Sixteen, the kid was, and bragged about "serving" in the Hitler Youth, and about his pals in the Regional Youth Headquarters, and about rifle practice at night in the woods belonging to Gneez. So that was evidently one way of being accepted into the Nazis: since 1932 young Böttcher had been sitting next to young Knoop in school. The Knoop boy was the son of Johannes Knoop, who was regarded as the leading figure among the 25,023 inhabitants of Gneez, coal, cartage, export and import. Johannes Knoop had a game preserve, and son Emil had free access to the gun closet. In 1931, on the strength of his father's weapons, Emil Knoop had already got his whole class, all members of the Christian Boy Scouts, into the Hitler Youth. Ever since sitting next to Emil in high school, Klaus Böttcher had acted as a kind of adjutant or sergeant to Emil.

Johannes Knoop had recently had to send his offspring away to boarding school, and the Hitler Youth of Gneez and Jerichow now took orders from Klaus Böttcher. He wore his uniform to school, and he wore his uniform to the dentist's. But in his father's workshop he was all thumbs. And this Klaus youngster had such a ridiculous way of talking. When the Austrian ordered half his Storm Troop leaders shot in June 1934, young Böttcher had said: "Well, the Führer can't be expected to know everything." When he said things like that he would look so cocky, as if he wanted to make the other person laugh or had no idea what he was talking about, and Cresspahl couldn't be bothered to decide which. It did not escape him that there was more than curiosity behind the boy's inquiries as to how Cresspahl came by the rank of noncommissioned officer, and that actually it was respect that made him question Cresspahl about his life in London, but that did not seem the right way to go about getting onto better terms with Willi Böttcher. No matter how cordial the boy's paramilitary good morning, Cresspahl would merely grunt his response. It struck him, incidentally, that Klaus did not greet him with the Heil Hitler which, as a Hitler Youth leader, must have been mandatory for him, but for the time being Cresspahl put this down to the silly way of behaving kids sometimes have.

Then Cresspahl had to deliver some papers to Böttcher, the ones proving his Aryan descent, and the boy was watching out for him. Again he was in full uniform, with a kind of leather thong knotted around his tie and a braided cord dangling on his chest, and Cresspahl eyed the boy's attire as if conducting an army inspection. "Yeah, the Youth Federation's all washed up now," young Klaus said in his easygoing, would-be sophisticated manner. "That I can see," said Cresspahl, pushing Böttcher's front door part-way open. Böttcher's entrance hall was half the width of a street, to allow a truck to drive up to the workshop. Young Klaus, talking away, managed to steer Cresspahl back to the yard. It sounded as if this time he really did want to tell him something. The story was all about a campers' hut which the Youth Federation had built on the south shore of Gneez Lake. In 1931 the Hitler Youth had been banned and had often rented the hut for secret meetings.

"We were once illegal too, see," said young Klaus in his offensive, man-of-the-world way.

"And now we're going to occupy it tomorrow night, and Heine Klaproth'll be hopping mad!" said the guild master's offspring.

"You just see what a long face he pulls the day after tomorrow!" said Klaus. Heine Klaproth was one of Cresspahl's apprentices, and it was true that he had once been a Christian Boy Scout. "You won't let on to him, will you?" said Klaus, looking genuinely anxious, all agog with delight at his Nordic cunning.

During the night Cresspahl, in Arthur's car, had driven very slowly and as quietly as possible along Adolf Hitler Street to Gneez, continuing along Schönberg Street and right around the woods as far as the south shore of Gneez Lake. It was October, and when he switched off the headlights he couldn't see his hand in front of his face. The lake was pitch black. Only by the lakeside promenade, on the far side, was lamplight reflected in the water. On this side the shore seemed very busy, and Cresspahl couldn't believe the scouts had that many members. "Those are fellows from the Socialist Workers' Youth," said Heine Klaproth. Apparently they had also borrowed the hut once.

So, in the darkness, without a sound, they dismantled the building. There were only three carpenters and two carpenter's apprentices among them; nevertheless, by three in the morning nothing remained but the bare ground where the hut had stood, and not even the posts of the landing stage had been left. One person had brought along a hoe, and another had swiped a sign from the rose gardens in Gneez, and what they left behind was a neatly hoed stretch of shoreline with a sign in the middle saying: KEEP OFF—FRESHLY SEEDED. And when early in the morning Cresspahl drove along the north side of the woods with his share of the lumber, he overtook a weary band of Hitler Youths who had carried out a maneuver that night, and this time Klaus Böttcher called out neither Heil Hitler nor good morning and apparently did not even see him.

The prank earned him more than the lumber. The Socialist Workers' Youth had been the youth organization of the Social Democrats, for whom it was now an established fact, from Gneez to Jerichow, that that fellow Cresspahl was putting on a show, just as they were.

And Heine Klaproth behaved like the son of the house. The boy had always been a hard worker, but now Lisbeth was almost overwhelmed with help as he tried to anticipate all her wishes. As soon as the woodbox was only half empty he was already on his way to the chopping block.

No doubt Lisbeth would have forbidden Cresspahl this kind of night work and reproached him with jeopardizing the family. Since she did not hear about it until morning, she found the escapade amusing and only regretted not being allowed to share the fun even with Aggie Brüshaver.

And the members of the carpenters' guild now made a point of inviting Cresspahl to their regular table. And they now taught him what the score was. For instance, he was not to have any respect for the German Labor Front of the Nazis. In the first place, those fellows had pinched their funds from the unions. And it wasn't only what they were doing to the wage scales. They were nuts with their "Beauty of Work." Flowers in the workshops! D'you know of any flowers that can stand carpenter's glue? Increase the window area! Are we gardeners? Seating accommodation for work breaks! I like to sit on my work, otherwise my lunch doesn't taste right. Plant lawns! And where's Gertrud to grow her radishes? But the dirtiest trick of all was that those idiots from the Regional Home Improvement Board of the German Labor Front specify the orders. That standardized furniture of theirs, mass-produced! Those were orders for factories, not for the carpenters' shops. We don't even get the bones of that fish! And that Irene Loohse, you have to watch out for her, she has a brother-in-law who's a le-gal coun-se-lor for the Labor Front, you might as well turn yourself in to the police right away. Now you know what's what, Cresspahl.

And they were saying, around the end of 1934: "Heinrich, there's something in the air. When the time comes, we'll cut you in."

At first Cresspahl had wanted only to adjust to life in Germany without losing his integrity. Now it turned out that things were not that bad. With the other fellows in the trade you could get along very nicely, drinking beer, discussing machinery and materials and workmen, playing tricks on the Nazis, just plain living. You really could.

Hold your tongue, Gesine. Hold your tongue.

December 14, 1967   Thursday

Dear Anita of the Red Hair,
Dear Doctor of Oriental Archeology,

Thank you for your letter and for actually returning the passport for Henri R. Faure by November 15, and Shakespeare thanks you for the Swiss stamps. Shakespeare's real name is Mr. Shaks with, as you can guess, Bill for a first name, an infinitely kind black gentleman from Brooklyn, a plumbing artist with the bearing of a hotel manager. And he lives up to his name by knowing not only half of *Hamlet* by heart but also *Richard IV*. Collects our European postage stamps.

It was a smart idea to have your "Henri R. Faure" write a thank-you letter to Henri Faure. Now the old Faures are convinced they haven't been played for suckers. And Henri examined his passport every which way and could find no traces and couldn't grasp the fact that such a small object can be the ticket to depart from a country that is out to prevent such departures.

And the Faures still believe we have done this for the Jewish cause and greet us from way off. They are quite an elderly couple, and he raises his hat with a stiff, elegant flourish. And they invariably stop us and get us into conversation. My French has Belgian overtones by this time.

I can see that you have no time now for research and excavations on this continent, which is sad. It would have been good to have someone like you around at Christmas. Someone who can recite the Fish's Night Song, for example. I can't stand Christmas. I don't know what it is. I have no deaths to remember during that time, yet I can't stop dreaming of deaths. And Marie expects the routine of the festive season, and I have to go through all the motions. Someone was asking for you here only yesterday: as a poet tells us.

This is the day on which the New York *Times* can finally report that the young man on the Greek throne has gambled away his seat and left the country. Sometimes I'm not so sure after all whether you and I would see eye to eye over such events. We haven't met for five years.

You can't come to see this country, but I can tell you about it. How your letter arrived. In the morning, around nine, a mail truck stopped outside our building, and the driver carried a small armful to Mr. Robinson and discussed union rates with him. By about 10:30 Mr. Robinson had sorted the mail and rode up in the elevator to the top floor. From there he walked down floor by floor, going along each corridor twice. The first time he threw the printed matter down outside the apartment doors. That is a slapping, echoing sound that merely announces the arrival of the mail. The signal that there's some mail for you is when the apartment door shudders gently in response to a soft thud. Then he takes the real letters and squeezes them between door and door jamb, at keyhole level. There, you see, they are more taboo than the junk mail on the stone floor. Sometimes he comes a third time, with a little package or a parcel, and rings the bell and says: "I've got NEWS for you!" Not at our place, at our place it would be useless, for I've been in the office for some time and Marie's already in school. I have never seen Mr. Robinson at this job. Ever since hearing, one Saturday morning, the sounds he makes, I have a mental picture and know that's how it is.

Now about how I can dispose of this letter to you. There are the ordinary mailboxes, blue, with red caps. But instead of being fastened to walls of buildings they stand all by themselves at street corners, and when you pull the handle of one beneath its half-domed brow, a great scooping maw opens up. They have olive-green siblings, but these are stepchildren, for their heads have no openings at all and they are obliged to announce to all and sundry: We do not accept mail. But they do, from letter carriers. In the mansions along Riverside Drive there are bronze plates, like coats-of-arms, set into the wall and they have a slot and tell you a zip-code number. In the lobby of our building the mailbox is merely an old cast-iron one, not elegant, but for our building only. I don't have to go to it. For in office fortresses as well as apartment houses there are flat glass shafts running from top to bottom and with mouths at each floor. Inside this glass the letter flutters down but on the very next floor the passer-by is startled by a plunging flicker of white, glimpsed out of the corner of one eye, as it hurtles down to our venerable coffer which the mailman in his truck visits several times a day, as now at nine o'clock at night. The truck, which I can see below my window, is blue and white, and when it reverses it lights up red eyes and it can emit shrill notes of warning. The driver steps down from his roomy cab and goes to the door of the truck, grabs a sack, enters the building, returns with the sack, steps inside the truck, and this time switches on the light, which to us up here appears as a yellow glow in the darkness of the truck roof.

Now about the postal system in general. The uniform of the letter carriers is a shirt of light blue-gray that interprets the occupation literally with an embroidered badge on the upper arm: The man inside is a letter carrier, it says. And we all know what Herodotus said about them. Since the mail is sacred, its buildings are modeled after classic temples, and since it belongs to the Federal Government WANTED signs hang on the walls of its branches. A mail truck even has right-of-way over a fire engine. In cities, post-office windows are carefully screened with wrought-iron grilles, in the country the desks and counters are open. But we don't happen to live in the country. And wish we could have gone there with you.

Marie asks to be remembered and says she knows all about you.

I'm not that presumptuous, but rather

Your very affectionate
G. C.

Your letter will bear the Grand Central postmark. The best is none too good for you.

December 15, 1967 Friday

In one thing, typographical errors, the New York *Times* reveals herself as the old lady she is. Today she speaks of a "Wost Important Target," the Longbien Bridge near Hanoi. If only the pilots' hands were as unsteady as those of the New York *Times*.

And the New York *Times* prints one story especially for Marie's benefit. On 48th Street near Fifth Avenue, His Honor John Vliet Lindsay saw an empty cardboard cigarette box come flying out of the driver's cab of a truck. He ran after the box and flung it at the three men in the cab. "I'm the Mayor," he said angrily. "I'm trying to keep the city clean. You ought to be ashamed of yourselves."

"Yes sir," said the men in the truck. They almost tipped their hats.

And invariably there are people who cannot apply the seriousness applicable to the occasion: a passer-by said to the Mayor, "Finders keepers, Mr. Mayor."

And, all unsuspecting, Marie falls for it and says: "John Lindsay's quite right! He's right, I tell you! I can't imagine what you're laughing about!"

Weather: Mostly fair, windy and colder today, tonight and tomorrow.

"Now I'm going to test you," says Marie. "I'm going to find out where you get your pasts from. We've had enough of these inventions. Tell me something about the child Gesine when she was two years old!"

"When she was two years old, the child Gesine could sit, stand, walk, talk a little, and she read the newspaper."

"There, I've caught you!" cries Marie. "I did that too! You've got that from me!"

"That's true, Marie, when you were two you used to read the *Frankfurter Allgemeine Zeitung.* But you weren't allowed to make the tiniest little tear in it, not even by mistake, and you learned that very quickly. Almost from the start you had a respect for the printed word. But the child in Cresspahl's house read the *Lübecker Generalanzeiger,* the official news sheet for Lübeck, Schleswig-Holstein, and Mecklenburg. And the grownups looked on indulgently when she tore the paper in half with a great swing of her arms, partly because this was at least one way of ridding the world of lies, and in that state the paper was at least good for lighting fires."

"One nothing," says Marie, crossly. Then a sudden idea can make her very crafty, she beams in happy anticipation as she says: "And the child Gesine held the paper upside down."

"Yes."

"Like me!" says Marie. "Like me!"

"One all. Congratulations, Marie."

"I'm not nearly through yet!" she says. "What kind of things did the child say, when she did say something?"

"The child considered the following words important and tried to imitate them: Cresspahl, bear, buttermilk, cat. And when her father's name came out as Esspaw, you can imagine the rest. Low German, incidentally."

"And not the word mother?"

"It's possible. Since it's probable, let's assume so."

"How about me?"

"It was your second word, and you used it in the form of my first name. You used to say: Ee-ne. Ee-ne."

"No score," says Marie, disappointed.

"No score."

"And the bear?" she says, as casually as she can.

"The child at Cresspahl's pronounced that th'beh. She had grasped that she had to leave certain holes open in speech, but not yet what had to go into the holes. Verbs like be, have, come, all took the same form. For these she just added on an s: 's'th'beh.'"

"And the bear wasn't by any chance called Edward and lived under the name of Sanders in gold letters in a forest all by himself?" says Marie. She is racing along now, she is quite sure of her victory.

"He certainly was, and in other circles the bear was known as Winnie-the-Pooh."

"Now I've got you," says Marie, relaxed, cool as a cucumber. "You've got that from me. We've got the German translation, remember? Over there in your glass bookcase, and it says: Copyright 1938. But we're talking about March 1935. It didn't exist then. You've stolen that from my life, and now the score's two to one. In my favor."

"Maybe not. There's another book on the shelf, remember? And in that one, under Milne, Alan Alexander, you'll find: Winnie-the-Pooh, 1926 (Pu der Bär, 1928)."

"Damn," says Marie. "Sorry, but isn't that maddening? By the way, I think we ought to deduct one point each time one of us makes a mistake. So that would make it one nothing, in your favor."

"You couldn't be expected to know that, Marie."

"Never mind, it's a principle, as of now."

"All right. A principle it is."

"How come we have the German edition of 1938? It belongs to you, doesn't it?"

"Because I didn't get it till 1939, Hilde Paepcke gave it to me for my birthday."

"Then how come the child Gesine knew about Mr. Sanders, Winnie-the-Pooh, way back in 1935?"

"Cresspahl told her. Cresspahl used to tell the child stories."

"I see."

"The child didn't know what name Edward Bear lived under in a forest all by himself, nor what pseudonym he used in social circles. The child only knew that her teddy was called Bear, and Cresspahl happened to be talking about that Edward, the one he had run across in 1929 among English children."

"That was a trick, Gesine."

"Yes, maybe it was. D'you want a point?"

"I come by my points honestly, and what's more I know the answer. The child knew the bear's English name. Like me."

"I used to read to you from the book Hilde Paepcke gave me. In 1959 we were living in Düsseldorf, and you still spoke your mother tongue. German."

"I laid a trap for myself there," says Marie, now very nearly confused. But she is brave, she says: "Minus one plus one. In your favor."

"I don't think we ought to deduct points after all, Marie."

"You're quite good as a mother, Gesine. Any other mother I know would have laughed. But that's enough. You mustn't coddle me."

"A tua disposizione, Fanta Giro. Minus one plus one. In my favor."

"How did I say my name, Gesine?"

"Ma-ee."

"And the child at Cresspahl's?"

"Gay-zeena."

"No points."

"Game stands."

"This isn't a game, Gesine!"

"As you were, Marie."

"Suppose there were some things the child in Cresspahl's house didn't like."

"Such as having her hair cut."

"Like me! Like me! One nothing, in your favor, though."

"But the child cried only once over the loss of her own hair. Then Cresspahl had an idea and took the child by the hand and went for a walk with her along Town Street in Jerichow."

"Along Adolf Hitler Street. No score."

"Along the street of the Austrian in Jerichow and bought a leg of mutton at Klein the butcher's and some corduroy trousers at Tannebaum's and a postcard at the post office, and the child followed right along, going into one store after the other, including Fiete Semmelweis's, Hairdressers for Ladies and Gentlemen, Superior Shave & Haircut. And the child watched while Cresspahl prematurely, less than two weeks after his last haircut, let them take a little bit off his hair. Cresspahl had murmured something to Semmelweis, to make sure he didn't clip him totally bald, and Semmelweis was very touched, delighted too in a way, and the child saw that for both men the business of haircutting was an enjoyable, entertaining affair, and next time she raised no objection to being deprived of a bit of her hair and probably thought it was a present for Cresspahl. For she turned her back on Lisbeth's scissors but went to Cresspahl's."

"Minus one plus one. In your favor."

"That's not how I meant it, Marie."

"That's how I mean it. I started this."

"But think about cutting nails, Marie."

"Just so you can invent a story about Cresspahl's child, how she cried too when her nails were cut, and right off I'll score a point. No funny business, thank you."

"It's not a fair contest, Marie. I'm bound to win if I don't cheat."

"I know something else. The child spoke so little."

"The child kept a somewhat resolute silence, even when she was two. She listened to the grownups, but seldom replied to questions. She behaved diplomatically. For example, if Aggie Brüshaver were to ask the child how she was, she would still have to guess the answer. When Heine Klaproth invited the child to come along and see his rabbits, he had to wait and see whether she was following or hadn't abruptly turned aside and the only evidence that she had been there a moment before would be a solitary wooden shoe. And Methfessel might stop the child in the square and inquire in his conspiratorial voice, with his quiet chuckles: How would you like to be a lion? Can you eat everything now? But maybe the child realized that this grownup no longer needed an answer. She would smile at him, and then give her father's hand a little tug, to make him look at her, and Cresspahl would look at her and understand that her negotiations with Methfessel were now ended and she was ready to walk on."

"Hm. Like me?"

"Like you. You were still like that when we arrived in New York. Nothing to one. In my favor, though."

"And Cresspahl's child loved going for walks."

"With him. With him she would go to buy lumber, to pay taxes, to the barber, to Wulff's. Cresspahl had explained Wulff's tavern as being an apple-juice store, and she must have understood. She learned something there too: she only liked apple juice, not soda pop, and when she shook her head Wulff would take away the pop and bring the apple juice. At home, with Lisbeth, this would have been out of the question. The child enjoyed going to apple-juice stores and knew them all in Jerichow. Lisbeth was made aware of this one morning when she was out shopping and the child tried to drag her into the Lübeck Arms. Lisbeth didn't understand what the child wanted, and tried to walk on. The child lay down in front of the steps to the Lübeck Arms, on the dusty paving, flat on her stomach, and could only be removed by force, to the accompaniment of screams. She expressed her defiance by refusing to walk, and Lisbeth had to carry her home all through town, and the child screamed until Cresspahl's door closed behind them, and so for the first time Lisbeth's competence as a mother became the subject of gossip in Jerichow. The child was always in her father's company, on walks, on drives, gardening, bathing in the Baltic, always, everywhere, whenever he made an appearance outside the workshop, and because you have never had any of this I shall promptly and irrevocably and under threat of serious consequences give you one point. One all and end of game."

"Please don't cry, Gesine. Do stop. Shall I bring you a drink of D. E.'s whisky? Please don't cry, Gesine!"

December 16, 1967   Saturday

Today is a bad day for the Union of Soviet Socialist Republics. Not only was Sergeant Ulysses L. Harris, of New Jersey, sentenced yesterday to seven years' hard labor for espionage on behalf of the U. S. S. R., but today the New York *Times* let all the world in on it. And in Italy the Union of Soviet Socialist Republics lost three of its spies to the penitentiary: Giorgio Rinaldi for fifteen years, Angela Maria Rinaldi for eleven, and Armando Girard for ten years.

Will compound interest be added to the continuing salaries?

The Air Force claims to have smashed two spans of the Longbien Bridge near Hanoi and to have knocked down a third. And Bob Hope has taken off for his annual Christmas tour of military bases in Vietnam, Cardinal Spellman being dead, and REMEMBER THE NEEDIEST!

And as for Sonny Franzese and his three friends, justice has been performed. They had caused a certain Mr. Walter Sher, a convicted murderer, to write a letter. The letter says that actually it was Mr. John Rapacki who was responsible for the fact that Ernest (The Hawk) Rupolo, with six bullet wounds and seventeen stab wounds in his body, was found floating in Jamaica Bay on August 24, 1964. Mr. Walter Sher's sentence has now been commuted by the Governor to life imprisonment, and Mr. John Rapacki says: It was a lie, and he could prove it. But never mind that, Franzese and his friends have been acquitted, and the New York *Times* has seen his wife, trim and blonde, sobbing, and knows why too: with emotion and relief. Have a nice Christmas, Mrs. Franzese!

Marie finds nothing extraordinary in the Cresspahl family's being picked up in the late afternoon at Riverside Drive and driven to Connecticut by chauffeur in a limousine. To judge by her behavior, this was no more than she expected. For now the Cresspahl family not only has a friend who shares a big car and a house in the country with them, which, after all, might be personal coincidence, if not merit; now it also gets invited to partake of such luxuries by the boss, by His Majesty the Vice-President himself, and Marie feels secure in a world in which ability receives its just reward.

As long as the car was in town she may have regretted that its windows are tinted a discreet dark green and offer no opportunity to any of her classmates to observe her being driven in such style; as soon as they are on the parkways she begins to experiment with appropriate behavior for a conveyance of this kind. She decides in favor of an upright, severe posture in the well-padded upholstery. Then a little camouflaged closet in the front panel of the passenger compartment becomes too much for her curiosity. She thinks there might be a bar inside. With the utmost casualness she pulls at the resplendent knob. For Heaven's sake, it really is a bar, with a refrigerator. This car has a radiotelephone! There's a television set no bigger than a little box! Marie is so busy with discoveries and how to behave that she fails to notice that Arthur is just waiting for an invitation to lower the dividing glass panel and start up the conversation of which he now considers this Miss Cresspahl to be worthy. But this Miss Cresspahl is talking to her child. This Miss Cresspahl has other things on her mind.

De Rosny's house stands close to Long Island Sound in a park-like area in which even the roads are privately owned. The area begins with a hump right across the road, the idea being that when it jolts the wheels the visiting driver's attention is drawn to the fact that he has crossed over into private property with its own rules and customs. The house has no less than five white columns in front of its two stories, and the only thing they hold up is the projecting roof. The wrought-iron gates open at an electronic signal from the car. Marie is only slightly embarrassed that Arthur holds the door open for her and remains standing, head bowed, his cap held at his chest. She thinks such customs are a matter of course, once they are observed and performed. She has time to dart a glance of thanks. She believes this is all due to her mother's work.

She has it all wrong. She regards De Rosny, this loose-limbed, hardy man, simply as a kind person with particularly credible manners. She does not realize that we are dependent on this person. Yet she has been told this more than once. She lets him take her through the lower floor, rooms filled with inflatable furniture, Colonial closets, hanging chairs, the walls hung with reproductions of comic strips and canned soups. So this is where the New York *Times* took pictures. Here, too, there are signs of preparations for Christmas. De Rosny has hung paper stars from the lamps, Eastern stars, the biggest and brightest to be found at New York stationers'. If one is to believe him, he has set up a medieval Italian Nativity scene especially for Marie, and Marie believes him. He so totally envelops Marie with the treatment accorded to a lady that she cannot help but adapt to it. It is all thank you and please and may I but of course. She wouldn't dare flutter her eyelids like that at me. Even her voice sounds different.

To Marie the whole evening is a visit among friends. To her it is possible for people working in offices to have power over one another through a chain of command and differing remuneration, and yet in their leisure time to associate as equals. She is so convinced of her welcome being without ulterior motive and on the strength of her personal charms that she will promptly admit the entire De Rosny family to her intimate circle, and the first thing she will ask me outside will be why Mrs. De Rosny stayed upstairs all the time, on the second floor, walking up and down through the rooms with a rather heavy tread. The New York *Times* won't have taken any pictures up there. Marie finds the transformation of Arthur into a manservant downright comical and winks at him when he wheels over the cocktails in a converted baby buggy, Paris 1908, and she accepts her orange juice, which Arthur has dubbed a screwdriver, as the joke he had intended.

Marie regards the conversation before dinner as lighthearted reminiscences of work in the far-off city and is not aware that in reality it is an exhaustive, ruthless test to see whether I have properly and fully understood the fiscal system of the Czechoslovak Republic, and by how much the Czechoslovak Government hopes to raise the national income with the aid of its new 1966/70 five-year plan, and in which areas, and in the chemical industry by 50 per cent, for example, and finally whether the Czechs and Slovaks will bring this off, and if not, for what reasons. What that Mr. Kouba said in February

1966 in the *Mirovaya Ekonomika i Mezhdunarodniye Otnosheniya* about the New System of economic management in the Czecho-slovak Republic, this I reeled off so fast that I had no time to find the German words for it, let alone the thinking behind them. The test appears to have been passed, perhaps with a B minus. All Marie has noticed is that once again her mother has known a lot of things, and she displays her pride with big shining eyes.

Yet it is by no means certain that the men in Prague seriously intend to restore the health of their economy with the aid of Western foreign-exchange credits. Still, it was not a Western financier who approached the Státní Banka Československá, it was that bank's president who paid a call on Karl Blessing of the West German Bundesbank. What a blessing there's a Blessing. The question put to me is not whether it can be done; or even whether I am willing. I know of no firm except the House of Revlon where a woman is even a minor executive, let alone of a bank, and De Rosny won't be able to swing that. That takes care of that.

All Marie notices about the dinner is how solemn it is. This is a result of the combined efforts of a housekeeper, a cook, and finally Arthur. Marie sees only that Arthur really does pour wine into one of her three glasses. She takes De Rosny's inquiries about my background for simple concern, as is only right and proper among friends. What he is conducting is an interrogation. He can do this, he is the boss, he is investing money, with all the risk entailed, he claims that right, no matter how courteous the phrasing, how pleasant the manner. He quite simply wants to know everything I have not told the Personnel Department, from Mecklenburg trade guilds to my present grasp of the principles of Marxist dialectic. De Rosny cannot understand that Cresspahl was once Mayor of Jerichow, and although he may find it amusing he still wants it explained. As for Jakob, he is satisfied with the facts of his occupation and death. You are ever so thoughtful, sir. But in the course of this conversation it transpires that Jakob never did represent the German Democratic Republic at an International Conference on Railway Timetables, was never even in Lisbon, and Marie is disappointed. She had been so sure. Well now, and how would the Czechs and Slovaks feel about me personally? How should I know? What he means is: the Government and Party of the Czechs and Slovaks. They are not likely to have any quarrel with me. After all, I don't need to rub it under their noses that I traveled through their country on a passport in which only the photograph was mine. But then again: the Czechoslovak Republic is on fairly close terms with the German Democratic Republic, and they might want to share the distress of that Government over the fact that I tried out living there for only three and a half years and then went to another Jericho. That does not bother De Rosny. On the contrary, he regards it as not unfavorable. True, there is no need for me to confide by registered letter either to De Rosny or to the Ministry of the Interior or Exterior of the G. D. R. that I have a friend by the name of Anita, Anita of the Red Hair, who assists private individuals to get out of the G. D. R. and so far I have not been able to refuse her anything. But then there is that job I had with the Maneuver Damage Compensation Department of NATO in the woods near Mönchengladbach. For De Rosny this was a frill, inclined rather to enhance my trustworthiness. Possibly, but the way I came by the job. If he doesn't ask I can't tell him. So that takes care of the second point on the agenda. It seems that, all in all, I have the right knowledge and the right background for the fishing expedition that our respected employer De Rosny has in mind for the Eastern European credit market. Now I would like to be allowed to go home.

But Marie has one more question. While my biography was being examined she was all eyes and ears, and indeed there was much that she heard about for the first time. Now it appears that throughout she was thinking of something else as well, and what comes now is nothing short of an interview with De Rosny. She produces her question somewhat diffidently, at first with lowered lids, restricting herself to generalities and without naming De Rosny's firm: "Is it true that the banks are making money out of the Vietnam war?"

Before De Rosny has even opened his mouth, Marie believes everything he is about to say. He resisted any impulse to a critical glance at the mother who prepares her child for life with such stereotyped Communist notions; he even refrained from allowing his expression to betray any amusement at the childishness of the question. He straightens himself in his chair, leans forward, his elbows resting on the damask arms, puts his hands together, almost clasping them, and gives Marie a long, serious look. He is making the effort of an actor playing the part of a doctor at the bedside of a very sick patient. Even his voice has become deeper. "We," he says, and stops, as if, for the sake of greater precision, he has to weigh everything once more in his mind. Now Marie is frightened. Money itself is talking to her, and Money is looking at her out of steady, concerned blue eyes while it talks to her face to face.

"We wish with all our hearts that the conflict in Indo-China would come to an end, one way or another, at least so that our country will cease to be involved in it. We don't believe there will be a peace with an American victory, not even in two years. And peace in Indo-China without a victory for our side, a peace we can have in two years, is what we want now. For war brings and fosters inflation. Inflation, young lady, is a terrible thing for a bank. In the long run, war enables the Government to tie the hands of the banks, to dictate to them down to the last detail what they may and may not do. Already it's going to require an appalling effort to cure the sicknesses that are concealed behind today's false prosperity. I'll tell you, young lady. If President Johnson were to announce defeat in Vietnam and that we were cutting our losses, the market would jump fifty points. Fifty? Sixty's more like it, and the very same day at that. And then there's the human side, the most important of all, my dear Mary. Bankers have human feelings too. Believe me," says De Rosny.

And Marie believes him. She complains with a look of surprise at her mother, who has shown things in a different light, but since her mother does not contradict De Rosny the matter is settled for Marie. Marie ought never to have been brought to this house.

As we leave, a box wrapped in a white cloth is carried to the car, and the Italian Nativity scene no longer stands where it did. When an employee turns out to be thoroughly suited for a profitable enterprise, it is legitimate to bind that person more firmly to oneself with a gift worth, say, a thousand dollars, even if the gift is intended for the child.

"We all wish you a pleasant Christmas," says De Rosny, and he really does stand in his inherited doorway until the car has left the drive. Marie continues to wave through the rear window until she is sure he can no longer see her.

And for Marie that's not all. There is no end to the false gifts that day. De Rosny wishes to start his fishing expedition discreetly. The purpose of my learning Czech is to facilitate my vacation in Prague, and should I be asked again about the bank's attitude toward credits to Eastern European countries, the more intelligent answer would be: The bank's policy in this area may be described as not aggressive, repeat: not aggressive. Strange, that Dmitri Weiszand should have spent a whole evening and a meal at the St. Wenceslas to draw out Mrs. Cresspahl with this question. And even for Marie it will be better to behave as if we had spent this evening with soda pop and popcorn at the Riviera Cinema and, predictably, Marie is thrilled.

"A real secret?" she says. "You mean a secret even the New York *Times* doesn't know?"

Yes, that kind of secret, and Marie enjoys this.

December 17, 1967   Sunday

Either it is because of the approach of the Christmas holidays, or that old lady the New York *Times* is definitely showing her age. Here she is, blatantly claiming the existence of a West German writer called Günther Glass. To begin with, th is wrong, and surely the other cannot be right. Doesn't the New York *Times* know that the Glass family is the lifetime companion of another author, Jerome D. Salinger, in Westport, Connecticut?

And the Air Force unloads all it has over Hanoi and even some Congressmen consider the Vietcong to be doing a better job of land redistribution than the government in Saigon and a charred package containing $44,000 in cash was found in the burned-out post office and the city burglars are now going into the suburbs and the cause of the common cold may be psychic depression rather than a virus and Sonny Franzese is back home again with Tina.

In 1935 my father started two things.

One was that he made himself a garden. Behind the house, from the back entrance to the front of the workshop barn, there was uncultivated, weed-choked ground, and one Sunday evening in March a whole group set to work digging over the compacted soil. Those who came, each bringing a spade, were: Hilde Paepcke, Alexander Paepcke, Aggie Brüshaver, Creutz Senior and Junior ("as good neighbors"), Arthur Semig, Meta Wulff, Albert Papenbrock, Louise Papenbrock, the two assistants, the two apprentices, Lisbeth Cresspahl, Cresspahl, and the child. They formed a long front against the land, and they dug, and they turned the earth over, and they threw the stones neatly onto a pile, and there was fun, as when Louise broke her spade, and around Heine Klaproth a fat mound spread in his wake, and there was laughter, as when Louise Papenbrock refused help with her portion, and in a few hours they had finished. Lisbeth was given the honor of treading the paths between the beds. The others were given beer and pea soup from the very largest pot in the house. Creutz had brought along ten fruit trees, but he did not want to plant the first one because that would not be quite the thing and so Cresspahl went over and planted a tree and watered it and hoped for good apples. Then he paced off Lisbeth's paths once again to see that everything was in order and the party at the windows laughed, for he did not know that the little tot was following him with her hands solemnly clasped behind her back, just like him. And in the cold cold month of May the ground was a garden. That had been started, and it was to last.

The other came from the guild in Gneez. They had promised to cut him in, and cut him in they did. What had been in the air was the placing of a contract by the Reichswehr, now known as the Wehrmacht, and it called for construction and road-building and subcontracts for carpenters and plumbers and glaziers and roofers and chimney masons and gardeners on a very large tract of land to the north of Jerichow, halfway between the town and the sea, where the land rose quite high above the water. Before they cut Cresspahl in there was one small matter to be cleared up.

I hear you have ten thousand marks in the Credit Union, Cresspahl.

You say so, Böttcher. I don't.

And even if it's fifteen thousand, Cresspahl. That's not the point.

I see.

Hm, yes. Well, it won't do. Take it out of there and put it in Wismar, Lübeck, wherever you like. I must be able to say: Cresspahl has no more than eight hundred in the Credit Union. I must be able to say that with a clear conscience.

I'll attend to it, Böttcher. And thanks.

Then they cut him in and invited him to the home of the guild master and calculated what each would get, the Reichswehr in Mecklenburg being known to favor small enterprises, and the Gneez guild wanted to get all the business. And in fact the tradesmen in the district of Gneez did have the construction of Jerichow North almost entirely sewn up among themselves. Only for the concrete work and steel construction were specialist firms called in from Berlin and Hamburg. This in turn yielded the hotel owners some extra revenue. So almost everybody was taken care of. Something was in the air, you could sense it, and there were those who even put it into words: Things are beginning to roll. And Köpcke the contractor had so much cause to rejoice that he started speaking to Cresspahl again, although the latter hadn't put a single penny in his way during his own rebuilding. There were plenty of pennies around now, and there were no complaints about marks either.

Not everyone, though, had it all his own way. Cresspahl, for instance, wanted more than anything else to get the order for the officers' mess. It mattered a great deal to him. An officers' mess has guests, people talk. Some of them are well-to-do citizens. What Cresspahl wanted to show off there were massive redwood bays on three sides. For the center he had in mind three tables that could be easily combined into a long dining table or removed to make way for a dance floor. That's how it was before, there used to be dances in the officers' mess. But Cresspahl did not get the contract to furnish the mess, and he could not insist either, it went to Wilhelm Bött-cher, master of the guild, since he was the one who had landed that particular fish. In the end Wilhelm Böttcher was not to be envied, for the Reichswehr, or the Wehrmacht as it was now called, sent him some fellow who mucked up his drawings in the worst way. So Cress-pahl contented himself with the beds, wall closets, sentryboxes, and the slatted platform the sentry has to stand on, otherwise he gets cold feet. And he now got almost more assistants and unskilled workers than he had room for, so he had hastily to convert the old fodder room in the barn into sleeping quarters. And when Else Pienagel appeared with a dining-room chair that she wanted fixed up as nicely as her sewing cabinet had been, he could not promise when she could come to pick it up, for now there was no time for deliveries either. And there was something to show for it, at last there was money to spare. By the end of 1935 he had been able to buy a belt sander and a chain mortiser and a veneer router and an angle assembly jig, and it was all very well to criticize the German Labor Front and that drunken bastard Ley, but in spite of that Dr. Erdamer had not been above accepting an important post in that outfit, and Dr. Erdamer wangled a bargain for Cresspahl to buy new machinery from the German Woodworking Machinery Co. of Schwerin and so for the whole lot he had had to pay only 9,500 Reichsmarks. Otherwise the machines would have easily cost 11,000 Reichsmarks. They were not called Rentenmarks any more, they were called Reichsmarks. And Lisbeth was so busy with cooking for all the workmen and with the house and the child; although she had two maids to help her who were learning what a Mecklenburg household was like, there were still many days when it was late evening by the time she was through, for often she was the one who had to take the train to Gneez to pick up forms at the Army construction headquarters on Station Street.

You can't expect me to do that, Cresspahl.
Can't expect you to do what, Lisbeth.
Go to Gneez and pick up the forms.
Yes I can. The less the maids know about it the better, and the child can't take the train by herself yet.

But that makes me guilty too, Heinrich!
Guilty of what?
War! The barracks are for war, aren't they.
Lisbeth, I can't help you there.
Couldn't we . . . can't you get out of the contract?
And how would we live, Lisbeth?
Oh Henry, live! Just think of the guilt.
D'you want to go to England?
No!
I don't know what you want, Lisbeth.
Cresspahl.
Can't you hear? The child's crying.

And the roads in Jerichow North had been laid out with surprising width in some places. And behind the barrier of Army barracks the area that had been fenced in was larger than was needed for a drill ground. The fences ran for miles toward the west. And the wide roads got longer and longer, there was no end to them. And for a long time the children of Jerichow learned to use the wrong word for airplane, they learned: fighter, and they learned: bomber.

December 18, 1967   Monday

In 1935 the German State Railway booth at the end of the steamer dock in Rande-on-the-Baltic still sold tickets to anywhere, to Lübeck as well as to London. Perhaps Cresspahl had put it out of his mind because the Government of His Majesty King George V had disappointed him. For although the Austrian really had reintroduced conscription and compelled every soldier to take an oath of loyalty to him, was it necessary for the English to aid and abet him with their permission to build up the German fleet to 35 per cent of the strength of the British fleet? They were in for a surprise over the twelve German submarines that were put in service at the end of June 1935, and over those still to come. And he probably thought he would no longer be welcome.

Brüshaver would have been forbidden by his Church to flee the country, and apparently Brüshaver saw nothing wrong in his son by his first marriage serving as a pilot in the Air Force of that Austrian who wanted to pocket the Church. The reason for Brüshaver's inquiring about the progress of construction in Jerichow North was probably that he wanted to have his son transferred there, perhaps as commandant.

Old Mr. and Mrs. Papenbrock could not be expected to leave now. For every suspect action of the Führer and Reich Chancellor, Papenbrock found, as he always had, one that he did not consider suspect. If it was a bitter pill that that fellow had banned the Mecklenburg flag, along with the flags of all the German states, the fact remained that the two Mecklenburgs were now reunited for the first time in three hundred years, and even the stuck-up Lübeckers with their Free Hansa City were included; and the reincorporation of the Saar territory with the Reich, let someone try a coup like that. It was annoying, of course, that the fellow called himself an author, and that he had not for appearances' sake continued a while longer as a member of the Brunswick legation in Berlin. And as far as he, Papenbrock, was concerned, the Austrian hadn't yet taken away or destroyed anything of his.

"How could Papenbrock ever have gone to the memorial service for Stelling? Had Stelling been in the Papenbrock party too?"

"Johannes Stelling had been a Social Democrat, but in 1920, as Minister of the Interior for Mecklenburg-Schwerin, he had not stood in the way of the Volunteer Corps who were quartered on the Mecklenburg estates and going after the workers. Without him, Papenbrock might easily have lost his Vietsen tenancy even sooner. Stelling had been Prime Minister of the state from 1921 to 1924. And a Reichstag deputy. Papenbrock probably wanted to do him honor, even though it was the last."

And at the end of 1935 Arthur Semig was still living in his comfortable, well-built house on the Bäk in Jerichow and receiving his retirement pay and found that quite fair. It was true that now it was even legally impossible for him to keep a maid for Dora, and in Jerichow there was no longer any person with whom he would have been permitted either marriage or extramarital cohabitation, and his German citizenship had also been taken away from him. But to make up for that he had the right to hoist the Jewish colors on his flagpole, and it was up to the municipal police to protect this flag from damage or desecration. Arthur simply could not bring himself to leave a country where everyone spoke as he did, even though in many respects they thought differently.

And Peter Niebuhr was serving in the Eiche school for noncommissioned officers near Potsdam and had been a member of the Communist Party of Berlin-Friedenau. Did he want to take revenge on Comrade Stalin, who now also had his dead friend Kirov, as Hitler had his Röhm, and was taking his time over putting down the putsch and continuing with his liquidations? Was it not to his liking that the U.S.A had finally taken up diplomatic relations with Stalin's state, that under these circumstances Stalin had been admitted to the League of Nations against Switzerland's vote? Peter's relatives did not understand him. Ever since Peter had started going to university in Berlin he had been hard to understand.

And even Martin Niebuhr now realized that the Department of Waterways would never offer him anything bigger than the lock near Wendisch Burg. And Gertrud Niebuhr would have liked to adopt a child, at least. And Lisbeth had had to promise to pay a visit to the lock, with the child Gesine, of not less than two weeks every year. And Horst Papenbrock had not only returned from "Rio de Janeiro," he had brought along his brother Robert. Jerichow did not see much of Robert, he had moved to Schwerin some time previously. And the military was still not much in evidence in Jerichow, but Pahl did well with his officers' uniforms made to measure. The trades complained rather more loudly and were doing well. Even Alexander Paepcke had been transformed into a businessman by the urgent demand for building material for Jerichow North, and he spent his days at the brickyard and the office and not on the tennis courts of Gneez. And in August 1935 the Paepckes had their second child, a boy, Eberhardt Paepcke, Paepcke Junior. And the brickyard still hadn't burned down. And only Methfessel had not been able to adjust. Methfessel had been obliged to make over his business to his oldest assistant; his sons were still children. It was a shame to see the big burly fellow walking the streets of Jerichow, looking for children and asking them: "How would you like to be a lion? Don't make me laugh!" And Dr. Avenarius Kollmorgen had given up his practice and was seldom to be seen outdoors and asked very few people nowadays whether they were getting along all right. And Dr. Hauschildt had grown into an almost competent veterinarian, now that an eye was being kept on him. And Methling had taken to his bed in Gneez and had died after doing all he could for race and Reich and wished to be buried in Jerichow and had actually succeeded in obliging Bishop Schultz to arrange for a ceremony more national than religious. And on the coffin lay a flag with the swastika, and six Storm Troopers carried it out of St. Peter's Church, and school was closed to enable the children to sing.

Dr. Berling had discovered relatives living in Sweden, when he went there in search of his Aryan descent, and now spent his vacations in Schonen. Swenson was running two taxis now and maintained a bus line from the Jerichow station to Jerichow North and was fighting the postal bus service over the license for a route to Rande. Erich Schulz had not come back to Jerichow-Ausbau; he was said to be in the Navy. The Plessens and the Bothmers and their associates had allowed themselves, together with their riding clubs, to be absorbed into the SS. And Friedrich Jansen had been mayor and district leader of the Nazi Party in Jerichow for almost two years now, and had learned to listen to old Papenbrock. There were still a few he could not quite cope with. Johs. Schmidt's House of Music still demanded payment whenever the Party ordered loudspeakers for national and National Socialist events; one day they'd learn. Another one was the Englishman, that Heinrich Cresspahl behind the church. The fellow turns up at the town hall asking for an application form for membership in the Party and doesn't bring it back and claims the form was for one of his helpers. The helper went to Wismar, and that much Friedrich Jansen had been able to find out, that the helper had in fact been a member of the Party since June 1934, but there was something fishy going on. That fellow Cresspahl would not admit to having had second thoughts when the Führer purged his Storm Troopers of traitors and vermin; and the only explanation he would offer was that he was still thinking it over. And he went on offering the same explanation over and over again. So far there was no way of getting at the man, so far there was no way of getting past Papenbrock. But one day Cresspahl would fall for Nordic cunning.

Cresspahl had now taken out another life insurance policy, with the Alliance Company. Cresspahl could now be reached by telephone at Jerichow 209. It was always the wife who answered the phone, he seemed to be too busy to walk the few steps from the workshop into the house. Now it was 1935, and they still did not have their second child, or a third. Lisbeth Papenbrock had not looked like that sort of person. The saying about the walnut trees had proved to be right, the volatile oils really did keep the gnats away. They just had the one child, Gesine; by Christmas 1935 she was a little over two and a half. She still did not talk much, but she kept her eyes wide open.

Hold on to the fence, the sky is high.

December 19, 1967   Tuesday

Oh how indignant the New York *Times* can get! It is nothing very extraordinary, only that the Commissioner of Water Supply, Gas, and Electricity resigned last week because he had an arrangement with Antonio Corallo, "Tony Ducks" of the Mafia, involving the private distribution of, for example, $835,000 of city funds. Two articles begin on the front page and the whole of page 52 is given over to them. Another article begins on page 1 and continues on page 53. And the newspaper does not miss this opportunity of giving us a review of corruption in the city "over the last century." And in the editorial the voice seems to tremble, yet the old lady does not lose her head and advises us to regard the case in its proper perspective and tells us how to do so.

And who thanks her for this, other than with ten cents?

We would like to, because it's Christmas.

Thank you kindly, dear lady.

It must be because of Christmas that people seem so stimulated. It can't be anything else.

It began with Marie, who wanted to express her gratitude for an apartment in which in the morning she can see a wintry river and the sunlit cliffs of the far shore. She is devious about it, she assumes a patronizing air, she says: "Nice apartment you have here." Anything else, and she might have betrayed an emotion. Then she said: "Some kids are lucky."

And Shakespeare and Jason were almost beside themselves as they went on and on about Mrs. Cresspahl's appearance, and this may be because they will shortly receive envelopes with bits of green stuff inside, and that can't be the only reason.

The black mechanic in the middle garage on 96th Street, the solemn man who approaches a broken-down car like a dedicated doctor, waved at Mrs. Cresspahl with his whole hand, in a brotherly manner, as if to say: Watch out, sister, take care of yourself. Have a good day. He can do that without smiling.

And on West End Avenue outside the liquor store there was again one of those frayed men who invariably have a sick aunt in New Jersey because that means they need at least 35 cents bus fare, and Mrs. Cresspahl would not relent and gave him a measly subway token instead of cash, and he actually said: "God bless you, lady." It's impossible.

The old man at the newsstand held up Mrs. Cresspahl by being positively talkative and asking: "Don't you want your *Spiegel?* It just came up." Until now he has always behaved as if the customers with their never-ending requests were a nuisance, and today he looks up at the sky and looks this customer in the eye and says: "Nice day." This went beyond a statement of fact, this was not far from being a wish. Might someone have given him a drink?

And at least on the twelfth floor of the bank they could not get over the fact that on December 19 the temperature was all of 55 degrees. It seemed it had not been that for decades. It seemed the last time that happened was in 1931! Each good morning comes close to being an embrace. And no one pays any attention to whether Mrs. Cresspahl obeys the rules and returns the compliment on her appearance with a compliment of her own. They may have meant it; but is that possible?

And all day the weather was what is known here as balmy, sunny and mild, and perfect strangers smiled at Mrs. Cresspahl, on the sidewalk, in the subway! The light feels solid. One could run up against it with one's whole body, not just one's eyelids.

And in the cafeteria Sam intervened personally when I started reading his menu for the second time. "Take the pot roast, it's delicious, I promise you!" he said, kissing his fingertips with pleasure. Then in his opinion the waitress was unduly slow, and Sam called out personally through the hatch to the cooks: "One pot roast, for the lady here, the one with the smile!"

And whoever I saw, Amanda, James Shuldiner, Mrs. Kelly, Mrs. Ferwalter, Marjorie, they all wanted to know how Mrs. Cresspahl was, and they all wanted a true, straight answer!

And Marie telephoned the office, against regulations, and reported that there was mail at home from Kliefoth, from Karsch, from D. E. And the man who sells us cheese would like to ask Mrs. Cresspahl something today, after some two and a half years' acquaintance. The man always has a sour expression, or else his pale complexion makes him look that way, because by afternoon it is already made conspicuous by a telltale five-o'clock shadow. His store is so popular that the customers have to take numbers so as to be served in turn, and he has never once given any sign of recognition. But this evening he was alone.

"O.K., then I'll ask you, ma'am."

"Go ahead."

"You come in here sometimes with a child."

"That's right. Sometimes there are two of them."

"Actually I mean just the one child."

"The one with the braids."

"Right. That's the one I mean."

"And what was your question?"

"Is that your child?"

"That's my child."

"I see."

"Yes."

"Then I'd like, if you don't mind, to ask one more thing."

"Yes."

"Well—. Are you married?"

"The answer is in the affirmative."

"Hm. Well. That takes care of that."

That took care of that.

And Marie had borrowed the elevator from Mr. Robinson and was riding up and down in the building and waiting for the elevator doors to open in front of Mrs. Cresspahl, as I am called, Mrs. Cresspahl, who was not expecting to see her child here, Gesine, as I am to Marie.

One day the child will resemble me at first glance, but the world will come to like her at second glance, and she will not even know that she smiles back like Jakob.

December 20, 1967 Wednesday

The water is hidden deep down where the street has to pass over a hump of rock, chlorine-green, tepid, tight water in a tiled basin beneath the Hotel Marseilles on West End Avenue, Manhattan, Upper West Side, New York, New York. The water is noisy, bursting and shattering as the swimmers dive into it; it slaps against the sides, gurgles in the overflow gutters, tosses the walled-in echo wildly back and forth. On your toes. Arms outstretched. Ankles raised. Head between your arms. Keep your feet together. Now the water strikes the crown of your head. The swoop under the water, in the wake of the hands, passes through a purblind twilight.

The kids at the shallow end of the pool greet the head as it surfaces among them. "Beautiful header, Gesine," they say. But they say: Jee-zine, and maybe what they mean is that they learned to dive differently. A curious header, Mrs. Cresspahl.

The kids from West End Avenue, Riverside Drive, pre-empt the Mediterranean Swimming Club at this hour between the end of the working day and the last meal. They tolerate the presence of the old ladies gamely paddling away in their flowered swimcaps, they keep an eye on the youthful athletes who are trying to prevent physical deterioration by underwater forced marches, and it is less noisy in the corner where a solitary married woman is standing, motionless, conscientiously and shyly holding a pre-toddler against her hip. But the kids are more likely to keep the diving lane clear for one of their own kind, letting the grownups wait up there on the board, and boys like David Williams get a kick out of suddenly diving in among the grimly flailing musclemen.

They learned to dive differently. The jolt given to the whole body by the forward-thrusting arms, right down to the ankles, is not apparent. Just look at that Marie Cresspahl, she came to this country only six years ago, and in one single continuous movement she glides from the edge of the pool into the water like a fish returning to the more familiar element. She seems just to let herself drop; there is no visible kick-off as she jumps. Marie practices diving with her friends, with Pamela Blumenroth, Rebecca Ferwalter; but instead of throwing coins onto the bottom of the pool they throw locker keys, which are camouflaged by their dull color. Without their keys they would not be able to leave the pool, in their exultant shrieks there is apprehension, and when Marie surfaces from the bottom, preceded by a hand holding the salvaged key, there is undeniable relief in her small, wet, broadly beaming face. Later, when she pulls off the tight cap, her long winter-blond hair will make her look older than her ten and a half years. In the white frame of her cap, the immature curve of her eye sockets is exposed beneath the foreshortened brow as if stripped of all protection.

Above the noisy water, halfway up the blue-tiled expanse, a balcony runs around two walls, the back of the Marseilles Bar, where there are tables for two. That dates the hotel. For the customers of 1895 it was enough to look down from above, from a distance, on the bathers, the scantily clad; in a contemporary building the drinkers would want their stools placed at the edge of the pool, or alongside it, behind a transparent panorama wall. Yet Mr. McIntyre hardly ever has a moment to spare up there in front of his ninety-nine bottles of firewater; in this part of town there are enough people who like to meet in the dark-paneled bar, who spend a little time each day on well-worn shiny leather, polishing the venerably gleaming rounded bulk of a mahogany counter with their elbows. Up there on that balcony, six years ago, one Gesine Cresspahl sat too long, trying by way of Irishisms to find a wrong access to life here, often not far from Mr. Blumenroth, who in those days did not look like a father of Pamela. The Jews still have not quite abandoned the Upper West Side, Jews are welcome here; but not once in six years has the head of a black citizen shown itself at the fretted balustrade, and just as up there it is not Mr. McIntyre's prices that deter the blacks from visiting the Marseilles, so down below it is not merely the annual dues of sixty dollars that account for the whites having the water to themselves.

On this particular evening it is two hotel guests who are swimming up and down the south side of the pool, stubbornly keeping to their lanes, two young foreigners who pause almost insolently upon reaching the old ladies who prefer to swim the short distance across the pool, and they swallow water and rage at the kids plunging into the water right in front of their noses. Perhaps they are Germans, technical trainees taking a course with the New York parent company, for they are talking German, although the Jewish swimmers as well as Gesine Cresspahl manage to understand their rather bewildered comments and calls. They haven't realized where they are; their voices are uninhibited, loud. This place is not clean enough for them. At home a new indoor swimming pool has just been built. Many of the swimmers, they feel, look as if they would pass unnoticed in European countries. And at last Marie arrives, swimming with smooth supple strokes underwater, and reports triumphantly: They're talking about you! They said you were the right size! That your bustline was too low! That maybe you hadn't had a child yet but that you sure did have round heels! That to judge by your hair, your cheekbones, you must come from Poland! From a Slav country! she says. For German is spoken by the Cresspahls only when they are sure of not being overheard. Marie insists on this, and her green and gray eyes have become quite solicitous in the belief that she has conveyed a compliment to her mother, something that would please her.

And if you have kids, let's hope they don't have your bones, Cresspahl! I mean, if it's a girl, see she gets Lisbeth's legs!

The pool at the Mediterranean Swimming Club, sixty feet long, with eight lanes, is perhaps larger than the military one in Jerichow, the "Mili," where Gesine Cresspahl learned to swim, the child that I was. Memory magnifies, say those who have gone back. That's one place I must not go back to. It's a long way from here: 4,500 miles and more, even after eight hours' flying you still have to travel till dark and you're not there yet. It's more than 6,000 kilometers. That's Wendish country, Mecklenburg, on another coast. That's where I lived, for twenty years. Afterward you'll be stuck here, on your beam ends, in some American forest. . . .

Thirty years ago my father, Heinrich Cresspahl, born 1888, erected rain shelters at the "Mili" in Jerichow North. He had turned his back on the German wars and gone to the Netherlands, to England, yet he had returned to Mecklenburg with my mother so that I could be born in Germany, only a few years before the next war. That's how miserable my mother, Lisbeth née Papenbrock, was even in those days. Because the airfield above the high Baltic coast near Jerichow, where my father worked as a carpenter, was designed for a modern war, a measly little ditch of a river was halted on its way to the sea and diverted so it could replenish the water in the military swimming pool. The installation was dubbed the "Mili" by the school kids, but only after the war when the Soviet occupation powers blew up the whole Jerichow North complex, razing it to the ground, and forgot the swimming pool. Long before 1953, Cresspahl's rain shelters had passed through Jerichow's furnaces, and rotted stumps were all that remained. It was February, the pool had been drained, and the driving snow had neatly carpeted the bottom in white. Without hesitation Jakob climbed down after me. We walked up and down in the pool until all the lanes were filled with our footprints. Jakob's face that day eludes my imagination; I would have to invent it. We were out of sight, protected by the walls of the great pit, hidden beneath the whirling sky, in the buzzing silence. And though he knew what it's like to live abroad, he couldn't teach me.

The Administration is now permitting American pilots in Vietnam to fly through the buffer strip along the Chinese border. Fourteen American scholars assure the nation that a Communist victory is likely to lead to larger, more costly wars rather than to a lasting peace.

That's Mrs. Cresspahl, waiting at the end of the springboard till the diving lane becomes free. Lives around the corner here, Riverside Drive and 96th Street. Thirty-four years old. She holds her neck stiffly, pulls in a stomach. It won't be long now before she buys her shoes for comfort rather than smartness. When she gathers herself for the dive her eyes narrow, her lips tauten. The sharp impact of the water against her skull results in a momentary unconsciousness, blindness, absence; not for long.

"Quite a header, Jee-zine!"

December 21, 1967   Thursday

In the Senate Foreign Relations Committee some members doubt whether the Administration and General Staff were telling the truth in 1964 when they claimed that on August 4 the destroyers *Maddox* and *Turner Joy* had been attacked by vessels from North Vietnam. According to John W. White of Cheshire, Connecticut, who at that time was serving on the tender *Pine Island* and monitoring the radio messages from the destroyers, the latter were uncertain as to whether they were being fired on or not. Incoming torpedoes were being signaled, but no torpedoes arrived. Was the radar actually showing the approach of a bevy of small craft? Was there any evidence of antiaircraft fire, were illuminating flares sighted? Was it possible for such minimal wakes to be distinguished by aircraft at night? At the time all this was regarded as true and sufficed for the President to be empowered to tackle this foreign war in all seriousness.

"A president can't lie," says Marie. "He'd be found out, wouldn't he?"

She is standing in the kitchenette in the hallway of our apartment, wearing an oversize apron, a cloth over her arm, turning the meat in the pan, and with a bent forearm pushing back the hot hair from her temples just as her grandmother and her grandmother's mother had done, not like a child who is helping out by playing housewife but as a member of the household who understands and assumes her share. Photographed like this, in ten years she would judge herself to have been a child who grew up in happy circumstances, in an era of peace. She takes her time, her lower lip slightly drawn in, her eyes narrowed, and when she spoke she no doubt wanted to show her mother that she was listening but also to relieve the grownup of her needless misgivings. What she lacks in terms of the war is seeing it.

She cannot see the war in Vietnam. Only too minutely has she heard from me of the outward manifestations of war. She has never heard of a family from her school to whom the Government has sent a filled coffin. She is familiar with the ruins between Amsterdam and Columbus Avenues, but these are being knocked down not by the bombs of that enemy but by the wrecking balls of real-estate speculators. The small businesses along Broadway are dying not because of war casualties among the heirs but because of rent and Mafia dollars. The Government is not requisitioning automobiles, and gas stations reward the purchasing of gasoline with free gifts. Marie need not remember to lower her voice at the sight of a policeman nearby. She could not conceive of Mr. Weiszand being wakened at six in the morning by four plain-clothes policemen and taken off to jail for having publicly inveighed against the far-off war during the demonstrations at Columbia University. She knows about railways, ships, and airplanes, that in order to travel she needs money, not a travel permit from a government department. I would have a hard time naming a single article that could not be bought in New York. No war is necessary for our telephone to be tapped. In fact the Army would have to occupy Riverside Park across from our building and seal off the approaches to the promenade along the Hudson with bazookas for Marie to be halfway convinced. It is possible that, basically, she regards the things I can tell her about Germany as nontransferable. That may be the way they conduct a war in Europe, not here; but she is here, and has enough to think about.

Marie is against wars because people can get hurt in them. And she can't attack my information outright; she doesn't even want to hurt my feelings. She went to school and started an argument in class with a teacher about the justice of the fighting in Southeast Asia; she has previously sounded out her friends Marcia, Pamela, Deborah, Angela, less to stockpile solidarity than to avoid jeopardizing their friendship. In the presence of Marcia's parents, Mr. and Mrs. Linus L. Carpenter, she wouldn't even be able to bring up the subject; the Carpenters donate money for civil-rights workers, would like black citizens to have a decent place to live anywhere but at their own address, and consider the subject of Vietnam hackneyed and that to talk about it has by now become tactless, if not in downright bad taste. Linus Carpenter III, Georgetown, Harvard, Colonel of the Reserve with a helicopter battalion, Carpenter of Allen, Burns, Elman & Carpenter, has explained to Marie that in a democratic constitution each person has his job to do and the business of war is part of the President's job. When Marie repeated this at home, cautiously, to test her mother, it was also revealed that she had worn her GET OUT OF VIETNAM button for just as long as the fad lasted in her grade. She is as insincere as I have brought her up to be.

She cannot maintain herself against this country with my equipment any better than I can. She has been living here six years. She wouldn't want to live anywhere else. She wouldn't want to live in a country she doesn't trust. This one she trusts.

Her courtesy, however, is almost inexhaustible. While setting the table and bringing in the dishes she was still wondering, and before she had taken her first mouthful she said: "D'you mean that when it gets out that a president has lied it's too late for us and late enough for him?"

She can look like such a little sophist. Her chin propped on her folded hands, her head amiably to one side, that's how she looked at me. She had proved to me that she listens to every word her mother says. In addition to the one answer she had provided me with another, and she wasn't in the least shocked at either.

December 22, 1967   Friday

What a paper we have in this city! The New York *Times* reports the astronomers' statement that today the sun in the Northern Hemisphere will be above the horizon for the shortest period of time, and that winter began seventeen minutes after 8 A.M.

And it also reports that in August 1964, in the Gulf of Tonkin, four crew members of the *Turner Joy* did in fact sight the wake of a torpedo from North Vietnam some 300 feet off the port side, but that the Administration had already prepared contingent drafts of the resolution empowering the President to a full prosecution of the war long before August 1964.

And Marie says, in a rather pert, tense voice: "I can't live that way, the way you want me to! I'm not supposed to lie because you don't like lies! You'd've been out of a job and I'd've been out of school long ago if we didn't lie like three American presidents in a row! You haven't stopped your war and now I'm supposed to do it for you! When you were a child they were getting ready for their war all around you and you noticed nothing!"

"They told me nothing, Marie."

"But you could see it! Apologies are in order, Mrs. Cresspahl."

"Stop crying, Marie."

"Say: ' 'Scuse me,' like I used to when I was little."

" 'Scuse me, Marie."

My war was well hidden. Even the name of the town of Jerichow was remote in Germany. The summer visitors driving through it on their way to the seaside resort of Rande, what did they see? Four hundred yards of rough cobblestones that made the cars jolt and bounce. Barns. Farmyards. The red eastern façade of the brickyard with its two genuine and fifteen fake windows. Cool gravestones in the shade. A narrow village street flanked by low two-storied houses, plastered fronts, timbered sides. Topped by a monster of a church with a spire like a bishop's miter, treetops massed around it all the way up to the level of the gables. Numerous shops displaying goods in what had once been parlor windows. Karstadt's concrete cube of a rural department store. Or they arrived by bus from the railroad station and started out from the market square with its almost seigniorial buildings. Papenbrock's house, like the Lübeck Arms, less modest than the town hall. Horse-drawn carts on their way to the town scales. Hardly any local automobiles. Holiday peace and quiet. At the point where visitors started to expect the actual town to begin, they found themselves already bowling smoothly along the bare highway to the Baltic. On the left, some distance off, clusters of barely completed houses could be made out, no doubt yet another agricultural workers' housing project, as it said on the billboards, "New Soil of the North." Where an unaccountably wide cement lane went off, the highway dipped, and beyond the densely embowered hotels of Rande spread the sun-striped sea. What had been left behind and forgotten in the west was the military airfield of Jerichow North. 1936.

But the airfield was not called by that name in Jerichow. For over a year the town's craftsmen and tradesmen had been working and making money at it, yet the installation was called "Mariengabe," after the village that had been wiped out by it. The region had always been a Customs border area so that now the restricted military zone did not seem strange. Summer visitors directed by obsolete guidebooks to rewarding walks were stopped and warned by Army patrols at a suitable distance from the construction site.

The local aristocracy had retained its regular table at the Lübeck Arms; there the Olympic Games at Kiel were discussed, possibly even the drought of 1934, more reluctantly still the Four-Year Plan. For Friedrich Jansen, mayor and local leader of the ruling party, had established a table of his own, by the windows overlooking the stable yard, usually whiling away long evenings in conversation with strangers. Quite often these were gentlemen from the Secret Police in Hamburg, in black uniforms, some of them actually with heavy leather overcoats to hang up on the pegs. In September 1936 the workers at Mariengabe had refused to work for half a day and there had been talk of Communist pamphlets. Von Maltzahn had found one in his woods and lost no time in handing it personally, "unread," to Friedrich Jansen. These days Von Maltzahn referred not to an airfield but to "our revenge for Versailles." Von Lüsewitz had received satisfactory compensation for the part of Mariengabe that had been on his property and since then liked referring to his "sacrifice." Friedrich Jansen came right out with the words "Nordic cunning" and apparently knew about a "bunch of wine-guzzling aristo-crats."

In Peter Wulff's tavern the subject of the airfield was circum-vented by such expressions as "fat cow" and "bloody marvel," but not when strangers dropped in for a drink, no matter how far out of earshot they might be or how convincing their Low German dialect might sound. Stoffregen, a schoolteacher, also preferred to switch from the airfield to the Jews and the attempted assassination of the Swiss regional Party leader Gustloff that he considered an "unmask-ing." As to Kliefoth, a high-school teacher, it was regarded as a cer-tainty that he had not for nothing sneaked from Berlin to an area in which the Nazis had been in power six months longer than anywhere else and would be more inclined to forgive him, but for what? And the tale was being told that, on the train to Gneez, Kliefoth had interrupted some other passengers who had been discussing "con-struction work" with the remark: I'm warning you. He was said to have given no explanation for this notion of his.

Swenson, with his transportation business, had made such a "moderate" profit with his bus line from the station to Jerichow North that he had now been able to acquire a second truck, and Swenson described his share in the building of the airfield as "his duty." Pastor Brüshaver attempted a joke and referred to it as the "Reich Project People's Sport," after the billboards that had been erected at the western end of the construction area; and Pastor Brüshaver's son was flying in Spain against the troops of the legal government and as a reward might perhaps earn the command of an airfield, which merely had to be completed, that was all. And my father had the saws going in his workshop from early morning till evening and at dinnertime tried to rid his ears of the noise by shaking his head and had a bank account in Rostock and one in Lübeck and also accepted payment through the Hamburg post office for the labor of eight employees and had obediently joined the Labor Front and, law-abiding citizen that he was, let Heine Klaproth off once a week for his Hitler Youth service and had twenty ears at the midday dinner table, including mine, and talked about Mariengabe.

He found the name appropriate. Mariengabe: a gift from Mary. If someone made a gift one didn't mind accepting. Water was harder than stone, and whatever fell from a great height into the Baltic he wasn't going to take as a gift. He had seen airplanes in England too. Lisbeth had even been up in a British plane. She couldn't deny that now, could she? Jerichow had never yet been famous, except for

Friedrich Jansen, and that would certainly change with the bombs the English were obviously going to drop here first. That had been as good as agreed upon with the British.

Heinrich, you'll be the death of us! Heinrich, the child! Heinrich Cresspahl!

Instead of talking about bombs my father talked about "unloading shit," and whatever he uttered in the way of unexpected ideas, in a casual, almost relaxed manner, all found its way, but not as the crow flies, to Friedrich Jansen and his morocco-bound notebook: first next door, then across the yards and into the gardens and onto the fields, and only after Jerichow had been catered to did Friedrich Jansen get his turn. Party member Jansen then passed it on word for word to the Gestapo in Gneez. That proved to be a mistake; for in his mayoral office he received a stern official letter from a Luftwaffe department in Hamburg, complete with emblem and seal, advising him to stop his complaining, because by including his own name he had betrayed the fact that he was grinding his own personal ax and the German Luftwaffe declined to operate the grinding stone for him. Moreover, science had confirmed, the letter went on, that water received a falling airplane with a harder impact than land, and finally it was not incumbent even upon a person prominent in political life and with the rank of district Party leader to insinuate that the Luftwaffe Command underestimated the potential enemy; and as a matter of fact the conviction was current in the Luftwaffe circles concerned that many a tradesman was making a greater and more effective contribution toward the development of Germany's air defense than some persons employed in the ranks of Administration and Party. Heil Hitler! And Friedrich Jansen sat there and had to hold his tongue, even when told how that Cresspahl shook his head during his speeches. As if he had water in his ears. And although someone always came to sit for a while at Friedrich Jansen's regular table, partly to cheer him up with Cresspahl's insinuations but also because it really *was* irritating the way that Cresspahl talked so naturally about the war, as if it were a foregone conclusion. The man was a regular spoilsport. He really was.

"Mariengabe," says Marie, in a voice of brooding annoyance. "I hope the British unloaded plenty. It'd suit me fine."

" 'Scuse me, Marie."

What a paper we have in this city! It acknowledges even us as customers and is careful to remind us to register our addresses with the Federal Government during January.

And that very day, in the late afternoon, Marie goes to pick up the registration forms from our post office on 104th Street. Just imagine if we were to be deported!

December 23, 1967

243 Riverside Drive,
New York, N. Y. 10025

Dear Dr. Kliefoth,

Thank you for your kind inquiry about my child. I will try to tell you something about her.

My daughter Marie is ten and a half years old and four feet ten inches tall. She is considered tall for her age. I have no recent photos of her; in earlier ones she usually tried to pose. In other words, she sees herself as someone observing those behind the camera in an inquisitive and at the same time solicitous manner. A passport official would note the shape of her head as elongated-oval, but it is not as long as an egg and in profile her head actually seems somewhat round. As winter progresses her hair turns almost sandy, especially her eyebrows. Her eyes are gray and green, depending on the light. Clear. Long wide-spread eyelashes, not from me. In her face I see her father (whom you never met), my friends see me; although I do find in it much that is Mecklenburg, irony in the cocked head, sidelong glance from lowered brow, stony inscrutable expression, the general air of plotting and mischief. And all this in a foreign language. This is middle-class American, disciplined by a traditional school, careful with slang. But what she speaks is what she lives. Many times, in spite of my interpreter's certificate, I have to look up a word. Serendipity. At the moment she is addicted to circumlocutions: "I scorn the action," when it is a matter of a disagreeable job to be done. Recently it has been a form of apology: "I stand corrected," and this in the accent of New York's Upper West Side, which you would not find it easy to classify.

She speaks German as if she had a sore throat. Probably she had to sacrifice the language she brought with her in order to take root more easily on the street, in school, in the city. Düsseldorf, Berlin, Jerichow, for her all that is geography. She finds it easier to recall vacations in Denmark. To make her revert to German would be a greater misfortune for her than the shift to American. She would rather we had a proper passport, one of this country.

This afternoon on Fifth Avenue we got caught up in a demonstration against the Vietnam war, not afternoon in your terms, it wasn't yet one o'clock, but it was after twelve. Sentences like that must have been quoted in your English classes as being genuine Kliefoths. Did you know that? Participating in the demonstration were some three hundred demonstrators and certainly no fewer policemen. We were heading toward Dunhill's in Rockefeller Center to buy you your early-morning tobacco, and the police were assiduously guarding the Mall, the Rockefeller Center promenade, since it was private property. The police were doing their best to appear relaxed and were trying to stop the demonstrators on the sidewalk with bullhorns, as if all they were worried about was controlling the traffic, and the demonstrators had forgotten their megaphones. It wasn't until a word had been trumpeted three times into my ear that I grasped what it was. LOVE, that's what he wanted. They called themselves Santa's Helpers, and instead of wearing ordinary clothes they had got themselves up in oddments, half from boutiques and half from army-surplus stores. What's more, they had long hair, and the law-abiding public, laden with last-minute shopping parcels, smarting and sweating because of all the money they had been spending, this public shouted comments about baths and cleanliness. That aroused Marie's indignation. She has been taught that everyone must be free to express his opinion in public; and now here were people trying to dictate to others how they should dress and wear their hair.

The leader of the demonstrators was a young man with a great mop of fair hair, carrying an American flag and a placard on which was written, in the same colors, the word KILL. The last I saw of him, he was trying to break into Saks department store with his friends. And the Salvation Army calmly went on tootling, and fellows in red hooded suits and fake beards were still waiting to have their pictures taken with kids. Finally we were pushed all the way to Madison Avenue. The police did not show their anger, merely their irritation at the prolonged effort of appearing to be unmoved; mind you, they still called me Lady, but they rebuked me for walking about through these goings-on with a child, and rather sternly sent me "home." For the second time Marie became indignant for, although there may be moments when she feels like a child, this was not one of them. In her anger she forgot herself and called the policeman, although sotto voce, a pig. The term was new to me. Then she apologized for her unconsidered choice of words.

I hope you won't mind my asking you, but would you go to the cemetery and see whether the Creutzes have covered my three graves for the winter? It's not that I wish to defend the custom of grave care. It's just that, although Erich Creutz may well want to do something in return for my money, Emmy Creutz has already tried to stop him, and I begrudge her the satisfaction of feeling that, although she was unable to cheat old Cresspahl, she can cheat his daughter all the more.

Wishing you a happy New Year, your eighty-second—and an otium cum dignitate,

Yours very sincerely,

G. C.

December 24, 1967 Sunday

Immediately under the date line on page 1 the New York *Times* publishes two pictures, as if they were neighbors, relatives: President Johnson pinning medals on American soldiers yesterday at Camranh Bay, a base in South Vietnam, on the left; President Johnson looking past the Pope yesterday as the latter is speaking, the President's face wreathed in smiles, on the right.

Because it's Christmas?

As its Quotation of the Day it prints his statement: "We are ready at any moment to substitute the word and the vote for the knife and the grenade in bringing an honorable peace to Vietnam."

Because it's Christmas?

Christmas 1936 my mother was not yet dead. Even Christmas 1937 Lisbeth Cresspahl was still alive.

December 25, 1967 Monday

Christmas. Still a day to be celebrated, and not even the New York *Times* reckons with more attention than for a mere 44 pages.

On Christmas Day 1936, Lisbeth Cresspahl was taken from her home and driven to the county hospital. For Cresspahl it all happened so unexpectedly that it was noon before he suspected it had been planned.

He had seen her for the last time early that morning, asleep between her arms as they lay extended along her body, breathing shallowly, frowning as if she were already compelled to defend the kindly anesthetic of dreams and sleep. She looked like herself, as she often did when she was not awake. He still regarded her as the person he had married five years earlier; for him she was young, for herself as for him perhaps she enjoyed being alive. He even placed the things she had said in those days above the things she now kept secret from him. There had been many a morning when he had chosen to assume that she was deceiving him with those closed eyes; by this time he no longer liked to ask her.

My father was in the kitchen, lighting the stove for the child ensconced among her many pillows and blankets in the high chair from Vietsen, watching him in happy anticipation, friendly, unsuspecting. The child had often had breakfast with him before. The kitchen had retained the warmth of the previous evening, the big window toward the south formed a glassy frame for the black morning sky. The light from the hanging lamp that had been pulled down low over the table made reflections in the Dutch tiles. When Dr. Berling arrived at the house it was barely daylight.

Dr. Berling may not have realized that Cresspahl knew nothing of his wife's telephone call. Came through the front door, announcing his arrival by stamping his feet on the steps, was in the kitchen, with an impatient greeting walked past the father who, apparently unalarmed, was feeding his child sweetened warm milk, pulled the bedroom door shut behind him, tugged it shut again when Cresspahl tried to follow him. Came back, suddenly comforting, gentle, moving swiftly in spite of his bulk, keeping Cresspahl on the run with one instruction after another: get some blankets; get some hot-water bottles; pack her night things; alert the county hospital in Gneez but on no account order an ambulance; find something waterproof to take care of the bleeding; step lively now, step lively. The child did not begin to bawl until she was left behind alone in the kitchen and Cresspahl was carrying his wife across the snow-covered yard to Berling's car, a clumsy limp package. Her head hung down, painfully it seemed, and he was unable to support her by extending his elbows still farther. With her pupils rolled back like that she could see nothing now, let alone him.

The Berling who took leave of Cresspahl that morning was no longer the man of 1933, the man who slapped people on the shoulder "prophylactically," the man with the casual manner of speech, who had infected the sick with health and rounded on complainers as if they had insulted him. Today's Berling observed as closely as ever, but his efforts at encouragement were less vehement, he listened more patiently, even nodded, his fleshy face impassive, and there were times when he would look downcast. He no longer went out for a drink where he could be overheard; he spent the evenings sitting at home. So many little blood vessels had burst in his cheeks that he was sometimes called a "blue devil." A heavy man, nearly six foot seven, two hundred and twenty pounds, powerful as a butcher, a man who had turned melancholy with the years that should have been his best. And it was not from Berling that Jerichow found out that young Mrs. Cresspahl had just lost a child; all he would say was what he suggested and prescribed to Cresspahl with a final nod before starting up the car: she had eaten something. Something bad for a person's stomach.

For a long time Cresspahl regarded it as a case of bad luck; moreover, he welcomed the fact that the bad luck had not come at a more unfavorable time. It was the quiet season, the time between the holidays. The workmen had left for their homes; he had no one to look after but the child. And Lisbeth's last strength for the call to Berling could just as well have been the last ounce, not the deliberately conserved one. If he had no mind to, he did not even have to tell the Papenbrocks anything right away, or the Paepckes. They were still asleep, Jerichow was still asleep. Later he could not understand all that Berling tried to explain to him about Lisbeth's feverish talk; by that time work was under way again in the workshop; by that time Lisbeth had long since been in charge of the household again, tired, unyielding, and, true enough, her face as pale as if she had been poisoned by something that did not agree with her.

Dr. Berling said:

With the loss of the second child my mother had hoped to lose her own life too, in order to escape her guilt.

On that drive through the snow and during the operation, she knew of many kinds of guilt, and some were not hers at all, and yet they were hers.

She was guilty of having accompanied my father to England in 1931, in the secret knowledge that she did want to live with him but not abroad. My father, of course, was to blame for having trusted her. A person could not carry that much trust.

She had wanted to flee from her guilt and went back to Mecklenburg for the birth of the child. But a Christian should not flee from guilt, and Cresspahl was guilty of having allowed it.

Her guilt had then acquired many ramifications. Not only had she gone back to the multiple guilt of her father, who loaned money to impoverished people and demanded their houses as repayment, with the result that they were now his employees. (Here she may have been referring to Zoll the master carpenter, whom Papenbrock had "bought out"; but who else could there have been?) She had then wished to remain in a country whose new government was harassing the Church, with a family that could still be said to be making money from the new rulers and in which her own brother was said to have helped beat Voss to death in Rande. Cresspahl, on the other hand, was guilty of not having prevented such an extension of her guilt. He had given in to her over the move; but it is the husband who is supposed to decide. As the Bible says. He had decided, wrongly, the way she wanted it.

Cresspahl was guilty of the fact that her guilt was not enough for him. He wanted to bring a share of it into the world, not only for this one child Gesine but for three more. As she had promised. But doesn't the New Testament tell us to forgive a light debtor? But then Cresspahl was guilty of not releasing her from her promise; and she, of course, for not being able to express her need for this. But he made her conscious of her guilt by spending the evenings over his ledgers and drawings and a bottle of kümmel until he was able to forget the promise.

She was guilty of not living with him as she had undertaken to do before the Church, her hand on the Bible. But doesn't the Bible also say: that man should "crucify the flesh with the affections and lusts"? Galatians 5, 24. Cresspahl was guilty of not being prepared to relieve her of that; and she was guilty of doubting the words of Holy Scripture.

In order not to retain so much guilt and not to multiply it, she had wanted to be guilty of one of the greatest sins of all: to preserve an unborn child from guilt, true, but to give away her own life. Granted that God was not to be bargained with, nevertheless it would have represented some kind of payment. Also for Cresspahl's guilt.

Which, when you got right down to it, remained hers; for she hadn't wanted to let herself be saved. She had not been obedient to her husband. In 1935 when he had wanted to turn his back on Germany's new war, why had she not accepted it as a command?

From weakness, in other words, guilt.

Guilt, she felt, was not for a doctor's ears, even if no man came after him. And she apologized for that. For if her latest, greatest guilt should come to the ears of the Church, she would have to forgo the last blessing. In this way, however, dead of the unrevealed guilt, she could be sure of a Christian burial.

So all that remained was the guilt of deception, but not of deceit. One of the little ones, the venial ones, the kind a child has. And only thus would Cresspahl remain ignorant of his guilt and, at least until his death, be able to live without that guilt.

And Dr. Berling said:

"She's forgotten all about it by this time. Just feverish talk. Not a soul knows about it."

And he said:

"Always this sentimental nonsense at Christmas. Candles; all that singing! It's to blame for a lot of things, you old rascal. Just put the money on the table."

He said:

"She'll get over it. Just wait a couple of years, Cresspahl you old rascal. After a couple of years she won't be able to stand it without that second child."

And:

"Happy New Year, Cresspahl!"

December 26, 1967 Tuesday

Christmas is over, and already the New York *Times* considers sixty-eight pages necessary in order to bring us good buys as well as the world. Air strikes have been resumed in North Vietnam. Fire on a Norwegian freighter in the harbor. The Free State of Bavaria sees itself as a bridgehead to Eastern Europe. Peking remains silent on its nuclear explosion. Mayor Lindsay regrets mistakes, promises improvement, and in the office at his official residence has a hidden television camera that allows him to appear on six New York channels. Now we know; who knows what for.

One day Marie will say of me: My mother was a New York *Times* reader; meaning to be descriptive rather than indiscreet. She will then compare me with Cresspahl in London, who tried to hear the Labour Party speaking through the *Daily Herald,* and with Lisbeth Cresspahl, who did not bring home the *Manchester Guardian* accidentally, who in Mecklenburg was quite content that the only paper one could now subscribe to was the *Lübecker Generalanzeiger* and not the Social Democrats' *Volksbote,* banned, looted.

Marie, it wasn't like that. When we arrived in New York in April 1961, the papers we could choose from were the *News,* the *Journal-American,* the *World-Telegram & Sun,* the *Post,* the *Herald Tribune,* the *Wall Street Journal,* the *Long Island Press,* and the *Times.* I bought the *Times* because of its British origin, without even knowing that it was one of the minority which, in opposition to Richard Nixon, had wanted John Kennedy for President. At the bank they had advised me to take the *Times:* because of the rental ads every day, not only at weekends. With the aid of the New York

Times we found our apartment in New York, five windows overlooking river colors, Riverside Park, unimpeded sky. I didn't realize I had become accustomed to the New York *Times* until one day when it was sold out at Lexington Avenue and a courteous child, not yet four, with a turn of the head at Seventh indicated what I was looking for: a newsstand, although without the *Times*; and I didn't feel like buying the *News*. Once again you realized that grownups are very strange, yet you couldn't let go of my hand in a place where the language, the colors of the automobiles, the height of the buildings, were unfamiliar to you, to say nothing of your mother.

Explain what you like when you are over thirty: My mother was fooled by the conservative appearance, while imagining that she wasn't fooled by the inch-high report of nothing, embarrassing photos of nobody. Say if you like: My mother wanted to learn to speak the American of property and education rather than that of workers and thieves and policemen. You may be right, but if I needed that kind of language for false pretenses, then I needed it all the more to cope successfully with my superiors who had been to university. Have your fun over the fact that I learned about New York from the *Times:* not only who happened to be senator, but how he got his votes; not only the name of the mayor, but at what point his authority stopped; the difference between a misdemeanor, a felony, and a violation of the law, and to what extent the letter of the law protects you from the police. Claim that even at twenty-eight I was inclined to make allowances for age, and maybe that's how I was: No. 4230 on the occasion of Lincoln's assassination seems to me worthy of respect on account of tradition, just like today's issue, No. 40,148 of Volume CXVII; but don't accuse me of: not examining tradition. Not: of replacing a lost authority by evoking a new one. For in that case I would have to look on the paper as a father; I look on it as an aunt.

There may be some admiration in this. The mirror of daily events, blind in only a few, unavoidable spots. The completeness of many reports. The scoops, the successes: over the San Francisco earthquake in 1906, the sinking of the *Titanic* in 1912, the ten pages by August 7, 1945 (out of a total of only 38) on the dropping of the atom bomb on Hiroshima; I may kowtow to the *Times*'s self-eulogy more than is necessary. Perhaps I attribute merits to it that seem so only to me: to the *Times*, Barry Goldwater's candidacy appeared to be a "disaster," totally; for three or four days in a row the *Times* brought John Kennedy's assassination to the people in headlines across its front page. But I have also been with you in the lobby of the Times Building and have seen the motto above the bust of Adolph Ochs, and although it may have become a saying in our household it is scarcely used with reverence.

"TO GIVE THE NEWS IMPARTIALLY,
WITHOUT FEAR OR FAVOR,
REGARDLESS OF ANY PARTY,
SECT OR INTEREST INVOLVED."

It is in keeping with the flags flown at half-mast by the City of New York when this most loyal nephew of the *Times* was carried to his grave in 1935, and with its self-image as an "honorable human institution." During working hours, however, the aunt runs a business whose job it is to procure news and disseminate it through sales; the strikes of 1962 and 1965 would have brought this home to me then if no sooner. One per cent of the New York *Times* shares, and we would be trapped in New York's Social Register, Marie!

One auntlike trait that struck me (as soon as I was able to read it) was its inability to do good without talking about it. When the *Times*, never prepared to support any political party, supported a politician, it did so expressly because his party's platform was deemed by the *Times* and not, say, by Kennedy, to be correct. The conscience of the ideal U. S. A.: the *Times* had that in its safekeeping, and how it allowed its feelings to be hurt by Kennedy so shortly after his election as senator, and how devastatingly it struck back with the suspicion that he had not written his own book! When a citizen sought nomination as a representative of the people and the *Times* caused this to be described, step by step and by a friend of the office-seeker at that, this was not aid and comfort, this was keeping the public instructively informed of political processes; and just as it regards a murder in the *News* as outright reader-snatching, so the *Times*'s own murders are, item for item, sociology. In fact a general auntlike behavior is evident in the paper's unremitting pedagogic compulsion. It is impossible to count how repeatedly it quotes the Staten Island Ferry fare as being an astonishing five cents, a fact known to local inhabitants qua inhabitants and visitors qua guidebook readers, as one of the wonders of the world. Finally even I noticed the careless repetitions, became suspicious of patriarchal turns of speech, mentally suggested more precise expressions that were still far short of vulgar. (Had I not also picked up some of the American language of the *News* I would hardly have been able to find my way around Broadway.) These were symptoms of old age, yet not ludicrous, not contemptible. In fact it was quite touching, the shock this auntie got from the swallowing by a competitor of three newspapers at once, the way she tried to wiggle out of the dilemma of trying simultaneously to educate and interest her readers! How she took the historical explanation of an incident and bravely proceeded to wring from it its contemporary functional relevance, and then, chin in air, behave as if it were the most natural thing in the world!

We'll show our readers which way the cat jumps. The public can then proceed to worry about the cat.

Who, at that age, undergoes such a rejuvenating cure and no longer sends her people to watch only the mouseholes of police, government departments, embassies, news service, maternity home, and crematorium, after the dignity and comfort of letting others lay the spoils at one's feet to observe them conscientiously and then, conscious of its responsibility, to describe them! No, this auntie sits down, crosses her legs, accepts a cup of tea spiked with rum, chews on her ubiquitously respected cigarillo, and ponders the matter. Aha, she's got it! Until now, by and large, the *Times* has reported with infinite accuracy the goings-on in the cities of the world both large and small: what was happening, who was involved, what the weather was like, and what came next. But surely there was something missing, something missing—? Right, what people were talking about in those cities! And from that moment on the *Times* offered, for immediate delivery: the Number One topic of conversation in Hanover, or in Moscow, in order that the forty airmail subscription issues sent daily to these cities might acquire a quite unexpected relevance. Carrying on from there, henceforth always in stock: the Man in the News, his biography, primary occupation, secondary occupation, goals, opponents. And as if that were not enough, this auntie goes in search of things of which she does not presuppose her readers to have a satisfactory knowledge, in their own city! And holds forth, concisely, at times charmingly: on the life-habits of various disadvantaged groups, Upper West Side, Lower East Side: on the mixture of structural problems and real-estate problems in White Plains, "Stranger, When Thou Camest to White Plains . . .": on the emotional entanglements of those of other complexions in the ghettos not only of Harlem but also of Williamsburg and Bedford-Stuyvesant, that can be interesting too, you know; and she straightens herself in her chair and invests this non-news with the rank of news! It is not so much that she is more than willing and well able to document the facts; the point is that she has found them, this old Auntie Times. One always thinks that young people will soon quit shirking their duties and responsibilities, but no, one must do everything oneself! Granted, she had to think of her reputation and did all this not exactly on the front page but well forward in the second section; although this might bespeak an apology, the exemplary moral attitude was surely indisputable. And here again Auntie Times was doing good, delicately pointing out that no one else would bring himself to do it: on the subject of the police we suddenly learned not only about discharges, arrests, corruption, and promotions but how the police feel in their hearts, whom they must unfailingly obey and when, what rights those accused by them actually possess, and that at least 800,000 *Times* readers are bidden to elect those politicians who are seriously concerned with subordinating the police to the control of civilian committees, word of honor.

That didn't come off, because the other seven million inhabitants of the city think in a language which the New York *Times* would not dream of using, because they live with things that a society lady does not permit to occur even as words in her customers' advertisements: nudity, homosexual, carnal lust, naked, nothing on, panties, pervert . . .: don't you see that she could never maintain her role of aunt in any other way, Marie?

She spares me all that astrological rubbish, Marie. She is not invariably tangled in the enlightenment meted out to her in 1896 at a Geneva finishing school.

No comic strips for you, I'm sorry to say. Do you expect her to live like an ordinary citizen of the U. S. A., who has parents instead of ancestors, and tolerates, enjoys using, household articles which . . .

The old-fashioned, indeed, the indispensable fairness of eschewing cartoons because a cartoon can only say: On the one hand. But not: On the other hand.

Marie, your mother was a person who read the *Times* of New York.

With respect. Without respect. Figure out the synthesis for yourself. (I'll make you a suggestion: defenselessly.)

I leave it to you to prove that my upbringing forced me, by way of the *Lübecker Generalanzeiger*, the *Völkische Beobachter*, the *Tägliche Rundschau* of the Soviet Union and the *Junge Welt* and the *Neues Deutschland* and the *Frankfurter Allgemeine* and the *Rheinische Post*, to spend one hour every day conversing with an old aunt.

For if the Free State of Bavaria sees itself as a bridgehead toward Eastern Europe, she'll tell me about it. She reminds me that starting January 7 the post office is going to demand higher postage from us. And whether I believe it or not, this auntie passes on to me what she heard an American soldier say in Vietnam: "Christmas and war are a contradiction in terms." Finally she does not withhold from me that yesterday the family of President Johnson spent "a wonderful, wonderful day."

And when I have finished with her I go and wash my hands.

December 27, 1967 Wednesday

The New York *Times* has discovered the inventor of napalm. (The New York *Times* explains what napalm is.) The inventor is a professor emeritus of Harvard, Louis Frederick Fieser (pronounced Feezer). In the fall of 1941 he was commissioned by the National Defense Research Committee, by mid-1942 he was ready. What he says is:

"You don't know what's coming. . . . You can't blame the outfit that put out the rifle that killed the President. . . . I don't know enough about the situation in Vietnam. . . . Just because I played a role in the technological development of napalm doesn't mean I'm any more qualified to comment on the moral aspects of it."

Is there such a thing as anti-fascist napalm?

Marie plays: "Taking my mother to the subway." The iron steps of the winding staircase sound xylophonic when she jumps on them. On the street she walks beside me at a most polite distance, her hands thrust comfortably into the pockets of her London coat, entertaining me with her plans for the day: she might take her skates to be sharpened, she might make another trip to Queens Plaza, she might go to Macy's and have a look at what's new from Lesney of Britain Limited. . . . She does this skillfully: in actual fact she will go back to our apartment and continue to work on the "secret" that she has promised me for New Year's. She walks on my right, thus scaring away the old man waiting at the top of the steps going down to Mr. Fang Liu's laundry, a man who was once a gentleman, whose only visible lapse from neatness so far is his frayed trouser legs. He stepped back as soon as he saw Marie.

He had already tried it once. He is without experience, he always has to start with a Please reminiscent of his earlier days, tends to break off: Please. Madam. I am sorry to stop you, you are very kind madam thank you madam: thank you. This morning he has to take off his hat and greet us because he is ashamed in front of the child.

"Another twelve years and I'll go to work so you won't have to," says Marie, unexpectedly sobered. She is shy about being embraced on the street, even if only for a moment and cheek to cheek; this morning she wanted it.

In the camphorous, creaking, careening subway the New York *Times* reports in her controlled, ladylike voice that on September 26, 1967, Mr. Gostev of the Moscow K. G. B. put the following question to the physical chemist Pavel M. Litvinov: "Could you possibly think that now, in the fiftieth year of Soviet power, a Soviet court could make a wrong decision?"

Can you imagine that?

At the bank, the Christmas poster has disappeared from the public rooms, the evergreen wreaths from the hallways, the greeting cards from the desks. The teletype machine rattles as if it had never stood still. By eleven o'clock Miss Cresspahl has to prepare two letters to Frankfurt, to the Deutsche Bank, one to the Banco di Spirito Santo in Turin, one to the private office of Giovanni Agnelli. By noon a draft of an Italian/French contract is expected from her, at twelve thirty she has an appointment with the Vice-President. And that afternoon, if possible, she is to help with the backlog of letters of credit in the South America Department, although purely out of kindness. I'd be delighted, Guarani. The Vice-President regrets having to cancel his appointment, he has flown to Mexico. No, to Canada for hunting. On the contrary, today he is helping to buy Xerox.

Unseeing through repetition. At one place one is known as Antipasto, at another as Gauloise, at another as Large Black Coffee. At the child's-size tables in the Thousand Delicatessen, jostled by the hurrying lineup of lunchers, two soft-mannered gentlemen were comfortably seated, Italians apparently; they had come to some agreement and were drinking to each other, in beer out of paper cups, with rather affectionate smiles, trustingly. For poisoning is not the custom of the country, it is shooting, shooting.

Dear Sirs: We hereby establish our IRREVOCABLE credit in your favor, available by your drafts drawn at 90 (ninety) days sight for any sums not to exceed a total of about U. S. $80,000.00 accompanied by commercial invoice describing the merchandise as indicated below. . . . Dear Sirs. And you learn something else new every time, Gesine.

There's a message for you, Mrs. Cresspahl. Your daughter called. She said you looked so worn out that we ought to send you home.

A medium-heavy rain, supposed to be snow, penetrates the evening crush at Third and 42nd, the citizens press through the entrance to the subway, gusts of wind catch them in the back of the neck, and a cheerful voice addresses them from the left. There's a man at the newsstand there, tossing stressed syllables into the air, swallowing the weaker words: GOOD EVEning! It's a PERfect EVEning! It's a PERFECT EVENING for a NEWSpaper. We have the LATEST NEWSpaper in NEW YORK! The voice follows you down the escalator into the cavern of the Flushing line. They haven't killed him yet. That fellow with his happy disposition, he's new here. They'll kill him all right.

At the vegetable store the salesman (from Galicia, four weeks in Berlin in 1923, Berlin has the best ice cream in the world): "Lovely things you bought today." For the bill comes to $3.85.

Amsterdam, you great big town,
You're all built up on posts,
And if you fall about our ears
Who's going to pay the costs?

December 28, 1967   Thursday

The New York *Times* cannot hear the grass growing in Prague. It has to rely on Frankfurt for the information that in addressing his Central Committee last week, Antonín Novotný did not speak kindly of Antonín Novotný and no longer considers him worthy of presiding over the Communist Party of the Czechs and Slovaks. But the New York *Times* gives this Czechoslovakian grass only twenty-seven lines, albeit on page 5; no doubt it considers it small.

Later on, Cresspahl felt that Lisbeth's life with him was known to people in Jerichow like a story at whose beginning they had been present, a story they had watched grow, could predict bit by bit, and that they had placed bets on its twists and turns which, although they might wish to deflect them, they no longer wished to halt, in which they no longer took a hand, of which they knew the end more than approximately, more so than he did, he who had to live that life.

The idea that someone might have wanted a say in his marriage amazed him so much that he would have forgotten to listen. Later on he realized that it had been his fault if they approached him so casually, cautiously, as the master craftsmen chatted over their lunch breaks at the airfield, in a slow exchange of words in which they answered each other at such long intervals that the reply finally came as a surprise, and a storyteller had first to reckon with disapproving looks no matter how sure he might be of his reminiscences being welcome. Cresspahl had not lived long enough in the area, he did not feel involved in the stories, he was merely a listener; there was no reason he should notice right away that these tales contained information for him. There was one about an exchange of horses in Gadebusch, then the tale moved on to a beet cutter in Rehna and lingered in a yard in Gneez and there was a man who tried to set fire to an adulterer's woodpile and finally the tale returned to Jerichow on horseback and cast a glance at "our Lisbeth" and petered out reluctantly in the Gräfin Forest when the lunch break was over. They didn't say "your Lisbeth" or even "his Lisbeth," which meant he had to keep quiet like someone being told things he has never heard before.

For Cresspahl these were things he had never heard before: besides, sometimes he thought he heard a warning, an apology. And yet these were all familiar things, seen merely from a different viewpoint, seen afresh. Much of what Dr. Berling had told him about Lisbeth's feverish talk at the hospital was already known to him, only it was said differently, put in a different way; now this too was not clear, not palpable, not put into words.

More than anything else, it had been what Dr. Berling had told him that made him brood darkly, set to work frantically on monotonous jobs. He was not inclined to accept everything Berling said. As for strange talk, Berling was hardly the person to comment on that. He addressed every reasonably husky-looking fellow as "you old Swede," meaning "you old rascal," long before the Nazis gave him cause to dig up relatives in Sweden. Before settling in Jerichow he had evidently been reading local historical tracts, and to excess about a General Oxenstierna under whom the Swedes had ravaged the area during the Thirty Years' War. Another rascally Swede. And his sinister references to "focal spots of disease in the heart of the nation" had not begun until his wife had left him and was living with someone else in Schwerin, granted that the other man wore a peacock uniform and served as an interpreter between Governor Hildebrandt and the Army. Berling would probably have done better to choose a different time for his grumblings against the Nazis, or at least a different occasion. These days he spent his evenings at home alone, his Rhine wine being delivered to him by the case, trundled from the station into his cellar; during too many drunken evenings he had had time to rearrange Lisbeth's words for Cresspahl's consumption. That had been eight weeks ago, and how did he address Cresspahl? You old roué, is what he said, although he also said: Well, you old Swede? In this part of the world what was strange did not seem strange. The part of Mecklenburg best known to Cresspahl was Malchow; things had been different there.

It was simply that Lisbeth took the Church too seriously, and that in the long run a person couldn't reconcile the two things, the teachings of the Church and the demands of the Nazis. She had learned it a certain way as a child, in a house like Papenbrock's a child could spend a long time growing up in that belief.

He once asked her about the family cleric employed by Louise Papenbrock in the days when they had leased an estate near Crivitz and later at Vietsen. He began quite casually, asking as if it were something that had slipped his mind. Did she remember him? And Lisbeth, Lisbeth laughed, turned part-way from the stove and took a half-step forward until she could comfortably stroke his brow and temples, as if he were a child to be comforted. If she was to be believed, she had even forgotten the name of that clerical candidate. She laughed quite naturally, looking at him gaily and frankly in the eye as if she had secretly guessed somthing of which he didn't even know whether he had concealed it. They still had these unspoken understandings, they didn't even have to be alone for that; at such times he was happy at least to be living with her, and far from demanding that he too should be happy.

In the evenings he sat in the kitchen and got himself drunk to the point where all he was conscious of was fatigue. Didn't even have to search in the pantry, the kümmel stood right up front on the shelf as if put there in readiness.

So it was Louise Papenbrock who, with her blindly pious training, had not succeeded with any of her children except this one. He couldn't forbid Lisbeth her mother.

He could have forced Lisbeth to go away from Jerichow, maybe not all the way across the water, only as far as the Netherlands. But she had never become used to the strange church in Richmond, and with the Dutch one it was not likely to be any different. And he did not care to force her.

He looked for guilt in himself too, and in 1937 he was finally ready to admit that he should not have married a girl with an upper-class education and background if all he had to contribute was primary school, his trade, and what he had learned on the streets; and he could hear Lisbeth's voice of 1931 saying: I don't want to quiz you, I want to live with you, with you and the children, four of them. You're doing your part, I don't think I'll fail in mine.

There were times when he reached the point of wanting to rouse Pastor Brüshaver from sleep and challenge him about that St. Paul of his who is said to have believed that it is good for a man not to touch a woman. Brüshaver with his three new children. During the day what was left over from such notions was that he would drive past Brüshaver as if the latter were invisible, just occasionally touching a finger to his cap, or at the last moment, sullenly; Sundays he would sit with folded arms beside Lisbeth in the church pew, marveling at a strong, not even narrow-minded man who chose to earn his living by interpreting a book that laid down such rules for man and woman. Cresspahl had looked it up, St. Paul had written it down in an open letter.

And there were often times when he could almost forget Lisbeth's strange moods. Those were the mornings when she would wake him not absent-mindedly, in a listless voice, but cheerfully, with jokes harking back to their time in England; days when she would carry on until evening, working steadily, never complaining, and with a readiness to joke and tease that relaxed the dinner-table crowd, suspicious though they had been at first, almost to the point of jocularity; that could last for months.

He didn't always quite trust her in this mood, however much he longed for her to be like that. He had already told her back in Richmond about a Mrs. Elizabeth Trowbridge; Lisbeth had not asked for a confession, she had merely listened calmly, nodding when he had finished as if at something expected, as if she were satisfied. In Germany he had to add a bit more and announce that, of the money being held for them in England in the bank, a certain sum would have to be deducted every month for a little boy whom Mrs. Elizabeth Trowbridge had produced without his knowledge. He had waited a long time for the right moment, not deciding until after supper whether it had been a "good" day. On evenings like that, work done, house and child taken care of, they chatted together as if they had grown up side by side: rapidly, almost without caution, always on the qui vive for the other's teasing, never at a loss for the right repartee, in half-sentences of which the other anticipated the answer, each welcome to the other, each never looking past the other for hours on end. For Cresspahl those were memories of their first years, before she had known anything about guilt and the places in the Bible that made life not worth living; but these too were pretense, performances, for the end remained the same, she would be the first to go to bed, and alone.

She had wanted to know the birth date of the other child. May 1932, she did not seem to mind. Then she had said: Heinrich, if only she could live here; not too close to Jerichow, not too far away. Then you could live with her, and yet with me.

And no matter how often he compared and made a mental note of how her moods switched, he never discovered what triggered them, or whether it was he who did it. It happened from one day to the next, and by evening she was already kneeling beside the child's bed praying about the war about which he had been prophesying that noon. By this time he had learned that whatever he said now would have no effect on her, and that she would emerge from limbo only when she was able to, and could show it.

Pray, child, pray,
The Swedes are on their way,
Old Oxen-Steer will come the morn
To spear and toss you on his horn.

December 30, 1967   Saturday

In 1937 Cresspahl was still not sure who he really was in the little town of Jerichow, who he might be in the eyes of the other inhabitants, by this time numbering two thousand four hundred and ninety.

He was not regarded as pro-Semitic, although he still associated with the veterinarian Semig, a Jew, as if he had never been told anything about April 1, 1933. It could be interpreted as obstinacy, the fact that several times a week Cresspahl would stop in front of Dr. Semig's imposing villa on the Bäk in Jerichow and carry in something in baskets, but then remain longer indoors than was necessary merely to deliver fruit or game. Possibly he did this for the sake of Dora Semig, née Köster, who was not more "non-Aryan" than he was. Besides, when you got down to it, Arthur Semig was only *one* Jew. Perhaps the thing was that in England a person learned to associate with Jews as if they were friends too.

"The Englishman" was how Cresspahl was known in Jerichow.

He liked that, as if they were glad he had married Lisbeth but had forgiven him Lisbeth's family. He wouldn't have liked to be obliged to speak for the Papenbrocks. For one thing they had only been living in the town for fifteen years, and they hadn't started out tactfully. Papenbrock had set up house in the former property of the Von Lassewitz family, as if he bore their name, and he seemed to be pretty intimate with the local aristocracy, who had their hands not only on the countryside but also on the town itself, with rents, leases, interest, mortgages. But if he wanted to make himself the secret king of Jerichow, then it was time he stood up and made himself known, instead of allowing a Friedrich Jansen to be mayor; the town hadn't much to be conceited about but then neither had it deserved that fellow. Papenbrock preferred to rake in his shekels on the quiet; it made no difference that shrewdness stood for something in Jerichow. And Papenbrock's wife Louise behaved not only as if the town belonged to her but also as if St. Peter's couldn't hold up its spire without her. His girls, as long as they remained girls, passed muster. They had given away not only clothing but toys. And their Low German dialect, despite its southern overtones, was, after all, what they had learned as their first language from poultry maids and stable boys. Our Hilde had sometimes been pert, not outright, but perceptibly. Our Lisbeth, too pious alas, was the best of the lot. Lisbeth hadn't cared whether the children she brought home to play in Papenbrock's garden were the mayor's or the cobbler's. Papenbrock had brought up his two daughters almost as an example of what should be permitted and given to children (in Jerichow). It was hard to be envious of the children, even if your own lacked much of what Papenbrock's had.

When the old man had married them off it once again became obvious that he intended to make his property more secure by splitting it up. Hilde's husband Alexander Paepcke did not remain a failed attorney in Krakow for long, Papenbrock having installed him as the lessee in the Jerichow brickyard. In a way it seemed like justice that things should go wrong for Papenbrock there. For Alexander Paepcke had managed, despite an assured, insatiable demand for bricks for the airfield at Jerichow North (a demand for which no end appeared to be in sight), to get red dots, red holes one might say, in his ledgers, and, intimidated, had taken himself off to the easternmost corner of Military District II, to the Stettin Army Ordinance Department; and it was probably true that Papenbrock in his rage did secretly give Hilde a little something toward her housekeeping; all Alexander was aware of was the stringent salary he was now bringing home. Podejuch, what a name for a place, if it existed at all, if it wasn't in fact a "Rio de Janeiro."

And as for Papenbrock's Sonny Boy, that fellow Horst, from the very beginning Cresspahl hadn't wanted to answer for him. While the old man had tried to keep him down, Horst had wanted to throw his weight around with that Storm Trooper gang of his; he was over thirty and drove about the countryside in trucks, shouting and

singing with his Party cohorts at the trees along the highway because
he had sworn some kind of oath to a foreigner by the name of Adolf
Hitler. At Cresspahl's and Lisbeth's wedding he had wanted to go to
the church in that shit-brown uniform of his. True enough, since his
return from his overseas trip he was lying low. The Jerichow Storm
Troopers had positively to remind him that he had formerly been
their leader. Since then he occasionally joined in maneuvers and
marches, but he had not insisted on receiving payment for his share
in the Nazis' victory in the form of promotions and medals. Those
had been distributed during his absence. Once again he learned to
work in his father's yard and granary and in so doing had ruined his
brown boots. He had been traveling for over a year, had come back
broader in the shoulders, no longer the eager beaver, and now held his
head erect, not tensely but relaxed; he might well turn out after all to
be the kind of Papenbrock the old man wanted. He might well be
unable to accept the fact that his Hitler had found it necessary to
shoot down half the Storm Troop leaders like mad dogs; or he had
seen something in America. And when he insisted on marrying that
Elisabeth Lieplow, suddenly it was all right by Papenbrock, and he
couldn't even reproach him with spending half a week at a time in
Kröpelin; for Horst had done himself out of his inheritance in
Jerichow.

What he now refused the Nazis, the Nazis got from Robert
Papenbrock, the brother who was supposed to have disappeared, for
whom Horst had gone to look in "Rio de Janeiro"; he had eventually
turned up and was now holding an official position in a confiscated
villa in the provincial capital, and rumor had it that, besides his
brown, i.e., "official," uniform, he had another, the black one of the
Secret Police. Another brother-in-law.

Of him Cresspahl used to say: Don't know him; not our sort; far
as I'm concerned, he died.

It wasn't necessary: on the day of Horst's wedding in Kröpelin,
Cresspahl had been putting in windows at Jerichow North. If
Cresspahl was to be found anywhere, it was not at the Lübeck Arms,
where the aristocracy went, nor at the station restaurant, where the
Nazis drank, but perhaps at Peter Wulff's tavern, known to Regional
Party Leader Jansen as a rats' nest of Social Democrats. He got all the
work he wanted on his own, neither needing nor using old Papen-
brock for that. Bit quiet, that fellow. In the midst of a conversation
he will fix his eyes on the middle distance, and has taken off. An
Englishman.

They knew very well that it wasn't until 1922 that he had

worked in the Netherlands and still later in England, that he had been born in a village on Lake Müritz and had been declared a master carpenter in Malchow; that same Malchow-by-the-Lake, the clothmakers' town, from which Kliefoth the schoolteacher came, having moved to Jerichow after Cresspahl. They called Cresspahl the bur-picker, after the burs that the people of Malchow had to pick out of the sheep's wool before they could start making their cloth; for them Cresspahl was the man from England, not in any bad sense, sometimes jokingly, sometimes confidentially. (The fellow who knew all about the English. In case the English should win the war.)

This much was a fact, that he usually knew about English matters from that same paper, the *Lübecker Generalanzeiger*, to which they also subscribed; apparently he spent longer reading it.

This much was correct, that he had sounded off with a kind of contempt, if not rage, at the cowardice of the English in letting the German Army occupy the Rhineland. He was probably embarrassed on behalf of the English.

This much was true, that he dismissed as childish the visits of the Lord Privy Seal, Lord Londonderry, and of Lloyd George and the Marquess of Lothian. Apparently he wished the English would do something more, or other, than crossing the Atlantic in their *Queen Mary* for the sake of a blue ribbon. Couldn't blame the man for that now, could you.

This much was true, that the law concerning the reconstruction of the German Reich had invalidated his Weimar Republic passport. That he had had two years in which to go to the county office in Gneez and apply for a passport with a swastika. That he had not done so.

This much was to be expected, that he did not leave Semig in peace until the latter had gone to Gneez and returned with a passport for himself and his wife.

This much was possible, that Cresspahl would rather they had called him something else.

Well, you old bur-picker?

December 31, 1967   Sunday

Braised beef. Take a cut from a well-aged rump of beef, lard it with bacon strips, rub with salt and allspice . . .

Married life, Marie's not going to learn about that from me.

What she gets are performances; not even the way it would be. These are the visits of D. E., known as Mr. Erichson, professor of physics & chemistry, adviser to the U. S. Air Force in matters of radar research, guest and host of this Cresspahl family for the last five and a half years and far from being the man of the house, which is how the neighbors regard him because they see him arriving with elaborately wrapped parcels, with a suitcase after a trip, using the same phrases he has been using for years for as long as the front door is open.

True, once the door has closed behind him he seems completely at home, finding his way around with hardly a glance, with almost casual signs of affection that Marie scarcely notices. All the same, he won't completely empty his suitcase today either, and as he was about to put it in the south room he made sure by a glance that it was all right for him to go in there. He's not here for long and won't stay beyond tomorrow evening, even if Marie should ask him to. Which she might.

This suits her too. She likes the way he sits at table as a guest between the two windows, asking her about school because he is genuinely interested and not from any sense of duty because of being her guardian. They have a lot of little codes: skeptical sidelong glances with lowered head, or attempts at lying with a deadpan expression, or whether he or she is obliged to say at certain stages: Which I undertook solely to help keep New York clean; whatever the routine calls for. She would even like to live with him permanently, in his house, yet on her own terms. It never occurs to her to compare D. E. with the husbands who visit her friends' homes in the evening as fathers; she looks on him as a friend, in one sense her mother's, even more specifically her own. It is through her that he has the name D. E. from his initials, and although this may be interpreted as Dear Erichson, she does not use his Christian name to show her affection but the other, which everyone uses. "Well, D. E.?" she says. "And how's business in your business?"

So that, cheerfully and patiently, he tells her about the radar centers of the U. S. Air Force in Greenland, about the ritual words spoken nowadays in Thule before a meal, invariably lapsing into the history of the Goths which Marie doesn't always instantly recognize, although she has been watching for it like a hawk. Kneeling on her chair, rocking on her elbows, not taking her eyes off him, his relaxed expression, the amused movements of his lips, his skin tautened by cold air, the forty-year-old gray hair, the sober, dispassionate look, the Mecklenburger who has become an American. Using English without a thought, with their subdued laughter, they behaved as if they were enjoying themselves.

Meanwhile, the housewife is standing at the stove attending to her duties: Flour the meat, brown it in butter, pour on simmering water to a depth of two thirds, add a few stale crusts of bread, a few vegetables (carrots), an onion, a bay leaf, a few peppercorns, and simmer everything for two and a half hours; but D. E., like a typical middle-class father, has taken the child out into the black evening, into the soggy snow in Riverside Park, to walk up an appetite. Married life, Marie's not going to learn about that from me. An exception for a celebration, just once, not forever, not every day. When we have something to celebrate.

"What's there to celebrate?"

"The date, Gesine. Although astronomically speaking unsatisfactory."

"Yes. That the year's over. That we've survived it."

"October went by too fast for me."

"Everyone has their own things to celebrate, Marie."

"O.K. Because this year Senator Kennedy has overtaken the President. Because he's going to end the war in Vietnam."

"Bugs Bunny? Against more than half the population, who want to see the war continued? Bugs Bunny?"

"Senator Robert Francis Kennedy."

"I stand corrected, Marie Cresspahl."

"Marie Henriette Cresspahl, at that."

"Sorry, M. H."

"The astronauts who got burned up in January. The Soviet astronaut who crashed in April."

"Your summer dress, the yellow one, with the tortoise-shell buttons."

"Two hundred and three more days and I'll be eleven."

"That we'll have to celebrate."

"That it had to be that gang from the CIA who saved a comrade of Che Guevara's from being shot to death."

"That Guevara might still be alive if he hadn't slapped a Bolivian officer during the interrogation."

"And our dear old Auntie Times, long may she live!"

"Now the New Year's resolutions. That I go on getting A's from Sister Magdalena, even if the beast never has a good word to say for me! Now it's your turn."

"That we stay in New York and can live here."

"That's a wish, not a resolution, Gesine: you're only allowed to say something you can do something about."

"That I don't become like my mother."

"Now you're talking wildly, Gesine."

"Wildly or not; now let's hear how Professor Erichson proposes to improve himself in the New Year."

"By you both marrying me in the New Year."

"Wrong! That's a wish again."

"For me it's a resolution, dear Mary, quite contrary."

"Which I undertook solely to help keep New York City clean."

"Right. Once upon a time, when wishes still came true, there lived a woman with many blessings who was bonny and sound of limb. . . ."

"Now she hangs there in St. Mary's Church in Lübeck, no bigger than a mouse, and makes one little movement each year."

"She wished to live forever, Marie."

"What a stupid thing to wish!"

"Happy New Year! Happy new year."

January 1, 1968   Monday

Three inches of snow; 24 degrees Fahrenheit, swept against the windows by a wind that is colder still.

Marie manages to contain herself until after breakfast, but then she can no longer keep her gift from me, her New Year's present. I've no idea what it is. For over six weeks she has turned her room into a restricted zone, betraying herself only by the sounds of sawing, hammering, and drilling, much of which she concealed by playing records. Early in December I saw her emerging from one of the side streets in the hundreds onto Broadway, carrying perforated boards and laths under her arm; maybe it's something made of wood. She says it's something I want without knowing I want it. D. E., all dressed up on a holiday and early in the morning as if for his restaurants and conferences, is leaning by the window, a relaxed spectator, arms folded, speaking of his own day. In his day, children who did fretwork occasionally produced a lighting fixture for a passageway.

The gift, covered by a sheet, has been set up between the double doors to Marie's room and is as large as a dog, larger than the chow dog that used to live under Dr. Berling's desk. But white sheets are laid over something that is dead, something that is finished, that will never come back.

"It's our house, Marie."

"It's not supposed to be your house! It's only what I've managed to pick up about it!" she says. And she walks restlessly up and down beside me, as if to keep me away from the model.

It is the house transferred by Albert Papenbrock to his grand-daughter in the spring of 1933 in order that Heinrich Cresspahl would do what Lisbeth wanted and return from England to Jerichow. It is a low building, weathered red beneath the steep red mossy roof complete with sloping eaves. There are the three sets of window bars, painted white, to the left of the front door, one to the right of it. The door is correct, set into a beveled frame, with mitered corners, both doors with a lower panel of wood, an upper one of glass. Both halves are hinged, each has a knob and a latch.

"I can't help it if the only photo we have shows the walnut trees hiding the front of the house and half the door!"
"You even remembered the doorstep."

The entry had red tiles, like this one. A person going in would turn to the door on the left, into the room used by the farmers before Cresspahl's day as a front parlor. Cresspahl had tried this too, with the table that could almost seat eight and that he had brought from Richmond, setting it up in the middle as a festive board. By the time the house, together with yard and garden, had been fixed up, there were no more feast days to celebrate. The table was then placed across the room, one end by the window. This was where he kept his tax records, his order books, drawings, rulers. By the other window stood Lisbeth's desk, given her by Papenbrock on her marriage, with her books on the shelf mounted on top of it. But Lisbeth did not come here to read, and she no longer had any letters to write. Cresspahl had moved out the chairs as well as the chest of drawers and distributed them among the workmen's rooms; for now he slept in this room on a leather-covered sofa against the wall, it was bare enough for that.

Next door, in a room not quite so big, heated by an extension of the tiled stove, slept the child.

"Was there really only one door, going from the child's room to Cresspahl's office?"
"You never mentioned any other."

Then it had been Cresspahl who had looked in on the child at night. Without Marie I would have forgotten that.

From his desk he could walk through a door at the end of the long wall into the room with the big bedstead built by him the way Lisbeth had wanted it and in which she now wished to lie alone. From there one went straight into the kitchen. But when Cresspahl went in for breakfast he had used the entry and the back passageway into the kitchen, merely in order to avoid Lisbeth in her sleep. It was here, at the long tiled table, that they had their meals, even on Sundays.

"If the right half of the house isn't the way it should be, it's your fault," says Marie, still a bit worried as to whether she should have built the past from memory.
"Because I didn't tell you about it."

Why not? Why did I never say anything about Paap, Alwin Paap, who had the front room to the right of the door? He had lived in the house until 1939, head journeyman. That's why he always went to his room around the outside of the house and through the back passage, regarding himself more as a servant. Marie has divided up the rest of that half into two small rooms, just as it was. One of them, the one across from the kitchen, was used as a large storeroom. The other had been fixed up for two workmen in 1935. They stayed until the beginning of the war. Then came the French, the prisoners of war. In three years' time they will be sleeping there in bunks one above the other.

January 3, 1968 Wednesday

In the early-morning darkness today, enemy forces attacked the United States air base at Danang with about 30 rounds of 122-mm. rocket fire, wrecking an F-4 Phantom fighter-bomber.

In Jerichow things had not reached that stage yet; the airfield was far from complete. First Jerichow wanted to get at least one Jew out of the way.

They did this for Arthur Semig, Doctor of Veterinary Medicine, owner of a house, owner of a bank account.

They did not do this for Oskar Tannebaum, who lived on Short Street in two rooms overlooking a courtyard, the shop bell seldom summoning him these days to make a sale. Rubber boots, blue jackets, green caps, all this could be picked up in Gneez, Wismar, Lübeck. Mr. Tannebaum paid his taxes just like Semig, but he had no friends among the better-class families, he sent his children out in clothes that had been mended too often, his wife did her shopping as frugally as if she were afraid of being cheated. He had had rich relatives in Gneez; but for the relatives he had not been sufficiently respectable for them to take him along to Hamburg or Holland or wherever they had ended up. Oskar was not from Mecklenburg, his wife came from the lost Eastern territories. And to cap it all the Tannebaums had settled in Jerichow ten years ago at the very most.

Dr. Arthur Semig, on the other hand, came from western Mecklenburg, one was tempted to think of Ludwigslust and the grand-ducal residence, his wife had been a Köster from Schwerin and from a Protestant family to boot; Arthur had started his practice in Jerichow seventeen years ago, he had been asked not only into the stables but also to the coffee tables; whether at the Bülows' (the "Oberbülows") or at Dr. Erdamer's, Arthur had been part of the Establishment, a man of property, of education, with his friendly little anecdotes, his discretion, his endless fund of rhymes for every child that came running up to him. Nothing must be allowed to happen to Arthur. He had already realized something when he removed his little square mustache; now he could not fail to realize that it was time to leave.

Papenbrock started it. No, this time it was started by Axel von Rammin. Or was it Avenarius Cold Morning? Avenarius Kollmorgen? It had been Cresspahl.

They descended on him from all sides, it was useless to show his annoyance, and they listened to his embarrassment with such persistence that it was always he who had to say the next word. He could not very well ask a Von Rammin, a baron for centuries, to leave his house when the Baron had made an appointment to consult him about rebuilding his cow barns and had left his carriage not in the yard but on the Bäk, hitching it right there on the street, visible to every eye. Von Rammin actually did listen for half an hour to what Semig could tell him about the most up-to-date methods in cattle-breeding. Then, without lessening the severity in his craggy face, he started to talk about a friend in Austria for whom Semig had once fulfilled a request, Count Naglinsky, known as Nagel, Beatus Nagel for short. Beatus, according to the Baron, was as relieved as ever that his Weimaraner had recovered so well after Semig's treatment, Beatus controlled a great deal of land and, what was more, was above the stupidities of a Hitler and would never dream of regarding the German Reich Chancellor as a true compatriot. Now a thought had struck Naglinksy. He had his dogs; but he also kept dairy cattle, maintained horses, he had losses among his pigs as well as his poultry.

For all this he had to send for a veterinarian from town. So it was not just for economy's sake, it made good sense that he should have his own resident veterinarian who, as far as he was concerned, would be free to carry on a practice on the side in the village. And in his family, professional men shared his table and lived at the manor house. Baron von Rammin asked that an account be sent for the consultation, wished to be remembered to Mrs. Semig, and left with an original remark about the climate of Lower Austria. And it was Semig, not the Baron, who was obliged to pass his hand over his hair as he stood in the doorway watching the uninvited counselor leave.

Papenbrock wanted no part of it. Papenbrock refused to have the funds in Semig's bank account transferred to his own account in settlement of a loan; this would be acting under false pretenses and an immoral action. Papenbrock refused to consider buying Semig's house; he already had plenty of property in Jerichow, and he needed his ready cash for a promised security in Lübeck.

Papenbrock was scared. The old man sat there hunched up, laid aside his cigar in distaste, chewed his knuckles, and finally reached the point where he began to rail against the Jews, in a shrill, fretful voice, with contemptuous gestures, longing for the interview to end. He was too embarrassed to look at Cresspahl.

Semig was quite satisfied. This was no way to persuade him. He had become used to living without a telephone. The driving about the countryside, the night work, really had been rather tiring; now he had time to read. Dora was also managing better with her housekeeping, with the regular hours. He didn't mind giving up his games of skat with Dr. Berling; Cresspahl was a better player anyhow, and they'd manage to find a third. He wasn't going to let himself be sent away from Jerichow.

Then came Dr. Avenarius Kollmorgen, attorney. Instead of going to the Bäk, he invited the Semigs and the Cresspahls over for an evening of red wine.

Kollmorgen had given his maid the evening off, and he drew his guests personally, with outstretched hand, into his living room, where he made a speech on his feet, rocking on his heels, massive head held high atop the short, squat body. He spoke about the law. The upshot of it was that he needed a loan, among other things to purchase a house on the Bäk that "is familiar to all of us," and because he was not too sure of his ground in the rules and regulations governing foreign currency he had always had such matters handled by a "trading house" in Bremen that he could recommend. He arched his eyebrows as learnedly as during his most famous cross-examinations, he looked Dora Semig almost affectionately in the eye, he was really making an effort. Then he drank very rapidly, was soon no use for a game of skat, stared glassily at his guests, the corners of his mouth drooping. Cresspahl, who had come alone, thought he looked like an elderly child unable to swallow a hurt.

For Semig wouldn't see it. He took exception to any interference. He let Dora criticize him for his tone. He gave Dora time to have her say. And Dora looked at him, tightened her mouth a little, and nodded. She had not even sighed.

Cresspahl offered Semig his account at the Surrey Bank of Richmond in exchange, and Arthur refused to discuss it. Cresspahl said: "We'll keep a faithful account of everything, there won't be a penny missing," and Semig said: "My dear Mr. Cresspahl! If I'm not good enough for you —."

Axel von Rammin had seen to it that his friend Beatus wrote the appropriate letters, and now his feelings were hurt that a veterinarian should presume to refuse to proceed in a matter which had, after all, been initiated by a person of no ordinary standing.

And Avenarius, on meeting Cresspahl, sometimes forgot to greet him with that charming upward twist of his head and to say with mysterious significance: "Getting on all right, Cresspahl? Getting on all right?"

Lisbeth Cresspahl said: "Christ was a Jew too. So that makes us all Jews. Leave Semig in peace."

And Papenbrock said: "If you're all determined to get rid of him, he won't go the easy way. So try the tough way!"

January 6, 1968 Saturday

Senator Kennedy is far from satisfied with the training offered American Indians and in the previous year the Vietcong had killed 3,820 civilians and President de Gaulle had not meant to insult the Jews by characterizing them as an "elite people" and there had been a fire at the Hotel Alamac on Broadway and the Christian Democratic Party of West Germany has attacked the Social Democratic Party because of the latter's appeal to the U. S. A. for a cessation of the bombing of North Vietnam and Antonín Novotný is no longer the First Secretary of the Czechoslovak Communist Party but has had to step down in favor of Alexander Dubcek, and a Slovak at that, after a thousand years of Bohemian-Moravian rule; the New York Times has accurately calculated it.

In Jerichow a rumor persisted that it was old Papenbrock who was going to rid the town of Semig the Jew; so another rumor had it that Papenbrock intended to acknowledge his new-found son Robert only so long as Governor Hildebrandt's word was law in the province of Mecklenburg; then never again; it wasn't his son.

The identity of Robert Papenbrock in 1935 or 1937 was something to which not even the family could absolutely swear. He had made one visit to Jerichow, perhaps only because Horst insisted on it, for he stayed over Saturday and left on Sunday for the regional headquarters in the provincial capital and sent a picture postcard from Berlin, and since he hadn't married that woman who shared his villa in Schwerin he couldn't send an announcement through the mail. It was hard to visit him, for when not entertaining a visitor himself he was off on some official trip. First class, sleeper.

It might have been he. The Robert who ran away from Parchim in May 1914 might rather have been expected to turn into a bony fellow; this man was tall, heavy-set, with a white fleshy face. And he was the right age, by now Robert would be a bit over forty. The Robert who had grown up in Vietsen and Waren had been a quick-witted, dexterous kind of person; this one was easygoing, leisurely, slow-spoken. It was very odd that he didn't even ask about the child with which he had saddled the French teacher's daughter. The Robert whom the Papenbrocks remembered had had no compunction about scattering debts throughout the town of Parchim; this one had come to terms with the estate owner whose two riding horses he had not delivered to Schwerin but borrowed in a manner that even in these days is still considered theft; possibly the victim had complained to Robert's party about him. Robert affected surprise over the affair and had evidently expected Papenbrock to regard it as an honor to pay for the horses too. In discussing those times he was inclined to pussyfoot. Was it possible for someone to forget the Low German dialect so hopelessly in a mere twenty years? A Mecklenburg child? Granted that foreign languages might have an eroding effect. What Louise Papenbrock found hardest to accept was the bald head, not even her bald husband had quite such a rounded forehead. And when she thought of Bobby's little-boy hair, the wiry shock of hair of those days . . . but abroad, of course, one contracted diseases more dangerous than any existing in Mecklenburg. Yes. But tell us one thing, Bobby. How come you never wrote?

In his new, easygoing way, Robert spoke about a person's pride, and Louise on the sofa could no longer remember whether her eternal malediction had been included with the two hundred gold marks she had sent the "poor lad" in Hamburg, to the underworld quarter where he lived. In the advertisement in the *Hamburger Fremdenblatt* she had put it differently: Come back, all is forgiven, Mother, née U. from G. Papenbrock had arranged himself in his chair in such a way that his stomach lay comfortably uppermost and he could devote all his attention to the tall slow-moving fellow who was dislocating his mouth on a wooden toothpick. Papenbrock was thinking of a pride that had not sufficed for a return to Germany at a time when the country had been at war with half the world.

Cresspahl sat at the table next to Horst, trying to get a glimpse of his expression other than in profile, but Horst was leaning forward looking at his hands as if some disagreeable job had to be got through. Cresspahl was watching Lisbeth as she scanned the face of the new arrival, her chin propped on folded hands, kindly but to an even greater degree astonished, and in neither case the erstwhile little sister; Cresspahl was more interested in enjoying her and in how their child wandered around the table, sitting down sometimes beside him, sometimes beside her mother, in a solemn game. Then all eyes would turn swiftly and surreptitiously toward Horst; nothing was to be got out of him beyond a nod that seemed to confirm something to himself more than to the others. Horst was probably regretting the loss of his inheritance to the first-born, and he hadn't been around at the time, had he.

Well, O.K. So Robert *had* been unable to swallow his pride. But why *hadn't* he been able to think of anything better than buying false papers and signing on on an American ship to Montevideo? This happened in too many books. And forever upholding the honor of the German nation, our glorious Kaiser, proud Mecklenburg-Schwerin, and if anyone said anything, immediately asking: Want me to beat you up! Just step right up! In German, of course, what else.

It was because Robert had first passed himself off as a Norwegian, then as a U. S. citizen, later as a holder of a Mexican passport, that his brother had had such a hard time finding him. Very much later, Horst repeated that first storytelling afternoon as he saw it, but not directed against his parents, and not until the point had been passed at which someone might have interpreted it as resentment over the lost inheritance.

The family knew about Montevideo through one of Papenbrock's army buddies (later killed), whom Robert had approached for a loan. Nothing could be found out about Robert in Montevideo. In Porto Alegre, Paranaguá, Santos, Rio de Janeiro, there had been many transients who might at one time have resembled the youth in the photograph. Meanwhile Horst had picked up enough Portuguese to fend off at least the greediest of the informants and, since he was spending Papenbrock's money with a certain amount of defiance, his hotel addresses recommended him to the German communities. Robert had kept his distance from the Germans.

At one time Robert had been an inspector on the hacienda of a family of German origin. Five hours' drive from Salvador, also known as Bahia.

In Vietsen, Robert had learned no more about agriculture than could be picked up from watching others work. Robert could not drive a car.

With a chauffeur. The same thing when he was manager of a factory in Colón. On the Panama Canal. Where he learned his first American phrases.

He learned Spanish as a taxi driver in Mexico. Mexico City. The heights and depths of life.

At this point, about four in the afternoon, Robert asked for a schnapps; and Lisbeth took the child by the hand and went off to see to the household duties that she had thought up for this time of the day.

Canal Street in New Orleans; what a sight! The yellow waters of the Mississippi. The noble Indians of Arizona.

How Robert helped build Golden Gate Bridge. Pushing a wheelbarrow full of rocks across a narrow plank. The sneaky nigger who gave him a push. A boy from Mecklenburg, can you see him drowning? And in San Francisco Bay?

And always saving. His money in a bag on his chest, when he rode the east-bound freight trains. A hobo. The others, lying with him on the roof, their resentful looks. Occasionally one would roll off the edge, and if the tracks happened to run above a three-thousand-foot cliff, too bad. And yet never dishonoring the image . . . the memory . . . the faith in our dear old Mum. But the main thing was to survive.

A trucking company bought in Hoboken with his capital. Three employees. All gone in the Depression. Then, that mighty Manhattan always before his eyes, he was bound to make it. Longshoreman in the harbor, yet a down payment made on a house in Long Island City. Partnership in a restaurant with a former member of the Schwerin Rowing Club, on Broadway somewhere in the nineties. Then Germany's rise from the ashes of democracy. By the time Horst found him he had already applied for his passport. Or as good as. All Horst had to do was swear he was a Mecklenburger. Just a technicality. *You* know.

Nothing but a bunch of Jews and niggers, those Americans. This is one war we're going to win.

Learning to stand on his own feet. Not to be a burden to the family. Putting his shoulder behind the victory of National Socialism in the rest of the world.

On the back of that postcard with the view of the New Reich Chancellery he had written: In Berlin they'd put him through the wringer, but they had to accept him, regardless.

As early as September 1936 he made a speech in Erlangen at the Reich Conference of the Overseas Organizations of the National Socialist German Workers' Party "in front of 5,000 Germans from all over the world."

But in Jerichow people were saying that Pastor Brüshaver's sermon the morning after Robert's arrival had made no mention of this happy turn of events; the Papenbrocks could have asked for it. It was being said that Avenarius Kollmorgen must know whether Papenbrock had had his will redrawn, and that when referring to the Erlangen speech Avenarius spoke only about his own time in Erlangen and what had been regarded as decent behavior at the time. It fitted that Papenbrock didn't show off this Robert. The old fellow had always been a smart one. They didn't exploit him, and although by this time Robert had been back nearly two years he was almost forgotten when people thought of the Papenbrocks. What difference did it make whether it was he or not.

Lisbeth had not liked the way this stranger wanted to embrace her after more than twenty years as if she were not his sister. But then Lisbeth had turned queer about anything to do with embraces.

January 7, 1968 Sunday

The underpass beneath the Henry Hudson Parkway was so brimful of scintillating lights that Marie expected the river to have been frozen into a smooth mirror for the sun. But beneath the cloudless illuminated sky the great river was on its powerful way to the Atlantic, sparkling in countless ice floes, no longer Hudson's river, so poisoned by industrial effluent that the fish are already dying far up in the North; the memory of a river. Across the deep plain that it had eaten into the land, a wind was tearing along faster than an automobile is ever permitted in built-up areas, and the 10 degrees

Centigrade below freezing had penetrated so deeply into the promenade railing that fingertips stuck instantly to the iron. Marie stomped happily along through the repeatedly thawing and freezing snow, toward the sun, which was feigning heat somewhere over Hoboken. She looked at approaching pedestrians as gaily as if half inclined to pass on to them some of the fun she was carrying around with her. When she spoke, the wind sometimes caused little clouds of her breath to hang in the air before being whisked away by the cold. "Hoboken!" she said, and actually lifted her nose as if wanting to have a good look at the wool that nobody was going to pull over *her* eyes.

"A trucking company in Hoboken, a staff of four, and what else? City councilor at least, that's for sure!" she said, pretending to be indignant, so amused was she at the idea that Robert Papenbrock might have made a bourgeois living and acquired bourgeois honors in our area, only on the other side of the Hudson. She refers to him as "your uncle," as if this dissociated her from the relationship.

"During the twenties, the ships from overseas were still docking in Hoboken, Marie. There was certainly work for a trucking company."

"Oh, I agree. He dreamed up something pretty good there."

"What d'you find dreamed up about it?"

"His excuse is too pat."

"But still possible."

"About as possible as the restaurant 'on Broadway somewhere in the nineties.' In 1930! In the Depression! When he'd have been lucky if his Schwerin friend had let him wash the dishes, if he hadn't had to wipe the scraps off first, and with his own hand too!"

"You don't believe him because you only see him at a distance. You've got a pretty low opinion of him."

"That's the way you told it."

"I just wanted to explain the way it was. The way it might have been."

"It sounded more as if you were disgusted by him."

"Cresspahl was, I guess."

"And you're on your father's side."

"No. Whenever I do understand him, it's a tour de force."

"Second proof, Mrs. Cresspahl: Mrs. Cresspahl is upset because everyone in her family associated with the people then in power in Mecklenburg (and in Germany, I know). 'Robert Papenbrock,' or his murderer, didn't even begin at the bottom with that lot, he started right at the top!"

"You just refuse to believe it was him?"

"Aren't I supposed not to believe it?"

"I'm only telling you how it looked at the time."

"Why not the way it was?"

"Because it wasn't till years later that it became known whether his story was true. D'you want me to tell you the tale in the wrong order?"

"No. Though I don't sort out that Jerichow of yours by years."

"How else?"

"By the people you tell me about. What I know about them. What I'm supposed to think about them."

"O.K. Let's hear it."

"O.K. At first he wasn't, but by now Albert Papenbrock is almost my favorite. To begin with, he's my great-grandfather, a great rarity to know about, certainly in my grade. Maybe because I feel sorry for him. The Nazis won't let him be king any more, neither in the town nor in his own home. Let him boast that he's taking splendid care of his family—part of it is that he does want to take care of them. That's a different feeling, and not a nice one to lose."

"Did you learn that from your association with Francine? 'The exemplary manner in which the Cresspahl girl lends a helping hand to a black classmate who is disadvantaged by race and family background?' "

"I don't boast about it; apologies accepted. All the same, I can recognize Albert's position now and again."

"O.K. Now Loveesing."

"Who? Albert Papenbrock's wife Louise? No comment."

"Because she lived one way and prayed another?"

"No comment, Gesine!"

"Any comments on Lisbeth?"

"Your mother. Because she's your mother I've almost always made excuses for her when you told me about her. By this time she's ill, and nobody's going to help her. In a country like ours, in New York, she'd have gone to a head shrinker long ago, and been cured. She'd no longer be all locked up in her church, she could look at it from the outside. And because she's going to be the next one to die. You're easy on her yourself."

"Go on."

"You see? The workmen, Böttcher the carpenter, Köpcke the mason, Pahl the tailor, I don't hold it against them. They haven't even understood their first war, what else were they to do but build for the new one? The man who sawed the plywood for me to make

your house, that man in the West Nineties off Broadway, he'd been
in Korea, wounded too. You should hear him talk about Vietnam!
But those professional men of yours, Dr. Hauschildt, Dr. Semig, Dr.
Avenarius Kollmorgen, Pastor Brüshaver, Dr. Kliefoth, Dr. Berling,
Dr. Erdamer —"

"Hi, Mr. Faure! Mrs. Faure!"

"Yes indeed! It's a perfect winter day."

"Take care on the steps."

"You can count Brüshaver out. His son from his first marriage
was returned to him from Spain in a soldered box."

"Sorry. But that's a coincidence, all the same. In Semig's case I'll
take into consideration that he couldn't believe in the possibility of
what we now know to be possible. But the others, the ones with
diplomas from universities, those professionals, those heroic farters!"

"I like your language, Miss Cresspahl."

"I'm not even trying to insult them!"

"Cresspahl."

"That's someone I'd despise if he weren't your father. I'm very
sorry. I really am. I didn't mean to say that. I do take it back, and I
mean it."

"Your grandfather?"

"Him. He was the only one who had his eyes wide open, he'd
learned his lesson from the first German war—what had he been
doing anyway?"

"Bayonet attacks in honor of a Kaiser's birthday, on the Western
front. That a person can stick bayonets into people and enjoy it. And
that gas attack near Langemarck."

"That's what I mean. If at least he'd tried the Netherlands, after
all in those days that country didn't look as if it was going to be
involved in a war; if he'd tried that he'd have been in my good books
forever. And he had a child, one called Gesine, and he let her stay
right there where he was expecting the bombs to fall. I often think
it's terrible the way you can believe that all those people in Jerichow
made you what you are; that today you're what you are because they
were what they were!"

"If Cresspahl hadn't accepted the house from Papenbrock, in
1945 the Cresspahls would have been in England, though maybe
interned, and Jakob would have asked some other people for a room.
And if Dr. Berling had known his way around in other people's
minds rather than only in his own . . ."

"O.K. So that's why we're in New York?"

"That's why."

"And right there and thirty years ago it was all decided that you'd rather feel a dime in your hand than half a dollar?"

"Yes. Maybe because there's a Dutch coin that feels like a dime."

"I find that unbearable. But I'm what I am because of you?"

"It happens. We've forgotten one person. Horst."

"I've almost come to terms with him. Don't laugh. He'd made a mistake. Then he saw something. For regardless of who he identified, he's still been to New York."

She walked comfortably beside me in the cutting wind, well wrapped up in her heavy London coat, her peaked cap, herself. We had the sun behind us, and she was trying to keep step with her shadow. In winter, when the buildings along the steep New Jersey shore are hidden under snow and blinding reflections, Henry Hudson might after all have recognized his river from the mottled white cliffs. Marie thinks this is possible. And she is absolutely sure that a person in this city of hers, even if at the very lowest end of Broadway and not along Park Avenue where the West Germans are showing off today—she is convinced that if a person comes to New York he must also come to his senses.

The things she believed as a child ought to be written down for her.

January 8, 1968   Monday

You can depend upon it that we did not escape the New York *Times.* "And residents of Riverside Drive found the Hudson River glutted with more ice floes than they had seen in many years at this time of the winter." As if they had seen us, asked us.

And the Cresspahl apartment is occupied by a lot of family for whom it would be too small even without us. Marie has decided that we are good enough friends with Annie Fleury and her children for us to live together, just the way they turned up out of the blue, from the Far North, from Vermont, from the Greyhound bus. Marie had explained the subway route from the bus depot to our 96th Street so carefully over the phone that, although they did not arrive much before the bank closes, they had been in the apartment for some time, the three children all in Marie's room behind closed doors, Annie on the sofa, as timid as an uninvited guest who immediately gets up and wants to go right off to a hotel. Surely you don't want to leave us and go rushing off to the Marseilles, Annie? You're so jumpy, Annie, why d'you keep your knees so tightly together, why on earth are you sitting there so uncomfortably, all hunched up like that and twisting your hands! If you don't feel like laughing we won't try to make you. We'd rather you had come to us the way you used to be, that your colors of wind and forest were of some use to you, that your peasant girl's brow were smooth, that amusement were sparkling from your eyes; but we'll accept you the only way you could come. Don't look around as if we couldn't help you. We can help you; we'll get Mr. Robinson up here in his elevator, Mr. Robinson will bring up some bedsteads from his inexhaustible supply in the basement, we'll bring the suitcase in from beside the door to wherever you're going to sleep.

You're here now, Annie.

Because I didn't know anyone I could trust, Gesine.

None of your suitors of five years ago, just because one of them now has something reassuring to say about the news and another still wants you to move in with him in his official apartment at the Finnish Consulate? Not F. F. Fleury, who wanted to live with you as in Thoreau's day? He'll find that hard to take, sitting there alone in a creaking house in the snow by the mountains, abandoned by an Annie who for more than four years worked at creating a life in the country, with three children and venerably splintered floors, his typist, his secretary, and the admirer of his genius as a translator from the French, who finally ran off early one morning, taking along three children, to the Plymouth Union bus depot. What shall we do now, Annie? Weep, divide up the property, tear our hair? So we won't do anything. I guess we can admit to having a serious problem on our hands, and perhaps share somewhat; not in front of the kids. We and Mr. Robinson, from his hiding place we'll bring up a TV set for the kids, for Frederic F. Junior, for Annina the apple child; for Francis R. too, aged two and a half? If that's the only way to satisfy them. We'll keep the kids from knowing that you're not just on a little trip. You want us to hide you too? Not say on the phone where you are? Anything to please you, Annie. You're not here. No, you're not here.

Because I knew you wouldn't push me.

The things you're saying, Annie, remember where you are. You're in New York, to your right ships are passing by, to your left the subway's running, Lines 1, 2, and 3, behind you your kids are sleeping off the trip, they're sleeping like freight, across from you sits

Marie, a child of not yet eleven, and d'you want her to hear it? Tell her about it, and me, if you think it's educational material.

So Marie is to hear that Annie Killainen wants to run away from a marriage with F. F. Fleury because of Vietnam? Because of Vietnam. And both of them over twenty-five, and both reciting their programs, he about the Domino theory, the greed of China, the honor of the U. S. in Southeast Asia, the continuation of the French heritage in Vietnam, the liberty of man and peace on earth; you about the seventh commandment, the commandment about foreign markets, the honor of the U. S., the self-determination of small nations, plus the liberty of man and peace on earth. How did you both do it? At breakfast too? Whenever the kids weren't around. That's too often. Or in French. Annie, that's the way it used to be done forty years ago in Mecklenburg, you can't go back to that, you know! And now F. F. doesn't want a wife who signs antiwar petitions, who belongs to antiwar associations, he doesn't want to drive to the shopping center and recognize his wife carrying a hand-written antiwar placard; he wants a wife at home, with the kids, in the kitchen, in the bedroom. He says you've disgraced the name of Fleury. And where you pause, Marie's not supposed to think such things possible, but I'm supposed to be able to imagine them. Well, Annie.

Because I knew you'd understand, Gesine.

Yes. No. Annie, stay here. Stay a week, stay two, scare him. If you spend even one day in our apartment I'll not recognize it in the evening, it'll be so spick and span. It'll be great for me. We'll go to the opera, movies, concerts; and Mr. McIntryre at the Marseilles Bar can wonder about us. Marie also knows the tales about your—our—Baltic Sea, the tales your kids want to hear; she'll take them to the park, the Bronx Zoo, Broadway. We'll have a great time. Three weeks, whatever you like. Then talk to him, to F. F. He'll be very humble, ready to eat humble pie, Annie. No matter where he's lived he's been waited on; he can't cook, he doesn't know how to work a washing machine, and by this time he's even forgotten how to prepare a typescript for the press. He'll have realized not only what he needs you for but—also that he needs you. I'll explain the business about Vietnam to him, if you insist. But go back. The kids. Your five years together. Let him beg, if you like; he'll be less able to forgive himself that than to forgive you. Then let him come and get you. It's no concern of mine; you're my concern.

You live a married life once in a while, when you feel like it, as if
you were putting on a play, Gesine. You don't know what it's like to
be married all the time.

O.K., then An-nie. We'll find an apartment for you in New
York, we won't particularly recommend Riverside Drive. We'll find a
job for you in New York; I won't recommend too strongly the bank
that has me. Or go back to United Nations, they still only take on
the pretty ones there. But don't do that, take a boat to Liverpool and
Hamburg and Stockholm and Helsinki and Kaskinen, or Kaskö.
What kind of Finnish do your kids speak? Francis R., his is still the
best, Annina could just about get by. But F. F. Junior, it's almost too
late to undo all that American. Don't write your parents yet. Stick
around for a while. All right. Another five days. If by then you're still
talking the way you are today, I'll go along with you to buy the
steamer tickets.

Because you're my best friend, Gesine. Didn't you know that?
No. Sorry: I did. I mean: Yes.

January 9, 1968 Tuesday

In this cold cold city, 165 people died last week of pneumonia, 70
more than expected, and blood for operations is running short.
Charles Gellman, executive director of the Jewish Memorial Hospital: "The Vietnam war doesn't help either, because there is a lot of
blood sent there."

Since yesterday, the playground bounded by Hudson, Ganse-
voort, West Fourth, and Horatio Streets, at the level of Pier 52, has
been named after John A. Seravalli. A boy who used to play
basketball there. He entered the Army on May 26, 1966. On February 28, 1967, at the age of twenty-one, he was killed while on patrol
near Souida.

In the summer of 1937 Horst Papenbrock wanted to enlist in the
Army.

On going to tell Lisbeth he found her cleaning the cutlery. She
had spread towels over the kitchen table, and the work seemed to slip
through her hands, so deftly did she turn three knives at once between her fingers, dab the cork in water and then in the emery
powder in the open drawer, rub the blades clean, and place them in

the bowl alongside for rinsing. It was a warm afternoon in late July, the light in the garden, divided into rectangles by the window, already slanting. Nearby, the starlings were being a nuisance and going for the ripe cherries; from a distance Paap could be heard rearranging piles of planks. It was a Saturday, a sense of resting from the week's labors was already in the air. Horst was reluctant to come right out with it, so Lisbeth took it for an ordinary visit and began talking about the trip she had had to make that morning to the military construction headquarters in Gneez, and about conversations on the train. To herself she was thinking that she should have washed her hair and was annoyed that Horst should now also be getting an illustration of the Jerichow gossip that she neglected her appearance. Horst was thinking in terms of going away, and he looked at his sister more closely than usual, did indeed notice the wispy, loose braids but regarded Lisbeth as the child, the youngster, of whose reputation for being pretty he had often been proud. Then he told her, acting the complete big brother with his mysterious and impressive decisions, and saw her give a start as if she had cut herself and were trying to contain the pain with compressed lips. Then he forgot about it because she reacted as he had expected her to. What he heard was the innocent girl asking him how far it was from the barracks to Jerichow, the kid sister who was feeling sorry for him because of the row Albert Papenbrock was going to have with him. "You chump," she added, the way she used to when they were kids, only that the mutual understanding in challenge and teasing was lacking. No doubt Horst did notice that the cutlery flew somewhat vehemently to one side, but he interpreted it as haste, and he also noticed that Lisbeth was now wearing gloves because of the black from the silver polish, and that it was the Güstrow family silver in which she was making dents. Horst was surprised that the child had sneaked off from the table and finally trotted away along the back passage. Lisbeth may have wanted to bear in silence the fact that once again her family was helping Cresspahl to place guilt on its shoulders, but she was unable to do so patiently.

You advised him to do that, Cresspahl!

Oh come on, Lisbeth. The lad wants to hide. The Army's not such a bad place to hide.

For the time being. And if war comes?

Lisbeth. I'm not giving your brother any advice. Either good or bad. Because they're not going to take him.

Papenbrock could not find the words for a row. In his helpless rage he flailed blindly about him, from one day to the next. He summoned the Schwerin son to Jerichow, and even with the harvest in full swing this son managed to come, in a big car with a chauffeur; Papenbrock summoned Avenarius Kollmorgen, who appeared with surprising compliance, self-importantly carrying his brief case, the furrows on his brow significantly but helplessly arched; Papenbrock summoned Cresspahl as a witness. He did not come. He must have realized that the old man wanted to ease his conscience by giving Cresspahl part of the load to carry; he didn't have that much pity. Dr. Berling was obliging enough to come. After he had hung the slack loop of the last letter of his name onto the well-rounded B, the group in Papenbrock's office hardly knew what to talk about; and even Avenarius confessed to himself that as a rule a Moselle like this did not make him tired. But no suitable remark occurred to him, the sultry dark cavern of the market square outside the windows did not lure him out of the building, and before he could manage, out of sheer cautiousness, to take his leave he heard Horst recounting before witnesses what Lisbeth Cresspahl had picked up the previous Saturday on the train, at Wehrlich station, of the conversation between Warning the farm laborer and Hagemeister the head gamekeeper, something about a high-level Party comrade associating with a Jewish veterinarian before the Nazi take-over. Horst had merely wanted to fill in a pause, and his brother from the two Americas did no more than shake his head, in boredom, as if he too had had enough of this stupid gossip in or between small towns. Robert, incidentally, had shown surprise and embarrassment, and when it came to shaking hands his look of emotion had been unsuccessful and had slipped down off his face.

Horst and his wife Elisabeth moved to Güstrow at the end of August. True enough, the Army rejected him. They could have appointed him a lieutenant of the Reserve since he had emerged from the war in 1919 as an officer-candidate; if at almost thirty-seven he hadn't been a bit old for a lieutenant. Horst could sense his father's plump fingers behind the notice of rejection; he never returned to Jerichow. The advance settlement of his legal portion sufficed for his wife Lisbeth to furnish a respectable apartment in Güstrow, not far from the new housing settlements of the Regional Farm Bureau, where he took on the job of allocating seed according to National Socialist principles. Alexander Paepcke had got the job for him through his buddies in the Leonia Corps; Papenbrock hadn't been able to stop that. The old man had actually had to find a manager for his granary, just as he had wanted to in March 1933, and he couldn't speak his mind to that Waldemar Kägebein who knew by heart many things from Aereboe's *Manual of Agriculture* that Papenbrock had to look up. Robert Papenbrock, on the other hand, once again served his country by taking an official trip overseas, not to Rio de Janeiro this time but to Chicago, Illinois. To judge by the postmarks.

And once again people in Jerichow were convinced that this proved that no one could beat the Papenbrocks for craftiness. For the local Storm Trooper authorities had run aground with their suspicions, none of them would have tried to chase after Horst any place where rifles were being used in earnest. And Horst's job with the Regional Farm Bureau wouldn't exactly hurt the family business.

It was a pity, of course, that old Mr. Papenbrock now had to act so contrary to his nature, hardly ever opening his mouth and with scarcely a moment for those long-winded, wily conversations at which he had been such an adept. But needless to say the inns weren't safe in times such as those.

In September Lisbeth, née Papenbrock, residing at 3-4 Brickyard Road in Jerichow, received a summons to appear before the County Court at Gneez as a witness in a court action against Warning and Hagemeister. The defendants were accused, among other things, of libeling a National Socialist Party official by alleging that he had derived advantage from associating with a Jewish citizen.

The summons was delivered at the Cresspahls' on the very day for which the Mecklenburg Christian Family Almanac recommended the reading of St. Paul's Letter to the Romans, 5, 1–5.

Lisbeth would not budge from her assertion that she had heard it. What she had heard was Hagemeister saying: And just look at fellows like Griem. Then Warning saying: He and Semig used to be as thick as thieves, always in each other's pockets. Now Griem is a big shot in the Reich Labor Service.

Dr. Semig said: What kind of advantage can a veterinarian procure for a prosperous farmer, and then Griem of all people! My dear Cresspahl —!

Griem made a survey of the Great Friedländer Meadow for improvement purposes, and it really did look as though he didn't get his mail.

Robert Papenbrock, who had filed the denunciation, was not expected back from the States before early in 1938.

Avenarius Kollmorgen was prepared to recollect nothing. Papen-brock was willing to say he had been well and truly drunk. But Dr. Berling had still not got over who it was that his wife had run off with, and he spent the whole of August passing the story around among those of his patients whom he credited with agreeing as to the "corrupt rabble" among the leadership of state and Party.

Lisbeth had heard it all right.

Our Lisbeth under oath, in court, what next?

January 10, 1968   Wednesday

Mr. James R. Shuldiner has made up his mind to get married.

Mrs. Cresspahl would never have expected James Shuldiner to start a conversation in this way. She has known him since he once called on someone in the office next to hers at the bank, then from chance encounters on the way to the subway, finally from hasty meals in snack bars in the forties; it was always he who phoned, Mrs. Cresspahl invariably paid for her own meal, and there had never been any mention of what he expected or derived from such half hours. Perhaps he wished to include a German among his acquaintances; maybe others did not lend the necessary ear to his concern over the behavior of statesmen; possibly he keeps coming back because of that afternoon in early summer when he ran into us at a concert in Central Park and Marie solemnly insisted on his explaining mathe-matical processes to her; Marie has by now forgotten that she did not number him among her friends for long, and Mrs. Cresspahl should think more carefully about what such an association could lead to. For if the usual pattern were followed, today would be the day for discussing the Pentagon's once again covering up for the President with statements concerning August 1964 in the Gulf of Tonkin, or that actually De Gaulle meant it as a compliment to the Jews when he called them an "elite people, sure of itself and domineering." But no, we are to devote ourselves to Mr. Shuldiner's wedding, and he is in such a hurry that he can't wait until tomorrow noon but has actually come into the bar of the Marseilles. Sits there rather awk-wardly, one elbow on the railing above the swimming pool, pleasure inadvertently flickering around his eyes, but still far from being the radiant bridegroom, his forehead still drawn tight as if weighed down by some pressure.

Mr. Shuldiner is asking us to do him a favor. His wife would like to live in this area, and could we help. Another Bloody Mary, Mrs. Cresspahl?

No thanks, and unfortunately not. Mrs. Cresspahl is in no position to do so. For her the Upper West Side, as an area, has become fragmented into more and more scenes and views, the better she has come to know it in almost seven years; she has no opinion to give on it. The response to this address has usually been a vague nod, an unseeing look from which comprehension fades. Greenwich Village to the south is well known in the city at least as its own myth; Riverdale, in the Bronx, seems equally familiar with an aspect composed of memory and intimidated imagination. What surrounds the Upper West Side is familiar; the area itself, hardly. To the north, Morningside Heights looks across from a safe distance to Harlem, Columbia University snatches building after building and street after street under its honorable cloak; there is the Church of St. John the Unfinished and that of Rockefeller, known as Riverside, there is also St. Luke's Hospital, also frequented by New Yorkers who are far from being on their last legs. The district south of our area even manages to get itself into the supplements of European papers with opera and Philharmonic, the subway stops at what is undeniably a new station, homes are being not merely rehabilitated but seriously renewed. The boundaries of the area are well known. What lies in between, the Upper West Side, is an unknown hole, and in this pot swim the most ill-assorted fish, anything goes, Mr. Shuldiner. Why don't you stay with your girl in New Jersey.

That's the point. She doesn't want to live near his Orthodox relatives.

But does your girl want to fall among heathens and Christians, Mr. Shuldiner? First of all, this is a white-skinned area, and at the very utmost there are thirty thousand Jews living among twice the number of Anglo-Saxon Protestants, Irish and Italian Catholics, and the two Germans with no religious affiliation on Riverside Drive. Without doubt there are Jews here who do their laundry on the Sabbath and those who are the pride and joy of their Rabbi; just ask for Mrs. Ferwalter. And they're not, like the future Mrs. Shuldiner, from Rapid City but from Western Europe and the Slavic countries. Will a bride from South Dakota feel at home here? And how about the other fifty thousand, the Puerto Ricans, the Negroes, and the sprinkling of Japanese and Chinese? The unknown races? They may all be Americans, but each group clings to its own language, they don't mix readily; the confusing mixture doesn't even remain constant, so unexpectedly do people move house here. Wouldn't your wife prefer to be in a community where the people don't only resemble each other more but also feel they should get along together?

Yet Mr. Shuldiner would have something to offer his wife here. A metropolis does have its price, you know.

Of course, Mr. Shuldiner. For a life of comfort there are still the streets of Central Park West, West End Avenue, and Riverside Drive, stubbornly defended heirlooms of old-fashioned dignity. Central Park West may continue for a time to overlook the elaborate artificial landscape, the man-made lakes, reflected clouds, the rolling lawns under the snow, the meandering paths, across an open sky to the (as yet) more snobbish address of Fifth Avenue, squatting there complacently under its water pots, irradiated with monotonous regularity by every evening sun. Or take West End Avenue, down by the Hudson, that gloomy chasm between walled monsters, but the cages in the windows are not for birds, they are machines for air-conditioning, and you have to pay for it yourself. Perhaps among all those homes of the aged you will find a house for a bride from the country. Or in one of the numbered side streets, where single-family houses are still polished like precious stone. There, as along Riverside Drive, the sidewalks are swept clean, heavy truck traffic is prohibited, living there would seem to be desirable. In this area it is easy to find a building erected before February 1, 1947, in which the rents have been frozen; there is not much new building here. Then all you have to pay is 15 per cent above the old rent; Mr. Shuldiner can afford that. Of course.

Right. And he would know his wife was safe.

Not quite, Mr. Shuldiner. Here the opposite is true too. In many of the side streets there are slums. Where the poorest of the poor have to live, the fire inspections are even less strict with their regulations; why shouldn't buildings burn there as they now do in Harlem? Why shouldn't sidewalks collapse there as they do in Harlem? There are plenty of houses there in which the tenants, whole families in one room, have to bang on the pipes because the owner is economizing on heating. Who complain to the city with a phone call every two minutes, they live here too. Why shouldn't those people snatch your wife's handbag, hold a knife under her chin? And don't rely on Mrs. Cresspahl. For a whole year she regarded two apartment buildings on 95th Street as cheerful because of the movement in passageways and windows, because of the Spanish voices, calling out and singing, the life on the sidewalk; she couldn't understand why her child wanted to walk only on the other side of the street. The child had recognized the buildings as poor, as full of anger; only after that would Mrs. Cresspahl be able to prove something to you with the pots and bowls which those inhabitants have placed on windowsills in the cold because they can't keep their food safely indoors.

Now let's not beat about the bush, Mrs. Cresspahl. You live here.

We can recite the whole thing to you as if from a geography book, Mr. Shuldiner: You are now in the northwest portion of Manhattan Island, between 70th and 110th Streets, between Central Park to the east and, to the west, the river that was discovered by Henry Hudson before his crew put him out to starve. Between south and north run avenues such as Riverside Drive; that's misleading. You should see it from the air, Mr. Shuldiner. An irregular jumble of towers and huts, hemmed in by high-rises. Nearly a thousand people live in one block, few of them singly in apartments, too many of them cheek by jowl, closer than the law permits. The Upper West Side doesn't even have a name. At one time the Dutch founded a village here and called it Bloomingdale, but it has not become a valley of flowers. In speaking of this part of town among themselves, the inhabitants call it "the area," as if it were nothing but a haphazard conglomeration of buildings, a meaningless juxtaposition of people rather than neighbors. You enter the area most easily through the park at Broadway (where Verdi stands with pigeons on his head), now know as Needle Park, after the hypos, Mr. Shuldiner. You turn up Amsterdam Avenue, you note the resemblance to bombed-out streets in World War II—

"And I admired you so much, Mrs. Cresspahl," says Mr. Shuldiner. He sits there for a long time, his head bent, both elbows on the table, his shoulders hunched, twisting his glass as if there were, after all, some answer written in the swaying surface of the liquid.

"I don't know my way around here, Mr. Shuldiner."

"That wasn't what I wanted. I had been hoping you'd be of help to my wife."

"Like supplying her with information?"

"And the little things one does for a friend, Mrs. Cresspahl."

Later that evening Annie, née Killainen, said: "Now you've got your second client within three days. I can see why. You must've been like that even in school."

And she refused to believe the contrary from Mrs. Cresspahl, saying that, if you look a certain way, that's what you're responsible for.

On the front page, next to the continuing report on deaths due to the cold (so that we will believe it), the New York *Times* presents us with a photograph of the harbor, showing a sturdy tugboat, tiny amid the dense clusters of ice floes that floated down the Hudson yesterday afternoon. The water is so full of poison that a person can die just from swallowing a bit too much of it, he wouldn't need the cold.

At the time when Cresspahl took over the farm behind the Jerichow church, it stood more or less open to the path running alongside the brickyard; now it had long since been closed off.

The farmers before his day had had an entrance in the middle, in order to reach the open coach house on the left and the cesspool, manure heap, and stable doors on the right; Cresspahl had dug it up and planted it with quick-growing shrubs. He had also planted lilac in among the sparse row of elderberry bushes, from the maple at the corner as far as the smaller path, which he had made into a road. The latter was open to the view, but it was closed off by a gate of horizontal boards, although secured only with a latch, and anyone trying to go through the bushes was confronted, in the midst of branches and foliage, by a wire-mesh fence surmounted by spikes. He had allowed everything to grow wild, and to anyone who knew nothing about the house at the back the road stopped right there, since beyond the brickyard it petered out in the sand and there was nothing but fields.

This was no longer a property from which a small child could inadvertently run out onto the motor road, nor could any of the chickens get out. It was not until Cresspahl attached a padlock to the gate, in the summer of 1937, and from then on Lisbeth hardly set foot in town, that people in Jerichow started talking about the prison where he kept his wife, although the latch was only padlocked at night. In daytime it could still be opened, except that it unhooked with a clang loud enough to scare a person. He'd thought of everything! And even when there was noise in the workshop, the uninvited visitor would get as far as the third door and from the fourth would emerge Paap or Cresspahl or some other hefty fellow who had no need of a dog. Now just try and explain that you were making for the workshop and didn't go through the door in the barn where the sign hangs. There was just no way of getting to the front door of the house, nor would it have done much good as it was kept constantly locked. Anyone whom Cresspahl allowed to go through to see Lisbeth was taken there to her by Heine Klaproth; anyone else had to remain standing beside him, staring at nothing but the curtained windows, the bare yard, the little lawn for the child, till a person could get dizzy from the smell of the fresh-cut woodpile. And Cresspahl, that Englishman, stood there so deceptively like some innocent artisan, sweating in his dusty work clothes, his neck bent, then suddenly lifting his head and directly meeting the other's gaze with his suddenly hard eyes which in recollection had been merely watery blue. And those who then preferred to leave the yard without delay hadn't even picked up anything worth the telling.

It wasn't only Warning's or Hagemeister's relatives who came to appeal to Lisbeth's conscience. Avenarius Kollmorgen turned up too and banged on the workshop door with the crook of his cane, incessantly brushing imaginary bits of fluff from his broad shoulders as he announced, in the midst of the noisy machines, that a person cited as a witness was at liberty to testify or not. Cresspahl took him along to the house, to his desk, and when Avenarius took his leave at the gate half an hour later he struck the dusty hedgerow so wildly with his cane that the chickens whirred up into the air out of their hollows in the sand. Papenbrock was allowed to proceed alone to his daughter's and on his way back chose not to show himself in the workshop. However, when Cresspahl stepped into his path the old man looked dazed. With his favorite child he had tried the method that had always worked with Louise, and Lisbeth had refused to be treated like that, saying that she had never been shouted at, and that if he were her own father three times over he'd better watch out for Cresspahl! Papenbrock found it inconceivable that a man would not shout at his wife, but his good advice evaporated when his son-in-law gave him a sidelong look of almost friendly attention.

Others came too, including Brüshaver. Cresspahl put one over on the pastor by asking him about the Christian significance of an oath before letting him enter the house, so that on seeing Lisbeth this visitor started off less forcefully, turning into a request what he had envisaged as a kind of instruction. What he did achieve was that Lisbeth now made the lie depend solely on her mother. Old Mrs. Papenbrock had roughly understood what her husband and Cresspahl had told her, but then she felt too important in the affair and her imagination got onto the wrong track and wandered off to Romans 5, 1–5. When Lisbeth told them about this at home, she sat leaning back as languidly as she had at her mother's, her hands limp in her lap, nodding so submissively that a chair back broke under Cresspahl's hand. It could not be glued on again later. Warning's wife promised Cresspahl that God would visit a double punishment on Lisbeth's head. Hagemeister came personally, making no attempt to go beyond the workshop, in fact he inquired casually about the trees in the garden, discussed the sheep-shearing in Rande, and appeared to have no further request. When Cresspahl let him go, it looked from the workshop as if he were promising him something. He had sent a message to Warning that he had no use for people who, while sitting in a public train, on a day during this Nazi period, sat gossiping about the Shitbrowns. Criminals, that's what they were. A sheep would have more sense. And a sheep wouldn't drink up a whole bucket of water in a year.

Then Dr. Arthur Semig, veterinary surgeon, who had fought in World War I and been awarded the Iron Cross, was taken into custody in Jerichow, driven through town to the railway station, and kept in the cellars below the Gneez County Court.

It was the end of September, the holiday season was over but the weather was still good for swimming, when Lisbeth Cresspahl handed over her child to Aggie Brüshaver. She told Aggie, as she had told Cresspahl, something about a visit to the dentist, and she did in fact walk to the bus stop on Station Street, but the bus she boarded was the one to Rande.

When the sun was beyond the horizon and the water of the Baltic not only was but looked cold, an outgoing fisherman noticed a swimcap a long way from shore. It was a couple of miles out in Lübeck Bay, far beyond the fifty-foot line. Out there the water was seventy and seventy-five feet deep. She was already too weak to resist when Stahlbom and his boy dragged her on board.

Stahlbom turned his boat around because she was shivering so violently and couldn't get warm even in three blankets. His mind was more on the lost catch, for back in August 1931 another young woman, a kindergarten teacher, had swum way out, well over a mile, although in that case it was because the battleship *Hannover* had been lying at anchor, and the young woman had promptly turned back. As soon as Cresspahl arrived that night to pick up his wife in Rande he asked the fisherman how much he owed him for his services, and Stahlbom would most likely have forgotten the incident had he not been asked to do so.

"The swimcap, that was my undoing," Lisbeth said next morning, lying almost comfortably ensconced in her fatigue, with a playful, absent-minded smile which then vanished behind lips taut with anger.

"It was my vanity. The punishment for it," she said.

Don't ever do that again, Lisbeth!
No, Cresspahl. I won't do it again. Not that way.

January 12, 1968   Friday

It's a good life, sharing the Cresspahl apartment with Annie Kil-lainen and her three children. The rooms are not large, and the middle one with its four doors lacks privacy, yet even on the fifth day the young Fleurys are not clamoring for their lost big rooms in Vermont, and Francis R., with his game leg, has already fixed up places for himself, where he can be alone, at the Danish girls' desk, or in the clothes closet. Maybe at home they had had to live more quietly than they manage to do here unprompted. Marie also gets along very well with the big family, thanks to an arrangement whereby she voluntarily offered the other children her room, also thanks to the fact that Marie is often treated as the head of the household and is constantly being asked "how your mother does it." She hasn't yet noticed that Annie goes off with the kids, into the icy park, or shopping, or to the swimming pool at the Marseilles, when-ever Marie comes back from school with her homework. What she does notice is that I am treated like a breadwinner, breakfast is served to me almost as soon as I come out of the bathroom, the early WQXR news is switched on punctually, my coat and scarf are held ready for me as if Mrs. Cresspahl were a husband and father. Let's hope she doesn't insist on copying this later. In the building, too, Annie has made herself known in her own way; Mr. Robinson knows each of her children by name and face, and Jason has hinted that on the eleventh floor an apartment like ours might become vacant. For that, an outsider would have to drape a whole pile of greenbacks over his hand. Annie's contribution to keeping house is unobtrusive; all of a sudden the aluminum window frames have been polished to a shine with steel wool, the bookcase gleams as if fresh from the hands of the refinisher; she does not draw our attention to this, it is not a re-proach, not even a compensation. It would never occur to her to interfere by adding to the flatware chest or the linen closet; but she has provided an inordinate supply of candles because "New York can so easily go dark." In saying this she draws her head down between her shoulders in mock alarm over her prejudice, until everyone is ready to laugh, and she laughs. The tape-recorder remains firmly fixed at yesterday evening's figure, letters are not gone through; she may well use a duster here, or polish the lock of the drawer. Of Annie's presence there is much that we won't notice until she has left. But of course we don't want her to leave.

It's unbearable, living with her. Isn't it, Gesine?
I don't mind.
You can hardly stand it.
Seeing her, listening to her, and it's O.K.
And when you're sitting in your office at the bank, thinking about her.
Not so good.
Admit it, Gesine.
All these questions! Just because for you it's all in the past!
You've got a job to do for us, Gesine.
I admit that.
Give it some more thought. Without sparing yourself.
I couldn't do that.
There you go again, trying to dodge the issue, Gesine. That's not what we mean.
As if it were nothing! After five years of living with a person, to run away leaving no letter, no forwarding address, taking your three children with you! If I had five-year-old habits, could I give them up? Easily?
You're twisting things around, Gesine. You're exploiting your own objections to marriage.
All right then, you begin.
You can't stand it; you can't bear thinking about it. Annie marches with her antiwar posters in a ridiculous little procession along the main street of a small provincial town, stared at by the bank manager and the mayor's grandmother and the store help, and all of a sudden she's no longer the respectable Mrs. Fleury but a foreigner, a Communist.
I chose not to enter a prison from which I would have wanted to escape.
But the real prison, where Annie spent a night, side by side with the town drunk and the local shoplifter?
What the shoplifter stole, she needed; or else advertising en-

couraged her to steal. How does spending a night next to her promote peace for Vietnam?

Gesine, Annie did something.

Without success.

She didn't just do nothing.

I'm a guest in this country.

Well, Annie wasn't born here either.

I went out once too, carrying posters in the cold, walking up and down for hours outside Cardinal Spellman's palace because he blessed U.S. soldiers in Vietnam.

You did that out of curiosity, and you didn't do it again.

I didn't do it again because I don't want to be forced to leave the country.

How can you want to live in a country like this, Gesine?

Because it's become Marie's life.

The child, the child. Your emergency parachute, your sacrosanct excuse.

I want my child to have what I didn't get.

And not what children in Vietnam get.

Prove it to me! Prove it! Show me how I could be sure of helping a single one of them! Now!

If you don't begin in a small way, in five years you'll still have the war.

Well, supposing I do try something more than words and walk up and down Riverside Park with a poster and go around at the bank waving a Vietcong flag and send checks to Students for Peace?

Even that would be better, Gesine.

D'you guarantee peace in five years?

Of course not. That's impossible.

And you're impossible too!

That's how we like you, all worked up, Gesine. You must admit it's no ordinary husband-and-wife quarrel.

I wouldn't even like this one.

You wouldn't like it, you wouldn't let yourself be slapped at a birthday party, in front of your guests, at the festive table with the family silver, by candlelight, and all because you've said that the President's policy toward Vietnam was murderous?

No F. F. Fleury from Boston is going to slap my face.

You're envious, Gesine.

Embarrassed, that I'll admit.

Well, that's something anyway.

If she wants to fight her husband she doesn't have to use that excuse. She can disguise it.

Stop it, Gesine. You're accusing Annie Killainen of not carrying on her quarrel at its roots—

This is her fifth day in New York, and she still hasn't gone to the place where the students are collecting money to end the war, where pamphlets are being printed and distributed.

—but in our case there's no doubt. "Papenbrock did not want to help Semig the Jew to leave the country and was satisfied with having a low personal opinion of himself." Period. Not a word about the rest.

Is that how it was?

Even if it's true, you'd invent it!

I'll fix it up to make it intelligible.

In your case we're supposed to believe you. But when it's a living person, an Annie Killainen, you're suspicious.

I'd be only too glad to be otherwise.

And you can't because you know yourself.

Not because I've caught myself lying without wanting to. Because I've no confidence in my confidence.

And now Annie is to carry on the way she's begun just so as to conform to your image of consistent behavior? What you lack in the way of logic, she is to demonstrate in her life?

I'm not telling her what to do.

Yet there you sit in the empty apartment, full of uneasiness, waiting for her to come home after doing nothing against the war?

Yes.

And she has only to open the door, pushing the children in front of her like a hen with her chicks, pink-cheeked as she'll be from the cold, from her memories of the Finnish countryside, bubbling over with news of people she's met on the walk, all of them transformed by her into friendly faces, into opportunities for a laugh—and you're not envious?

That's when I know why I get along with her so well.

Yet you still hold it against her that you slip into her mood, into the games, into the stories, into the fun around the big common dining table, willy-nilly, as it were?

It makes me uncomfortable.

We're sorry for you, Gesine.

You won't manage to make me feel sorry for myself.

You'll regret that, Gesine.

January 14, 1968   Sunday

Gaetano Gargiulo has a store in Queens, on Farmers Boulevard. A young man, Nellice Cox, tried to rob the store and pointed a pistol at Gargiulo's son. Gargiulo slipped out of the back door, borrowed a pistol from a nearby hardware-store owner, confronted the holdup man, pressed the trigger once. Nellice Cox won't be returning to his home at 109-82 203rd Street in Hollis, and Gaetano Gargiulo is being held on a charge of violating the Weapons Law.

"Listen, Gesine," Marie says. "Now I'm going to play back the last thing you said on Thursday evening:

'However, Fretwust did not enter Semig's war decorations in the list of personal effects. He was not counting on the Jew being given back his medals. Besides, Fretwust had not been a police sergeant for very long; actually, he should have been drawing off the sludge at the Gneez pumping station. And Fretwust was not embarrassed by his name; on the contrary, he was proud of it.'

"O.K. Isn't that an ending?"

"Not for the other story, Gesine. That's what I'm going to prove to you. You said, at 266 on the tape:

'No doubt the girls from the Labor Service Corps had not yet learned how to buy meat, and Lisbeth would rather have everyone at her table wear their teeth down than make a trip herself to Town Street in Jerichow.'

"That's where it really begins, Gesine!"

"May I join in?"

"Annie, you won't understand it."

"Mrs. Fleury, this is something we can't explain to you. You'll never understand it."

"I come from a small provincial town too, you know."

"O.K. What do you say to the fact that in 1937 a veterinary surgeon was arrested for having allegedly broken a law prior to 1933?"

"Isn't that all water under the bridge?"

"That's the whole point, Mrs. Fleury!"

"He was arrested as a witness, Annie."

"That can happen. Danger of collusion, or whatever you say."

"We don't say anything at all. His wife's parents lived in Schwerin, her mother had friends who associated with the ducal family, her father still had friends with whom he had worked at the Mecklenburg Savings Bank. Those were the Kösters. The Kösters saw to it that their son-in-law was arrested."

"A stuffy crowd."

"They did it for the sake of their daughter; you see, it wasn't the regular police who conducted the investigation."

"Hm. The political police."

"Whether the Gestapo in Gneez wanted to clear Griem, the Reich Labor Service leader, of the suspicion of acquiring an illegal property advantage with the help of a Jewish professional man, or whether they wanted to frame him, was something they probably didn't even know themselves to begin with."

"But surely that shows up in the evidence."

"Evidence was something they had too much of rather than too little. Following the movements of a veterinary surgeon during nearly twenty years of practice, from estate to estate, from farmer to cottager to Grandma Klug: all kinds of things came to light. A Baron von Rammin spoke to the investigators in his yard, holding his horse by the bridle; the Bülows, the "Oberbülows," asked them into the house. The Bülows had a son in England who preferred to go to university there than do his military service in Germany. And if a farmer lost a head of cattle in 1931 because he didn't want to spoil his Saturday evening at the tavern and failed to call the vet until Sunday morning, how much did he still remember after six years, and maybe by this time he was quite glad to lay the blame on Dr. Semig. Since the fellow was already in jail anyway."

"And Griem?"

"At first Griem didn't want to come across."

"Couldn't remember anything?"

"Because he knew there wasn't anything. And he couldn't understand why those fellows in Gneez wanted a trial; he would have liked to know, in the first place, who was gunning for him and why. He had acquired his rank not as a reward but because he was a good farmer and one for whom a small part-time farm in Jerichow was not sufficient. To think in terms of large areas, to plan work for years ahead, to train workers, for this he had a real gift. True, he had accepted money when he saw to it that a soggy meadow belonging to the local aristocracy was improved to the point where it benefited the national economy, that's to say, at the expense of the German Reich; more than one meadow, in fact. But since he was able to substantiate his decisions his conscience hadn't bothered him. But if the Gneez District Court wanted to put him on the witness stand side by side with a Jew, an inquiry into his bank account could not have been very far off."

"As far as he was concerned, Semig could have continued to carry on his practice?"

"As far as he was concerned not even the Tannebaums needed to flee from Gneez. Griem wanted to be left in peace; for the time being he restricted himself to rejecting all those rumors 'as a cowardly attack on the Party.' "

"Stuffy bunch."

"Meanwhile the fellows in the black uniforms had had time to find out a lot. In Jerichow they could go from house to house. Albert Papenbrock, grain wholesaler, had remitted fees to Dr. Semig for services for which a casual worker would have received less. Heinrich Cresspahl, entrusted with important war-essential contracts, had bought an automobile from Dr. Semig and couldn't produce a bill of sale. Mrs. Methfessel would not budge from her statement that the health department would never have cleaned up the slaughterhouse had it not been for Semig's letter to Schwerin. Whenever he was ill Dr. Semig had treated himself, whereas he had sent his wife to Dr. Berling; Berling had been in and out of the house all the time when Dora had that broken ankle, but when it came to his account the figure had been more of a nominal one, as between friends."

"Without counting all the other things they turned up."

"Berling's speeches about the Fatherland in its hour of need. That fellow Cresspahl, of course, was suspected of being pro-British."

"And Kollmorgen had wanted to buy the house in the Bäk."

"That they hadn't yet discovered. But they held it against Semig the Jew that he had rejected an offer to purchase on the part of a veteran fighter of the National Socialist movement, a Party regional group leader, none other than Friedrich Jansen."

"And the documents relating to Kollmorgen's appearance in court against a member of the Storm Troopers—"

"Turned up just at the right moment."

"Is the trial coming next?"

"By the middle of October the trial was still not under way. What the Gestapo failed to dig up in the way of evidence was supplied them by means of anonymous letters. And Griem still hadn't softened up. Griem sat there at his headquarters, District II, and held forth: he had all due respect for those thick skulls the Mecklenburgers were so proud of, but not for the closed minds. He behaved as if he couldn't imagine that all the Secret Police needed was two men and a car to come and take him away."

"Did Papenbrock consult an attorney?"

"That would have seemed to him like admitting to the accusations. And apart from him and the Cresspahls there were five others in Jerichow who could expect a summons to Gneez; with so many witnesses truth was bound to triumph in the end."

"So your Semig—"

"Ours?"

"Well, all right, Marie. Mine."

"—must have been full of good cheer."

"In the cellars of the County Court."

"He was safe there till the trial, and the trial was properly and thoroughly prepared, not at all like what one always reads about those times."

"He wasn't even accused of anything, Annie."

"Now you're both looking at me as if I hadn't understood a thing."

"There's nothing about it to understand, Annie."

"Mrs. Fleury, d'you know something? Sometimes I think I understand it and can't believe what I understand. And yet it's from the life of my own mother."

January 15, 1968   Monday

You wanted to know why there is so often a popping sound in the streets these days. The New York *Times* has found the explanation for you. Yesterday evening's rain, the snow showers of noon today, not only caught you in the back of the neck, but the water, mixed with the salt that had been sprinkled on the streets, also seeped into cable shafts, caused short circuits, and set off gas explosions. It was the sound made by the manhole covers: Pop.

And whether you want to or not, the New York *Times* makes you aware that your presence was lacking yesterday evening among the fifteen hundred persons at Town Hall who wished to join forces to combat the draft. You could have signed the scroll with your name and address and promised "to counsel, aid and abet" youngsters who refused to be inducted. If you still wish to do this, you will find the group at 224 West 4th Street. Will Annie do this? Will you do this?

You have always wanted to know the background of your child's new doctor, what sort of man this is who shines a light in Marie's mouth, listens to her breathing, questions her about her sleeping habits in a comfortable American, a nimble German with a Polish accent. Who is he, this dignified gentleman in his sixties, his back stiff to the waist with age, what lies behind the kindly slightly deaf expression on that plump face? Do you really want to know? Why not settle for the Latin diplomas on the wall, as long as Marie trusts him?

"The one on the left is from Bratislava, the one on the right from Warsaw. The one in the middle from Germany," says the old gentleman, with rather strained politeness. You shouldn't have looked across like that to the solid oak frames, as if you wanted to find out something. Now you can't get out of the introductory conversation, out of the formalities of a first visit. "Isn't Cresspahl a German name?" he says, turning away from the desk, head cocked, alert. The impassive, smooth face, the thin gray hair combed back in two swaths over the ears, we wouldn't know it again if we hadn't seen the care with which he handles and speaks to a child, to be quite sure of not frightening it.

"Cresspahl is a German name, Dr. Rydz."

"Germany was a good place to live, in those days, Mrs. Cresspahl."

In those days was 1931. Germany was Berlin, when he was working at the Charité and "in the hospital on Reinickendorfer Street." He lived at Friedrich-Wilhelm-Platz in Friedenau. Took streetcar 177 to the Zoo station. What did it look like in those days?

Friedrich-Wilhelm-Platz in Friedenau, Mrs. Cresspahl, was a charming place to live, at that time. If one had two rooms on the west side which were quite dry in the mornings from the sunshine, and in the evening full of the breath of the dense foliage outside the windows. Friedenau was a good place for walks, the little streets with the old countrified houses, the solid respectable apartment buildings, the bushy green treetops. Nied Street, Schmargendorfer Street. And the chestnut trees thick with blossom, close-ranked on Handjery Street. Some city councilor must have given way to a craving for chestnut trees.

The people sitting quietly, sociably in the beer garden by the post office, helpful, even toward foreigners. A happy year, Mrs. Cresspahl. In the evening one returned to the quiet parklike square as if one were coming home. The streetcars were boxes, ugly, sturdy, efficient. Do you know Berlin, Mrs. Cresspahl?

Friends have written to us from Friedenau that a subway is being built through the square.

"What a pity the church has to go!" says Dr. Rydz. He has laid aside his writing things, has turned right around to face his visitors, his voice is animated, his fingers are laced, relaxed. The church was a

shade too small for the square with the result that it looked a bit
deformed, standing there like a little red-brick hunchback. Ugly,
sturdy, efficient, a creation of the Empress, who consecrated a new
abode for her God every three months. The name will come to him
in a minute: Auguste Viktoria von Schleswig-Holstein-Sonderburg-
Augustenburg. Doflein was the name of the architect.

Unfortunately the church is to remain, Dr. Rydz.

But he is relieved. At least one fragment of the past intact. In
those days it was not easy to choose between Berlin and other
European capitals. Trips to Paris, to Vienna, to Prague, yet no sighs
on returning to Friedenau, to the Church of the Good Shepherd,
whence stuffy comments on the night life of Dr. Felix J. Rydz penetrated to Mrs. Rabenmeister who, as a landlady was—

A smasher, Dr. Rydz?

A corker, Mrs. Cresspahl. That was the expression in those days.
In other words, one lived the good life. The man who then returned
to a small but prosperous country town in Poland to settle there as a
general practitioner, one must admit he had really seen life and knew
for all time a country where his annual vacation would one day
become a right to permanent residence.

Now has your curiosity evaporated, Mrs. Cresspahl?

The girl from Berlin who wanted to spend the 1939 vacation
with him, although not in Charlottenburg, settled for Cannes (did
you know a family called Von Lassewitz, Dr. Rydz?); four years in a
French military hospital; 1943, escape across the Pyrenees; 1945, by
ship to the U.S.A., where all his degrees were worthless, where it was
five years before he was able to set up practice again, and then right
away on Manhattan's Upper West Side so as to benefit at least to
some extent from his command not only of Polish and German but
also of Czech, French, Spanish, and American. A practice entirely for
children. It was in New York that he realized for the first time that
he understood children best, or better than adults.

Now you know, Mrs. Cresspahl. The conversation went so well
because you regarded him as a European such as you feel you can
more readily understand; now you're pretty sure he is Jewish. What
happened to the girl from Berlin-Charlottenburg? Don't say it. Ask
him something else, but not that. Ask him whether he has ever been
back to Poland.

"No. Never," says Dr. Rydz. His reply comes with surprising
swiftness, terse, the soft face tightens, the eyes narrow and then stare
into space. He will never go back to Poland. More calmly, as if

wanting to make amends, he adds: "You see, Mrs. Cresspahl, all the Poles I need come flocking to my doorstep on the Upper West Side."

You needn't ask him whether he went back to Berlin-Friedenau for a visit. Why should he seek out the Germans who exterminated his family in Poland as if they were nonhuman? Isn't Cresspahl a German name?

"Mrs. Cresspahl, are you sure you're in good health? Is there anything I can do for you?"

"Are they going to take this one away from me too and send him to Vietnam?" says Marie.

"He can't even walk properly, Marie."

"Even if the war spreads?"

"He'll be allowed to stay with us, Marie. We're not going to be deprived of Dr. Rydz."

"Gesine, have you noticed they're fixing up the burned-out building on 96th Street? They've set up a huge crane, you should see how it works! They've finally realized that our area mustn't be allowed to go to the dogs, so we can live here."

"And supposing we left here, Marie?"

"Never! Never! You mustn't even think of such a thing, Gesine."

January 16, 1968   Tuesday

In the dazzling, low sunshine slanting down 96th Street in the morning and against which it was hard to walk with one's eyes open, there was something missing along Broadway. It was the motley herd of taxis, whose drivers are on strike, and their customers, jammed into the subway and most of them men in sober business suits, looked around uncomfortably, repelled by the crushing proximity of others.

Dr. Walther Wegerecht, County Court judge in Gneez, forty-eight years of age, with a reputation for candor and cunning, respected for his wondrous career and a rich wife, derived no pleasure from being in charge of the action against Warning and Hagemeister. He had had enough of such affairs by now, if only because it was difficult to know what was going on in them. That's how I imagine it. Some friends from his student days, now in the Ministry at Schwerin, had hinted at promotion; and early in his career Wegerecht had married above him, a Schwerin girl who never let him forget her boredom with life in a county capital, and did not consider the attainment of such favors as an official residence on Berlin's Tiergarten to be out of the question.

Meanwhile he had begun to doubt whether he should continue to regard his advisers as his friends. At first the Chancellery of the Mecklenburg Reich Governor had let it be known that the honor of the Party and its affiliations took precedence over all else, etc.; and this could have been achieved quite cheaply and without too much effort, for a reward of that kind. On first acquaintance with the inquiry he had expected to find it indirectly aimed at Dr. Semig; however, he was now forced to acknowledge that the Jewish veterinary surgeon was merely a steppingstone and that the inquiry was in fact directed at Griem. If the Commissioner of Criminal Investigation who had been shunted to the Gestapo was to be relied upon, those fellows also had a line to Schwerin which was directly connected to the Reich capital. At the Hanseatic Supreme Court in Hamburg the affair was dismissed as trifling, and he did not like to make any inquiries at the Supreme Court in Rostock.

Wegerecht, an endomorphic type who kept his round Mecklenburg head shaved, had been late in joining the ruling Party, almost too late, and more from a sense of duty. He came from the German National People's Party, had read the *Deutsche Tageszeitung* with more appetite than the *Mecklenburgischer Beobachter*, and would have preferred the revival of the imperial (also the grand-ducal) house; moreover, he was uneasy at what he heard about the spreading influence of Hitlerism in the Army. The program he brought with him from his old Party program included an aversion to the Jews in Berlin, an aversion based on economic reasons, not to a Jew who had fought on Germany's side in the 1914–18 war, was a homeowner in Jerichow, and spoke good Mecklenburg Low German dialect. He merely wanted to teach this Jew a sharp lesson so he would finally come to his senses and get out of the country. That would have been his patriotic deed, the one meriting promotion. Moreover, Kraczinski, the prosecutor, was prepared to acknowledge this as a side benefit. But otherwise Kraczinski made out that with this one trial he could produce about seven others, a veritable "Jerichow" conglomerate. And furthermore he was quite serious in his prosecution of Griem; Wegerecht felt uncertain of his ground here. It was so difficult to have any kind of insight into the Reich Labor Service. It was like the forest at night, where behind every tree there might be someone holding a club. What Wegerecht knew for sure was that he had to emerge from this affair with flying colors so that his stance in the Zentner case might be forgotten (Dr. Zentner, industrial engineer,

traveling with a fierce dog, mistakenly harassed as a Jew, despite
Zentner's warning that the dog was dangerous; versus the Storm
Troopers, who had demanded compensation for their injuries). He
must come out of this like a knight in shining armor, for with one
false step he might break his neck.

Walther Wegerecht well knew that his wife, Irmgard née Von
Oertzen, cared less for what he was than for what he signified for her.
His good mood signified that the money would be paid into the bank
on the thirtieth; his worries were, in her view, irresponsible as being a
threat to their style of living. He could not discuss these worries with
her; at such times he saw little of Irmi, and she did not even chalk it
up to him that he turned a blind eye to male visitors from the
garrison whose numbers then increased. She wanted him independent, clever, supremely confident; only thus, he felt, could he be sure
of her. That also meant the children, and Wegerecht was a doting
father. He wore his head shaved not because of a bet but because his
four-year-old daughter, the latecomer, enjoyed feeling the thick
carpet of stubble against the palm of her hand. He was not a well
man. His high color gave him the reputation of being "a picture of
health"; he refused to be surprised at listlessness, or even bouts of
bad temper, as long as his work kept him up till all hours; his doctor
chatted with him over the Friday game of skat at the City of Hamburg Hotel, but not about essential hypertonia. From time to time he
dreamed he was driving with the car windows closed, he felt short of
air and was too weak to wind the handles; sometimes he felt in broad
daylight as he did in the dream. He did not like to consult his doctor
with such imaginings. If it was not feasible to proceed against Griem,
Irmgard would never return to Schwerin or, if she did, it would be
without him. If he started something against Papenbrock, Irmi would
lose many of her Jerichow friends, and as far as Gneez affairs were
concerned the citizens would leave him to grope his way in the dark
by himself. If it were only a matter of cautioning Warning and
Hagemeister he should have stopped the case earlier, and once again
people would have been reminded of the reputation he had. And the
annoyance of the Jew in Jerichow would still not have been removed.
And Irmgard wouldn't let him rest, no matter what the doctor said.

He knew he was losing his grip and told Ramdohr he was
coming to see him. He had not felt easy about being promoted at the
same time that Ramdohr was obliged to retire from the bench on
account of his Social Democrat friends; for four years now he had
been making his heavy work-load an excuse. Ramdohr, now no longer
Judge Ramdohr, came to meet him at the door, introduced him

around the family, to his wife, to all four daughters, as if the friendship had been in continuous use since 1933, and he insisted on his family's staying. The company sat on the terrace in the still-warm October evening, with a view over Lake Gneez, drinking a Moselle that used not to be so generously dispensed in this house, and the talk was about maritime law, a recent interest of Dr. Ramdohr's. It was clear, from the Horch automobile outside the house, from the newly acquired furniture, even from the wallpaper, that his colleague Ramdohr ("former colleague," interjected Ramdohr) was earning more than he needed from his Hamburg consultations and, annoyingly enough, was not suffering in the least from the punishment that his dismissal was supposed to represent. When Wegerecht, late that evening, was seen out onto Gustloff Street, not comfortably but annoyingly drunk, he had got absolutely nowhere with the Jerichow affair, a chance to recuperate in reconciliation and good company had slipped through his fingers, and he could not even blame Günti Ramdohr for having his revenge.

A chance to recuperate, at least to get away and forget his worries, was what he was hoping for from the Mecklenburg Army maneuvers at the end of September 1937, to which Irmgard had procured him an invitation through friends in the Army regional command at Schwerin, yet the very first day was ruined for him. He was present while a senior official of the Reich Labor Service created a scene with some Army officers of whom one was his superior in rank. The subject was a cord road which the infantry wished to have laid, contrary to their own instructions and drawings of yesterday, and they wanted it laid by tomorrow 22:30 hours. Wegerecht watched the brawny, violent fellow succeed in obtaining the apology he demanded, which he did simply by stubbornly and vociferously insisting that he was right, and Wegerecht had little desire to have any truck with him. Then he found out that the name was Griem and that the name Griem enjoyed popularity and respect. (The next night, at 20:00 hours, the cord road lay across the marsh, and it even had a kind of railing for which the Army had no longer dared to hope.) (And because Wegerecht had allowed himself to be held up by this scene, he also missed the sight of Mussolini, who had been driven through a few miles to the west. He had been more curious about Mussolini than about his companion, the Führer and Reich Chancellor. Mussolini had at least got where he was in his own country.) Then there was an invitation to dinner at an estate on Lake Krakow which Wegerecht did not attend when he saw Griem standing on the entrance steps in his Labor Service uniform, a boorish country bumpkin who had meanwhile learned to offer the ladies his arm and to tell stories in such a way that career officers listened to him, and laughed obediently.

Shortness of breath, palpitations, dizzy spells, diminishing output, irritability.

Was there any connection between Robert Papenbrock, originator of the denunciation, and Walter Griem? The Nazi Party's foreign organization versus the Reich Labor Service?

If he knew Papenbrock at all, Papenbrock would persuade his daughter to refuse to testify. To tone down. To reduce the substance of her testimony. Leaving Wegerecht holding the baby.

How about charging Lisbeth Cresspahl with failing to denounce? With spreading rumors hostile to the interests of the state? With aiding and abetting? Under the law against insidious attacks on state and Party? Article I, Paragraph 1: with malice aforethought? Paragraph 2: with gross negligence? Imprisonment not less than three months. Up to three months, or a fine.

How about that?

January 17, 1968   Wednesday

Stalin's daughter, his little Svetlana, can't keep her mouth shut. Sits in Princeton, N. J., and wants to involve herself in the protests against the sentencing of four young citizens of Moscow for writing without permission. Does she suppose that a Soviet court will listen with particular attention to the voice of a defectress? Perhaps she is trying to defend Papa's patented rights to the social justice he invented; a justice that has cost more people their lives than can ever be counted; in the present case the severest sentence was seven years. "In the face of suppression of fundamental human rights, wherever it takes place, we must not remain silent," Svetlana Hallelujah has told the CBS news service; why doesn't she get Dial-A-Flower to send flowers to the graveyards where her father's comrades are buried, if they are buried? "We must give all possible support to those who remain honest and brave under unbearable conditions" is another of her inspired sayings; next thing she'll be surprised that Isaac Babel's daughter or Ossip Mandelstam's widow fails to thank her for assistance rendered. "A wild mockery of justice" is what she sees happening. When she's right, she's right.

Wegerecht was saved.

He did not believe it, right to the end. His Schwerin friends (in particular Theo Swantenius, the lawyer among the four brothers) also turned out to have a direct line to a Reich ministry and although everything came through loud and clear it was the opposite, so that it all looked just as treasonable as the reverse had looked, without even a promise of benefit from it. By now it was too late to drag the former Miss von Oertzen into the affair; he had Gisela prepare his breakfast as soon as he woke up these days, so that he could see the children but not his wife. On one occasion his thoughts strayed, and he mistook the maid for the wife, and sighed; but Gisela came from Thüringen so was unable to pass on the condition of the County Court judge to interested parties in Jerichow, or even in Gneez.

The first direction came in the form of a reproach: Would the presiding judge kindly recollect the names of the accused? Since when were witnesses being arrested as long as the accused were running around loose, etc.?

Wegerecht could not summon the courage to send Semig home. He believed he had grasped that he was to lock up Warning and Hagemeister. This was during the last third of October.

With Kraczinski matters went as expected. The prosecutor had merely wanted to give Wegerecht time to get on the bandwagon of the prosecution and dismissed almost contemptuously any of the judge's new ideas regarding the conduct of the case. Kraczinski was confident of victory. Wegerecht did not like this, nor did he like the pursed lips, the crafty glances, the relaxed humming. There was something calculating about Kraczinski. He had figured something out for himself in that schoolboy pate of his.

Wegerecht wanted to get the thing over with and opened proceedings on October 29.

Pushed his judge's cap back on his hot head, straightened his gown, seated himself. He was bright red in the face, looked as healthy as a spoiled child, but hurt. He was very watchful. He could not see well that morning.

His oldest boy had told him something at breakfast about the first period in school being canceled. It was the birthday of the Reich Minister for Enlightenment and Propaganda, Dr. Joseph Goebbels. One day earlier, and the judgment could have been passed more as Erasmus of Rotterdam would have conceived it.

While the indictment of Paul Warning, agricultural worker, and Siegfried Hagemeister, forestry employee, for infringement of the "law of insidiousness," was being read out, Wegerecht was searching among the spectators for unfamiliar faces. He found no visitor from the provincial capital, either in uniform or otherwise. That was good; unless, of course, he had been written off to such an extent that a local observer sufficed. It was of little consolation to him to have seen those Jerichow people sitting in the witness room like sheep in the rain.

The denunciation, presented by the prosecution and emanating from a patriotic German citizen inspired by a sense of national duty, had been properly formulated, sworn to, signed. Someone had helped here, advised, filled in the cracks. Who?

Warning and Hagemeister became quite carried away in their eagerness to admit that they had held a conversation as claimed in the indictment. Both had got the shock of their lives at being taken into the cellars and placed beside Semig the Jew, as if it were not only he who was in danger but their own skins too. Hagemeister was casual, dependable, so like himself that what he said sounded not like a repetition but like the start of a further conversation, when he said: "And look at people like Griem."

"Yeah," said Warning. "Used to be thick as thieves with Semig, couldn't get them apart. Now Griem's some kind of a big shot in the Reich Labor Service."

The prosecution had no questions. Damn.

Dr. Wegerecht was surprised to find that not even his palms were moist although his whole body felt hot. His head was aching as if something inside the temples wanted to get out. He pressed his stomach against the desk as if he could hold on that way. The old County Court judge Wegerecht used to wave his arms with gusto as he talked; this one held his hands flat on the papers. Seen from below he was a stern, angry representative of the law when he asked: What had they been thinking of.

Warning hadn't been thinking of anything.

Hagemeister had not considered this anything worth overhearing. Considering the silence beyond the other walls of the train compartment, one would have thought the whole coach was empty.

Now the prosecution did have a question, but as unexpected and proper as if Dr. Kraczinski had suddenly started up from sleep or as if with the best will in the world he had forgotten a firm intention. What was it that had drawn the attention of the accused to Griem? What statements had been made prior to the one attested to?

First of all, said Hagemeister: Kraczinski stopped him with a gesture as if he had just thought of something. It had just occurred to Hagemeister that in Griem's own farming days Warning had worked for him, and Warning was most eager to confirm this, but before they could get going the eyes of both men had swung back in bewilderment to Wegerecht because Kraczinski did not seem to be listening.

Wegerecht called the witness Lisbeth Cresspahl. Kraczinski acted surprised.

Lisbeth was not the tradesman's wife, slow-witted, eager or stubborn, whom Wegerecht had expected; the woman now approaching, face not lowered, sure of step, wearing a black cloth coat with a velvet collar: this was a daughter of Papenbrock, unintimidated, studied in both dress and demeanor. Which form of oath, Mrs. Cresspahl, secular or religious?

Religious. And Lisbeth had not only recalled but looked up what the Mecklenburg Christian Family Almanac recommended for October 29, 1937: Matthew 10, 34 to 42.

She had heard it at that time, she said. (Think not that I am come to send peace on earth: I came not to send peace, but a sword): By "at the time," what she meant was that she merely remembered the words from the depositions of the police. (He that loveth father or mother more than me is not worthy of me: and he that loveth son or daughter more than me is not worthy of me.) She would deny nothing except that she remembered; and if her brother Horst said that's what she told him, then that's what she heard, and it's true. (And he that loseth his life for my sake shall find it.) On the contrary, the opportunity for overhearing had been excellent, a Saturday in mid-July, noonday quiet, the train from Gneez to Jerichow almost empty, and when it stopped in Wehrlich the wind was swallowed up by the Gräfin Forest; she had even been able to hear the scratching of the stationmaster's chickens. (And he that receiveth me receiveth him that sent me.) She couldn't understand the question. Why hadn't she filed a denunciation herself? Because it was stuff and nonsense. Rubbish. Drivel. Crazy. Only someone who knew nothing about Jerichow could ever harbor such stupid suspicions about Dr. Semig or Griem, and Hagemeister knew this as well as she did. (And he that receiveth a righteous man in the name of a righteous man shall receive a righteous man's reward.) That had nothing to do with favoritism toward Jews, only with the truth. (And whosoever shall give to drink unto one of these little ones a cup of cold water only . . .)

After Wegerecht had thanked her she remained standing in front of him. She had to be led to the bench. Suddenly she looked as if she had been prepared for a long journey, for something uncertain. The gesture with which she pulled out her scarf from under her coat collar had something of surprise in it.

Griem, beefy, jovial, his podgy, weatherproof face lending him almost an air of gaiety, his uniform endowing him with the power of the state: Not that he knew of. Idle talk. He could only feel sorry for poor sods like that. He was not going to lay a charge. A lesson. A sharp lesson. Without wanting to anticipate the court.

The prosecution requested that the witness Griem be reprimanded for offering unsolicited advice to the court. That had been the Kraczinski of only ten days ago, quick off the mark, rapacious, pouncing like a chicken hawk. The Kraczinski who then had no further questions did not match that one.

Dr. Semig entered the courtroom with lowered head, not humbly but like a grown man who has caught himself out in some childish error and does not need others to supply him with the reprimands he administers to himself. He chose the religious form of oath. After that he sat up very straight, looked the judge full in the face, turned without haste toward Kraczinski. They had given him back his Iron Cross. He spoke rather slowly because he had been alone for so long.

Did he abide by his version, he was asked, that Griem, in his former occupation of farmer, had not derived any illegal pecuniary benefit as a result of his (Dr. Semig's) having given a veterinary certificate for a sick cow to be destroyed with the result that the said Griem had obtained from the Mutual Cattle Insurance an amount of eight hundred former Rentenmarks, a sum which he might not have been able to realize from an ordinary sale? And moreover, without Dr. Semig's having participated in the proceeds as the dispenser of a favor to the recipient of the favor?

Semig passed his hand over his brush of gray hair as if embarrassed to have to explain yet again to an educated person something that any child should have grasped at first hearing. Hepatitis was hepatitis, he said. It had never been within his power to direct the Bacteriological Institute in Schwerin to falsify its findings. Not even in 1931 had his financial circumstances been such that . . .

This was not clearly audible because, as soon as Kraczinski directed his first question at Semig, Griem had begun shouting, firing off half-finished sentences that were interrupted by violent slaps wherever his hand happened to land, on his knee or on the arm of the chair, as if he were incapable of feeling pain.

Kraczinski had no questions.

A fine was imposed on Griem for contempt of court.

Semig was allowed to go free, in a subsidiary paragraph.

Warning was sentenced to four months' imprisonment for un-warranted suspicions directed against a Party official and hence against a Party organization.

Hagemeister was fined two hundred marks.

Wegerecht went home, so staggered by Kraczinski's change of mood that he took him along for lunch. In broad daylight he sent Gisela down to the cellar for some wine, and the pleasant relaxation he derived from the sense of relief and the first glass was only slightly marred by Irmi von Oertzen's flirtatious behavior with the new guest and by her asking why they had consented to handle such trifling matters.

Hagemeister came to express his thanks. He insisted on shaking Lisbeth's hand. "That was an expensive conversation, that was," he said.

Cresspahl mumbled a reply that might have turned into an offer.

"Nonsense!" said Hagemeister. He was quite willing to pay a hundred marks for learning his lesson. But he'd collect the second hundred from Robert Papenbrock without ever having to go and see him; that fellow would have to come crawling to him! Nothing personal, Mrs. Cresspahl!

"I don't like it," says Marie. One can tell from her voice that she is lying on her back; since the arrival of the Killainen family she has been sleeping in the Swiss girl's room with Annie and me. She speaks slowly, thoughtfully, dissatisfaction in her voice.

"The fact that they got off so lightly? It's not finished yet."

"The fact that harshness was promised, and didn't happen."

"Thwarted expectations?"

"Yes. And that there's no ending. And that the end is not explained."

"Marie, how could the people of Jerichow know who might be phoning on Griem's behalf and who against him?"

"You mentioned Ministries."

"They were far away, and even if they'd been near neither Cresspahl nor Papenbrock could've known what was going on there. The Jerichow witnesses, Dr. Berling, Avenarius—who was an attor-ney, mind you—were so in the dark that someone had to go to the witness room and tell them they wouldn't be needed: the bailiff had forgotten them, while they were still rehearsing their digressions and excuses."

"O.K., Gesine."

"Now how about if I tell you something about Peter Niebuhr?"

"Oh no, not Peter Niebuhr. A brother-in-law of both Lisbeth and Cresspahl. A young man. He doesn't even come into this story."

"But supposing he did, Marie? Supposing he'd long since been given leave from the school for noncommissioned officers near Potsdam and was working in an office under Eugen Darré, head of Farm Production, and that while there he had run across a Nazi who had been bribing people with money and favors—and a Nazi from Jerichow at that—and supposing he'd imperceptibly steered his department head to the phone and impressed on his superior the honor of German agriculture, so that at least within the immediate circle of his in-laws up there on the Baltic a Nazi would get it in the neck, until it dawned on Peter that the denunciation originated from a Papenbrock, and that he wasn't giving Cresspahl his brother-in-law or sister-in-law the pleasure he had imagined and was now obliged to switch the orders to Schwerin and, mind you, between different departments, and then had to swallow not only a self-administered rebuke but also one from friends who, if he'd been successful, would have commended him, increased their confidence in him. . . ."

"Yes," says Marie. "Yes," she repeats, in the deep-throated, voluptuous tone of utter conviction. "I don't doubt that for an instant."

January 18, 1968 Thursday

The face of the New York *Times* betrays nothing. Incorruptibly, agilely, she holds forth for our benefit on efforts to save the British pound, on gold coverage of the dollar, as well as the churches' good will extended toward the Negroes, wherein Henry Ford II will not be outdone. In her own personal transcript, her energy unimpaired by night work, our reliable Auntie publishes President Johnson's State of the Union Message ("seeking, building, tested many times this past year, and always equal to the test"). She does not suppress the news that Prince Sihanouk of Cambodia despises the American nation for, as she quotes, "cynically" breaking its promises. She has the latest news on the Mafia scandal in New York's water department, on tax agents caught out in corruption, on stolen credit cards, on the narcotics raid at the Stony Brook State University Center; in a tone bordering on consolation she points out that, if Pavel Litvinov is not happy with socialist justice in Moscow, he is likewise not allowed to work as a physicist. All this on the front page, as if it were all there. Such honest knitting of brows.

If only we had restricted ourselves to reading the continuations of these items, and not the new beginning which she hides on page 28! Such a dignified old lady, allowing herself to be caught out in such awkward circumstances! If she were to report such things about other people, she would be embarrassed. But she shows herself as she is. It is . . . it is a confidential matter.

The beginning, while not innocent, is no surprise. Yesterday afternoon a Federal inquiry commission reviewing the situation of black and Puerto Rican employees met again at Foley Square and charged the news media with giving a false image of those minorities: just like that—with no sign of doubt, no quotation marks, in the *Times* headline; and surely our tried-and-true dispenser of reality must be above such suspicions.

The commission finds that the communications industry is giving Americans a false image of the society in which they live, and Negroes and Puerto Ricans a distorted view of themselves. No doubt. But surely not the New York *Times*; want to bet?

Of course not. The communications industry has an enormous influence on the nation, and it is the proprietors of this industry who, in less than no time, are able to create the climate for substantial changes in the social structure. There is no question but that the New York *Times* is capable of this. If there are those who have shirked this responsibility, our dear old Auntie—just, helpful, the ethical figurehead—will not be among the culprits. She knows what it means to be among the opinion- and taste-makers in this "grave period of our national history"; she will do her duty. And immediately she gives us the percentages of these minorities in the State of New York (Negroes, 18 per cent, Puerto Ricans 10 per cent), so that we may go to work well furnished with facts and figures.

The competition, the minor competition, the New York *Post*; what can you expect? Caustic, no less, was the commission's attitude toward the *Post*, the New York *Times* goes on to tell us in her sweet-and-sour way: 450 employees, and only 24 Negroes or Puerto Ricans among them. 5.3 per cent. Tsk-tsk. Did it bother the New York *Post*, a basically liberal newspaper, that there was virtually a segregated press in New York City, the commission had been obliged to ask? And the *Post* could only come up with a flippant, typical reply: Any type of segregation bothered the New York *Post*. Ha-ha. And only four black reporters among its total of 53: 7.5 per cent. Hm. There you are, you see? And not one of the editors is a Negro. What a hypocrite the *Post* is.

This really demonstrates why we have riots and explosions of despair in the cities, says the commission.

Anyone wanting to get in ahead of the New York *Times* would have to get out of bed a lot earlier than she did. She has already looked in on the police of Los Angeles, Detroit, Virginia, Philadelphia, Chicago, and Atlanta, on the armaments factories in Memphis and Springfield. Orders have even been placed for armed helicopters of the type used in Vietnam. Next time the police are going to use the chemical known as "banana peel," which makes the streets so slippery that it is difficult to walk, let alone riot, on them. And the New York Police Department has bought 5,000 riot helmets at a cost of $20 each—$100,000.

That's on another page.

Now it's the *Times's* turn. Three cheers for the favorite!

All honor to the truth. The *Times* didn't emerge from this unscathed either. But the commission was not caustic—biting, scathing—toward her. Critical, yes. Perhaps in order to spare her. To save an old lady from embarrassment as she sits there before the judge in her neat black dress, her discreetly preserved youth, the dignity of old age, twisting her hands in her lap, agitated after all now that she has to admit that of her 200 reporters not more than three were black: 1.5 per cent. Yes.

We may imagine the ensuing silence.

Hurriedly the New York *Times*, née Ochs-Hays-Sulzberger, adds: This applies only to the New York offices of the *Times*.

That's not much help either. The same was true of the *Post*. And the old lady fails to demonstrate that the comparable figures in the Washington and Paris offices represent any improvement; she implies this, mind you. It's possible, of course. Isn't it? It's possible.

Now she is back on course. Head held high again, she looks the commission full in the face and says firmly: She is not proud that only 7 per cent of the *Times's* white-collar employees are from the minorities now being reviewed by the commission. Thus she can at least be commended for her integrity.

Then she ruins her moral advantage by putting her foot in it with her mania for fuller explanation, saying: A year ago it was only 6 per cent.

Oh dear, oh dear. Less than the *Post*. And her 7 per cent are only "about." Does the *Times*, we wonder, employ a Negro as editor?

She may have given this information, but she is not telling her readers. Let's skip that question.

There she sits, an old lady, humiliated, exposed, no respect for her age, her merits. She looks at her toes. She blows her nose. All to no avail; the commission has an unfair question to put to her.

Did she not want to retract part of her prepared statement? The part described by the *Times* as trying to "practice what we preach"?

"No, I don't want to," she says.

Did the *Times* see itself as a leader in the newspaper field?

"Possibly," she says. There she goes again, chin up, gaze proudly fixed on the middle distance, her tone a haughty young girl's.

That was a good deal of modesty, was the commission's rejoinder. And it was to be hoped that a newspaper like the *Times* would extend its leadership in the field of equal opportunity for employment.

"We will vigorously attack the problem," says the New York *Times*. It is the last account she gives of herself. Is it a promise? But the tears softening her voice are audible.

Now quickly off to Time Inc., Columbia Broadcasting, to American Broadcasting, Doubleday & Co., book publishers, to the J. Walter Thompson, the Grey, advertising companies. There'll be skeletons in their closets too. And they don't come off much better either. Just draw a veil over the terrible, the intolerable, scene that has just taken place, a veil of something that is true. It's not enough. Now she turns to the Jews.

But the Jews are not the object of this investigation!

Never mind. There's enough there for at least two paragraphs. Nothing but the facts; in other words, justified. 25 percent of the inhabitants of New York City are Jews. But only 4.5 per cent of the 2,104 officers of 38 major corporations are Jews. Yes sir. If you're going to talk about the beam in my eye, I'll talk about the motes in yours. The concerns least inclined to employ Jewish executives are banks, insurance companies, shipping firms, and law firms. There you are. And the hearings continue today, and we'll see what kind of things they turn up!

I've never known her like that.

A shrewish, crafty old woman with a guilty conscience. You let her tell you what's going on in the world when you're not there to see. And many times you can't be there to see, Gesine.

Won't you take into account that she exposed her own disgrace?

It seems she prefers to let herself be accused of lying by evasion rather than by suppression.

But she didn't hide it, did she? She draws attention to it in the Contents.

Have a good look, Gesine. It's not the way the headline has it. She couldn't resist this last opportunity. The Contents says nothing about reproaching the news media with giving a false image of society. It says "false image."

If I kick this Auntie out of the house, who's going to take her place?

You mean you expected nothing better from her.

If I admit that her behavior surprised me today, what am I saying about myself? No.

January 19, 1968   Friday

Fifty ladies were invited to the White House yesterday to discuss crime in the streets; among these were the New York *Times* and Eartha Kitt, the singer. Miss Kitt had an answer to the question, why young people rebel in the street, take pot, and don't want to go to school: "Because they're going to be snatched off from their mothers to be shot in Vietnam." "You send the best of this country off to be shot and maimed."

The President's wife was pale, but she rose and declared, her voice trembling and tears welling in her eyes, that not all problems could be solved by force.

Eartha Kitt: The other guests knew the ghettos as crusaders; but she herself had lived in the gutters.

Mrs. Johnson: "I cannot understand the things that you do."

Miss Kitt: The speakers had "missed out on something."

The *Times* is almost the first with the story. Shall we be friends again?

Lisbeth Cresspahl now believed herself to be at odds with Jerichow too, a place where over two thousand people lived, not counting the cattle. She had no desire to be forgiven for testifying in court against others; in this way she could hang on to her guilt. She even went so far as to forgive Robert, who had had the nerve to involve her in this court action, and once again she forgave Cresspahl, who had calmly told her that he would throw the denouncer out of the house and through the barbed wire. This merely added one more to her store of ordeals. The trial over, there was nothing to show that she was depressed, and again Cresspahl believed that a period of reason was due (illness was something he did not wish to think of). It was rather that Lisbeth was no longer overcome by alternating confusion and peace of mind; there must often have been a blend of these two states in her head. For it was not as easy as it had been to persuade her to go for walks into town. To have others condemn her by their glances, no, she did not want that, yet in that way she could have added to her list of sufferings. To take care of the shopping which, however much she might have wanted to, she could not palm off on Louise or Aggie Brüshaver, she did not stop at Gneez but took the train there to Lübeck, and in a first-class compartment too. This was how she avoided getting into conversation with people she knew in and around Jerichow; this was how she earned herself a reputation for extravagance.

In Lübeck she did not have many chance meetings to fear, either in the shops or in the department stores. Often she stayed longer than was necessary and on her return home could tell about the altered appearance of the Holstenhaus, to which the Nazis' Public Works Department had added some new gables, just as they had done to the old Gothic buildings on König Street, Meng Street, and along the Schrangen, as if to prove that Germany was building less for the war than Cresspahl knew. He did not fall for this, he had learned to mistrust that teasing tone of voice; he looked at her. Then he thought of their time in England, of her leisurely, carefree walks through the strange town, of the clear gaze with which she had once walked past him in Richmond. It was the gaze of someone who knows herself to be alone; now it had grown more fixed, more stubborn, clouded with perplexity. There was still that gentle line of eyesocket to brow and cheekbone, and a person seeing her like that, sitting in her first-class compartment, occupied perhaps with a secret little smile, would often open the compartment door and address her as Madam before he realized that the young woman was not as amiably inclined as she looked, and that actually there was something a little uncanny about her smile. Then Lisbeth would pull her coat around her, stiffen, and turn her face toward the window, just to prevent anyone from challenging her with Warning's hundred and twenty days in jail.

This would not have happened to her even while traveling between Gneez and Jerichow, where none of the trains had a first-class compartment. For in Jerichow the talk was quite different. Our Lisbeth. Our Lisbeth behaved quite properly. Our Lisbeth wasn't a man, now, was she; perjury, that's something for men. What could Lisbeth do for a fictitious brother like that? Anger was directed at

Warning, first because he hadn't had enough sense to keep his trap shut in the train and then because he had put Lisbeth into such an awkward position. And people kept saying that Warning was one of those fellows who'll lean on his spade while right next to him a cow is bellowing, and that behind his amiable, quite tolerable grumbling there was no proper get-up-and-go. His wife was being helped out with odd jobs, even getting paid for work not done; as for him, his homecoming to Jerichow was going to turn out rather differently from the one he might be imagining at Dreibergen near Bützow. And look at that Hagemeister. All he had really wanted to hear was that Griem had meanwhile got as heavy as a fattened sow, or that a top hat is a splendid hat, but that it won't look good on someone who can't handle it. And Warning opens his big mouth to talk about ancient history. And Hagemeister was fond of saying, in his sleepy way, but then quite enthusiastically: Cresspahl's wife sure got me out of that one nicely. Lisbeth Cresspahl got me out of that one.

That was the point the people of Jerichow had reached. Lisbeth was no longer regarded as Papenbrock's daughter, now she was Cresspahl's Lisbeth.

It seemed she was ill. One hardly ever saw her around. All the more reason to give her credit for telling a real live county judge, right to his face, that he was wasting his time with stupid nonsense. Nothing but the truth. That's what she said: Stuff and nonsense. Just you try that.

She heard nothing of all this; nor would it have been any help to her.

"And now the story about the water butt," says Marie.

"What water butt? You don't know anything about it."

"What I do know is that the day before yesterday James Shuldiner was at the Mediterranean Swimming Club and told me: 'Your mother's not going to let *you* fall into the water butt.' "

"No."

"Come on, Gesine."

"Anyhow that was in the summer of 1937, and we're way past that."

"What is a water butt, anyway?"

"Annie's sure to have one."

"Annie's not here."

"A water butt, Marie—"

"Yes?"

"Most people have them in the country, preferably standing

away from a wall but in such a way that leaves and pollen don't drift into them. The idea is for the barrel to collect rain water, because that's the purest kind that occurs in Nature. While it does contain nitrogen, carbonic acid, ammonium nitrate, and all the other things it draws from the atmosphere, it doesn't contain calcium carbonate or the salts contributed by the soil. It's just condensed steam. Soft to the touch, that's why it's called soft water. The purest kind of country rain. Ours contained more ammonia because we got sea spray in it too. Ammonia makes water softer. So it foams better. For the laundry, you know. If the barrel's made of wood, the water that collects in it is inclined to turn brownish because the ammonia absorbs organic substances. So that's your water butt, or rain barrel."

"You're trying to avoid that story more than you do Robert Papenbrock."

"You'll wish you'd never heard it."

"Sometimes you treat me as if I weren't ten years old. Ten and a half."

"Cresspahl had set up a water butt next to the barn. Although it was a long way to carry it from there, no purer water could be got from the sky. In all other respects, too, until 1938 the property was equipped and maintained as if it were to serve as a textbook model. No clamp remained loose for long, and the well water, instead of running back into the ground, ran into a wooden tub where a child could play boats with pieces of wood, or cool her feet. There was nothing niggardly about the way things were run either; a pane was taken out again from the new window above the back entrance so that the swallows could keep to their old habits and fly in to build their nest on their usual beam. While they were there, the red flagstones below were simply scrubbed that much more often, since they didn't always aim accurately at the pages of the *Lübecker General-anzeiger* spread underneath. And that was the kind of water butt which the previous owners, the Pinnows, had set up by the kitchen window under a pipe leading down from the eaves. Cresspahl left it there. Anyway, it would probably have fallen apart if he'd moved it. Since it wasn't watertight it was always surrounded by long lush grass and flourishing weeds. I liked that. But because the rain water from the roof carried down moss and dust, it was hardly ever used for the laundry, and the lid was hardly ever taken off. But the lid was new, Cresspahl had made it so I wouldn't drag over a kitchen stool and use it to climb into the water."

"If the lid wasn't there, it might have been an oversight."

"On a stranger's part, yes. But anyone belonging to the household knew all that about me and the cat. It was a huge gray creature, fat and lazy. When Cresspahl was turning the Pinnows' barn into a workshop and slept in the fodder room next to his tools, the cat had come visiting and had stayed on. Lisbeth and the child were still living at the time in Papenbrock's house, and when they arrived the cat insisted on its prior rights. It didn't like me. I tried to persuade it to play; but it preferred lying on the sill inside the window, watching the birds. It was old too, not just lethargic. The child used often to stand outside, head tilted back, looking up at the cat and talking to it, and the cat would look at me as if it knew a secret but wouldn't let me in on it."

"Carelessness. After all, your mother couldn't tie you to her apron strings, and I know that much from the four-year-olds, they vanish like baby rabbits."

"See?"

"But first you had to climb up onto the lid to get level with the cat's head and then you fell into the water, Gesine!"

"Just as you say."

"And your mother, your mother stood looking on?"

"Yes. No. If I don't focus my thoughts, I can see her. Then she's standing outside the back door, drying her hands on her apron, wringing her hands, one can be the other. She watches me like a grownup being amused at a childish prank, waiting to see what happens; she watches me quite solemnly, approvingly, as if she were confident I'd do the right thing. When I try to force my memory, I can't see her."

"And she didn't move."

"By that time I was below the surface. I could still see her in my mind's eye; then I realized that in the round shaft of the barrel only the sky was visible."

"Then she pulled you out."

"Then Cresspahl pulled me out. He had come up behind her around the corner of the house, and had watched her watching me. After the war he didn't want to tell me too much about it, just that she stood there 'as if rooted to the spot' when he carried me, a dripping bundle, past her into the house."

"Taking off wet clothes from Cresspahl and a child, washing the child, drying her, dressing her, I can't picture that."

"But she did, that's why he called her into the house. And by the time I had a fresh dress on and was cheerful enough to forget about being submerged in the barrel—"

"He beat her."

"Never. He let her watch while he gave me a hiding. He didn't bother to hit me lightly; the idea was for me to remember the water butt once and for all. That was the only way he could protect me from Lisbeth."

"And she didn't hold back his hand?"

"Heavens no. Now she had something else to offer up to her God—the unjust suffering of her child."

"Have you ever hit me?"

"No. And what I found so terrible about the beating was not the injustice but the fact that my father was angry with me. That's why all through dinner I was looking for something with which I could start a reconciliation—and it had to be under the table so I could be safe from his eyes. Then I saw the cat coming in from a walk outside the house and going under Cresspahl's chair and settling down across his feet and wooden clogs. And I said: Dad, the cat! And he said: Never mind the cat! And looked at me as if he shared my surprise about the cat, and was with me as he always was."

"She wanted to kill you!"

"She wanted to pass me on, Marie."

"She must've hated you."

"It wouldn't have taken long, the drowning."

"But she wanted to get rid of you!"

" 'Whoever loves his child,' Marie, 'will . . .' She would have known the child was safe, far removed from guilt and the acquiring of guilt. And that would have been the greatest of all her sacrifices."

"You're trying to say she loved you."

"That's what I'm trying to say."

"Next time you don't want to tell me a story, Gesine, don't."

"Now you don't trust me."

"I do. You're your father's daughter, aren't you?"

"Yes, Marie. I'm Father's daughter."

Lisbeth I'll kill you.
Kill me Hinrich. I'm past helping.

January 20, 1968   Saturday, South Ferry Day

The New York *Times*, our moralistic Auntie, refuses to let Eartha Kitt get away with answering Mrs. Johnson back. The *Times* speaks of a "rude confrontation." And how much it was to the credit of the President's wife that she candidly realized that she could not understand the things and the life which Miss Kitt understood. And that one could learn from that. To understand them. After centuries of psychic injuries, the accumulated venom poured out, she said, often rude and irrational, often self-destructive. But it was there and must be faced with compassionate understanding.

It'll be a while after all before we're friends again with Auntie Times.

January 21, 1968   Sunday

Once again the New York *Times* has sold a whole page to herself in order to report to her readers on her own progress. Since May she has been the owner of the Microfilming Corporation of America, she boasts about her niece Hallelujah, she has gained weight; but the most important thing in her eyes is the 117-year-old period after her title which she has now discarded. The reason for this was not the annual $41.28 for printer's ink, but the wish to make Auntie more legible and enjoyable.

In other respects, once again it seems to be all there. She has not even overlooked the fact that shortly before Christmas the Government sent a Deputy Secretary of Defense to Senator Fulbright. Would Senator Fulbright kindly call off the inquiry by the Senate Foreign Relations Committee as to whether U. S. destroyers had in fact been attacked in the Gulf of Tonkin in 1964. The Administration had its proof, and the bombing strikes during the preceding three and a half years were justified. Senator Fulbright is still not convinced.

Dr. Semig had been convinced. The first week of December he left town.

Still it was not fear that prompted him. In the cellars below the County Court he had been no worse off than a thief whose guilt has not been established. Dora had been allowed to bring him reading matter, and she had not been refused permission to visit him out of hours. On many days he had been allowed out in the prison yard for half an hour, although alone. He had been interrogated only twice. Throughout his imprisonment he had felt secure, not only because Dora had greased Alfred Fretwust's palm until he was soft as butter but because of the conviction that what was happening to him was not possible. Since it was not lawful it had to be a mistake. He left for his wife's sake.

When Dora came to see him she would tell him about the progress being made with the stamping of their passports. She did not tell him what the authorities had promised her if she divorced him. They talked about the house in Jerichow, about selling their belongings, about matters just barely within Fretwust's comprehension. She did not tell him that Friedrich Jansen had occupied the house for several hours with his guard of bullyboys so that he could measure the rooms. Once she turned up without her coat, in late October, and he forgot to ask her why. At the station in Gneez she had been spat upon by Frieda Klütz, and she had taken off her soiled coat and laid it neatly in the arms of the shrewish old maid. But Arthur did notice she was not getting enough sleep, that each time she seemed to have got thinner, those great burning eyes. He did not feel like waking up many more mornings without her, he gave in. The point on which he felt he had to dig in his heels was his insistence that they talk of taking a trip, not of emigrating. Even Fretwust could see there was no difference and entered in his monitoring notes: Plans to leave the German Reich. As far as possible Fretwust avoided Arthur's name in making his notes, after Dora had once burst out in anger: anyone speaking of her husband was to call him "Doctor." This had confused Fretwust. The man was called Doctor because he had gone to university, no one could take that away from him. The man had been an officer, and in being addressed by his first name he must surely recall that during the war he had addressed his subordinates like that. A Jew, yes, but a Jew on top of everything else. The veterinarian's wife still classed herself as among those to whom he used to raise his cap. She was capable of stopping at a door so abruptly that a bailiff of the New Greater German Reich positively ran to open it fast enough for her. When she instructed him how to treat her husband he would try to grin, without success, even from his mother he would not have tolerated so severe a tone, such relentless looks. When the visit was over, Fretwust, contrary to regulations, would stand up and turn for a few seconds toward the wall. When he glanced over his shoulder, the two would be sitting facing one another exactly as before, and although they may have tried to pass each other something he never caught them in an embrace. When, over a beer, Fretwust later talked about the lusting couple, his conscience would be confused, yet he was almost certain, when recalling the afternoon, that Mrs. Semig had placed her hand on the Jew's as if she had to offer him comfort. That was after she returned from Schwerin with the hint that life for the Semigs in Germany would have been easier if they had children.

It was not only his wife whom Semig wished to spare what he regarded as a mistake, but also those in Jerichow with whom he had remained on speaking terms. It was not his fault, but it was on his account that they had received visits from police, both political and criminal. He had exposed them to this, and that was no way to show one's gratitude; hence he had to absent himself from them. That called for two visits.

The first was to be to Cresspahl; except that Cresspahl immediately suggested coming to Semig's house. Once again Lisbeth found it unnecessary to announce to all of Jerichow that they were on their way to the Bäk. But she let Dora Semig hold her in her arms like a child that has cried itself to sleep.

Kollmorgen came to the house too. That short gentleman had prepared a speech, and while making it he insisted on holding one of Semig's hands in both of his, which obliged him to look upward rather too steeply and Semig to look down from too great a height. The speech began with the topic of departure but then veered off at a tangent. It was almost four hundred years, he said, since Jürgen Wullenweber, Mayor of Lübeck, had been executed. From that September 29, 1537, he proceeded to December 20, 1712, the day the Swedes had won a battle against the Danes near Gadebusch, and although both dates had, in a remote and vague way, something to do with surviving in bad times, eventually even Avenarius lost confidence in the analogy, and his listeners were bound to notice that this was not what he had come to say. He was very embarrassed, afterward standing, whenever possible, with his back to the others and pretending to examine the Köster family Biedermeier furniture. The fact that he revealed his hands clasped behind his back, the helpless intertwining of his fingers, was something he probably overlooked.

That was the last case ever pleaded by Dr. Avenarius Kollmorgen, attorney.

Dr. Semig did not call to say good-by to the Tannebaums, Jewish clothing merchants in Jerichow. He had never had any dealings at all with them; not even as a customer.

Both of them—Dora as well as Arthur—refused to be seen off at the station. They were planning to take the first train next morning to Gneez, the milk train.

The train was due to leave at two minutes past seven, and at a quarter to seven Dr. and Mrs. Semig were standing outside Cresspahl's kitchen window, Dora in the light, Arthur farther back in the dark, by the milk platform. When he came into the kitchen his face was still a familiar one, the once comfortable creases around the mouth, the slightly pouting lips, the once thoughtful eyes that had always brightened when he had an amusing thought, even when he refrained from uttering it. But it gave Lisbeth quite a scare because she had already written off that face. So now Cresspahl had to drive them to the milk train after all, in the car that had belonged to Semig.

"What had they forgotten?" says Marie. She had inquired about the mechanics of the move, from time to time asking what had been done with the used household linen, the breakfast china, the house keys; in her eyes, all was over and done with once those good-bys had been said the evening before in Semig's yard.

"They wanted to see the Cresspahl child just once more."

January 22, 1968 Monday

The New York *Times* is still calling Eartha Kitt to task. This Negro obviously refuses to see that her statement on the Vietnam war was a breach of etiquette in that she had opposed the wife of the President. For Miss Kitt calmly told radio station WEEI in Boston: "I don't know why. I am very surprised. I raised my hand and was called on to explain my views. That's what I did."

January 23, 1968 Tuesday

"Are you the lady who called ten minutes ago about the weather in North Germany during Easter 1938? Crassfawn? You can take this down:

Flensburg

April 17: 8 degrees Centigrade, high winds, sleet showers.

April 18: morning—1.5 degrees Centigrade, highest daytime temperature 7 degrees, snow showers.

Putbus

April 17: 5 degrees Centigrade, no night frost, no precipitation.

April 18: no change.

Königsberg

April 17: 5 degrees Centigrade, snowfall.

April 18: no change.

We have nothing on Wismar or Stettin; can you still get an over-all picture? It's wonderful of you to say so, Mrs. Cressawe. The bill to go to Apartment 204, 243 Riverside . . . is that New York 25? No, not at all. You know, I also found out that March 1938 was the warmest of the century in that area; that's certainly not a thing I'm likely to forget. Yes. You've been talking to Herbert H. Hayes. The pleasure's all mine, Mrs. Crissauer!"

Which means that the daffodils, snowdrops, and forsythia in Hilde Paepcke's garden must have been destroyed by the frost, and no leaves were in sight, when her younger sister, accompanied by husband and child, arrived in Podejuch from Jerichow for a visit. Invitations for Easter in '35, '36, and '37 had been brushed aside by Lisbeth; now here she was, arriving in a renewed winter, and her insistence had been such that Alexander had had to cancel arrangements with some of his friends in the department. What was going on, that Lisbeth had become such an enigma, as was reported by one person after another coming from Jerichow?

On Saturday morning the Cresspahls arrived in Gneez by bus, he with a light-tan leather suitcase that was conspicuous among the bags and baskets of the other passengers, the child beside him with one hand on the suitcase handle, not beside her mother, who, empty-handed and unhurried, stepped after them onto the platform. The three took a second-class, not third-class, compartment in the Hamburg-Stettin express, which a few minutes after ten passed Gneez-Ausbau. Scarcely a quarter of an hour later and they stopped for three minutes above Lake Schwerin and could see, close by in the cold water, the northern tip of Lieps Island, not completely bare but covered with a brownish fuzz of trees. Here they could have changed trains onto the Rostock line and been in Copenhagen at their usual supper hour. It was the father who explained such connections to the child, and it was beside him that the child sat, patient and silent beneath her dark-brown coxcomb that looked as if she had rolled it under and pinned it herself. The two other passengers in the compartment, an elderly couple from Hamburg, stole furtive glances from time to time at the young woman, who was leaning her head back as if exhausted by something, often closing her eyes as if that released her from hearing too, and otherwise looking without curiosity out of the window so as to reveal nothing to those glances. To strangers it looked like a matrimonial tiff, yet again it did not when Lisbeth, with an affectionate and encouraging smile, suggested that her child and Cresspahl take a walk through the train. After a while she also left the compartment because she had been asked about common acquaintances between Hamburg and Schwerin; but she turned in the other direction.

Cresspahl was pleased that for once Lisbeth had asked for something to be done that could be done, although he could have used the Saturday for work. He expected Hilde with her questions to take the younger woman's mind off her preoccupations; he was almost looking forward to seeing his brother-in-law again and to the chance of drinking purely for pleasure. Cresspahl stood by the window and pointed out the Warnow to his child, the little river meandering along over stones and broken branches, whose right bank the train had been following since the town of Warnow, and then on the other side the canal between Bützow and Güstrow which had once been intended to go all the way to Berlin. At Güstrow the name of the station was painted on the sides of the square lamps. The child wanted to know why they had to wait here for five minutes. Cresspahl thought it was because of the connection to Neustrelitz and on to Wendisch Burg, where some other relatives lived, the Niebuhrs. He forgot about Horst in Güstrow. By then it was already eleven thirty, and they were passing through the forest east of Güstrow, the Priemer Forest, where beyond a thin wall of pines the Army Ordnance Depot, Northern Command, was being developed. He knew that Schmidt was shipping lumber supplies there from Güstrow. And Kröpelin from Bützow. For someone whom an Englishman might question, Cresspahl knew a lot of state secrets. While the train ran level with the High Wood outside Teterow, the Hamburg couple chatted with a new passenger about Austria's *Anschluss* with the Greater German Reich, grumbling a bit but in qualified agreement, and Cresspahl told the child about the pike which the people of Teterow dropped back into their lake because they were sure they could find it again by the notch they had cut on the edge of the boat. Just after twelve thirty the Cresspahls went off to the restaurant car, and at Malchin the child caught a glimpse of a small harbor with laid-up boats and boatbuilding sheds. But as the train passed Leuschentin Forest they were already on their way back because the restaurant car had been too crowded, mostly with military personnel who were obviously taking their time as they sat over their beer and wine. At Neubrandenburg the train stopped for five minutes, and Cresspahl was able to buy some lemonade for the child to drink with Lisbeth's sandwiches. By now it was already a quarter to one and they were passing through Pasewalk-on-the-Uecker and shortly, before two, between Grambow and Stöwen, they crossed the border into Pomerania. At two thirty the train stopped at Stettin, and in another quarter of an hour they had covered the five miles along the Greifenhagen line to Podejuch, and there at the station was Alexander Paepcke with his children Alexandra and Eberhardt, and Alexander said: Well, Hinrich, it's about time we got outside a few.

Hilde, who had stayed home with one-year-old Christine, gave her brother-in-law Cresspahl a lengthy embrace, keeping one eye on her sister; Lisbeth's expression was friendly, rather encouraging. She found Lisbeth little changed, if one discounted her fatigue. She got through her work with the same old efficiency, only now it was without enthusiasm and without enjoyment. So she did not necessarily notice that Lisbeth hung almost fearfully on Alexander's lips when he talked that evening about the Army Ordinance Department at Stettin. Alexander was a major in the Reserve now, would you believe it! The Podejuch house was only rented, mind you, and was costing a packet, but quite impressive, you'll admit! Yes indeed. After Austria it might be Poland's turn, or Czechoslovakia might be the next to join Germany. Of course it's going to be a real war, Lisbeth! What did you imagine? And one couldn't be too careful about aircraft, he must agree with Heinrich. It wasn't so bad to live close to an airfield, like in Jerichow; there they did their best to land all in one piece. But out in the open, the stuff that comes down there! Sometimes there were holes in the ground big enough to put this house in! Including basement and chimney. Things with such incredible explosive power would surely be better transported by rail than by the Luftwaffe. Eh? You bet. Prost, Hinrich! Lisbeth had gone upstairs very early and, because Cresspahl would not accept the Paepckes' bedroom either, Hilde found nothing strange about his sleeping three houses down the street in Widow Heinricius's back room while Lisbeth slept in their attic room with the children.

Next morning Paepcke shouted across the back gardens for Cresspahl, so that the surrounding eight houses were aware that Paepcke was shaving and had visitors. After breakfast Lisbeth insisted on going to church, so that Alexander finally decided, with an irritated laugh, that then they might as well all go. Over a grog at the Podejuch forester's house he began to extol Lisbeth's sister in whatever aspect occurred to him; he could not get Cresspahl to speak about Lisbeth. ("We're both outsiders among these Papenbrocks, you know," said Alexander. "True," said my father. He still didn't know it was urgent.) Driving out onto the heath, the Buchheide. In a clearing, damp between pitch-black pines, there suddenly lay, amusingly hidden, gaily painted Easter eggs; Alexander Paepcke, who knew the art of living and of conjuring. The edge of the heath lay surprisingly high over the river valley and the new barracks. Another evening over beer. Moselle, and prospects of the coming war. Each time a fresh glass was brought, Hilde plunked it down on the table; but that wouldn't bother a Paepcke. Cresspahl had no opportunity to talk to Lisbeth alone; he would have liked to take the sting out of Alexander's remarks. And once again Alexander, with suds on his chin, stood early in the morning at the window and shouted to Mrs.

Heinricius, widow of a senior government official, to wake Cresspahl. A walk beside the east arm of the Oder. A drink at eleven and lunch in Stettin at the Terrace Hotel with the stepped tower (at the foot of Haken Terrace); at three thirty the train left for Hamburg, and at eight thirty that evening Cresspahl carried his sleeping child home from Jerichow station. Cresspahl had much enjoyed the little trip; and, what was more, Lisbeth had got her way.

You went to see whether they had room for me there.

And it didn't turn out to be so, Gesine? Alexandra was four months younger than you, so you'd have had an advantage over her. She had the soft fair hair, you the dark, she would always have been considered the prettier and wouldn't have become jealous of you. With her you let yourself go as never at home; how you talked! With her you could live. And as for that shrimp Eberhardt, you could have ganged up with her against him. You should have drawn Christine to you. There was room for you there.

So why didn't you do it right away? Why did you wait so long?

I didn't want to do it. That didn't mean preparing the ground. I wanted to hold out if I could.

And suppose your sister hadn't been willing to take me?

She would have taken you from Cresspahl, Gesine. You are Father's daughter.

Rest comes not easily to him
Who once our Auntie Times displeased.

Once again Eartha Kitt has to defend herself for telling Johnson's wife that the war was a fundamental cause of the nation's criminality, and against the fact that this had brought tears to Mrs. Johnson's eyes. Miss Kitt still doesn't understand. As an actress, a Negro, whoever, she is entitled to her opinion, she said, particularly when it is asked of her. But the New York *Times* remains adamant and concludes by mentioning, not the telegrams that agree with Miss Kitt, but those intended to comfort the President's wife.

Well, Miss Kitt?

January 25, 1968   Thursday

The apartment is empty. The beds occupied by the Killainen children have vanished, even the television set has been returned by Mr. Robinson to his basement. All the furniture is back where it was two and a half weeks ago when the fatherless Fleury family descended upon us, some pieces slightly out of place. It is as if the family had never been here, were it not that in the warm air there hung a vestige of the perfume Annie used to cool her forehead. Can you explain it, Marie?

Marie thinks it happened like this: Annie didn't like to remain with us after she had read a letter not addressed to her. She cannot bear herself because the letter wasn't even hidden, making the breach of confidence all the greater. She can't bear to know that Mrs. Cresspahl must now believe that she has also figured in Annie's conversation with F. F. Fleury as a disagreeable person with nothing but Vietnam and the tormenting of children in her head. She can't get along with herself because she didn't like to stay until she had a chance to deny at least that.

Yesterday the President's wife was harassed between limousine and club entrance by youthful picketers carrying placards reading: WE SUPPORT EARTHA KITT. "The nation's First Lady pulled her mink coat around her, threw her head back, and made no response." She won't speak to people like that.

Try again, Marie. That's no explanation. O.K. then: Maybe Annie can't bear the knowledge that you didn't tell her the letter was from her husband. She knows she had no right to expect that, but she holds it against you that you have decided without consulting her what she may and may not be told about you. She holds it against herself that you're now going to regard her as a reader of other people's letters, but she didn't like to admit that she knows that you don't know that she knows. So then I had to get her a taxi from West End Avenue, and with all three children she drove off south down West End Avenue, and maybe then she did turn north. Is that clear?

The Foreign Office in Moscow gave an immediate rebuff to the United States request that the Soviet Union use its good offices with the North Korean authorities in connection with an intelligence ship. Deputy Foreign Minister Vasily V. Kusnetsov did not even accept the United States message for use as a memorandum for consideration by the Kremlin.

No. Can't you try again, Marie? If you insist: She holds it against you that, by saying nothing about the letter, you prevented her from consoling you. She would like to have told you that you're not as Fleury describes you. In particular that you're not perfect and had no such ghastly aspirations. Now she holds it against herself that she has put herself in a position where she can no longer say this. She holds it against you that you didn't even hide the letter. She holds it against herself that she's not the way you think she is. Now I can't understand it myself.

A young woman who was attacked by a man with a knife as she started to open her mailbox in her apartment building on 75th Street, while thirty yards away a policeman failed to hear her screams or the doorman's loud whistles, sums up the incident in one question: "If the police don't help a citizen here, what do they do in the slums?"

I suppose Annie said some things in Finnish, Marie. No: she was upset at having to wait because I got home late from school, so all I could actually gather was that she held it against you that you didn't want to advise her. She holds it against herself that she is doing it, although she knows that, after a letter like that, you could no longer talk about returning to Fleury's house. She holds it against you that you didn't even advise her against it, as if you knew it had already been decided. She can't bear herself because she is letting you think that she is going back not merely to Fleury's house but also to his opinions about you. She holds it against you that you didn't go with her to Vermont, and she holds it against herself that she would have used you to help in the house and to cope with her fear. And if you don't accept this eighty-five dollars without argument she never wants to see you again. But she likes you, and if you went to Vermont she'd like that too. She simply thought I wouldn't understand what she was saying and wouldn't be able to explain it. And what does it mean anyway?

And what are we to make of the fact that a straitlaced aunt such as the New York *Times* publishes an advertisement today for a studio where naked women can be photographed?

January 26, 1968   Friday

Yesterday evening, in the crowded bus terminal on Eighth Avenue, a man threw a nineteen-year-old coed to the ground on the landing of a staircase that led to the lower level, threatened her with a pistol, and prepared to rape her under the eyes of numerous spectators, who did not intervene. Then a man by the name of William Williams came along and freed the girl.

In April 1938 Wilhelm Brüshaver, Protestant pastor in Jerichow, heard his wife telling him that Lisbeth Cresspahl had said there was no place in Holy Writ where suicide was forbidden. Mrs. Brüshaver couldn't believe that; was it really true?

This occurred to Aggie Brüshaver at the moment her husband,

returning from visiting a sick parishioner, was putting down his muddy boots in the kitchen, and she asked him as the thought crossed her mind while she was doing the children's laundry, so that once beyond the door he had half forgotten it. He had his sermon to think about; he didn't even mean to be surly as he went off without answering.

Pastor Brüshaver had meanwhile taken to drafting his sermons on paper. Fridays and Saturdays he would sit writing by lamplight far into the night, and in the pulpit on Sunday mornings he would look gray, his face puffy, no longer speaking as one who has seen something and gives his account of it simply following the truth, but as if he doubted his recollection. It was not merely reading aloud his sermon that caused him to stumble; before many sentences he actually wondered whether he had sufficiently hedged them. There was at least one person in the congregation who took down his sentences not for himself but for others. Then one of the pleasant gentlemen from the Gneez Gestapo would turn up at his house, order coffee as if he were in a requisitioned inn, help himself from the cigars as if they had been offered, and inquire about the significance of the sermon on the penultimate Sunday before Easter. They were not satisfied with being told that in St. John, Chapter 8, Jesus really did rebuke the people for seeking to kill Him because He spoke the truth; they wished Brüshaver to explain which deaths he had been referring to. The fact was that he had been thinking vaguely of Methfessel the butcher, who on account of a few words had been beaten into imbecility in a prison camp, and of the executions being reported from Hamburg; he felt uneasy when he later managed to extricate himself by explaining that what was meant was Divine, not secular, truth; see verses 40 and 41.

He would have liked to be courageous, stand his ground. But he still hadn't recovered from not being allowed to open his son's coffin. He had not been permitted to have the body taken to the Lalendorf cemetery, where his first wife lay buried. And the funeral was not permitted to take place in Jerichow, it had to be at the Gneez cemetery, which meant that the cortege would be smaller; moreover, it turned out that not only the strangers in the cortege but also the pastor summoned from Berlin had been in the employ of the police. And it did Brüshaver no good to remind himself that he had sacrificed a son for the Fatherland. Not even the fact of having been an officer in the 1914–18 war kept him above suspicion. That did not prevent the visits of these gentlemen and their accusations concerning a call on Alfred Bienmüller, who had not wanted to have his son confirmed. Brüshaver had spoken to Bienmüller in the tone of one seeking information, and Bienmüller had politely placed the tongs on the fire and come to the front of the smithy to supply the answer. He didn't have the money, first of all. Secondly, not for that. Thirdly, the boy had been forbidden by his Hitler Youth to be confirmed. Was it possible that Bienmüller had subsequently filed a complaint of harassment? Or had Bienmüller talked about Brüshaver's visit, and someone listening, whose business it was not, had made it his business? The Monday after Palm Sunday, Bienmüller had been working in Creutz's hothouses, and his greeting over the pastor's fence had been perfunctory but not indicative of any complaint.

Now on the first Sunday after Easter, Chapter 20 in St. John was due. He could be satisfied with Mary, who was no longer allowed to touch Her son. But there was also Thomas, who wanted to see and touch the print of the nails in Jesus' hands before he was prepared to believe. And the writing down of the sermon in advance was no help either. Two people testifying against him would be proof of his having said what he did not say.

No ban on suicide in the Bible. He was willing to believe that this Lisbeth Cresspahl had read both books of Holy Writ from beginning to end. But how ridiculous, the sight of an ordinary layman's daughter, Cresspahl's wife, engaged in thorny theological questions. To be sure, Samson had pulled down the temple over himself as well as over the Philistines. Abimelech had seen to his own death in order to avoid the disgrace of being killed by a woman. Ahithophel and Judas had hanged themselves. See also Acts 16, 27; Revelation 9, 6. Simri burned himself to death, and it was declared a consequence of his sins against God.

Brüshaver ended up noting down such places instead of getting on with his sermon for April 24. He fell asleep over it, and by the time Aggie came after midnight to persuade him to go to bed he had forgotten what he had learned at the seminary: that suicide was not wicked in the eyes of men or for moral reasons; suicide was a falling away from God.

If Lisbeth had found out that there was this hurdle, it might not have occurred to her to climb over it.

January 28, 1968   Sunday

John Ramaglia, of 211 North 6 Street, Newark, announces by way of the *Times* that he needs the help of an attorney in a matter of life or death. His telephone is being tapped. Then he gives the number: (201) HU 5-6291.

At the Jerichow post office an observation list was pinned to the sorting shelves, to the continuing annoyance of Mr. Knewer, senior clerk, who had persisted in citing the professional ethics of a German postal official until Edgar Lichtwark hinted at dismissal from the service and loss of pension. When Knewer knuckled under, he was punished with demotion from the personnel department and was no longer even considered worthy of handling long-distance calls or registered mail, being now obliged to sit in the back room, stamping the outgoing mail and checking both it and the incoming mail for sender and addresses. His official telephone calls were now restricted to reporting to the Secret Police in Gneez whenever mail was received from or for a person under observation. Berthold Knewer put up very little resistance these days, as when he listened to Party Comrade Lichtwark with an attentiveness intended to express contempt at being forced to take orders from a person whom he regarded as a work-shy letter carrier from Berlin-Lichtenberg. Knewer looked like a parrot with ruffled feathers, the way he wrinkled his nose, and this earned him a nickname instead of the promotion now five years overdue. Actually, he was concerned with the principles underlying his position, and he would never have withheld, out of consideration for the addressee, any letter that he had been directed to submit for checking, particularly since he believed he was being watched by one of the two apprentices whom he now had to teach how to hold the stamp-hammer in such subtle balance that the Jerichow postmark would land fair and square on Hitler's head. In Knewer's eyes, however, mail surveillance remained a matter of professional secrecy, and it was with this that he dismissed Papenbrock's attempt to ask him why many letters were now taking two days to reach Hamburg.

Papenbrock was not on the list. Cresspahl was not on the list. Semig was, as sender, and at the sole instigation of Friedrich Jansen, to whom the political police were indebted for the favors he had done them. Jansen found Dora's first letters galling. The Jew was supposed to be having a hard time of it, and there he was comfortably ensconced with his wife in some place in Lower Austria where Jansen would never get to even for a vacation. They were staying at a country mansion, they could dine at a count's table. And the letter betrayed nothing. Dora uttered no word of thanks to Lisbeth Cresspahl for assistance rendered; and once again there was nothing to be proved against the Cresspahls. And Friedrich Jansen would have dearly liked to know what the Semigs had done with their money. He did not believe they had each crossed the frontier with ten marks in their pockets. Surely they must have owned more than house and stable and practice! When Jansen had wanted to take over the house he had found himself confronted by a furniture van, and the packers showed him some documents stamped in Schwerin according to which, in his disgusting smartness, the Jew had made over the property, including movable and immovable objects, to his wife's parents. Friedrich Jansen had made a rental offer to these high-and-mighty Kösters and was dismissed with two lines: the house had been leased for ten years to the Luftwaffe. He could not prove that Kollmorgen the attorney had found no young veterinarian in Erlangen for Semig's equipment. Whenever Jansen thought up a new chink, he would find it had just been stopped up; he felt himself to be positively under observation. Dora Semig wrote about deer in the snow, about snow-capped peaks, about soil conditions and alpine streams that tossed out "gravel and pebbles," of shopping trips to Vienna! Pebbles. And the non-Aryan left it to his wife to convey his greetings, thus depriving Jansen of any grounds for claiming that the Cresspahls were associating with Jews. The letter he started looking for on March 28, 1938, did not arrive.

The letter did not carry the foreign stamp for which Knewer had to watch; the stamp was a Greater German one, and the postmark was from Pirna and bore the obsolete message of "Your Vote for the Führer!" However, it was possible that this time Knewer had deliberately not been on the lookout, the sender having given her name as D. Köster and her address as Adolf Hitler Street in Radebeul. Lisbeth did not open this letter on its arrival but left it lying on the table for Cresspahl. Cresspahl, not she, was to read it aloud, although it was addressed to her, no longer to both.

So it was only during the first three weeks that the Semigs had had an easy time of it at Count Naglinsky's. After that Dora ceased to feel safe going into the village and cared only to go for walks in the woods, which Beatus had barred to outsiders. In the village Arthur had only been given work twice, then he was recognized as a Jew, and his wife too. "Which is true." She had been spat at. "In Austria they have a nose for it." Naglinsky had pretended to know nothing about it, and the evenings spent over records and discussing people like Galsworthy had become unbearable. The first week in March, Arthur gave up the position that had not been a position, and in his relief Naglinsky paid over their money to them although he had not yet picked up the equivalent in Germany (from "Raminsky," perhaps Baron von Rammin; that was only guesswork). In Vienna they had wasted almost too much time, because "my husband" could not make up his mind to go to France, and there were some rather ominous reports circulating about the Customs officials at the Swiss border. On March 10 she had finally managed to get him to Bratislava. Up until the last moment Arthur had put his faith in the Austrian plebiscite and the Treaty of Saint-Germain. True, the Czechs had let them enter their country, but "in Austrian fashion." All the reports from Vienna were true: the enthusiasm for the invasion, the looting of Jewish stores. One had only to look at photos of Jews being forced to clean the sidewalks with toothbrushes. As a city Prague had been more reasonable than Vienna. Dora was allowed to do mending and alterations for the rich émigrés, and Arthur had found a job as an orderly in a veterinary clinic. "We certainly don't need any help." The only problem was an address: again and again hotel rooms slipped through their fingers, maybe because "we are Jews," maybe because they had to economize. Arthur didn't want to learn Czech. The letter was dated the end of March, and it had taken over a month to get to Jerichow.

Lisbeth spoke of the guilt with which Dora Semig was trying to saddle her. Cresspahl had a talk with Kollmorgen, but even with two pairs of eyes they could not find a concealed address in the letter.

Whatever the letter to the Kösters—both in their late eighties—had contained, they had committed suicide in Schwerin with sleeping pills.

They were cremated secretly by the police, and no outsiders had been allowed to watch. In Jerichow it was said that the two coffins had been very small ones. In former years Privy Councilor Köster used to spend his vacations by the sea near Jerichow.

January 29, 1968   Monday

In the 20th Precinct, between 66th and 86th Streets on Manhattan's West Side, the following were reported by the inhabitants in ten months: 14 murders, 37 rapes, 552 robberies, 447 felonious assaults, 2,200 burglaries, 1,875 grand larcenies, and 371 auto thefts. These figures are incorrect. The numbers of rapes, burglaries, and felonious assaults are likely to be double or triple since many of the victims refrain from reporting them to the police, perhaps from fear, or lack of confidence.

Would a foreign visitor to Cresspahl in May 1938 have been able to notice that the country was in the hands of criminals?

Would Mr. Smith have noticed anything?

When Cresspahl thought back to the workshop yard with the elm tree in Richmond, his mind no doubt went to England and to a time when Lisbeth had still been enjoying her own life and a life with others; he also thought of Mr. Smith—of his small secretive face where the sawdust clung to the roughened creases, of the skinny, spry little man who spent his days in anticipation of the evening's drinking—if not as a friend yet nevertheless as of someone on whom he could count on the other side of the Channel with no need to exchange Christmas cards or letters. If he felt he would like Mr. Smith to come for a visit, it was not for any particular purpose, just so that someone like that would see what life was like these days in Jerichow, in Mecklenburg, in Germany. He would have been less concerned about conversations with Mr. Smith.

Mr. Smith as a tourist in foreign parts?

Mr. Smith in a dark suit, wearing a hat, not a cap, as a traveling subject of His Britannic Majesty, would not have looked poor or awkward. Mr Smith's eyes could gaze out so imperturbably that his cheap spectacles could have been a whim. The roughness of his complexion might have been caused by the sea wind. Surrounded by a foreign language he would have been more laconic than ever, and the Customs officials at the port of Hamburg would probably have taken him for a man of dignity. In their use of English he would still have heard courteous attention and respect for his country. And since Mr. Smith had the ability to forget himself, he would soon have noticed that his German fellow travelers, who had been treated as equals on board, were now treated with rudeness and suspicion by the officials, like escaped convicts who turn themselves in to their guards, but not with a light heart.

Mr. Smith would have said nothing about this in Jerichow; he would have been more likely to ask: What was all this about dogs? Was it a good idea to have a dog along with you when you traveled in Germany if you wanted to make sure of a friendly reception and good service? A foreigner doing his best to understand native customs.

Cresspahl, cheerful and relaxed about this kind of start to the visit, would have said: Quite, Mr. Smith. Oh, quite.

But Mr. Smith would have suspected a garden path up which even Cresspahl was not going to lead him, and along the beach promenade in Rande, as well as in Jerichow, he would have kept an eye on passers-by with dogs, wondering whether they represented that kind of German whom the English Cresspahl had not suggested.

Cresspahl was meanwhile taking care of someone else's dog, but he would have introduced it to Mr. Smith even more casually than the feline members of the family who were resting up in the wood shavings after their night's labors. He would have said: I'm just looking after the dog while its owner is away.

What would Mr. Smith have brought for Cresspahl's child? Something useful. Not exactly a pocket knife perhaps, but a sailor hat.

The child would have imperceptibly grown used to him because he would not have bothered her with questions or attempts to play, his presence marked only by a cautiously observant glance that was then swiftly concealed, as if this foreigner were embarrassed.

Lisbeth would have wanted to know all about George V's Jubilee procession through the streets of London on June 14, 1935, the outriders in their red tunics and the yellow-robed heralds with their fanfares, and finally the King in his red field-marshal's uniform, with his graying pointed beard, raising his hand in the military salute like an overworked machine, preoccupied, in the radiant summer weather and amid the crowds of citizens lining the streets, with his own death. From her searching questions Mr. Smith would have first thought that Mrs. Cresspahl was pining for her life in London. He would have done his best to ignore the hesitancy in her English and so would not have heard that in places where she was unsure she would sometimes use turns of speech to be found in the King James Bible.

Cresspahl as a tourist guide?

He would not have been allowed to take Mr. Smith to the Jerichow North area; but he could tell him about it. The number of inhabitants in Jerichow had dropped by at least four hundred since the construction battalion of the Luftwaffe had been transferred and the tidying and cleaning up of the construction site had been left to the local tradesmen. From the description of the barracks, from the quantity of housing that had been built for civilian employees, Mr. Smith would have had no difficulty in imagining an airfield whose uses went beyond mere weather observation. Nor would he have let on to his former employer that he preferred the work Cresspahl had done in England, when he had worked on the wood piece by piece instead of, as he now did, putting it together with powerful machines and a regular team; Mr. Smith would have decided to advance his departure.

Just as he saw Cresspahl do, Mr. Smith would have raised his hand when Storm Troopers marched by with a flag, and each time he would have glanced over his shoulder expecting to find everyone laughing at his gesture.

Then again he would have compared the flag that Cresspahl sometimes attached to the barn door with the one that was run up outside the house across from the property, a kitchen towel as against a bedsheet.

The evenings with these Cresspahls would hardly have gone down well with Mr. Smith. Some were more bearable. Then Mrs. Cresspahl would have her mending on the table, Cresspahl his cold coffee, and for the guest there would have been more than water. In May the sun did not set until after eight, and outdoors it stayed light a long time. By lamplight the boss's wife looked more like her thirty-two years than she did during the day, when she went through her housework like a machine, experienced and knowledgeable in every familiar procedure, nervous and erratic when a visit or delivery departed from the norm. Mr. Smith's initial shock at her appearance would have subsided at the sight of their behavior together, the tolerant, often teasing tone. In Mr. Smith's presence, that would have worked one more time. Mr. Smith would have adopted one end of the kitchen table and almost looked forward to going off to sleep and dream on the wings of "kümmel" and "Kniesenack," and would have plunged suddenly from his gentle flight at Lisbeth's resuming the topic of George V's death in January 1936 at Sandringham and suddenly darting out of the door, in tears. Mr. Smith would not have understood that. He would have compelled himself to plead fatigue.

Where would Mr. Smith have slept? On the leather sofa in Cresspahl's office, and Cresspahl once again beside his wife. There Mr. Smith would have found some Marine Sport cigarettes, and a bottle of schnapps, thoughtfully opened, so that the guest was provided for until long past midnight. He might have given some thought to marine sports, which in this country too were usually beyond the means of the average smoker.

During the solitary evenings with Cresspahl, when Lisbeth kept to her room after supper, they would have got into conversation. Mr. Smith, in his recent amazement over German greeting customs, would have recalled that George VI had been horribly shocked when the German ambassador had shot up his outstretched arm right under the King's nose. Brickendrop they called him, because he was forever putting his foot in it. And George VI had a hard enough time of it as it was, what with his stammer.

And no, Cresspahl would have said. It is to be hoped that Cresspahl would have talked about the seven Mecklenburg clergymen

who in 1938 were either in jail or in prison camps. It is to be hoped
that Cresspahl would have said something about the dog that slunk
around the yard, still confused and lost, still unwilling to adopt a
permanent sleeping place. That was the dog called King, whose name
had been Rex in the days when his job had been to guard the home
and yard of a Jewish veterinarian in Jerichow, an animal that had lost
its master. If only Cresspahl had told his guest the story from the
beginning up to its most recent ending.

And yet: Mr. Smith might have answered. All that prosperity.

And no, Cresspahl would have said. He would put the number
of ruined tradesmen's businesses in Germany at over 50,000. And
that now every tradesman had to pay compulsory insurance pre-
miums, it looked as if the Government even wanted to make money
out of those bankruptcies. And even now it was impossible to get
steel frames for machinery because the Government had been so
greedy in gobbling them up wherever it could; just let Mr. Smith try
and imagine a rough plane on a wooden frame.

Yes, I can see that, Mr. Smith might have replied, tucking away
the information behind that low, lined forehead without betraying
whether, once inside, it became lost or hidden. Would have
smoothed the parting of his graying black hair with eight fingertips,
pushed his cheap spectacles closer to his eyes, and gone off to bed
without giving Cresspahl a chance to stop him. For Mr. Smith skillfully arranged his departures to look like consideration for others.

Mr. Smith would not have stayed long in Jerichow. For, if it had
been May 1938, the Germans had already marched up to the Czechoslovak frontier, and the Government of Czechoslovakia had proclaimed partial mobilization, and Mr. Smith was needed by his
detachment if his Government were to keep its promises to the
Czechs and the Slovaks.

Once again Mr. Smith would have been seen standing at a
second-class window in the milk train, a stunted, wizened figure who
removes his hat to reveal a narrow face sufficiently impassive to
conceal distress at leaving or relief that the visit is over.

And where would Mr. Smith have found the money for a dark
suit, a hat, new shoes with still unscuffed toecaps? Who would have
paid for these things?

(It wouldn't have been Mrs. Trowbridge.)

And what aim and object would Mr. Smith have found in
Jerichow anyway? What food for thought did it offer?

Nevertheless, even he would have noticed something.

January 30, 1968   Tuesday

Here we have Mr. Weiszand. Dmitri, who so often offers us his first name so that he can say: Gesine. "Gesine," he says, planting himself so bulkily in the midst of the herd of pedestrians as they start across to the south side of 96th Street that it is not easy to get past him. "Gesine," he says, and we are certainly glad to interpret his surprise, his warm smile, as pleasure at the encounter; but he runs into Mrs. Cresspahl quite often on Broadway, and more often than not the meeting is limited to three words about the weather and Marie's school. "Jezinnay," he says, it's not likely he will ever learn to cloak his Polish-Russian linguistic heritage in American, he is liable to embrace Mrs. Cresspahl in front of store windows and passers-by, as one Slav to another, for in his eyes Mecklenburg is Slavic. Better to pull him into Charlie's Good Eats for fifteen minutes over a cup of coffee and whatever else he has on his mind. Hi, Charlie!

Right, Charlie. It's certainly damp weather. Black coffee, this morning's. Would you mind calling Marie and telling her I'm held up here? This is Mr. Weiszand. Professor Weiszand? O.K., not Professor, then. So this gentleman in the short-sleeved butcher's jacket, he of the nimble forearm, the face of a theologian under the severe brush-cut, is New York's Champion Buckwheat Pancake Maker, Charles Charlie himself.

This was not what was preoccupying Mr. Weiszand. He obviously considers it more pressing to tell Mrs. Cresspahl confidentially that she is looking ill. Not ill exactly, but tired, overworked, with lackluster eyes. What a way to begin, Mr. Weiszand!

Hard work, Mrs. Cresspahl?

Just work.

What kind of work is it anyway, Mr. Weiszand would like to know, his head so firmly propped on his wrist, looking so devoted, so solicitous, as if he really wanted to hear that Miss C., bank employee, rides the subway from here for ten minutes as far as Times Square and from there for another five to Grand Central and, just before nine, after a twelve-minute walk, removes her typewriter cover, five days a week until 5 P.M., up until this very moment in fact, when she is still prevented from going home, Mr. Weiszand. It is an IBM golf-ball typewriter, in case that was it.

That wasn't it.

And why are you growing a beard from ear to ear, Mr. Weiszand?

If Mr. Weiszand is to be believed, he is not growing his beard for a bet; it is unhappiness that is causing the red stubbly fuzz to sprout. In order not to hear more about that, we will throw our job of foreign-language correspondent at him as food for thought. Well?

German, French, Italian—?

And American, and English, Mr. Weiszand.

He fails to see why a bank should employ someone for such a job. He drinks a little of Charlie's black coffee, puts down the cup, puzzled, adds sugar, tries it again, puts it down with a shake of his head. It's a mystery to him.

The coffee?

The bank.

Mrs. Cresspahl writes to a French credit company in French, conveying her employer's wishes. To an Italian company she writes in—

As a courtesy?

As a service, Mr. Weiszand.

And you mean to say that the psychological gains offset the salaries—?

It's not exactly a business secret, merely that it's not the person doing the work who knows that but the person who profits by it. Ask my superior, Mr. Weiszand.

De Rosny, Vice-President. Mr. Weiszand states this casually in order to keep the ball rolling, he has not noticed that he has betrayed an item of knowledge.

Not De Rosny. A vice-president and a secretary—! No, the department heads for Italy and France, less often for West Germany. In West Germany they have already mastered the American language.

And is there no one to check Mrs. Cresspahl's phraseology?

There had been a Miss Gwendolyn Bates, Vassar 1918, rescued from the Depression and the marriage market by the bank, so devoted to the bank that she made work for herself where none existed. Liked to summon the translators to her office and with long pencil and raised wrist draw strokes through the French that had not been spoken in her day, not maliciously, merely from a sorrowing urge to dominate. Then one day at a conference in Bern she insisted too stubbornly on her own phraseology, all for the good of the firm, and on her departure was presented with the President's Silver Medal, and no banquet. Now living with relatives in Colorado, writes proud, nostalgic letters. She still hasn't learned that we can manage without her, and the Scandinavian and Spanish sections too. If you should ever go to Denver, Mr. Weiszand, take Federal Highway 25 for Pueblo, turn left at Greenland—

That's not what Mr. Weiszand is after. Doesn't Mrs. Cresspahl speak Russian too?

Oh come now, Weiszand. Our class had six years of Russian, and in the entire town there wasn't a single Russian we were allowed to speak to. They were quartered behind high green fences, the officers never used public transport, and if an ordinary soldier climbed over the boards and all he was after was a bottle of schnapps—

Mr. Weiszand knows that. Whenever a fact can be understood or misunderstood as being anti-Communist, he forestalls it with a brief, curt nod, feigning agreement and administering a rebuke. And does he want to hear again that this New York bank is not hungry for business with the Soviet banks in Europe but would rather wait until it was approached by them, whether it was the Vokshod in Zürich, the Moscow Narodni in London, or the Banque Commerciale pour l'Europe du Nord in Paris? The firm's policy in this regard cannot be described as aggressive; repeat: not aggressive.

But surely in regard to Czechoslovakia? Mr. Weiszand is still leaning back in his chair as comfortably as ever, his gaze amiable, childlike, good will, co-operation, and warmth written all over his face. He has heard about Mrs. Cresspahl's Czech lessons with Mr. Kreslil, innocently enough through our Mrs. Ferwalter, his sole motivation is sympathetic interest, a desire for the truth, among friends a right.

My trip to Prague this summer will be a private one; that's all, Mr. Weiszand.

Mr. Weiszand finds it exceedingly thorough to learn an entire language just for a vacation. He still can't be accused of pestering her; except that his gaze has become a shade more attentive, almost triumphant.

If you were no longer allowed to go to your own country and had to meet your old friends in a foreign one, and for three weeks wanted to understand what was going on around you—what would you do, Mr. Weiszand?

Mr. Weiszand would learn any language you care to name if that would enable him to get a friend out of Poland. But he had been brought up short, for an instant his guard had been down. The solicitous expression in his eyes was wiped out, as with a liar caught in the act, so that it takes him a while to get going again with nods and ponderous breathing and the conveying of his admiration. Thinks it's wonderful of her.

That wasn't put into words.

Mr. Weiszand insists that he had understood everything, desires nothing less than a handshake, in his embarrassment wallows helplessly in compliments, says he has made a mistake, thinks Mrs Cresspahl looks the very picture of health tonight. "Jezinnay," he says.

Here we have Mrs. Cresspahl, tired, not enjoying her work, eyes lackluster, a bit deafened by the long-winded detailed conversation going on between Charlie and his customers, cheerful broad-shouldered men who were downing their meal as deliberately as if they had just got out of bed and had all day ahead of them. The voluptuous skill with which Charlie turns his steaks and hamburgers on the charcoal grill, the spicy smell of broiling, the companionable warmth, it is all very far away. She can hardly endure the five minutes that pass before Mr. Weiszand strides off alone on Broadway into the damp twilight, equipped with a magnificent trenchcoat of British design, his high bald forehead raised in brooding annoyance, on his way to his sociological studies, not those of international finance, a man given to emotional greetings and good-bys, a friend who has become unrecognizable.

"What did Dmitri want?" asks Marie, who has been waiting at the swimming pool below the Hotel Marseilles, disguised in her tight-fitting white cap.

"Has he found some more Nazis in West Germany?"

"No. What was bothering him was that out of every dollar in the national budget 13 cents go for education and social projects while 14 are spent on the Vietnam war and 43 on defense."

"He'll soon be organizing another demonstration at Columbia," says Marie, taking her key from her wrist, throwing it into the water, and diving in after it in one smooth oblivious movement.

We apologize, Mrs. Cresspahl.
I'm not concerned with finesse.
But we are, Gesine, and we wouldn't have started off like that.
And if I'm mistaken?
Then you've made a mistake, Gesine.

The photograph of Senator J. W. Fulbright in the New York *Times* shows a serious, thoughtful man who knows what he is asking. Now he wishes also to summon Secretary of Defense McNamara before the Foreign Relations Committee with the question: whether those destroyers in the Gulf of Tonkin three and a half years ago had been attacked, if at all, by North Vietnamese vessels because they were on an intelligence mission and zigzagging in and out of nonterritorial waters. He may receive no other reply than that at the time it would have been possible to avoid the war in which today American troops have to attack their own embassy in Saigon because it has been occupied by Vietcong.

Friedrich Jansen, in referring to the theft of the Sudetenland, called his Führer a statesman of genius, and Cresspahl agreed with him.

My father was not joking. Whenever he pulled anyone's leg, that person was supposed not only to notice but to enjoy being made a fool of, so they could share in the fun. In the case of this local Party leader and Mayor it would have been a waste of time; he had no desire to be on such terms, or any terms, with him. In 1938 Friedrich Jansen had been Mayor of Jerichow for five years, and Cresspahl had been observing him long enough. He would have described him as a pig. Not in any metaphorical sense, simply on the basis of physical similarity. Take Jansen's long pink body, covered with whitish hairs, take the heavy thighs, pudgy rather than massive, the thick arms, handsome at first sight, soft of muscle at second, and over the whole body the tender nervous fat accumulated in thirty-five years devoid of any real hard work. That was not enough for Cresspahl to call him a pig; perhaps he did not want to waste the Mecklenburg word on him. He called him by his full name, with a certain solemnity. That way he could do the representative of the Hitler party more harm, and at less expense.

The usual German misuse of the animal's name would not have been unbecoming to Party Comrade Jansen, even if Cresspahl only wanted to count what he would have to put up with and face from him. Take the kidskin notebook he was so fond of trotting out, the one he now and again opened up and showed to his drinking pals: by this time the notes in it under the letter C had consumed half the section for D, although there was only one other name in Jerichow that began like Cresspahl's. Take the zealous reports to the Gestapo headquarters in Gneez about which Cresspahl learned not only from questions but also from warnings. Take Jansen's speech on May 1, 1938, in which he said that Jerichow must be cleansed not only of Jews but also of the friends of Jews. Take the hypocritical inquiries about the application to join the Party that Cresspahl had requested three years earlier for one of his workmen, and still not for himself. There was not even hostility, there were merely petty attempts to trip him up for the sake of the attempts, and there were times when Cresspahl was glad he was a head shorter than Jansen. That way he did not have to look into those innocent, unsteady eyes, could look away from that large, unformed, pleasantly ruddy face, and only his ears needed to endure that hearty pompous manner. In Jansen's case, Cresspahl did not even stop to wonder why he found him so repulsive.

He did not even give Friedrich Jansen credit for sparing neither voice nor emotion in publicly proclaiming his faith; Cresspahl regarded that as life insurance. If the time should ever come for Jansen when he would have barely enough to eat for a week, no liquor to drink, and with the possibility of having to dig with spade and bowed back, Jansen would soon be finished. Whether or not Jansen suspected that in 1933 he had been rescued by the skin of his teeth from a life of starvation wages or the workhouse, he would now no longer have been able to do without his new life, with breakfast shortly before noon, office hours of his own choosing, joyrides and drunken nights. Even the knowledge taught him by his civic office would be of no use to him. He had no conception of how the various municipal departments were dovetailed, what the town could have recouped for its taxes from provincial government and regional administration, what, with a plan, he could have garnered for Jerichow out of the airfield construction; the department was run by the civil servants whom Dr. Erdamer had trained, and for the time being Friedrich Jansen managed well enough with his notion that it was enough to have cronies in the right places and that all the rest would look after itself. So far it had. And Cresspahl was convinced that the fat fellow was scared of the war he was always carrying on about. On his return from a stint of voluntary military training during which, instead of being able to rest up behind the front, he had had to hoist his bulky person hurriedly over high walls, he was for a few days as friendly as if asking for sympathy. What an ordeal it had been. In military matters he was ignorant of all save one item: when giving reconnaissance instruction to his Storm Troopers in the Gneez municipal park, he could plant himself with legs wide apart and call that one yard.

That's the way I saw him, legs straddled, behind sticking out, bending forward from the hips, while a subordinate measured the distance between his brown boots with a yardstick. No doubt about it, that was one yard, and Jansen was once again free to raise his crimsoned head.

Lisbeth would say: Friedrich, as if of a child who never learns and is forever getting itself in a mess; and sometimes: Friederich, after an irredeemably wicked figure in a children's book. The Cresspahl child knew the lines about that terrible villain by heart, yet without being afraid of him. Whenever Lisbeth recited them, it seemed to the child to be about a puffed-up fellow who never achieved anything in spite of all his threats and flailing around.

When the Semigs left the country, Friedrich Jansen had wanted to buy the dog which the Jew used to keep in his yard. Stood outside Cresspahl's gate, sweating in the sharp sea wind, as guileless as you please. On his refusing to believe that the dog was merely in Cresspahl's care, Cresspahl whistled for King. The dog came running out from behind the house, dashed across the yard, sat down beside Cresspahl, and looked up at him, not yet in blind devotion but friendly enough and prepared to obey. He was six years old, sturdy of body, swift, strong, and equipped with nice shiny white teeth. "Well, Rex?" said Jansen, on the other side of the fence, in a veritable falsetto of bonhomie. The dog parted its jaws slightly, just enough to allow a warning growl to escape, and gazed alertly at the stranger. "Rex!" said Jansen reproachfully, and again his voice went too high, cracking on the vowel. Since Cresspahl did not move, the dog growled again in its hearty bass voice but remained sitting. Now Jansen wanted more than ever to become the owner of this perverted creature which had betrayed the Aryan race to Jews, and Cresspahl was obliged to sell it—too soon to suit the child—to an engineer from Berlin who had also taken a fancy to it. When the dog was safely away and living in a garden in Grunewald, Jansen returned and demanded to see at least the pedigree, and Cresspahl told him again that the animal had been only temporarily in his care. So many questions proliferated simultaneously in Jansen's head that all he could get out was: "I just thought—"

He did not exactly wish to be abusive. He had become Cresspahl's neighbor. The Jew's house had remained just as much out of his reach as the Jew's dog; for five years he had had to live in Dr. Erdamer's house on the Rande road as a tenant, now at last he was in the brickyard residence, one of the most respected houses in town because it had been remodeled by a Schwerin banker, before the turn of the century, as a dwelling, a roomy, handsome enough edifice, under a coat of thick white paint, with generous windows, unusually high garden gates, and an immaculate tiled roof. It was in front of this house that Friedrich Jansen now hoisted the flag bearing the Indian good-luck symbol.

With the villa went the brickyard, and the Van Zelcks had sacrificed the property merely in order to satisfy the heirs to a disputed inheritance by converting it into cash. That was their story. During the years following Paepcke's lease, orders had declined because by that time almost all the brick buildings needed by Greater Germany for the war had been completed, and anything left over was planned in concrete. They did not tell Friedrich Jansen this. Jansen derived little more ownership from the villa than the title deed, so much room being taken up by mortgages, and in order to acquire the brickyard he had had to enlist the help of some Party comrades, for, as much as he would have liked to make a fortune from his political office, he lacked the brains to do so. Now he spent his evenings poring over figures extracted for him from the ledgers by his trustee, and found them depressing, and thought anxiously of his pals. Old Mr. Jansen, an attorney in Gneez, had accepted the fact that in 1933 his son Friedrich had expressed contempt and similar filial harshness to his father for the latter's mistrust of the new rulers, and the old man refused even to discuss the Jerichow Party leader, let alone listen to any appeal for help from him. But a sociable get-together at harvest-time, with festive lighting and Party cronies cheek by jowl around the trestle tables on the noble lawn, with songs and shooting contests and toasts until after midnight: there was no doing without that.

The Von Bobziens (the same family who refused to put their Gräfin Forest at the disposal of the Storm Troopers for their maneuvers) owned a stud bull by the name of Friedrich der Grosse. This was the way the animal was listed in the official livestock records and, since the regional cattle-breeding department had raised no objection to the name, Friedrich Jansen could do nothing about it. The Bobziens were happy to display the animal, even when the visitor did not bring along a cow in heat. It was a great hefty beast, sluggish and cunning, a bit too torpid of eye. "The way bulls are."

This fellow Jansen recalled two movie reviews which during his student days he had been allowed to submit as specimens, and spoke of "brilliant stage management" when enumerating the various phases of the Czech crisis in his high, officious voice. It was here that Jansen was heard to call his leader a statesman of genius, while for

Cresspahl the Führer was someone with whom he had no contact, who stole the shirt off his back, who would never think of *his* good but always of the good of the state, an out-and-out enemy. And so he said, to Friedrich Jansen's delight: That's something everyone has to admit, whether they like it or not.

Then he walked on a few steps, turned, and such was his hold over Jansen by now that the latter not only re-emerged from his front garden but positively ran after him. Cresspahl had one more philosophical question. The territorial gains also included human beings, didn't they, more than five million of them? Jansen spoke of a liberated border-people and so on, at great length, although he had been just about to set off for his morning-after beer. Cresspahl refused to be sidetracked. There were other countries, weren't there, countries with German-speaking citizens, like Brazil or Switzerland: how did Jansen suggest that they were going to become part of Greater Germany?

"Switzerland," said Friedrich Jansen. "We'll take care of them too!"

February 1, 1968   Thursday

Mrs. Anne Deirdre Curtis, a slender woman five feet one, was seen yesterday about 4 P.M. by a neighbor when she returned from her grocery shopping with her thirteen-weeks-old child. When her husband, a twenty-seven-year-old medical student, returned to the apartment, 297 Lenox Road, Brooklyn, at six thirty, he found his wife sprawled on the bed, covered with blood, and dressed only in a blouse and bra. The towel with which she had been strangled was wrapped around her neck. Marks on her wrist indicate that she had been bound. Around the body lay broken glass and a smashed clock. In the opinion of the police, Mrs. Curtis defended herself before being raped and killed. The baby lay unharmed in its carriage. The carriage also contained the bag of groceries.

February 2, 1968   Friday

There must be plenty of new arrivals at the Hotel Marseilles who get a shock when, after finally getting into the elevator, they are taken, bag and baggage, not up but down into the basement, simply because among the passengers there is one whom the man at the controls wishes to put off down below and of whom he takes leave in a decidedly practiced manner. He addresses her as Mrs. Cresspahl, mentions a child in the pool, and only then closes the elevator doors and starts the journey to the floors above ground.

From the wicket at the entrance to the Mediterranean Swimming Club, a dry corridor, carpeted in green felt, leads past some freshly varnished benches to the "Women's Area." The door shuts tightly, and beyond it damp air envelops the prospective swimmer like a second skin. A lot of noise is enclosed here, the sound of flowing and slapping water, the shouts of children in the pool, casual conversations over the partitions, and murmuring beyond the white walls of the sauna. How had it been in Germany—had they walked about naked in the dressing room so uninhibitedly, schoolgirls, matrons, and old ladies alike, eyeing one another under the hissing showers, with occasional praise for a bosom or a word of comfort for a still red operation scar? It is forgotten. Forgotten. How had it been?

"What you don't know you'll leave out, and I won't be a bit the wiser," says Marie mildly. She is squatting on the stone bench under the clock, her knees drawn up under her chin, pleasantly tired, preoccupied. She has already been in the water for half an hour. But she still keeps gliding from her crouching position to dive in a lizard's leap from the edge of the pool the moment an eight-yard lane opens up in front of her, turns around as her head emerges, and keeps the diving space free for her mother. She goes back at once to the bench, and each time the conversation goes on as if there had been no interruption. The bench is safely out of earshot of the other swimmers, and Marie condescends to speak German.

"What you don't know in your story you fill up with other stuff, and I believe it anyway," she says.

"I never promised to tell the truth."

"Of course not. Only your truth."

"The way I imagine."

"Gesine, there are some things you do know."

"Like Friedrich Jansen's straddled yard. But I don't know why my memory has stored that up. Why not some other sight, a more meaningful exchange of words?"

"The cat called Memory, as you say."

"Right. Independent, incorruptible, intractable. And yet a comfortable companion, when it puts in an appearance, even if it stays out of reach."

"In September 1938 you were . . . five and a half."

"And by the time I was eighteen I had forgotten what I never wanted to lose and retained what I have no use for. The way Cresspahl clears his throat, and not the things he said."

"What Cresspahl did in '51, wouldn't it have to match the Cresspahl of '38?"

"More or less, Marie."

"Who can decide that better than you?"

"Let's go in the pool."

"I don't mind knowing that the only thing you're sure of is the way Friedrich Jansen stood in the Gneez municipal park and that the rest of the story gradually grew from that. I'd just like to know how you do it."

"Although Jansen's story is merely a possibility?"

"It's a possibility that only you can think up. Whatever you imagine of your past must in the end be reality."

"You're calling the shot, Marie."

"Right. How do you do it?"

"Water butt—"

"Attempted murder."

"The dog Rex, and what Cresspahl said after the war about Dr. Semig—"

"The Semigs' emigration."

"Books, you know."

"Old movies. The exhibition at the Jewish Museum."

"Letters from Kliefoth."

"Yes. But are you stealing from the present year too?"

"No."

"The rain in January '68, you haven't used that. All those fires in Harlem—"

"Marie, if I need a burning building for 1938 I don't have to borrow it from New York."

"But the airplane with the hydrogen bomb which the Air Force lost near Greenland eleven days ago? That same day you told about plane crashes near Podejuch, about enormous craters."

"The story's in the family, Marie. It was never forgotten because of the rocket tests in Peenemünde, later."

"But the way Cresspahl's child pulled itself around the kitchen table by hanging on to the edge with its raised hands until it could walk by itself, you got that from other children, not yourself."

"From a child whom I knew personally."

"And what else from today?"

"The things I couldn't see then. Things I never learned and have to catch up with. Take today's pictures from Saigon in the New York *Times*—"

"Don't start that again!"

"No, I don't want to pester you about the war. I'm just trying to answer you."

"Which pictures? The one showing the officer coming out of the house carrying the body of his child that's been shot?"

"No. The series."

"The execution."

"(The murder. I don't want any argument.) I mean that series of events in three stages. The first picture shows a young man being led off by a marine. His hands are behind him, bound maybe. He looks as if he's off work, because of his checked shirt and because he's wearing it outside his pants. His mouth is open, as if he were talking earnestly but not angrily to the soldier, who has turned his face in a friendly manner toward him, although it's overshadowed by his helmet. The American seems to be leading him by the arm, rather than forcing him. According to the caption, this is a Vietcong officer, and he'd been carrying a pistol. Number One."

"Number Two."

"Caption: 'Execution.' On the left stands a man, seen from behind in profile, in what is obviously not a civilian vest, his shirt-sleeves rolled up. This is Brigadier General Nguyen Ngoc Loan, South Vietnam's police chief, and in his outstretched right arm he is holding a revolver a hand's breadth from the prisoner's temple. The prisoner is still upright, but his head is tilted toward his left shoulder, his eyes are half closed, his mouth is gaping like a wound. Otherwise the head appears intact. Hands behind him, doubtless bound. 'The prisoner's face shows the impact of the bullet.' Number Two."

"Number Three."

"The victim is lying in the road, his bare legs at a crazy angle. The Brigadier General is holding open the holster at his belt with his left hand, with the other he is putting away the weapon. He is not looking at the dead man, he is gazing at the ground before him, as if mentally reviewing the incident. In the background, store fronts and, unexpectedly, a man in American uniform, disguised by sunglasses, who has stopped in his tracks and turned part-way around, but not as if he intended to intervene. After all, the man had been handed over to the Brigadier General."

"I know all that, Gesine."

"No. I've never seen a man being shot. The second picture shows the prisoner's moment of death."

"If someone gets shot in your story, you won't have to describe it to me now, Gesine."

"It can happen differently, Marie."

"But if you have someone shot in your story, I'll know what you're thinking about, and I'll think that too. Is that what you wanted?"

"Partly."

"O.K. Now will you show me the dolphin dive again?"

"Now I'll show you the dolphin dive again."

February 3, 1968   Saturday, South Ferry Day

"What did Cresspahl look like in September 1938?"

"Age: fifty. Height: six feet two. From a distance, erect posture; close up, drooping shoulders; a defect caused by work or discouragement. Longish skull, full head of hair still—coarse, iron-gray, crinkly. His expression when silent: so imperturbable that the impression of attentiveness can hide all other expression; when talking or working: directed at the matter in hand, severe, speculative, acute. Color of eyes: light blue to gray to green. Lips no longer slightly protruding, as in the early 1930's, tightly closed, making them look thin. Deep, heavy creases on either side of his mouth. Mouth expressing no expectation, merely vigilance now, a slight disgust. Yet still unsuspecting. Clothing: usually blue mechanic's overalls, in the workshop wooden clogs. His age was at one time known as "the best years of one's life.""

"Gesine, I mean: what did he look like!"

February 5, 1968   Monday

One day, when the city was blanketed by snow, De Rosny conducted some West European visitors through two floors of the bank and stopped outside Miss Cresspahl's cubicle, saying: All we need is a few wolves, and we'll look just like your native country!

Miss Cresspahl had remained seated, since she was being merely shown, not introduced, to the visitors, and she politely made up some story for his benefit about foxes exchanging good nights near Beidendorf, and right up until noon she was refreshed by the ideas entertained by the Vice-President about a Communist country in general, and about Mecklenburg in general.

Today he sympathized with Miss Cresspahl because in yesterday's newspaper he had seen a picture of West 97th Street, a collection of full garbage cans with bags of refuse piled on top of them, results of the city sanitation strike. He does not know that in our quarter, besides the neglected buildings, there still remain those whose management looks after the burning of tenants' garbage. No doubt he drives into town along shut-off freeways, and knows no more than an eighth of it. This amusing skepticism as to the omniscience of her highest superior must not, despite its tension-relaxing qualities, find form or voice. Miss Cresspahl has been summoned for a report.

A person finding himself in De Rosny's office has a feeling of being in an apartment building rather than above roomfuls of typewriters closely surrounded by cubicle after cubicle containing people shut up with their work. For his own office in the bank, De Rosny has created a spacious living room, the Danish sofa next to the captain's writing desk from sailing-ship days, intimate lighting from green-and-gold lampshades, heavy royal-blue curtains facing the patio. In the midst of all this, De Rosny moves around like a guest in a hotel, lounging about as if in almost foreign surroundings, ready to be called away at a moment's notice, with unshakable confidence in his directives. He likes to conceal his directives, by temporizing if need be. The weather-beaten face, comfortably relaxed, the leisurely blue gaze, this is how he feigns invitation and welcome, speaking not only of the effects of the garbage workers' strike on the Upper West Side but also of the Vietnamese war, so as to make his subordinate believe that he is even prepared to take an interest in what he regards as one of her obsessions.

De Rosny has watched the shooting of a bound suspect by Brigadier General Nguyen Ngoc Loan on television and declares himself finally converted to Mrs. Cresspahl's opinion. (She has not expressed any opinion.) The basic brutality of war. And, he goes on, when one sees on the screen what the Vietcong is up to, and hears that Washington declares the offensive to have been a failure, the credibility gap is not exactly diminished.

That's right, Mr. De Rosny. That's what the New York *Times* says too. And about the work assigned to me—

When one got right down to it, the *Times* was in fact against the continuation of the war. De Rosny is not inclined to relinquish the steering of the conversation, shakes his head incredulously and at length, and anyone wishing to make a guess would see him finally arriving at the conclusion that Miss Cresspahl was genuinely concerned over the Vietnam affair. Has come across similar remarks that very morning on the last but one of the seventy pages. What had Mrs. Cresspahl been going to say?

In regard to the Czechoslovak Government, it seemed that the cat had at least got its tail out of the bag, and that possibly a person by the name of Dmitri Weiszand was trying to catch it, sir.

"Well now!" said De Rosny, in a gratified voice, as if at a plan that had worked. All of a sudden he ceased to be the expert host, he was a hunter choosing his next trap, with narrowed eyes, a crafty frown. "Thank you," he said solemnly, repeating it with something like emotion, but he remained seated, lost in thought, massaging his temples with his knuckles. The secretary who brought in the coffee set out the tray and its contents as quickly as possible, hurrying out again through the door as if escaping from an embarrassing or unseemly scene.

And then De Rosny said:

"You'll never guess, D. E."

"That he knew all along, Gesine."

"Yes. Squirming in his chair, embarrassed in spite of himself, and thanking me—"

"Because you volunteered the information."

"I let him believe that, but—"

"—first of all Miss Cresspahl stands right up to him, as well as she can while sitting down: she refuses to be under surveillance! At the very least she must be told; she has a right; she has half a mind—etc., etc."

"I managed quite well sitting down, D. E."

"And he was enjoying himself."

"You're guessing!"

"No, Gesine. I've been an employee myself for quite a few years too; I have to live with bosses just as you do."

"Now you're going to tell me you're better at that too."

"When did Weiszand try to see the cat, Gesine?"

"On Tuesday. Six days ago."

"From what you've told me of De Rosny, I'd have imagined him quicker."

"Why won't you have anything to do with the men I tell you about, D. E.? Like F. F. Fleury, D. W. Weiszand, De Rosny?"

"You would feel you were being watched, Gesine."

"No."

"No."

"The long, long leash, D. E."

"Does De Rosny think it's true?"

"Do you?"

"You yourself have called the Council for Mutual Economic Assistance a kindergarten, Gesine. Is the kindergarten teacher going to like it if one of the children suddenly wants to keep a cat? Isn't the International Bank for Economic Co-operation in Moscow at least going to want to know whether the Czechoslovak Government wants to borrow secretly in the States?"

"Yes. But it can't happen to me."

"Well, what did happen to you when you were with NATO at Mönchen-Gladbach?"

"That was a personal affair, D. E.!"

"And how did you get that job?"

"Through an ad in the *Frankfurter Allgemeine Zeitung*, D. E."

"In 1955?"

"In 1955, D. E. And now we're here in New York. In 1968."

"Exactly."

"This Weiszand is a sociologist, D. E.!"

"That makes no difference, Gesine."

"A Pole, a Jew, whom the Soviets kept sitting on the farthest bench at school before handing him back to the Germans for the concentration camps, why should he lift a finger for the Soviet Union?"

"He doesn't have to like what he's doing."

"Now you're going to start in on the psychology of the traitor, Professor."

"No. On the hypothesis that personal misfortune doesn't count against the victory of socialism."

"Dmitri Weiszand is not going to betray me."

"It need not be called betrayal. Perhaps he wishes to do you a good turn."

"'Any person organizing demonstrations against the Vietnam war is an agent of Soviet economic espionage.' I must say, your equations used to be more polished, D. E."

"I didn't know about his connections with Vietnam, Gesine."

"You consider it possible."

"According to your stories, Gesine."

"That De Rosny is having me watched."

"He'll talk about protection, and not mean you but his investment."

"Oh no. Not again."

"Hand in your notice. Take the child and come and live with me."

"That'll be the day. You'll eat your words, D. E."

"What would De Rosny say if you quit?"

"I can't do that now, D. E."

"He invited you to dinner."

"To the Brussels."

"Brown damask on the walls, soft light, Waterzooi de Volaille à la Gantoise. But that's not where the bankers go."

"Selle d'Agneau Rôti à la Sarladaise, D. E."

"From a distance you must have looked like lovers. D. W. Weiszand can now come to this conclusion too—that you'll be promoted, on trial, two floors up, to a newly inaugurated desk called not 'Czechoslovak Republic' but 'General Contacts,' with a phone number not listed in the house directory. Mrs. Cresspahl as a protégée."

"But you'd let me out on loan, Erichson."

"You'd be loaning yourself, Gesine."

"Would that be so bad? After all, this time it would be a socialist system that would be getting aid."

"No."

"Well then."

"And it won't work, Gesine."

"We'll see about that."

"It's a deal. And if it fails and you come out of it in one piece, you'll marry me."

"A bet?"

"A bargain."

"If this doesn't work either, I give up, D. E."

"That's not the way I want it."

"You have to take me the way I am."

"I'm the proverbial bad penny, Gesine. I'll always be around."

"Good night, D. E."

"I really mean it."

February 6, 1968   Tuesday

In West Germany there is a millionaire who was simultaneously a member of the West German Free Democrats and of the East German Communists and who wanted "to keep a hole in the wall dividing Germany" by supplying intelligence. The New York *Times* goes on to say that the East German military intelligence service had tipped off the West German Federal Government about his activities because he would only work with a rival agency in East Germany, the State Security Service.

In Warsaw the composer of an operetta is to be prosecuted in a secret trial because, according to a law of 1946, he has disseminated "false information" in it.

Lisbeth Cresspahl had already had to endure listening to her husband talk about the coming war; in the fall of 1938 she was forced to observe that his actions were suited to his words. She could no longer assume that his sole motive for such talk had been to persuade her that they should return to England; she saw that he was following her wishes and preparing to remain in Germany, but also preparing for a war. Cresspahl took the train to do some shopping.

The first list was one he had drawn up himself. It started off with all the steel, iron, and brass items: saw blades, nails of all sizes, axes, files, planing blades, rasps, clamps, spades, fittings for furniture, doors, and windows. These were followed by machine belting, gasoline, oil, grease. He actually bought a motor that did not run by electricity, took it apart, packed the parts in oiled paper, and carried everything down to the basement under what had once been the living room, placing it behind a newly erected wall that looked like a partition for junk. His purchases went unnoticed in Jerichow since he obtained his supplies in Lübeck, Hamburg, and Schwerin, also because a master carpenter was allowed to buy fuses in packs of one hundred if obliged to work with an inadequate electrical system.

Lisbeth tried to stop him because he was thus turning into reality his anticipation for the coming years, and Cresspahl pointed to the scrap-iron collection on October 19 which was designed to clean out the last vestiges from people's homes for armament purposes. Cresspahl had been astute enough to contribute a large quantity which, while considerable in terms of weight, was negligible in terms of usefulness, and had carefully preserved the receipt. Lisbeth wanted to keep at least two kerosene lamps as an unnecessary reserve, and Cresspahl spoke of a single bomb dropping on the Lübeck-Herrenwyk power station, which supplied Jerichow with electricity. Cresspahl went about all this in his usual deliberate, imperturbable manner, regardless of how long it took; and she could not even laugh at him for making a fuss or a commotion over it.

She found it even harder to accept the necessity of making her own list, as directed by Cresspahl. This would mean admitting that the town of Jerichow, her home and household, her own child, were facing times in which shoes, clothing, even kitchen knives, would be unobtainable; she was so reluctant to do this that Cresspahl had to spend a whole evening questioning her as to what she would need in these annoying circumstances of his, and she was not prepared to comply until she had found large cartons containing candles, tobacco, and shoe leather in the storeroom. She said it gave her a headache, so that Cresspahl would have a guilty conscience, but he refused to be satisfied with linens and cottons and insisted on sewing-machine needles too.

When she went off to do her own shopping, she would often return from Lübeck or Schwerin in good spirits. She enjoyed giving presents, and there was often an apron or a head scarf for the Labor Service girls; she found her own amusement in some dainty embroidery scissors or a patent lemon squeezer that she would never use. Her mood was often that of the time just before her wedding, when Louise Papenbrock had completed her trousseau for her; and again and again she was reassured by the displays in the store windows. There she saw no sign of shortage, of war; on Sundays, the *Lübecker Generalanzeiger* published sixteen pages of advertisements which included Underberg Schnapps, Mercedes typewriters, Attika cigarettes (pure Turkish tobaccos), Junker & Ruh gas ranges, Karstadt's department store, safety-glass manufacturers, as if all these firms could not unload their products—or put new ones on the market—fast enough. Maybe it really was a tiresome mistake on Cresspahl's part, and harmless enough, since after all his activities amounted to no more than a slightly exaggerated stocking up of supplies; Cresspahl himself appeared amused when she returned with a hat that she could not wear until next summer; indeed, Cresspahl seemed to understand that she was thumbing her nose at him.

There were other days. Days when she was tired even before she began. She would not feel like going into the stores, could spend half an hour sitting in the station restaurant at Lübeck, and a movie ad would eventually keep her from her shopping. Walking from the cashier's window into the movie made her feel very uncomfortable, as did the wait in the dim light, but her headache would vanish as soon as the images appeared on the screen. On her arrival home in Jerichow in the evening she would still be bemused, absent-minded, yet still refreshed by the hour and a half's oblivion, by having been off in a world of pretense and illusion, with no trace of Cresspahl's war.

These were the films being shown in Lübeck in the third week of October 1938:

Mazurka, with Pola Negri, no admittance under 14.

Vanished Traces, with Kristina Söderbaum, restricted.

Thirteen Chairs, with Heinz Rühmann and Hans Moser, unrestricted.

The Little Sinner, with Rudolf Platte and Paul Dahlke, restricted.

A Girl Goes Ashore, with Elisabeth Flickenschildt.

The Jungle Princess.

Petermann Says No, with Fita Senkhoff.

Love On The Run, with Clark Gable.

Clark Gable?

And Coca-Cola existed then too, daughter.

The same as here?

The same one your Marie drinks, daughter.

Did I drink it as a child?

Certainly, daughter. On Schüsselbuden Street in Lübeck, and you didn't like it.

And you went to see those movies the way I used to go during my first year in New York?

Just like you in New York, daughter.

To dull the senses.

It was a stupid feeling. But for as long as it lasted I felt safe. For as long as it lasted no one could find me. I couldn't even find myself.

Did you take me along?

Sometimes I did try to do you a favor. Don't forget that, daughter.

I won't.

She told Cresspahl about her visits to the movies, about the wasted hours. She would have liked a rebuke from him, not merely in order to reproach him with being unjust but also to help her cope with such dereliction of duty, such attempts at escape. Cresspahl was glad for her to have what he regarded as her amusement. As long as she let him believe that she had no secrets from him, he was almost reassured.

February 7, 1968   Wednesday

Dear Mary, liebe Marie, dorogaya Mariya,

There is something I want to keep from you for another eight years.

One reason is that we only have three hours a day together,

when I come home from work, and when we ought to have been talking about your school today you were busy.

You were busy with the pictures you had cut out of the New York *Times*. One was a view of the Chinese section of Saigon. The bombs, fires, and street fighting had left more or less identical ruins, and since the photograph is not clear you did not realize that those were the remains of human habitations, you took them for a garbage dump, with flames and dense smoke rising from the background, which looked something like a forest. And once again you said, it couldn't happen to us in New York; already it was less real to you.

So today you would have accepted what I would like to prove to myself with the latest news on the death of Charles H. Jordan, whose body was found in the Vltava River on August 20 of last year. Mr. Jordan, an executive with the Jewish charity organization JOINT, left his hotel in Prague on August 16 to buy a newspaper. Friends and acquaintances have ruled out the possibility of suicide. A Belgian scientist who was subsequently on a visit to an East European country complained of being constantly followed, and he was given the reason that this was so that Soviet agents should not be able to do to him what was done to Jordan. If it was not the people from the K. G. B., the Soviet security police, it might have been Arab agents who were responsible. The Swiss pathologist Ernst Hardmeier, who had been retained by JOINT to perform an autopsy on the dead man, was found on December 10 several hundred yards from his locked automobile, frozen to death in a snowy forest near Zürich, and he had not completed his examination. That was how it was up to now.

Now we see that a socialist Czechoslovak Government has given the United States a report on the circumstances surrounding an American citizen. The report is an interim one, investigations may be continued. So far the Czechoslovak Government has established that Mr. Jordan died on August 16 between 11 P.M. and midnight, and that his body fell into the river at a certain point on the First of May Bridge in downtown Prague. The manner of death is stated to be suffocation from drowning, the body showed no signs of major trauma, the choice of words does not rule out a blow by a sandbag or some other similar object. Attached to the report are photographs of the scene and drawings of the river currents, which were measured by means of a dummy of Mr. Jordan's size and weight.

Supposing this were to be reintroduced in a socialist country:

that a death for reasons of state is not automatically lawful;

that a murder must be accompanied by a murderer;

that the dead at least have a right to the truth about their death;

that deaths by violence, at night, in secret, behind locked doors, are forbidden and, if not prevented, condemned:

then a socialism might begin with a binding constitution, with freedom of speech and movement, and freedom to decide on the use of means of production, even for the individual.

Something is missing. No, it has not been answered: was the dead man killed and, if so, by whom, by whose orders, why, and for what purpose?

Dorogaya Mariya, it might still be a new beginning. For that beginning I would work, of my own free will. I am sitting here alone at the table with your pictures from the *Times*, alone with the lamp and your sleeping breath, which is louder than my pen, and alone with an absurd confidence in this year. I have written this down for you so that you will understand, late though it will be, what I may begin this year—at the age of thirty-five, so help me—one last time. So that you won't have to guess, as I do.

Sincerely yours,

February 8, 1968   Thursday

The American-led camp at Langvei near Khesan was overrun yesterday by Soviet PT-76 tanks. Street fighting in Hue. The town of Bentre was destroyed by shelling and bombardment from the southern allies; this was necessary "in order to save it," according to a U.S. major. And Captain Bacel Winstead said in Hue, at the sight of some U.S. marines riding to the front on motorcycles "liberated" from private ownership: "The American military is the damnedest military in the world."

On about October 20, 1938, a man in Dassow, near Jerichow, was sentenced to eight months' imprisonment and costs; he had not been a member of the Nazi Party. He had, however, worn the badge of that Party in order to express his "inner conviction." In view of his many former sentences, the court found his behavior "that much more despicable."

When Lisbeth got hold of some idea, Cresspahl was usually soon aware of it. Once Lisbeth had discovered that the boys of the Hitler Youth stood with their collecting boxes outside the church waiting for churchgoers, she pinned to her hat such little buttons with portraits of outstanding Nazis as the Winter Assistance Program gave in return for donations, so that she could then say to the collectors, her forefinger pointing daintily to her brow: I've already got one.

Cresspahl talked her out of this, yet he enjoyed the knowledge that she was capable of a joke and had also shown good sense, albeit on the wrong occasion. She behaved similarly with her old gold coins that were supposed to be turned in at the Reichsbank: Lisbeth had a five-mark coin set as a brooch by Ahlreep the jeweler, and was sending her daughter Gesine with this new pin to a children's party at Party Comrade Lichtwark's. Cresspahl talked her out of that.

It was not always fun. When the *Lübecker Generalanzeiger* devoted a whole page one Sunday to the topic of London messenger boys, she became so deeply absorbed in reading about the boys in their uniforms and looking at their pictures—showing shoulder strap, cap with chin strap on back of head, number badge over left breast— that it ended with suppressed tears, and that evening she had already completed the first three lines of a letter to the editor in which she intended to expose the cruelty of English capitalism, although her only motivation was the memory of her time in London and the desire for self-chastisement. This did not escape Cresspahl's notice, despite all her attempts at secrecy, and he talked her out of it.

That Lisbeth was letting her child go hungry was something that only dawned on him gradually.

In those days the child was still asleep when he got up; he breakfasted alone and would not have had the time that the older Gesine would have liked to spend on the first meal of the day. He had to be off as early as in the days of his own childhood when he had had to go out into the fields with the Von Hasses' day laborers; he had to take the milk train to Gneez to connect with the train to Lübeck, he might have to do some preliminary work at the airfield, or in the hour before breakfast replace the shaft of the flagpole which some unknown experts had sawn part-way through during the night in Friedrich Jansen's front garden. When he finally sat down at table, Gesine was up too, and he probably enjoyed the way she watched him so attentively as he ate. Had he asked Lisbeth, she would have answered that the child had already had something to eat, and Gesine could not have contradicted her except that it had not been enough.

It was the same at lunchtime, it was the same in the evening. Cresspahl saw to it that Paap and the workmen had their slices of meat on their plates, and he was also satisfied with his own portion; the child sat beside Lisbeth, two stools away from him. Why should a five-year-old doubt that her mother calculates her portions to the best of her knowledge and ability? How could she appeal to her father when she had been expressly cautioned not to bother him? During the Easter visit to Podejuch, the Cresspahl child had had meals with the Paepcke children, and Hilde may have noticed that Gesine would quietly and furtively assemble onto her plate and into her apron pocket everything she could lay hands on; she spoke of it later. The Labor Service girls knew quite well that the master's child had an inordinate appetite and was merely too scared to steal the soaked pieces of bread from the cat's bowl; Lisbeth kept her store-room carefully locked, and whenever she caught the girls slipping something to the child she would, with a withering glance, forbid any meddling in the child's upbringing. The girls used to say later: When she looked at you like that, so coldly, never moving her eyes, it was quite scary. Apart from laymen, there was also Dr. Berling who observed the Cresspahl child on Town Street, a thin, if not precisely emaciated, little creature who seemed not to have grown at all in six months and looked out upon the world somewhat bemusedly. Louise Papenbrock no longer waited on customers at the bakery, the child did not like to go begging from the salesgirls, and when old Papen-brock slipped her a candy these days he did so secretly, after Lisbeth had pointed out in no uncertain terms the possible danger from sweet things to the teeth, once again in the severe, distant manner she had adopted. Whenever the child stuffed herself with unripe apples, the stomach upset was a reason for keeping her in bed. The first time the child was allowed to lick the remains of cake dough from a bowl she was six years old; but Lisbeth scraped out these remains with a white rubber spatula that left nothing behind. It was not only food that she wanted to deny the child but also pleasure. If she was not as yet permitted to sacrifice the child, then at least she wanted to do her a good turn by making her suffer. There were exceptions, such as that bottle of Coca-Cola in Lübeck when Lisbeth had felt sorry for herself as well as for the child dazed with hunger; not very often. By October 1938 this had been going on for more than a year.

In October 1938 Hermann Liedtke complained to Cresspahl that he was often finding his lunch sandwich nibbled at as if by a cat. Liedtke preferred to have the money rather than share the Cress-pahls' lunch and brought along his own sandwiches from home. Cresspahl had the cat-flap in the workshop door nailed up, but Liedtke could still confront him with teeth-marks in the bread, really as if from a cat. Cresspahl was on the point of passing out padlocks for the clothes lockers, being more inclined to believe in quarrels among the workmen than in the cat, until one day he came upon the child in the empty workshop. She had slipped away from the breakfast table, had seen Liedtke go off, and was now standing at a locker and cautiously nibbling at his bread, so frightened of being discovered that after each little nibble she would fold up the wax paper with both hands. At the time she was no more than 3 feet 3 inches tall, and she was very scared when all of a sudden she looked up to see Cresspahl. She held out the packet, which was too bulky for her fingers, and said abjectly, with lowered lids and a deep sigh: I didn't mean to do it.

Lisbeth looked kindly at the child, who was very ashamed of her confessions; but she did not wish to discuss it. Cresspahl sent the child out of the room; Lisbeth did not wish to discuss it. Looked at him clear-eyed, head uplifted and undaunted, a faint smile at the corners of her mouth, as if Cresspahl would not understand her anyway, the point that she had reached. By force he could have wrung from her: I've gone hungry too, Cresspahl; he did not attempt force.

This time it was Cresspahl who initiated the silence and held out for a week; and Cresspahl now took the child along on his shopping expeditions or to the airfield, and when he had a meal at home the child would sit beside him, in Lisbeth's place. He was very embarrassed when he held bread out to the child and received a shamelessly grateful look as a reward. In Jerichow there was talk of his wanting to take away Our Lisbeth's child, and after only three days Lisbeth asked him to leave the child with her, promising "Whatever you want, Heinrich"; but Cresspahl enjoyed having the child close to him all day and, above all, talking to the child, explaining his work to her. After he finally did supply the lockers with padlocks, Hermann Liedtke knew one more cat story to tell and did not suspect the child, who now waited patiently half the day under the projecting roof of the workshop, until the machines were shut down or Cresspahl stepped outside. Cresspahl kept the child with him, although he no longer doubted Lisbeth's assurances; later on he admitted to himself a desire for revenge and wished he had given in on this occasion too.

Thanks, daughter.
I don't deserve any thanks.

Yes you do. Because you didn't tell your Marie about it. It's
almost as if now you could forgive me.
I've forgiven you! I've forgiven. I've forgiven!

"Sold out! All gone! Finished!" says Mrs. O'Brady, who has bent
down behind her counter and knows only that yet another customer is
there, but not which one.

"Matches all sold out?"

"No! Oh, it's you, Gesine. Those goddamned pictures!" says
Mrs. O'Brady, who now has an excess of blood in her sturdy forceful
head and is annoyed about that too.

"No. Never filters."

"Here! Here you are, here's the stuff that's dangerous to your
health! That's the way I imagine a bush fire! They simply tore the
issues out of my hands!"

"Go ahead and tell me, Mrs. O'Brady."

"*Time* Magazine, Gesine! The one with the pictures. That's how
some people get their kicks!"

"It doesn't turn me on," says Sam. His restaurant is almost
empty by now, and he has time to chat with a fat, morose-looking
individual in a leather jacket, evidently a friend of his to judge by the
familiar terms they are on. The new issue of *Time* lies under the
customer's elbow, open at the color pages and already considerably
crumpled. Sam does not think it right that John Stewart should have
taken a picture of a wounded G. I., a husky black M. P., in a semi-
kneeling, apelike position, staring dully from under the pink blood-
soaked bandage around his forehead "at the enemy." For, as Sam
said, he was actually staring into the camera. And instead of waiting
the few seconds until the man keeled over dead, John Stewart might
well have shot with something other than his camera.

"Fair enough," says the other man. He must have an extraordinary talent for keeping a conversation going like this without saying
anything. It sounds as if he had agreed; he could easily dispute that.

"And anyway it's faked," says Sam. He pulls the magazine
toward him from under the other man's arm, looks at the pictures,
lays them aside. He looks gloomily and good-naturedly at his bald-
headed friend, the gray creases in his furrowed brow are closer
together than ever, and Sam says: "The colors aren't right. Ever see a
color photo with natural-looking colors?"

"Nah," says the other man. " 'Course, everyone has his own idea of what's natural."

"Right."

"Maybe it's true at that."

"Sure—but just one obvious moment of truth."

"And an obvious truth isn't just merchandise—"

"—it's hot merchandise," says Sam, obviously gratified that once again they had managed to exchange a ping for a pong. Then he sees Mrs. Cresspahl, who has come in to pick up her afternoon tea, and starts an affectionate abuse. The solitary customer buttons up his scruffy leather jacket and, without turning around, slides from the stool and heads for the street.

" 'By, Sam," he says.

"Take care," Sam calls after him; and now he lets fly: "Don't you dare do that again to me, you chick you! Standing around waiting while we're chewing the rag. If I don't notice you, beat me over the head! That's an order! As of now! Tea with lemon. Twenty! Thanks, Gesine. What a day it's been again."

"These Fridays."

"Right, Gesine. And now you're going back to that cubicle of yours where you'll sit down comfortably and not do another thing. You've had enough for today too."

"Have a good rest at the weekend, Sam."

"You too."

"Hello?"

"Mrs. Williams, Foreign Sales."

"Oh, I thought it would be Mrs. Cresspahl."

"One moment, I'll connect you."

"Hello?"

"Yes?"

"It's Eileen."

"Eileen?"

"See? You've been buying your damned cigarettes from me for close on two years, and you still don't know my first name. Mrs. O'Brady."

"I didn't want to seem familiar, Eileen."

"That's quite all right, Jee-zine. Listen, I've been able to hunt up another batch of *Time* Magazines. D'you want me to put one aside for you?"

"No thanks, Eileen. Wait! Eileen! Yes, please do. Would you mind?"

February 10, 1968 Saturday, South Ferry Day

On October 26, 1938, a Wednesday, the Luftwaffe took over Jerichow North.

This time Johannes Schmidt's House of Music did not ask for financial reimbursement: at his own expense he undertook to blare out the orders-for-the-day throughout the town, using a panel truck equipped with a loudspeaker. Johannes Schmidt intended this to be interpreted as his contribution toward national honor. He spent the whole of Tuesday afternoon personally driving up and down the streets and even out into the villages, announcing in stilted High German that buildings were to be flagged and that the show would start at 10 A.M.

Jerichow's market square was filled with more people than there were inhabitants. A long rectangular space had been marked off in the middle by newly painted white flagpoles garlanded with evergreens. A police detachment from Gneez held the thrusting crowds back from the flimsy barrier, but old Creutz kept on managing to slip through in order to admire his own handiwork. Just before the ceremony was to begin he fastened a loose garland back in place, grumbling openly at those bastards who had tried to damage his artistic reputation. He was referring to the policemen, who had not been all that careful and who, since they were less emotionally involved than he, reacted with smiles instead of a warning.

The Luftwaffe troops arriving by train did not come as far as Jerichow itself. Jansen had deemed Station Street to be too narrow for a bang-up parade. The soldiers had left the train unobtrusively at the Knesebeck station, two miles outside Jerichow, thus seeming to arrive from nowhere. When they reached the brickyard, the band intoned the first march, the "Hohenfriedberg." There, at the point where a path met the road, stood a man of about fifty, holding a child by the hand and observing the new arrivals in a calm, appraising manner. The paving stones of Town Street snapped and flashed under the iron-shod heels, and at the rear of the parade boys were already beginning to search for fragments of iron among the cobbles. Standing on the sidewalks, girls in the uniform of the League of German Girls threw flowers at the soldiers. Papenbrock's Edith craned her neck as high as she could, sometimes trying to jump in the air; she was in such an ecstasy of laughing and shouting that she suddenly grabbed Stellmann by the arm. "Oh! Oh!" she cried,

causing Stellmann to wobble and spoil two pictures. In the wake of
the troops, windows were shut and the inhabitants came running out
onto the street, toward the market square, leaving the houses deserted.

At thirty seconds to ten, the Blues were drawn up on the market
place, forming a square with the Storm Troopers, the National
Socialist Reich Veterans' Association, and the Naval Storm Troopers.
Only Friedrich Jansen, standing on the flag-draped dais, knew why he
opened his mouth as if to speak, closed it again, jerked it open again.
Then he realized that Pastor Brüshaver was actually daring not to
have the bells of St. Peter's rung. In his rage, Friedrich Jansen pulled
himself together and hurled a preliminary word from his throat. It
remained a secret, for now the Catholics were pulling at their bell
ropes. Despite the obvious effort, it was hardly more than a tinkle
and stopped immediately, as if startled. After a few sentences, Friedrich Jansen saw no more. He spoke of the happiness felt by the town
at having its own garrison (measured; determined). How they had
had to beg for soldiers in the past (self-pitying; threatening)! How,
however, the Führer, anticipating—nay, knowing—their wishes, had
made the town a gift of them (preaching, humble). When Jansen
came to quote from the Rostock speech of Heinkel, the national
award winner, his overpowering awe caused him to flub, and he gave
as the present maximum speed for aircraft a figure of 900 kilometers
per hour. Heinkel had spoken of 700. "And if a dastardly foe now
wishes to raise arms against the German people" (pityingly). "Then
we won't turn a hair" (Grand Hotel). "We're certainly not going to
ignore it" (the professional, both feet firmly on the ground). "Then
we'll simply say: 'Down, boy!' " (bulging-eyed dog-owner). " 'Down,
boy!' " he shouted. Each time he uttered the word "Luftwaffe,"
saliva welled from his mouth, and he could not have told you what
he was saying. While Georg Swantenius from Gneez was expressing
gratitude to the Führer for this proud day in the name of the local
Party organization and the district administration, the sweetness
somewhat soured by envy, Jansen was still red in the face and breathing heavily. Next day Stellmann sold more photographs of Jansen in
this state than of any other subject.

As the commanding officer of the troops stepped forward, the
people fell silent, like students in a classroom who are ready to
confront an inept teacher but not the school board. The Lieutenant
Colonel spoke in a normal tone of voice, relaxed, in fact he sounded
almost like a civilian. He introduced himself. He looked around, in

such a way that many people imagined that his eyes had lighted on them. He thanked them for their reception; as was only right and proper. The troops would make every effort to deserve full acceptance by the community; he knew the rules of hospitality. He rejoiced in this day, using no stronger words than those. When the Catholics rang their bells, he had composed his face and bent his head a little; he was showing respect for the Church. He spoke with a slight Hanoverian accent, like a neighbor. From the good-natured way he kept his mouth open whenever he paused, he might have come from this very area. Long-boned, muscular, with a drooping left shoulder where he had been wounded. As he gave the command to present arms for the playing of the two national anthems, the syllables were clear and distinct; it sounded incongruous and, to their discomfort, peremptory. The fellow was not easy to figure out, and for the time being this made him rank high with the people of Jerichow.

In the photographs prepared by Horst Stellmann of the ensuing events, Cresspahl is no longer visible, either at the handing over of the keys outside the main guardhouse, or during the wreath-laying ceremony at the World War I war memorial, or at the open-air concert given by the Luftwaffe and the Storm Troopers on the market square. Cresspahl kept to his property, tidying up in the workshop, going through his ledgers, oddly annoyed by the aircraft which were making friends with the population by flying noisily around over the town. But he did step outside and look up at the flight formations. He stood outside his barn and looked at the flag hanging from the north gable across the way. He wandered back and forth about the property, chin in hand, through the empty rooms, through Lisbeth's too.

It's all my fault, Cresspahl.
Now it's mine too, Lisbeth.

Gala balls had been organized for that evening at the Lübeck Arms, the inn, the Rifle Club, and the Foresters' Tavern. The Cresspahls attended the one at the Rifle Club. Our Lisbeth did not miss a dance for two and a half hours. She was so gay, laughing all the time, quite different from what people said about her. When she did sit down, it was always beside Cresspahl, one hand as if casually, but firmly, on his shoulder.

I wanted to sleep with you just once more, Heinrich. Before it's all over, I mean.

February 11, 1968 Sunday

Since yesterday afternoon, a black child has been living at the Cresspahls', and it is not to everyone's liking.

We took the child Francine out of the confusion of squad cars and ambulance and strewn garbage on 103rd Street, away from a knifing and an argument as to who was in authority between policemen, social workers, and building superintendents, away from the indifferent spectators who were standing around her bleeding mother and the screaming infant. The latter was taken away by the ambulance driver, the police sergeant was reluctant to hand over Francine to white people.

"Are you sure you know what you're doing, lady?" he said.

Mr. Robinson, who once again had to produce a bed from his secret vaults, was less satisfied with this billeting than he had been over the arrival of the Fleurys. He brought in the bedstead, set it up neatly in Marie's room the way she wanted it, but in saying good-by he stood in the doorway with a puzzled look, not patting the crisp waves of his hair as he does when normally in doubt but with bent head, which he was actually scratching in his puzzlement. Thus his eyes were hidden. "Oh well," he said at last, now even dissatisfied with himself. "I guess you know what you're doing, Mrs. Cresspahl."

Does it suit Francine? She used to phone us. She has known Marie for almost six months in school, she knows the apartment from visits. On those occasions, alone with Marie, her behavior had been trusting, cheerful, as if they were on almost equal terms. Yesterday afternoon, scarcely did we have her inside our front door than she was as shy with Marie as she had at one time been with Mrs. Cresspahl, whom she would run past to be sure to avoid a look or a word. Sitting down only when invited to, and then at a distance, her long, sticklike legs close together, hands tightly clasped on knees, staring at the floor. Having thanked her hostess for a mug of cocoa she said, addressing the spoon as well, "Thank you," softly, without hope, as if even so she was unable to lessen a threat. Once, because Marie was talking about D. E., she thought she was not being watched and attempted a wary glance that was quickly deflected. She arrived exactly as misfortune had struck her, in a shabby logging-type jacket, which for a long time she was reluctant to take off, as if the fact of her arrival here did not mean she was going to stay.

It was not necessarily because of her mother. She did not want to go to our phone when we finally managed to get a nurse on the other end. Francine accepted the news that her mother would fully recover from the stabbing; she nodded without relief, rather out of politeness. She nodded at the information that her older brothers and sisters had still not been located and that the youngest boy was in a children's home, as if there were no sense in taking special note of it. There was one more thing that Francine's mother wanted relayed to Mrs. Cresspahl: God's blessing. That won't suit us.

It was a mistake for Marie to try to distract the black child with a game; Francine did not know Mikado, was obedient enough to learn it, and was so unhappy over her lack of skill that she broke a stick by mistake and was inconsolable. "Now we can always think of you when we find this stick missing," said Marie, but what Francine heard was the heralding not of a kindly remembrance but of an angry one. Another mistake was a supper that is not eaten with the fingers, and it was no use for Marie to casually lay aside her knife and then, like Francine, attack the cutlet with the side of her fork. It was not a good idea to send Francine off for a shower; what she inferred was a suspicion of dirt and vermin. "We do this every night," said Marie; and what Francine heard was not information but instruction. Perhaps it was a good idea to give her a pair of Marie's pajamas and, for the next day, a complete set of clothing; it was not a good idea to put all her things right away into the basket for the washing machine, as if they could not be worn a single day longer. She was very relieved when bedtime came since now she no longer had to be conscious of the threat from the strange household, and she pulled the sheet right up over the tightly wound braids that stuck out all around her head; she lay there stiffly, not falling asleep for a long time, on the lookout for some unimaginable danger.

Rebecca Ferwalter did not like the idea of her friend's taking in a black child; the black girl came from a street, a house, about which the Jewish child had been expressly warned. Rebecca, the smart little miss in a bolero dress that was a small replica of a grownup's, Rebecca of the ladylike behavior and the masklike doll's face, felt trapped, and in the course of a rather stilted conversation she invented an order of Mrs. Ferwalter's which allowed her to stay with us for only ten minutes. Rebecca hears many times a day what suits her mother and, more often still, what does not.

It did not suit Francine that we took it for granted that a mother with stab wounds in chest and shoulder must have a visit from at least one of her children; when inquiries were made at the entrance and in the corridors of the hospital, she kept so much in the background that at first it was the Cresspahls who were thought to be visiting a black woman. Francine entered her mother's room reluctantly and after a very few minutes held the door of the ward open for us. And she seemed to be even more remote than we were from the woman lying there awkwardly dumped under the green institutional blankets, immobilized by heavy bandages, medicated into semiconsciousness, the broad gray face covered in feverish sweat. "She's a good child," she managed to get out, and it may have been a conviction rather than a plea, Francine all of a sudden staring morosely, even hostilely, past her. Nor did it suit us that the lack of space between the close-ranked beds, the smell of poverty rather than of illness, the guarded looks of the black neighbors, were soon more than we could bear. Francine stayed by the door until Marie turned around. Now the look in her eyes was timid, disdainful, her chin tucked in, and Marie innocently asked her what was the matter. Francine did not answer, refusing to budge as if Marie ought to confess something. So perhaps it was a good idea to shepherd her out of the way of other visitors; but Francine had not expected to be taken back again to Riverside Drive.

Now you've seen for yourself, Marie.
I've not seen anything. A sick woman.
Now you're lying, Whitey.
My lies don't concern you.
This one does.
It's no use, Francine, you won't get me to talk about it.
I'll come along, but I don't trust you.

It suited Francine to be left in peace with a pile of comics, and she gave a casual little push to one of Marie's double doors to keep out of sight. She carried pretense to the point of feigning sleep when Pamela Blumenroth came to pick up Marie to go to the Mediterranean Swimming Pool. And in fact she did fall asleep, and her scared little black face came peeking out from behind the door, jet-black eyes surrounded by huge whites, turned toward the other strange person who was blocking the exit in this strange apartment. Then, waking up, bent on humility and atonement, she said eagerly: "Shall I carry the newspaper down to the street for you, Mrs. Cresspahl?"

Then she could not understand that people living in a building like this would place their garbage in bags next to the elevator door every evening instead of having to carry it furtively out to the city litter baskets at the street corner. She accepted as one more incredible fact that every evening around ten Mr. Robinson would stop the elevator at each floor and pick up the garbage for the incinerator; that still had to be explained to her.

What could not be explained to her was why Marie has outlined a picture on the front page of the New York *Times* in red; beside a wounded U. S. marine in Danang, a chaplain in fatigues, with a cross on his helmet cover, staring up into the sky, watching for God and the evacuation helicopters.

"Vietnam," says Francine, unmoved, incurious, as if speaking of something useless, like the moon.

By tomorrow Marie will find it suits her less. She had quite liked being able to go swimming without Francine, who might have been the only black person there and hard to defend. Tomorrow, when she turns up at school with Francine, she will be relieved to desert her for her white friends.

There is one classical writer whom it would not suit. He has dealt with that kind of shelter in a book which he enjoins his readers not to lay aside,

> *I hear that in New York*
> *At the corner of 26th Street and Broadway*
> *During the winter months a man stands every evening*
> *Soliciting from passers-by, and obtaining*
> *For the homeless who assemble there a place to sleep*
> *. . .*
> *Don't lay aside this book, fellow man reading it.*
> *A few people have a place to sleep*
> *The wind is kept from them for one night*
> *The snow destined for them falls on the street*
> *But this does not change the world*
> *This does not improve mankind's relationships*
> *This does not shorten the age of exploitation.*

And there is no telling whether or not a certain person approves of Francine's accommodation: D. E., who arrives about 6 P.M. from Kennedy Airport, just back from Europe, bringing two dresses from Copenhagen for Marie, one of them now for Francine, for

"I know all about it," he says, and Francine believes him;

"Though I'm a stranger here myself," he says, and Francine laughs quite naturally, spontaneously;

"All the things I did to keep New York clean," he says; and Francine looks with shining eyes at this white man, eagerly listening to him talk about such mysterious objects as a "Magasin du Nord" and a "Kongens Nytorv" in "København," and is already jealous of the hours when she will have to share him with Marie.

D. E.; he would accept even a black child in loco parentis. But again on one condition.

February 12, 1968   Monday

Fog in London.

The profits Cresspahl had derived from the airfield construction had come to an end. Klein the butcher supplied meat for the garrison, Papenbrock baked the bread, the taverns made money out of the soldiers' weekends. The Rande hotels, formerly well mothballed at this season, were heavily booked with seminars, wives, movie shows put on by the Nazi Party. Pahl the tailor ran his business avertisements at a different spot every day in the *Gneezer Tageblatt,* waiting for the moment when they would catch the eye of an officer; the yard goods were already on hand. Jerichow's business world had welcomed the arrival of the troops in a joint advertisement. The Church was selling lot after lot around Jerichow. Köpcke the builder had orders for summer homes along the cliffs, he could hardly keep up with them; the carpentry work was given to Böttcher in Gneez. Cresspahl was now working with Alwin Paap and one young journeyman only; Kliefoth had not ordered his new bookcase in Wismar after all. The other orders were small stuff, chicken feed.

Cresspahl had time to go for walks. Sometimes he and Our Lisbeth were to be seen in the evenings on the seaside promenade in Rande, silently walking along with their faces toward the heaving sea. For this they were suspected not of city manners but of a desire to recall the year 1931, when they had walked there in secret, as lovers about whom not much was carried to Louise Papenbrock's ears.

The Japanese had captured and occupied Hankow.

The sea wind had plucked the trees bare not only along the coast but in Jerichow itself. Sometimes old Creutz would be standing there leaning on his fence when the Cresspahls returned to the light in their house. Had they already moved their dahlias into the cellar, he would ask? The Cresspahls had almost finished putting the garden to bed for the winter, they would say. October should have twelve fine days, like March, Creutz would say. Mightn't it have been only eleven this year, Lisbeth Cresspahl said, and Creutz heard her laugh softly. He could hardly see them in the darkness, but he confidently stayed where he was. They would wait until he had finished. The Cresspahls had always been easy to get along with as neighbors.

In August all Jews had had to retire from the occupations of broker and traveling salesman. Arthur Semig no longer needed to get upset over this. Now they were to be prohibited from practicing as attorneys, and medical appointments were also taken away from them. Arthur Semig had been spared this.

It served Warning right that his spades seemed to snap as if of their own accord, with no trace of a saw mark. What did it matter if his fence had more holes in it than boards? A bit of wood like that always comes in handy for burning. The latest, though, was that the leather for his pump had been stolen. Not even his dog would do anything for him these days. Jailbirds. What he had said about Arthur, only jailbirds talked like that.

Leather was supposed not only to shine but to have life. Erdal prolongs the life and beauty of your shoes. Hm, yes. Leather must have life.

Work-shy tramps are put into the workhouse. That's the way it goes.

All the benefits Jerichow derived from the airfield. Much of it did not become apparent until later. Of the sixty-four children baptized so far that year by Brüshaver, thirteen were illegitimate. But it was better to pay taxes for that than for—there's someone coming. Oh it's only Cresspahl. Cresspahl the bur-picker. Takes his wife along when he goes for a beer. Next thing you know, your own wife will be asking for the same English customs. A fellow can't even talk to him about illegitimate kids and such. Won't do for Our Lisbeth.

On October 27, Ernst Barlach, sculptor, draftsman, dramatist, died. Because he was taken for a Jew, he was spat at on the street in Güstrow. They had hounded him to such a degree by forbidding him to work and banning his exhibitions that he just lay down and died. The people of Lübeck had made an honorary citizen of one Alfred Rosenberg; but they had not erected Barlach's statues on the outer walls of their St. Catherine's Church. The *Lübecker General-anzeiger* had not wanted to publish any independent statement about his death, preferring to copy something from the *Berliner Tageblatt* to the effect that he had remained a problem for a generation that had taken other paths. For a long time Lisbeth was mystified by: The poet had had to wrestle more to find God than with God.

With God—but that's not allowed.

That's right, Lisbeth.

To find God; that's the way it should be.

That's right, Lisbeth.

When you were in Güstrow, did you ever see him?

No, Lisbeth. But I know Büntzel. Friedrich Büntzel, Lisbeth, now there's a man who understands wood. It was to him that this fellow Barlach turned for advice. But first he had to say of a block of wood: This one will split; and Barlach: No it won't.

Then it split.

And from then on Barlach listened to Büntzel the carpenter.

You'd have known too.

Not any more, Lisbeth.

Heinrich, it's a bad time to die. If it were only August. When the soil is light.

Yes, Lisbeth.

February 13, 1968   Tuesday

The Union of Soviet Writers has compared Alexander I. Solzhenitsyn with Joseph Stalin's only daughter.

And with whom did President Johnson compare himself on Lincoln's birthday? With Abraham Lincoln.

The New York *Times* also has a comparison to make, now that the sanitation men have begun to remove the garbage of two weeks from the streets: This time the city was Saigon and the crisis was the Vietcong disruption of the city at the beginning of the month. The paper means the New York garbage crisis. It means the losses in human life in Vietnam. It compares.

This day, Miss Cresspahl was repotted like a plant, restacked like merchandise, relocated like a tool bench.

The new pot, the new warehouse, the new machinery room, the new office: undoubtedly it is more spacious. Amanda Williams says: Very grand. It is very grand territory, the sixteenth floor, just below the executive offices. Here there is not only fluorescent lighting in the ceiling, there is also a reading lamp under costly Swedish glass, and over the typewriter there are two shaded white tubes to keep the golf-ball trough well lighted. Here the desk is no ready-made affair, like those supplied to such humble depths as Foreign Sales; this one is a slab of artistic design into which smoothly gliding jewel cases have been fitted. The room does not anticipate a visitor who would be satisfied with an ordinary chair; here there is provision for VIPs to sit on a sofa. Not only has this floor a covering of wool shag instead of the wall-to-wall on the lower levels: this office is in a corner of the building, has a window in each of two walls, and almost six square yards of light behind the Venetian blinds, although today there are dark clouds. The promotion is like an American fairy tale.

But Miss Cresspahl is sitting on the luxurious upholstery right next to the door, not like the occupant but like a visitor, prepared to leave, with no eyes for the documents and stationery that she should be putting away in the safe and the open drawers. The procedure has not been like a fairy tale.

Announcement of the move had been offhand, without notice, almost overlooked. Without warning, as she sat at her desk, in broad daylight, the herald of Destiny had stood at the door of Foreign Sales, more disconcerting than a window cleaner sliding in front of the windowpanes.

"A very good morning to you!" was Destiny's greeting.

The herald was a slight, curly-haired youth in grayish overalls, the bank's emblem embroidered on his left breast-pocket. He sized up Mrs. Cresspahl with a casual nod and pushed a cart on casters into the cubicle, effectively blocking the exit. He kept his hands on the vehicle as if it were a stretcher for the sick or the dead.

"What in the world—! And who do you think you are?"

He gave a slight start, not having been on the job long enough to be familiar with the prevailing tone among the employees. But he was not to be deterred from carrying out his orders. With a half-turn he leaned back and from the wall to the left of the door drew the plastic name-plate out of its slot and held it out to me, if not like a doctor at least like an orderly who has seen enough cases and knows his way around. Mrs. Cresspahl felt herself nod, and he casually threw my name into one of the trays piled onto the upper deck of his cart. And it was gone.

"It says so on this paper," the young man confirmed indifferently, like an executioner brooking no nonsense. Onto his Puerto Rican English he had welded the laconic speech-forms of Western movies, and the vehement contractions sounded incongruous with his dark skin, the skin of losers, or with his guileless expression, long practiced in the art of ingratiation. He also seemed shy, overtaxed by the remorselessness imposed upon him by his checklist. The list had thought of every item in the inventory, from the adding machine to the ash tray, and even a container for personal effects had been sent along. That was the only point at which the list suffered a defeat. For

Mrs. Cresspahl had merely to take a slip of paper off the bottom of the desk calendar, and it fitted into the smallest pocket of her suit. The young packer had never known anything like it, and it confused him. The name beside the door had been the sole personal item. He was tempted to ask for an explanation, but thought of his boss and took the room apart in scarcely more than twenty minutes. Then the drawers of the steel cabinet and the bookshelves shone in their emptiness, the cork board had been stripped, the chairs among the naked working surfaces might have been on display in a store window, the keys swung once or twice, and then the cubicle was free and ready for the next person.

The boy thanked her as he left. "Some folks go out of their way to make it hard for a guy," he said. Pushing the loaded cart, he moved off as if accompanying a coffin without a cortege.

The old office was lost. The new one was in alien territory. With no room, no tools, there was no further justification for remaining.

Miss Cresspahl sat outside the office that had only just ceased to be hers; but she sat beside Amanda, who, shrill and gloating, was telephoning all over the building, in sheer delight that once again an action had collapsed owing to overorganization. "The company should've gone broke long ago!" she said. "Don't you run after that boy, you're a lady!" "I wish to express my indignation on behalf of Mrs. Cresspahl!" she shouted into her telephone, and in less than fifteen minutes she had ascertained that the interoffice memo had been lying since yesterday morning in the outer office of Personnel, where it had seriously impaired a secretary's initiative, and finally the head of Personnel himself, Mr. Kennicott II, came on the phone. Each time he spoke, Amanda laid her hand over the mouthpiece and signaled the latest positions in the skirmish. "He's wavering," she said. "He's weakening!" "He's given in," she finished, for she had won. The excitement had done her good. Her voice was much deeper now, she felt a pleasant quickening in her circulation and, with a sensual gesture of both hands, patted her mass of black hair into place. Now she had balanced Friday's tiff in her favor, now she could say: "I'll miss you, Mrs. Cresspahl."

"I'll miss you too," Mrs. Cresspahl says lamely.

"Don't take it personally, by bloody Jesus!" said Amanda and Mr. Kennicott II made the same request when he arrived to pick up Mrs. Cresspahl in Foreign Sales and, while accompanying her to her new office, explained skillfully and illogically that any initiative, once split into three simultaneous steps, stood and fell by the planned irregular or regular flow of information, all with his most personal and abject apologies. When he ran out of things to say, he inquired about the origin of the name Cresspahl and mentioned one of his uncles, of German origin, who at the outbreak of World War I had dropped the name Junkers, not because he wanted to dissociate himself from anything German but on account of the neighbors, in a little village in Michigan . . . and when, secretly relieved, he was free to go, his face was totally forgotten, only his agreeably rasping voice remaining in the memory.

That was not right either, for after this he will expect to be recognized. How can he possibly imagine that he is forgotten? Send me a photo of yourself, Mr. Kennicott II.

Then De Rosny appeared in the new office, the Vice- President himself, as he lives and breathes, a genial godfather anxious to share in the pleasure over his gifts. Is everything all right, Mrs. Cresspahl? He did not think so, he had his doubts about the position of the desk and, with his own presidential hands, helped to shift it so that it now no longer stood at an angle between the windows but squarely in front of one of them. In doing so he noticed a drawer a fraction open and pulled it out, shutting it quickly with a look as if wishing to pass discreetly over something immoral. Then he realized that Miss Cresspahl had not had time to put anything away in this room, and he reopened the drawer.

"Shoes," he said in dismay.

Certainly, Mr. De Rosny. One pair of lady's shoes, white pumps, hardly worn.

"May I ask you, just for the record," he began, already on his way toward the chastising thunderstorm that he was planning to unleash on all the lower floors.

Miss Cresspahl wears a smaller size. White shoes in February, who wears such things in this country? No, Mr. De Rosny.

Miss Cresspahl was given the rest of the day off, on the grounds that the telephone in the new office had not yet been hooked up to the right number.

What must you think of us now, Mrs. Cresspahl!
What am I supposed to think?
You've got me in your power for all time, Mrs. Cresspahl!
I could never think that way.
That's why you're here: to learn such things!
And ladies' shoes in the desk—no one's going to believe me.
Then you needn't tell anyone.

Is that a deal, Mr. De Rosny?
That's a deal, Mrs. Cresspahl.

"You look like you're not feeling well, Gesine. What's the matter?"

"You won't believe me anyway."

"Tell *me*, Mrs. Cresspahl. Tell Francine."

"This afternoon I went to two movies, I saw two one after the other. I expect that's it."

February 14, 1968   Wednesday

In Darmstadt, in a small shabby room, a court has now been sitting for four months, examining the murders in the Babi Yar ravine near Kiev in 1941. The New York *Times* gives the number of victims at over 30,000 Jews and some 40,000 others. The eleven defendants, former members of the SS, appear interested, bored, amused, abstracted. None of them seems worried or sad at the evidence. One of them cannot remember, the next had not been responsible, yet another knew of it only by hearsay. When the walls of the ravine were dynamited and the rubble was shoveled over the victims, some were still alive. According to the testimony of one witness, one of the accused had been a specialist in stringing children up by the legs, shooting them with a pistol, and throwing them into the prepared ditch. This defendant did become excited: someone must have had the same name as his, he said. It hadn't been him. A mistake. The New York *Times* has counted the spectators on February 13. There were four. Mr. Bernd-Rüdiger Uhse, West Germany, one of the prosecuting attorneys, in a statement to the New York *Times* yesterday explained the lack of emotion at the trial as follows: "If you see a car accident today and look at the bloody victim, you are horrified. But if you talk about the same accident five years later you will not get very upset about it."

Early in November 1938, Herschel Grynszpan, aged seventeen, shot and killed the German Embassy Attaché Ernst vom Rath in Paris, "out of love for my father and my people, who are enduring untold sufferings." He regretted very much, he said, having injured someone, but he had no other means of expressing the strength of his feelings.

The space panic of early November 1938—that had been in the United States, after Orson Welles's broadcast of a radio play over

CBS. In the play, a spaceship had landed in New Jersey. Men with death-rays attacked. Orson Welles's listeners took this for an actual news report and fled from the cities. On the streets of New York, women knelt and prayed. People were running around with scarves and handkerchiefs over their faces to protect themselves from poison gases. The roads leading out of the cities were clogged. Princeton University dispatched a scientific team with student volunteers and death-defying professors. That was November 1938 in this country.

In the other country . . .

In Jerichow, Mecklenburg-Lübeck, the film section of the regional Party office presented two films at the Rifle Club early in November, *Sword of Peace* and *Jews Unmasked*. The first one actually drew spectators from the surrounding countryside, partly because it promised pictures from prewar days, and partly because, in spite of all the rearmament, it denied the possibility of a future war. Toward the end of *Jews Unmasked* the hall had become pretty empty, to the vexation of Prasemann the caterer, who had been hoping to sell beer and schnapps to the audience after the performance, and to the rage of Friedrich Jansen, who made up his mind that at the next performance he would post Storm Troopers at the doors. Whoever the regional Party film officer was, he was not familiar with the mentality of a country town. The film was a composite of extracts from movies that had at one time been produced by German Jews, and what they revealed was not "the disastrous effect of the Jewish influence on our culture" but the fact that what was shown could only have occurred in large cities; just try and imagine Oskar Tannebaum alone in a drawing room with a lady. However, the Storm Troopers in the front row stayed in their seats, and what they had imbibed by midnight provided some consolation for Prasemann.

On November 5 and 6, the Hitler Youth boys were once again running around for the second "Reich Street Collection," and they not only stopped people on the street but rang doorbells. Papenbrock, whom they had wakened from his afternoon sleep, made an almost soundless scene and boxed the ear of one lad who, regarding this as almost adequate punishment for his crime, once again held his collecting box out to the old man. That was Otto Quade, who on his return home got slapped again because August Quade, Plumbing & Heating, had taken up a loan from Papenbrock. The papers carried the picture of the christening of Edda Göring, the same person who is now arguing with the courts today over her right to Cranach's painting, "Madonna with Child," with which the city of Cologne had had to present her father on the occasion of that happy event, and the Gestapo in Gneez received a denunciation of several persons who had refused a donation, using this christening as an excuse. Later investigations revealed that the boy had held his collecting box under the noses of a group of chatting beer drinkers, that the insulting utterance had been an unrelated statement of fact, and that Alfred Bienmüller, who had not allowed his son to be confirmed, was perfectly entitled to declare that he would never spend money on a christening, whether or not he was still to be presented with offspring by his fifty-year-old wife. Lisbeth Cresspahl was indignant that the Second Reich Street Collection was even going to ignore the Sacred Feast of the Reformation. On November 8 the *Lübecker General-anzeiger* published the news of the killing of Vom Rath, adding that in National Socialist Germany not a hair of the head of a single Jew had been harmed, let alone attempts made on the life of any Jew. Lisbeth seized upon the remark about not harming the hair of any Jew, because Spiegel, the Kiel attorney, had been shot in the head, although she may well not have approved of the intention to kill. Cresspahl saw a brief agitation flare up in her, "like a matchstick fire" was how he described it ten years later, then once again a casual attitude, amusement almost, at a Hanseatic newspaper that did not know the truth. Then the child was summoned, Gesine, who meanwhile had learned to tear paper into squares as a substitute for toilet paper. For the sake of Lisbeth and the Reformation Day service, Cresspahl did not make the trip to Malchow and Wendisch Burg over the weekend, but he did not want to put it off any longer. It never occurred to him that this time things might be different from two years earlier, when David Frankfurter had shot and killed the Swiss Nazi, Wilhelm Gustloff. He wanted to see whether his parents' graves in Malchow were being properly cared for, he wanted to call on Schmidt and Büntzel in Güstrow, and also to look in at Wendisch Burg so his sister's feelings would not be hurt. "Why don't you take the child along?" said Lisbeth. The child was standing by the coal scuttle, tearing the newspaper into strips, solemn and dignified as in all the chores she had learned to carry out, such as feeding the chicken or picking berries in the garden. "Gertrud would like that," said Lisbeth, not attempting to coax or persuade him and, because once again Gertrud Niebuhr had gone without Gesine's promised visit that year, he and the child left the house together to catch the eleven o'clock train.

"Gesine!" she called when they were already beyond the gate. She was standing in the front door, leaning against a doorpost, her arms lightly crossed under her breast. She waved, several times, until the child raised her arm too and moved her hand slightly. But the child was pulling Cresspahl with her other hand, and later on he could only assume that she had smiled as she waved, and that she would have allowed herself to be embraced.

The next evening my mother was seen twice more.

What she was planning to do in Gneez at that hour remains a mystery. The Schauburg was showing a movie that she had already seen in Lübeck, *Vanished Traces*, with Kristina Söderbaum. The Capitol was showing *Heroes in Spain* that evening, preceded by *Nuremberg on Parade*, and it would have only reminded her of the war which Cresspahl believed to have been rehearsed there. The Gneez synagogue was off Horst Wessel Street, which led from the Capitol to the station. When Lisbeth was seen there, the roof of the synagogue was already on fire, but at street level men in shabby clothing, which bore the stamp of Methling charity, were dragging shining objects out of the entrance, as well as things in sacks. The air was bright from the fire, as well as from the light inside the synagogue, but all the windows of the two adjoining buildings were dark. Level with the dividing wall, police had cordoned off the street, also on the other side of the synagogue. Lisbeth Cresspahl was noticed trying to pass through the cordon toward the lower end of the street. A policeman did not even ask her her business: he advised her to go around the block and try from the other end. The spectators, a silent dark group, made room for her, but apparently she did not move away. She was still there when the fire brigade arrived from the lower end and took up their positions. By this time the flames were shooting out from the ground floor of the synagogue, and the truck with the looters had driven off. The firemen behaved with dispatch and according to regulations, as if this were drill practice, except that they stood drawn up in readiness when they might have been putting out the fire. Perhaps Lisbeth was still there to see Joseph Hirschfeld come running up from Horst Wessel Street, thrusting his way through the crowd with powerful arms, despite his sixty-nine years, and the same policeman who had so politely advised Papenbrock's daughter hurriedly dragging the rabbi off through the crowd. He had the old man firmly by the arm, and—also because he was taller—he seemed to be disappearing along Horst Wessel Street not so much with a man he had arrested as with a victim. Now the firemen did begin sporadically dousing the corners of the buildings adjoining the one that was on fire. When the synagogue roof collapsed and its debris flew into the air, burning sparks rained onto the street, and the spectators fell back. At this point Lisbeth was no longer to be seen. Perhaps she had gone off to the Jerichow train, the one leaving at eleven thirty.

It was said that in Jerichow, in Oskar Tannebaum's store, there were some of those present who had set fire to the Gneez synagogue. If that is true, she may have recognized them. The Jerichow police force did not have enough men to block off the street, hence Friedrich Jansen—mayor, police chief—was standing guard there with drawn revolver. The disguised Storm Troopers took their time over Tannebaum's store. It was such a very small opportunity, the pleasure had to be prolonged. The performance recalled amateur theatricals. Prasemann the caterer put a finger to his lips and, waiting for the narrow street to fall almost silent, he raised his ax and brought it down on the glass of the entrance door. Then they recovered in stifled laughter. Oskar Tannebaum still did not turn on the light. Next they carefully hacked the door to pieces. The spectators in Jerichow were more excited than those in Gneez, commenting on the spectacle, complimenting the men on their blows, or shouting derisively. "Can't even aim straight!" they called, or: "It's all for free, says the farmer and beats up his son." This was said by Pahl, for whom the Jew had been a humble competitor. It was intended less as an act of malice than as a lesson; once and for all the Jew was to be taught his place.

Inside Tannebaum's store the Storm Troopers found they had forgotten the show window and proceeded to throw chairs and shelves against the glass from inside. In a dry-goods store there are not many hard objects and they needed the cash register to do the job properly, and when this fell onto the sidewalk it broke open. There the money lay, on the street, a few bills, a handful of coins. "That's not right," said a female voice, obviously that of an old woman, worried and horrified at one and the same time. "Now we're off, says the mouse, as the cat runs off with it to the hayloft," said Böhnhase as Oskar Tannebaum was shoved out onto the street. He fell onto his knees but got to his feet again immediately. That didn't suit Demmler (Hansi Demmler, Jerichow-Ausbau), he had preferred the kneeling position. Tannebaum had to gather up the money on his knees and take it to Friedrich Jansen. Friedrich Jansen motioned Ete Helms over to him, and Ete Helms stood at attention but would not take the money. Jansen, crimson in the face, threatened him with punishment for refusing to obey a command, and Ete brought his heels together and would not take the money. If Jansen had then buttoned the money into his own jacket pocket, this would have been just as bad for his reputation as what he now did, which was to throw the money onto the cobbles and trample around on it.

The first shot was heard only by Peter Wulff, who had been standing silently to one side. Now ignoring the agents of state power, he called for quiet in a businesslike, military manner. Then came the second shot. Friedrich Jansen ordered the street to be cleared for the fire brigade, and the old-fashioned vehicle was pushed in front of the jagged hole in the building, although there was no fire there. Then Frieda Tannebaum emerged from the store, slowly, without being pushed from behind. In her arms she carried her oldest child. Like Oskar, she stood with her back to the wall. They looked at each other across the child. The child was Marie Tannebaum, aged eight, an unruly, withdrawn girl who had been roaming the Gräfin Forest ever since Stoffregen had refused to have her in his school. She had long black braids, which now hung almost to the ground. When she became too heavy, Frieda Tannebaum, with the child in her arms, slid to the ground, obediently keeping her back to the wall, and collapsed over her. She was still holding her as if the child were merely asleep and not to be wakened.

Lisbeth Cresspahl apparently arrived on the scene just as Friedrich Jansen was stamping on the money. She had slowly threaded her way among the spectators to the front, which she had just reached when the second shot was heard. Then she stood still, silent like all the rest. Only when Mrs. Tannebaum had slid to the ground did she step forward and walk around Friedrich Jansen, so that he got the first slap in the face without warning. She struck him several times, although she could not seriously hurt the big heavy man. She struck out like a child, awkwardly, as if she had never been taught how to. Friedrich Jansen simply grabbed her by the hands.

Ete Helms pulled her back into the crowd, and because he put his hand on her shoulder Friedrich Jansen must have assumed she had been arrested. Friedrich Jansen was now giving orders to the fire brigade. The men were ordered to play the hose on the building for half an hour, a building that was not on fire, because Jansen was standing behind the pump with his pistol.

Ete Helms had released Cresspahl's wife as soon as she was out of sight of the spectators. He let her go outside Papenbrock's building, touching his hand to his cap in salute. As far as Helms can remember, she went into the building, but he did not actually see this.

"Is this another of those things you don't want to tell me about?" says Marie. "Wouldn't Francine understand?"

"No, she wouldn't."

"Something like the water-butt story?"

"Something like that."
"Don't tell me about it, Gesine."

February 15, 1968   Thursday

The question was a broad one. Whether the use of atom bombs in Vietnam was being considered. General Earle G. Wheeler, Chairman of the Joint Chiefs of Staff, narrowed it down: Not in Khesanh.

There is also a news item from those who call me one of their own. Three East German girls were disqualified from the Winter Olympics at Grenoble for warming the runners of their sleds. But the West Germans are alleged to have been responsible.

And once again the New York *Times* has given His Honor Mayor John Vliet Lindsay a good thrashing, for it seems he is giving serious consideration to renting out loudspeakers in the subway for the relaying of commercials. A sample: "Times Square. Change for BMT and IND. And stop at Nedick's for an orange drink and hot dog." This to a captive audience! This added to the cacophony of clank, screech, and grind under the ground! It is incredible! It is the last straw! cries the New York *Times*, coming down with another whack on the Mayor across its knees. An unpleasant sight, a painful sound.

Cresspahl and his child traveled south via Blankenberg, Sternberg, and Goldberg, the last stretch from Karow to Malchow on a line that ceased to exist after the war. The child learned: Blankenberg-on-the-Lake, Sternberg-on-the-Lake, Goldberg-on-the-Lake, Malchow-on-the-Lake, and to this day the name Karow is a dry place in her memory because there was nothing there but the station, the street, and the Habben Inn. But they had their lunch on the train, Lisbeth's sandwiches, which the man cut up on his thumb into handy strips for the child. When he held the bottle of Mahn & Ohlerich beer under the child's nose, snapping open the cap, she made a face but then did take a cautious sip of the burning bitter stuff. At such moments they both looked quite used to traveling around together. Once Cresspahl was asked where he was going with "the kid," and he gave her a long look. Then he said sadly: "She won't tell me," and silly Gesine thought that once again her pride was being respected. Cresspahl was not asked very often.

At the Malchow cemetery, the graves of Heinrich and Berta Cresspahl were as neat and tidy as any client could wish, and he did not bother calling on the caretaker. The couple had a common gravestone, and right after her husband's death Berta had had her name

and birth date chiseled into the stone, so that the year of her death
stood out conspicuously in the dim light.

> *That's my Mom and Dad.*
> *Can't they get out of there?*
> *They're shut up in there forever, Gesine.*
> *Mamma says the dead will be free.*
> *Not here, Gesine. Not with us.*
> *I don't think I'll ever be dead.*
> *That's right, Gesine. Don't.*

Gesine Zabel, née Redebrecht, was now a waitress at a hotel on
Lake Malchow, and because Cresspahl did not know this he had
taken a room there (three marks; with child's cot, four marks).
Cresspahl left the dining room as soon as the child became tired, and
he sat down with his pipe at the open window beside the black water
that from time to time was swept by the waning full moon. Gesine
Zabel did not come until just before midnight. She was now forty-
nine. Her plentiful blond hair had become sparse and rather sandy,
and it was too short to braid. For eight years she had had to work
very hard, without having been brought up to it. The corners of her
eyes were all wrinkled from so many frightened glances. While waiting on table she had seemed harassed, defenselessly irritated, with
forestalling apologies in her expression. She was too tired after her
day's work to be able to stay for more than half an hour. Next
morning a plate with an apple and knife stood on the windowsill, the
excuse for going to a hotel guest's room.

> *You're drinking, Hinrich.*
> *I'm drinking, Gesine.*
> *Peter Zabel wasn't a bad sort.*
> *I never heard that he was.*
> *I wasn't allowed to marry you.*
> *We were just kids.*
> *Why ever didn't you stay in England, Hinrich!*
> *My wife wanted it this way.*
> *Is she a good woman?*
> *She's a good woman, Gesine.*
> *Is the child hers? She doesn't look like you.*
> *She takes after me, I think.*
> *And now you're drinking, Hinrich.*

Can I help you?
No, Hinrich. Try to help yourself.

Next morning Cresspahl's child was amazed to find she was supposed to shake hands with the woman who had brought her her breakfast, but she obediently stood up. And she had taken a lot of trouble to manage to get dressed and washed without her father's help, so she would do nothing to spoil their trip. She shook hands with the woman, bobbed a Papenbrock curtsy, and thanked her, not in dialect. It was a while before she dared ask the question: had the woman been crying?

After Wendisch Burg they changed to a branch line going southwest from Neustrelitz, and they reached the Niebuhrs by bus, the driver being kind enough to stop for Cresspahl in the middle of a leafless wood. Then, among the tree trunks, a low red roof came in sight, in the creeping mist. That was the Wendisch Burg Lock on the River Havel.

At the lockkeeper's house were not only Cresspahl's sister with Niebuhr, but also Niebuhr's brother Peter with his wife and child. It was with this Klaus Niebuhr, not quite five, a Berlin child who could scarcely speak the Low German dialect and understood little more, that Gesine was sent off to play behind the house. There was a swing there, and the childless Niebuhrs had built a sandbox. "But I don't live here, I live in Berlin!" said the boy. . . .

With modest pride Martin Niebuhr showed his brother-in-law around the property, pointing out the locks, the office, the two telephones, the beehives, but for the rest of the afternoon Cresspahl was alone with Peter Niebuhr, who was trying to fix up a boat in a shed across the river. It was a yawl, and not only was it storm-damaged and its mast broken away but it had lain outdoors all through the previous winter. Peter Niebuhr had bought it for a song, but his knowledge of boat-building was inadequate, with the result that conversation with Cresspahl was started off awkwardly.

Peter Niebuhr, then just thirty, took cautious stock of the older man. He could not understand a life spent in that way: Mecklenburg, emigration, return to the Nazis. He could not comprehend the patience with which the other man suppressed questions which must surely be occurring to him: why a card-carrying member of the Communist Party should have attended the Eiche school for non-commissioned officers in 1934 and from there gone to Darré's Reich Ministry of Agriculture. After they had been working silently side by side for a time, Peter brought up the subject of Dr. Semig, not without some defiance and prepared for only the slightest excuse. "My boy," said Cresspahl after a while, and the man of thirty, a university graduate, holder of a diploma, employed at a ministry in the Reich capital, found he could accept not only the mode of address but also the relaxed, speculative look in the eyes of this relative whom he scarcely knew, who amounted to nothing more than a master carpenter in some tiny place on the Baltic. Then Cresspahl recollected the other man's superior education and said, this time not in dialect: "It went off very well, the way you must have intended it. Without you, of course, we would never have got him out of the country."

Cresspahl liked the boy. Of the two Niebuhr brothers, he was the one who had as much intelligence, strength, and stamina as his older brother Martin lacked owing to his carelessness, dilatoriness, and inertia. What he liked in Peter was that he was uneasy about having not only abandoned his party but, in order to feed his family, gone over to another party. There were several things here that threw light on Cresspahl's own decision fifteen years earlier. With his profession, it had been less easy for Peter to go abroad than for Cresspahl. He also liked the woman whom Peter had chosen, Martha Klünder from Waren, still a girl, shy with everyone except her husband, with no trace now of the civil servant's daughter she had been when Cresspahl first met her. It was with some envy that Cresspahl looked on such a marriage, scarcely younger than his own. He thought also of Perceval, T. P., whom he had lost in England, and of Manning Susemihl. Maybe he would have one more try. He let Peter tell him his side of the Griem affair. Then he told Peter what it had looked like from Jerichow. He did not interrupt Peter when the latter complained at length of his superior, who had not wanted to back him unless he wore a Nazi badge in his lapel. After a while they quit working and walked along the river as far as the next village, returning for supper almost of one mind. As for the boat, Peter was to send it to Jerichow and, except for the cost of transportation, pay nothing to have it fixed up. In return Cresspahl wanted to learn sailing.

The children were put down to sleep in a little room off the living room. They had spent the day telling each other about their parents, their homes, their neighbors, and they soon fell asleep in spite of the murmur of voices in the next room, a sound in which laughter mingled too, and enjoyment and kindliness. Gesine had never before met so many new people in one day.

It was Gesine who next morning heard the telephone ringing. It was not the instrument that was connected to the internal circuit of the Water Board, but the regular telephone. She was just stepping through the door of the office as Martin Niebuhr handed the receiver to Cresspahl. It was a few minutes to six on the morning of November 10. My mother had already been dead for an hour.

February 18, 1968 Sunday

My condolences, Mr. Cresspahl.
G'd afternoon.
When did you learn of your wife's death?
This morning about six.
Who told you?
Jansen.
The Mayor, the local Party leader?
From Jansen.
In what form?
No form. Over the phone.
What was the exact wording?
"Good morning. Your wife is now dead."
What was the tone?
Jansen.
Are you and Jansen enemies, Mr. Cresspahl?
I don't make an enemy of Jansen.
On November 9, 1938, at 23:55 or 24.00 hours, your wife slapped Jansen's face.
Am I under arrest?
Why should we arrest someone like you, Mr. Cresspahl? There's plenty of rabble running around loose outside.
Then I wish to go to my wife now.
Soon, Mr. Cresspahl. A few more questions.
Then I must ask you now, Commissioner—
Why don't you just call me Vick?
How she died. What killed her.
That's what we'd like to hear from you, Mr. Cresspahl.
I've been away from Jerichow since Tuesday morning. You were the one who had me picked up from the Güstrow train, remember?
And what train did you take to Güstrow?
The Berlin-Copenhagen express.
And where were you before that? Since Tuesday?
In Wendisch Burg. With relatives.

The whole time?

Before that in Malchow-on-the-Lake.

You can prove that?

With the hotel bill.

Who did you get in touch with there?

I wanted to look up my parents. Their graves.

We'll find out, Mr. Cresspahl. We'll find out.

How did she die?

There was a fire at your place, Mr. Cresspahl.

Yes.

So you know about that?

No.

Your parents-in-law live in Jerichow, you have a telephone, Jerichow 209, and you're trying to tell me—

My own line was dead.

Ah yes. The fire brigade drove into a telephone pole and knocked it over.

Yes.

How do you know? You can speak freely.

From you, Mr. Vick. No one answered the phone at Papenbrocks'.

Because they couldn't. They'd already left for the brickyard.

The express had no phone, in Güstrow there wasn't time, and I intended to phone here in Gneez but you had me picked up.

There's been a fire at your place, and you say: Yes.

Yes.

Doesn't surprise you in the least.

All that lumber in the yard, that can burn easily enough.

But that's not where it started. That didn't go up till later.

Where was my wife?

At midnight she was in Jerichow on the market square, and before that at the scene of the accident at the Jews'.

What was she doing at the Tannebaums'?

Cresspahl, you can't pull the wool over my eyes. My eyes are pretty good. Don't you ever read the papers?

I do.

But not today.

Not today.

I see. And at Wendisch Burg you didn't notice anything. Your relatives live in the woods.

My sister lives with her husband who operates a lock in the woods.

Let me tell you something, Cresspahl. What happened last night all over the Reich—we won't go into that. I'd rather not know anything about it.

What kind of accident was it, Mr. Vick?

A Jewish brat got shot and killed.

Walter? Young Marie?

Young Marie, Mr. Cresspahl. Marie Sara Tannebaum. Your wife—

My wife doesn't own a gun.

It shouldn't concern you who did it, who happened to make the mistake. Your wife was merely at the scene.

Then she slapped his face.

That's right. Ah, here's the report from Wendisch Burg. You were there. You might have told us right away that your other brother-in-law is with the Reich Ministry of Agriculture. Here. Have a look at that. We've no secrets here.

Then the fire started.

We don't know when it started.

Where did it start?

The alarm was turned in this morning at 4:30 hours. The flames had just shot through the roof.

Through the roof of our home?

The roof of the barn. Where your workshop was. Have you any enemies, Mr. Cresspahl?

Was it arson?

We don't know. Everything was destroyed by the fire, everything west of where the stalls used to be. Three of the four doors on the east side of the workshop are burned through. The fourth, at the southeast corner, was locked and bolted. That was where the fire reached last. At that time the ceiling was still only smoldering, but the oxygen must have been all used up.

Where the fodder room used to be.

That's where your wife was lying.

Was she dead?

No. She died when she was carried outside.

Did she die from the fire?

She was not burned to death, if that's what you mean, Mr. Cresspahl. For the time being the medics are giving asphyxiation as the cause of death.

I see.

Maybe you can explain why the workmen in the house heard nothing. And saw nothing.

All the windows on the east side of the barn have shutters. If any of the windowpanes cracked they must have fallen inside, not onto the paving. If the fire consumed the threshing floor and the stall partitions first, that's to say the workshop and the work being done there, all the glare must have gone upward and westward. There's no one living on that side. If the fodder room is still intact, that means the glass in the south door was the last to go. In that case Alwin Paap must have been the one to hear it.

Just like you'd been there, Mr. Cresspahl.

Yes.

It wasn't Alwin Paap who turned in the alarm.

Then it must've been Friedrich Jansen from across the street. When the fire burned through the north door he may have noticed the glare.

It was Jansen, Mr. Cresspahl. Doesn't anything strike you about that?

Mr. Vick, can I go to my wife now? The next train won't leave for three hours.

You won't need that train, Mr. Cresspahl. Tell me something. You spoke of Jansen just now in a rather derogatory manner.

I said I had no quarrel with him.

You mean you're above that.

I'm a carpenter, and Jansen is the local Party leader. What would I have to quarrel about with him, Mr. Vick?

Let's suppose it was arson.

It can't be done from the outside. If someone tried to break into the workshop he wouldn't get far without making a noise. It's not like a fire that's contained by walls and a roof. My wife would have heard it. Paap even more likely.

Let's assume your wife does hear it. She gets out of bed, puts on a winter coat over—

No, a blue housecoat. A padded one. With a London label.

Just like you'd been there, Mr. Cresspahl. She surprises the fellow at one of the doors—

Which door?

Ah, we've no clues as to that! What d'you expect! The Jerichow fire brigade! They expect a blow from an ax to open a lock!

Yes.

Since they couldn't put out the fire anyway.

The fire brigade couldn't put out the fire.

They must have tried, Mr. Cresspahl. They managed to find the

hydrant in the brickyard and hook up to it and extend the hoses, but
it all took time, and then the pump wouldn't work. They had messed
about with the equipment at the Jew's place.

Who had?

Jansen, Mr. Cresspahl.

Yes.

Doesn't anything strike you?

So that's why the lumber in the yard was burned up too.

Everything's gone, Mr. Cresspahl, everything. The machinery is
nothing but twisted scrap. The walls had fallen in on them, and the
roof. You can think yourself lucky you've still got your house.

Yes.

The intruder, the arsonist, now takes the keys from your wife,
drags her into the workshop, hits her over the head—

Had my wife been beaten?

We don't know. She has a place on the back of her head that
might be from a sandbag.

I know who uses sandbags.

My dear Mr. Cresspahl, I prefer not to have heard that. This
isn't the Gestapo, this is the Criminal Investigation Department, but
I advise you not to take advantage of the fact. The fellow locks up
your wife, who is unconscious in the fodder room—

The fodder room has a double bolt. A child could unfasten it.

But there was no key in the lock.

The key is kept in the lock on the outside, and we don't lock up
with that.

There was no key there, Mr. Cresspahl. Now he has all the time
in the world to lay the fire, lock the door again, and make his escape.
He may not have had far to go.

It must be someone who objects to the work being done for the
Air Force base at Mariengabe. Or that was being done.

Mr. Cresspahl, if you're trying to exonerate someone simply so
that you can get your own hands on him—well, O.K. But that's no
use to me.

Then I can leave now.

You're not leaving, Mr. Cresspahl. You're going to have a look
at this rope.

That's not a rope. That's a piece of clothesline.

Might it be one of yours?

I suppose so.

Do you recognize it?

My wife kept her clotheslines in the house, to keep them dry.

And what did she use for small items, the day-to-day laundry?

A line is usually put up and not always taken down again at night. Along the garden fence.

That's the one we found cut, Mr. Cresspahl. Don't touch where it's been cut, that's an exhibit!

Some fellows steal a cow in one place and the rope somewhere else.

That fellow wasn't after a cow, Mr. Cresspahl. But he knew what he wanted all right. We won't find out whether this piece is part of your clothesline till we get the lab report. But we do know that your wife was tied up with this piece of clothesline.

There are no scorch marks on it.

But it smells as if it had been hanging in smoke for a year. She was bound at the ankles with this rope, and not only that—the rope was also pulled through a ring in the wall and knotted. Beside her lay another piece of rope, from which she evidently just managed to free her wrists.

I'm leaving now.

One thing more, Mr. Cresspahl. Did Friedrich Jansen actually say "Your wife is now dead"?

"Good morning," and then the other.

Not, for instance: "Your wife has committed suicide"?

No.

And what do you say to the fact that Friedrich Jansen tells everyone in Jerichow who is willing to listen that your wife committed suicide? What do you say to that?

It's none of his business.

Mr. Cresspahl. You don't understand. You don't want to understand. This is the Criminal Investigation Department. We are not the Secret State Police.

I don't mean to forget it.

And I've learned something from you too that I don't mean to forget either, Mr. Cresspahl! You may go now.

Is my wife at home, Mr. Vick?

Your wife is not at home. The body has been confiscated because of suspicion of a criminal act. There'll be an autopsy tonight. You may inquire at the hospital in Gneez tomorrow, Mr. Cresspahl. If you want to know the cause of her death. My condolences, Mr. Cresspahl.

G'd afternoon.

February 19, 1968   Monday

A victim with a name, Ngo Van Tranh, was suspected by a marine yesterday morning in Saigon of belonging to the Vietcong. Ngo Van Tranh, already seriously wounded, stated that the Vietcong had taken him from his home in Thuduc during the previous night and forced him to carry ammunition. He is offered some water, he seems to be trying to drink it. He is lying half under some boards. He is then questioned by another marine and threatened with a rifle. Then he is stabbed by a third marine who finally kills him with a rifle burst. Associated Press has had three photographs taken of this, and the last picture shows the former Ngo Van Tranh lying in the rubble almost completely covered by boards.

Cresspahl went not to search but to find.

Thursday evening he stayed in Gneez. He called on Wilhelm Böttcher, head of the carpenters' guild in Gneez County, and his visit was followed by one from Herbert Vick, who wanted to question Böttcher. If Böttcher was to be believed, Cresspahl had bought some of his best wood from him, light oak, aged for five years. "You realize I'm from the Criminal Investigation Department, not the Gestapo," said Vick in the challenging tone that he considered engaging, but Böttcher would not say whether he regarded Cresspahl as being somewhat too businesslike because he had made some purchases while his wife was still aboveground. Vick went away, his appetite whetted for the next incomprehensible factor.

Vick spent the evening in the dining room of the City of Hamburg Hotel, where Cresspahl had booked a room. Sitting over his expense-account beer, a relaxed, dumpy little figure kneading his plump chin and staring absent-mindedly toward the door whenever his nose was not in his fat notebook. Vick failed to discover what Cresspahl ordered up into his room because Alma Witte would not be intimidated. He had better luck with the staff members whom he furtively waylaid. For a long time Cresspahl gave no sign of life, as if he wanted no one to know where he was. After a while, Vick was asked over to the table of Wegerecht, the county court judge, feeling somewhat exposed there with his beer but reluctant to drink the red wine the others were drinking. At last the hall porter glanced into the dining room as if looking for someone, and Vick went out into the lobby. He stood next to the telephone operator, reading the sheets on which Cresspahl had written his telegrams and handing them to her one by one. They were ordinary death announcements for Timmendorf, Wismar, Wendisch Burg, Neustrelitz, Schwerin, Berlin, and Lübeck. He had her translate the one to London. "Mr. Cresspahl requests the presence of the addressee at the funeral of his wife," said Elise Bock pertly in German, smug over her linguistic talents, indignant at his prying, and Vick told her too that he was from a certain police department and not from another. His manner was especially gruff because he was annoyed by the certainty with which Cresspahl named the day of the funeral, as if the body would be handed over to him by then. Smith in Richmond, it sounded a bit fishy. Meanwhile Messrs. Wegerecht and Rehse made it quite clear by their questions that the only use they had for him was so that they could pump him about this new affair in Jerichow. Sheltering behind the lateness of the autopsy, Vick left earlier than he would have liked. At the corner of the market square he turned around, but Cresspahl's windows were still half open, and dark.

Next morning he intercepted his man at the Gneez station. Cresspahl had gone to the hospital at seven, and they had not shown him his wife. Vick could have told him this. "I wouldn't advise you to," said Vick. "Yes," said Cresspahl. "I mean, to look at your wife," said Vick. "Yes," said Cresspahl. He did not appear to have lost much sleep, but his eyes could not focus very well, they were more bloodshot than yesterday. Vick let him leave by the Jerichow train and got into his car, but during the long gentle climb up the narrow highway Vick found himself behind slow trucks, and he had no desire to tangle with drivers showing armed forces license plates. By now Cresspahl had gained more than half an hour on him.

The Jerichow fire brigade had stationed a guard at the ruined building which they had not been able to save. The workshop had collapsed, all except for the east wall, to which the remains of what had once been the stalls were still clinging, and at the south end the almost intact rectangle of the Pinnow fodder room. Wherever a piece of machinery had once stood, smoke still rose thinly from the ruins. They had torn apart the stacks of burning lumber, and the blackened charred planks lay jumbled together as far as the remaining wall. They had ripped away the barbed wire in the bushes and dragged it right across the path, like a barrier. It was a long time since the house itself had been visible in this way, hidden only by the bare walnut trees, dazzling white window frames in the neat red-brick walls. The sky, sunless, was pale, white. To Cresspahl it all seemed as silent as if there were no one about.

In the kitchen the fire was burning under the kettle as it was every morning. The door to Lisbeth's room was closed.

Her dress was hanging over the foot of the bed. She had intended to hang it up in the closet and then go to bed. The coverlet was turned back. She had sat on the edge of the bed, not for long. Here the air was almost smokeless.

In the kitchen she had taken the storm lantern down from its hook. She had opened the passage doors very quietly, so as not to attract the attention of those in the rooms on the west. Moved on bare feet.

In the storeroom was some spilled kerosene. By now she was hurrying. By the time she reached the back door she must have started to run.

She had left herself so little time that, instead of unknotting the clothesline, she had chopped it through with a pruning knife. The Labor Service girls had been taught by her to untie every knot. The pruning knife had been stuck into the top of a fence post, so it would be seen and not get rusty.

By the pump, where the path begins to slope down, there was a depression in the damp ground as if she had fallen there, on one knee. But there were all kinds of crisscrossing footprints here, and none to be seen of bare feet.

The south gable of the workshop building had broken off at an angle. There was nothing left of the entrance door but the frame. The doorpost had been hacked away with axes. The broken glass on the ground was blackened and greasy from the smoke. The two door panels were still firmly joined in the middle by the lock. Here she had managed to gain a little time.

On entering the workshop on Wednesday night, she had found it smelling of freshly cut wood, of stain, paint, machine oil, work. She had not switched on the light because Alwin Paap might have been wakened by the big square of light in the darkness. She had screened the lamplight with her own body and placed the lantern in the middle of the threshing floor under a piece of machinery so that from outside the barn looked dark again.

Then she had faced one more choice. She could unhook a ladder from the wall, stand it up against one of the crossbeams, climb up on it, kick away the ladder, tie herself with the rope to the beam, and jump. That way she would not have needed three hours to die. But maybe she did not want to be seen with a twisted head, a broken neck, by anybody. So she decided not to be found at all.

Then she laid the rope over the edge of a saw and cut it into short pieces that were no good for a hanging. Now all she had to do was knock over the lantern. Everything here would burn.

In five years the Pinnow barn had become a sturdy, windproof building. It was dry inside even in winter, and even on the coldest days the chill was off the air. She did not need to give the little fire much assistance. It was enough to lay a path for it from one of the long walls to the other, and in no time they were hot and wrapped in color.

When a flaring sheet of fire hung down from the third cross-beam to cover the north door, the flames were already thrusting their way into the little room containing the oil cans. By that time she was completely surrounded except for one place opposite, where from time to time the flames still parted. One leap and she would have been through it.

She had not wanted to escape. She had locked herself in the fodder room so that she would not be carried out immediately or easily. She had wanted to wait there.

When she went through the door she had hardly taken any fire with her. She had banged the key firmly into a crack between the floorboards so that it was no longer visible. The fodder room, later the workmen's room, was empty; it contained no tool with which she could have pried the key loose from the floor. The window had iron crossbars and was bricked into the wall. She could not even have let in any air; outside the window there was still the heavy shutter, bolted from the outside. She was now securely locked up inside.

The fire had not reached her from the floor but through the wall of the toolroom, and from above. At first the walls merely crackled, then the heat turned them black. The floor remained undamaged to the end. Then she had tied her feet together and knotted the rope through the ring so she could not run away. Had she been in a complete daze she might have tried to tie her hands. Cresspahl did not believe this. In falling she may have struck the back of her head against one of the projecting beams; perhaps that knocked her out and she never knew.

The firemen had not found her right away, the fire being too intense, too loud, for anyone to be alive in there. They had knocked the first door on the right, with its frame, out of the wall, because it was locked. The damp debris of this was still lying on the ground. Among the debris lay a broom with a broken handle, otherwise almost clean. Kneeling down, Cresspahl wiped over the place where he assumed Lisbeth to have lain. The chalk outline showed a figure lying on its side, arms along the body, like a sleeper's.

They had not hurried to carry her outside.

All around the fodder room they had doused the fire, with bucket after bucket from the pump, to preserve the evidence.

The inside walls had been burned thin, but they were still standing and the roof had not yet collapsed. So they still had time to pick her up and run with her through the open south door and along the path between workshop and lumber pile, which was only then beginning to catch fire.

Then she had lain on the ground, until she was dead.

"A complaint from you, Mr. Cresspahl, that's all I need!" implored Vick. He was standing on the brickyard path as if rooted to the spot, but he did not dare try, with his short legs, to get through the tangle of bushes and barbed wire, which meant that he could only watch Cresspahl walk away. He lifted one foot halfway across the barricade, pulled it back again. Now it did him no good that he had caught up with Cresspahl.

February 21, 1968 Wednesday

On Friday morning, after Cresspahl had left to catch the Gneez train, Pastor Brüshaver began work on his funeral sermon.

Cresspahl had not requested a funeral sermon.

He had come straight from the scene of the fire, soot on his face, his coat streaked with debris, and listened to Brüshaver's account. Sitting patiently on the visitor's chair, his eyes unseeing on the man across from him, his hands lightly clasped on his lap, not folded. These he had washed. His eyes were screwed up with the effort of remembering, and Brüshaver realized that he was the last of the witnesses whom Cresspahl would interview.

She had lain on the north side of the brickyard path, resting on a brown uniform coat, beside Creutz's fence. She had been surrounded by many people, not just Friedrich Jansen, Alwin Paap, the Labor Service girl, old Creutz, Amalie Creutz, Aggie Brüshaver, and Brüshaver. He did not know the names of the others. It was still dark, with light from the fire shining fitfully across. He decided not to say anything about Lisbeth's clothing. Cresspahl asked him. Lisbeth had been wearing a blue housecoat, but it had been open and burned spots in her nightgown were noticeable. As Brüshaver had stepped toward her, Berling had just removed his hand from under her head. But he remained on his knees and had closed her eyes before Brüshaver had got down. The face seemed quite unharmed, except for some fresh blood from her nose and a small patch of open skin under one eye. The right eye. Later, Berling had called the blood from her nose "pulmonary blood," caused by asphyxiation. Then Aggie had covered her up with her own coat. Friedrich Jansen obtained the Wendisch Burg telephone number from Alwin Paap and had then left. At six thirty the police arrived from Gneez. They had brought along an ambulance and, after inspecting the scene of the fire and the house, had driven off just before seven.

Cresspahl also wanted to know who had placed the body on the stretcher, was satisfied with its having been the two ambulance men, and stood up. Brüshaver had suggested Sunday for the funeral. Cresspahl said: "Monday, at three." Brüshaver had had a church funeral service in mind, and Cresspahl said: "She needn't be taken to the church." Brüshaver asked what text he should take for the graveside ceremony, and Cresspahl drew from his coat pocket the page that was now missing from the Bible of the City of Hamburg Hotel. It was the Thirty-Ninth Psalm, with some verses deleted. Cresspahl placed the page on the desk, as if he were not sure whether the pastor would find it in his own Bible. Cresspahl's next request did not upset him, he had faced it so often. The request did not concern Cresspahl himself, it was on behalf of Lisbeth, and Brüshaver felt rather that he was being asked some casual favor. He knew, said Cresspahl, that it was not customary. But his wife should forgo nothing at the grave.

And thou shalt not want.

This fellow Cresspahl had requested: Invocation, lesson, prayer, Lord's Prayer, consecration, benediction. This constituted three more rites than were permitted to suicides by the Regional Church of Mecklenburg.

Brüshaver followed Cresspahl into the kitchen, where Aggie had set out a washbowl for him and was brushing his coat. When Cresspahl had dried his face, Brüshaver asked about a blessing in the house. "No," said Cresspahl, and Brüshaver realized that the other man no longer wanted the Church in his house now that he was alone in it: there had really been no need for Cresspahl to hang the towel so neatly over a chair, like something he had used for the last time.

Then Brüshaver had to look on while his own wife threw herself on the other man's breast, as if wanting forgiveness for something.

Every two hours his wife placed a pot of fresh coffee on his desk, even bringing his meals in to him so that he would not have to leave his work even for fifteen minutes. A red-eyed wife and three kids slinking past the door as if they had been beaten, how was a man supposed to work in such a house!

Aggie wanted Lisbeth to be mentioned in his Sunday sermon. This was contrary to all custom and regulations. Once she was under the ground, she could be mentioned the following Sunday in the regular service. His wife knew this. He did not want to lose face in her eyes. This fellow Cresspahl wanted the Church to acknowledge partial responsibility for his wife's death. He would never see him in church again, no matter what he did; all the same, Brüshaver did not relish the idea of living alongside a neighbor who had no respect for him. That's vanity, Brüshaver. You can't bear the thought of someone cutting you in the street as long as you stay in this town. That's not vanity.

Before Brüshaver had as much as three words on paper, someone arrived to disturb him. Vick, from the Department of Criminal Investigation in Gneez (not from the Gestapo). He wanted to hear of quarrels between Friedrich Jansen and Cresspahl. He could not grasp the fact that the two men existed in Jerichow as if at opposite ends of the world, and that the conflict between them had been promoted and sustained by the inhabitants. Did Brüshaver consider Jansen capable of an act of vengeance? He was capable of an act of vengeance, but only when he was drunk and when Cresspahl was not in town; Brüshaver suspected a trap and kept silent. Why should a man like Vick suspect a, shall we say, worthy National Socialist fighter? Why did he need this particular denunciation, so that he could first get Jansen under arrest and then saddle him with the errors in the financial report of the town of Jerichow? "Because that bunch of scoundrels must disappear from our ranks!" "Because I'm a true believer in National Socialism!"

Nowhere does the Bible expressly forbid suicide. Young Mrs. Cresspahl had asked about this. On closer consideration, it was obvious that she had been asking loud and clear for help. There may have been others in the town from whom she had hoped for reassurance, support, information; but they were not obliged to admit this. The pastor had a duty to confess this. But a sermon for the Twenty-Second Sunday after Trinity can't start out that way.

About noon on Thursday, Brüshaver had called on the Tannebaums because they had failed to get in touch with him about a funeral for Marie. Brüshaver had wanted to offer them a burial (a "quiet one") at his cemetery, if Oskar had the say and his wife did not want to take the child to the Catholics. He found the family in the wagon shed in the yard. They were seated on chairs around the coffin, which they had placed on the ground. It was a mass-produced one, varnished with black shellac. The coffin had been sent by the Gestapo from Gneez, and that evening Swenson was to transport it to Gneez for a burial after dark. The child looked very long in it, the head tilted sharply back, arms along her sides. The blood that had run out of the hole in her temple had been so gently blotted up that a trace of it still remained, and they had shrunk from touching the wound itself. Oskar planted himself in front of Brüshaver, as if he wanted to bar the way to the dead child. He said in a gruff but not hostile voice: "Well, she died like a Jewish girl; so she's going to have a Jewish burial." When Swenson drove up that evening with his hearse, the house was empty, the inside still in the waterlogged mess in which the Storm Troopers had left it. The building belonged to the Von Bobziens; that was why Jansen had wanted to soak it and thus prevent the nonexistent fire. The Tannebaums had left town by Field Street, with the coffin and the dead girl's younger brother on a farm cart, the parents on foot, the wife beside the horse, Oskar beside the boy, who sat facing backward. If they were making for Lübeck, they would have to cover many miles of muddy roads before coming to a highway. It was now Friday afternoon, and they had not been seen at any farm, in any village. Brüshaver was now spared the fuss with the Church authorities and the Gestapo over a Christian burial for the Jewish child; now for Lisbeth Cresspahl he was to risk a good deal more than a warning.

There is no doubt that the Bible does not expressly forbid suicide. But in place of the prohibition is the reminder of God's mercy that is put to the desperate person. The fact was that suicide rendered remorse impossible and hence forgiveness; how could he deny Lisbeth that before the assembled congregation? Brüshaver started to read. He was searching for proof that God has pre-empted the right to determine the ending of a life because He alone knows to which end He will lead that life. There was a fleeting sense of uneasiness in this reading; it was excused by the task, it was a pretext for evading the task.

Late that afternoon it occurred to Brüshaver that he did not know for sure whether Lisbeth had ended her life deliberately and with premeditation. It was only Cresspahl who had admitted to a suicide by requesting the exceptional; that Wednesday night Cresspahl had been far away from Jerichow. The townspeople spoke of an accident, and even the rumor of a murder had been prompted by Jansen's stubborn insistence that Lisbeth had taken her own life.

Brüshaver took the six o'clock train to Gneez and found Cresspahl in the Böttcher workshop. Böttcher accompanied the Jerichow pastor only as far as the door. Böttcher could understand that Cresspahl wanted to build his wife's coffin with his own hands; but he could not help feeling a bit embarrassed about it, and he did not like the idea of anyone, no matter who, watching a colleague at this work.

Cresspahl looked pleasantly over to Brüshaver and rested his arms by placing them on the lower end of the box, which now, after eight hours, he had completely finished. Brüshaver put his question. He noticed himself adopting a pleading tone; moreover, Cresspahl was looking at him like a teacher at a schoolboy who still fails to understand even after a simple explanation. "Yes," he said patiently, with something like amusement in the corners of his eyes. Brüshaver repeated his question. Lisbeth had believed in God, hadn't she? Now Cresspahl filled his pipe, lit it, closed its lid, spat on the match. "Now maybe He'll believe her," he said. He stood up, not because Brüshaver had found nowhere to sit but in order to stretch, his pipe raised in his fist. He waited for the next question. Brüshaver looked with a kind of horror at the man who could attribute such a death to his wife, who was willing to accept the loss of insurance money for workshop and machinery just so this chosen death would be hers forever. He waited for Cresspahl to wish him a good night and left, but paused once more in the yard. Cresspahl had sat down again beside the coffin, hunched over, his hands inside the coffin and holding his pipe. Evidently he wished to use the tiresome interruption at least as a breather. He seemed perfectly at home in the other man's workshop.

So if God does not forbid suicide, does He not guide the desperate person's hand in that He permits such an end? If God pre-empts the right to life, is not the ending of that life also at His behest? Now Brüshaver had only the Saturday left, and not even half a page had been written.

On Saturday, Cresspahl's announcement appeared in the *Gneezer Tageblatt*. It was signed by the Papenbrock, Paepcke, and Niebuhr families, but the wording was Cresspahl's. There was no mention of a tragic fate, of God's (inscrutable) wisdom, or that Lisbeth had been taken (snatched) from this life. It said: Lisbeth Cresspahl has departed this life.

The police had released her. Early that morning Swenson took her to Jerichow, but before the news had got around town new barbed wire had been strung along Cresspahl's property. Anyone passing by as if out for a stroll would have seen Cresspahl, Paap, and

Heine Klaproth clearing a path to the front door of the house through the piles of charred logs and broken bricks; no one ventured up to the house itself. Apparently even Vick no longer considered the yard a potential crime scene. And Aggie Brüshaver went to her husband's study and told him she was being pestered about the exact time of the Cresspahl funeral, more out of curiosity than sadness, and that Frieda Klütz was having a new black dress made in the two days before Monday.

After that, Brüshaver found that the words flowed from his pen. At noon Aggie could sit down at the typewriter. That afternoon he paid calls, and all those who saw him so relaxed and friendly found it hard to believe next day.

The Government in Berlin had taken upon itself to declare the Twenty-Second Sunday after Trinity a "One-Dish Sunday." But Friedrich Jansen had gone off to something calling itself "proceedings of honor," and without him the Storm Troopers were afraid to check up, on the pretext of a social call, as to whether a family might have a roast on the table after all. The Church was no more crowded than usual. Cresspahl was not there.

Brüshaver began with Matthew 18, with the conditions for entering the Kingdom of Heaven: Except ye be converted, and become as little children. It goes on to speak of the person who offends a child, it were better for him that a millstone were hanged about his neck, and that he were drowned in the depth of the sea. (Brüshaver omitted the verse about the necessity of such evil in the world and the dire fate threatening him who commits it.) Then came the part about the hundred sheep. If one of these goes astray, does he not leave the ninety and nine in order to search for that one? And when it is found, it is beloved above all the rest. And until seventy times seven shalt thou forgive.

Then to the people of Jerichow he spoke the words that Cresspahl had not wanted to hear at the graveside. He spoke them for Louise Papenbrock, who even now could not resist conveying, with straight back and lifted chin, that, say what you might, no one else had lost their youngest daughter. He spoke them for Albert Papenbrock, who first gazed sternly at the pulpit as if performing a duty and an ignominious one at that, then looked thoughtful, as if pondering a suggestion. He spoke them for people like Richard Maass, who preferred to regard attendance in church that day rather as a reproach for bad behavior. He spoke them for the person who took copies of his sermons to the Secret State Police. He spoke them for Hilde

Paepcke, who was crying. He spoke them for Lisbeth, and apologized to her. He spoke them for Cresspahl.

It was no concern of the people of Jerichow how Lisbeth Cresspahl had died. Suicide was not to be condemned either before men or on moral grounds. It was a matter between Lisbeth and her God that she had expected more from Him than He had been prepared to give. She had been as free to die as to live and, although she would have done better to leave her death to Him, she had nevertheless offered up a sacrifice to atone for another life, the murder of herself to atone for the murder of a child. Whether or not that had been an error was not going to be discovered in Jerichow.

On the other hand, it certainly did concern the people of Jerichow that Lisbeth Cresspahl had died. They had been involved in the life she had no longer been able to endure. Now came the enumeration that formed the basis of the verdict against Brüshaver. He began with Voss, who had been whipped to death in Rande, he overlooked neither the mutilation of Methfessel in concentration camp nor the death of his own son in the war against the Spanish Government, until he came to the Wednesday night outside the Tannebaum store. Indifference. Tacit consent. The profit motive. Betrayal. The selfishness of a pastor who had seen only the persecution of his Church, who had kept silent contrary to his duty, under whose very nose a member of his own congregation had been able to seek her own inescapable, unhallowed death. Where all had not accepted God's everlasting offer of new life, a single human being had no longer been able to trust in it. Benediction. Choral. Amen.

February 22, 1968   Thursday

In 1938, St. Peter's Church in Jerichow had the following scale of charges: pastor's services at burial, ten marks; full peal of bells, six marks; precentor's services, five marks; use and cleaning of church, five marks; bellringers' wages for two hours, thirty marks; grave-digging, twelve marks. All fees payable in advance. For Lisbeth Cresspahl, everything from this catalogue was ordered except for use of church and the interfering singing; and when the bells, which had just been rehung by Ohlsson of Lübeck and converted to electricity, began to toll their d f g b, work was put down in many of Jerichow's houses. The Luftwaffe had obviously taken seriously the matter of meriting full acceptance by the community, and in its order-of-the-day for November 14 had pointed out that in this town it was customary for pedestrians as well as horse-drawn and motorized vehicles to halt at the approach of a funeral cortege; and today no one needed anything more than the acoustic signal, for Lisbeth was not going to pass through the town again.

As the bells announced the start of the funeral at three o'clock, the coffin was carried along the neatly raked path between rubble and the charred remains of the yard. The coffin was pale, smooth, unvarnished. It looked very durable. The pallbearers were Alexander Paepcke and Peter Niebuhr, both in Army uniform, Horst Papenbrock and Peter Wulff, Alwin Paap and Mr. Smith. Cresspahl walked behind the coffin with the child, then came old Mr. and Mrs. Papenbrock, then the invited guests. As Lisbeth was carried through the open mortuary into the cemetery, the waiting crowd began to push through the six-foot-wide gate; and there were people already standing among the crosses and headstones, black, silent, like hiding ghosts.

Our Lisbeth.
Look at the child.
There's nothing so unhealthy as being ill.
Ottje Stoffregen's well away.
I wonder they haven't picked up Brüshaver yet!
He won't dare give the blessing. He won't dare do that.
You're the one who doesn't dare do anything here, Julie.
No use putting an arm or a leg on the fire. It's got to be wood.
November—what a month to die.
The fog month.
For a Jewish brat.
It may do something for Marie, you know.
And it's not right, it's all wrong! If she killed herself she belongs
in the corner, with the suicides, where they put the unbaptized!
I wouldn't mind having such a lovely funeral myself.
Our Lisbeth. Will we ever forget.

When Lisbeth was set down on the burial plot belonging to the Cresspahl family, a boy started to wave in a dormer window far away, and another boy ran into the church by the north door, and the bells stopped so suddenly that the silence hurt. Now all those who had been standing a little apart gathered hurriedly around the open hole.

Brüshaver pronounced the Invocation. This was permitted by

the Church of Mecklenburg regulations. He spoke as he had yesterday in his sermon, matter-of-factly, as if he were a doctor prescribing, a little louder.

"In the Thirty-Ninth Psalm we read," said Brüshaver. That was the lesson, and for this death that was not permitted. Brüshaver had memorized Cresspahl's deletions so carefully that he did not once stumble. He began with Verse 4, which speaks of "the measure of my days." Cresspahl had eliminated the preceding pangs of death, as well as the heart being hot within, and the fire. From Verse 4 it went to Verse 8; omitted after that were Lisbeth's failure to speak, her plea for an end to her sufferings, and her confession to being consumed by God's blows. Hear my prayer, O Lord, and give ear unto my cry; hold not thy peace at my tears: for I am a stranger with thee, and a sojourner, as all my fathers were. O spare me, that I may recover strength, before I go hence, and be no more seen.

At this point the graveside sermon was supposed to be given. But Brüshaver took half a step backward to leave more room for the lowering of the coffin. The child looked up at Cresspahl, astonished that he was allowing her mother to be buried.

Then followed the prayer and Lord's Prayer, both permitted. While Brüshaver was negotiating with his God, he stressed that He alone knew what had gone on in the soul of this woman whom we are burying today. Mr. Smith, who was trying to replace the unintelligible words by English ones, was puzzled by the fact that in this country the men hid their faces while praying, and when the Amen came he felt a distinct relief that they had all held their hats in front of their faces.

Lisbeth got her benediction. Brüshaver threw earth onto the coffin three times, raised one hand over the grave, and pronounced the words about earth to earth, dust to dust; in sure and certain hope of Resurrection to eternal life, through our Lord Jesus Christ; Who shall change our vile body, that it may be like His glorious body, according to the mighty working, whereby He is able to subdue all things to Himself. What does that mean, mighty working? Surely they must have borrowed that from some theory of emanation. During the consecration, the person to be buried is addressed in the second person singular, and Brüshaver talked to Lisbeth in a casual, friendly manner, like someone promising a child that it is not going to die. Amen.

Then Brüshaver pronounced the final Benediction, which should not have been granted to Lisbeth either. Now he had burned his boats not only with the secular authorities but also with the Church.

Now the boy at the dormer window waved to someone below again, and the one below ran into the church. Ol' Bastian pressed the button for the bells that would toll over the town for the next two hours. Pauli Bastian was not happy with the newfangled electric methods; he used to have four assistant bellringers under him. And yet he was obliged to stand there throughout. And, for the fifth year, he was not satisfied with Pastor Brüshaver's calm, official manner; now with the Full Peal, Brüshaver had really put his foot in it, dug his own grave, and if that's how it's to be, someone's going to fall over backward and break his teeth.

Brüshaver took his time replacing his biretta. He simply stood in front of Cresspahl until the man had his features under control again.

I'm doing this for you, Lisbeth. For you. But can you see that?

The receiving line was as follows: first Gesine standing beside Cresspahl, then old Mr. and Mrs. Papenbrock, the Paepckes, the young Papenbrocks, the Niebuhrs from Wendisch Burg and Berlin. Cresspahl looked so intently at the guests that they could not get away with mumbled condolences, and there were some who were satisfied with a silent handclasp. Wulff said: She didn't deserve that; he meant not only her death but also the risk to which Cresspahl had exposed the pastor. For the next seven years Wulff would have to believe that this remark was to blame for Cresspahl's no longer coming to his tavern, cutting him on the street, not even looking at him. He did not know this yet. Käthe Klupsch stepped into the soft mud like a chicken into a puddle; she was so worried about her shoes. Mr. Smith said helplessly, in his embarrassment, "You know —"; and this guest got an answer from Cresspahl, who said: "I do." It must have taken twenty minutes for the procession of handshakers to go down the whole line.

Gesine had placed herself so close to her father that her right hand was hidden. When she realized that this meant everyone would take her other hand, although it was not the "proper" one, she put both behind her. Then they stroked her head. This greatly annoyed her. She did not understand why Martin and Matthias Brüshaver bowed to her, and Marlene curtsied. That was for grownups. The child was tired. After three days among strangers at the lock, she had left Wendisch Burg by train early in the morning. The Niebuhrs had not liked to say anything to her, and she had endured their melancholy behavior, their sympathetic caresses, out of sheer obedience to her father. Her father had been very slow in taking her to her mother. Then he had forgotten to tell her that the fire had been not just anywhere but in their own yard, and she had found it hard to recognize the property, the bare house. When Cresspahl led her into the emptied office, she found it darkened by people in black clothes. It was the relatives; those are the people I'm related to; but she did not recognize them all. On the big table in the middle of the room stood a box made of pale wood with something inside it, for some people were looking into it, some at her. Cresspahl lifted her up. There was someone lying in the box. The child trod once in the air, then again, until Cresspahl stood her on the table beside the coffin. It felt good that he did not let go of her. She had been told that that was her mother lying there, and she tried to imagine her. The person in there was bigger than she remembered. She had been covered up in a funny way, as far as the middle. She recognized the black jacket and the white blouse with the freshly ironed ribbons at the neck. The face was unrecognizable, so highly colored. And as if it had slipped into itself. That kind of smile was unknown to her. The hair, light and plentiful, looked artificial. She tried to walk along the edge of the table, at least as far as the folded hands, so she could touch them. Then Cresspahl led her by the arm as far as the unfamiliar hands. She looked at him, and his nod gave her permission. But the hands were not hot as if from fire, they were cold, like the handle of a spade in winter. Then she had been stood in a corner of the room, and Cresspahl had placed a lid on the box. The small bells had started to ring outside, as always at burials. Now she had to stand there in the cold, stuck to the wet ground, and her mother was to be shut up in the ground forever, quite different from what she had said. By the time Cresspahl carried Gesine over his shoulder away from the open grave, she was asleep.

By five that afternoon they had still not come for Brüshaver.

Brüshaver stayed at the Papenbrock house, where Louise had prepared a large table, for as long as propriety required. He did not remain long. Louise Papenbrock had begun to have doubts about her condescending manner toward the pastor and now attempted an exaggerated civility, which did not quite come off. Moreover, she switched too rapidly from her ensconcement as a grieving mother to the bustle of a housewife who is trying to feed twenty people and has to look out for the mouth the fingers the eyes of the cook as well as the maid in the kitchen on the stairs in the dining room. Brüshaver also noticed that the funeral guests were gradually becoming mindful of everyday life again, and he utilized Aggie's first gentle promptings to take leave of the company.

The silence at the long table was not a grim one, and it was hardly ever present for long; all the same, there were crosscurrents of hostility: Papenbrock toward his son Horst and his son's wife because they both intended to return to Güstrow that evening, which meant that nothing could be settled by discussion; if desire for revenge was the reason, old Papenbrock claimed that prerogative for himself; toward his son Robert, who had not even cabled from overseas, thus forcing Papenbrock to resort to a forged ribbon for the wreath to make it look as if Robert had sent his condolences. Louise toward Cresspahl because she had had to yield the place of honor at the graveside ceremony; toward the Niebuhrs from Wendisch Burg because they sat there looking so dejected and silent as if they knew more about grief than a hostess who had her hands full anyway; toward Lisbeth because she had inflicted on her mother what she had done to herself; toward Alexander Paepcke because he already had the second bottle of claret in front of him. Horst toward his father; above all toward Peter Niebuhr because this young fellow whom at Lisbeth's wedding he had considered lower class was now with a ministry in Berlin and presuming to instruct him quite competently on seed-selection. Hilde toward her mother's rattled behavior, and toward Cresspahl because he made such a fuss over his child and would not allow her to go back with them to Podejuch. Alexander toward Cresspahl because he was spending so much time at the lower end of the table with all those strangers from Lübeck, one of whom was called Erwin Plath; Alexander would have much preferred to drink with his brother-in-law than with that heavy-going Schmoog couple. Alexander toward himself because vanity had caused him to wear his uniform and now everyone could tell that he was an administration officer. Alwin regarded himself more as a servant and wished himself elsewhere. The Schmoogs, the Niebuhrs, and Heinz Mootsaak were surprised to see that, while Mrs. Papenbrock had prepared the better rooms for the Paepckes, laundry baskets had been left standing around or the washbasin was missing in the rooms allotted to them; they were not annoyed. Peter Niebuhr toward no one, except that he would have gladly cut short his conversation with Horst Papenbrock and gone for a walk with Martha. But he stayed for the sake of that Mr. Smith from Richmond who was so delighted with Martha's high-school English; now he could even be proud of his wife. No one toward Cresspahl.

When the first evening bells stopped, the people in Papenbrock's house stood up. Ol' Bastian pressed the button once again, and then came the special evening bells for her who had been buried that day.

They came for Brüshaver that night, four hours before dawn.

February 23, 1968   Friday

Today we lost Francine.

Twelve days was all she spent with us at the apartment, and we could have stood it longer with her. By that time she had become almost one of us.

For Francine it was a good thing that since Sunday Mrs. Cresspahl had not got out of bed, had slept away the days and nights in a fever, sometimes semiconscious, talking in her sleep, so they said. That was something for Francine, she knew about such things, this probably made her feel she was earning her keep. She worried about the patient, coming home with ice cream when it was her turn to do the shopping, continually placing fresh water with ice cubes beside the bed, always on tiptoe. Marie describes it. This morning Francine arrived with a bitter gray brew of a tea she had obtained not from the pharmacy but from an old man way up in North Harlem, a wizard with herbs, and she said categorically: If the medicines did not bring down the fever, only this would help. It did not do just to swallow one mouthful, for politeness' sake, Francine's long trip and great effort demanded that the patient sip the bowl clean down to the dregs. There was nothing left. Her throat opened right up. "When you wake up, it'll be gone," said Francine solemnly, and for a while accompanied the patient into a dream where she sported a dainty crumpled lace handkerchief between her braids, making her skin look somewhat darker. Her manner with the white woman was not trusting, and certainly not familiar, she tried to mask her timidity with nurses' parlance, with "we" must be obedient and "we" want to get well; then Francine's voice became quite high, firm, with an edge of gaiety to it, for it was meant to be a game too. She had changed.

She was no longer the child still trying to defend its place on a chair, to extend its property with defensive action in all directions, even if the newly won privilege means only that one has listened to her a minute longer than to the competition. And by now she could look at Marie's dresses in terms not of how she could wangle them for herself by flattering and wheedling but of whether or not she liked them. As soon as she realized she had the right to ask for something, and that she would even succeed, she found it easier to refrain. When she was certain of having her share in the common use of the apartment, her envy diminished, and her admiration for Marie too. Then she could look at Marie for what she is, not for what she has; Marie, it must be said, still drew much of her compliance from what Francine did not have, or ever will have, at home. Rivalry was not apparent. When suddenly faced with illness in the home, they were forced to set up a strict division of labor, each depending on the other for certain jobs, and in some Francine was more dependable. When the meal is over, Francine goes and washes the dishes, efficiently and unprotestingly simply because it has to be done; Marie first puts the dishes into the sink and indulges in a respite. When Mrs. Erichson arrived, she was expecting chaos in the kitchen as well as the other rooms, but she found a tidy, well-run household that almost met her Mecklenburg standards for the orderly home; it was only the inordinate supply of TV dinners and frozen chicken that for one moment took her breath away. For Mrs. Erichson, her days in New York became not a chore but a vacation; all she had to do was give the children instructions, and she had soon lost her heart to the little black girl who could say with such perfect docility: Yes, ma'am; certainly, ma'am; who nevertheless was not timid and could look her in the eye often enough in the spirited way that the old lady might have interpreted as defiance. A Mrs. Erichson does not allow herself to be defied, she has her sayings for that: Give them an inch and they'll take an ell. When she left to return to New Jersey she was almost tempted to invite this little Francine with Marie; but she did not say so this time. For Mrs. Erichson saw this home being run without any contribution from her, and she wanted to get back to her own; and since the patient no longer required her presence she took her car and must be far beyond Bayonne now. The fever came down around noon, and stayed down.

Francine and Marie were sitting at the table in the big room next door before supper, trying to catch up on as much of their missed lessons as they had been able to gather over the telephone. They were partially visible from the bed, the fair head next to the dark one, Francine's slightly more rounded back, Marie's habit of leaning way back when she is thinking about something, chin in the air, pencil at her lips, eyes fixed on the ceiling. Then the bell went, and the door to the patient's room was softly closed, but not quite, because of the hurry. The patient was meant to go on sleeping and now was fully awake.

The voice of the visitor was that of a young man, a drawling, vowel-accentuating tenor, about twenty-five years old. The stranger may have gone to university, but he could switch easily enough to slang, which coming from him sounded quoted, and the tentative, suspicious, circuitous manner betokened many years of practice. At first he and Marie held the conversation; and even later on Francine was not often heard.

"If this is the Cresspahl apartment, I guess I'd like to come in."

"Do you always act like this?"

"I always act like this."

"Then you can go away. You needn't think we're alone here."

"I'm from the City, my pet."

"You can look for your pet someplace else. And I guess you have identification."

"You're really fabulous, kiddo."

"From Welfare?"

"My, you can read!"

"We've got nothing to do with Welfare. My mother earns a salary."

"So how does she keep the family?"

"She works at a bank in town."

"Then it has to be the Chemical."

"It's not the Chemical."

"Does a fellow get a chair offered to him here?"

"Only because you're a gentleman."

"I didn't mean any harm, kids. Just you try running around all day in buildings with no elevator."

"D'you do it for nothing?"

"So we're going to talk business. I'm looking for a child called Francine, age eleven, colored, and I've even got a picture of her."

"O.K.—so?"

"That's her."

"Well?"

"Then I've come to the right place."

"It's completely legal for her to live here with us. The police know about it, and Francine's mother has the address too."

"Where else would I have got it?"

"Do you know what this is all about, Francine?"

"Your mother says to say hello, Francine."

"We were going to the hospital again tomorrow."

"Francine's mother isn't in the hospital any more."

"We'd know about that."

"You don't know about that. Otherwise you'd know that during a cold spell there's an even greater shortage of beds. She's been discharged."

"I just have to pack my things."

"You can't put Francine's mother back into that hole on 103rd Street after she's been so badly hurt!"

"It wasn't me. What's your name anyway."

"M'rie."

"Well then, Mary dear. O.K.! O.K! So you're not my dear Mary! I'm working on this case. Someone told me the story during one of my routine visits. And I made up my mind: If she comes back, then not into a hole. As you so aptly put it."

"It's extremely kind of you, Mr. Feldman."

"So I had the case shunted to a hotel."

"One of those where the City pays the rent?"

"You must admit it's an improvement."

"I guess a hotel like that's a bit better than 103rd Street."

"Now Francine's mother's all alone with a baby. The older daughter's run away from a children's home, they haven't been able to find her."

"And the older brother's missing too."

"That's the kind of family it is."

"I don't think they're to blame."

"Mary dear (O.K.! I know!), if I had to start wondering about that, I'd never accomplish anything."

"And now you're taking Francine away."

"If she doesn't want to come with me, I can have her picked up."

"I see."

"Mary, don't you believe in families staying together?"

"I do. And Francine's to take her mother's place looking after the baby so she—nothing. I didn't mean that."

"Maybe her wounds aren't properly healed yet. Her mother says she wants Francine."

"Why doesn't she phone us?"

"I don't know. But obviously she doesn't want to. Can't bring herself to. Something like that."

"And you've got a letter from her."

"I can leave that with you. And anyway it's a favor."

"For whom?"

"Mary, if your friend Francine has known for two days that she's supposed to go back to her mother, and even knows the new address—"

"I don't believe that."

"Francine, do you know a Mrs. Lippincott? She lives in your old building."

"Yes, Mister."

"Did she run into you the other day on Broadway?"

"Yes, Mister."

"Did she tell you where your mother is and that she wants you back?"

"Yes, Mister."

"Francine."

"It's true, Marie."

"Francine!"

"Now then: when does this Mrs. Cresspahl get home from the bank, the one that's not the Chemical?"

"She's here. She's sick."

"You're a weird generation, by bloody Jesus. Now I have to go through the whole thing again with her."

"No you don't."

"Maybe I should introduce myself to her."

"You can't go in there. If Francine would like to say good-by—"

"No, Marie. I'd rather not tell her."

"See?"

"Even you didn't understand. It wasn't a lie."

"So you're going."

"We can go now, Mister."

February 24, 1968   Saturday

Public Notice. Louis Levinson, brother of Sam, Isidore, Tillie, and Pearl Levinson, wants to be contacted by some member of family. IN 1-6565.

When my mother was a child, a doctor said: The child has a weak heart. And see that she walks more often with the stick.

Children used to have a stick placed across their backs, and they had to hold it in position with the crooks of their arms. To learn posture.

My mother had narrow hips. Even at sixteen she was still said to be "not strong." She always walked with a slight stoop, her shoulders sloping forward. She tired easily, even from a half-hour's walk. Then she learned riding.

When she passed a mirror she would say: I can't help it, I think I'm pretty. She was teased all her life about this. (Because once, when she was ten years old, she arrived fifteen minutes late from combing her hair.) Think you're too pretty? If I say so myself.

At eighteen she was the cream in everyone's coffee.

As a child she had said: I know a girl who doesn't believe in God.

God, who invented the atom bomb, also shoots at sparrows and makes them fall off the roof.

She trod so lightly that her shoes never wore out.

Her dresses were all knee-length when she was to marry the man from Lübeck.

Papenbrock to Cresspahl in 1931: I'm sure you can make my daughter happy. Man to man, you know.

A sentence, written in secret in Richmond, August 1932:

You know, I have secrets in my head, but I don't know what they are. Only my head can get at them.

A mania about being responsible even for the birds in the garden.

After the doctors found out what she had died of, they washed her hair.

At funeral services there was a desk by the north door of St. Peter's with a list for those attending to enter their names. Pauli Bastian stood by asking each one: Do you wish to view the body? This time he was not allowed to say that. This time he was asked: What! No viewing? No viewing?

She was a Protestant. "Protestants decide their own priorities."

The sound of the pebbles on the beach as the ebbing wave grinds over them. She could stand with her face toward that sound for a long time, especially in the fog.

When she removed the rings from the stove, she sometimes forgot she was still holding them with the hook, so lost was her gaze in the fire.

She never ceased to be surprised at her long neck. As a child she had had almost no neck.

She was gone so suddenly; she was never mentioned.

Seen no more.